"Maddie, I'd lil

She was uncomfortable with the message she saw in Dylan's eyes. It said, "I'm a man and you're an attractive woman." She didn't want to get that kind of look from her landlady's son. "You don't want the coleslaw?" she asked, deliberately misunderstanding him.

"I'm talking about last night. There's no point in pretending it didn't happen. But we did manage to live under the same roof without problems when we were teenagers. We should be able to do the same as adults, don't you think?"

She almost said no. Every instinct told her Dylan could be big trouble for any woman.

"I don't see why not," she lied.

As if he knew she wasn't being sincere, he said, "It's a big house."

Not big enough.

Dear Reader,

Welcome to 14 Valentine Place, a wonderful old Victorian house that is home to three special women. Walk through the front door and you'll meet Leonie Donovan, a mother who is very wise when it comes to affairs of the heart. Living upstairs are her two tenants, Maddie Lamont and Krystal Graham, two single women who try to be smart when it comes to romance, but occasionally need a little advice from their landlady.

One person who doesn't need Leonie's advice is her son Dylan. When he comes home for a visit, the last thing on his mind is romance. But as his mother is quick to point out, sometimes love happens when one least expects it—with or without any coaching.

I hope you enjoy reading about the residents of 14 Valentine Place as much as I enjoyed telling their story. I love hearing from readers and welcome your letters. You can write to me c/o MFW, P.O. Box 24107, Minneapolis, MN 55424 or visit me via the Internet at www.pamelabauer.com.

Wishing you a Valentine's Day filled with love and laughter,

Pamela Bauer

14 Valentine Place

Pamela Bauer

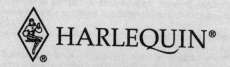

HARLEQUIN®

TORONTO • NEW YORK • LONDON
AMSTERDAM • PARIS • SYDNEY • HAMBURG
STOCKHOLM • ATHENS • TOKYO • MILAN • MADRID
PRAGUE • WARSAW • BUDAPEST • AUCKLAND

ISBN 0-373-71035-6

14 VALENTINE PLACE

This edition published by arrangement with Harlequin Books S.A.

Visit us at www.eHarlequin.com

Printed in U.S.A.

14 Valentine Place

CHAPTER ONE

Dear Leonie: I'm in love with a guy who doesn't even know I exist. Not that it would do me any good if he did notice me. He's popular and he's a senior. I just wish it didn't hurt so much to be in love. What am I going to do? Will I ever get over him?
Signed: Sad Sophomore

Leonie says: Time has healed many a broken heart. What you should do is enjoy being young and have fun. Boys will come and go in your life. When you meet the perfect guy, you'll be happy you forgot about this one.

"I SMELL CHOCOLATE."

The accusatory tone had Madeline Lamont glancing over her shoulder. "I plead guilty."

"I should have known it was you," Leonie Donovan said, pointing a finger at Maddie. "Krystal hates to cook. What are you doing up so late?" she asked in the maternal tone Maddie had come to expect from the woman who was more like a sorority house mother than a landlady.

"I'm making fudge. I found the recipe on the Internet. It's supposed to be the same one they use at the candy shop over on Seventh Street."

"I thought you gave up chocolate for New Year's."

"I did. I went four days without it before I realized the error of my ways." She stirred the dark brown mixture patiently. "You do know that some people consider chocolate a health food."

Leonie chuckled. "Some being us, right?"

"Of course."

"So when will this fudge be ready to help save our hearts?"

Maddie eyed the candy thermometer. "It's almost done. I'm surprised you're still up. You're not working, are you?"

"I am." Leonie stretched, rubbing the muscles at the back of her neck. "There were so many letters this week that I'm having a difficult time choosing which ones to use in my column."

"I would imagine lots of people want advice as to what they should do about Valentine's Day."

"That's what I was hoping, but most of my mail is from the brokenhearted. Unfortunately, there were an awful lot of people who made ending a relationship one of their New Year's resolutions."

"January is a bad time of the year for relationships," Maddie noted pragmatically. "No one wants to break up right before Christmas, so they wait until the holiday season is over and then they say goodbye."

"Is that the voice of experience speaking?" Leonie asked, propping a hip against the counter.

"As a matter of fact it is. I remember this one guy I dated. He had huge sideburns." She laughed. "You should have seen how my friends teased me about that.

They nicknamed him Elvis. Anyway, we started going out in July and by the time Christmas came along we—'' She stopped in mid-sentence as a hissing sound alerted her to the fact that the fudge mixture was bubbling over the rim of the pot.

''Oh no! It's not supposed to do that! I sprayed the edges with vegetable oil.'' She groaned, frantically lifting the pot off the burner. ''Now look at the mess I've made!''

Leonie reached for a sponge. ''Don't worry about it. That old stove has seen worse spills than that.''

''Be careful,'' Maddie cautioned as Leonie mopped up the gooey liquid. ''The burner's hot.''

''Ooh, this *is* painful,'' Leonie agreed.

''You didn't burn yourself, did you?''

''No, I just hate to see good chocolate go to waste.'' Leonie licked her finger.

''I should know better than to try to cook and talk about my old boyfriends at the same time,'' Maddie said with a sigh.

''Speaking of boyfriends, I saw Jeffrey in the post office this morning,'' Leonie said, rinsing out the sponge at the sink.

Jeffrey Anderson was a teaching assistant in the English department at the university, but he was more of a friend to Maddie than a boyfriend. In the past six months they'd grown closer and she'd been patient, hoping that what had started out as a friendship would turn into something else, but so far not even his poetry, which he wrote especially for her, could kindle the flame of romance between them.

''Were his eyes glazed over?'' she asked, her attention on the fudge. ‘‘He’s been working night and day on his thesis.’’

‘‘He did look a bit frazzled. He asked me to give you a message, but I’m wondering if it’s safe… I mean, we don’t want to lose any more of the fudge, do we?’’

‘‘No need to worry about that. It’s done.’’ Maddie peered closely at the candy thermometer before removing the pot from the stove and setting it on a wire rack to cool.

‘‘In that case, he said to tell you he misses you,’’ Leonie told her.

‘‘He misses his back rubs, especially now that he’s spending long hours bent over the computer working on his paper.’’ Maddie added a chunk of butter to the mixture.

‘‘You aren’t seeing him at all during semester break?’’

She shook her head. ‘‘We’re both too busy, although we might go to the Saint Paul Sunday Chamber Music Series next week.’’

‘‘He mentioned that his parents were coming for a visit.’’

‘‘Another reason we won’t be together. His mother has a way of seeing things in a relationship that aren’t there. I call it wishful vision.’’

‘‘She’s hoping that you and Jeffrey are more than friends?’’ Leonie asked with a lift of her brows.

Maddie began clearing away the measuring cups and spoons that littered the counter. ‘‘He’s an only child and his mother is ready to be a grandmother. Need I say more?’’

Leonie smiled. "Then it's a good thing she lives nine hundred miles away, isn't it?"

"Yes, it is," she said, rinsing the dirty dishes before putting them into the dishwasher. "Jeffrey and I don't need that kind of pressure."

"So he's uncomfortable with her attitude, too?"

"Of course he is. He knows I'm not ready for that kind of a relationship. And neither is he."

"Are you sure? About his feelings, I mean?" Before she could answer, Leonie held up one hand. "You don't need to answer that, Maddie. I'm not supposed to wear my romance coach hat when I'm out of the office and you certainly don't need advice when it comes to love."

"You weren't wearing your business hat. You were just being you," Maddie insisted. "And looking out for the daughter of an old friend."

Leonie smiled affectionately. "You are so much like your mother. I think she'd be happy to know that you're staying here with me, don't you?"

Maddie nodded, a lump forming in her throat. Even though it had been four years since her mother had died, she still couldn't think about her without feeling the pain of her loss. "When we were kids she used to always tell us that if we ever were in trouble, we should call you."

"Well, I'm glad you came to me—even if you weren't in trouble," Leonie said. "If you hadn't suggested I rent out some of the rooms in this big old house, I'd still be a lonely, grieving widow. Sharing my home with women was exactly what I needed to move on after Frank died."

The women Leonie referred to were the college students who'd rented rooms in the house at 14 Valentine Place. At one time there had been four of them, but now there were only two, Maddie and a hairstylist named Krystal Graham, who had moved in while she was a student at a cosmetology school nearby.

"You did all of us a favor, Leonie. Finding affordable housing near the university can be a nightmare," Maddie remarked.

"But if it weren't for you girls, my life would be quite different than it is today," she said with a grateful smile. "I don't think I'd be a romance coach if you hadn't been here to encourage me."

"Oh, I bet you would have. And the reason you're so good at what you do is that you and Frank had such a wonderful marriage."

Leonie sighed. "It's hard to believe he's been gone over two years."

The sadness in her eyes tugged at Maddie's heart. "He'd be proud of you if he could see what a success you are. And I doubt he'd be surprised."

"You mean unlike my sons? I don't think any of them expected their mom would get paid for dishing out advice on romance," she said on a chuckle.

"No, but they're all very proud of you, too."

"Three of them are anyway. Dylan doesn't really know the extent of my business."

"You haven't told him?" Leonie's oldest son wasn't exactly the black sheep of the family, but he was a stray one, having left home at eighteen. Seeing how close Leonie was to her other sons, Maddie found it puzzling that her landlady's relationship with her firstborn was strained.

"It really hasn't come up. When we do talk on the phone, there are always so many other things to catch up on."

"You're not worried that he won't approve, are you?"

"What's there not to approve?" she said, spreading her hands in the air.

"I like that attitude," Maddie said with a grin. "I was only fourteen the last time I saw Dylan, but if I remember correctly, he was a pretty smart guy. I think he can deal with the fact that his mother's a successful businesswoman."

"I'm going to find out. He needs to have surgery on his rotator cuff and has decided to have it done by an orthopedic specialist here at the university hospital."

"He's coming back to Minnesota?"

"Mmm-hmm. Next week." Leonie went on to explain how he'd injured his shoulder while working as an engineer for an overseas construction company. "Garret offered to have him stay at his place, but you know the crazy hours he keeps as a resident. I told Dylan he had to come here, that we have plenty of room." She fixed Maddie with an inquisitive look. "His being here won't make you uncomfortable, will it?"

"No, not at all."

"Good. I know I've only had women living here since you moved in, but I figured there's never been a problem when Jason's come home so there shouldn't be one when Dylan is here, either."

Jason, Leonie's youngest son, was a sophomore in college. Maddie could have pointed out that having a nineteen-year-old drift in and out was not quite the same as having a thirty-one-year-old man around, but she simply said, "Of course there won't be a problem. This is a big house and since you've remodeled the upstairs and put in the private entrance, it's more like separate apartments."

Leonie nodded in agreement. "I know, but I like it when you and Krystal share my house with me. I enjoy our girl time and I don't want you to feel as if you can't come downstairs because there's a man in the house."

"That won't change anything," Maddie assured her.

Leonie smiled. "Good. I've called the plumber to see if he can get the bathroom upstairs finished before Dylan arrives." She tried unsuccessfully to stifle a yawn, then glanced at the clock. "No wonder I'm tired. Look at the time. As much as I'd like to sample that fudge tonight, I'm afraid I'm going to have to wait until tomorrow."

Maddie nodded and wished her a goodnight's sleep. As she finished cleaning up the kitchen she thought about what Leonie had told her. In a week there would be a man in the house.

Not just any man, but Dylan Donovan. Memories of a tall, thin boy with brown eyes flashed in her mind.

She'd come to stay with the Donovans for the summer so that she could enroll in a dance program here.

For Maddie it had been a dream come true. A chance to leave her small town in North Dakota for the big city and to take a class at one of the top ballet schools in the Midwest.

The only down side had been that she had to spend a summer living with a family of four boys. She'd grown up in a house of women, and the thought of being around boys twenty-four hours a day had made her uncertain and shy.

Especially seventeen-year-old Dylan. Not only was he city smart, he was the cutest guy she'd ever set eyes on and that summer she'd spent nearly every hour she was awake fantasizing about what it would be like to be his girlfriend. Convinced she'd die of humiliation should anyone discover how she felt about him, she'd worked very hard to pretend she didn't like him at all.

Not that she had needed to worry. Dylan had no reason to notice a fourteen-year-old with braces and a shape not much different than that of his twelve-year-old brother Garret.

Unfortunately, it was Garret who had discovered how Maddie felt about his oldest brother. If she hadn't beaten him at chess, she was certain he would have told Dylan that she fancied herself in love with him.

Maddie sighed, thinking how silly those adolescent crushes were. Dramatic but silly. She finished beating the fudge until it was thick and creamy, spread it into the pan, then took great pleasure in eating a huge chunk.

Dylan's presence in the house would not create any awkwardness other than to cut in on what Leonie called their "girl time." As Maddie washed down the fudge with a glass of milk, she said, "Nothing like chocolate to put your world in order," then went to bed.

THE MAN SITTING NEXT TO DYLAN nudged him. "Did you hear that? It's two above with a windchill of seventeen below. And to think people actually like living here," the stranger said with a shake of his head as the plane taxied to the gate at the Twin Cities airport.

"Some people like the cold," Dylan noted.

The stranger made a sound of disgust. "Me...I like warm, tropical breezes and white sand beaches."

"Then you've come to the wrong place," a flight attendant said with a teasing grin as she handed the man his suit coat.

Dylan hoped *he* wasn't in the wrong place. When his brother had suggested he come home to have the surgery on his shoulder, his first instinct had been to say no. There were good doctors in Miami, which would have been a lot closer than Minnesota to Saint Martin.

Unfortunately, Miami was also where Andrea lived. Dylan knew that had he chosen to get medical treatment there, the flight attendant would have assumed he'd had a change of heart about their relationship. He hadn't.

That's why he'd allowed Garret to convince him to have the surgery on his shoulder at home. Now, as the plane taxied closer to the gate, Dylan wondered if he would have been better off going with his first instinct.

Saint Paul wasn't his home anymore. In the past thirteen years he'd seldom visited, and when he had come to see his family, he'd never stayed more than a few days. Now he was planning to spend six weeks in the snow and cold.

Again he had the uneasy feeling he'd made a mistake. Memories of the last time he was home flashed in his mind. There'd been arguments over things that now seemed unimportant. What was the best way to memorialize his father? Who should be in charge of what arrangements?

Accusations had been made, insults had been hurled. Not the kind of scene anyone wanted or needed when grieving.

As the oldest son, Dylan had wanted to make those few days of mourning easier for his mother. Instead he'd only made them more difficult. Now as he grabbed his carry-on bag from the overhead compartment, he realized she was the true reason he'd come back to Saint Paul to have the surgery.

Although Garret had emphasized the reputation of the medical staff available to him at the hospital, Dylan knew there had been an unspoken message in that phone call. Coming home would be an opportunity for him to put right what had gone wrong two years ago. This trip wouldn't be to simply mend his shoulder, but to try to fix his relationship with his family, as well. They both knew it and Dylan suspected that his mother did, too.

As he walked out of the jetway into the airport terminal, he searched for her face in the crowd gathered at the gate.

"Dylan! Over here!"

At the sound of the man's voice, he turned and saw

his brother Shane standing off to one side of the arrival gate. If there was one person Dylan hadn't expected to see at the airport it was Shane, not after the sharp words they'd exchanged the last time they'd been together.

Dylan knew that the grief over their father's death and the stress of the funeral were partly to blame for the tension that had existed between them after their father's death. He also knew that not all of the blame could be assigned to the difficult circumstances.

Of the four brothers, Dylan and Shane had always had the most tumultuous relationship. Being only eleven months apart, they'd been extremely competitive and had often found themselves at odds with each other. Whatever Dylan had done well, Shane had always wanted to do better.

It was a rivalry their mother had done her best to discourage, often telling the two boys they were supposed to support, not fight, each other. She was the peacemaker of the family, forever assuring them that one day they would be the best of friends.

Their father, though, hadn't seen anything wrong with their relationship. He believed it was healthy for the two of them to challenge each other.

Dylan wondered if that wasn't the reason Shane had reacted the way he had at the time of his father's death. When Dylan had tried to make decisions on behalf of the family, Shane had challenged his right to assume that responsibility. The friendship their mother had promised they'd have was nowhere to be found. He'd wondered then if she'd been wrong. Maybe they would never be friends.

When his brother greeted him with a smile, he had reason to hope they could.

"Welcome home, Dylan. How's the shoulder?" Shane asked, sounding more like the kid who had played catch with him in the backyard than the man who'd confronted him in anger at their father's funeral.

"Garret tells me it'll be fine in a few weeks. It's good to see you, Shane," he said, realizing that it was the truth. He had missed his brother.

"You look good. Your hair's lighter," Shane noted.

Automatically Dylan ran a hand through his hair. "That's from working in the sun. I'm surprised to see you here. I thought Mom was picking me up."

"She wanted to, but when your flight was delayed I offered to come so she wouldn't have to miss her class." Before Dylan could ask him what class, Shane looked to his right and said, "Mickey. Come say hello to your uncle."

It was then that Dylan realized that his brother wasn't alone. Standing only a few feet away, watching the airplanes taxi across the runway, was a small boy who looked like a miniature Shane. At the sound of his father's voice, he came running toward them.

"Remember Mickey?" Shane asked Dylan as the boy barreled into his legs.

"That's the baby?" Dylan stared at him in astonishment.

"I'm not a baby. I'm four," Mickey declared, holding up four fingers.

"Mickey, say hello to your uncle," Shane ordered.

"Hi, Uncle Dylan."

Dylan stooped so that he was eye level with his nephew. "Hey, Mickey. How's it going? Can you give me five?" He held out his hand and the four-year-old smacked it in delight.

"We saw your plane come down. It went really fast." His eyes widened at the memory. He glanced toward the window and said, "Look! There goes another one!"

Dylan watched him scramble over to press his face against the glass. "I can't get over how much he's changed."

"Yeah, well, kids grow up fast and it has been over two years since you were home," his brother reminded him, in a tone that held more than a hint of admonishment.

Dylan fought the temptation to defend himself, knowing it would only add tension to their conversation. He said simply, "He's a good-looking kid."

Shane nodded, then extended his hand toward his son. "Come on, Mickey. We need to get Uncle Dylan's luggage. Do you have your mittens?"

"They're in my pockets."

Shane looked at Dylan's short-sleeved shirt. "I don't suppose you own any winter clothes."

"It seldom goes below seventy-two in Saint Martin," he said with a half smile.

"You can probably buy a parka in one of the shops here at the airport. They've practically made this place into a shopping mall."

Dylan gave his brother's shoulder a playful punch. "You're dealing with an ex Boy Scout. Remember our motto? Be Prepared.'' He grinned. ''I have a leather jacket in one of my suitcases.''

''Then we better go.'' He looked down at Mickey. ''Take my hand so you don't get lost,'' he instructed as they merged into the crush of people heading toward the baggage claim area.

The four-year-old not only grabbed on to his father, but Dylan as well. His tiny hand felt soft against Dylan's palm. As they walked through the crowded concourse, Dylan thought about how familiar yet how strange he felt walking alongside Shane and Mickey. Looking at his brother, he felt that thirteen years hadn't passed, yet all he had to do was look at his nephew to realize how much everything had changed.

Feeling the need to make small talk, Dylan asked, ''How have things been going for you?''

''Not bad,'' Shane responded.

''How's Jennifer?''

''She's good. You'll see for yourself. She's at the house with the rest of the women. Maddie's doing her thing.''

Maddie. There was that name again. Whenever Dylan had spoken to his mother in the past two years, that name had crept into the conversation. Even Garret had mentioned her when he'd called.

He had to ask, ''Who's Maddie? One of the college students living with Mom?''

''She lives with Mom but she's not in college. You've met her...Maddie Lamont. She came and stayed with us one summer. Long hair pulled back in one of those big clips, glasses, real skinny.''

''Are you talking about that scrawny little Madeline

from North Dakota? The one who was always dancing even when there wasn't any music playing?"

"Yeah, only she goes by Maddie now."

"She showed me how to dance. Want to see?" Mickey dropped both hands and began to wiggle.

"Not now, Mick. We're in the middle of traffic," Shane said, grabbing his hand and getting them moving again.

"She was a couple of years younger than I was so she must be what...late twenties?" Dylan tried to remember the summer she'd stayed with them.

Shane shrugged. "Somewhere around there."

They passed another set of windows and Mickey said, "Oh-oh. It's snowing again."

Dylan asked, "You like the snow, Mickey?"

"Yeah, but Daddy's gonna get crabby because he hates driving when it's snowin' out."

Shane met Dylan's glance. "The roads are actually in pretty good shape considering the storm that passed through here."

Feeling as if he'd imposed on his brother, Dylan said, "You didn't have to come get me. I could have taken a taxi to Mom's."

"If Mom had thought you were taking a taxi, she would have changed her plans and come and picked you up herself."

Again Dylan wondered about those plans, but before he could ask, Mickey announced in an urgent tone, "Daddy, I have to go to the baffroom."

They had reached the baggage claim area and Shane turned to Dylan. "Why don't you find your luggage and I'll meet you back here after I've taken him to the men's room?''

Dylan nodded just as an alarm sounded indicating the bags would soon be tumbling down the conveyor belt. As he watched a steady stream of suitcases go by, his thoughts wandered back to that summer when Madeline Lamont had shown up at the house.

He remembered his mother giving him and his brothers orders that they were to treat her as if she were their sister. Dylan knew it was a warning not to think of her as a possible girlfriend—as if he, a senior in high school, would ever consider dating a freshman.

Once he'd seen what she looked like, he knew there was little chance of his being tempted to regard her as anything but a friend of the family's. Shane was right. She'd been as thin as a post and about as shapeless. She'd looked to be all arms and legs as she twirled and spun her way through the house.

As he hoisted his luggage from the carousel, he remembered something else about her, too. She was smart. She could beat Garret at chess—something neither he nor Shane had been able to accomplish. And when his mother had trouble doing the crossword puzzle in the Sunday paper, Madeline was the one she'd ask for help.

Skinny, smart, shy Madeline.

She'd never been particularly friendly toward him. Actually, when he thought about it, she'd treated him with a disdain he hadn't understood. Not that it had mattered at the time. She was closer to Garret's age than she was to his and those two had gotten along just fine.

"Got everything?" Shane interrupted his musings.

"Yeah. Just let me get my jacket out of my suitcase." When he had the dark brown leather jacket zipped up, he said, "Let's go."

On the way to his mother's house, Shane talked to Dylan as if he were a visitor, telling him about the local professional sports teams' successes and pointing out changes to the Twin Cities skyline. Listening to him made Dylan realize just how little attention he'd given to what had been happening to his family while he'd been in Saint Martin. It wasn't that he hadn't cared, because he had. But work had always taken precedence over everything else in his life, including his personal relationships.

Not wanting to be treated like a stranger, he said, "Shane, I can read about the basketball team in the paper. Tell me what's been happening with Mom and the rest of the family."

"What do you want to know?"

He shrugged. "The usual stuff. What's this new job Mom has? She said something about writing a column for the paper?"

"Yeah, she really likes it."

"What kind of column is it? Helpful household hints?"

"She hasn't told you what she writes?" he asked with a frown.

"Is it a secret or something?"

He shrugged. "No, but since it's her work, she should probably be the one to tell you about it."

His comment only intensified the feeling Dylan had that he wasn't a family member returning home, but rather a guest coming to visit. Determined not to be put off by his brother's attitude, he asked, "What about her renting out rooms to college students? Has that been working out all right?"

"Sure, it's been good for Mom. Are you worried about having to stay in a house full of women?"

Dylan chuckled and, before he could respond, his brother added, "Now *that* was a dumb question, wasn't it? Since when have you ever objected to being around women?"

"I love being around them. Living with them is another thing," he said with a sly grin.

"You still living alone?"

"Yup. I like having my place to myself."

"Well, you're not going to have much space to yourself at Mom's."

"I thought she remodeled the house and the tenants live upstairs?"

"They do. When she got rid of Dad's office, she had the workers put in a separate entrance for the upper floors."

"I didn't realize she got rid of Dad's office."

"There wasn't much point in keeping an office at the front of the house when the business had been moved. I work out of the office towers over on Lexington."

"Then you didn't have any problems taking over for Dad?"

He didn't answer, but cast a curious glance his way. "What's with all the questions? You've never expressed an interest in any of this in the past."

"Just because I haven't lived here doesn't mean I

haven't been interested.'' He knew that before they arrived at his mother's house, there was something he needed to say. ''Look, Shane. Now is probably as good a time as any for this.''

''For what?'' His brother didn't take his eyes off the road.

''I know that we've had our differences and that the last time I was home, things were said that neither one of us probably would have mentioned had the circumstances been different,'' he began, trying to find the words that wouldn't put his brother on the defensive. ''I guess what I'm trying to say is that I don't want our family to be one of those kept apart by hard feelings.''

Shane cast a sideways glance at him. ''Is that an apology?''

''Yes, it is. I'm sorry about what happened the last time I was home. I know your relationship with Dad was different than mine was.''

''Maybe we should just leave it at that,'' Shane said, then motioned with his thumb toward the back seat. ''Little pitchers have big ears, if you know what I mean.''

Dylan glanced at Mickey and then back to Shane. ''Point taken.''

''Dylan, we can't change the past.''

''No, but we don't have to repeat it, either.''

''I agree.''

There was a short silence, which Dylan broke by saying, ''You know, it really was good to see you standing there at the airport. It made me think of when we were kids and all the fun we had. I'd like to think there can be more good times for us.''

''I know it would make Mom happy.''

''There's Grandma's house!'' Mickey's tiny voice squealed with delight, as Shane pulled up in front of the big blue Victorian house Dylan had called home for eighteen years.

His mother may have remodeled the inside, but not much of the exterior had changed. It looked as familiar to Dylan as the day he'd left. The only thing missing was the small sign with the words Frank Donovan, C.P.A., written across it in bold letters. It had been on the newel post for as long as he could remember, a small lamp lighting it in the darkness. Now the only light came from the recessed fixture above the door where the number fourteen was painted on a tin frieze.

As soon as Dylan stepped inside the house, he saw the results of his mother's remodeling project. Gone were the accounting offices where his father had spent his days working. One room had been converted to a library, the other a dining room. Dylan hung his jacket on a coat tree, aware of two things: the aroma of freshly baked bread and the sound of Middle Eastern music.

Mickey noticed the latter, too, saying, ''Hurry up, Daddy. The music's on.'' He tugged at the snaps on his jacket while his father untied his boots.

''Are those bells I'm hearing?'' Dylan asked as he wandered down the hallway. He found his answer when he stepped around the corner. Gathered in the middle of his mother's living room, waving their arms and swishing their hips were at least a half dozen women dressed in what could only be described as harem apparel.

‘‘Remember, you’re drawing a circle with your hips, keeping your movement fluid.’’ A melodious voice directed the women. ‘‘Shift your weight from side to side, then back and forth.’’

‘‘Move, Uncle Dylan,’’ Mickey pleaded, pushing on his legs to get him to step out of the doorway. ‘‘I want to belly dance.’’

Activity ceased as six pair of eyes turned toward Dylan.

‘‘Oh my gosh, you’re home. I didn’t hear you come in!’’ one of the dancers exclaimed as she rushed toward him.

He stared in surprise at the woman wearing red harem pants and a matching blouse with poufy sleeves—or maybe he should have called it a half blouse since it didn’t cover very much midriff. She looked nothing like the woman he remembered. No brown hair peppered with gray, no glasses, no apron covering her matronly skirt and blouse. Nothing about her was familiar except her voice, and it told him in no uncertain terms what he found difficult to believe. This was his mother.

CHAPTER TWO

Dear Leonie: The nicest guy just moved into the boardinghouse where I live. I'd like to let him know I'm interested, but there's one small problem. He's my landlady's son and I'm not sure she'd appreciate me making a move on him. What should I do?
Signed: Don't want to be out on the street

Leonie says: How nice is your apartment? Are you willing to sacrifice it for something that might never develop into anything special? On the other hand, there are lots of nice apartments. Can you say the same about men?

DYLAN'S MOTHER WRAPPED her arms around him and gave him a hug. "It's so good to see you! Welcome home." She pushed him back a little and said, "How's your shoulder. I didn't hurt it grabbing you like that, did I?"

"No, it's fine. I—" he stammered, at a loss for words. Her dance costume was unlike anything she'd ever worn. He couldn't remember ever seeing his mother's midriff before. Even when she'd gone swimming she'd worn a one-piece. Nor had she ever been a blonde or had her fingernails painted bright red. She looked nothing at all like the mother he remembered.

"You're not wearing your glasses," he finally said.

"I don't need them anymore. I had laser surgery." She stepped aside and said, "Hey everybody, if you haven't figured it out, this is my son Dylan." Then she pointed to each of the women in the room in turn. "This is Krystal. She lives upstairs so you'll be seeing more of her, and this is Valerie, a friend of Krystal's, Jennifer you already know since she's married to your brother, and you remember my friend Jan, don't you?"

Dylan acknowledged the introductions with a nod and a few polite words.

"And this is Maddie Lamont, our instructor," his mother said when she'd reached the last of the belly dancers. "I know you remember her. She stayed with us one summer and practically became part of the family."

Dylan's eyes met those of Madeline Lamont and he had his second shock of the night. She was nothing like the scrawny kid who'd looked as if she'd wanted to bolt every time he tried to talk to her.

Quite the contrary. She was boldly looking him over with eyes full of the same surprise that was in his. He didn't remember them being such a bright blue, but then they'd always been hidden by glasses. When she smiled, he saw perfectly straight teeth instead of a mouth full of metal. Her long dark hair fell in soft, shiny waves down to her shoulders instead of being pulled back in a clip. And she'd gained weight. In all the right places.

Like the others, she wore harem pants, but instead of red they were a turquoise-blue and had a slit down the side of each leg. Around her hips was a scarf from which rows of coins dangled provocatively and on her fingers were tiny cymbals—the source of the tinkling sound he'd heard when he'd first entered the house.

"Hi Dylan. It's been a long time, hasn't it?" she said in a voice that made him think of moonlit nights on the beach with the sound of the surf in the background.

"Yes, it has," he answered, trying not to gawk at her like some bar patron ogling an exotic dancer, but that's exactly what he thought of when he looked at her. Instead of having a top with long sleeves, she wore a bikini bra, trimmed with sequins and beads and revealing a generous amount of cleavage.

"We've both changed a bit, haven't we?" she said, amused by his reaction to the changes thirteen years had produced.

"Just a bit," he agreed, still having a hard time believing that the skinny little kid who'd done cartwheels on the front lawn had matured into this beautiful woman.

"Can we dance?" Mickey asked impatiently, drawing Maddie's attention away from Dylan.

"Maybe we should stop for tonight," she suggested to Leonie.

"No, it's okay. You girls go ahead and finish. I'll take Dylan into the kitchen and make him something to eat," Leonie insisted. She linked an arm through Dylan's and motioned for Shane to join them.

"Smells good in here," Dylan said as he stepped into a kitchen that didn't look much different than it had the last time he'd visited. "You must have been baking."

She chuckled. "Not me. Maddie. She's the cook around here. She loves to make bread from scratch."

It was hard for Dylan to imagine the woman with the jewel in her navel and cymbals on her fingers as whipping up anything in the kitchen. She didn't exactly look like the domestic type.

Leonie put her hands on Dylan's arms and give him a thorough perusal. "Let me look at you."

"He's got all his limbs, Mom. I already checked," Shane quipped, grabbing a can of soda from the refrigerator. "Dylan, you want something stronger? Mom's got beer in here."

"No, but a cup of coffee would taste good."

"I'll get you a cup. You sit." She pushed him toward a chair at the table. "I have some cold chicken I can put in the microwave. How does that sound?"

"It sounds great, but I'm not hungry. Why don't you sit down so we can talk?"

"All right, but let me change first." She gestured to the costume. "I wouldn't want to spill anything on this fabric. It needs to be dry-cleaned. I'll be right back." With a wave she was gone, leaving him alone with his brother.

"Surprised by all the changes?" Shane asked, hooking a chair with his foot and sitting down across from Dylan.

"You could have warned me about that." Dylan gestured with his thumb toward the living room. He didn't intend for his tone to have an edge, but he was tired and it had been a shock to see his mother belly dancing.

Shane popped the top on his soda and took a drink. ‘‘I shouldn’t have had to warn you. If you called home, you’d know what’s been going on here.’’

So much for the truce they’d declared in the car, Dylan thought, wondering if he and Shane would ever be able to sit down and talk without the past coming between them. He chose to ignore his brother’s comment. He wrapped his fingers around the cup in front of him, appreciating its warmth. He’d been cold ever since he’d left the airport and it felt good to be in the kitchen drinking hot coffee.

Shane broke the silence with an attempt at an apology. ‘‘Forget I made that crack. I was out of line.’’

‘‘It’s forgotten,’’ Dylan told him, although they both knew it wasn’t. He didn’t expect that years of tension between him and his brother would fade away with a few sentences. It would take time to rebuild their relationship, but time was something Dylan had.

‘‘I meant what I said earlier, Shane. I have missed you. And this evening, coming home with you and Mickey in the car, listening to him talk…well, it’s made me realize I’ve missed a lot of other stuff, too.’’

Shane grinned proudly. ‘‘Mick’s quite a kid, isn’t he?’’

‘‘Yeah, he is. Smart little thing. Must take after his mother,’’ Dylan teased.

‘‘Who takes after his mother?’’ Leonie asked on her return. She’d changed into a pair of jeans and a red sweatshirt. Dylan again was surprised at how young she looked.

"Your grandson," Shane answered.

"I think he has the best of both of his parents," she said with an affectionate pat on Shane's shoulder. Then she looked at Dylan. "Are you sure you're not hungry? How about a nice turkey sandwich?"

"See? She hasn't changed as much as you thought. She's still the same old mom," Shane told Dylan with a sly grin. "Always trying to feed somebody."

"I'm supposed to. It's in a mother's job description," she insisted, arranging cookies on a plate.

"Belly dancing isn't," Dylan said. "What's up with that?" he asked, nodding toward the other room.

"Maddie suggested she teach us because it's such great exercise." She set the plate on the table in front of Dylan. "It's low impact and it releases tension. And the best part is, it's fun."

"Then you're only doing it to have fun?" Dylan asked.

"You don't think anyone would pay to see us, do you?" she asked with a laugh, pouring herself a cup of coffee.

"Then why the fancy costumes?" Dylan wanted to know.

"Maddie suggested we get them—to make it more fun. At first I was a bit shy about wearing something so exotic looking, but then I figured what the heck, why not try it? So I did and I liked it."

"Mom's tried a lot of new things lately," Shane pointed out.

"I've noticed," Dylan stared at her hair. "So tell me. Do blondes have more fun?"

She fluffed her curls with her fingers. "As a matter

of fact, I think they do. I probably should have done this years ago."

"I liked you as a brunette," Dylan told her.

"I did, too, but I wasn't exactly a brunette anymore. Salt-and-pepper gray would be more accurate. People have told me I took ten years younger because of the highlighting."

"Is that what you want? To look forty-two?" he asked.

"Thirty-two would be even better, but I'll settle for forty-something," she said with an impish grin. He must have frowned because her smile slid away. "You're looking at me as if you don't approve."

It wasn't that he didn't approve; it was just that she didn't look like his mother. She looked...well, young, for one thing. And so very different from the last time he'd seen her. Before he could say anything, Shane spoke up.

"I think you look great, Mom. And I won't be offended if anyone asks if you're my sister." He gave her an affectionate wink.

She flapped her hand at him. "As if they would. It was a change I needed and it's been a good one for me." To Dylan she said, "You probably haven't noticed, but I've lost weight since the last time you were here, too."

"I noticed."

As she sat down at the table she said, "Maddie's the one who helped me shed the pounds."

"Maddie knows about dieting, too, does she?" Dylan asked with a lift of one eyebrow.

"It's not really about dieting, Dylan. It's more

about living a healthy lifestyle,'' his mother corrected him.

''And I suppose that Maddie knows all about that, too.''

She frowned. ''Dylan, why that tone of voice? There's no reason for you to be sarcastic regarding Maddie.''

''I'm not trying to be sarcastic, just asking questions,'' he insisted, although he knew he was sounding churlish. He rubbed a hand across the back of his neck. ''Ah, don't mind me. I'm just tired. Maybe I should take my bags and go to bed. You want me to take the spare bedroom on this floor?''

''I'm going to put you in Jason's room. The spare bedroom is now my office.''

''If you needed a office, why didn't you just use Dad's?''

''Because she didn't want to use his,'' Shane said, coming to his mother's defense. ''Mom has a right to remodel the house if she wants.''

''I'm not criticizing her for making changes to the house,'' Dylan snapped at his brother.

''It sure sounds as if you were.''

Leonie held up a hand. ''You two stop. There's no need to raise your voices.''

Dylan could see by the set of his brother's jaw that he wanted to continue their discussion, but the look on his mother's face kept him silent.

Then she turned to Dylan. ''You won't be uncomfortable in Jason's room, will you?''

''No, not at all,'' he assured her. ''I guess I didn't

realize that you needed an office. I forgot that you were doing your column for the paper.''

''Yes, I am.'' She cast a rather furtive glance at Shane, who apparently found it necessary to come to her defense once more.

''Mom's not just writing a column. She has her own business,'' he said.

''Business? What kind of business?''

Again her eyes darted to Shane, as if she were nervous and needing his reassurance. ''You're going to be surprised when I tell you.''

''Come on. I've just seen you belly dancing. You think I'm going to be shocked at you owning a business?'' he asked dryly.

After one more glance at Shane, she said, ''I'm a romance coach.''

Dylan nearly choked on his coffee. ''A what?''

''A romance coach,'' she repeated. ''The column I write for the paper is an advice column on romance.''

''You mean people write to you about their problems with their love life?'' Dylan thought his voice must have gone up an octave.

She nodded. ''And I also teach classes on making relationships last.''

''Don't forget about the one-on-one consulting,'' Shane added.

Seeing his mother belly dancing was nothing compared to the astonishment Dylan felt at hearing this. ''But…'' he began, then stopped himself. His instinct had been to blurt out, ''How can you give advice on romance after what happened in your own marriage?''

He knew, however, that he could never say those

words to her, because she didn't know her husband had been unfaithful to her. Only Dylan had known. And it was a secret he would continue to keep even now, because to reveal it would mean shattering an illusion his mother still treasured—that his father had loved only her.

"How did all this come about?" he asked, trying not to sound disapproving.

"You know I've been renting out the rooms to the college girls since your father died?" When he nodded, she continued on, "Well, they would always come downstairs to eat and I'd listen to their problems. They'd ask my opinion on things and I'd give it. The next thing I knew, they were bringing their friends over and asking my advice about love. Questions such as, how did I manage to stay married for thirty years, how did I know when I was in love...those kinds of things."

It was something he could see his mother doing. She'd always been a good listener and her kitchen had often been the gathering place for the neighborhood moms. How many times as a child had he heard the phrase, "You should ask Leonie." Was it any wonder she was still answering questions? Only now they weren't about getting out grass stains but mending broken hearts.

"So you went to the newspaper and suggested you write a column answering people's questions about love?" he asked, still trying to figure out how it had all come about.

"Not without any training I didn't." She took a sip of her coffee. "Maddie suggested I take a writing class. She helped me put together a sample of what the column would be like and then, bless her heart, she took it to a friend of hers at the newspaper."

The ubiquitous Maddie. Dylan should have known she'd be behind this. "How did that lead to you having your own business?"

"Maddie suggested I branch out, you know, cover all the bases when it came to romance and relationships. So I began offering workshops and the next thing I knew, I was printing up business cards with the title 'romance coach' after my name."

Again *Maddie.* Dylan took a deep breath to keep from making another sarcastic comment about the woman. Was there any aspect of his mother's life in which she hadn't interfered? Only it didn't sound as if his mother saw it as interference.

"I never realized that running a business could be so exciting!"

From the glow on her cheeks, Dylan could see that it was a fulfilling career for her. He was about to tell her he was happy for her, but her next words kept him silent.

"What's really special about this job is that it makes me feel close to your father. Whenever I have to answer a question about love and romance, I think of him and the love we shared."

The love we shared. Dylan knew she'd been happy with his father. That had never been something he'd questioned. What he didn't know was if that love had been based on a lie. Would his mother's feelings for his father be the same if she knew he'd cheated on her? Was she basing her career on a lie?

They were questions he knew he could never ask. He sighed, and his mother mistook the sound for fatigue.

She reached across the table and patted his hand. ''You've had a long day. We'll have lots of time to talk once you catch up on your sleep.''

Dylan gently rotated his neck. ''Bed is going to feel good. I must have slept wrong on the plane because I've got a kink in my neck.''

''You should ask Maddie to give you a massage,'' his mother suggested. ''She's got the right touch when it comes to soothing aching muscles.''

''Tell me, Mom, is there anything that Maddie doesn't know?'' he asked.

''I don't know anything about living on a Caribbean island,'' she said, entering the room. She gave him a flirtatious grin. ''Maybe you could fill me in.'' Then she placed a hand on Leonie's shoulder and said, ''We're stopping for tonight. Do you want to come say goodbye?''

Leonie scraped back her chair. ''I do. Thanks for letting me know.''

''No problem,'' she said as left the room, the coins on her costume making a tinkling sound with every step she took.

Shane rose, too. ''That means Jennifer and Mickey will be wanting to go.'' He turned to Dylan. ''You need any help with your luggage?''

Dylan shook his head. ''No, I'm fine.''

His mother asked, ''Are you going to bed then?''

''No, I'll wait for you,'' he said, knowing that he needed to talk to his mother alone. His reunion with her hadn't gone as he'd hoped, and he needed to smooth things over.

Only it wasn't his mother who returned a few minutes later, but Maddie. She looked startled to see him, and he suspected that if she could have left without saying a word, she would have.

"Looking for something?" he asked.

"Just getting some water," she told him, pulling a bottle from the refrigerator.

"Belly dancing makes you thirsty, does it?" He didn't know why the words came out on a note of sarcasm. She'd neither said nor done anything to warrant it.

"If that's the tone you used with your mother I can see why she's upset," she told him, then unscrewed the cap and took a long drink.

He let his eyes travel over her figure and felt something stir deep inside him. Now he knew the reason for the sarcasm. It was a self-defense mechanism. He was attracted to her and he didn't want to be.

"Mom's not upset." He spoke the words with confidence, although he knew his reunion with his mother had had its share of tension. She'd wanted his approval and, instead of complimenting her on her new look, he'd put her on the defensive, asking questions with a critical eye rather than an understanding one. He wasn't, however, going to admit that to this woman.

"Now why doesn't it surprise me that you didn't notice?" Maddie shoved a fist to her waist, which only caused Dylan's eyes to focus on her flat stomach and the turquoise jewel in her navel. It was almost the same color as her eyes and seemed to wink at him.

He forced his eyes back to hers. ''My relationship with my mother doesn't concern you, although I'm sure you think it does.''

She stiffened, her chin lifting slightly. ''Actually, I don't, but I happen to care about your mom and I don't like it when people hurt her.''

''People meaning me?'' he asked in disbelief. ''I didn't come home to upset my mom.''

''I'm glad to hear that. I'd like to think that we can get along while you're here.''

Her attitude annoyed him. Who was she to stand there like some champion of the mistreated, looking at him as if it were her duty to protect his mother from him?

He was about to tell her that *if* they were going to get along, she was going to have to get rid of that attitude. Only his mother chose that moment to return.

''So here's where you disappeared to,'' she said to Maddie. ''Are you and Dylan reacquainting yourselves?'' She looked from one to the other.

''Yes, I was just telling Dylan how fond I am of you.'' She put her arm around his mother and gave her a squeeze. ''He's lucky to have you for a mom.''

''Thank you, Maddie. I do believe I'm quite lucky to have him for a son, too,'' she responded, giving Dylan an affectionate glance.

Only he saw the look in Maddie's eyes. It told him there wasn't even a slim chance she shared that sentiment.

''Well, I'm off to bed,'' Maddie announced, then she turned to Dylan. ''Hope the cold doesn't get to you.'' It was said in a cheerful way, but he knew there was a hidden message. She wasn't going to spread any warmth his way.

"I'm sure I'll survive. You forget. I lived here eighteen years. This is my home."

"Yes, it is," his mother agreed happily.

As Maddie passed him on the way out, she said in a voice meant only for his ears, "And we all know that home is the place that has to take you in."

MADDIE LAY ON HER BED flipping through the glossy pages of the latest edition of a gourmet food magazine. Not even the lure of scrumptious desserts smothered in chocolate could take her mind off what had happened this evening. No matter how hard she tried, she couldn't put Dylan Donovan out of her mind.

She wished she hadn't confronted him in the kitchen. He was right about one thing: his relationship with his mother wasn't any of her concern. Still, she'd grown very fond of Leonie and it had seemed natural to come to her defense.

Despite Dylan's claim that he hadn't intended to upset his mother, Maddie knew that whatever they'd discussed in the kitchen had taken the sparkle out of Leonie's eyes. It didn't take a psychologist to know that the joyful reunion her landlady had hoped to have with her son hadn't materialized.

Maddie didn't understand why it hadn't. As hard as she tried not to be curious about their relationship, she couldn't help but wonder what had caused Dylan to become the stray sheep of the family.

She supposed it could be his personality. He wasn't exactly the easiest man to get along with. She resented his implication that she had somehow stuck her nose into business that didn't concern her—as if being a friend to Leonie was a devious plan on her part. If Leonie hadn't come into the kitchen when she had, Maddie might just have set him straight on the subject.

A knock on her door had her looking up with apprehension. Maybe he regretted his mother's appearance, too, and wanted to continue with his warning.

Then she heard a woman's voice. ''Maddie, it's Krystal. Can I come in?''

Maddie threw her legs over the side of the bed and sat up. ''Sure. It's open.''

''I saw your light beneath the door and figured you were up,'' her housemate said as she padded into the room in her robe and slippers. ''I just had to come in and see what you thought about Dylan. Is he gorgeous or what?''

That was something she hadn't wanted to think about—Dylan's looks. He was every bit as good-looking now as he had been all those years ago and, to her dismay, when he'd walked into the living room, her body had behaved as it had all those years ago when she'd practically melted whenever he'd pass by.

''He's all right,'' she said, trying to sound disinterested.

''All right? Maddie, are you blind? That sun-streaked hair and that golden tan and those muscles.'' She sighed dreamily. ''Leonie said he worked with concrete. No kidding. He must lift a ton of blocks to get that kind of a bod.''

''I'm going to have to get you a bib if you keep talking that way,'' Maddie said dryly.

Krystal playfully punched Maddie's shoulder. "Come on. Admit it. You think he's cute."

Maddie didn't see much point in denying the obvious. "Yeah, he's attractive."

"But is he smart? Does he have a nice personality?" Krystal wanted to know. "You talked to him, didn't you?"

"We only talked for a few minutes in the kitchen," she said, not wanting to say what she really thought about the man. Krystal was single and so was Dylan. As Leonie often said, romance could happen when you least expected it and what Maddie didn't need was to say something negative about Dylan and have it end up coming back to haunt her later. "But he can't be dumb if he's an engineer," she pointed out.

"That's what I figured, too. I was hoping I'd run into him when I went downstairs to use the shower tonight, but he'd already gone to bed."

Which was exactly what Maddie wanted to hear. She'd avoided going downstairs to the bathroom for that very reason. She didn't want to risk bumping into him again this evening. One unpleasant confrontation was enough.

"It'll be nice when we don't have to use the shower downstairs," she remarked. "Having only a half bath on this floor could result in things getting a bit awkward."

"Or interesting," Krystal said with a wiggle of her brows. "I wish I'd listened more closely all those times Leonie talked about him. I thought he'd look like Shane or Garret." She held up her hands. "Don't get me wrong. It's not that I don't think they're cute, 'cause I do. It's just that Dylan is so..." Her eyes got all dreamy as she searched for the right word.

Maddie could have supplied it. *Hot.* There was no denying it. The man had *it,* whatever *it* was. Not that she cared. She wasn't fourteen anymore and she didn't respond to *it.*

"He hasn't been married, has he?" Krystal asked.

"Not that I know of."

"I can't believe he doesn't have someone waiting for him back in Saint Martin," Krystal said, sighing heavily. "Leonie says he doesn't, but look at him. Good-looking guys like that are rarely unattached."

"Just because he hasn't told his mother doesn't mean he doesn't have a girlfriend," Maddie pointed out. "But does it matter? I thought your heart belonged to the bodybuilder over at the gym."

"T.K.? I'm thinking it may be time to move on."

Maddie wondered if she was planning to move on with Dylan. Before she could ask, Krystal said, "I suppose it could get sticky, though, if I messed around with Dylan. I mean, Leonie's a dear, and I wouldn't want to create problems...you know what I mean?"

"I think you're right on with that one," Maddie agreed. "Mothers can get funny over their sons."

Krystal nodded her head in agreement. "I once dated this guy who had a really neat mom. She treated me just like a daughter until she found out we'd been talking about marriage. Then she went ballistic. Started cussing at me and telling me I wasn't good enough for her little boy."

"I don't think Leonie would be like that."

Krystal thought for a moment, then said, "No,

you're probably right, but I still wouldn't want to screw up a great housing arrangement.'' She sighed. ''At least Dylan will make good eye candy for these cold, gray days of winter.''

As much as Maddie wanted to deny it, she knew her housemate was right. Only she wasn't going out of her way for any visual treats. She'd do her best to avoid him, even if it meant disappointing Leonie by being absent in the kitchen. She was determined that when she shared a house with Dylan, this time she was not going to become infatuated with him.

Once in a lifetime was enough for her. Besides, she already had one man in her life. Jeffrey, who was a dear friend. That's all she wanted in a relationship right now. It was all she could handle. She needed to figure out what she was going to do with the rest of her life before she could look at men as anything other than friends.

Unfortunately as she drifted off to sleep, it wasn't Jeffrey's face in her thoughts. It was the man she wanted to forget—Dylan.

CHAPTER THREE

Dear Leonie: It's been fourteen years since I had my first crush on a guy. Now I'm twenty-eight and he's back in my life and all those old feelings have come rushing back. I don't want to feel anything for him. What should I do?
Signed: Wanting to forget the past

Leonie says: You're only attracted to him because he rekindles those adolescent feelings of first love. My bet is once you spend a little time with him you'll realize that's all it was—puppy love.

THERE WAS ONLY a two-hour time difference between Minnesota and Saint Martin, yet Dylan awoke feeling as if he had jet lag. Maybe it was because he'd had a restless night. Strange beds often did that to him.

Or it could have been his guilty conscience that had caused him to toss and turn last night. He should have apologized to his mother before saying good-night to her, but his confrontation with Maddie had left him in a sour mood and, instead of focusing on the matter of most importance—his mother—he'd been preoccupied with thoughts of the belly-dance teacher.

But that was last night and today would be different

he vowed as he showered and shaved. When he walked into the kitchen his mother was alone at the table, reading the paper.

At the sight of him she smiled. "You look much better this morning. See what a good night's sleep will do for you?"

He chuckled to himself. *If she only knew.*

"Smells good in here. Like oranges." Before she could speak he held up his hands. "Don't tell me. Maddie made orange bread before she went to work this morning."

She clicked her tongue in admonition. "No, she did not. I just ate an orange. The peeling is still on the counter." She nodded toward the cabinets.

"Sorry." He gave her apologetic smile. "Mom, about last night..." he began. "There's something I think you should know."

"If it's about you and Maddie having words, Dylan, I already know about it. She told me this morning."

So Maddie had already talked to his mother about their confrontation. Dylan could see she was going to be a more formidable opponent than he'd expected.

"Well, I can see one thing hasn't changed. She's just as annoying now as she was at fourteen," he remarked.

That had his mother gasping. "She most certainly is not annoying!"

He held up his hands in surrender. "All right. She's not."

"She's a dear and if you must know, I'm surprised by your behavior toward her last night," his mother chastised him.

"*My* behavior toward *her?*" He should have known she'd come to Maddie's defense, not his. "In case you hadn't noticed, Mom, it takes two to disagree."

"And just what was this disagreement about?"

"She didn't tell you?"

"No."

So she hadn't run to his mother with her version of what had been said. She went up a notch in his estimation, but only a small notch. He still found her irritating.

"It was nothing important, Mom. We just rubbed each other the wrong way, sort of like what happened the summer she stayed with us. Remember how she'd always bristle when I'd talk to her?"

"No, I don't." She gave him a blank look. "I only remember her being very sweet and shy and having to put up with the roughness of four boys who at times could be a bit overbearing even for their own mother."

"Well, there's only one Donovan boy at home now, so that shouldn't be a problem. I know you're very fond of Maddie. I'm sorry about last night and I promise I'm going to do everything I can to not repeat what happened."

His mother stared at him, her finger on her chin. "You know, that's nearly the same thing she said to me this morning."

"Great. Then we're in agreement on something." He went over to the refrigerator and pulled out a carton of milk.

"I know you had a long day yesterday because the plane was delayed, and you weren't yourself. Why don't we just forget about last night and start over?" she said with her usual optimism.

"I'd like that. I know I said some things I shouldn't have," he told her as he poured himself a glass of milk. "Not just to Maddie but to you as well. If I upset you, I'm sorry. I was tired and I wasn't expecting to find so many things had changed around here. I had the weird feeling that this wasn't home anymore."

"It hasn't been your home in a long time, Dylan," she reminded him gently.

"I know and I had no right to act as if you'd done something wrong by getting on with your life. The house looks great and so do you. I should have said that as soon as I saw you."

She smiled warmly. "Thank you." Then she got up to give him a hug. "Have I told you how happy I am that you decided to have the surgery here? As long as I own this house you'll always be able to call it home."

"I appreciate that, Mom."

"Being home will be good for you. You'll see," she said with confidence. "I know there have been a lot of changes, but there's a lot of things that are the same."

"I can see one thing that hasn't changed. You still know how to make a kid feel better with words," he said with an affectionate grin.

She smiled, too. "I've had lots of practice. Now, would you like me to make you some breakfast?"

"No, I'm fine. I don't eat much in the morning," he answered, then drained the milk from his glass.

"That hasn't changed, has it? You were always in

too much of a hurry to take time for breakfast when you were a kid. I still make a pretty good omelette.'' She tried to tempt him.

''I'm sure you do. Maybe another morning? Now tell me why you're all dressed up,'' he ordered with a cocked eyebrow. ''You look nice, by the way.''

''Thank you. This is a new outfit. I have several appointments today.''

''Ah, business,'' he said in a knowing tone.

She fixed him with a questioning gaze. ''Does it bother you that I'm a romance coach?''

He didn't want to tell her the truth, yet he couldn't lie to her, either. ''I'm not exactly bothered by it, Mom, but I wasn't expecting to come home and find you so involved with your work.''

''I needed something to fill my days. Dad's gone, you kids are all gone...'' She trailed off. ''I like people too much to sit home by myself.''

''I thought maybe you would have gone to work for Shane when he took over the business.''

She wrinkled her face. ''I never really liked doing tax forms.''

''Then why did you do it all those years?''

''Because I liked working with your father.'' A contented look came into her eyes. ''Sometimes even the most tedious tasks don't seem so bad when they're shared with the one you love.''

Talk of her love for his father always made him uncomfortable and this time was no different. Ignorance may have been bliss for his mother, but for Dylan, knowledge of his father's infidelity continued to color his perception of his parents' marriage.

He didn't want to think about that, so he said, "Then it's a good thing you tried something different. It's obviously been good for you because you seem happy."

"I am happy, but I still miss him," she said, a note of sadness in her voice.

He placed an arm around her and gave her a gentle hug. "I'm sorry I couldn't be here for you those first few months after he died."

"There's no need to apologize," she said, patting his hand. "I understand why you kept your distance."

At the time he had thought he had, too, but now he wasn't so sure. He'd told himself that if he were to spend any time with his mother, there was bound to be more tension between him and Shane. Yet now that he was actually home, he wasn't sure if there hadn't been another reason for his absence. Maybe he had stayed away because he hadn't wanted to share in his mother's grief, hadn't wanted to hear her eulogize his father as an ideal husband.

"That's all in the past," his mother continued. "You're home now and I want to enjoy every minute of your stay. Will you be seeing Garret today?"

"I have a doctor's appointment this morning, but then I'm going to stop by the hospital so we can have lunch."

"You can take Dad's car. It's in the garage. Jason's been using it when he's been home, so it's in good running condition." She reached for a set of car keys dangling from a hook on the wall and set them down on the table, saying, "I have a favor to ask you."

"Ask away."

She pulled several plastic gallon containers from under the sink. "Maddie left this morning without taking these. Would you be a dear and drop them off for me?"

"Drop them off where?"

"Remember Ken's Market, that small family grocery near the hospital? It's now community owned."

"It's a co-op?"

She nodded, setting the jugs on the table next to the keys. "They sell spring water, but you have to supply your own containers."

"You want me to fill them and bring them home?"

"Or you can leave them with Maddie and she'll take care of it."

"She works at the co-op?"

"Mmm-hmm. In the deli."

So Maddie was a belly-dancing teacher at night and a deli clerk during the day. Not exactly what he had expected she'd be doing for a living.

"You need me to pick up anything else?" he asked.

"No, that'll do it." She placed her fingers on the upper portion of the refrigerator. "There are frozen dinners in here and there are cold cuts, too, if you want to make yourself a sandwich for dinner."

"Dinner? Aren't you going to be here?"

She shook her head. "Tonight's my class at the community center. I would have canceled, but it's my first one and I thought I'd better not."

"What class is that?"

"The keys to making love last."

"They actually offer a class like that through community ed?"

She gave him a look of admonition. "Love is a very important thing in people's lives. If you look at the statistics, Dylan, you'll see that most people still believe in marriage." She gave him a gentle shove so she could get to the door. "I'll tell you more about it when we have more time. I have all sorts of interesting statistics I can share with you."

Dylan didn't want to tell her that he really wasn't interested in hearing any numbers when it came to love and marriage. Fortunately, the phone rang and he didn't have to come up with a response.

The call was brief and as soon as she'd hung up, she said, "I have to get going. I have an extra stop to make. Try not to leave the kitchen a mess, will you? We have a rule around here. Everyone cleans up after herself."

"Mom, I haven't become a slob since I left home," he told her.

"I didn't think you had, but I need to consider my tenants."

He frowned. "Are you saying they'll be eating their meals in the kitchen?"

"Krystal won't be home tonight. She's going to a convention in Saint Cloud and will be staying overnight, but Maddie should be back after she finishes her classes."

He wanted to ask his mother about Maddie's classes, but swallowed his curiosity. He didn't think she would understand the reason for his inquisitiveness.

He didn't understand it himself. All he knew was that since he'd seen Maddie in those harem pants with that turquoise jewel winking at him from her navel, he'd had trouble forgetting that she lived upstairs. And now that he knew she ate her meals in the kitchen, his imagination was already working on possible scenarios in which he might see her again.

As he left the house, he made sure he took the plastic jugs.

DYLAN WASN'T QUITE SURE what kind of a reception he'd get from Garret, but he was glad when it turned out to be a warm one. As the young doctor came down the hall toward him, he wore a big grin.

"I can tell you're a doctor now, Garret. You're late," Dylan said with a teasing grin.

The younger man smiled, then gave him a bear hug. "There literally aren't enough hours in a day in this profession. Welcome home, Dylan. It's good to see you. How's the shoulder?"

"Your friend Pete says it'll be as good as new after he goes in and does his handiwork," he answered, stepping aside so they were no longer in the center of the corridor. He studied his brother. "You look tired."

"That's the way I'm supposed to look. I'm a resident." He nudged Dylan toward the stairs. "You look like you've been leading the good life."

He spread his hands. "What can I say? I live on an island in the Caribbean. I thought by now you would have come to visit me."

"Don't think I wouldn't have liked to, but I'm short on two things. Time and money. And until I'm finished with my residency, that's not going to change."

"I could help you out in the money department," Dylan offered.

"Thanks, I appreciate the offer, but time is the real villain here. Speaking of which," he glanced at his watch. "We need to make this lunch a quick one."

"I guess that means we don't get to pop across the street for a big thick juicy burger?" he quipped.

Garret smiled apologetically and said, "The hospital cafeteria makes a great tuna hot dish."

Dylan grimaced, then followed his brother into the dining area. "I guess I should get used to this," he said as they passed a section of Jell-O and pudding. "It's going to be my diet while I'm here."

Garret chuckled. "I hope you're going to be a better patient than Jason was. You should have heard the moaning and groaning that kid did when he had his appendix out."

Since Garret had mentioned their youngest brother, Dylan decided to steer the conversation toward family. As they sat down at a small table, he asked, "Is Jason doing all right? I know he was in some trouble last semester with his grades."

"Mom told you?"

He nodded. "Yeah. It's not a secret, is it?"

Garret shrugged. "No. I just didn't think you knew about it, that's all," he said as he removed the items from his tray and set it aside.

"So is Jason doing all right?"

"Yeah. He's just trying to figure out what he wants to do with his life. There are so many opportunities, so many choices to make. It isn't easy being nineteen."

"As we both know," Dylan agreed, slipping his jacket over the back of the chair before sitting down.

"It's that emotional tug-of-war every college kid goes through—wanting to be independent, yet liking the security of still being able to be a dependent on the folks. One minute he's saying, "I can take care of myself. The next he's calling Mom and moaning about the latest crisis in his life."

"You mean like when he needs money," Dylan remarked dryly.

"It's not just money. Mom handles things pretty well, but it's too bad Dad isn't here. Jason could use a good role model," he said, ripping open the cellophane wrapping on his soda crackers and crumbling them into his soup.

Dylan would have liked to point out that their father wasn't exactly a good role model, but he didn't want their reunion to be spoiled by the animosity such a remark would create.

So he let the comment about their father slide and said, "I'll talk to Jason while I'm here and see what I can do."

"You don't need to worry about it. Shane and I are keeping an eye on him."

"You don't want me talking to him?"

He shrugged. "I didn't say that. I just think it might be better if you didn't try to be an authority figure."

Dylan frowned. "Why not?"

"He's belligerent enough the way it is and you two haven't exactly been close. You left home when he was only six."

Dylan felt the hairs on his neck raise. He knew he

had no reason to be defensive, but that didn't matter. "It's not my fault that there are twelve years difference in our ages. I left home at eighteen because it was time for me to leave."

"Yeah, I know. I didn't say you abandoned him," he reminded Dylan. "I just said you weren't here when he was growing up."

"He's still my brother and I care about him."

"All of us do. And as I said, Shane and I have already had a talk with him about his grades."

So you don't need to, was the unspoken message that came through loud and clear. "I still would like to take a drive over to Wisconsin to see him. I'll have the time once the surgery's over."

"Mom would probably appreciate it if you did, but you'd better be prepared to get a lecture from him on how he's not a kid anymore and he can take care of himself. He doesn't want anyone checking up on him," he warned.

"I'm not going to check up on him," he said with a hint of impatience. "I just want to visit him and see how he's doing. Any other warnings you want to give me?" Dylan tried to keep his voice light but failed.

"Actually, there is. It's about Mom." He set his spoon down and stared at Dylan. "She was really upset by the way things went the last time you were home. The stuff that went on between you and Shane—"

Dylan interrupted him. "I've already had this conversation with Shane, and we've worked things out, so let it rest, okay?" He was disappointed to sense that Garret seemed to be on Shane's side.

"Good. I'm glad to hear that. We're brothers. We should act like it."

There was a bit of an uncomfortable silence, which was broken by a nurse who stopped by to give Garret a message. When she eyed Dylan curiously, Garret made the introductions.

After a few minutes of small talk, she was gone and Garret said, "I can see you haven't lost the touch."

"Touch for what?"

"If you'd patted your knee she would have sat on your lap." He shook his head. "Man, you have always had a quality that women respond to."

"She stopped by to talk to you," Dylan pointed out.

Garret chuckled. "Yeah, and if you believe that, I have some nice oceanfront property in South Dakota I can sell you." He took a sip of his coffee, then said, "I don't suppose these northern girls have the same appeal as those sun-kissed, bikini-clad island beauties running around on Saint Martin."

Dylan smiled. "A beautiful woman is a beautiful woman, no matter what the climate."

"And you've always had an eye for one, haven't you," he said with a sly smile. He took a bite of his sandwich, then asked. "How many are there in your life? Still juggling more than one at a time?"

"What makes you think I have any?"

He chuckled. "Come on. I may be five years younger than you, but I did know what was going on when we were kids. By the time I hit junior high your reputation with women was legendary."

Dylan couldn't suppress his smile. "All right, so I

made the most of my youth and the opportunities that presented themselves.''

''Are you saying you don't have those opportunities now?''

Dylan shook his head. ''If I had kept going at that pace, I'd be dead.''

''So it's one woman at a time now?''

''It always was. They just came closer together back then,'' he said with another grin.

''Come on, be serious. Is there a special woman in your life?''

''Not at the moment.''

''I thought Mom said there was someone named Andrea.''

''*Was* is the correct word. That didn't work out,'' Dylan said, not wanting to tell him the details of a relationship he had already put in the past.

''What about you? Last time I was home you seemed pretty serious about another med student. A Sarah with auburn hair, nice legs.''

He shook his head. ''It didn't work out, which is probably good because I really don't have time for anything but medicine right now.''

''Then Mom hasn't tried to find you the perfect mate?''

''She's not a matchmaker, Dylan. She only responds to those who seek her advice. Mom would never try to interfere in our love lives. She's not like that.''

''I'm glad to hear that. The last thing I need is to have Mom trying to fix me up with someone. It's going to be difficult enough staying in a house full of women. I'm used to living alone.''

Garret shook his head. ''It's hard to think of you living alone. I mean, I guess I just assumed you lived with some woman but didn't tell us.''

Dylan chuckled. ''I've had a few try to move their things into my closet, but they haven't made it past the front door.''

''At least with the remodeling Mom's done, Maddie and Krystal shouldn't get in your way. What do you think of what she's done to the house?''

''It was a bit of a shock at first, but I think it looks good.''

He nodded in agreement. ''It was a good project for her. Shane offered to deal with the contractors, but she insisted on doing it all herself. And she did just fine, although I think Maddie helped her.''

Mention of the other woman gave Dylan the opportunity to ask the questions he hadn't wanted to ask his mother. ''How did Madeline Lamont end up renting from Mom? I thought she only took in college students.''

''Maddie was Mom's first boarder. She came here shortly after Dad died. She was with some theater production that came to the Twin Cities.''

''She's an actress?''

''A dancer.''

''Is that what she does for a living?''

''She's not performing anymore, just teaching.''

Again the image of Maddie dressed in the harem pants flashed in Dylan's memory. ''There's a big demand for belly dancing in the Twin Cities?''

''Not belly dancing. Ballet,'' he corrected. ''The belly dancing is something she does on the side.

Mainly she teaches kids ballet and tap at a studio just a few blocks from here.''

''Mom said something about her working at a food co-op, too,'' he went on. ''Is she one of those health food nuts who won't eat anything that isn't organically grown?''

''Just because she's conscious about her health doesn't make her a nut. And why all the questions about her anyway?'' He paused with his fork in midair. ''You're not thinking that she might be a pleasant distraction while you're here, are you?''

He clicked his tongue. ''If she's a distraction it won't be the pleasant kind.''

''Why not? She's hot and she's smart. What more could a man want? And she can still beat me at chess.''

Dylan agreed with his brother about her being hot but kept his opinion to himself. ''She may be your type, but she's definitely not mine,'' he told Garret, wanting to dispel any notion Garret had that he was interested in the woman.

''I'm glad to hear that, because she's taken.'' There was no mistaking the warning in his brother's voice.

''By you?'' Dylan asked with a sly smile.

''No, but she does date a very good friend of mine.''

''Well, your friend has nothing to worry about from me. Even if I were looking for a woman—which I'm not—I wouldn't be looking in Madeline's direction. If anything, I'll be doing my best to avoid her as much as possible.''

He stared at him in amazement. ''That's the first

time I've ever heard anyone say that about Maddie. It might be a good idea if you didn't share your opinion of her with Mom. She regards Maddie as the daughter she never had.''

''So I've noticed.''

''You sound as if you disapprove.''

''I'm just worried about Mom, that's all. I'd hate to see her be taken advantage of by anyone.''

Garret laughed. ''You don't need to worry about that with Maddie.''

''You sound awfully confident.''

''That's because I am.'' He'd already finished his lunch and shoved aside his plate, resting on his elbows as he asked, ''Have you met Krystal?''

Dylan shrugged. ''Other than a brief introduction, we haven't talked,'' he answered honestly. ''Why?''

Just then Garret pushed his lab coat aside to reach for the beeper on his waist. ''I'm being paged. I have to go.'' He quickly drained the remains of his coffee and was about to load his dishes back on the tray when Dylan stopped him.

''I'll get them. You go attend to your emergency.''

Garret smiled. ''Thanks.'' Before he left he said, ''I'll try to stop by the house tonight, but if I don't, I'll see you in the morning before you go into surgery.''

Dylan nodded.

As he walked out of the cafeteria, he called over his shoulder, ''Don't worry about a thing. Pete's the best.''

Dylan hadn't been thinking about his upcoming surgery. He was thinking about Maddie.

As he climbed into his father's car, he noticed the plastic water jugs in the back seat of the car. He didn't have to give them to Maddie. He could fill the jugs himself and leave without even seeing her.

There were only two problems. One was that he didn't want to stand in line to fill water jugs. The second was, he wanted to see her.

MADDIE NOTICED Dylan the minute he entered the store. He wore khaki slacks and a dark brown leather aviator jacket. Despite the below-zero windchill, his head was bare, his sun-streaked hair in disarray from the wind. Just as it had last night, when she first saw him, her heart skipped a beat.

"I'd like half a pound of baby Swiss cheese," a customer said, drawing her attention back to the deli case in front of her.

Maddie lifted the cheese from the refrigerated case and slid the block onto the slicer, aware that Dylan was headed in her direction. Before she had finished the woman's order, he was at the deli counter.

She could feel his eyes on her as she worked. As hard as she tried, she couldn't keep from sneaking a peek at him. He looked like a surfer who'd taken the wrong flight and ended up in the land of snow and ice instead of sunshine and beaches.

When her customer left, she had no choice but to give her attention to him. "What can I do for you?" she asked, trying to keep her voice level, which wasn't easy considering the way her breath wanted to catch in her throat.

"Mom asked me to drop these off." He held up the

plastic jugs. "Said you'd know what to do with them."

When she took them from him, their fingers touched. His were cold, hers warm, which she figured accounted for the tiny shiver she felt. "Thanks."

"Mom never bought water when we were growing up," he commented. "We drank it straight from the tap."

"No one realized the problems with lead pipes back then," she responded, setting the jugs on the floor behind her.

"So this is where you work," he said, giving a cursory glance around the store.

She spread her arms. "This is it."

"The store's changed quite a bit since I was a kid." She didn't comment, but waited for him to speak again. He turned his attention to the food in the refrigerated case. "Why don't you give me one of those small cartons of coleslaw."

She reached for a half-pint container and filled it with coleslaw. Her movements were sharp as she slapped a couple of spoonfuls into the cup. She could feel his eyes on her and she hurried so he could take his purchase and leave.

As she set the carton on the counter, she asked, "Anything else?"

"Yes. I'd like to start over." His eyes were a warm brown and the message in them made her uncomfortable.

It said, "I'm a man and you're an attractive woman." She didn't want to see that kind of look in his eyes. He was her landlady's son and that was how she planned to regard him. ''You don't want the coleslaw?'' she asked, deliberately misunderstanding him.

''I'm not talking about the coleslaw. I'm talking about last night. There's no point in pretending it didn't happen, Maddie. If we're going to live under the same roof for the next month or so, don't you think it would be a good idea if we made a fresh start?'' The words were delivered with the ease of a man who was no stranger to negotiation and compromise.

She knew that to do anything but agree would be ill-mannered. ''All right. I'm willing to forget about last night.''

''What about fourteen years ago? Can you forget about that, too?''

She frowned. ''I don't know what you mean.''

''You didn't like me very much back then, either.'' He didn't look offended by the statement, but rather amused.

She folded her arms across her chest. ''That's not the best way to make a new beginning—by bringing up the past.'' She didn't see any need to correct him regarding the feelings she'd had for him as a fourteen-year-old.

''We're not exactly strangers, Maddie.''

She didn't need him to tell her that. The minute she'd seen him last night, memories of that summer had come flooding back. She knew more about Dylan Donovan than she cared to admit.

''How do you suggest we make a new beginning?'' he asked. Again there was that interest in his eye that had the nerves in Maddie's body rising to alarm status.

''Maybe we say we both misunderstood each other last night and just start over,'' she suggested.

He stared at her, those penetrating brown eyes making her want to squirm. She didn't. She stood her ground, arms folded, chin up, meeting his eyes squarely. She was twenty-eight, not fourteen. She didn't need to run and hide from any man.

''I can do that,'' he told her with a grin that made her stomach do a funny little flutter.

''Good. Then we start over,'' she stated evenly.

''We start over,'' he repeated.

She wondered if that meant he'd finally pick up the coleslaw and leave, but he didn't. He said, ''I know we agree on one thing.''

''And that would be—?''

''We want my mom to be happy, right?''

''Right,'' she agreed.

''You must know I didn't come home to upset her,'' he said with a questioning look in his eyes.

''And I haven't lived with her the past year and a half so that I could take advantage of her.'' The look in her eyes dared him to challenge that statement. He didn't and she added, ''That is what you were thinking, isn't it? You don't like the fact that your mom and I are close, do you?''

''I didn't say that,'' he denied.

''You don't have to.'' She took a deep breath to steady her emotions. ''Dylan, your mother's not some helpless, naive widow. She not only runs a boardinghouse, but she runs her own business, too. She's nobody's fool.''

To her surprise, he said, "I do believe you're right."

"I am."

He grinned then and Maddie's heart skipped more than one beat.

"You and I managed to live under the same roof without any problems when we were teenagers, Maddie. We should be able to do the same as adults, don't you think?"

She almost said no. Every instinct in her told her Dylan Donovan could be big trouble for any woman.

"I don't see why not," she lied.

As if he knew she wasn't sincere, he said, "It's a big house."

Not big enough.

"And it's only temporary," he added. "Who knows? My shoulder may heal faster than expected and I might not even be here this time next month."

She should be so lucky.

"I'm used to living alone, fending for myself. I don't need to be entertained," he continued.

As if she was even interested in trying to entertain him.

"I only say that because, knowing my mom, she may have different ideas." He smoothed a hand over the back of his neck. "It's going to be embarrassing if she tries to arrange social activities for me."

"She hasn't done it for any of your brothers, so I don't think you have anything to worry about," she assured him. Not that he needed any assistance from anyone in that department. She doubted he had trouble finding female companions.

Noticing a customer approaching, Dylan finally picked up the small container of coleslaw. ''I'd better pay for this. I'm glad we cleared the air, Maddie,'' he said with a grin that gave her a glimpse of the charm he could exude if he chose.

She didn't like what that smile did to her insides. She had no doubt that Dylan Donovan, should he choose, could be one irresistible man.

''Me, too,'' she said, grateful for the customer waiting for her attention. ''It's good we settled this.''

''Yes, it is.'' He extended his hand to her.

Unlike the first time their fingers had touched, his hand was warm. She'd barely placed hers inside his when she pulled it back. She hoped he thought the brevity of their handshake was due to the fact that there was a customer waiting for service. What she didn't want him to know was that it'd been an instinctive defense mechanism. She didn't like the pleasant sensation that contact had created.

She wasn't fourteen and he wasn't some heartthrob who could make her go weak in the knees. He was nothing at all like the kind of man she wanted to arouse her interest.

If he thought she'd be seeking his company while he was home, he was sadly mistaken. She'd do whatever she could to avoid having to spend any time with Dylan Donovan, even if it meant volunteering for extra hours at the co-op.

''How much is the farmer's cheese?'' A voice interrupted her musings.

Maddie was forced to turn her attention back to the

deli case, but not before she took one more glance in the cashier's direction. She noticed Dylan was smiling at the woman behind the counter. Maddie was certain that the woman smiled back.

CHAPTER FOUR

Dear Leonie: I'm attracted to this guy and I don't want to be. I'm doing everything I can to avoid running into him, but it's as if fate keeps putting him in my path. What can I do?
Signed: Wishing I could be invisible

Leonie says: Are you sure you really want to get out of his way?

ONE OF THE THINGS Maddie liked best about living in Leonie's house was that Leonie made her tenants feel as if they were part of her family. Although Maddie and Krystal both had their own rooms on the second floor, there were many nights when all three women would gather downstairs in Leonie's living room. It's where Maddie and Krystal were when Leonie returned from the hospital the following evening.

"How's Dylan?" Maddie asked when she entered the room.

"He's doing fine. The doctor says he'll be able to come home tomorrow," Leonie said, shrugging out of her coat.

"We were just going to watch a chick flick. Want to join us?" Krystal asked.

Leonie glanced at the big bowl on the coffee table. ''Is that popcorn buttered?''

Maddie grinned mischievously. ''Yes, and we're drinking real Coke, not diet. It's so much fun to be bad.''

''Come on, Leonie. Join us,'' Krystal urged. ''We've rented a romantic comedy starring Joseph Fiennes. He is sooo cute.'' She sighed. ''And when the popcorn's gone, we're going to have hot-fudge sundaes.''

Leonie chuckled. ''Oh, you girls do want to be bad, don't you?'' Maddie could see her resolve weakening. ''All right. You convinced me, but first I need to take care of a few things. Will you give me fifteen minutes to change my clothes?''

''Take your time,'' Maddie called out to her departing figure.

But she didn't take very long at all. And when she returned, she hadn't changed her clothes.

''You're never going to believe who I just talked to,'' she said in a breathless voice. ''The producer of the Rob Lerner show. He wants me to come to California and tape a Valentine's Day segment.''

Krystal shrieked. ''Oh my gosh, that is so cool! Do you know how many people watch that show?''

Maddie didn't watch a lot of TV, but she did know that Rob Lerner was a comedian who hosted a late-night talk show that consistently scored high in the ratings. ''That is good news, Leonie. What exactly did he say?''

''I'm so stunned I can hardly remember. Luckily I took notes.'' Leonie waved a pink slip of paper in midair. "Apparently they're going to be doing a special segment for Valentine's Day and they want me to be a part of it. I'm supposed to give tips on how to make the day more special for the one you love." She paused, pushing her finger to her lips. "Of course, just because I'm there for the taping doesn't mean I won't get edited out before the program is aired."

"They wouldn't fly you out there if they didn't intend to have you on the show. They'd interview you over the phone," Maddie said reassuringly. "When do they want you?"

Her face fell. "Well, that's the problem. They want to tape the segment this weekend."

Krystal looked at her anxiously. "You're going to go, aren't you?"

"How can I? Dylan's going to be here," she reminded them. "He came home mainly because I told him he could recuperate here."

"Can't he go to Shane's?" Maddie asked.

Leonie immediately shook her head. "Oh, no. That wouldn't work. The house is small and Jennifer works those odd hours. Besides, Dylan wouldn't want me to ask Shane. No, that definitely wouldn't work."

"What about Garret?" Krystal suggested. "You said he offered to let Dylan stay at his place when he first suggested he come home for the surgery."

"He did, but realistically, it wouldn't work." Again Leonie shook her head. "You know the kind of hours Garret puts in as a resident. Dylan would spend most of his time alone." She glanced down at the slip of paper and sighed. "This would have been fun, but the truth is I'm not the Hollywood type and I don't need to be on the Rob Lerner program. Dylan's probably right. I should decline."

"You've already talked to Dylan about it?" Maddie asked.

She nodded. "I called him right away to get his advice. He told me the decision was mine to make, but he had his reservations."

Maddie wondered if they weren't motivated by his desire to have his mother nurse him back to good health. If they were, Leonie needed to hear another opinion.

"I don't think you should pass up such an opportunity," she told Leonie. "Do you realize what a few minutes of TV exposure could do for your business?"

Leonie nodded. "I know millions of people watch the Rob Lerner show and it would be exciting...." She trailed off.

"So why are you hesitating?" Maddie asked. "Leonie, you can't not go just because Dylan doesn't think it's a good idea."

"But I asked him to come here to recuperate. It wouldn't be right for me to leave him alone so soon after he's out of the hospital," she said with a look of regret in her eyes.

"He won't be alone. We'll be here," Krystal pointed out. "We can make sure he gets something to eat and anything else he needs, for that matter."

Maddie wanted to say, *Speak for yourself,* but held her tongue. Krystal's words produced a spark of hope in her landlady's eyes that had Maddie remaining silent.

"It's generous of you two to offer, but—" began the older woman, only to have Krystal cut her short.

"But nothing. With everything you've done for us, you're not going to tell us we can't do you a favor." Krystal looked at Maddie. "Isn't that right?"

"Yes," Maddie had no choice but to agree because she knew it was the truth. When she'd twisted her ankle, Leonie had canceled her plans to spend a few days with friends at a resort in northern Minnesota so that she could take Maddie to physical therapy.

"What about work? You both have jobs to go to this weekend." Leonie's brow wrinkled in concern.

"The shop is close enough that I can come home on my breaks to check on Dylan," Krystal stated.

Curious, Maddie asked, "How much care does he need?"

"With his arm in a sling, he only has use of one hand and unfortunately it's his left one," Leonie answered. "Plus he needs help with his exercises."

"What kind of exercises?"

Leonie shrugged. "I don't know. Whatever they have you do after shoulder surgery."

"I'm sure we can do it." Krystal's voice had a confidence Maddie didn't share. "Leonie, you have to go to California," she stated emphatically.

Leonie hesitated, her teeth sinking into her lower lip. "You're sure you don't mind looking after Dylan while I'm gone?" She looked from Maddie to Krystal.

"Of course we don't," Krystal spoke for both of them.

"Do you really think it'll be okay?" Leonie sought

reassurance and Krystal gave her a gentle nudge in the back.

"Go make that phone call," she ordered her landlady, who acquiesced with a smile and went scurrying out of the room. Krystal looked at Maddie and said, "This is so exciting, isn't it?"

Maddie truly was happy for Leonie, but she had a hard time sharing Krystal's enthusiasm. It might turn out to be a great weekend for her housemate and her landlady, but she didn't see how it could be anything but a big headache for her—unless she left all the nursing duties to Krystal and saw as little of Dylan as possible.

But she knew that at some point during the weekend she was going to have to either help him with his exercises or get him something to eat. The latter would be the easier task, as she could prepare the food ahead of time and put it in the freezer. She smiled to herself at the thought of him sitting alone in the kitchen with a microwaved frozen dinner on his plate.

At least he'd get *good* frozen dinners. It was more than he deserved. Much more. Especially after trying to talk Leonie out of going to California. *That* still annoyed Maddie and she thought it would serve him right if no one lifted a finger to help him all weekend.

Except someone would wait on him—Krystal. Maddie should have been happy that her housemate wanted to play Florence Nightingale. It meant Maddie wouldn't have to spend much time with him. And that was what she wanted.

Wasn't it? That was a question she didn't want to examine too closely.

NOT SINCE HE WAS A CHILD had Dylan needed anyone to help him put on his clothes or eat his dinner. For the past thirteen years he'd traveled the world, lived in foreign countries and worked a variety of jobs in which he'd relied on nobody but himself. And that's the way he liked it. He didn't want to be dependent on anyone for anything, which was why he hated being in the hospital.

He wanted to feel like his old self again. To be in control.

However, he discovered independence didn't necessarily come with his signature on a hospital release form. The staff insisted he leave the building in a wheelchair, which made him feel even more helpless. Then his mother picked him up at the front door, fussing over him as if he were an invalid.

"You're in pain, aren't you?" she said, when he winced as he fastened the seat belt.

"Mom, I'm fine," he assured her, determined not to let his shoulder prevent him from doing the simplest of tasks.

"I don't think you are. Maybe I should cancel my trip to California."

"No, you don't need to do that. I said I'm fine and I mean it. I'm fine," he barked at her and then immediately felt remorse. "I'm sorry, Mom. I didn't mean to snap at you. I just hate that I can't take care of things myself."

She made a soothing sound and patted his hand. "You're just like your father. He didn't want to be dependent on anyone, either."

The comparison to his father only fueled his frustrations. "You're wrong. I'm not like him."

She didn't say anything but started up the car. The silence stretched uncomfortably and again he found himself apologizing. "I'm sorry, Mom. I should probably have had this surgery in Florida. You don't need me grumbling."

"You'll feel better once you're home," she said in her usual cheery way. "Everyone gets a little testy when they're in pain. They say the first few days after surgery are the hardest."

"If that's true, it's a good thing you're going to California this weekend. If I'm going to be ornery, I might as well be alone."

"I'm still wondering if it's a mistake for me to leave," she said apprehensively.

"Don't give it a second thought. I'll be fine."

"It's not you I'm worried about. It's Krystal and Maddie. If you treat them the way you've treated those nice nurses at the hospital..." She shook her head.

"There's an easy solution. Tell them I don't need their help."

She clicked her tongue. "Now you're being ridiculous. You know as well as I do that you need someone to help you with your exercises. You heard what the doctor said about the importance of doing them correctly."

"It's not that big a deal. I have the diagrams. I'm sure I can manage by myself."

"And will you manage to cook for yourself, too? Seeing as it's your right hand in the sling, how do you plan to do that?"

"I can eat frozen dinners. It only takes one hand to punch a microwave button. Mom, I just want to be left alone for a few days. I can take care of myself until you get back."

"Now you're being stubborn."

"No, I'm not," he denied. "I just don't want anyone hovering over me as if I'm some kind of invalid."

"Maddie and Krystal won't hover. They won't even be around that much. They have work to do."

He shifted in his seat, unable to get comfortable. "I just wish you hadn't asked them to look out for me."

"I didn't ask. They volunteered."

He cast her a sideways glance. "Are you sure Maddie volunteered?"

"I didn't ask her to look after you, if that's what you're thinking. I don't understand why you get so touchy whenever I mention her name."

He knew there was no point in answering, so he simply leaned his head back and closed his eyes while she recited a list of Maddie's virtues. He would have preferred to forget about his mother's tenant, but he found himself thinking back to his encounter with her at the co-op.

He'd thought the reason he'd found her attractive the first night he'd come home was her belly-dancing costume. But then he'd seen her with her hair pulled back in a net and a large butcher's apron covering nearly all of her, and he'd realized that it hadn't simply been her state of dress that had aroused his interest.

She had an appeal that had nothing to do with her physical appearance. There was something in the way she looked at him, a silent message that told him if he wanted to do battle, she was ready. She wasn't exactly feisty, but she certainly wasn't the shy kid he remembered, either. It had been a long time since he'd met a woman who truly intrigued him.

And as much as he hated to admit it, Maddie did pique his curiosity. But that didn't mean he wanted her nursing his injured shoulder. He shuddered. He needed rest, not to have his blood pressure rise—or to have any other kind of physical reaction every time she came in the room. It was the latter response that bothered him most.

"The next couple of days are important to your recovery, Dylan." His mother's voice broke into his musings. "You need to remember that and follow the doctor's instructions. Maddie and Krystal have been kind enough to help you do that, so please be gracious and accept their help."

"I won't do anything to embarrass you," he promised even though he knew that when it came to Maddie, he shouldn't be making any such statement.

He sighed as he thought about the weekend ahead of him. It didn't matter if his shoulder was out of commission. He didn't need a woman to take care of him. He could take care of himself. He always had and he always would. Maddie Lamont would discover that for herself.

LEONIE LEFT Friday morning. Maddie offered to take her to the airport, but Krystal insisted she be the one to see that their landlady caught her plane on time.

Before she left, Leonie sat them both down and explained that Dylan was not the best of patients. Krystal tossed off the warning with a flip of her hand, saying, ''Men can be such babies when it comes to their health, but don't worry. We can handle it.''

Maddie remained quiet, knowing that if Leonie were apologizing for her son, then he probably was like a bear with a sore paw. Not that she didn't think Dylan had a right to complain. Surgery and rehabilitation were never accomplished without pain.

Instead of giving him the opportunity to moan and groan about his predicament, she avoided going down to the lower level, deciding to stay in her room until it was time to leave for the dance studio. She stretched out on her bed with a good book.

While she was reading, Maddie heard a loud clang, as if a pot had been dropped on the kitchen floor. She wanted to ignore the sound, but visions of Dylan doing further injury to himself while trying to manage the basics of cooking had her going downstairs. When she walked into the kitchen, he was at the counter trying to open a can of soup.

''You don't have to do that,'' she told him. ''Didn't you see my note? I left a sandwich for you in the refrigerator.''

''I ate that earlier.''

She watched as he struggled to hold the can of soup with his right hand, which was in the sling, and use his left to attach the opener to the lid. He wasn't having any luck.

She walked over to him and stuck out her palm. ''Let me.''

He relinquished the can and the opener. In only a matter of seconds she'd completed the task. Instead of giving the can back to him, she poured its contents into the pan and set it on the stove. "Sit down and I'll make it for you."

"You don't have to—" he began but she interrupted him.

"Yes, I do. Now sit," she ordered. To her relief, he didn't protest. Neither did he look happy.

He shuffled his feet as he walked over to the table and plunked himself down. Today he wore a pair of jeans and a lemon-yellow crew-neck sweater. He looked good. Too good, Maddie thought, wishing she could ignore the little sensations of pleasure that always seemed to tickle her stomach when she was around him.

"How's your shoulder?" she asked, trying to focus on his health, not his looks.

"Do you care or are you just making polite conversation?"

"Both." She broke eye contact, grateful she had the excuse of watching the soup.

"It's fine as long as I don't move it."

"Have you been icing it?"

He sighed. "Please tell me my mother didn't leave you a list of things I should and should not do."

"She's worried about you."

"I can take care of myself."

"You mean the way you took care of the soup?" she asked, arms folded across her chest.

"All right. So I can't do everything I'm used to doing, but I don't need a baby-sitter."

"You don't need to worry. I don't baby-sit grown men even if they behave like children." She was losing patience with the man. "Maybe you should watch your own soup."

Then she went over to the refrigerator, thinking that as long as she was in the kitchen she might as well get her own lunch. She pulled out the fixings for a salad and began tossing them together. Dylan didn't say a word. When she stole a glance in his direction, she saw that his eyes, however, followed her every move.

When she'd finished, she set the bowl on a serving tray, added flatware and a can of iced tea. She was about to take it to her room when he stopped her.

"Where are you going?"

"Upstairs. It's where I live," she added, not wanting to sound defensive but knowing she did.

"Mom said you eat your meals in here."

"Sometimes."

"Then you should stay. I promise to be good." He gave her a smile that said he knew exactly how bad he could be. It was the kind of smile that made her want to revise all the nasty opinions she held of him.

When she hesitated, he added, "What do you think Mom would say if she knew you were carrying your lunch upstairs just because I was eating mine in here?"

Maddie quirked one eyebrow. "She doesn't need to know, does she?"

"Then don't do it for her. Do it for me."

It was a silky smooth plea that had Maddie's nerves shivering in a pleasant way. "Why do you want me to stay? We both know we don't get along very well."

Normally she wasn't so blunt, but with him it seemed to be necessary.

"Maybe it's time we do something to change that." There was a provocative glint in his eye that dared her to take him up on his offer.

She cocked her head to one side. "You think by eating lunch together we'll become good friends?"

"I'm not sure friendship is an option with us. What do you think?"

She could see that they were getting dangerously close to flirting. It was a side of Dylan she would be foolish to encourage. "There's a difference between being friendly and being friends," she said carefully.

"Then come sit down and I'll do my best to be friendly," he urged her.

Again he smiled and Maddie found herself wanting to give in to the temptation to be with him. Ignoring the voice in her head that told her she would be wise to go back to her room, she set her tray on the table.

"That looks good," he said, eyeing her salad.

She was tempted to tell him there was plenty more in the fridge. But if they were going to be friendly, she needed to make an effort to avoid that kind of comment.

"Would you like me to fix you a salad?" she offered.

"I can get it myself." He started to rise, but she stretched out a hand and stopped him.

"It'll take me a fraction of the time it would take you," she told him. "I'll get it."

He sat back down. "Thank you. I'd appreciate that."

As she chopped cucumber and carrots, he spoke to her. "You're pretty good with that knife."

"I've taken a few cooking classes," she admitted.

"From the way Mom talks about your cooking, it sounds as if you could do it for a living."

She shrugged. "I've thought about it, but decided it's not what I want to do to pay my bills."

"You'd rather work at the co-op?"

"There's nothing wrong with working at the co-op. Lots of good people work there." Normally she didn't allow anyone to put her on the defensive when it came to her personal life, but with Dylan it was different. She felt as if she constantly needed to justify herself to him.

"I'm sure they do. I just expected you to be doing something different."

"Such as?"

"Maybe coaching the U.S. chess team."

She couldn't hide the smile his compliment produced. "Garret told you I can still beat him at chess, didn't he?"

"Yes, but even if he hadn't, that's one of the things I remember from the summer you stayed with us. Not many fourteen-year-old girls play chess the way you did." Admiration tinged his words and pride had her smiling inwardly.

"My uncle coached the chess team at our elementary school. We won the state championship the year I was in sixth grade." She set his salad on the table in front of him, then went over to the stove and ladled the soup into a bowl. "As long as I'm up," she said, when she placed it on the table.

"Thank you." He gave her another smile and she knew that one thing hadn't changed since that summer—he could be very charming when he wanted to be.

And he was definitely making that choice now.

"You'll have to forgive me if I spill on myself. I haven't quite got the hang of using my left hand yet," he said as he raised his spoon, a hint of a smile creasing his cheeks.

Maddie would have thought she was the one who had spilled something, the way his eyes were on her while they ate. She tried making small talk but felt extremely self-conscious. Finally she asked him, "Do I have something caught in my teeth?"

"No, why?"

"Because you've been looking at me as if I do."

He apologized. "I'm sorry. It's just that you look so different from that fourteen-year-old girl who used to twirl her way through the house."

She chuckled. "I should hope so. I was all arms and legs back then."

"And you wore glasses and had braces on your teeth."

"I don't know what was worse...being called four eyes or tinsel teeth." She shuddered at the memory.

He looked surprised. "That's what kids said to you?"

"A few. The price you pay for having bad eyes and bad teeth."

"They both appear to be fine, now, or are you wearing contacts?"

She shook her head. "I had laser surgery."

"I should have known there was a reason Mom had it done."

That had her pausing with her fork in midair. "You think I told her to do it?"

"Didn't you?"

"No. It was the other way around. When she told me how painless the procedure was and how happy she was with the results, I decided to try it, too." She could see it wasn't the answer he expected to hear. "Your mom does have a mind of her own, Dylan."

She expected him to give her another skeptical look, but instead he said, "It's good you took her advice. You have beautiful eyes."

The compliment was unexpected. She didn't want to be flattered, but she was. Heat spread through her and she took a drink of her iced tea, then managed to say, "Thank you."

Again a silence stretched between them and it was all because of the change in his attitude. He wasn't simply trying to be friendly. He was flirting with her. She should have known how to handle it. After all, she hadn't reached the age of twenty-eight without having men come on to her, yet this wasn't just any man. It was Dylan, her landlady's son, the guy she'd fantasized about when she was fourteen.

She needed to bring the conversation back to safer ground. It was important that she remember why she was having lunch with him—Leonie. "I hope your mother's trip goes well."

"Time will tell," he said in an almost ominous tone.

"Is there a reason why you think it wouldn't?" she asked.

He shrugged. "Rob Lerner can be brutal with his guests if he doesn't agree with what they're saying. That's why I didn't think she should go."

"And that's the only reason?" she asked with a lift of one brow.

"Yes. What did you think? That I was against her going because I wanted her here to make me lunch?" There was a note of incredulity in his voice. "Have you ever seen the show? The guy can get pretty nasty."

"I know, but he asked her to come specifically to talk about romance. Why would he give her a bad time?"

"Because she's a romance coach. It's a job a sarcastic male comedian could make fun of without any reservations, don't you think?" There was no mistaking the skepticism in his voice.

"And would you be one of those laughing?"

"Not at my mother's expense," he stated unequivocally.

"But at someone else's expense?" She set down her fork and leaned her forearms on the table, sensing a battle of words was about to ensue. "Tell me. Why don't you think being a romance coach is an occupation to be taken seriously?"

"I didn't say I don't take my mother's occupation seriously. I just wish that she wasn't talking about it on national TV," he corrected her.

"Why? Does it embarrass you that she's a romance coach?"

"No." Again the denial was firm.

"But you don't want her talking about it on TV." She didn't give him a chance to respond. "Would you have felt better if you had come home and found her helping people with their taxes instead of giving romance advice?"

"She worked for over twenty-five years helping my dad with taxes," he answered. "She knows the accounting business. I'm not sure she has the kind of credentials needed to withstand a verbal attack by someone like Rob Lerner."

"What better credentials than experience? She put in the same twenty-five years with your father working on love and marriage," she countered.

"You talk as if anyone who's been married is qualified to give advice on romance."

"Not everyone, but your mom has good instincts for the subject. And she's constantly gathering more information—going to workshops, attending seminars, reading journals. She knows what's she's talking about, Dylan."

She could see he wasn't convinced and wondered if it wasn't the subject matter that disturbed him more than his mother's qualifications. Garret has said he doubted his brother would ever give up his bachelor lifestyle. If Dylan didn't believe in marriage, why would he want his mother helping others find the road to happily ever after?

"Tell me, Dylan. What bothers you more? That she might not be the authority you think she should be or that she deals in a subject you haven't much interest in?" She challenged him with a direct stare.

"I'm not against romance," he responded with a dangerous glint in his eye. "Just the opposite. I like women, Maddie." The look he gave her left her in no doubt that he liked them very much.

"But you don't need to ask anyone's advice on romance, do you?"

"Most men I know don't."

"Oh—so you think it's only *women* who need help in that department?"

"Uh-uh." He leaned back and held up his left hand palm outward. "You're not going to trap me in that corner. I'm not going to make some sexist observation that you can jump all over."

"Your mother has both men and women clients," she informed him.

"Maybe she does, but most men I know wouldn't be caught dead hiring a romance coach and I can imagine what kind of questions Rob Lerner's going to ask Mom on the subject."

Maddie could see his concern was real and felt a bit guilty that she herself hadn't thought about such a possibility. Probably because she hadn't wanted to think that Leonie had been invited to be on the show for any reason other than to be her charming self.

"I hope he doesn't ask difficult questions or make her uncomfortable, but if he does, I think your mom will know how to handle it," she stated evenly.

"I hope you're right."

He didn't look convinced and Maddie wasn't sure there was anything she could say to change his mind, so she didn't try.

Having finished her lunch, there was no reason for

her not to return to her room. As she cleared away her dishes, she said, "I'm going to leave for work shortly. Is there anything else you need?"

He shook his head. "I'm fine." As he flexed his fingers on his left hand, she remembered Leonie had said he was supposed to exercise his arm at regular intervals.

"What about the exercises? Do you want me to help you with them?"

"No, it's all right. I can do them myself," he stated stoically.

Maddie knew that wasn't true. If there was one thing Leonie had stressed before she left it was that Dylan needed an assistant when it came to his passive motion exercises. Still, if he wanted to do them alone, what was it to Maddie?

Glancing over her shoulder, she saw that he'd eaten everything she'd made for him. He pushed back his chair and carried first the salad plate over to the sink, then the soup bowl.

"I'll take care of the cleanup," she offered.

To her surprise, he didn't protest. "Thanks for lunch."

"You're welcome."

She watched him leave, then finished with the dishes. She was about to go back upstairs when Dylan returned.

"I guess I need your help after all," he said as he entered the kitchen.

Maddie could see by the look on his face that he wasn't happy he had to ask her for anything.

"I tried doing the exercises by myself and it didn't work," he confessed.

And now she was going to have to help him. Trying to sound as detached as possible, she asked, "What do you need me to do?"

He slipped his hand out of the sling and let it drop to his side. "You have to lift my arm forward until it's at a ninety-degree angle to my side." Just before she was about to touch him, he added, "Gently."

She wasn't sure where to put her hands and ended up slipping one beneath his elbow and the other on his wrist. Carefully she lifted the arm forward. She was close enough to smell a hint of his aftershave. It lent an intimacy to an act that should have been strictly therapeutic.

"Hold it there for a few seconds, then let it down again," he told her.

She did as he instructed, repeating the exercise three more times, asking in between sets, "Am I hurting you?"

"Yes, but it's necessary. Otherwise my shoulder will stiffen up."

She could tell by the look on his face that it was painful for him. There were several more exercises, each one causing him to grimace.

When they'd finished, he breathed a sigh of relief. She helped him put his arm back in the sling, again sensing an intimacy that she found disturbing. She wondered if he'd noticed it, too. When his eyes met hers, she could see that he had.

He didn't say another word, however, but simply thanked her and headed back to his room. As Maddie watched him walk away, she found herself remembering the smile that had been on his face when he'd asked her to stay and have lunch with him.

"I promise to be good," he'd said.

That's what made her nervous. She had no doubt that Dylan could be very good—at winning a woman's heart.

CHAPTER FIVE

Dear Leonie: I made a bet with this guy that I could beat him at a board game, certain I would win. And I would have—had he played fairly—but he didn't and I lost. Now he expects me to honor my wager and have dinner with him. Do you think I should have to pay up?
Signed: Wishing I'd turned down the challenge

Leonie says: What part of the game wasn't fair? If he was dishonest, then no, you don't have to honor your wager. But if all he had was an unfair advantage, and you knew about it from the start, then I'm afraid you're stuck.

DYLAN WAS RESTLESS. He craved physical activity. A few miles away from his mother's house was a health club, but he was a prisoner of 14 Valentine Place. Not that he would have made use of the recreational facility even if he could get there. He couldn't use the pool, not with the stitches in his shoulder. He couldn't even take a shower without putting a plastic bag over the bandage.

He'd discovered there wasn't much a guy could do two days after having rotator cuff surgery. Until his shoulder healed, he didn't have a lot of options as to how to pass the time and that was the part he was having trouble accepting. It didn't help that he had an abundance of energy.

It had always been that way, even when he was a little kid. He'd been the first one up in the morning and the last one to bed at night. It had been a source of irritation for his dad—but then nearly everything he did had created friction between him and his father.

He picked up the remote and turned on the television, hoping to find something of interest. After several minutes of channel surfing, he tossed the remote aside. He didn't want to sit and watch TV. He wanted to be up and moving around. To be outdoors.

He glanced outside and saw that snow was falling. Across the street the mail carrier's truck was stuck in a snowdrift. A neighbor stood on her step shivering as she watched several men try to free it.

Dylan frowned, wondering how he'd ever lived in such a climate. It was a constant struggle with nature at this time of year. As he let the curtain fall back into place, he noticed the photographs his mother had displayed on the table below the window.

They were proof that he had indeed grown up in the Midwest. There was a picture of him in his hockey uniform, a snapshot of him and his brothers building a snow fort, another of his dad ice fishing. As he glanced around he realized that the room was filled with family photos.

Like a visitor to a museum, he examined each one. He picked up a silver frame with a picture of the six of them—Frank and Leonie Donovan and their children, smiling as they huddled together around the Christmas tree. He and his brothers had had a good childhood. There had been a lot of reasons to smile.

As he set the photo down, he noticed his parents' wedding portrait. Etched on the frame were the words "Only you, forever."

His father had certainly made a mockery of those words, Dylan thought as he stared at the picture of a groom gazing in loving adoration at his bride. What bothered Dylan most was that he knew the emotion hadn't been fake. As a child he'd often seen his father look at his mother with that same devotion. So how could a man who'd been so much in love with his wife do what he had?

It was a question Dylan had stopped asking himself because he didn't like the answer. He wanted to forget that his dad had been unfaithful to his mother. But no matter how he'd tried over the past thirteen years, the memory of that spring day—when he'd seen his father with another woman—refused to fade away.

Even now he could recall the afternoon perfectly. He was supposed to have been on a road trip with three of his buddies. Four guys in a 1972 Mustang on the highway headed for the Gulf of Mexico. Only they'd never made it past Iowa. The car had literally fallen apart. At odds as to what to do, two had voted to continue on their way, hitching rides. Dylan and his best friend, Kevin, had decided to catch a bus home.

Dylan hadn't called to tell anyone of his change in plans. His mother and his brothers had gone to visit his grandparents in Wisconsin, which meant only his father would be home. He figured he might as well hear his father's "I told you so" face-to-face rather than over the phone, for his dad had warned him not to attempt such a long trip in an old, run-down car and Dylan knew he'd waste no time in reminding him of the fact.

Determined not to ask his father for help, Dylan had hitched a ride home from the bus station. Expecting his dad to be in his office, he used the side entrance, wanting to avoid the inevitable lecture.

Only his father wasn't in his office. He was in the living room and he wasn't working on anyone's taxes. He was in the arms of a woman Dylan had never seen before.

"What are you doing home?" his father demanded, his face paling at the sight of his son.

At first Dylan was too stunned to say anything. He simply took in the scene before him. A man and a woman on the sofa in the family room, arms wrapped around each other. His *father* with his shirt unbuttoned, the woman next to him with only a black bra covering her. It didn't take a rocket scientist to know what had been going on.

"I'd better go," the woman said in a low voice, reaching for her blouse, which had been flung carelessly over the arm of the sofa.

"Dylan, it's not what you think." His father, too, reached for clothing tossed aside in the heat of passion.

Dylan knew it was exactly what he thought it was. He felt sick at the sight of his father with a woman who was closer to his age than his parents. As she scrambled to button her blouse and slip her feet back into her high-heeled shoes, Dylan could think of only one thing. He needed to get away. To forget what he'd seen.

Without a word, he left the house, ignoring his father's attempts to call him back. There were still six days of spring break left. He wasn't about to spend them in the same house as his dad.

He'd ended up at Kevin's. All he told his best friend was that he'd had a fight with his old man. Knowing that Kevin's would be the first place his dad would come looking for him, Dylan persuaded his friend to head to Texas as planned.

Using money he'd put away for college, he bought two airline tickets and flew to South Padre Island. He spent five days on the beach trying not to think about what he'd unexpectedly walked in on back in Saint Paul.

By the time he returned from spring break, his mother and brothers were home. Although his father made attempts to talk to him alone, Dylan refused to let him. He didn't want to think about his father's infidelity, much less discuss it with him.

Yet he was constantly reminded of it. Every day, when he'd see his dad sitting at the dinner table. And when his mother would shower his father with affection, Dylan wanted to scream. But he couldn't. Because his mother didn't know what her husband had done. So Dylan suffered in silence.

Until the day he could take it no longer and he confronted his father. He vented all of his anger, all of his frustration, thinking it would make him feel better. It didn't. Because no matter what his father said about having made a mistake and promising it would never happen again, Dylan couldn't forget that the man who'd vowed to love his mother faithfully had betrayed her with another woman.

The affair may have been over for his father, but for Dylan it never went away. As the summer passed and he continued to live with the secret, he felt more and more as if he was part of his father's lie—and he resented it. He hated living in his father's house, hated having to take orders from him and hated having to watch him act as if nothing had happened.

Something big had happened, although his mother didn't have a clue as to what or when. She went blissfully about her job as a wife and mother, unaware of her husband's betrayal.

Often Dylan thought about telling her the disgusting thing his father had done. He wanted his father to suffer for his sin, yet he knew for that to happen, his mother would have to suffer, too. *That* was something Dylan wouldn't allow.

So when she'd asked him what the problem between him and his father was, he'd told her he was tired of being treated like a child. It was easier to let her assume that the constant friction was caused by his need to feel like an adult.

Just as he was getting ready to leave for school, Dylan realized he couldn't go to the same college his father had attended. He didn't want to be a chip off the old block. He didn't want to do anything that would further connect him to his father. So three weeks before classes started, he joined the Marines.

When his father had heard what he'd done, he'd

called him into his office. They'd argued. The rest of the family had thought the tension between them had to do with his rebelling against parental authority. Dylan didn't see any need to tell his mother or his brothers anything different. All he wanted was to be gone, far away from Saint Paul, far away from a secret he wanted no part of.

And he had thought he had forgotten it—until the night his mother had called with the news that his father had had a heart attack. He'd rushed home, the memories of that summer at the forefront of his mind. But when he'd seen his father's weakened state, that summer ceased to matter. What was important was that he'd arrived in time to talk to his father. Although they'd only had a short time together before he died, they were able to be a father and son one last time. When his dad had asked him if he'd forgiven him, Dylan had answered yes, because he had. Although he still didn't understand why it had happened.

Dylan set the wedding photo down, wishing that it hadn't stirred memories of that summer thirteen years ago. Looking at the number of photos his mother had on display of her and his father, he knew she still believed that her marriage had been made in heaven. His father had taken his nasty secret to the grave with him, leaving his mom blissfully unaware of what had happened all those years ago. Only Dylan knew how imperfect their marriage had been.

"What you don't know won't hurt you," a voice in his head said.

Dylan wished he hadn't known. If only that rat trap of a car they'd taken to Texas hadn't fallen apart in

Iowa. If only he hadn't walked in on his father. If only he could be as blissfully unaware of his father's infidelity as his mother was.

"Dylan?"

The sound of Maddie's voice had him turning toward the doorway. She stood there in a navy blue jacket with a red scarf wrapped around her neck.

"I just wanted to let you know that I'm leaving. Krystal should be home around six-thirty," she told him, pulling on a black pair of gloves. "Can I help you with anything before I go?"

"No, I'm fine," he told her.

She nodded. "I left the number of the dance studio on the notepad next to the phone in the kitchen...just in case."

He nodded. "When will you be back?"

"I get off work at eight, but I'm not coming home. I have a date."

With Garret's friend, no doubt. Dylan found himself wondering what kind of man would hold Maddie's interest. Where would he take her on a date? To a club? To dinner and a movie?

He found himself asking, "With your Jeffrey?"

"He's not *my* Jeffrey, but yes, I am going with him to a lecture at the university. Gerald Dawber is leading a panel discussion on Shakespearean sonnets."

Shakespearean sonnets. Was that the way to Maddie's heart? he wondered. Not that it mattered to him. He had no intention of pursuing her. He was already in the doghouse with his brothers. Garret had warned him to stay away from Maddie, and Dylan knew it was unlikely that Shane would stick up for him should it be thought he was hitting on a woman Garret regarded as taken.

He'd come home to patch up things with his brothers, not to put a distance between them. As attractive as he found Maddie, he knew that his family would hardly be his champion should he show an interest in her.

"There's some lasagna in the freezer you can have when you get hungry. All you have to do is pop it in the microwave. I've left a note on the counter with the instructions," she said.

He could see she was all business. She made very little eye contact with him, all her concentration on her preparations for her venturing into the cold outdoors.

Unfortunately, the more distant she was with him, the more intrigued he was by her. He wished she would stay and keep him company. He shook his head, realizing how ridiculous a thought that was. He didn't need Maddie Lamont to keep him entertained and he was relieved when she said a curt goodbye and left.

Hearing the door slam, he walked to the windows on the back side of the house so he could watch her head to her car. But it wasn't a car that she climbed into. It was a sporty red pickup. She started up the engine, then got back out to brush the snow from the windows.

Watching her, he wondered about her date that evening. Who was this Jeffrey? He thought back to his father's funeral and didn't remember meeting anyone by that name, yet Garret had said he was a close friend.

He discovered he didn't like the idea of Maddie having a date. Here he was stuck in the house, bored and unable to do much of anything, and she was going to work and going out on a date.

As the sporty red pickup disappeared down the alley, he chastised himself for even giving her a second thought. Normally he didn't pay attention to women who made it obvious that they had no interest in him.

But was she really as indifferent to him as she wanted him to believe? He hadn't missed the look that had been in her eyes when she'd touched his arm during his exercises. She'd been as aware of him as he'd been of her.

And how could he not be aware of her when her hair smelled like strawberries? And when her dark lashes lowered provocatively when their eyes would meet.

Having a beautiful woman under the same roof was not something he'd expected to find on his trip home. Yes, it would be tough spending the next four weeks cooped up in his mother's house, but maybe it didn't have to be such a long recovery period after all. A smile slowly spread across his face at the thought.

ANY HOPE MADDIE HAD that Dylan wouldn't notice her return vanished when she pulled into the alley behind Leonie's house. He stood in the snow wearing a pair of work boots, his leather jacket bulging awkwardly because of the sling on his arm.

"You're back early," he said as she climbed out of the pickup.

''They canceled classes and closed the studio because of the heavy snow warning,'' she explained, wishing he didn't look so attractive with his stocking hat cocked at an angle on his sun-bleached hair.

''What about Jeffrey and the sonnets?''

She thought she detected a hint of mockery in his tone. ''Postponed as well.'' She tried to sweep past him, intending to go directly upstairs, but he blocked her way.

''I'm glad you made it home safely. From what they said on the radio, the roads are in terrible condition and there have been a lot of accidents. I was worried about you.''

She didn't like that his words made her feel warm inside. ''As you can see, I made it safely home.'' She stepped around him and saw that the walk had been partially shoveled. ''You didn't do this, did you?'' She gestured toward the cleared area.

When he reached for the shovel leaning against the house, she knew that he had.

''You're not supposed to be doing any physical labor.'' She tried to grab the shovel away from him, but he refused to let her take it.

''I'm not using my right arm. I'm using my left,'' he told her. ''It still works. See?'' He demonstrated.

Maddie thrust her hands to her hips. ''Do you know what your mother would say if she saw you right now?''

He grinned. ''Oh, I think I can imagine. Lucky for me, she's not here.''

Again she reached for the shovel, trying to still his motion. He stopped and stared at her, his eyes holding a challenge. "You honestly think you can take this from me?"

She tried, but even with two hands she was no match for his strength. She finally conceded defeat and with a sound of frustration let go of the handle. She knew her muscles were no match for his, but she figured her words might be.

"Dylan, you've just had surgery. You're not supposed to be using that arm. If you tear open those sutures you're going to be sorry," she said in a pleading tone.

"I'm not using my right arm, so I won't rip any stitches. I can shovel with my left hand," he said with an annoying twinkle in his eyes.

"It takes two hands to shovel snow," she declared sternly.

"No, it doesn't," he boasted, showing her once more how easy it was to push the snow away from the walk.

"You don't need to be doing this. Krystal and I take turns clearing the snow. It's in our rental agreement," she informed him.

"I don't care what your rental agreement says. As long as I'm here, I'll take care of it."

Maddie could feel her patience slipping away. "Leonie said you were a lot of things but she never mentioned bullheaded."

Instead of getting angry, he grinned at her. "I'm sure I could fill you in on a whole lot of stuff my mother hasn't told you about me."

The provocative statement sent a tiny shiver of excitement through her. "You know the doctor said no lifting."

"I'm not lifting anything, just pushing it to the side."

"Dylan, please stop."

He paid no attention but kept working.

"Do you realize how ridiculous you look? You have your arm in a sling and you're trying to shovel snow."

He paused then, holding her eyes with his. "I'm not worried about how I look, Maddie."

She realized he didn't need to be, because he didn't look ridiculous. He looked incredibly sexy.

Disturbed by the direction her thoughts were taking, she was tempted to go inside and leave him be. If he was foolish enough to risk injuring his shoulder, why should she care?

The problem was, she couldn't in good conscience leave him to do the job alone. She went to the garage and got another shovel and started at the opposite end of the walk.

She didn't look at him, but worked steadily until they met in the middle. She expected him to make some sarcastic comment, but he didn't. He simply said, "Thanks. At the rate it's coming down, it's almost too much for one person to clear."

She could see the sweat on his brow. It had cost him a lot to shovel the small section of walk and already a thin layer of freshly fallen snow hid his efforts.

She glanced up at the sky as huge, fluffy flakes continued to fall. "We could be here the rest of the day. I say we stop."

He, too, looked up at the clouds. "For now, anyway."

When he grimaced she asked, "Are you sure you're all right? Maybe I should put the shovels away."

"I'm fine," he insisted, but this time he didn't protest when she took his shovel from him. He climbed the front steps, then leaned against the door as if trying to muster enough energy to open it.

After returning the shovels to the garage, Maddie could have easily gone in the side entrance and avoided seeing Dylan.

She could have, but she didn't. Concern for him had her using the front entry.

She kicked off her boots, then hung her jacket and scarf on the coat tree next to his. On any other day she would have taken off the warm-up suit she wore over her leotard, but the thought of Dylan seeing her in her dance attire made her uneasy.

Which was ridiculous. It practically covered her from neck to toe and she'd danced on stage wearing far less. She started to unzip the nylon jacket only to zip it back up again.

"Dylan?" she called out tentatively as she wandered down the hallway.

"In here." The sound came from the kitchen. She poked her head inside and saw him next to the stove. "I thought I'd have some hot chocolate. Want to join me?"

Chocolate. If he'd said a cup of coffee, she wouldn't have had any trouble saying no, but chocolate…it was a temptation she couldn't resist.

So was he. With his cheeks rosy from the cold and

his hair mussed from the hat he'd worn, he had a boyish appeal that Maddie found hard to ignore.

"You need someone to make it for you, is that it?" she asked with a lift of one eyebrow.

"No, that's not it. Come inside and see for yourself." He smiled and crooked a finger in her direction.

She walked over to him and saw that he'd already put the milk on the stove to warm. "Not bad for a one-armed guy," she noted.

"Piece of cake compared to shoveling," he said, his eyes meeting hers in a look that said they shared a secret.

She forced herself to look away, turning her attention to the cupboard, where she reached for two mugs. "Come on. Admit it. You're tired, aren't you?" She cast a glance in his direction and was rewarded with another smile. This one had her breath catching in her throat.

"Invigorated, is more like it. A little work never hurt anyone."

"I beg to differ. In your case, it could have hurt you," she chastised him, glad to focus her attention on finding the cocoa in the cupboard.

"That little bit of time I spent outdoors did more for my healing process than two days of rest," he told her. "I was going stir-crazy sitting around here. I'm not used to lying around and doing nothing all day."

"There are things you could do."

"What? Read or watch TV?" He made a derisive sound. "Do you realize what kind of programs are on during the day?"

She did actually, but she didn't comment. ''Some people call that entertainment.''

''And it is...for some.''

''But not for you.''

He shook his head. ''I need a little more action.''

''Like parasailing over the Caribbean?''

He grimaced. ''I can see Mom's been talking about me.''

''In a nice way. I'm sure life is much more exciting in Saint Martin than it is in Minnesota.''

''I haven't ruled out having excitement here,'' he said in a tone of voice that intimated she could be the reason for his excitement.

Annoyingly, heat rushed through her. ''With your arm in that sling you'll probably have to postpone the speed skating and downhill racing for a while,'' she said dryly, trying to make light of his remarks.

''That wasn't exactly the kind of excitement I was hoping to have,'' he admitted.

Maddie didn't think it would be wise to ask what exactly he had in mind. She reached for the cocoa and stirred a generous portion into the milk, sniffing appreciatively. ''Marshmallows or whipped cream?''

''Whipped cream,'' he answered.

''Good choice.'' She opened the refrigerator and pulled out a can of compressed whipped cream, adding a generous squirt to each of the mugs. Then she carried them over to the table, where she noticed the weekend entertainment section of the newspaper was open. Several items had been circled in red.

''Are you planning to go out?'' she asked him.

"If it ever stops snowing," he answered. "I don't suppose it's easy to get a cab in this weather."

"Most people stay home during a snowstorm," she told him, wondering where he planned to go and if he were planning to go with anyone.

"Some do, some don't."

"Why do I get the feeling you don't?" she asked.

"Maybe because you know I like a challenge." The words held a double meaning, as evidenced by the look in his eyes. He slid the newspaper in her direction. "So tell me. What do you recommend for excitement?"

She shrugged, then lifted the mug to her lips, licking the whipped cream from the surface of the chocolate. "Depends on what your interests are."

"What about you? What do you do besides go to lectures on Shakespearean sonnets and play chess?"

She stared at him over the rim of her cup. "I'm afraid my life is boring compared to yours."

"Maddie, if there's one label I would never pin on you, it would be boring. You were always doing something out of the ordinary the summer you stayed with us. Putting on a puppet show for Jason, enlisting Garret's help to learn Russian, making paper mobiles to hang all over the house." His eyes were wistful with the memories. "Are you still like that?"

"Like what?"

"Full of curiosity. Always looking for something new to try?"

She was, and it was the reason she'd changed her major so often in college and had worked so many different jobs. Her father had said she was like a butterfly, flitting from idea to idea, always searching for something but never quite finding it.

"I've given up trying to teach myself foreign languages," she said with a grin, not wanting to admit that she hadn't changed all that much from the fourteen-year-old he'd known.

"What about reading the encyclopedia?"

He knew about that, too? She inwardly groaned. "I guess I was quite the nerd, wasn't I?"

He tilted his head to one side, as if seeing her in a different light. "Knowing what I know now, I'd say that wasn't a bad thing."

Before she could ask him what he meant, the phone rang. "That's probably your mom calling to say she arrived. Do you want me to get it?" she asked. When he nodded, she walked over to the counter where the cordless rested on its base.

Except it wasn't Leonie's voice on the other end. It was a woman asking for Dylan and Maddie promptly handed him the phone. "For you."

Instead of sitting back down at the table, she picked up her mug, drained the remains of her chocolate and took it over to the sink, not wanting to listen in on his conversation. Not that she needed to worry about that. He left the room with the phone close to his ear. The only words Maddie heard were, "I didn't expect you to call me here," before he disappeared out of sight.

As hard as she tried not to be, Maddie found herself curious as to who it was he hadn't expected to call. The voice on the phone had sounded sultry and kittenish, and immediately Maddie imagined a beautiful woman decked out in a sleek-fitting sheath with an enormous wide-brimmed hat pulled low over her sensuous eyes.

She shook her head. What did it matter who was calling him? It was nothing to her. She should be grateful the woman had called so she could go upstairs and leave him alone. But the phone call was brief and, before she could get out of the kitchen, Dylan was back.

"Your girlfriend?" she found herself asking, much to her own surprise.

"I'm not currently seeing anyone," he answered, his eyes sending her a message that clearly said he was free if she was.

She didn't want to be asking him questions about his personal life and knew the sooner she was away from him, the better it would be. "I should go upstairs."

"Are you sure you wouldn't rather stay down here?" he asked in a tone of voice she thought could have melted the snow off the roof.

"I have work to do," she said weakly.

"You can't do work on a day like today," he argued. "Remember when we were kids and we'd get a snow day? We didn't go home and clean our rooms. We played."

The way he said the word *played* sent a shiver of anticipation through her. "And what would we play if I stayed?" She could hardly believe she'd asked the question.

"What about chess?"

She folded her arms across her chest. "You must

be desperate for company if you're willing to let me beat you in chess."

"You're awfully confident that you can beat me, aren't you? How do you know I haven't become a member of the Saint Martin chess club and been playing three times a week?"

"Have you?"

"No." His mouth spread into a grin. "That doesn't mean I can't beat you."

"You couldn't fourteen years ago," she reminded him.

"We only played once."

Ah yes, how well she remembered that game. She'd nearly drooled all over the chess pieces just having him so close to her. It had been hard to remember everything her coach had taught her about keeping her mind sharp to battle her opponent, especially when he'd smelled of some delicious aroma that made her want to swoon.

And she nearly had swooned. He'd looked at her with those eyes and smiled at her with that charming smile and her heart had banged against her chest. But she'd known that she was never going to wow Dylan with her looks. The only chance she had of impressing him was with her wit and it was for that reason she'd been able to focus on the game.

She'd come a long way since then, definitely beyond the stage when a man's presence could cause her to lose her concentration.

"You lost," she reminded him, feeling a bit smug at the memory.

"Then I ought to have a chance for revenge, shouldn't I?"

There was a challenge in his eye. She should have walked away from it, but she'd never been able to turn down the opportunity to beat a man at chess. "All right. One game."

Satisfaction gleamed in his eyes. "Great. Mom should have a chess set around here somewhere."

"In the living room in the cabinet under the television," she told him. "When Shane and Jennifer went to Mexico last year they brought her back an onyx set. I'll get it."

He followed her into the living room, saying, "Why not play in here? We can sit in front of the fire."

Maddie thought it was a bit too cozy a setting for a competition of the kind she intended, but she didn't object. She sat down on the floor next to the coffee table and put the chess set between them.

"What are we playing for?" he asked as he lowered himself to the carpet.

She arched one eyebrow. "Your pride?"

"That's a given," he said with an easy grin. "We need to have something else at stake. What about dinner?"

"If I lose I cook you dinner?" She shook her head. "I already promised your mom I'd do that."

"I'm not talking about you cooking for me."

"Oh, *you're* going to cook for *me* if I lose?" she said on a note of amusement.

"I didn't say that."

She shot him a puzzled look.

"If you lose, you have dinner with me—not here, but at a restaurant," he suggested.

"You don't like my cooking?"

"This isn't about cooking, Maddie. It's about me wanting to take you to dinner," he said in a velvety smooth voice.

He was looking at her the way a man looks at a woman he's interested in getting to know better and she found it exciting. Yet she knew not to regard it as anything but flirting on his part, shrugging off the comment as if she hadn't understood the message in his eyes.

"What if I win? What's my prize?" she asked.

"You're absolved from your nursemaid duties for the rest of the weekend." He extended his left hand over the chessboard. "Do we have a deal?"

It was a wager she couldn't refuse. To not have to spend any more time helping him would be a great relief. And as for him taking her to dinner…she doubted that he'd be able to beat her. She may have had trouble figuring out what it was she wanted to do with her life, but if there was one thing that didn't confuse her it was the game of chess.

She placed her hand in his and gave a gentle squeeze. "Deal."

Maddie thought it would only be a matter of minutes before she had his king in check. She was wrong. He'd improved since the last time she'd played him and she realized she was going to have to plan her strategy carefully.

Whenever he'd capture one of her pieces, he'd look at her in a way that made Maddie feel as if there was more at stake than a dinner and nursing duties. The longer they played, the more intense his gaze became.

She knew he was trying to unnerve her, to get her to forget logic and resort to emotion. She remembered the techniques her uncle had taught her, thought of the practice she'd had at school. Only this wasn't a school match and Dylan was no boy. He was a man who was looking at her in a very provocative way—as if this wasn't about capturing her king but about capturing her.

"You're not playing fairly," she said as he removed one of her bishops from the chessboard.

He shot her an innocent look. "Why do you say that?"

"Don't think I don't know what you're doing."

Again, the look of guilelessness was in place. "Doing? I'm sitting here quietly waiting for you to make your next move."

No, he was trying to make her squirm by using the tactics of seduction. "You think I can't tell when a man undresses me with his eyes?"

He clicked his tongue in amusement. "Maddie, Maddie. What would my mother say if she were here?"

"That I'm right. She'd probably say you're looking at me as if I were that king piece and you were that queen." She pointed to his queen and her king.

He smiled devilishly. "Shouldn't I be the king and you the queen?"

She moved her knight into position and said with a sly smile, "Check."

His mouth popped open, as if he were surprised and

she felt a moment of triumph. It was short-lived, however, for a slow smile spread across his face as he moved his queen. ‘‘Checkmate.’’

She frowned. He couldn’t have! She was certain she’d had a foolproof strategy. He continued to stare at her smugly as she mentally replayed the last few moves, trying to figure out what she had done wrong. All the while she could feel his eyes on her.

‘‘Want a rematch?’’ he asked.

‘‘No, thank you,’’ she said, scrambling to her feet. ‘‘It’s getting late. Krystal will be home soon and she’ll want to cook dinner for you.’’

‘‘Does that mean I don’t get to take you out to dinner tonight?’’

She shoved her hands to her hips. ‘‘Maybe you haven’t noticed, but we’re in the middle of a snowstorm. Nothing’s happening on those city streets.’’

‘‘Then how will Krystal get home?’’

‘‘By bus. They manage to get through in any kind of weather,’’ she told him, sounding like a commercial for mass transit.

But when Krystal phoned, Maddie discovered her housemate wasn’t on her way home. She was at the hospital with a co-worker, relieved to hear that classes at the dance studio had been canceled and Maddie was at home.

‘‘Shannon got this really bad pain in her side and couldn’t drive herself to the emergency room, so I had to drive her here. The roads are awful! Anyway, she’s with the doctor right now.’’

‘‘Is she going to be all right?’’ Maddie asked.

‘‘They think it’s her appendix. That’s why I

called—to tell you I won't be home to make dinner for Dylan. I'm waiting here until Shannon's sister gets here from Fergus Falls.''

''When do you think you'll be home?''

''Gosh, I'm not sure. I'll call you when I know more, okay? You will make sure that Dylan has something to eat, won't you? I wouldn't want to disappoint Leonie.''

''I'll take care of it,'' she said, casting a glance at the subject of their conversation.

As soon as she'd hung up the phone, Dylan looked at her. ''She's going to be late?''

Maddie nodded, then gave him a brief explanation as to why.

''I guess that means I can collect on our wager after all, can't I? Where should we go for dinner?''

Maddie could see he was determined to collect his prize, yet she wasn't about to give in easily. ''We can't go out in the snow. Krystal said driving is terrible.''

''That doesn't mean we can't walk somewhere. Unless things have changed, there'll be a pub open over on Snelling Avenue, snow or no snow.''

''I...'' she began, trying to think up an excuse as to why she couldn't have dinner with him. Nothing came to mind.

''Come on, Maddie. Humor me. It's been a long time since I've walked anywhere in snow.'' When she still hesitated, he added, ''I'm going to have to collect on that bet sooner or later. Why not get it out of the way tonight?''

She knew he was right, yet Garret's words echoed

in her head. Just before Dylan had come home he'd told Maddie, "The only thing Dylan takes seriously is his work. Mom likes to think it's just a matter of time before he settles down, but I know my brother. When it comes to women, he's like a kid who collects seashells on the beach—always looking for the next one."

Not that it mattered to Maddie. She had no plans to become the next seashell. Nor was she under any illusions as to why he wanted to have dinner with her. He was simply tired of being cooped up in the house. He'd made that perfectly clear and she'd seen the advertisements for nightclubs circled in the newspaper. All he was looking for was to be with people, to have some *excitement.*

It was that last part that made her wary. She wondered just what kind of excitement he expected to find having dinner with her.

She didn't want to admit it, but it was that very thought that had her saying, "All right. I'll go with you, but I need to change my clothes. Shall I meet you down here in say, half an hour?"

His eyes gleamed at her acceptance. "Half an hour will be fine. You'll have a good time, Maddie. I promise."

CHAPTER SIX

Dear Leonie: There's this really cute guy who's been coming on to me. I'm not interested in him because I'm dating this really nice guy who's more my type. The problem is my roommate likes the really cute guy and the thought of her with him is making me crazy. What's wrong with me?
Signed: Really Confused

Leonie says: Are you sure you don't like the really cute guy?

WHEN MADDIE CAME BACK downstairs she had changed into a pink vee-neck sweater and a pair of black slacks. Her hair hung loose around her shoulders.

"You look good." Dylan hadn't intended to compliment her. She'd made it clear that she only thought of him as the landlady's son.

"Thanks." She looked uneasy and quickly reached for her jacket, which hung on the coat tree. "Are you sure you want to do this? The snow's going to be deep."

"I think I can handle a little snow," he said, bending to slip his feet into the work boots he'd worn earlier.

But it was more than a little snow, he discovered, as they walked the short distance to Snelling Avenue. By the time they reached the pub, Dylan's pant legs were wet and his fingers were a bit numb. He welcomed the warmth that greeted them as they stepped inside.

"I can see no one's taking the weather advisory seriously," he commented, surveying the crowded restaurant. "I'm not sure there are any vacant booths."

"I think there's one in the back," said a passing waitress who'd heard his comment. She directed them to a high-backed booth in a corner that was far away from the noise of the bar. It had leather seats and a wooden table that had a candle burning inside an amber glass centerpiece.

Dylan helped Maddie as she shrugged out of her coat, then hung it on a hook on the side of the booth. He watched her slide across the bench seat and wished he could slip in beside her. Nothing in her body language told him she'd appreciate such a gesture.

He removed his jacket and hung it next to her coat, then sat down. She looked so beautiful in the dim candlelight, with her cheeks rosy from the cold, that he found it difficult to take his eyes off her.

She was staring at him, too, but for another reason.

"Your ears are red," she told him.

"It's cold out there, in case you hadn't noticed," he said in good humor.

"I bet you wish you were back in Saint Martin."

"No, I'm glad I'm right here." It was the truth. He liked being with her.

She raised an eyebrow. "You'd rather be in an Irish

pub in Saint Paul in the middle of a blizzard than in the fresh air on a beachfront restaurant in the Caribbean?''

He jerked his thumb over his shoulder. ''The air out there is fresh.''

''Yes, and if it keeps snowing at the rate it is, we might know all of these people quite well before the night's over,'' she noted with a quirky smile.

''I guess there are worst places to be stranded than in a pub.''

She didn't need to comment because a waitress arrived. When Maddie asked for a Killian's Red, Dylan said, ''Make that two.''

As soon as the waitress had gone, he picked up one of the menus and asked, ''What do you recommend?''

''I like the corned beef and cabbage, but they also make wonderful potato-leek soup.''

It was while they were going over the menu choices that someone called out, ''Well, for goodness' sake. Look who's here.''

Both Maddie and Dylan turned at the sound of a woman's voice. Approaching the booth was a gray-haired woman, a grin on her face, a balding man at her side.

Maddie smiled in recognition. ''Hi, Elaine.''

The woman tugged on the arm of the gentleman at her side and said, ''This is the girl I told you about, Leo—the one who's organizing our prom night at the co-op.'' Then she looked at Dylan and said, ''Finally I get to meet your beau. You must be Jeffrey. I have to tell you, I think the world of your Maddie. She's the best,'' she said, casting an affectionate grin at Maddie, who shifted uneasily.

''Elaine, this isn't Jeffrey.''

The older woman covered her mouth with her hand. ''Oh my, I'm sorry. I just thought...forgive me,'' she said contritely to Dylan.

''No problem.'' He rose to his feet. ''I'm Dylan Donovan. I'd offer you my hand but, as you can see, it's out of commission.'' He pointed to the sling.

Elaine expressed her sympathy and concern, which had Maddie adding, ''He's recovering from shoulder surgery, which is why we're here. Dylan's mother is my landlady and she's out of town so I'm playing Florence Nightingale.''

''How sweet of you,'' the older woman said, giving Maddie's arm a pat.

While the four of them made small talk, it was obvious to Dylan that Maddie was trying to dispel any notion Elaine might have that they were anything but casual acquaintances. Several times she mentioned his mother's absence and her role as nurse for the weekend. She looked relieved when the waitress returned with their beers and Elaine and her husband said goodbye.

When they'd gone, Dylan asked, ''So what is this prom day at the co-op?''

''It's a fund-raising event the store is sponsoring this spring. Employees dress up in old prom dresses and formal attire in an effort to raise money and donations for the emergency food shelves,'' she explained, then took a sip of her beer.

"And you'll be wearing one of your old prom dresses?"

"Not one of mine. They're long gone, but Elaine found one for me at a consignment shop."

"She's a good friend of yours?"

"More of a professional acquaintance. She's one of the founding members of the co-op."

"Who obviously hasn't met your Jeffrey. I'm not sure she believed that I was your landlady's son."

Maddie shrugged. "It doesn't matter. It's not like we're on a date and didn't want anyone to see us together."

No, it wasn't exactly a date, but Dylan found himself wishing that Maddie was having dinner with him because she wanted to be with him, not because she'd lost a wager. He didn't want to be an obligation to her, yet that was exactly how she saw their time together and it bothered him.

"Your Jeffrey has nothing to worry about from me. I don't make it a habit of going after other men's women—no matter how tempting." And she was definitely a temptation, especially the way her tight pink sweater clung to her curves.

"I wish you wouldn't call him *my* Jeffrey. People aren't possessions."

"Ah, so it's that kind of a relationship, is it?"

"What kind?"

"Politically correct."

"It has nothing to do with being politically correct. It has to do with respect."

"Is that what you think?"

"Yes. There's no place for possessiveness in a healthy relationship," she stated firmly.

"You really believe that?"

"Yes. Obviously you don't." She made it sound as if it were a defect in his personality.

"Maddie, the very nature of physical attraction demands that people regard each other in a possessive way." As he said the words he wondered if she'd ever had the kind of physical relationship that made one want to possess another's heart and soul.

"I disagree. Love isn't possessive."

"Who said anything about love? I'm talking about physical attraction."

"Look, it really doesn't matter, does it?" The impatience in her voice told him she was uncomfortable with the topic of discussion. Her next words confirmed it. "We've already established we're not on a date here, we're just having dinner. Maybe we should talk about something else."

He didn't want to. He wanted to ask her about her relationship with Jeffrey, but he could see it was a subject she didn't want to discuss with him. Instead he asked, "Have you ever lived anywhere but North Dakota and Minnesota?"

The fingers wrapped around her glass relaxed their grip. "Yes. I was in a traveling theater production before I moved here. Every six weeks we moved on to a different city. I saw a lot of the United States during those two years."

"And did you enjoy it?"

"I did. It was a great experience."

"Then why did you leave?"

"Because I got tired of dancing in pain. I had an injury that kept recurring and decided that being a professional dancer wasn't for me. Although I'm not sure how long I would have continued had my knee held up. It may appear to be a glamorous lifestyle, but it's actually very difficult."

"Teaching is easier?"

She nodded. "Oh yes. I enjoy the students. My youngest group is four-year-olds. They're so cute and so much fun. Your nephew's in that class."

He chuckled. "Mickey takes ballet lessons?"

"And tap."

And just when he thought he'd seen all the surprises coming home had for him. "Whose idea was that?"

"Not mine," she was quick to point out.

"I can't believe Shane would have suggested it."

"It was Jennifer's idea but Shane didn't object so I don't think you should, either."

"Did I say I objected?"

"You don't need to. I can see it in your face."

"What you see on my face is surprise. Knowing Shane, I'd expect Mickey to be playing peewee hockey, not dancing with a bunch of little girls."

"There are other boys in the class."

"How many?"

"One."

"Exactly my point."

She went on the defensive then. "There's nothing wrong with men learning how to dance. Believe it or not, women actually like it when they do."

"So I've noticed."

"Do you dance?"

"Only when there's music playing...unlike a certain fourteen-year-old I remember," he said, unable to resist teasing her.

It had the desired effect. She smiled. "The music is often playing in my head."

He lifted his glass in salute. "To those who dance."

She clinked her glass against his before taking a sip. Then she asked, "Are you good at it?"

"I haven't had any complaints thus far, but then I haven't had an expert's opinion yet. Maybe you could evaluate me once this shoulder is healed," he said provocatively.

She was spared from having to answer by the return of the waitress, who took their food orders. As soon as she'd gone, Maddie said, "Mickey loves to dance."

"I know. He tried to show me in the airport. What about your friend, Jeffrey. Does he like to dance?"

She looked as if she wasn't going to answer, then finally said, "No, he doesn't."

So they didn't have that in common. Again Dylan found his curiosity aroused. "I understand he's a friend of Garret's."

She nodded. "Your brother's the one who introduced us. He and Garret were roommates during their undergraduate days."

"And Jeffrey's a graduate student at the university?"

"Yes. He's very well respected in the academic community."

"Is he fun to be with?"

That question had her stiffening. "I wouldn't go out with him if I didn't enjoy his company."

"How long have the two of you been seeing each other?"

"About six months."

"I see." He'd hoped that she'd say only a few weeks. Six months increased the chances that it was not only a monogamous relationship but an intimate one as well.

Her eyes narrowed. "Just what is it you think you see?"

"That my chances of getting you to go out with me are slim and next to none if you're that serious about him," he said candidly.

"We're not serious in the way that you think. At this stage we're just *very* good friends."

Friends? Hope sprang to life. "How close are you?"

"And why should I answer that?"

"Because you know I'm interested in you and would like for this to be a real date." He didn't see any point in not being direct.

She lowered her eyes. "That's not possible."

"Because of Jeffrey?"

She avoided his eyes, her finger tracing the rim of her glass. "Because of a lot of things."

He frowned. "Tell me what things."

"Like the fact that you're only here for a short time."

"You don't date guys just to have fun?"

"I have fun with Jeffrey," she repeated with a hint of exasperation, then she rolled her eyes heavenward. "I knew you wouldn't understand."

"Understand what?"

''Why Jeffrey and I work and why you and I wouldn't.''

''And that would be because...'' He was eager to hear her answer.

''Because you see relationships as physical attractions and Jeffrey and I see them as companionships.''

Companionships? That had him assuming he was right—that there was no passion in her relationship with the other man. ''Is that what you really look for in a relationship—companionship?''

''And friendship, yes. It's a good basis for a relationship and it certainly will last longer than if you base it on...'' She seemed embarrassed to finish.

He wasn't the least bit reticent about supplying her ending. ''Sex?''

''I was going to say physical attraction,'' she corrected him.

''So you look first for friendship in a relationship—because you're worried that physical attraction will fade.''

''Physical attraction does fade. You know that. You wouldn't still be single if it didn't.''

''Yes, but when the chemistry is there, there's nothing more exciting.'' Which was what his own body was telling him right now. Just being with Maddie was enough to energize every muscle and nerve inside him.

''I'm not saying there isn't, but it's not the foundation for the kind of relationship I want,'' she stated rationally. ''I think if you're good friends, chemistry will follow.''

''So you're not going to risk putting the cart before the horse.''

"Exactly."

"So you're going to go with the horse and hope the cart shows up, is that it?" The thought annoyed him. That this unknown Jeffrey had this gorgeous, sensual woman at his fingertips and was content with companionship.

"Jeffrey's not a horse."

"But he's satisfied with the two of you being just friends." He raised a brow.

"Yes. Is there a reason why he shouldn't be?" She sounded a bit annoyed and her next words proved that he'd flustered her. "I'm happy, he's happy. Satisfied?"

The waitress arrived with their food, putting an end to what had become a tense moment. After she left, Dylan did his best to keep the conversation impersonal, but it was difficult. He knew that Maddie was fooling herself if she thought there wasn't a physical attraction between the two of them.

He'd noticed it the first night he'd come home and she'd confronted him with so much passion. He'd thought it was her defense of his mother that had aroused so much emotion, but every subsequent time they'd been together he'd seen that same fire in her eyes. They couldn't be in the same room together without tension arcing between them.

That's why he couldn't resist asking, "How often do you and Jeffrey see each other?"

In between bites of corned beef, she said, "Whenever our schedules allow us to be together."

"Did you see him last weekend?"

"No. He's been working on his thesis for the past

two weeks and he's been very busy. Could we not talk about Jeffrey?'' she asked on a note of impatience.

He shrugged. ''Suits me. I'd rather talk about you.''

''Maybe we should be talking about you and why your brother feels he needs to protect me from you,'' she suggested.

He frowned. ''Which brother?''

''Garret.''

''I should have known. And what was his warning?''

''Not to take anything you say too seriously. That you like to flirt with women. Not that I needed the warning. I did spend a summer here, remember?''

''Meaning what? If I remember correctly, I was on my best behavior,'' he protested.

''If that was your best...well, I guess it was a good thing I was a skinny little fourteen-year-old who could have passed for a boy,'' she said dryly. ''How many girls did you date that summer?''

''A few,'' he confessed with a grin.

She nearly choked on her food. ''A few? As in few hundred?''

''Now *that* is an exaggeration.''

''Is it? Is that why you were voted biggest class flirt in your senior class?''

''How did you hear about that?''

''Your mom has all the yearbooks on one of the bookshelves in the living room.''

He liked the fact that she'd been interested enough in him to look him up. Then she said, ''Krystal was browsing through them one day and pointed it out. I told her it didn't surprise me.''

"I think some of my buddies set me up for that one," he said with a sly grin. "They stuffed the ballot box."

She simply raised one eyebrow. "I hear you left a trail of broken hearts when you went off and joined the military."

"Now who would have told you that?"

"Actually, it was your mother."

"Mom?"

She nodded. "She talks about you often."

Dylan wondered what kind of things his mother had told her. Did Maddie know about the tension between him and his brothers? Suddenly he felt at a disadvantage. She knew a lot more about him than he did about her, which was evidenced by her recitation of his accomplishments over the past thirteen years.

"My mom told you all that?" he asked.

She nodded. "And more."

Throughout dinner she told anecdotes his mother had shared with her. To counter, he related the same stories but his versions—which he could see she didn't believe. The evening came to an end much too soon and he was disappointed when she declined his invitation to have an after-dinner drink.

When they stepped outside, the snow was still falling. The path they had taken earlier was now drifted over and Dylan automatically reached for her as they made their way home. He liked the feel of her gloved hand in his.

She had not wanted to prolong the evening at the pub, but he was determined that once they were back at the house they'd have a nightcap. His plans shattered though, when they stepped into the entry and found a duffel bag, a backpack and a pair of athletic shoes.

"What?" he wondered aloud only to have his unspoken question answered. Around the corner came his brother Jason.

"Hey, Dylan."

"How did you get here?"

"Some friends dropped me off."

"You're home for the weekend?"

Jason didn't answer, because he'd noticed Maddie and greeted her with a hug. "Hey, Maddie. How's it going? You got anything in the freezer I could heat up?"

"Are you hungry?" she asked. Before he could answer she said, "Silly question. College kids are always hungry, right? Why don't you go on into the kitchen and I'll be right there." She removed her coat and hung it on a hook.

This was not how Dylan had expected the rest of the night to go…sharing Maddie with his little brother. "What exactly are you doing here?" he asked Jason. "I thought the semester had just started."

"It did, but I came home." Then he turned to Maddie. "Hey—do you think you could give me a massage later this weekend?"

"You having trouble with that neck again?" she said in a sympathetic tone Dylan realized had been absent when she'd attended to his injured shoulder.

Jason started to follow her into the kitchen, but Dylan stopped him. "I'd like to talk to you for a few minutes."

"Can't it wait? I have to meet my friends and I really need to get something to eat."

"I'll be in the kitchen," Maddie said with a touch on Jason's arm, then discreetly left.

"What is it?" Jason asked impatiently as she walked away.

"I just wanted to know how things are going at school," Dylan said.

"Fine," he said abruptly. "Now can I go?"

He wanted to say, *No, you're going to stay right here and have a conversation. I'm your brother.* But then he remembered what Garret had said. Maybe tonight was not the time to get into a confrontation with him.

"All right. We'll talk in the morning. Go get something to eat," he said with a nod toward the kitchen.

Dylan could have gone with him, but he took a seat in the living room, envious of his younger brother and the attention he received from Maddie. Dylan wanted to be the one who was the recipient of her smile, the one she wrapped her arms around in a bear hug.

Then he stopped himself. That was not what he wanted at all. He wanted Maddie to smile at him all right and he especially wanted to have those beautiful arms wrapped around his body, but not the way it had happened with Jason. She'd treated his brother as if he was a long-lost relative who'd come home. Dylan definitely didn't want Maddie to regard him as a member of the family. He wanted to be something entirely different. Now he only needed to convince her she wanted the same thing.

MADDIE EXPECTED Dylan to come into the kitchen while she made Jason something to eat. When he didn't, she was disappointed. As much as she'd hated to admit it, she'd enjoyed their evening together and was sorry to see it come to an end.

"You know I'm interested in you." She could still hear his words in her head, and she couldn't pretend that she hadn't found them exciting. Maybe it was because all those years ago she'd longed for the seventeen-year-old heartthrob to notice her. Or maybe it was simply because he was a very attractive man.

Whatever the reason, she knew that she wasn't immune to his charm. If they'd been alone in the big house when they'd returned, she didn't doubt that she'd have found a reason to spend more time with him. That's why she was relieved that Jason had come home.

After fixing him a grilled ham and cheese sandwich, she'd gone up to her room where she'd put a Bonnie Raitt CD on the stereo and sat on the love seat near her window, watching the snow fall. She didn't want to think about Dylan, but she found it hard to think of anything else.

A knock on her door startled her. Her first thought was that it might be Dylan. Maybe he wasn't going to let her go to bed without saying good-night. Then she heard Krystal's voice.

"Maddie, are you in there?"

"Yeah, come on in." As the hairdresser poked her red head around the door Maddie asked, "How's Shannon?"

"She was in recovery when I left. It was her appendix as they suspected. I stayed with her until she got out of surgery.'' She flopped down onto the love seat next to Maddie. ''So what are you doing up here? I thought you'd be downstairs watching a video or something.''

''No, I'd rather sit up here and watch it snow,'' she said, glancing out the window.

''We've had so much it's getting to the point where it's not pretty,'' Krystal said with a yawn. ''I'm sorry I wasn't here to pull my share of the nursing duties with Dylan. Did everything go okay?''

''Yeah, it was fine,'' she answered.

''What did you make for dinner?''

''I didn't cook. We walked over to that Irish pub on Snelling Avenue. It was his suggestion, and to be honest it suited me just fine.''

''Leonie must not have told him what a great cook you are.''

''I think he's getting a bit claustrophobic.''

''And who could blame him?'' She pulled her feet up beneath her. ''So tell me. What's he like?'' Eyes that had been sleepy only moments ago now widened in interest. ''Did you ask him if he has a girlfriend?''

''I don't care if he has a girlfriend.'' She avoided answering, not wanting to be having this discussion. She could only imagine what her roommate would say if she knew what the actual subject of their conversation had been.

''Now that just goes to show you how unfair life can be. I mean, there I was stuck at the hospital when I could have been having dinner with that gorgeous specimen of man. And here you were, not giving a hoot about getting to know him better....''

''I thought you'd decided it wouldn't be wise to get involved with Dylan because of what it might do to your relationship with Leonie,'' Maddie reminded her.

She gave her a mischievous look. ''I didn't say I wanted to get involved, but I wouldn't mind having a little fun. And Leonie's not here this weekend.''

The image of Dylan with his arms around Krystal flashed in Maddie's mind and it wasn't pleasant.

''Well, you'll be happy to know that the beauty shop's not going to be open tomorrow because of all the snow. That means you won't have to do a thing for Dylan because I'll be here. I'll play nurse.'' She rubbed her hands together enthusiastically. ''Ooh, it's going to be so much fun!''

Maddie didn't doubt for one minute that Krystal would relish every moment in Dylan's company or that she'd do whatever she could to make sure that he received a lot of attention.

Krystal glanced at her watch. ''I'm hungry and it's not that late so I think I'll go downstairs and get something to eat. I should probably check on Dylan, too.'' She looked at Maddie. ''You want to come down?''

''I think I've done my duty for today,'' she replied. ''You know, you don't have to wait on the guy hand and foot. It's only one shoulder that's not working.''

''Maddie, you're looking at someone who's spent her life waiting on people. And very few of them have looked as good as Dylan. This is no sacrifice, believe me.'' With a wave, she was gone.

Maddie could hear her singing along to one of the

Bonnie Raitt songs as she went down the stairs. She closed her door, hoping to drown out any sounds that might come from the first floor. But even with the stereo playing, she could hear muffled voices. Every now and then laughter echoed up the stairs.

Maddie tried not to picture Krystal with Dylan, but she couldn't prevent the images that went through her head. Krystal was not shy. Maddie could imagine her placing her hands on Dylan's shoulders, getting close to him as she spoke.

A strange uneasiness fluttered through Maddie. So what if Krystal and Dylan were cozying up on the sofa? It was nothing to her. She had no reason to be jealous. She wasn't interested in the man.

She picked up the phone and dialed Jeffrey's number. She got his answering machine, which she knew meant he was in his study working on his thesis. With a sigh she returned the phone to its cradle.

Again she looked outside. It was still snowing. Chances were the dance studio would be closed tomorrow as well. The storm would have effectively shut down most of the city and she'd have to spend the entire day in the same house watching Krystal flirting with Dylan.

It wasn't a pleasant thought. Again she dialed Jeffrey's number. After hearing the answering machine's beep, she left her message, "Jeffrey, it's me. I hope the snow won't keep us from seeing each other tomorrow. Call me in the morning, all right?"

"There. That takes care of tomorrow. As for tonight," she said softly to herself. "I'll just go to bed."

She changed into her pajamas and slid between the

sheets, determined to put Dylan out of her mind. It shouldn't have been difficult to do. After all, the mumbled voices and distant laughter had disappeared.

Which only made it worse for Maddie, who now imagined Krystal in Dylan's arms. Kissing him. Touching him. Maddie wondered if he was telling Krystal the same things he'd said to her earlier that day...that she had beautiful eyes...that he was interested in her.

Maddie punched her pillow. What did it matter what he was saying to Krystal? He was a free agent—he'd admitted he was without a girlfriend. If Krystal wanted to be the latest seashell he added to his collection, that was her business. Maddie had better things to do. And tomorrow she'd show him that.

MADDIE AWOKE to the sound of Krystal's voice. She glanced up and saw her friend poking around the door.

"I'm sorry to have to wake you, Maddie, but I feel awful."

Now that Maddie's eyes were wide-open she could see that her housemate didn't look well and she sounded stuffy. "What's wrong? Do you think you're running a fever?" she asked as she climbed out of bed.

"I ache all over and I have the chills. I think I might have the flu. Do you have anything I can take for it?"

Maddie padded over to her desk. "Maybe these will help," she said, handing her a small bottle of pain relievers.

"Thanks. I'm feeling really weak." She clung to the door, looking as if she might keel over any minute.

"Then go back to bed," Maddie ordered, giving her a gentle shove.

"But I'm supposed to make breakfast for Dylan this morning."

"He can get his own."

"No, he can't. Haven't you seen how difficult it is for him to use his left hand?"

Maddie had seen his attempts in the kitchen and knew she had no choice but to say, "I'll help him. You just go back to bed and don't worry about anything. I'll bring you some juice and a pitcher of water so you can take those tablets."

Krystal murmured a weak thanks before shuffling slowly back to her room. She hadn't gone far when she turned and said, "Oh…as long as you're going downstairs, would you bring me my watch? I think I left it on one of the end tables in the living room."

Maddie nodded, then pulled on her robe and headed down the stairs, hoping that Dylan wasn't up. To her relief, it was still dark, the arrival of dawn allowing just enough light for Maddie to see without flicking on a switch. She carefully made her way into the kitchen, where she put a pitcher of water and a glass of juice on a serving tray. Then she headed for the living room, tiptoeing as quietly as she could.

Because there were fewer windows, the room was darker than the rest of the house. Maddie padded across the wood floor toward the sofa. Just before she reached it she realized there was a body there. A large body with sun-bleached hair. It was Dylan.

She stopped suddenly, nearly spilling the water. She

should have known. Jason had come home unexpectedly and Dylan had been using his room.

She glanced at the end table near the sofa, debating whether to continue searching for Krystal's watch. The gold band winked in the early morning sun, tempting her to come pick it up, yet there was a sun-streaked head nearby that made her hesitate.

Carefully she tiptoed over to the table, conscious of the man asleep on the sofa. Holding her breath, she reached for the watch, snatching it up without making a sound. She glanced at Dylan's face, serene in slumber. He was even more attractive than he'd been awake.

One stray lock of hair had fallen across his forehead. Her fingers itched to brush it back. That wasn't all they longed to do. Curiosity had her wondering how those slightly parted lips would feel beneath her fingertips, if the slight growth of whiskers on his jaw would be bristly to her touch.

The only other part of him sticking out from the blanket was his left hand, which clutched one edge of the blanket. He had big, powerful hands roughened from hard work and the sun.

He shifted, causing the blanket to move as well. As he struggled to make himself comfortable, it became apparent that his chest was bare. Except for the bandage across his shoulder, there was nothing but tanned flesh. Maddie's breath caught in her throat. She could see the results of his having worked with concrete. There was nothing but firm muscle.

For several seconds she stared at him, imagining what was under the rest of the blanket. At the direction her thoughts had taken, she felt her cheeks warm. When he stirred a second time, she hurried out of the room and back up the stairs.

After she'd given Krystal her watch and the tray with the liquids, she returned to her own room, where she collapsed onto her bed, her cheeks still stinging with heat from her encounter with the sleeping Dylan. What in the world had she been thinking?

But she *knew* the answer to that question, and it was definitely something she had no business contemplating. She'd been lucky to get out of the room without waking him. If he had caught her staring at him like that it would have been the ultimate in humiliation. And she had no doubt he would take great pleasure in reminding her of it.

She still couldn't believe she'd gawked at him as if she'd never seen a naked chest before. Well, she hadn't seen one that looked like that—at least not one that wasn't in a magazine or on the movie screen.

Her body warmed again at the memory. She groaned. Just what she didn't need—to revert to adolescence.

All right. So the inevitable had happened. She couldn't live in the same house as Dylan and not expect to see him without a shirt.

She'd done that and survived. And the best part of all was that he didn't know she'd done it. It was time to move on. She'd made it perfectly clear to him that she was in a relationship with Jeffrey and had no interest in seeing anyone else.

She'd give him no reason to think she regarded him as anyone other than her landlady's son. She'd treat him the same way she treated Jason. Like a brother. And as for those fanciful thoughts running through her head—she'd keep them to herself, just as she had all those years ago.

CHAPTER SEVEN

Dear Leonie: There's this girl I can't stop thinking about. I want to ask her out, but she's seeing another guy. She says they're just friends and I believe they are. Why else would she react to me the way she does? Signed: Itching to make a move

Leonie says: Until she tells you she's not involved with the other guy, you're going to have to find another way to scratch that itch.

DYLAN WOKE the following morning feeling stiff and out of sorts. His shoulder didn't ache, but other parts of him did. He pushed aside the blanket and sat up, rubbing the back of his neck with his left hand. As comfortable as the sofa in his mother's living room was, it couldn't take the place of a bed.

He staggered down the hallway to the bathroom only to discover it was occupied. He leaned up against the wall and closed his eyes. Since his brother's bedroom door was shut and there was a one-in-a-million chance that the teen would be out of bed before noon, he figured it was either Maddie or Krystal in the shower. He longed for the days when the only people he shared a bathroom with were his brothers. At least with them he could pound on the door and say, "Hurry up in there."

With a sigh he went back to his makeshift bed. He reached for the remote and flicked on the television. Scrolling across the bottom of the screen was a list of events canceled because of the snowstorm. With two fingers he spread the blinds on the window and saw that it was still snowing. Mounds of white had drifted close to the window ledge. Not since he'd been a kid had he seen such a sight.

He grinned, remembering how he and his brothers would pray for days like this so that school would be closed. He imagined a lot of kids were waking up and wishing this particular record-breaking snowfall hadn't happened on a Saturday.

As the public service announcements continued to appear on the TV, he realized that other activities had had to be postponed. Dylan didn't pay much attention to the names rolling by until he saw Diandra's School of Dance and the word *Closed* behind it. That was the studio where Maddie taught, which meant she would be at home today rather than at work. Again Dylan grinned.

When he heard movement in the hallway and on the stairs, he knew the bathroom was now free. When he stepped inside the hot, steamy room, he could tell who'd been in the shower before him. The air was thick with the aroma of strawberries, the same fragrance he'd noticed in Maddie's hair. Only today it was more potent, teasing his senses and arousing his hormones.

It lingered while he showered and shaved, a constant reminder of her presence in the house. Not that Dylan needed any reminders. She was already in his thoughts far too often and with good reason. She was beautiful, sexy and smart. And taken.

Thoughts of the unknown Jeffrey had him grimacing. Any man who chose to spend two weeks writing a paper when he could be with a woman like Maddie had to be one card short of a full deck. Or suffering a shortage of testosterone.

It was probably the latter. Maddie was not the kind of woman to put up with any man who wasn't her intellectual equal. From the way she spoke about her relationship with Jeffrey, Dylan got the impression that it was more of a convenience than a passion. He shook his head. He didn't understand how any man could look at Maddie and be content with simply being friends, or how she could settle for anything short of an all-consuming love. He wondered if she even knew what she was missing?

A short while later when Dylan found her in the kitchen, he had to remind himself that it wasn't his responsibility to show her. Not that the thought hadn't crossed his mind.

Today she wore a ribbed turtleneck sweater in a shade of purple that was the perfect foil for her dark hair. A pair of black knit pants hugged her legs like a second skin and on her feet were a pair of black satin slippers.

"Good morning," she said when she heard his footsteps.

"Hi. What are you reading?" he asked, noticing she had a book open on the table.

‘‘It’s a biography of Eleanor Roosevelt.’’

‘‘Interesting lady.’’

‘‘Yes, she was.’’ She closed the book and rose. ‘‘What would you like for breakfast?’’

‘‘You don’t need to get it for me.’’

‘‘If you’re expecting Krystal to help you, she’s got the flu. I doubt she’ll be out of bed today.’’

So she’d only offered because Krystal wasn’t available. He should have known. She hadn’t missed a chance yet to let him know that she was only helping him as a favor to his mother.

‘‘I don’t eat much for breakfast,’’ he told her. ‘‘I’m sure I can manage to pour myself some cereal without creating any havoc.’’

‘‘Probably, but why don’t you let me get it for you?’’ she said, going over to the cupboard and pulling out a bowl.

‘‘Because I’d rather get it myself.’’

His brisk tone had her shoving her hands to her waist, looking as if she were contemplating arguing with him. She didn’t. She simply shrugged and said, ‘‘If that’s what you want to do.’’

‘‘If I did what I wanted to do, it would create all sorts of problems, especially for your Jeffrey,’’ he couldn’t resist saying.

Color brightened her cheeks. She walked over to the table, scooped up her book and pulled it close to her chest. ‘‘I’ll be upstairs if you have any problems,’’ she said coolly.

She started out of the kitchen, but he stopped her. ‘‘Aren’t you forgetting about my exercises?’’

She gave him an impatient glance. "I thought since Jason's home he could help you."

He snickered. "If he were up. I'll be lucky to see him before noon. The doctor said it was important to exercise regularly. It's been more than twenty-four hours since I last did them."

She sighed and set the book down on the table. "All right."

As she came closer, he caught another whiff of the strawberry shampoo that had permeated the bathroom. Her hair was still damp from the shower, falling to her shoulders in loose curls. He wondered if they felt as soft as they looked.

As she had done yesterday, she provided a gentle touch, carefully moving his arm and providing the passive resistance he needed. And his body reacted to her nearness. He liked being close to her, watching her move with the grace of a ballerina. Most of all, he liked being touched by her.

"I see the snow canceled your dance classes again today," he said, wanting to engage her in conversation while she went through the exercises with him.

"It sounds as if the whole city is pretty much shut down," she remarked, keeping her eyes on his arm.

"So what are you going to do all day?" he couldn't resist asking.

"Oh, I have things to do," she said as she lifted his arm forward.

"What things?"

"Laundry, for one."

"What about after the laundry's done?"

"Housework."

He groaned. ''Please tell me my mom didn't ask you to pick up after me.''

''No, I'm sure she thinks you're old enough to straighten your own room.''

''I don't have a room. Jason came home, remember?'' he reminded her. ''So after you do this housework, then what are your plans?''

She shrugged. ''I'll probably finish my book.''

''Want to watch a movie with me? I've got a stack of DVDs in my suitcase,'' he suggested, wishing she'd look at him instead of focusing on his arm as if it needed all of her concentration.

''You're bored again, are you?'' She still didn't look at him.

''You think I only want to spend time with you because I'm bored? Maddie, I don't need a companion to become engrossed in a film.''

For one brief moment her eyes met his, then she quickly looked away. ''Thank you for the offer, but as I've already said, I have other things to do.'' As they finished up the last of his exercises she said, ''There. How's that?''

He slipped his arm back into the sling. ''Better, thanks.''

''If you don't need me for anything else, I'll go upstairs.'' She again reached for her book. ''What time would you like lunch?''

''Lunch?'' He shrugged. ''Whenever you eat is fine with me.''

''All right.'' And without so much as a glance in his direction, she left.

Dylan wasn't sure whether he should be pleased or

not. Maddie was going to make him lunch. That part pleased him. The fact that she was only doing it because Krystal had the flu was the part that didn't.

MADDIE CLEANED her closet and her drawers. Then she stripped all of the linens from her bed and laundered them. Every time she went downstairs to the laundry room, she expected to see Dylan in the living room. Only he wasn't there.

She'd looked in the kitchen, but it was also empty. She didn't want to be curious as to where he was, but she couldn't help herself. Certainly he hadn't gone outside to try to shovel? She pushed aside the curtains on the window over her bed and looked to the sidewalk below.

There was no sign of him. What was he doing? she wondered. On her third trip to the laundry room she wandered down the hallway leading to the bathroom and noticed that Leonie's office door was ajar. Tentatively she craned her neck around the edge to peek inside.

"Looking for anyone in particular?" a voice said from behind her.

Startled, she turned to face Dylan, who carried a laptop in his left hand. "Yes—you. I wanted to tell you that lunch will be ready in about half an hour. Is that convenient?" It wasn't what she'd planned at all, but she couldn't tell him the truth because she knew he'd take great pleasure in the fact that she'd been looking for him.

"Half an hour will be fine, thanks," he said in a very businesslike manner.

"Good. You like chili?"

"Texas style?"

"No, North Dakota style."

He gave her a half grin. "Never had it, but I'm not worried. So far I've been impressed with everything that's come out of North Dakota."

He was flirting with her again. She wondered if he was able to *not* flirt with a woman? "I'll see you in about half an hour." She stepped around him, determined not to respond to the charm that was as tempting as a hunk of chocolate.

She hurried back upstairs, where she put the freshly laundered sheets on her bed, then checked on Krystal. Her roommate's health hadn't improved.

"Feel like eating anything? I could heat up some chicken soup," Maddie offered.

Krystal flung an arm over her forehead. "Just let me die in peace, Maddie."

"Is it that bad?"

"It's worse. Thank God we have half a bath upstairs. It would be awful if Dylan saw me like this."

Maddie chuckled to herself. How like Krystal. No matter how miserable she was feeling, she still worried about her appearance.

"I can't believe I got sick and missed my big chance at impressing him," she said with a groan.

"You'll have plenty of time. He's going to be here a whole month." Maddie didn't want to ask, but she couldn't resist saying, "Besides, didn't you do that last night? I heard a lot of laughter coming from the first floor."

"Don't I wish," she said on a sigh. "That was Jason you heard laughing. Dylan spent most of last night in Leonie's office using his laptop. Jason says he's a workaholic."

"Maybe in the eyes of a nineteen-year-old he is."

"I don't know, but I would have liked to have had the chance to get him to think about something other than work." She reached for the tumbler of water and took another sip. "He didn't get this flu bug, did he?"

"I saw him this morning. He looked fine," Maddie assured her.

"What about Jason? He's the one who shared my pizza."

So it had been Jason, not Dylan, she'd been with in the kitchen. Maddie couldn't prevent the tiny beam of satisfaction the information gave her.

"I haven't seen him this morning. Are you telling me Jason ate pizza after I had already fed him a ham and cheese sandwich?"

"You know guys. Bottomless pits when it comes to food."

"I thought he was going out with his friends last night."

"He did—after the pizza was gone." She reached for a tissue and blew her nose. "Maddie, you should leave. I don't want you catching this."

"Are you sure I can't bring you something to eat?" she asked.

"Maybe later. Right now I just want to sleep." And with another groan Krystal turned her head into the pillow.

Maddie knew as she left the room that any hope she'd had that Krystal would make a miraculous recovery was gone. More than likely, she was going to get stuck taking care of Dylan tomorrow, too. It was both a pleasant and disturbing thought.

When she went downstairs to make lunch, it wasn't Dylan, however, sitting at the table. Jason was eating a bowl of cold cereal, the sports page of the newspaper spread out on the table in front of him.

"Hi, how are you feeling?" Maddie asked.

"I'm feeling good, thanks."

"I'm glad to hear that. Krystal came down with the flu this morning. She was worried that she may have given it to you last night," she said as she reached into the freezer for a packet of frozen chili.

"Uh-uh. I feel fine. Although, I'd probably feel a whole lot better if I had some of your homemade bread." He gave her a smile that had the potential of being as dangerous as his older brother's.

"Sorry. I think your brother scarfed down the last of it yesterday." She placed the freezer bag of chili on a plate and set it in the microwave. "There should be bagels in the fridge. Or if you want, you can have some of this chili I'm heating up for Dylan."

"Thanks, but it's a little early for chili. A bagel would be great, though. I don't suppose you'd want to toast me one, would you?" Again there was that cajoling smile.

"You want blueberry or cinnamon and raisin?"

"Blueberry with cream cheese and jam," Jason answered.

"Could you make that two?" Dylan's deep voice startled Maddie.

"Sure. The chili's in the microwave," Maddie said,

opening the refrigerator so she could focus on food and not Dylan. Out of the corner of her eye, she watched him walk over to the table and sit down next to his brother.

"What did you do? Have a fishing accident?"

Jason made a face. "That's almost funny."

Maddie could see by the teasing grin on Dylan's face that's exactly how he meant the words to be taken.

"Don't those things hurt?" he asked, motioning toward the two gold rings in his brother's eyebrow.

"Not as bad as when I had the tattoo put on my butt," Jason shot back.

Maddie was curious to hear what Dylan's response would be, only he didn't get a chance to continue the brotherly ribbing because the phone rang.

"Hi, Mom. How's it going?" he said when he'd picked up the cordless, causing both Maddie and Jason to look in his direction.

Jason, however, didn't just look at his brother. He jumped up from the table and ran over to Dylan. He was shaking his head and motioning in a gesture that said he didn't want his mother to know he was home.

Dylan paid no attention. "Jason's here. He came home for the weekend. You want to talk to him?"

The teenager reluctantly took the phone, but not before glaring at his brother. Maddie popped a bagel into the toaster and pretended not to notice the looks being exchanged between the two brothers.

Neither son talked to Leonie for very long, nor did either of them ask Maddie if she wanted to say hello.

As soon as the conversation had ended, Jason faced

Dylan and demanded, "Why did you tell her I was here?"

"Is there a reason I shouldn't have?"

"Yeah. The semester just started. She's probably thinking something bad happened if I'm home already."

"Did something bad happen?" When his brother didn't answer, Dylan said, "Jason, are you in some kind of trouble."

"No."

"Then why didn't you want Mom to know you're here?"

Again there was a hesitation. Maddie could see by the look on Jason's face that he had something to tell his brother.

"It's none of your business, so butt out," he finally said sullenly, then sat back down at the table and returned to the sports page.

Dylan wasn't about to let the matter end. "If it concerns Mom, it's my business. Maybe you'd better tell me what's going on."

"It's nothing to you," he said. "Next month you'll be gone again and it won't matter."

"It matters now." Dylan calmly stood over him. "Why don't you tell me what the problem is."

"Because it doesn't concern you," Jason said stubbornly, then began eating the bagel Maddie had toasted for him.

"Is it your grades?" Dylan asked, but his brother didn't answer, so he pulled out a chair and sat down. "Look, I'm not asking because I want to give you a hard time. I'm your brother. If there's something I can do to help you, I'd like to do it."

Jason eyed his brother suspiciously, as if contemplating whether or not he should confide in him. Finally he said, "If you must know, I've decided to quit school."

Maddie expected Dylan to explode in anger. To her surprise, he simply said, "In the middle of the term? Hasn't Mom already paid for this next semester?"

"She'll get some of the money back. It's still early."

"Then you've already officially withdrawn?"

"No. I'm going to do that on Monday when I go back to get Brandy."

"Brandy?"

"She's my girlfriend," Jason explained. "She's going with me to California."

Just then the timer on the microwave sounded. Maddie was forced to give her attention to the chili and didn't see the look on Dylan's face.

"California? And how do you plan to get there?" she heard him ask.

"In my car."

"*Your* car?"

"Dad's old one. Mom said I could have it. I'm not supposed to take it to school, but she never said I couldn't take it to California," he stated, using the logic of a nineteen-year-old boy.

Maddie sneaked another glance at Dylan. His face showed no emotion, leaving her to wonder what was going through his head.

"Just why are you going to California?" he asked evenly.

"To get jobs."

"What kind of jobs?"

"We don't know yet, but we'll figure something out. Brandy wants to be an actress. She's been in all the school plays."

"So now she's ready to head for the big time." Dylan's voice remained calm.

Maddie didn't think it was going to stay that way much longer. He looked as if he was about ready to let his younger brother have it. Not wanting to be present when that happened, she said, "I'm going to leave this chili on warm until you're ready." She started toward the door, but Jason stopped her.

"No, Maddie. Don't go. You understand what I'm talking about. You told me you dropped out of college to be a dancer." He looked at her with an appeal in his eye.

"My situation wasn't quite the same as yours, Jason," she told him, aware of Dylan's eyes on her as she spoke.

"But you understand, right?" Again he looked at her like a puppy wanting to be comforted.

"I know it's tough to make the kind of decision you're making," she evaded. "You want to do what you think is best for you."

"That's right. I have to do what's best for me," he declared confidently.

"And what makes you so sure leaving school is the right thing?" Dylan asked. "Getting an education is important."

"You're a fine one to talk," Jason said. "When you were my age, you weren't in college."

"No, I was in the Marines. I put in my time, Jason. Instead of four years at college I spent six years busting my butt following orders and taking every class offered to me. My education came from the military," Dylan told him.

"And I'm going to get my education from living my life the way I want to," Jason boasted. "College is not for me and I'm not going to continue doing something that's a waste of time."

"Getting an education is never a waste of time," Dylan contradicted him.

"It is for me and I'm not doing it, so get off my case." He grabbed the bagel and his glass of milk. "Thanks for breakfast, Maddie. I'll be in my room where I won't get hassled."

"If you're going to take food into that room, make sure you clean up after yourself," Dylan called out to his retrieving figure.

"Jeez! You're not my old man, so why don't you quit acting like him," he grumbled as he stormed out of the kitchen.

Dylan said to Maddie, "Thanks for keeping the chili warm. I'll be right back."

She watched him leave and wondered just what he was going to say to the youngest Donovan. She decided not to wait to find out. She left a note on the table, telling him all he had to do was pour the chili into a bowl and eat it. Then she hurried upstairs, away from the Donovan boys.

DYLAN WASN'T SURPRISED to find Maddie gone from the kitchen when he returned. He wished she hadn't witnessed his argument with his brother. Even though she treated Jason like a brother and was more than likely aware of his problems at school, he hadn't wanted her to hear their discussion of family matters. He especially didn't appreciate that Jason had brought his past into the conversation.

Even if he did suspect that Maddie already knew more about him than the average tenant usually knows about her landlady's son. She'd lived with his mother for the past year and a half and had become like one of the family. It was rather unsettling—wondering just how much she had been told about him.

He decided to find out. He had just finished the chili she'd left for him when he saw her pass through the hallway carrying a basket of laundry.

"Maddie, could I talk to you for a minute?"

"What is it?" She stood with the basket propped against her hip, staring at him with an impatience that warned him she didn't have time for any fun and games.

He would have liked to have proved to her that she'd enjoy playing with him, but he didn't. He simply said, "Do you think you could sit down for a minute?"

She hesitated, then with a sigh put the basket on the floor and took a chair across from him at the table. She'd tied her hair back with a scarf and wore no makeup, but to Dylan she couldn't have looked more attractive.

"I'm sorry you were stuck in the middle of what

happened between me and Jason earlier,'' he apologized.

She shrugged. ''It's all right. I understand. I have two younger sisters. One's the same age as Jason and at times she sounds an awful lot like him. Whenever she doesn't like what I have to say she uses that 'You're not my mother' line on me.''

''Where is she now?''

''At the University of North Dakota studying to be a nurse.''

''It sounds as if she at least has some direction in her life.'' He washed the last of the chili down with Coke.

''It's hard for any nineteen-year-old to know what career to choose. I struggled with the same issues that Jason's facing.''

''Did you really quit college?''

She nodded. ''Middle of my junior year. I was short on money and I had an opportunity to do something I love to do so I took it.''

''Any regrets?''

She shook her head. ''No. As I already told you, being in the traveling dance company was much harder than I expected, but it was a good experience. Maybe Jason will be able to say the same thing a few years from now.''

''You could be right, but I know my mom's not going to be happy. She told me he was having problems adjusting to college, but I don't think she expected him to quit without discussing it with her.''

''It hasn't been easy for him since your dad died,'' she said, her voice full of compassion. ''Losing a parent is like losing a compass. It takes a while to learn how to figure out in what direction you should be going.''

Dylan wanted to tell her that as a compass his father had been off center, but he knew he couldn't make such a comment without taking their conversation in a direction he didn't want it to go. ''Kids change a lot during their adolescence—physically and emotionally.''

''He's still trying to figure out who he is and what's ahead for him,'' Maddie said in his brother's defense.

''I've been there and done that,'' he said on a sigh. ''It's hard for me to fault him for wanting to set out on a different path than what he's expected to do. I did the same thing when I was his age.''

''Is it true you turned down a scholarship to join the Marines?''

Dylan figured Garret had done more than warn Maddie to be careful around him. ''So you do know about that.''

She gave him an apologetic smile. ''Our mothers were the best of friends, remember?''

So it wasn't Garret who'd told her. ''You knew way back then?'' When she nodded, he added, ''Then you must also know I never got along with my father.''

''Things were okay the summer I was here. What happened?''

He was tempted to tell her exactly what had been the turning point in his relationship with his dad, but he knew he couldn't, for it would mean sharing a secret that could come back to hurt his mother. Instead he gave the answer he'd been giving his family for the past thirteen years.

"My father had rules and expectations...probably because I was the oldest. I didn't want to have to march to anyone's beat but my own."

"You don't strike me as the rebel type."

"At eighteen I was, so I left."

"That must have been hard on your mom."

"It was. Over the years she did her best to get us to reconcile, but it just never seemed to work out. My dad and I couldn't talk to each other without there being antagonism." He shook his head at the memory. "I guess we just weren't meant to get along."

He was surprised when she said, "I can understand that. I don't get along with my father, either. I seldom see him."

"Why?"

"Mainly because he and my mother divorced when I was fifteen."

"That couldn't have been very long after you were here."

She shook her head. "It was the reason I stayed with your family. All three of us girls were sent away for the summer. My two sisters went to stay with my aunt in Wisconsin. She didn't have room for me, so my mom asked yours if I could stay here while I attended the dance camp."

"Did you know your parents were having marital problems?"

"No fourteen-year-old wants to believe her parents have fallen out of love." She got up to get herself a can of Coke from the refrigerator. "I'd hoped they were just going through a rough spell, as my mom always called it, but after I got back the inevitable happened. My dad moved out of the house.'' She popped the top on the can as she sat back down at the table. ''I thought you knew.''

He shook his head. ''Mom never mentioned it. She was too busy trying to make peace between me and my dad.''

She smiled weakly. ''And she's very loyal to her friends. She's so considerate when it comes to other people's feelings, and it was a very humiliating time for my mom. At first she didn't want anyone to know that she'd been dumped for a younger woman, but when he remarried a few years later, there wasn't much point in denying it.''

''So your stepmother is closer to your age than his?''

She took a sip of the soda. ''Yes, but she's not the woman responsible for breaking up our family. He had several women before finding the one he wanted to bear his future children.'' There was bitterness in her voice.

Dylan felt a rush of empathy for her. Her father had been an adulterer, just like his, breaking vows that should have been sacred. Again he was tempted to tell her the secret he'd kept for thirteen years, but thoughts of his mother stopped him.

''Do you have any contact with him at all?'' he asked.

She nodded. ''He calls every now and then, but my sisters and I know that it's more convenient for him to pretend we don't exist. We remind him of how old he is and he wants to think he's young like his second wife."

"I'm sorry."

She shrugged. "I've accepted that my relationship with him will never be what I'd once hoped. I can't change how he feels about me."

Anger for the man who'd always been just a face in a picture in his mother's photograph album rose inside Dylan. He understood all too well the bitterness Maddie felt toward her father. He'd had those same feelings.

"I don't know why some men have to be so stupid," he remarked, thinking of his own dad.

"Fathers aren't like friends. You don't get to pick the one you want," she stated with a sadness in her eye that made Dylan want to put his arm around her in comfort. Then she said, "That's why you're lucky, Dylan. You had parents who honored their commitment to each other. You didn't have to deal with the issues divorce forces a family to face."

No, but he'd had to deal with the frustration and anger he'd had for his father and keep a secret that could cause his whole family to suffer. He wanted to tell Maddie that she wasn't the only one who'd suffered because of a father's infidelity, yet if he did, he would put her in a difficult position.

"No one has the perfect family, Maddie," he said soberly.

"Maybe not, but yours looks pretty good from where I sit," she said, lifting her Coke can in salute.

"I can see why Mom thinks of you as a part of it," he said sincerely.

She looked totally taken aback by his comment. "What a nice thing to say. Thank you."

He reached across and took her hand in his. "I can be nice, Maddie. I wish you'd let me show you just how nice I can be."

"Dylan? You here?"

Maddie snatched her hand out of his at the sound of Shane's voice. Dylan wasn't sure she was quick enough as his brother came into the kitchen, an oblong glass baking dish covered with aluminum foil in his hands.

"I brought you something," he said, eyeing the two of them suspiciously. He set the dish on the table in front of his brother. "Jennifer sent dinner over. All you have to do is stick it in the oven. The directions are on the top." He gestured to a three-by-five note card that was taped to the aluminum foil. "She said this way Krystal and Maddie wouldn't have to worry about fixing something for you. They might want to spend the evening with their guys if the roads improve."

"Tell her I appreciate her thoughtfulness," Dylan said, although relieving Maddie of her cooking duties was not a favor he needed. Nor did he like to think of her spending the evening with Jeffrey.

"That was sweet of her, although I doubt if Krystal will be going out even if the roads do improve. She's got the flu," Maddie said, leaning closer to Dylan to read what was on the note card.

"How bad are the roads?" Dylan asked, hoping that Maddie wouldn't be able to go anywhere else for dinner.

"They're a mess," Shane answered. "It wasn't too difficult for me because I borrowed my father-in-law's four-wheel-drive pickup. It has a plow, too, which is the other reason I stopped over. I'm going to do Mom's driveway."

"I did the walk once yesterday, but it'll need to be done again," Dylan told him.

When Shane stared at him in disbelief, Maddie said, "He insisted on shoveling. I tried to tell him, but..." She ended with a shrug.

"No need for that today. I'll take care of it," Shane announced.

"If you need any help, you can get Jason out of bed," Dylan said.

"How come he's home?" Shane wanted to know.

Maddie must have seen the introduction of Jason's name as her cue to leave. She got up, taking the baking dish with her. "I'm going to put this in the refrigerator and then get back to my chores. Tell Jennifer thanks for me, will you, Shane?" She hurried from the room, pausing only to pick up her laundry basket.

Dylan hated to see her go. What he didn't want was to discuss Jason with his brother, yet he knew he didn't really have a choice.

"So now what did Jason do?" Shane asked when they were alone. "That is the reason why Maddie rushed out of here, isn't it? She knows he's in some kind of trouble?"

Dylan grabbed two beers from the refrigerator and handed one to Shane. "Sit down and I'll tell you what he told me."

When he'd finished, Shane said, "He's not going to

California. He's going to stay in school.'' He slammed his bottle down on the table, then jumped to his feet. ''Where is he now?''

''In his room.''

Without another word, Shane walked out of the kitchen. Dylan listened for voices raised in anger. There were none.

A short while later, Shane returned. Alone.

''Any broken body parts?'' Dylan quipped.

Shane sunk down onto a chair and said in amazement, ''I don't think he listened to a word I said.''

''I thought I was the only one Jason figured was clueless,'' Dylan said with a crooked grin.

''He thinks he knows more than both of us put together.'' Shane took a long drink of the beer he'd left on the table. ''It sure would be a lot easier if Dad were here.''

Dylan knew there was no point in bringing their father into the conversation, so he simply said, ''But he's not.''

''So what do we do?''

''I'm not sure there is anything we can do,'' Dylan said calmly. ''He's nineteen. Legally he's an adult.''

''That doesn't mean we should let him make a big mistake,'' Shane protested.

''We don't know it's a mistake.''

That drew another look of disbelief from his brother. ''You're kidding me. You're on his side?''

''No, but I'm trying to see both sides of the issue. Believe me, I don't want to see him quit school, but I'm not sure that's our decision to make,'' he reasoned.

"If he quits now, he'll never go back."

He shrugged. "It's a possibility." He didn't want to argue with Shane, especially not over Jason.

Shane shook his head. "I don't know what's happened to that kid. He's got more pierced body parts than I have shoes, and he looks as if he dropped a bottle of bleach on the top of his head."

"Could be worse. It could be purple," Dylan said with a grin.

"It *was* purple. Last summer. You weren't here."

Dylan wished he had been around more for his youngest brother. "I think the way he looks, the way he's behaving…it's all part of being nineteen and trying to figure out where to go next."

"That may be, but college is important. I think Garret should talk to him." Shane suggested. "He's closer to him in age."

"He's just warned me not to come down too hard on Jason. Do you really think he's going to want to play the heavy?"

"You can ask him. He's going to stop by when he finishes at the hospital."

"I hope he doesn't think he needs to come by and check up on me."

"I'd say it's more likely he's using you as an excuse to see a certain redhead," his brother said with a wiggle of his eyebrows.

"He's interested in Krystal?"

"You didn't know?" Shane rolled his eyes. "Oh, please tell me you didn't treat her as if she was fair game."

"No, I didn't," he denied emphatically. "She's

Mom's tenant. What do you think I do? Hit on every woman who happens to be in the same room as I am."

"Then you *have* changed, haven't you."

Dylan held up his fist as if he might punch him, then allowed a smile to spread across his face. "She is good-looking, isn't she?"

"Very."

"Then what's keeping our little brother from making his move?"

"You'll have to ask him that question." He finished the rest of his beer and then stood. "I better go plow the drive."

"Thanks for stopping by, Shane, and tell Jennifer I appreciate the food," he said sincerely.

"No problem." He started toward the door but stopped. "About Maddie..." he began.

"What about her?"

He looked as if he wasn't sure he should say what was on his mind. Finally he said, "I just thought you should know Mom thinks of her as a daughter."

"I know. You already told me that. So did Garrct. And Mom."

He shrugged. "Then you know."

"I know," Dylan repeated. That didn't stop him from thinking of her as something else, too. But he wasn't about to tell Shane that. His feelings were for Maddie's ears only. And he would tell her. Soon.

CHAPTER EIGHT

Dear Leonie: I've always prided myself on making smart decisions when it came to men. I thought I could handle an innocent flirtation with this guy I know, but then he kissed me and nothing's been the same since. I like him but I don't want him to want me. Or do I? Why won't my brain tell me what to do?
Signed: Knocked for a loop by a kiss

Leonie says: Flirting is never innocent and it sounds as if you're not listening to your brain.

MADDIE WAS STANDING on a chair trying to hang the curtain back on the window above her bed when she heard a knock on her door. Expecting it to be Krystal, she automatically called out, "It's open."

She was startled when a man's voice asked, "Need some help?"

She glanced over her shoulder and saw Dylan standing in the doorway. "Oh! I thought you were Krystal."

"Does that mean I can't come in?"

"No, it's all right." She attached the rod to its bracket, aware that with her arms raised, the shirt she wore crept up, exposing her midriff. Before she could step down, he was at her side, offering her his hand as she climbed off the chair.

"Thanks," she said, trying not to let him see how his nearness affected her.

Not that he would have noticed. He was too busy surveying the room. "This certainly doesn't look like the place where my brothers and I used to wrestle."

"Your mom wanted to give the house a more contemporary look," she told him as he made a 360-degree turn. "What do you think?"

"It looks good…and much neater than the way my brothers kept their room." He gave it one more quick appraisal before saying to her, "I like it."

Although she knew he referred to the room, the look in his eyes told her he meant the double entendre. "It's actually bigger than an efficiency apartment. I've plenty of room."

"I can see that." He stared at her treadmill, which was draped with damp garments. "Do you always use that as a clothes rack?"

"Only on the days I do laundry," she answered.

"If you lived in Saint Martin you wouldn't need a treadmill. You could walk beside the ocean every morning."

"Is that what you do?"

He nodded. "It's a great way to start the day." He strolled over to her bookcase, taking time to browse through the titles. Then he wandered over to her desk, pausing in front of her computer. "You on the net?" Seeing her nod, he asked, "What's your e-mail address?"

"Why? Are you going to send me an e-mail?"

"I might," he said with a smile that held a tempting promise.

"Is that what you've been doing on your laptop? E-mailing your friends?"

"Mostly I've been working, although that hasn't always been easy to do. Mom gets a lot of phone calls, even on weekends. There must be an awful lot of lovesick people in Saint Paul," he remarked with a shake of his head.

"People like to talk to her about relationships. They don't have to be neurotic to do that."

"And do you talk to her about your love life?" She could see the curiosity in his eyes.

"No."

The curiosity changed to admiration. It was obvious that he didn't see the need for anyone to seek advice on romance. She decided it would be wise to change the subject. "Why are you working? I thought you were on a short-term disability leave."

"I am, but I like to be available to answer any questions that might come up. That's what's so great about modern technology. An answer to a problem is only a click of a mouse away."

She gave him a look of admonishment. "Then you're not really bored here, are you?"

"I guess *frustrated* would be a better word to use." He lifted his incapacitated arm as far as the sling would allow. "I'm used to being able to do everything for myself."

Maddie folded her hands in front of her. "Is that why you came up here? Because you need my help with something?"

"No. I just wanted to see you." This time there was no mistaking the message in his eyes.

"I'm rather busy," she told him, shifting uneasily from one foot to the other.

He again made a survey of the room. "Looks to me like the housework is done." He extended his left hand. "You can take a short break, can't you? I want to show you something."

The smile on his face and the hand reaching out to her were a temptation she didn't want to resist. Cautiously she asked, "And what is that?"

He pulled her over to the love seat. "Let's sit down."

She knew she shouldn't, but he could be so very charming when he wanted to be. "Okay, I'm sitting. Now what?"

"You need to reach into my pocket," he said with a gleam in his eye.

"Uh…I don't think so," she said leaning away from him.

His grin told her he knew exactly what effect his request had had on her. "All right. I'll get it myself." With his left hand he managed to reach under his sweater and pull a small black rectangular case from his shirt pocket. "Have you seen one of these before?"

She leaned closer and watched as he opened it to reveal a small game board. "Electronic chess?"

"I found it in Jason's room. It's pretty cool. You can play by yourself or with a partner. Here. It's probably easier if you hold it since you have two hands."

He leaned close, explaining the various functions of the electronic device.

Maddie found it difficult to concentrate on the game. He smelled good, he looked good, and being so close to him made her breasts tingle.

''So do you want to go it alone or do it with me?'' he asked, his breath warm on her cheek.

''I...'' she began, but wasn't sure what she wanted to say. All she could do was stare at him. At his lips. She wanted to feel his mouth on hers, to know if his kiss could possibly be as fantastic as she'd imagined it to be all those years ago.

''Maddie, what is it you want me to do?'' His voice was husky and inviting.

Her lips parted, and she inched even closer to him. In the blink of an eye his mouth was on hers. Her teenage fantasy had finally come true. And just like the fourteen-year-old Maddie would have done, she sat as stiff as a board. His lips moved over hers, coaxing and tantalizing her until she could no longer ignore the response her body longed to give.

Any inhibition she may have harbored disappeared, her instincts guiding her as she deepened the kiss by letting her tongue find his. She slid her arms around his neck, pulling him closer, her body moving against his in an intimate invitation.

''Oops, my fault. Pretend I didn't come in.''

The female voice was like a bucket of cold water on a newly built fire. Maddie opened her eyes to see Krystal backing out of the room, an apologetic look on her face.

Maddie pushed herself away from Dylan with a

groan. "Just great. Now she thinks something's going on."

"Something *is* going on, Maddie," he said in a voice that caressed her skin just as the kiss had caressed her lips.

She jumped up from the love seat. "No, it's not. It most definitely is not," she said through lips that still tingled from the pressure of his. "You really need to go back downstairs." She didn't look at him as she spoke.

"Come on, Maddie," he pleaded, placing a hand on her forearm.

She snatched it away. "I mean it. I have a boyfriend. It may not matter to you, but it matters to me."

To her relief, he didn't try to convince her to let him stay. He slowly walked toward the door, but paused before leaving. "It *does* matter to me, Maddie, but that doesn't mean I'm going to apologize for kissing you."

She looked at him then and desire spread through her the way fire spreads through dry grass. She couldn't let him know. "I don't expect you to. I would just appreciate it if you'd remember that I'm not looking for that kind of entertainment."

"Go ahead and tell yourself that, Maddie, if it makes you feel better," he said, and before she could think of a suitable retort, he was gone.

Maddie stood for several moments, her fingertips on her lips, trying not to remember how good it had felt to have his mouth on hers. He was right. She'd wanted him to kiss her—but only to fulfill a teenage fantasy she'd had for fourteen years. She was just like hundreds of other women who'd been kissed by Dylan Donovan.

And there would probably be at least a hundred more in the future. She didn't want to think about it. She *wouldn't* think about it. She shook her head, as if the simple motion could erase what had just happened. She returned to the window to drag the chair back to her desk. At the sound of her housemate's voice, she turned toward the door.

"I heard footsteps on the stairs so I figured it was safe to come in." Krystal didn't wait to be invited in, but padded into her room in her slippered feet, saying, "I am so sorry I barged in on the two of you. I had no idea you were doing that."

"We're weren't doing *that,*" Maddie denied stridently.

"You weren't? Then what were you doing?"

"Playing chess."

That produced a laugh from Krystal. "I don't think I've ever seen the game played that way before."

"It's not what you think." Maddie knew her words sounded lame. "All right. He kissed me, but not for the reason you think."

"Maddie, dear, there's only one reason a man kisses a woman," she said, sounding more worldly than Maddie ever could. "He likes you. I picked up on it last night. Every time Jason or I mentioned your name his ears perked up."

"That's nothing new. His ears do that whenever a single woman's name is mentioned. It's like he has radar," she grumbled.

"Uh-uh. I flirted outrageously with him and got nowhere.'' She walked over to the love seat and sprawled across it. ''So what are you going to do about Jeffrey?''

''I'm going to do nothing.'' Maddie flopped down on her bed, placing her chin on her hand.

''I'd give you advice on how to juggle two guys at the same time, but my head's plugged and I'm not sure I'd make any sense,'' she said with a sniffle.

''I don't plan to juggle two men.''

Krystal groaned. ''Please don't tell me you're going to let a great opportunity like this pass?''

''I don't regard juggling two men as a great opportunity,'' Maddie said dryly.

''I'm talking about Dylan. Maddie, he's gorgeous and he wants you.''

''Well, I don't want him.'' She knew it wasn't exactly the truth.

''It figures. I'm the one who'd kill for a chance with such a guy and you're the one who has him following you to your room.'' She let out a long sigh of injustice. Then she sat up. ''Why *was* he in your room kissing you if you didn't want him to be here?''

Maddie exhaled a gust of air that ruffled her bangs. ''I told you. He wanted to play a game of chess.''

She chuckled. ''I don't think the game he's interested in is chess. The game of love, maybe?''

This time Maddie was the one who chuckled, but without humor. ''I'm not sure he and I have the same rule book when it comes to that one. In fact, I'm positive we don't.''

''He's definitely not the kind of guy looking to

make friends with a woman before he gets romantically involved with her."

"If that's a dig at Jeffrey..." she began.

"Just the truth, Maddie, dear," Krystal said placatingly, draping an arm across her forehead so that the sleeve of her robe covered her eyes.

"I'm comfortable with my relationship with Jeffrey."

"Maybe that's the problem."

"I didn't say there was a problem."

She lifted her arm to stare at Maddie. "You're attracted to Dylan. Isn't that a problem?"

"Not if I don't act on that attraction."

"Why wouldn't you?"

"Because Dylan's like a hummingbird. He goes from flower to flower, always in search of something sweeter."

"Uh-huh. That's the attraction. He's a real bad boy."

"Exactly. The kind of man I avoid."

"Maybe you shouldn't avoid this one. You know what Mae West said—a woman has to love a bad man once or twice in her life to be thankful for a good one."

"I don't think I need that particular life lesson, thank you."

"Looks to me as if you may be too late to stop it." She pushed herself up from the love seat and headed toward the door. "I feel lousy. As fascinating as this conversation is, I'd better go back to bed. I hope I can get up for dinner. It could be very interesting."

Not if Maddie had anything to say about it. As soon

as Krystal had gone, she reached for the phone and dialed Jeffrey's number.

"Have you been out? How are the roads? They're not too bad? Great. I'm coming over to make you dinner."

DYLAN SPENT MOST of the afternoon in his mother's office, going over an estimate of materials needed for a future project. But he found it difficult to concentrate. His thoughts were on Maddie and how sweet she'd tasted. Just thinking about her made his body ache with longing.

Despite her protests to the contrary, she'd wanted him to kiss her. When it was over, she'd told him that she wasn't looking for *that* kind of excitement.

He smiled. It definitely had been exciting. There was no denying the chemistry between the two of them. He didn't know what kind of a relationship she had with Jeffrey, but Dylan would bet that the English professor didn't leave her breathless the way his kisses had.

He, on the other hand, had a pretty good idea how to win her heart. For that was exactly the part of her he needed to reach. He needed to convince her that there was more to a relationship than being comfortable.

He closed the file on the concrete estimates and reached for the yellow pages. He found the listing he wanted, then picked up the phone and dialed the number.

"Are you open? You are, but you're not making deliveries? No problem. I can walk." He grabbed his coat, pulled on his work boots and went out into the cold.

Besides plowing the driveway, Shane had shoveled the walk in front of the house, as had the rest of the neighbors. Getting to the floral shop was easier than Dylan had expected it to be. Picking out the right flowers for Maddie, however, was much more difficult.

He decided on a colorful mixture that included exotic-looking tiger lilies and traditional carnations. He smiled to himself as he watched the florist put together purples, oranges, reds and yellows in a combination that reminded him of Maddie—vibrant and exciting. He wondered what she would say when he gave them to her.

He never found out. When he got back to the house, he discovered a note on the kitchen table. It read, "Dylan, I'm having dinner at Jeffrey's. The casserole Jennifer prepared is heating in the oven. All you have to do is take it out when the timer rings. If you need help, Jason told me he'll be home for dinner."

Dylan crumpled the note and tossed it in the wastebasket. He was tempted to do the same with the flowers, but then he realized that just because he couldn't hand the flowers to Maddie personally, it didn't mean he couldn't give them to her.

He climbed the stairs to the second floor and set the box outside her closed door. He was about to leave when he heard a voice.

"If those are what I think they are, they should probably be in water."

He turned to see Krystal standing in the doorway of her room. She had on a bright pink robe that covered her from head to toe and a pair of pink slippers that had bunny heads on their toes.

''Your mom has several vases. Want me to find one for you?'' she offered.

''Are you up to it? Maddie said you weren't feeling well.''

She dragged a hand over her hair. ''It's the flu. I suppose I look like a wreck,'' she said on a nervous giggle.

''Not to me you don't. You look like someone who's kind enough to offer to help a person in a similar predicament.'' He motioned to his injured shoulder. ''I'm not full speed, either.'' He gave her a smile of understanding.

She came toward him. ''Then maybe we can help each other.'' She swung the sash on her robe as she stood before him, as if it were a lariat. ''Here's the deal. You help me downstairs, and I'll find that vase and put those flowers in water for you. I can also put them in Maddie's room.'' She smiled slyly. ''I have a key.''

He returned the smile. ''You have a deal.'' He scooped up the flowers, then allowed her to loop her right arm through his left one before escorting her downstairs and into the kitchen, where he sat at the table while she tended to the flowers.

''It's too bad Maddie's not here to see how beautiful these are,'' she said as she snipped stems and placed them in a crystal vase filled with water. She sniffed a purple hyacinth appreciatively. ''They smell good, too.''

''You know Maddie pretty well?''

"Well enough to know when she's running away from something."

"And what would she be running away from?"

She gave him a coy look. "As if you don't know."

Dylan smiled knowingly, then sobered. "Unfortunately, the last thing I wanted to do was to send her running to the poet."

"You mean Mr. I'll-give-you-all-the-space-you-need," she said in a disapproving tone.

"You don't like him?" he asked, wondering if he'd found an ally.

"Jeffrey? He's nice enough, but somebody should light a match under the man."

So he'd been right in his initial assessment of Maddie's boyfriend—Jeffrey might know poetry, but he didn't understand women. "He shouldn't need a match. He's got Maddie."

"Exactly my point," Krystal said, jabbing at the air with the stem of a carnation. "You know, as lovely as these flowers are, I'm afraid they might make her run even faster."

"Then I guess it's a good thing I've got long legs. I don't do too badly when it comes to racing," he told her with a smug grin.

"I bet you don't."

"Anybody home?" a man's voice called out just moments before Garret stepped into the kitchen.

"It's a good thing you're here," Dylan said as his brother looked at Krystal and then at him as if sizing up the situation. "Krystal's not feeling well."

"It's just the flu," she answered, then jabbed a finger in Dylan's direction. "He's the one who needs the attention."

"Not true," Dylan interjected.

"I tend to agree with you, but I wouldn't want to face Mom if I didn't make sure everything's okay," Garret said, his eyes on Krystal. "Are you sure it's just the flu?"

Dylan could see that Shane was right. Garret may have wanted everyone to think he'd come over to check up on him, but the truth was he'd wanted to see Krystal.

She nodded. "A couple of people at work had it earlier this week. Maddie gave me some over-the-counter tablets this morning that seem to have helped."

Garret walked over to the sink, where she stood arranging the flowers. "Sometimes over-the-counter works just as well as anything I could prescribe. Are you feverish?"

"I don't think so."

He pressed the back of his fingers to her cheek. "You're warm. You shouldn't be out of bed."

"I know, but I hate staying in bed on a day off. I'm going crazy cooped up in my room."

"I know the feeling," Dylan piped up.

"And I'm hungry," she added.

"You're welcome to have some of my dinner," Dylan spoke up. "Jennifer sent over a hot dish. It's in the oven."

She smiled gratefully. "Thanks, but I think maybe I should just go back to bed. You don't need my germs around while you eat."

Garret continued to stare at her. ''I can bring your dinner upstairs to you.''

''I can't let you do that,'' Krystal told him, oblivious to the signals Garret was sending her. ''You put in all those long hours in at the hospital. You don't need to wait on me during what little time off you have.''

''We could get Jason to take a tray up to her,'' Dylan suggested, which had his brother shooting a nasty glance his way. ''I'd offer, but as you can see—'' he gestured to his sling ''—I'm short one hand.''

''Please. I don't need anyone waiting on me,'' Krystal insisted then promptly sneezed. ''Oh! Excuse me.''

''You really should be in bed,'' Garret repeated.

''All right, but first I have to finish arranging these lovely flowers. It would be a shame to see them wilt after Dylan walked through all that snow for them.'' She put the final stem in the vase, then wiped off the bottom with a paper towel. Then she looked at Dylan and said, ''Don't worry. I'll put them in a place where they're sure to be noticed.''

She padded out of the room, carrying the vase.

As soon as she was gone, Garret confronted him. ''You didn't waste any time, did you?''

Dylan straightened in his chair. ''What are you talking about?''

''Hitting on Krystal.''

He patted the chair next to him. ''Quit looking like a bull ready to charge a red flag and sit down. I'm not hitting on Krystal.''

''I suppose the flowers were to cheer her up because she's not feeling well,'' he said on a sneer.

''The flowers weren't for her. I bought them for Maddie, only she's gone, so Krystal offered to put them in water,'' Dylan explained.

If he'd expected Garret to be appeased, he was wrong. ''Maddie? Why are you giving her flowers?'' he asked, his eyes narrowing to even tinier slits.

''Maybe because she's been nursing me for the past two days,'' he answered, not wanting to admit the true reason. If he did, he knew Garret would have reminded him of Jeffrey's existence. He didn't need the reminder. ''They're simply a thank-you.''

His words didn't chase the suspicion from Garret's face, but his brother did sit down at the table. ''Where is Maddie anyway?''

''Over at her boyfriend's.''

That finally seemed to placate Garret.

''You want to stay for dinner?'' he offered. ''There's more than enough.''

Garret shrugged. ''Sure. You could probably use an extra pair of hands.''

''And you can make sure that Krystal gets dinner in her room,'' Dylan said with a sly smile.

He tried to look innocent but failed. ''I can take a tray to her.''

''You'll make the sacrifice, eh?'' Dylan said dryly. ''Hey—what's with this, little brother? I've been home almost a week and I need Shane to tell me that you've had your eye on her? Why didn't you just say something that day we had lunch at the hospital?''

''Because I haven't got a snowball's chance in hell

of getting her to look twice at me. Do you know what kind of guys she dates? Those guys who spend more time at the gym than they do at work and have arms the size of my head. She's not interested in a tired and wimpy resident whose idea of a good time is eight hours of sleep."

"You're not wimpy," Dylan argued. It was true that of the four brothers, Garret had the slightest build, but he was in no way a weakling.

"You, Jason and Shane all have Dad's physique. I had to take after Mom's side," he said on a note of disgust.

"Yeah, the ones with all the brains," Dylan reminded him. "None of Dad's relatives are doctors. And what makes you think Krystal doesn't value brains over brawn?"

He gave him a look that said, *Are you kidding?* "Have you talked to her at all?"

"No, but maybe you should. If you want her, go after her," Dylan urged him. "If you want some advice, I'd be happy to—"

He cut him off. "Just forget it. I don't need my big brother helping me get a woman."

Just then the timer rang. "That's dinner." Dylan raised his arm in the sling. "I'm at your mercy."

That brought a smile to his brother's face. "If you think you are now, wait until I help you with your exercises."

Dylan liked the easy camaraderie that followed. It reminded him of what life had been like when they'd been kids and on kitchen duty together. Jason didn't come home for dinner, but he did return about the same time that Shane stopped over. When it looked as if Jason was about to bolt rather than listen to his brothers try to convince him to stay in school, Dylan suggested the four of them play cards.

To his surprise, they all agreed to a friendly game of poker. One of the ground rules was that there be no discussion of any issues that might cause a difference of opinion. It was the first time Dylan had had a chance to enjoy the company of his brothers as adults, and he found he liked the experience.

By the time Shane and Garret left, it was after midnight and Maddie still wasn't home. Dylan sat up watching music videos with Jason, waiting to hear the sound of her pickup in the alley.

When his youngest brother went to bed and she still wasn't home, he accepted that she was spending the night with Jeffrey. As he lay awake on his makeshift bed, he chastised himself. What had he thought? That just because they were friends and they had a nonserious, companionable relationship that she didn't share a bed with him?

The truth was he'd hoped that was the case. He punched his pillow and tried not to think about her with another man.

Moments later, he heard a key in the lock, followed by a door opening and closing. Then footsteps on the stairs. So she hadn't spent the night with Jeffrey after all. A smile spread across his face and he closed his eyes.

MADDIE WOKE Sunday morning determined to act as if nothing out of the ordinary had happened to her yesterday. She'd pretend Dylan hadn't kissed her, that he hadn't left her the biggest and most beautiful bouquet of flowers she'd ever received and that she felt no different toward him today than she had last week.

Only it wasn't easy to do, not when the first thing she saw when she opened her eyes was the bouquet of flowers. He'd left no card. If it hadn't been for the note Krystal had put next to the vase, Maddie wouldn't have known who had left them.

Well, that wasn't exactly true. When she'd seen the flowers sitting on her nightstand, she'd had a funny sensation in her stomach. And when she'd looked among the flowers for a card and found none, she'd known they weren't from Jeffrey. He always included a poem when he sent her flowers. There was no poem, only a long slender stick protruding from the vase with "You're Someone Special" written in blue across the top.

Then she'd found Krystal's note. "So the kiss didn't mean anything, huh? He walked to the florist to get these for you. Lucky you. K."

Maddie didn't feel lucky at all. She felt confused. She'd gone to see Jeffrey with the hope that being with him would have its usual calming effect. But he'd seemed a bit on edge because she'd come on a night when he'd planned to work. She'd cooked him dinner, then finished the Eleanor Roosevelt biography while he'd immersed himself in his research. She frowned at the memory.

It was no wonder her neck was stiff this morning. She'd fallen asleep on his couch and he hadn't bothered to wake her until he'd finished working. If she'd known she'd spend the evening alone on his sofa, she could have gone home after dinner.

Only then she would have had to see Dylan. Dylan, who never missed an opportunity to tell her how much he wanted to be with her. Dylan, who could make her tingle by simply looking at her. Dylan, who'd walked all the way to the florist to get her the flowers.

She'd always taken great pride in not letting her emotions get the better of her, yet this morning she felt as if she had very little control over herself.

She only hoped that she could get downstairs to the shower without having to see him. Once she was dressed, she'd go to church, stay for coffee and donuts, and maybe even stop by to see her friend Natalie on the way home. Jennifer and Shane were picking Leonie up at the airport at two. It would be much easier to face Dylan in a room full of people than one-on-one in the hallway.

She tiptoed down the stairs with her towel and shampoo in her hands. She wanted to peek to see if he was still asleep, but didn't think she should take the risk of being noticed. When she reached the bathroom without bumping into him, she breathed a sigh of relief.

Showering as quickly as possible, she wrapped a towel around her head, pulled her robe back on and opened the door. No one was in the hallway and the house was quiet. She returned to her room to dress for church. She was just about to pull on her full-length coat when there was knock on her door. To her relief, it was Krystal.

"You going to church?"

"Yes. How are you feeling this morning?" she asked, buttoning her coat.

"Better. My head's still stuffy but at least I don't ache all over." She looked past Maddie's shoulder into the room. "How did you like the flowers?"

"They're lovely," she answered honestly.

"I thought so, too. Did you have fun last night?"

"Yes, I always enjoy myself when I'm with Jeffrey." She told the white lie, not wanting to get into a discussion about her love life. "I'd better go or I'm going to be late. Do you have everything you need? I can stop at the drugstore if you want me to get you more flu pills."

"No, I'm good. I'll see you when you get back."

Maddie nodded, then started for the stairs, pausing to ask, "Do you feel well enough to make lunch?"

"Sure, but Maddie, that's not the answer."

She feigned innocence. "Answer to what?"

"You're going to have to face Dylan sooner or later," the younger woman warned.

"I know. I just prefer it to be later," she said, then started down the stairs.

Maddie used the side entrance, which meant she could leave without having to go through Leonie's living quarters. The sun was shining, the air bitterly cold as she unlocked her pickup and climbed inside. To her horror, the inside dome light was on.

She inserted the key in the ignition only to hear a sickening grinding sound when she tried to start the engine. She groaned, angry at herself for not noticing the light was on when she'd come home.

She got out of the pickup and headed back up the

walk to the house. Before she could reach the door, she saw Dylan. He had on his leather jacket, but no gloves or hat.

"Having trouble?" he asked.

She rattled her keys. "Truck won't start. I think the battery has run down."

"I can give you a jump. There are booster cables in the garage." He looked at her inquisitively, waiting for either a yes or a no to his offer.

She knew it would be silly to refuse. "You sure you don't mind?"

"I don't mind." He stepped around her and headed toward the pickup. "We'll use Mom's car to get yours started. I'll move it next to your truck."

She followed him. "I thought you weren't supposed to drive?"

"It won't hurt me to back the car out of the garage and pull it alongside yours," he insisted. He reached into his pocket. "Good thing I brought the keys."

Concerned about his shoulder, she said, "Maybe I should pull the car out."

"I can do it," he stated confidently, then opened the garage door.

To Maddie's relief, he had no problem, and in only a few minutes he'd hooked up the booster cables between Leonie's car and her truck.

"You're all set," he told when her pickup was running.

"Thank you. I'm on my way to church." She didn't know why she said that. She didn't owe him any explanations.

"Now you can get there."

"Yes." She knew she needed to say something about the flowers. "Thank you, too, for the flowers. They're lovely."

"I'm glad you like them. Did you have a nice time last night?"

She didn't miss the way he emphasized "nice," as if to equate it with dull. "It was very nice, thank you. And you?" She thought it was a little absurd how they were talking to each other as if they were polite strangers.

"Shane and Garret came over. We all played cards—even Jason. We had a good time. All got along. No fighting." A hint of a smile curved his lips, as if he were proud of the accomplishment.

"Good. I'm sure your Mom will be happy to hear that." She glanced at her watch. "I'd better get going or I'm going to be late."

He nodded in understanding. "I'll see you later?"

"Sure. Thanks again...for the jump."

She climbed into the truck and backed out of the driveway, thinking how silly it had been for to her to spend so much energy fretting over seeing him again. He hadn't said a word about their kiss. He had treated her as if she were simply a woman renting a room from his mother.

She should have been relieved, but she wasn't. She was disappointed. And she knew the reason why. She liked being with him. He wasn't just someone who made her heart beat a little faster. He was a nice guy, and that was something she knew could be more dangerous than good looks.

CHAPTER NINE

Dear Leonie: I don't want to hurt my boyfriend, but I met this guy who wants to take me out for dinner—no strings attached. He's only in town for a few weeks and my boyfriend and I have always agreed that it's okay to see other people casually, but I'm feeling a bit guilty about seeing this guy. What should I do? Signed: Needing permission

Leonie says: If you're feeling guilty, this is more than a casual dinner. Be honest with your boyfriend.

DYLAN SUSPECTED THE REASON Maddie stayed away from the house most of Sunday was to avoid seeing him. Late in the afternoon she put in a brief appearance to welcome his mother home from her trip, but it wasn't long before she was once more driving away in her pickup. Dylan wondered if she was going to meet Jeffrey.

Later that evening Krystal noticed his preoccupation with looking out the back window toward the alley. "Awfully interested in what's happening—or maybe I should say what's *not* happening—in the back, aren't you?"

"Garret said he might stop by," he told her as he let the curtain fall back into place.

"Really? Then you're not looking for Maddie?"

"Has she been gone?" he asked innocently.

"As if you didn't notice." She leaned up against the counter and watched him move restlessly about the kitchen. "In case you're wondering, she's not with Jeffrey."

He shot a dubious glance her way. "What makes you think she's not?"

She gave him a mischievous grin. "This." She reached into her pocket, pulled out a slip of paper and dangled it in midair. "He called looking for her earlier this evening and we had a nice little chat."

"Then he doesn't know where she is, either?"

"No. He did tell me—"

Before Krystal could finish what she about to say, they were interrupted by Jason, who looked anxious to talk to his brother.

"You didn't say anything to Mom about California, did you?" He kept his voice low, as if fearing his mother would come into the room.

"It's not my place to tell her anything, Jason. You're an adult, responsible for your own life," Dylan told him.

"Yeah, I am. I wish you'd tell that to Shane." He opened the refrigerator and got a soda.

"He's just worried about you." Krystal spoke up on Shane's behalf. "You're lucky. Not everyone has three big brothers looking out for him."

Dylan could see that Jason didn't regard his older siblings as being his good fortune in life. "So what are your plans?" he asked his brother.

Jason shrugged. "Mom won't let me take Dad's car

back to school because she thinks you need it.'' There was no mistaking the hostility in his tone.

''I do need a car. Once I get this sling off, I'm going to have to drive myself to physical therapy on a regular basis, but that doesn't mean I couldn't get a rental car to use while I'm here.'' Dylan told him.

His face brightened. ''You'd do that?''

''Sure, but it might take me a day or two to make the arrangements.''

''That's okay. I can wait a week before leaving,'' he said. ''Do you think you could talk to Shane, too. He's been giving me a hard time over all of this.''

''I'm not sure there's anything I can say that will change his mind. He feels very strongly that you should stay in school.''

''Well, it's not his decision to make.'' Once more the defensiveness was in his voice.

Dylan held up his hands. ''I didn't say it was, but no matter what you decide, you need to discuss it with Mom,'' he stated evenly. ''You owe her that much since she's been paying thc bills for you to go to school.''

''I know, and I will,'' he said a bit impatiently. ''I need some time to figure it all out.''

Just then Leonie came into the kitchen. ''Do you want to take some food with you, Jason?''

The sound of a horn had him reaching for his backpack. ''No, it's okay, Mom. My ride's here. I've gotta go.''

''Give me a hug.'' She opened her arms and he went into them. ''You sure everything's okay?''

Jason met Dylan's eyes over his mother's shoulders. "I'm fine."

When he'd finished hugging his mother, he approached Dylan, his arms tentative as they reached for him. Dylan wasted no time in giving him a brotherly half embrace.

"Everything will work out," he said next to his ear. "You have a good head on your shoulders. Use it."

"I will," he mumbled, then pushed him away. "I better go."

As soon as he hurried out the door, Krystal said to Leonie, "You look like you could use a cup of tea. How about if I brew us a pot?"

"Tea would be nice. It's been a long day." She took a seat at the table, then looked at Dylan and asked, "Do you think I was wrong not to let him take the car back to school?"

He walked over to the table and gave her shoulder a pat. "If I'm the only reason you don't want him to take it, you might be. I can always get a rental car."

His mother sighed. "That's only one of my concerns. I'm not sure he's responsible enough to have it at school. He seems so young."

"Mom, when I was his age I'd been on my own for over a year and a half."

"I know that, but Jason's not as mature as you were at that age. I always knew that you would be all right no matter how far away from me you traveled, but Jason's had to deal with some pretty tough stuff for a kid his age." She finished with concern in her eyes.

Dylan knew she referred to the death of his father.

Again it was Krystal who spoke. "But look at the

support group he has...you, Dylan, Shane and Garret. And he's a smart guy. He'll be fine...you'll see,'' she stated reassuringly.

As she filled the kettle with water, she launched into a story about one of her cousins who'd had trouble in college and now was a high school teacher. Dylan was grateful that Krystal veered the conversation away from his brother. The less they talked about Jason, the easier it would be to keep quiet about Jason's plans.

Before long Krystal had successfully turned the conversation in a completely different direction. Instead of worrying about her youngest son, Leonie was answering questions about her trip to Hollywood, a subject that held great interest for the hairstylist.

''I still can't believe you met Shania Twain when you were at the TV studio,'' Krystal exclaimed, her face animated at the thought. ''Maddie is going to die when she hears that.''

''Maddie likes Shania Twain?'' Dylan found it surprising that someone who taught ballet and tap would be a fan of country music.

''She has all of her albums,'' his mom answered.

''And she even waited in line for five hours to get tickets to her concert, but they sold out before she made it to the front of the line,'' Krystal added.

''When's the concert?'' he asked.

''Two weeks from today.'' Krystal answered. ''It's probably just as well that she didn't get the tickets. She wanted me to go, but as it turns out, I'm going to be out of town that weekend.''

''Wouldn't she have gone with Jeffrey?'' Dylan asked.

That produced a chuckle from his mother. "Good heavens, no. Jeffrey will do just about anything for Maddie, but he draws the line at country music."

So no dancing and no country music. That was good as far as Dylan was concerned. The less they shared, the better.

"As much as I'd like to stay and listen to more of your stories, Mom, I think I'll leave you two to finish your tea. I'm going to make a few phone calls," Dylan said as he rose to his feet.

"What about your shoulder? Do you need me to help you with your exercises?" she asked.

He shook his head. "No, I'm finished for today. You sit and relax." He turned to Krystal. "Thanks for your help. I appreciate it."

"Anytime," she said with a knowing grin. "And Dylan, good luck."

Luck was something he definitely needed if he were going to accomplish his goal. Back in Jason's room, he pulled out his laptop and accessed the Internet. In a matter of minutes he'd found what he was looking for. Two tickets to the Shania Twain concert to be held at the Excel Center in Saint Paul. They were expensive, but worth every penny.

FOR TWO DAYS Maddie managed to avoid running into Dylan. It helped that on Monday the plumber finished working on the second floor bathroom, which meant she no longer had to shower downstairs.

On Wednesday morning, however, he was seated at the kitchen table reading the newspaper when she went in for breakfast. Maddie's heart thumped like crazy at the sight of him in blue jeans and a gray sweatshirt. She thought about backing out of the room before he noticed her, but she was too late. He glanced up and smiled, which made her heart beat even faster.

"I was hoping I'd see you today," he said, folding the paper and putting it aside. "I have something for you."

She didn't want to ask him what it was but found the temptation too great to resist. "And what would that be?"

"Come sit down and I'll show you."

They were words that reminded her of another time, when he'd encouraged her to sit beside him on the love seat in her room. Her body warmed at the memory.

"I'm going to toast myself a bagel. Would you like one?" she offered.

"No, thanks. I've already eaten. But you go ahead."

She could feel his eyes on her as she moved around in the kitchen, first getting the bagel from the refrigerator, then popping it in the toaster.

"I haven't seen much of you the past couple of days," he said as she poured herself a glass of orange juice.

"I've been busy," she said, deliberately keeping her back to him.

"With Jeffrey?"

"No, work," she said as the bagel popped up. She spread cream cheese on it, then took it and her glass of juice over to the table, where she sat down on the chair that was furthest away from his.

''I've been busy, too,'' he said.

He reached into his jeans pockets and pulled out a small folded piece of newsprint. ''This is what I wanted to show you.'' He slid it across the table in her direction. She stared at the paper for several seconds before reaching for it.

''Go on. Look at it,'' he instructed her.

She picked it up and unfolded it. Inside was an advertisement for the Shania Twain concert that was going to take place at the end of January.

''I have two tickets to her concert at the Excel Center.''

She stared at him in disbelief. ''How could you get tickets? They've been sold out for months.''

He lifted his brows. ''Guess I got lucky.''

Suspicious, she asked, ''Lucky how?''

''I went on the Internet and...'' He spread his hands. ''Found two just like that.''

She released a long sigh of envy. ''I didn't think about the Internet. I almost entered a lookalike contest to try to win tickets. I figured with my hair I'd have a chance, but the other part—having to sing in front of a mall full of people...'' She shook her head. ''Not me.''

He leaned closer to her. ''What about getting all dressed up and going out with a guy with a bum arm? Would you do that to get to see the concert?''

She was about to take a sip of her orange juice, but paused with the glass in midair. ''Are you asking me to go with you?''

''Yes.''

She shook her head and set the glass back down on the table. "I can't."

"Why not?"

"You know why not."

"Don't say because of Jeffrey."

She lowered her eyes to the bagel on her plate. "I don't want to discuss him."

"Good, because I don't either. I want to talk about taking you to see a concert. Two people, riding in one car, sitting next to each other at the concert hall so they can enjoy the music together," he stated in a matter-of-fact tone.

It was tempting and if it had been anyone else asking her, she wouldn't have hesitated. She had a pretty good idea that he wasn't going to the concert because he liked Shania Twain's music.

"What's your favorite song of hers?" she asked, a challenge in her eye.

He gave her a choirboy's smile and said, "I like all of them."

"Who are you discussing?"

Maddie turned at the sound of her landlady's voice.

"I'm glad you're here, Mom. You can help me convince Maddie that she must accept my thank-you for all the cooking she did for me while you were gone," Dylan stated easily.

So that's what it was? A *thank-you* for taking care of him? Maddie didn't believe him for one minute. After all, that was supposed to be the purpose of the flowers. Maddie would have mentioned them, but she didn't want Leonie to know that Dylan had given her the beautiful bouquet.

''And just what is your thank-you?'' Leonie asked, pouring herself a cup of coffee.

''I managed to get two tickets to Shania Twain, only Maddie doesn't think she should go,'' Dylan explained. ''She thinks Jeffrey will object.''

''I don't see why he should,'' Leonie said taking the chair next to Maddie. ''He's made it clear that he's not interested in the concert. Jeffrey doesn't strike me as the type who wouldn't want you to go simply because he doesn't appreciate country music, would he?''

Maddie could see that Leonie was going to be no help in this discussion. ''That's not the reason I don't think I should go,'' she began. ''Those tickets cost a lot of money. I can't accept such an expensive thank-you, not when I really did very little to help him.''

''She helped me with my exercises and she didn't just feed me. She fed Jason, too,'' Dylan countered.

Leonie put a gentle hand on her shoulder. ''Then you must accept, Maddie. Be gracious and say yes. You love Shania Twain.''

She did love the country singer's music. And it might be good to spend an evening with Dylan. She could see if the attraction she felt for him was more than the leftover remains of a schoolgirl crush.

''If you're that concerned about how Jeffrey's going to react, why don't you just call and ask him if he'd mind if you went,'' Dylan suggested.

''I don't need to ask him for permission,'' she scoffed at the idea.

''Of course you don't,'' Leonie agreed. ''But if you'd feel better discussing the matter with him first,

I'm sure Dylan will understand, won't you?'' She looked at her son with a query in her eyes.

''Absolutely,'' he said, amused by the whole conversation. He knew exactly what kind of response his suggestion would evoke in Maddie and he was enjoying every moment of her indignation.

''I don't need to discuss this with Jeffrey. I've already made up my mind. I accept your generous gift,'' she told him in a voice that sounded to her own ears very prim and proper.

''Smart girl.'' Leonie patted her on the arm. She didn't see the gleam of satisfaction that entered Dylan's eyes, but Maddie did. It frightened and excited her at the same time.

She took another bite of her bagel but found she no longer was hungry. It was as if she were fourteen again and just being in the same room with Dylan could make her lose her appetite.

Fortunately, he decided he had something to do and excused himself. Maddie thought, as he exited the kitchen, he looked like a cat who'd just found a bowl of cream. To Maddie's relief, Leonie didn't appear to notice.

''I'm glad you're here this morning,'' she said over the rim of her coffee cup. ''We haven't had much time to talk since I've been back from California.''

''I know and I'm sorry, but I'm been really busy,'' Maddie told her, wondering what her landlady would say if she told her the truth. That she'd deliberately stayed away because she hadn't wanted to see Dylan.

''Are you sure that's all it is?''

Maddie could feel Leonie's probing eyes on her. "What else would it be?"

Leonie continued to hold her gaze. "You do know that you can talk to me if something's bothering you, don't you?"

Maddie reached for her hand. "Of course I do."

Leonie gave it a gentle squeeze before releasing it. "Good. It helps to talk. I can listen without giving advice."

Maddie smiled. "I know that. You've done it often enough for me."

Leonie took a sip of her coffee, then asked, "*Is* something bothering you, Maddie?"

She hesitated, wondering if she should confide in her. She didn't need to bring Dylan's name into the conversation, but she could tell Leonie the concerns she'd been having lately about her relationship with Jeffrey.

"Yes. It's about Jeffrey," she began, wondering just how much she should tell her landlady.

"Is everything all right between the two of you?" she asked, worry furrowing her brow.

"I wish it were," she said soberly. "You know we've been good friends and I've been hoping that in time we would take our relationship to the next level. Well, I'm not sure there is another level for us. It's been over six months, yet nothing's changed."

"Love doesn't have a timetable, Maddie."

"I realize that." She wanted to ask Leonie how long she should have to wait before her heart beat faster when Jeffrey walked in the room or she would ache with longing just thinking about him.

That had only happened with one man. And that man was Dylan. Unfortunately, that wasn't something she could discuss with her landlady.

"Has Jeffrey said something to you that indicates he wants something more?" Leonie asked.

She shook her head. "All he can think about right now is his thesis."

"Ah." Leonie nodded in understanding. "That's what the problem is. He's spending so much time working that you haven't had time for your relationship."

She could have said, *No, the problem is your son has me questioning my feelings for Jeffrey.* Until Dylan had come home, she and Jeffrey had been plodding along— She stopped herself. *Plodding?* It wasn't a very romantic description.

But she feared it was accurate. For so long she'd been content to have a comfortable, nondemanding relationship. How many times had she told herself she wasn't ready for a passionate relationship, that she needed to figure out what to do with her life before she got seriously involved with a man?

Dozens, if not hundreds of times, she answered herself. Because she thought she knew what she wanted in a relationship. Only now Dylan had her wondering if she was wrong.

"I'm not sure this is about the amount of time we spend together, Leonie," Maddie admitted to her dear friend. "I'm concerned about the future. What if we continue seeing each other and later I discover he's not the right man for me?"

"That is a possibility, but on the other hand, you

could end your relationship and then a few years down the road realize that you let Mr. Right get away,'' she pointed out. ''Maddie, love takes time. Some of the world's greatest romances began as friendships. Didn't we have this discussion when you first starting dating Jeffrey?''

She nodded. But back then, Dylan hadn't been around, stirring all sorts of feelings inside her. ''In my head I know you're right. Jeffrey's my intellectual equal—that's important.''

''Yes, it is. You know I'm very fond of both of you. I'd like nothing better than to see things work out.''

''And if you didn't know both of us, if I were one of your clients, and I said I'd been seeing this guy for over six months hoping that a friendship would turn into something more, but so far nothing's happened…''

''I'd say don't give up. He's a terrific guy. Steady, reliable and one who's not going to run out on you when the water gets a little rough. He has staying power.''

Something Maddie was pretty certain Dylan didn't possess. Not that it made a difference. He'd made it clear what his intentions were. He was looking for someone to have fun with over the next few weeks.

Maddie wasn't so sure that she didn't need the same thing. Instead of listening to her head, she could follow her instincts. Go with the bad man so that when the right man came along, she'd recognize him.

''Thanks for listening, Leonie,'' she said to the older

woman, giving her a hug. "I think I know what I need to do."

YLAN'S POSTOP VISIT to the orthopedic surgeon didn't result in his getting rid of the sling as he'd hoped. One of the activities the doctor said he would allow, however, was driving, as long as he only used his hand and not his shoulder. Tired of being chauffeured around like an invalid, he managed to convince his mother to let him drive them home from the clinic.

"You're awfully quiet," Leonie remarked as he navigated the city streets.

"That's because I've been thinking."

"About your work?"

"About a lot of stuff," he said, evading her question. He didn't want to tell her that ever since he'd accidentally overheard part of her conversation with Maddie that morning, he'd been troubled. As much as he respected his mother, he couldn't help but feel that she'd given Maddie the wrong advice.

If he thought there was a way he could have told her she was wrong without arguing with her, he would have. It wasn't right for his mother to encourage her to stay in a relationship that obviously wasn't working.

And it wasn't working. Dylan knew that, but his mother didn't. Which was why he wasn't going to bring up the subject, because it would only make things more complicated than they already were.

"I'm going to have you stop at the co-op so I can pick up a few things," she said as he drove down streets made slushy by the thawing temperatures.

"Why don't you just have Maddie bring home whatever you need?"

"She's not working today. She's at the dance studio."

"Isn't that on the same block as the co-op?"

"Yes, but she doesn't get off until eight and I need a few things for dinner. You don't mind stopping, do you?"

"No, of course not." *Most certainly he did not.* Ever since this morning he'd been contemplating what he should do about Maddie. Now an unexpected opportunity presented itself. He'd be a fool not to make the most of it.

"Do you want to come in?" his mother asked when he'd parked the car in the lot next to the co-op.

"I think I'm going to take a walk up the block. There's a computer shop I'd like to check out," he told her, nodding toward the street. "How about if I meet you back here in say…twenty minutes?"

"Is that enough time for you to get what you need?" she asked.

"I think so." He handed her the keys. "Just in case it's not, why don't you take these?"

She pocketed the keys, then headed toward the co-op's automatic doors. Dylan went in the opposite direction. He crossed the street but didn't stop when he reached the computer shop. He kept on going until he came to a window that had "Diandra's School of Dance" written across it.

When he pulled open the door, a bell jingled, causing the woman seated at the front desk to glance up at him.

She wore a black leotard, her dark hair tucked up into a knot on the top of her head. In her hands was a piece of satin to which she was gluing sequins. Music could be heard in the background, a tune that sounded slightly familiar to Dylan, as well as the clicking of tap shoes on the floor. He could hear a woman's voice calling out, "Brush and stamp, brush and stamp, and turn."

"Can I help you?" the receptionist asked.

"I'm looking for Maddie Lamont. Is she here?"

"Yes, but she's with a class." She glanced up at the clock. "She'll be finished in about five minutes. You're welcome to take a seat if you'd like to wait."

Instead of sitting down on the narrow bench that stretched the length of the lobby, he stood in front a wall that was covered with photographs. Children wearing brightly colored costumes that resembled jungle animals posed with their toes turned out and their arms pointed upward. His eyes moved across the wall until they landed on a picture of the instructors. There were four women all wearing leotards with skirts made from yellow, orange and green feathers. Maddie was by far the most striking of the group.

The sound of children's voices had him glancing toward the black velvet curtain separating the studio from the lobby. It opened and a steady stream of little girls, all wearing leotards and tap shoes, filed through, followed by moms carrying backpacks and jackets.

The woman from the reception desk motioned to him. "It's going to be noisy out here until they get their shoes changed." She pushed aside the curtain, indicating he should follow her.

‘‘Maddie, someone’s here for you,’’ the young woman called out, then slipped back through the curtain, leaving them alone.

Maddie stood in the opposite corner of the room next to a small table holding a tape player. Dylan thought she looked fragile and delicate, her slim figure covered by a black leotard, a sheer pink skirt around her waist. On her feet were black ballet slippers and her dark hair was tied back in a ponytail. She had her back to him, but watched his approach through the floor-to-ceiling mirror that lined the wall. As usual, when he saw her, he felt the stirring of desire.

‘‘Is something wrong?’’ she asked, looking at his reflection in the mirror as he came toward her.

‘‘No. I just wanted to see you,’’ he answered honestly.

She was uncomfortable with his directness. ‘‘I have a group of eleven-and twelve-year-olds coming in a few minutes,’’ she told him, breaking eye contact to sort through a stack of cassette tapes in front of her.

‘‘That’s okay. I’m only going to stay for a few minutes.’’ He kept walking toward her until he was standing next to her. ‘‘What time do you finish today?’’

‘‘My last class ends at eight.’’

‘‘You get a dinner break?’’

‘‘Normally I do, but we’re short-staffed this week so I’m not taking one.’’

‘‘Then I guess we’ll have to eat dinner after you’ve finished work.’’

She looked up then. ‘‘We?’’

"I need to talk to you, Maddie. We might as well do it over dinner."

"That's not a good idea," she protested.

He stepped closer until his face was only inches from hers. "What? Talking or eating dinner."

She made a sound of impatience. "Both."

"You're wrong. It *is* a good idea." He longed to touch her but knew she wouldn't appreciate it. She looked past his shoulder, as if worried that the other woman might walk in and see something she wasn't supposed to see.

"What is it you want to talk to me about?" she asked.

"My mother."

She frowned. "Are you sure that's all?"

"Yes. I wouldn't lie to you, Maddie." He stared into eyes that reminded him of the ocean on a clear hot day. He wondered if she even had a clue as to the power in them. "I mean it. I want to talk to you about my mother."

She made him wait for her answer. "All right. I'll talk to you, but we're not having dinner together. For one thing, I didn't bring a change of clothes. All I have is my warm-up suit to put over this."

"Okay, so dinner at Forepaugh's is out. What time are you finished here?"

"I'm done at eight, but I usually stay an extra twenty minutes or so."

"Okay, I'll pick you up here at eight-thirty."

"That's not necessary. I have my truck. Why don't I just meet you at home?"

"Because we're not having this talk at the house."

The sound of giggling alerted him to the fact they were no longer alone. He glanced in the mirror and saw three gangly schoolgirls had entered the studio.

"Can we come in, Maddie?" one of them asked.

"Yes. It's okay," she called back. Then she looked at him. "I'm really not prepared to go anywhere for dinner."

"Sure you are," he told her with an appreciative glance up and down her slender body. "Don't worry. I'll take you someplace where you won't have to take off your coat." Then he whispered in her ear. "Be happy I don't kiss you right here and give those little girls something to really giggle about."

"ALL RIGHT. So where are we having this talk about your mother?" Maddie asked Dylan as they stepped out of the dance studio and into the cold air.

He took her hand in his and led her toward his father's car. "Someplace where you won't need to worry about being seen with me."

"And why should I worry about that?"

He looked her in the eye and said, "Maybe you should tell me the answer to that one."

She didn't say another word until they were seated in the car. "As far as I'm concerned, we could have had this discussion at home in front of your mother."

"No, we couldn't."

"Why not?"

"It just wouldn't be a good idea. You'll see," he said, then closed the door on her and went around to the driver's side.

Once he was seated behind the wheel, he started the

engine and Shania Twain's voice filled the inside of the car.

She tilted her head and asked, "So you really are a fan of hers?"

"I am now. I bought this CD this afternoon and I like it. She's good."

"Yes, she is." Maddie didn't want it to matter to her that he'd bought the CD simply because he knew she liked the singer, but she couldn't help feeling good about it. Jeffrey always rolled his eyes whenever she mentioned country music, and he refused to let her play any of her tapes when he was with her.

Not in the mood for conversation, Maddie sat quietly while Dylan drove, content to sit back and listen to the music. It wasn't long before he pulled into a parking lot next to an arena.

"This is it," he announced, turning off the engine.

"You brought me to an ice arena to talk about your mother?"

"And to eat." He jumped out of the car and came around to open her door. "I love the hot dogs here." As she climbed out of the car he added, "Don't worry. You can keep your coat and warm-up suit on."

"It's going to be an expensive hot dog," she told him as he slid several bills under the glass window of the ticket booth.

"We'll get a little hockey along with the dogs," he said with a wink. "A friend of mine coaches the team I played on when I was in high school. If we're lucky, we'll get to see most of the third period." He ushered her into the concessions area. "What's it going to be?

Chili dog or plain dog?'' he asked as they stood in front of the food vendor.

''Plain.''

''What about a soda?''

''Anything diet.''

While he placed the order, she went to the condiment counter, pulling napkins from the metal holder and getting straws from the dispenser. When he set his cardboard tray down on the counter next to the condiments, she noticed he had ice-cream cups sandwiched between the paper cups.

''Dessert.'' He wiggled his eyebrows. ''It's chocolate.'' He unwrapped the hot dogs. ''You like relish and mustard?''

She shook her head. ''Just ketchup.''

''Me, too.'' He squirted a generous amount of ketchup on the hot dogs, then wrapped them back up in the foil. A roar from the arena had him saying, ''Somebody must have scored.''

If Maddie had expected he'd talk to her about his mother once they were seated, she was wrong. With the game tied, he only wanted to focus on the action on the ice. She could understand why. It was an exciting finish with Dylan's alma mater coming out on top.

When it was over, he led her down the steps to the ice where he introduced her to the winning coach. Maddie didn't protest when he continued to hold her hand, even though she knew the other man would assume she was his date.

When the coach suggested they get together for dinner before Dylan went back to Saint Martin, Maddie knew that he meant the four of them—he and his wife, Dylan and Maddie. Dylan agreed it would be fun, then ended with, "It's up to Maddie. She's the one with the busy schedule."

As they made their way to the exit, she confronted him about his remarks. "You led him to believe that we're a couple."

"Did I? It wasn't intentional."

She made a sound of disbelief.

"All right, I confess. I like having you at my side. I think we could make a pretty neat couple, Maddie."

She didn't want to admit to him that the thought had crossed her mind more than once this past week. "Dylan, you got me to come out with you tonight because you told me you wanted to talk about your mother."

"That wasn't a lie."

"And how is going to a hockey game and being introduced as your girlfriend talking about your mother?" she asked as they waited for the crowd to slowly disperse through the exit gates.

"We're just getting to that point. We needed to eat and watch the hockey game first," he answered, placing his left arm around her protectively as they were jostled slightly in the crowded corridor.

"And now we've eaten and watched the game." She looked at him expectantly.

He pulled her out of the mass of people making their way to the exit into a corridor that was nearly deserted except for a few maintenance workers who were getting ready to sweep the floor.

''Mom shouldn't have been your romance coach,'' he stated evenly.

She wrinkled her nose. ''What are you talking about?''

''This morning. When she told you to stick with Jeffrey. She gave you bad advice.''

A sick feeling snaked its way through her stomach and up into her throat. ''How do you know about that?''

''I had to get something out of the basement and, when I walked past the kitchen, I couldn't help but hear some of your conversation,'' he told her.

''How much?''

''Enough to know that Mom shouldn't have said what she did.''

Maddie folded her arms in front of her. ''And what did you hear that you think she shouldn't have said?''

''That if you stay friends with a man long enough you'll discover the love of your life. Maddie, you're a passionate woman. You deserve more than companionship.''

Not wanting to admit she didn't have passion with Jeffrey, she said, ''I don't think you heard all of our discussion.''

He didn't argue the point but asked, ''Did you tell Mom about us?''

''There is no us.''

She saw his eyes darken, then he removed his arm from the sling.

''What are you doing?'' she asked, although the look in his eyes left her little doubt as to what was going to happen. It didn't matter that they were only a few feet from a steady stream of people making their way to the exit. She knew, before his mouth ever touched hers, that he was going to kiss her. She also knew that she was going to do nothing to stop him.

Because she wanted it as much as he did. There was no point in trying to resist the powerful longing that had her lips parting and her hands reaching for him.

It was a kiss that made her body tremble and her mind question how it could feel so right when it should have felt all wrong. Yet she didn't want to think, only to feel. His mouth beneath hers. His tongue touching hers. The delicious tremors of desire spreading through her, telling her that she needed him.

A loud whistle brought the kiss to an end. Maddie blushed as she realized that although most of the crowd had left, some teenagers waited in the lobby for their parents to pick them up.

Dylan didn't look the least bit embarrassed. He brushed her lips lightly one more time, then pressed his forehead against hers, his breathing ragged.

"You shouldn't listen to my mom," he said quietly.

"And who should I listen to?"

"Your heart." He reached for her hand and shoved it through the opening in her jacket so that it lay close to her breast. "Feel how it's beating? Doesn't that tell you something?"

"Now feel mine." He moved her hand until it was against his chest.

She liked the pulsating rhythm beneath her fingertips.

"Ever since that night I walked into my mother's living room and saw you standing there, I haven't been able to stop thinking about you, Maddie.'' His eyes roved over her face, studying it as if it were an artist's masterpiece. ''Something happens when we're together. You feel it, too, don't you?''

She nodded. ''It's a little scary,'' she admitted.

''For me, too. I didn't expect to come home and find somebody who makes me feel this way.'' He lifted her chin with his fingertips and stared into her eyes. ''I only have a few weeks to be here. I'd like to spend them with you, but if you tell me that's not what you want, I'll respect that. I won't send any more flowers. I'll give you thc Shania Twain tickets. I'll stay away from you, Maddie.''

She could have told him she was in love with Jeffrey and had no interest in him.

But she couldn't, because it wasn't true. ''I like being with you, Dylan,'' she told him, causing his eyes to gleam in satisfaction. ''And just for the record, I believe I told you a while back that I didn't need a romance coach.''

''Does that mean…''

''I didn't take your mom's advice. I followed my own instincts. Before I went to the dance studio today, I stopped at Jeffrey's and told him I thought we needed some time apart.''

''You're not friends anymore?''

''I hope we'll always be friends. He's a good man,'' she told him.

''Believe it or not, there have been occasions people have actually referred to me in those terms,'' he told her, the corners of his mouth quirking into a grin. ''I can be good, Maddie.''

It was said with such a devilish glint in his eye she couldn't help but grin. He planted a quick kiss on her lips, then his face grew sober.

"Our being together isn't going to make it awkward for you with my family, is it?" he asked.

She wasn't sure and admitted it. "Your mom's very fond of Jeffrey and he's Garret's friend, too."

He pulled her fingers to his lips and kissed them. "I'll do whatever I can to make it easier for you." Suddenly the lights dimmed. "I think that's our signal to leave," he said with a wry smile.

She looped her arm through his and they headed toward the exit. "Thanks for bringing me to the game. I like hockey."

"Good, because I do, too."

"So we have something in common."

"Maddie, I think over the next few weeks you're going to discover we have a lot more in common than you realize." It sounded like a promise.

She hoped he was right.

CHAPTER TEN

Dear Leonie: I can't explain it, but I've never felt such a strong connection to anyone before as I do to this guy I've been seeing. It scares me. I don't want to fall in love with him, but I'm afraid that's what's happening. What should I do?
Signed: Not ready for love

Leonie says: Falling in love isn't always a choice. Sometimes it finds you whether you're ready or not.

"YOU'RE UP EARLY," Maddie remarked when Dylan entered the kitchen on Saturday morning. She had on her warm-up suit and her hair was in a ponytail, which he knew was an indication that she was going to the dance studio.

"I could say the same about you. What time do you start work on Saturdays?" he asked as he poured himself a cup of coffee.

She stood at the sink washing up the few dishes she'd used for breakfast. "My first class is at eight."

He moved closer until they were side-by-side, though he had his back against the counter while she faced it. He liked the way she looked in the morning, her face freshly scrubbed, the faint hint of strawberries in her hair.

"You haven't been around the past couple of days," he noted.

"I've been busy." She kept her attention on the dishes she was washing.

Impatience pushed its way to the front of his thoughts. He was done with the small talk. He wanted to talk about them.

"I've missed seeing you."

A light pink colored her cheeks, then she looked up at him with a flirtatious tilt to her head, "Would you like to see more of me?"

His body responded to the provocative gleam in her eyes. "You need to ask?"

"Just checking," she said, looking smug as she lowered her eyelashes. "Are you free this evening?"

"Are you asking me out?"

She looked at him once more. "Yes." She dried her hands on a dish towel, then reached into her pocket. "I thought maybe you might want to make use of these." She held up two tickets. "They're for the Wild game tonight. One of the guys at the co-op has season tickets. When he said he couldn't go, I told him I might know someone I could take." She slowly waved the tickets in midair.

He snatched them from her, his eyes widening as he read the small print. "The second row?"

She smiled impudently. "I guess he's crazy about hockey."

And Dylan discovered that he was quickly becoming crazy for Maddie. It was only because his mother chose that moment to enter the kitchen that he didn't pull her into his arms to show her the effect she had on him.

"Good morning." His mother, as perceptive as usual, walked up to him and said, "You've got that look in your eye. Did you just find out that you have the winning numbers for last night's lottery?"

"You're close, Mom."

Maddie took the tickets from his hand and said, "I have tickets for the Wild game tonight. My boss at the co-op gave them to me because he had other plans for this evening."

His mother looked surprised. "And you're going to go with Dylan?"

"He's the only other person I could think of who might be interested in going. None of my friends are hockey fans."

From the way his mother was looking at the two of them, Dylan suspected she wasn't quite convinced that was the only reason Maddie had asked him to go with her. It wasn't much later that he discovered he was right.

"I guess you won't be around for dinner this evening, will you?" she remarked when Maddie had left for work.

"We'll probably grab something to eat after the game," he answered. She was looking at him as if he were a twelve-year-old in need of a warning to stay out of trouble.

He decided to take the offensive. "Does it bother you that I'm seeing Maddie?"

In a resigned tone she said, "I should have known

something like this would happen. I saw the way you were looking at her."

"In case you haven't noticed, Maddie's been looking at me the same way, Mom," he said, aware of his mother's unspoken accusation.

She looked at him with a look that only mothers knew how to give—the one that said you'd better listen to me because I'm your mother and I know best. "You're not going to like what I have to say—"

"Then don't say it," he cut her off, ignoring that look.

"I have to say it or I'd be breaking a promise I made to Nancy Lamont," she said, still holding his eyes.

"To do what? Protect Maddie?"

"You have been known to be a bit reckless when it comes to women's feelings," she chastised him gently.

He rolled his eyes. "So this isn't about Maddie, it's about me and my lifestyle. You don't think I should show an interest in any woman unless I have plans to put a ring on her finger."

He didn't realize he'd raised his voice until she said, "I don't want to argue with you, Dylan."

And he didn't want to make things more awkward than they already were. "I'm sorry. I don't want to argue about this, either. And I don't want to hurt Maddie. I just want to spend some time with her and she wants to spend some time with me."

"That's what has me worried."

He rubbed a hand across the back of his neck, wishing that his desire to be with Maddie didn't have to cause tension between him and his mother. "Mom, I know you only want what's best for Maddie. So do I."

She arched one eyebrow. "You think that starting something up with her when you know you're going to be leaving is what's best?"

"We have tickets for a hockey game. It's not like I'm taking her away for the weekend."

"And you think that because you both know the score, that nothing's going to go wrong?"

"What could go wrong? We're going to a hockey game." He struggled to be patient. "Look, I appreciate your concern, but we're two adults."

"Yes, you are," she agreed, looking as if she wanted to say more. To his relief she simply said, "Please promise me you'll be careful. You are both very dear to me."

He held up his hand, as if taking an oath. "I promise to be extremely careful." Then he leaned over and kissed her cheek. "There's nothing for you to worry about. Trust me."

"ISN'T THIS A GREAT GAME?"

Maddie liked the feel of Dylan's warm breath tickling her skin and was grateful for the enthusiastic hockey fans who made so much noise that it was necessary for him to speak the words close to her ear.

"It's exciting," she answered, bending closer to him and catching the aroma of his aftershave.

She knew the way to a man's heart was supposed to be through his stomach, but with Dylan she was convinced that it was through the Excel ice arena.

Never would she have guessed a hockey game could be such a great date. It was fun, it was exciting and it was surprisingly intimate. It didn't matter that there were thousands of people around them, they sat with their heads together, their arms entwined, and Maddie liked it.

It had been that way ever since they'd left the house and walked into the garage to get the car. Before he'd even opened the door for her, he'd pulled her into his arms and kissed her until she'd ached with longing for him.

Then he'd said, "I've been wanting to do that ever since you waved those hockey tickets under my nose this morning." He'd pulled her even closer to him and said, "But then every time I see you I want to take you in my arms. You've managed to captivate me like no one has ever been able to do, Maddie."

They were heady words, ones she hadn't expected to ever succumb to, but the truth was she felt the same way. Normally she wasn't a demonstrative person, but with Dylan she discovered she liked his hand at her back, his arm around her shoulder and his fingers clutching hers. He made her feel cherished and she missed his touch when he went to the concession stands.

When he did slide back into the seat next to hers, he wore a Minnesota Wild sweatshirt.

"I thought we should look the part," he told her as he handed her an identical sweatshirt. Maddie glanced around and saw that many of the fans around them wore clothing with the Wild insignia.

"You know I've never done this before," she told

him as she pulled the dark green sweatshirt over her head.

"Worn a sweatshirt with a professional hockey team's logo on it?"

"No, worn the same shirt as my date."

He grinned. "Me, neither. They say there's a first time for everything." Then he signaled a vendor, purchased two beers and proposed a toast. He raised his paper cup to hers and said, "Here's to all the firsts that wait for us, Maddie."

She tipped her glass against his and added, "To new things."

If she'd had any doubts that she'd made the right decision to ask him out, they were gonc by the end of the game. She supposed the exhilaration she felt could have been due to the atmosphere inside the arena when the Wild beat their opponents in overtime, but she suspected it had more to do with being with Dylan. Whatever the reason, as they walked out into the cold night air, she felt as if it was as close to a perfect night as it could be.

Before reaching the parking lot, they saw a small diner with a large neon sign in the window that said, "Comfort Food Inside."

"Appropriate for those times when the Wild lose," Dylan had commented as he held the door open for her.

Since the Wild had won, they hadn't needed comforting, but that hadn't stopped Dylan from ordering meat loaf and mashed potatoes. "It's been ages since I had this," he'd told Maddie when the waitress had set their plates before them.

"The same for me," she'd said, eyeing her plate piled high with a hot roast beef sandwich, mashed potatoes and gravy. Then she'd told him how her mother would cook a beef roast for dinner on Sunday, then on Monday pile the remaining leftovers onto slices of bread and smother it with gravy.

He'd mentioned that roast beef had often been on their Sunday dinner menu as well, but with four boys there were never any leftovers. That had led them to compare stories of what it had been like growing up in families where the siblings were, in his case, all boys and in hers, all girls. They'd had chocolate pie for dessert, then talked over coffee until they'd realized they were the last customers in the place.

"Another first for me. I've never had a waitress ask me to leave a restaurant because she wanted to go home to bed," Maddie said when they were once more back in the car. "I didn't realize it was so late."

"You tired?"

She shook her head. "I know I should be, but I'm not."

"Me, neither. Want to go for a drive?"

"Sure."

He slipped another CD in the car stereo system. This time it wasn't a country album, but the soft, soothing sounds of a jazz quartet. Maddie leaned back and closed her eyes, content to listen to the music.

When the car came to a stop, she discovered they were parked at the top of a hill with a spectacular view of the city. Millions of lights outlined the Saint Paul skyline, including the dome of the state capital.

When she sighed at the beautiful scene, he said, "I

love this view. This was one of my favorite spots when I was a kid. We'd park up here to watch the fireworks they have at the Taste of Minnesota festival every summer.'' He paused, then added, ''Saint Paul is a pretty good place to spend a childhood.''

''Don't you ever miss it?''

''It's not my home anymore, Maddie.''

''Is that a warning?''

''Maybe it should be.'' He reached across and brushed her cheek with his fingers. ''Work has always come first in my life and that work is in Saint Martin.''

''I know,'' she said, wishing she could have more contact with him than just the touch of his fingers.

But instead of pulling her into his arms, he straightened, putting more distance between them. ''I like you, Maddie. I like you a lot and while I'm here I want to spend as much time with you as possible.''

''But you're not going to make any promises,'' she finished for him.

''Do you want promises?'' he asked.

''No.'' There was no hesitation in her response. ''I'm not ready for promises from any man.''

''You're not.'' He sounded skeptical.

She shook her head, then went on to explain that she was still trying to figure out what she should do with her life. ''Until I have a career that I love, I'm not going to get seriously involved with a man.''

''You're still looking for the right job?''

''Yes. I like teaching dance, and working at the co-op is fun, but I feel as if there's something out there I should be doing and I can't seem to find it. That's why I keep taking continuing education classes,'' she told him, sharing with him feelings that, until now, she'd been reluctant to reveal.

"So you're okay with us taking things as they come?" he asked.

"Yes. Why wouldn't I be?"

"It was just something my mom said this morning."

"She's not happy we went out tonight, is she?"

"She's worried about you."

"About me?"

He nodded. "Thinks you're going to be hurt. That I'm going to break your heart."

She closed the distance between them, sliding her arms around his neck. "Maybe I'm the one who's going to break your heart."

"The way it's been acting lately, it wouldn't surprise me," he said, his breath warm on her face as he gazed at her. "I don't know what's in store for this heart of mine, but I'm looking forward to the ride."

She placed her lips on his, moving them slowly and softly, inviting him to find out for himself just what dangers lay ahead. A groan came from deep in his throat as he pulled her against him. Gone was the sweet temptation of her kiss. Their mouths were demanding and determined, expressing the hunger they had for each other.

Maddie wasn't sure what happened to her coat or how Dylan's fingers found the warm flesh of her midriff. Lost in the sweet sensations his touch created, she whimpered as he worked his way beneath the satiny fabric of her bra.

As if it were the most natural thing to make out in the front seat of a car, he pulled her on top of him. With her body so close to his, she could feel his arousal and suddenly all she could think of was what it would be like to make love with him. Brazenly she inched her fingers inside the waistband of his jeans and his breathing became ragged.

"We're going to be so good together, Maddie," he said thickly as his hands explored her soft, heated flesh.

His words were an aphrodisiac, making her forget everything except the need he stirred inside her. She wanted him. He wanted her. Nothing else seemed to matter.

Except the bright spotlight illuminating the car. Stunned at first, Maddie didn't move, but then Dylan gently pushed her away so he could sit up. He rolled down the window to see an officer standing outside his door. He squinted at the light shining in his face.

"Sorry. I thought you were a couple of kids," the officer said in a voice that held a bit of admonition, too. "This isn't a good place to park at this time of night."

"We just stopped to get a look at the view," Dylan told him while Maddie scrambled to rearrange her clothes.

They exchanged a few more words, then the squad car pulled away. Dylan turned to Maddie. "I guess he thought we were a couple of teenagers."

Maddie felt like one. "At least he didn't ask us for an ID."

Dylan didn't say another word, but started the car.

The ride home was accomplished in silence except for the music on the CD player. When they reached the house, he walked her to the side entrance that led to the rooms upstairs. When she unlocked the door, he stepped inside the entry with her.

"I had a great time tonight, Maddie."

"Me, too."

He reached for her hand. "I'd like to see you tomorrow."

"I'd like that, too."

"It's a good thing that cop came when he did." His eyes were dark as they stared into hers. "When we make love for the first time, I don't want it to be in my dad's car." And with those last words, he kissed her lightly on the fingertips and said good-night.

DYLAN ACHED SO BADLY for Maddie he had a hard time falling asleep. He still couldn't believe that he was thirty-one years old and he'd almost made love to a woman in a Chevy. Now he was one flight below her, taunted by thoughts of her lying in the bed above him, wondering how they were going to find the time and privacy to be together.

And that was definitely his plan. She'd made it perfectly clear that she wanted to be with him as much as he wanted to be with her. Now he had to figure out a way to make that happen without causing any friction in the family.

He hoped this Sunday wasn't going to be like the last one when Maddie had been gone the entire day. He wanted to see her. To talk to her. To laugh with her. To make love with her.

It was that last sentiment that had him thinking of places they could be together. If Garret weren't a friend of Jeffrey's, he'd have asked his brother if he could use his apartment while he was on night duty at the hospital. The only other alternative seemed to be a hotel room. He wondered how Maddie would respond to such a suggestion.

It was the final thought on his mind before he fell asleep. He awoke the next morning to the sound of someone knocking on his door.

"Dylan, I need to talk to you. Could you open up, please?"

He heard his mother's voice through the door. He glanced at the clock and groaned. Surely this couldn't be about how late he'd been out with Maddie? He stumbled over to the door. "What is it, Mom?" he said on a low grumble as he propped himself against the jamb.

"I'm sorry to wake you, but you need to call Shane," she told him. "Jennifer's grandmother passed away last night and they're going to have to go to Michigan for the funeral."

So it wasn't about Maddie. He immediately felt contrite. "I'm sorry to hear that. I'll call and give them both my condolences. Is there anything I can do to help out?"

"As a matter of fact there is. That's why I had to wake you. They need someone to take care of Cookie, their golden retriever. That's why Shane wants to talk to you before he leaves."

Dylan shrugged. "No problem. Is he going to bring the dog over here?"

"He'd rather have you stay there."

Stay there? Even in his sleepy state it didn't take Dylan long to realize that was the perfect scenario. He'd have an entire house to himself. He wouldn't have to worry about running into anybody in the kitchen. He'd be alone to do whatever he pleased whenever he wanted. He'd have a place where he and Maddie could—

"I'm on my way to church, but I wanted to let you know what had happened because Shane and Jennifer want to get on the road," his mother interrupted his musing. "They're making the trip by car."

"I appreciate you telling me, Mom. I'll call Shane right away."

She nodded. "Leave me a note if you decide to go over there before I get back."

"I will." He closed the door and reached for the phone next to the bed.

"Shane, it's me. I'm sorry about Jennifer's grandmother. Mom said you'd like me to stay at the house while you're gone?"

"I figured it would be a chance for you to get away from the women for a while. You like dogs, don't you?" Shane asked.

"Of course I do. And you're right—it'll be nice not to have to worry about whether or not I've got my pants on when I run to the bathroom. When do you need me there and how long should I plan to stay?"

"We'll probably be gone until next Saturday. Jennifer would like to leave as soon as possible, but if you have plans for today, Cookie can be on her own until this evening."

"No, I've got nothing planned. I'm sure Mom won't miss having to feed me," he said, but it wasn't his mother who was on his mind.

"There's plenty of food in the house so feel free to help yourself. I'll explain where everything is when you get here."

"Sure. I'll just take a shower and then I'll be right over."

MADDIE COULDN'T BELIEVE what time it was when she awoke on Sunday. She knew she'd crawled into bed only a few hours before dawn, but she hadn't expected to sleep so late. The sun shone brightly through her curtain as she stretched in bed.

She'd slept blissfully, but then there was no reason why she shouldn't have. She'd had a wonderful time with Dylan and her body tingled at the memory of what had happened at the lookout. A delicious shiver of pleasure echoed through her. Just thinking about the man could cause her to body to ache with longing.

Never had she experienced such intense feelings for a man. She'd always taken pride in the fact that she'd been able to control her emotions, yet last night, had the police officer not interrupted them, she and Dylan might have…

Heat spread through her body at the thought. She needed to shower and get dressed so she would be ready for whatever today would bring. Anticipation churned inside her as she thought about seeing Dylan again.

As she climbed out of bed and reached for her robe,

she noticed a piece of paper had been shoved under her door.

"Maddie, thanks for last night," the note said. "It was great, but today is going to be even better. I have a surprise for you. If you meet me at Shane's, I'll see that you get your surprise and breakfast. Dylan." Beneath the message was a roughly drawn map with an *X* marking his brother's house.

She wondered what were they going to do with the married couple? Not that it mattered. Sharing Dylan with Shane, Jennifer and Mickey would be better than not seeing him at all. But he hadn't specified a time that she should be there...and she'd slept later than usual. Had she caused all of them to wait?

She quickly showered, then pulled on a purple sweater and a pair of black slacks. Not wanting to answer any questions about last night or today, she was grateful that Krystal's door was still closed when she passed through the hallway.

She'd been over to Jennifer's on several occasions and had no trouble remembering how to get there. That didn't keep her from smiling as she glanced at Dylan's crudely drawn map.

The closer she got to the house the more curious she became as to just what Dylan had planned with his brother and sister-in-law. When she pulled into the driveway, she didn't see his car. Puzzled, she parked and then went to the front door.

Before she could even knock, it opened. It wasn't Shane or Jennifer who greeted her, but Dylan. "I was beginning to worry that you weren't coming."

"I'm sorry. I slept late," she said as she stepped inside.

He helped her out of her coat, eyeing the purple sweater appreciatively. "You look great."

"Thanks. I hope I didn't hold up breakfast."

"I'm in no hurry."

"What about the others?" She craned her neck, expecting to see either Jennifer or Shane in the living room, but all she saw was the golden retriever who moseyed over to Maddie to rub against her leg.

"That's the surprise," he answered, hanging her coat in the hall closet while she petted the dog. He put his arm around her waist and steered her into the kitchen. "The others have gone. There's no one here except you and me...and Cookie." The retriever nosed her way in between their legs, seeking affection.

"Where's everyone?"

"They had to go to Michigan for Jennifer's grandmother's funeral. I'm taking care of the place for them while they're gone."

"Oh, I'm sorry to hear about her grandmother." She glanced around and noticed that there were a couple of suitcases near the back door. "Does that mean you're going to stay here instead of at your mom's?"

"Not a bad arrangement, is it? Shane gets someone to take care of Cookie, I get a whole house to myself so I can do this—" he kissed her neck "—and this—" he slid a hand under the hem of her sweater and rested it on her waist, causing her to tremble.

"Definitely not things you'd want to do in your mother's kitchen," she said as exquisite sensations of pleasure rippled through her. ‘‘How long are they going to be gone?’’

‘‘Until next Saturday.’’ She shivered as his hand began to slowly work its way across her back. His eyes held hers as he found the fastener on her bra.

‘‘Six days,’’ she said, her voice sounding breathy.

‘‘And nights,’’ he murmured, sliding a finger beneath the narrow band of fabric.

She held her breath as she waited for him to undo the hooks holding the garment together. He managed it using only his left hand.

‘‘I promised you breakfast.’’ His breath was warm against her skin.

‘‘It’s almost lunchtime.’’ She moaned when his hand cupped a breast.

‘‘Does that mean you don’t want breakfast?’’

‘‘Not right now.’’

It was all he needed to hear. He took her by the hand and led her up the stairs to the bedroom.

‘‘TOMORROW’S YOUR DAY OFF. Where should we go? To a movie? To the mall?’’ Dylan asked Maddie as they lay wrapped in a blanket in front of the fireplace sipping hot chocolate.

She shrugged. ‘‘We can decide tomorrow. Tonight I just want to think about what a fabulous day it’s been.’’

Dylan knew she was right. It had been an incredible day. Not even in his wildest fantasies had he expected that making love with her would leave him feeling as if all of his life he’d been waiting for her to come along and bring out the best in him.

And she did. Not only when it came to sex, but with everything else they'd done. She'd taught him how to make a French pastry he couldn't even pronounce, how to do card tricks she'd learned from her grandfather, and how to two-step. Together they'd read the Sunday paper, worked the *New York Times* crossword puzzle and taken Cookie for a walk in the cold sunshine.

As he stared at her face in the firelight, he thought she must be a siren, for she certainly had cast a spell over him. When the grandfather clock in Shane's living room struck midnight, Maddie groaned.

"It can't be that time already!" She buried her face in her arm. "I have to go."

"Go? You're not staying here?"

"I don't think it would be a good idea."

"Of course it's a good idea. What's a bad idea is you driving home alone at midnight," he said, pushing himself up on one elbow. "You're not worried that my mom might find out you were here, are you?"

He could see by the look on her face that he was right. He lifted her chin with his finger. "You *are* worried, aren't you?"

"I'm not exactly worried, but it's awkward. She's very fond of Jeffrey and she wasn't exactly thrilled that you and I went out last night."

"She gave you bad advice regarding Jeffrey," he reminded her.

When she moved away from him, he didn't like the feeling that went through him. "Do you always confide in her about your love life?" he asked.

"Not in her capacity as a romance coach. I don't

need help with my love life—at least I didn't until I met you."

He wasn't sure she saw that as a positive or a negative.

Then she said, "Ever since I met you I felt this connection between us. I didn't understand it. I still don't."

He reached for her hand. "I feel it, too."

"Then maybe you can explain it to me."

"Sometimes it's better not to analyze, but to simply go with your feelings." He kissed her, hoping to prove his point.

"But I want to understand what it is," she said, unconvinced.

He rolled over and stared up at the ceiling, where the shadows from the fire flickered. He didn't understand why he should feel so connected to her, either, but he suspected one reason was that she'd confided in him about her father's infidelity. He debated whether or not he should tell her about his dad.

She leaned over him. "Why haven't you ever married, Dylan?"

"I thought my brothers would have told you the answer to that one," he said, uneasy that she'd even brought up the subject.

"I'm not asking your brothers. I'm asking you."

He could see by her eyes that she had no ulterior motive in asking such a question. She was simply curious. "I haven't wanted to get married."

"Me neither," she said, then rolled onto her back.

He decided they'd talked enough and in one smooth move he was on top of her. He covered her mouth with his, kissing her until they were both breathless. "We're two of a kind, Maddie. That's all that matters."

"Yes," she agreed, then gently pushed him away. "I need to go."

"I wish you wouldn't." He tried to tempt her to stay by planting kisses on her shoulder.

"I have to. I have no clothes to wear tomorrow."

"You won't need them," he said with a devilish glint in his eyes.

"You said you were going to take me to the movies on my day off. I need to put on clothes for that," she said as she fastened her bra.

He fell back onto the floor. "I can't convince you to change your mind, can I?"

"Tomorrow will be just as special as today," she told him.

"If it is, I will be a very happy man."

She pulled the purple sweater over her head, then kissed him. "And I a happy woman." She eluded his grasp and finished dressing.

He watched, thinking how graceful she was in everything she did. She could make tying shoes look like a work of art. The thought of her driving home alone had him reaching for his jeans.

"What are you doing?" she asked as he reached for his keys from the end table.

"I'm going to follow you home."

"You don't have to."

"No, but I want to. I know you're used to taking care of yourself, but humor me. Please?"

He liked the fact that she was independent. Most of

the women he'd dated had expected him to be at their beck and call. Maddie made no demands on his time. If anything, he was the one who waited for her.

He thought it was the reason that his interest in her hadn't waned. With each passing day he found it more difficult to share her with her work, with his family and with the rest of the world. With Shane and Jennifer returning on Saturday, he knew he needed to find another way for the two of them to have privacy. Because if there was one sure way to kill a romance it was conducting it under the watchful eye of a mother. That was something he wasn't going to let happen.

"WHERE HAVE YOU BEEN? I've hardly seen you all week," Krystal remarked to Maddie as their paths crossed in the hall outside the bathroom Friday morning.

"It's been a hectic week."

Krystal's mouth spread into a grin. "Hectic at work or hectic trying to spend all of your free time with a certain guy?"

Maddie didn't see any point in denying she'd been with Dylan. "You know, don't you?"

She nodded. "I knew it was just a matter of time before it happened. Anyone with half a brain could see there was going to be a spontaneous combustion. How does Leonie feel about it?"

"I guess she's fine with it. I haven't seen her all week." Something that bothered Maddie. She and Dylan hadn't exactly been sneaking around, but because they hadn't seen his mother, it almost felt as if they had been.

"You don't think she's going to object, do you? For Pete's sake, Maddie, she adores you. She'll probably be tickled pink that you and her son are hitting it off."

"And romance *is* her business," Maddie added, trying to convince herself as well as Krystal. "She understands why this kind of stuff happens."

"It's not like you're a couple of teenagers," Krystal pointed out.

"No, you're right."

"Just face her and get it over with. I know it's awkward, but Leonie is such a dear. It'll be fine. You'll see," Krystal said with her usual optimism.

Maddie knew what her friend said was true, yet she couldn't shake the uneasy feeling that her relationship with Dylan was going to change how Leonie felt about her. One thing she did know. She needed to talk to Leonie about what was going on and do it soon.

But when she went downstairs, Leonie was nowhere to be found.

Later that day when she arrived at Shane's, she found Dylan sitting on the sofa with his laptop open. She was about to express her concerns to him about his mother when he pulled her down onto his lap and kissed her thoroughly.

"I put in a request to extend my medical leave," he told her when the kiss ended.

"Because of me?"

"It sure as hell isn't because of the weather," he teased.

"You can get an extension?"

"I need to continue my physical therapy. I'd be

crazy not to—especially after the way this week has turned out.'' He nuzzled her neck with a trail of warm kisses.

She sighed. ''It has been incredible, hasn't it?''

''Beyond my wildest dreams.'' He stopped kissing her and looked at her, his eyes cloudy. ''Unfortunately, tomorrow we lose our privacy.''

''What happens when you're back at your mother's?''

''Actually, I've been thinking about not going back to her house.''

She straightened. ''What?''

''I'm used to living alone, Maddie. As much as I want to be close to you, it's going to be sheer torture trying to sleep when I know you're upstairs from me. That's why I've been checking into taking a room at a hotel.''

''It would be great…for us, but…''

''You're worried about my mom's feelings, aren't you?''

She nodded. ''It's awkward. I know it shouldn't be but it is.'' She got up from his lap. ''I need to have a talk with her, Dylan.''

''We're adults, Maddie. We shouldn't have to get anyone's blessing before we can see each other.''

''I know, but I'll feel better if I've talked to her about us.'' She folded her arms across her chest, suddenly chilled. ''I need to do it before Tuesday. That's her birthday and everyone's coming over. I don't want there to be any uncomfortable surprises.''

''Then tomorrow it is. Now come here and let's

enjoy our last night alone.'' He started to undo the buttons on her blouse.

''I thought you wanted me to make dinner,'' she said as her breath caught in her throat.

''Not necessary. I've ordered dinner to be brought here.'' He trailed kisses across the flesh her open blouse exposed.

When the doorbell rang, he glanced at his watch. ''If that's dinner it's early. They weren't supposed to be here until eight o'clock.''

Maddie watched him walk over to the front door and open it. A chill traveled across her arms, and she didn't need for Dylan to tell her who was at the door. It was Leonie.

CHAPTER ELEVEN

Dear Leonie: I met this guy who was only going to be in town for a month. I told myself I wasn't going to be upset when he left again, but I've gone and fallen in love with him and now I don't know what to do. Signed: Wishing I could turn back time

Leonie says: Hindsight is always twenty-twenty. Either forget him or get used to big long-distance phone bills.

''I STOPPED BY to see if you wanted to join me and Garret for dinner, but I can see you've already made plans,'' she said coolly. Leonie looked at Maddie. ''I figured this was why I haven't seen much of you this week.''

''He can go to dinner with you,'' Maddie said, wishing her dear friend didn't look so disappointed at finding her with Dylan.

''No, I can't because I've already made plans for dinner,'' he spoke up. ''But thanks for thinking about me.''

Maddie couldn't believe Dylan's ease. It was as if he didn't see any reason why there should be awkwardness between the three of them.

''Then I'll go,'' Leonie said.

"No, Leonie, wait. We should talk about this." Maddie spread her hands nervously.

Again it was Dylan who spoke. "Mom's fine with everything, aren't you?" He cast a glance at his mother, who Maddie thought was anything but fine.

Leonie's next words proved it. "As you already told me, what you and Maddie do is none of my business."

"You said that to your mother?" Maddie gawked at Dylan. Then she walked over to Leonie and put an arm around her shoulder. "Leonie, I'm sorry I didn't talk to you earlier about me and Dylan. I should have. I wanted to, but..." She knew there really was no reason why she couldn't have told her friend about her feelings for Dylan.

"I had to learn from Garret that you'd broken up with Jeffrey," Leonie said.

The disappointment on her landlady's face only added to Maddie's regret. Until today Leonie had never looked at her with anything but affection and understanding. Maddie wanted to right what was wrong between them, but she wasn't sure she knew how.

"I'm sorry" were the only words she could find to say.

To her relief, Leonie accepted her apology graciously. "I understand, Maddie. Now if you don't mind, I'd like a few words with my son."

Maddie nodded and excused herself, going into the kitchen where she flipped through the pages of Jennifer's cookbooks and tried not to think about what was being said in the other room. It wasn't long before Dylan joined her.

‘‘She’s gone,’’ he stated.

‘‘What happened?’’ she demanded, jumping to her feet, worried that he’d only made the situation worse, not better.

‘‘Nothing happened. We just talked. Everything is going to be all right.’’

‘‘That’s easy for you to say. You’re going to get on a plane and leave here in a couple of weeks. I have to live in her house.’’

‘‘Maddie, what’s with you? This isn’t that big a deal. So Mom knows you and I have been seeing each other. So what?’’

She made a sound of exasperation. ‘‘That is such a typical male response. Your mother has feelings.’’

He raked a hand over his head. ‘‘I know and I did my best to be considerate of them. You’re getting all upset about this when there’s no reason to. She’s not mad at you.’’

‘‘Well, she’s not feeling very motherly toward me. I can guarantee you that,’’ she retorted, pacing the floor.

‘‘Do you want to go home and talk to her?’’

She stopped. ‘‘You think I should?’’

‘‘At this point I’m not sure I should say what I think.’’

She realized then how emotional she’d become. She went to him and wrapped her arms around him, pressing her head against his chest. She needed to feel his strength, to feel the sense of rightness that always came over her when he held her in his arms.

‘‘I’m sorry I’m being so silly,’’ she said, swallowing back the tears that threatened to break loose.

He put a finger under her chin and lifted her face so he could gaze into her eyes. ''I'm the one who's sorry. I've made you cry.'' He swiped at the lone tear that trickled down her face. ''None of this would have happened if I'd listened to Garret and left you alone.''

''I didn't want you to leave me alone.''

''I'm not sure I could have had I wanted to,'' he said, smoothing his hand over her hair.

She saw the look in his eye and knew what he said was true. Krystal had been right. Eventually the spark would have ignited between them. ''This feels right to me.''

''It feels better than right.''

''Yes, it does,'' she agreed, then once more burrowed her head into his chest, loving the strength and security she found there. It was a new feeling for her—trusting someone enough to cry in his arms.

What she felt for Dylan was so very different from the feelings she'd had for other men. It gave her a great sense of contentment, but it also frightened her because of its intensity. In a few weeks he'd be gone, out of her life. The thought sent a chill through her.

''Are you cold?'' he asked. ''I can think of a good way to warm you.''

As always, his words were enough to send heat rushing through her. It had been that way ever since she first saw him. A look, a touch, a few provocative words and she'd melt.

It was only after they'd made love later that evening that she noticed the chill again. Leonie's visit had forced her to acknowledge that their relationship wasn't as simple as they'd hoped it would be.

She'd told herself right from the start that when Dylan's time was up in Minnesota, she would let him go. It was what she wanted. He was the one who was supposed to teach her how to recognize a good man.

Only it hadn't exactly worked out that way. She'd expected him to be shallow and self-absorbed, but he'd been compassionate and generous. She'd discovered she could talk to him about things she'd never thought she'd share with anyone. The more time they spent together, the more she began to think that he was good for her.

When she was with him, her world didn't seem so uncertain. She finally felt as if she'd found the direction in which she wanted to be going.

Only tonight she'd had to face the fact that it was temporary. For a little while longer she'd have her compass, but after that…

She wouldn't think about what lay ahead. She and Dylan had made a pact—they would enjoy each day they had together. And she was determined to do just that.

DESPITE DYLAN'S ASSURANCE that everything was all right with his mother, Maddie knew she needed to have a good talk with Leonie. For Maddie, who hated to have any unsettled feelings between her and her friends, it was important that she do it as quickly as possible. That's why she decided that, as soon as she'd finished her classes at the dance studio on Saturday, she would talk to Leonie.

To her surprise, she found Leonie waiting for her when she arrived at work.

"I know you're busy, Maddie, but I'd like to speak to you," she said in a serious tone.

Maddie led her into the small office at the back of the studio. As soon as she'd closed the door, Leonie was saying, "I owe you an apology. I did something I swore I would never do to any of my sons. I interfered in Dylan's personal life. I had no right to come over there last night and I'm sorry."

Maddie felt a lump form in her throat. "I'm the one who should be apologizing. I don't know why I thought I had to keep my feelings for Dylan a big secret."

"You don't?"

Maddie gave her a puzzled look. "No, do you?"

She nodded. "You didn't want to hear me tell you I thought you were making a mistake."

Maddie didn't want to ask the question, but she couldn't resist. "Do you think I've made a mistake?"

She sighed. "I honestly don't know. I'm afraid I can't be an objective romance coach in this particular situation…not that you need one."

No, she didn't need a romance coach, but she could have used a mother. Trouble was she couldn't say that to Leonie. Maybe once Dylan was gone, she could confide in her again, but right now Dylan stood between them.

Maddie sighed and leaned back against the desk. "Dylan doesn't understand why this is so complicated."

"No, he wouldn't, would he," Leonie said with a shake of her head.

"Does it have to be complicated?"

"Not as far as I'm concerned. Dylan's my son and you're like a daughter to me. I love you both."

"But you don't think we should be seeing each other." Before Leonie could respond, she held up her hand. "It's okay, Leonie. I've been thinking the same thing myself. We shouldn't have become involved."

"But it's too late, isn't it?"

Maddie looked down at her hands. "It didn't exactly work out as I expected it would. I thought it would just be this fun, exciting—" She stopped, uneasy that she'd said as much as she had.

"When it comes to romance, fun and exciting usually come with a price."

Maddie nodded solemnly. "I think I've been in a time warp. I've been acting more like a fourteen-year-old with a crush on a high school senior than an adult."

"But your feelings aren't that of a fourteen-year-old, are they?"

"If only they were," Maddie said on a long sigh. "I'm sorry. I shouldn't be talking about this with you. So what happens now?"

"We go on as usual," Leonie said in her cheerful, reassuring way. "Nothing's changed, Maddie."

A knock on the door preceded a woman sticking her head in briefly to say, "The second-graders are just about ready to start, Maddie."

"You need to get to work, so I'm going to say goodbye." She tugged on her gloves.

"Thank you for coming. I wasn't sure you'd want to talk to me."

Leonie spread her arms then and Maddie went into

them. "Of course I would. Maddie, dear, you're like one of my own."

Maddie choked back the emotion in her throat and said, "Thank you. I feel much better now that we've talked."

"Me, too. Now you go be with your kids." She started to open the door but stopped. "If it's any comfort to you, I think Dylan got more than he bargained for, too."

DYLAN DIDN'T CHECK INTO a hotel when he left Shane's house. He told Maddie it was out of consideration for his mother's feelings. She said she understood, but she couldn't help but wonder if he'd had second thoughts about their relationship.

Not that anything in his manner toward her had given her reason to think he had. Although he was less demonstrative around his mother than he was in private, he treated her as he had for the past week—as if she were the best thing that had ever happened to him.

On Tuesday Krystal and Maddie had planned a surprise birthday party for Leonie. Besides Dylan's brothers, guests included several of Leonie's friends, two cousins and a handful of neighbors. Normally Maddie wouldn't have been anxious about the party, but it was the first time she and Dylan would be together as a couple in front of the rest of the family.

The company arrived in bunches, which suited Maddie just fine. In the excitement of getting the happy birthday banner hung, the balloons inflated and everyone's coat hidden so as not to spoil the surprise, there wasn't time for anyone to notice that Dylan couldn't keep his eyes off Maddie.

At least she didn't think anyone had noticed until Jennifer approached her in the kitchen as she filled the punch bowl and said, "You and Dylan aren't—" She broke off, but it was obvious what she was asking.

Maddie couldn't prevent the blush that colored her face.

"Oh my gosh! You are." She looked at Dylan who'd just walked into the kitchen.

"It's not what you think," Maddie said.

"Yes it is," Dylan disagreed over her shoulder, then as if to prove his point, grabbed her around the waist and placed a kiss on her cheek.

Mickey gasped, then ran through the house repeating, "Uncle Dylan kissed Maddie!"

"So that's why there were all those wonderful leftovers in the refrigerator when we got back from Michigan. Maddie had been cooking," Jennifer said. When Shane came into the kitchen, she tugged on his sleeve. "I was right about these two."

Again Maddie blushed and Dylan grinned.

"That was pretty fast work," Shane told his brother. Maddie wasn't sure if it was admiration or apprehension in his eyes. However, there was something more important on Shane's mind than Dylan's love life. "Jason's here."

"It *is* Mom's birthday," Dylan reminded him.

"Yes, but he's here with all of his stuff. He's moved out of the dorm." Shane raked a hand over his head. "Just what Mom doesn't need on her birthday. To discover her kid's quit school."

Krystal popped her head into the kitchen. ‘‘Jan just called. She and Leonie are leaving the restaurant now so they’ll be here in about ten minutes.’’

The announcement created a commotion as everyone hurried into the other room to wait for the moment of surprise. Maddie finished mixing the punch. When some spilled over the edge of the bowl, she swore.

‘‘You’re not nervous, are you?’’ Dylan asked, reaching for the sponge.

‘‘Of course I’m nervous. Aren’t you? Can you imagine what your mom is going to say when she sees Jason and all of his stuff?’’

He shrugged. ‘‘She’ll deal with it the same way she dealt with me running off to join the Marines. Are you sure that’s all that’s bothering you?’’

‘‘What else would there be?’’ she asked innocently.

‘‘The fact that you’re going to have to see Garret. You haven’t talked to him since you split with Jeffrey, have you?’’

‘‘No. Is Garret here?’’

‘‘He called and said he was going to be late. He’s the reason you’re so fidgety, right?’’

He was, but she didn’t want to admit that to Dylan. Nor did she tell him she was worried that Garret might bring Jeffrey to the party.

‘‘No, and I told you I’m not nervous. I always get a little edgy before a party—especially when I’m responsible for the food.’’

‘‘Which tastes great.’’ He smiled sheepishly. ‘‘I sampled the hors d’oeuvres. Did I tell you you look wonderful?’’ He eyed her appreciatively and her face warmed even more.

"Please don't look at me like that. I'm already hot."

"What a thing to tell me when there are twenty people in the next room."

"Maddie, hurry!" Krystal called from the doorway of the kitchen. "Leonie's going to be here any minute."

It turned out to be more like five minutes before Leonie and her friend Jan returned from what Leonie thought would be her only birthday celebration. As the room full of people shouted "Surprise," she looked at Maddie and Krystal and said, "I told you I wasn't celebrating my birthday this year."

"You don't have to, Mom," Dylan gave her a kiss on the cheek. "We're doing it for you."

To Maddie's relief, the party was a success. When Garret arrived, he was alone. The only moment of tension came when Leonie opened her cards and gifts. Jeffrey had sent her a poem he'd composed himself. Maddie could feel both Garret's and Dylan's eyes on her.

After everyone had had cake and ice cream, Maddie and Krystal headed into the kitchen to begin the cleanup, leaving the Donovan family members to see to their guests. They hadn't been there but a few minutes when Garret joined them.

Thinking he wanted to talk to Krystal, Maddie said, "I think I'll go see if anyone needs more coffee."

"Maybe Krystal could do that," Garret suggested. "I'd like to talk to you if I could, Maddie."

Krystal reached for the silver coffee server. "Sure.

I'll take care of it,'' she said, and with a curious glance at the two of them, left.

Maddie turned her attention back to the serving plates she'd been washing. ''Are you enjoying the party?'' she asked Garret, making small talk, hoping she could avoid the real reason he'd asked to speak to her, because she was fairly certain it involved Jeffrey.

Shc was unsuccessful. He said, ''You and Krystal did a nice job, but I don't want to talk about the party. I want to know what's going on with you and Dylan.''

Before Maddie could answer, she heard a male voice say, ''Do you really think that's any of your business?''

She turned toward the door and her stomach jumped at the sight of Dylan.

''I was talking to Maddie, not you,'' Garret said quietly.

''When the question involves me, you should be talking to me.'' Dylan moved closer to Maddie.

She thought he looked like a tiger she'd seen on the nature channel, prowling the perimeter of its territory. She hoped he wasn't going to act like some caveman defending his conquest. Not now.

She tried to ease the tension. ''Garret and I have been friends for a long time, Dylan.''

Only Garret didn't look very friendly at the moment as his glance darted back and forth between Maddie and Dylan. ''Whatever you want, you go after, no matter who gets hurt.'' The accusation was directed at his brother.

''This really doesn't involve you,'' Dylan told his brother calmly. ''And even if it did, now is not the time to be having this conversation. It's Mom's birthday.''

He sneered. ''Oh, that's right. And you, her oldest son, have always been the one who's been most considerate of Mom's feelings, haven't you?''

Maddie could see the sarcastic bullet had hit its target. Dylan's eyes darkened. She expected him to shoot back an angry retort, but he simply said, ''I am right now, which is more than I can say for you. If you've got something to settle with me, fine. We'll settle it another time, another place, but leave Maddie out of it. It's not her fault.''

''I agree with you about that,'' Garret shot back. ''She didn't have a chance once you'd made up your mind to go after her.''

''What's going on in here?'' Shane's voice had all three of them glancing toward the doorway.

''Nothing's going on,'' Dylan spoke first. ''Garret and I were having a discussion, but we've decided to continue it another time.''

''*We* haven't decided anything,'' Garret contradicted him.

Shane extended a hand to him. ''Come on, Garret. You've worked too many hours and you're tired.''

''Yeah, tired of him acting as if just because he's the oldest he can do whatever he wants to this family.''

''Garret, that's enough,'' Shane spoke up. ''We're having a party for Mom. It's bad enough that Jason's going to drop his bombshell on her. She doesn't need more trouble.''

To Maddie's relief, Garret didn't continue. He

stepped around Dylan and headed toward the door, but not before saying to Shane, ‘‘You know I’m right. He did the same thing when Dad died. Came home, stirred up a bunch of trouble and left. This visit is no different.’’

Shane gave Dylan a long, hard stare then walked with his younger brother out of the kitchen, leaving Maddie and Dylan alone. She wasn’t sure what he would say to her.

‘‘Shocked?’’

‘‘About what I heard?’’ She shook her head.

‘‘I have been the black sheep of this family, Maddie,’’ he warned.

‘‘You’re not to me,’’ she said in a quiet voice.

‘‘There’s stuff that you don’t know about. The last time I was home, my brothers and I didn’t get along very well.’’ Again his voice carried a warning.

‘‘That’s to be expected at such a difficult time. All of you were upset by the loss of your father,’’ she said in understanding.

He reached for her hand. ‘‘It goes back further than that, but I don’t want to put you in the middle any more than I already have.’’ He nodded toward the other room. ‘‘I should get back. Are you going to be okay?’’

She nodded. ‘‘I’m going to keep working in here.’’

She thought he might kiss her, but he simply pressed his fingers to her cheek and said, ‘‘Don’t worry. Everything will work out.’’

Maddie wanted to believe him, but deep inside her a kernel of doubt kept growing. And growing.

MADDIE KNEW that what had happened the night of Leonie's birthday party had changed things between her and Dylan. Although they continued to see each other, their relationship held none of the urgency that had driven them to be together the previous week.

Maddie wanted to blame it on the fact that they were living in Leonie's house, but she realized that had he wanted to make love with her, he would have figured out a way to make it happen. She wondered if he'd tired of her already, or if he'd simply decided it would be easier to part company if they were friends instead of lovers.

She wasn't about to ask. She had her pride. When she found herself alone on a Saturday night, however, she knew she had to face a fact she'd been trying hard to ignore.

She was in love with Dylan.

When Krystal arrived home around nine, she took one look in the gathering room and asked, "What are you doing here? I thought you'd be out with Dylan."

She shook her head. "One of his high school buddies called and asked him to get together."

She plopped herself down next to Maddie on the sofa. "And you couldn't go along?"

Maddie shook her head. "No chicks. It was a guy thing."

"Oh, that must be what's going on at Shane's. Garret mentioned that a bunch of guys who used to live in the neighborhood were all getting together to shoot pool and watch the hockey game on TV."

"You talked to Garret?"

"He stopped in to get his hair cut yesterday. I didn't

realize Dylan was going to be at Shane's though. I thought after what happened the night of Leonie's party..." She didn't finish her thought. "They must have resolved things. Leonie said she was going to make them sit down and talk things out."

"Leonie said that? When?"

Krystal nodded. "The day after her party. I know they thought they could keep their feuding from her, but you know how moms are. They can smell trouble a mile off when it comes to their kids."

Maddie clicked off the TV and set the remote down with a thud. "It's my fault. I should have known better than to get involved with Dylan."

"Even if you hadn't fallen for him, it sounds as if there would have been trouble. It's no secret that the Donovan boys haven't always got along. We've lived with Leonie long enough to know that."

"Unfortunately, it seems to me that Dylan is the one who doesn't get along with his brothers. There never appeared to be any trouble between the other three," Maddie observed.

"That's not true. Look at how Shane and Jason have been at each other over his dropping out of school. Dylan's actually the one who's been trying to put things right for Jason."

"He has?" Maddie wasn't aware of his efforts. "I know Leonie was pretty upset."

"Yeah, which is why Dylan's been talking to her about it, trying to get her to understand that college isn't for everyone."

"He did that?"

Krystal nodded. "Garret told me."

Maddie's brows lifted. ''You've been talking to Garret an awful lot, haven't you?''

''Not really, but I keep my ears open when I do,'' she said with a grin. ''I think the Donovan boys are pretty cool guys and if they're all together at Shane's tonight, they must be getting along.''

''Or knocking each other down,'' Maddie said dryly.

Krystal reached over and patted her hand. ''At least you know all the trouble wasn't about you. You just got stuck in the middle.''

Maddie felt stuck all right, but she wasn't sure where.

''So how much longer does Dylan have before he goes back to Saint Martin?'' Krystal asked.

''He leaves the eleventh of February.''

She pulled a face. ''Right before Valentine's Day? That's a bum deal. What's going to happen after?''

She shrugged. ''Probably nothing. Why?''

She crossed her arms and stared at Maddie with a look of disbelief. ''Why? Because you're crazy about the guy and he's crazy about you, that's why.''

''Not quite.''

She harrumphed. ''I have eyes in my head.'' She sat forward. ''And just think how romantic it would be to have a long-distance relationship with a guy who lives on an island in the Caribbean. Très sexy,'' she said with a bad French accent.

''Très stupeed,'' Maddie countered.

''Why?''

''Because that's not me.'' She tried to keep any emotion out of her voice. ''We had fun and I'm glad we had the time together, but when it's over, it's over.''

Krystal eyed her suspiciously. ''You really believe that?''

She wanted to say yes, but the word stuck in her throat.

Krystal noticed. ''You don't! I knew it! You've fallen big time for him, haven't you?''

Maddie nodded miserably. ''And I didn't want to. It just happened.''

''Does he know?''

''No! And I'm not going to tell him. You'd better not, either,'' she warned. ''We both agreed from the start that we weren't looking for a long-term relationship.''

''No, but maybe you found one.''

''And maybe if I say something he'll just ignore me the rest of his visit and then things would be really awkward.''

''I don't think he can ignore you.''

Maddie wanted to tell her that he was already doing a pretty good job, but she didn't want to share that information with anyone. ''I'd rather not find out.''

''I bet you're going to find that absence makes the heart grow fonder.'' Krystal snapped her fingers. ''I have an idea. You've been together nearly every day now since you went to the Wild game, right?'' When Maddie nodded she continued, ''Maybe what you need to do is not be so available. Give him a preview of what it's going to be like to miss you.''

''I don't play games when it comes to relationships,'' she reminded her.

"You don't need to play a game. Just come with me to Saint Cloud and be my hair model. I could use someone with great hair, which you have. Plus, we could do some girl stuff together—hang out at the mall, maybe go to a chick flick."

Maddie considered the invitation. Dylan hadn't made any definite plans for the two of them and during the past week he had more or less taken it for granted that she'd be right there for him. Mondays were her day off, which meant she could stay overnight and not have to worry about getting back in time for work.

"What do you want to do with my hair?" she asked.

"Fun stuff. No tints, no cuts, I promise." Krystal could see Maddie was tempted. "Come on. We can get our nails done, have a facial. What do you say?"

Maddie hesitated for only a moment before saying, "What time do we leave?"

"YOU'RE LOOKING a little rough around the edges," Dylan's mother said to him as he stumbled into the house on Sunday morning.

"We played pool half the night."

"Must have had a good time."

"Yeah, it was good to see everybody," he said, opening the door to the refrigerator and pulling out the carton of milk.

"Need something to settle your stomach?"

He shook his head. "I'm not hungover, just hungry." He found a box of cereal in the cupboard and sprinkled some into a bowl.

"I thought when you didn't come home that you'd

wisely decided to sleep at Shane's rather than risk driving.''

''I wasn't intoxicated, Mom, just tired...which Garret tells me can be equally deadly behind the wheel,'' he said, pouring milk onto the cereal.

''Garret spent the night, too?''

He sat down next to her. ''Take that worried look off your face. When I told you we'd cleared the air, I meant it. Everything's cool with your sons. We're all getting along just fine. Even Jason was talking to Shane.''

Concern lined her face. ''What if Jason's making a mistake leaving school?''

''Then he'll live with his mistake. We all make them, Mom,'' he stated philosophically.

She smiled and patted his hand. ''That's true. Thank you for working so hard to make peace with your brothers. I know you did it for me and I appreciate it.''

''You're welcome, but it wasn't just for you, Mom. I don't like the fact that there's been this distance between me and my brothers...and I'm not talking about the miles between here and Saint Martin.''

''I hope that means you'll be coming to visit more often?''

''You're not sick of me?'' he asked in between spoonfuls of cereal.

''You know better than to even ask that question,'' she scolded him.

She didn't seem to notice that he didn't answer her original question and he was relieved. The truth was, he didn't want to think about what would happen once he returned to Saint Martin. Right now he wanted to concentrate on the time he had left...and how he would spend that time.

"Have you seen Maddie this morning?" he asked.

"She and Krystal went to Saint Cloud."

"For what?"

Leonie shrugged. "I'm not sure. All I know is that there was a note for me when I got up that said not to worry if they didn't come home tonight."

That news had Dylan frowning.

"Didn't Maddie mention to you that she was thinking about going?" his mother asked, eyeing him curiously.

"No, but then we're not exactly in each other's pockets," he told her. He knew that he should be pleased he could say that. It was exactly what he wanted their relationship to be. For the past week he'd done his best to make sure she understood that, as much as he enjoyed her company, he didn't *need* her. He wanted her, yes, but need her? Uh-uh.

So why did he feel so awful knowing that he wasn't going to see her the rest of the day? Or possibly not until tomorrow?

"What are your plans for today?" his mother asked.

He shrugged. "Maybe watch the basketball game on TV. Unless you need my help with something?"

"No, you watch the game. Jan and I have plans."

"Going shopping?"

"No, we're going snowmobiling."

He nearly dropped his spoon into his cereal bowl. "You're kidding."

"Don't you think fifty-three-year-old women can ride snowmobiles?"

"I didn't know that you *had* a snowmobile."

"I don't. We're going to visit some friends who live up near Silver Creek. They're the ones with the sleds." She looked at the clock, then quickly finished her coffee. "I didn't realize it was so late. I'd better get going. Enjoy your day, dear," she said with a wave and was gone. She popped her head back through the doorway to add, "There's some leftover chicken in the fridge you can heat up in the microwave if you get hungry."

"What time are you planning to come home?"

"Oh, not too late. Maybe nine or ten-ish," she said, and again disappeared.

Nine or ten-ish? Dylan sat in the empty kitchen, slowly shaking his head. He had the entire house to himself and Maddie was in Saint Cloud. Had she known that his mother would be out all day?

Had she gone with Krystal because she was tired of being with him? He frowned. Women generally didn't complain that they were seeing too much of him. It was usually just the opposite.

But Maddie wasn't like most women. She didn't like it when a guy referred to a woman as *his*. She'd told him she didn't belong to anybody.

He wanted her to belong to him. Not that he saw her as an object to possess, but he'd be lying to himself if he didn't admit that he wanted part of her to belong to him. And he was a little bothered that she'd never showed any possessiveness toward him.

Which had him wondering if she hadn't gone to

Saint Cloud because she'd needed some time to herself. He knew if he spent the day alone he'd just keep asking himself that same question over and over. He picked up the phone and called Shane.

"Want to go to the Timberwolves game?"

"I can't. Jennifer's going to a baby shower so I've got Mickey. I promised him I'd take him to Camp Snoopy."

"Does he want his uncle to go along?"

He heard a muffled "Hey, Mick! You want Uncle Dylan to come with us to Camp Snoopy," then a "Yeah, and Maddie, too."

"He says—" Shane began.

"I heard him. Tell him he gets his uncle. Maddie's in Saint Cloud with Krystal."

"What's she doing up there?"

He admitted he didn't know, then said, "I'll be over as soon as I've showered."

Chauffeuring a four-year-old through an amusement park wasn't what he'd call a perfect Sunday, but it beat sitting home thinking about a woman. Not just a woman, a voice inside his head reminded him. Maddie.

But he found it hard not to think about her even in an amusement park where screams from the passengers on the roller coaster drowned out nearly all rational thoughts. It would have helped had Mickey not mentioned her name on a regular basis. Ever since his nephew had seen Dylan and Maddie kissing, he'd become like a broken record, repeating the same question.

"Are you going to marry Maddie?"

Shane could only lift his eyebrows and shrug as if to say, *Don't look at me. I didn't put the idea in his head.*

Someone had and Dylan guessed it was Jennifer, since when they got back to the house, the first question she asked was, "I'm surprised you're not with Maddie today."

Although his sister-in-law invited him to stay for dinner, he declined, not wanting to be put through an inquisition about Maddie. He had no doubt that she wanted to ask the same question Mickey had, even if she would take a more subtle route to finding the answer.

So he went back to an empty house, where he sat alone watching TV and thinking about Maddie. He wondered where she was staying, if she and Krystal had gone barhopping—a pastime he knew the younger woman regarded as entertainment. He frowned. He didn't like to think of Maddie in a bar without him.

When she wasn't home by noon the following day, he began to get surly. His mother noticed and asked if his shoulder was bothering him. He lied and said it was, but the truth was that he couldn't stop thinking about Maddie.

That's why, when she finally waltzed through the door with her arms full of packages, he had to leave the room or risk grabbing her and kissing her senseless. He waited until he heard Krystal leave for work before he went upstairs to pound on her door.

When she opened it, she looked startled to see him.

"Have fun in Saint Cloud?" he asked.

"Yes, we did. Is something wrong?"

"Yeah, something's wrong. I've been going crazy missing you," he said, then practically devoured her mouth with his.

Frantically they tugged at each other's clothes, their lips pulling apart only long enough for Maddie to say, "Your mother..."

"Won't be back until after five," he finished, then captured her mouth one more. He couldn't think of anything except the aching inside him, an ache that only she could relieve.

Clothes went flying, limbs tangled, and they fell onto her bed as the urgency of their desires overcame them. Each time he'd made love with her he'd expected it couldn't possibly be as good as it had been the last time, and each time he'd been wrong.

Today was no different. They came together in an incredible explosion of passion and something else he didn't want to examine too closely.

When it was over, he held her tightly, loving the feel of her naked body next to his, needing the feeling of connection that flowed between them. The thought of not having that made him shudder.

She thought he was cold and reached for a blanket to cover them. Cocooned together, they didn't talk, content to listen to each other's breathing.

Finally Dylan said, "I don't know how I'm going to leave you, Maddie."

She kissed his naked chest. "It's only three-thirty. Your Mom won't be home for another hour and a half."

"I'm not talking about now. I mean when my medical leave is up."

"Then don't leave. They must need concrete specialists in Minnesota." It was said in a light tone, but he knew she wasn't joking.

He propped himself on an elbow to look at her. "I don't want us to end, Maddie, but I can't stay here."

She stared up at him with eyes full of honesty and sincerity. "I haven't asked you to stay, have I?"

"No. That's just it. You don't make any demands on me at all."

"Because we have an agreement."

He let his head fall back against the pillow. "Why did you go to Saint Cloud?"

"Krystal had a hair show and wanted me to be a model."

So she hadn't wanted to get away from him. He felt incredible. "It's so good between us, Maddie."

"What is?" she asked a bit impatiently. "Sex? Being together? What?"

"Everything!"

She smiled then, and kissed him. "Yes, everything is good. It's as if we have this connection. I don't understand it, but it's there."

He felt it, too, but unlike her, he did understand. There could be only one explanation—she knew what it meant to have a father who'd cheated on his wife.

"I may know what it is," he told her, looking into eyes that brightened with curiosity at his words.

"Then you have to tell me," she ordered.

"I want to, but if I do, I'll put you in a position that could make you uncomfortable. You'll know something none of my brothers or my mother knows."

She placed her hand in his. "What is it, Dylan. You look so serious."

"It is serious."

In her expression he saw trust and understanding. After thirteen years he felt as if he could finally let go of the burden created by the secret. As unemotionally as possible, he explained what had happened spring break of his senior year.

When he'd finished, her eyes were thoughtful. "And you've never told anyone else."

He shook his head. "I couldn't let my mother find out. You've heard the way she talks about my father."

"You're still angry at him, aren't you?"

"Aren't you angry at your dad for what he did to your mother?"

She sighed. "Part of me will always be sad about what he did to my mother and my family. He left us."

"So because my dad remained with my mom I should forget what he did to her?"

"I didn't say that. It's just that you're letting something your father did thirteen years ago affect your relationship with your family. Dylan, I've seen the tension that comes between you and your brothers whenever your father's name is mentioned."

"Because they always think of him as this great dad," he said in frustration. "He wasn't."

"But he wasn't a monster, either," she said quietly.

He stiffened. She didn't understand. How could she not when her own father had done the very thing to her mother?

He pushed aside the blanket. "I shouldn't have told

you. This isn't your problem.'' He rolled off the bed and began to dress.

She jumped up and tried to stop him. ''Dylan, I'm sorry. You have every right to feel the way you do about your father. I'm not criticizing you.''

He sank back down onto the bed, his shoulders sagging. ''We had fathers who screwed up big time, didn't we?''

''Yes, but that's not the only reason we connect with each other. We're good together, Dylan,'' she said, rubbing her hand across his bare back.

''You think so?'' he asked with a crooked smile.

''Yes, although I was starting to have my doubts this past week. You didn't exactly seem interested in being around me.''

''There hasn't exactly been an opportunity. Both of us have rooms in my mom's house,'' he reminded her.

''And that's the only reason why we didn't...''

He nodded, although he knew it wasn't exactly true. ''And believe me, it was hard to keep my hands off you.''

''I thought—'' she began, and then shook her head. ''Never mind what I thought.''

''Tell me.''

''I thought maybe something that was said when you talked with your brothers made you think twice about being with me,'' she told him. ''I'm sorry I came between you and Garret.''

He sighed. ''It's resolved. Not that there won't be something else that'll come between us.''

''Is that why you choose to live thousands of miles away from your family?''

He got up again, aware of the direction the conversation was going. ‘‘I like living in Saint Martin.’’

She scrambled off the bed and came to stand beside him. ‘‘Why?’’

He stood with only his pants on. ‘‘I can’t stay here, Maddie. Don’t ask me to.’’

‘‘You just said we’re good together, Dylan,’’ she reminded him. As if she sensed what he was going to say, she turned her back to him. ‘‘Just forget it. You don’t need to explain.’’

He turned her around to face him. ‘‘Yes, I do.’’ But he didn’t know what the explanation was. ‘‘I didn’t say I didn’t want to see you again.’’

‘‘You want to have a long-distance relationship?’’ He could see the idea didn’t exactly thrill her.

‘‘Would that be so bad? You could come visit me. I could come visit you. Other people manage to do it.’’ He was trying to convince himself as much as he was her.

She thought about it for a minute, then said, ‘‘I don’t like the idea of not being able to see you every day. I’ve gotten used to you living downstairs from me.’’

He’d gotten used to it, too. ‘‘I don’t think I can go cold turkey and just stop seeing you altogether. Weekends are better than not at all, aren’t they?’’

Her face brightened. ‘‘You mean that?’’

He answered her with a kiss, leaving her in no doubt that what he said was true.

‘‘Wouldn’t you like to come visit Saint Martin?’’ he asked, nibbling on her ear.

‘‘If you’re there, yes.’’

"Then you'll come."

"It'll get expensive," she warned him.

"Don't worry. I have lots of frequent flyer miles. I'll take care of everything. I promise."

And he would. He'd be in control, as usual.

CHAPTER TWELVE

Dear Leonie: I'm in love with a wonderful man who says he loves me. The problem? He carries around the burden of being the only one who knows that his father cheated on his mother. It's a secret he's kept from his mother and the rest of his family. Now I'm afraid this destructive secret has destroyed our love.
Signed: Sad in Saint Paul

DYLAN'S MEDICAL LEAVE was not extended. The doctor was so impressed with his recovery from the injury that he was told he could return to work ahead of schedule if he wanted. Dylan hadn't wanted to do that, which was a first for him, since work had always been the passion in his life.

That was before he'd met Maddie. Although he suspected that once he was back on the island life would return to normal. Work first, women second.

But until then, he wanted to make the most of his time in Minnesota, which was why he intended to make sure their last night together was one she'd never forget. As he reached for the phone to make sure all of the arrangements were in place, he thought ahead to what was in store for the two of them.

He'd wanted to spend the entire day with her, but

she'd had classes to teach at the dance studio and then there was his mother's appearance on the Rob Lerner show. Instead of airing the segment on Valentine's Day, as had originally been planned, the network had moved the show forward.

In honor of the occasion, Shane and Jennifer had invited the family over to their house to watch the program. As everyone waited for the program to begin, Maddie said to Dylan, "Isn't this exciting?"

He had to agree. "Mom looks nervous."

"Anyone would." She squeezed his arm. "Oh look! Tom and Judy are here with their new baby!" She dropped his arm and went hurrying toward the unknown couple.

"Who are this Tom and Judy?" Dylan asked Shane.

"Judy used to live with Mom. She was one of the first boarders," he answered, handing his brother a beer.

Dylan watched as his mother, too, fussed over the couple, but it was Maddie who held his attention. She had the baby in her arms and was gazing down at the infant with a look on her face that made Dylan's throat go dry.

Shane, noticing the direction of his gaze, said close to his ear. "Looks like Maddie found something that makes her smile."

Dylan wasn't sure what comment to make, so he made none. Shane drifted away and Dylan stood still, watching Maddie cuddle the baby. It was a sight that disturbed him so much he finally left the room. He went into the kitchen where he found his sister-in-law chopping away at a block of ice.

"Need some help?" he asked.

"This bag was supposed to have cubes, but they must have thawed and refrozen because they're all stuck together," she answered as she jabbed away at the ice.

He extended his hand. "Let me." It felt good to hack away at the frozen cubes, as if he were chipping away at the doubts that were racing through his head.

Seeing the way Maddie had reacted to the baby made him realize she would make a great mother someday. It was there in her eyes, in her smile, in her gentle manner. But he wasn't ever going to be a great father. He chopped at the ice with a vengeance, sending pieces flying in every direction.

"Whoa! I think you have it," Jennifer said with a giggle.

Someone hollered from the other room. "It's show time!"

Dylan followed Jennifer into the family room, where everyone gathered around the TV. He noticed that Maddie still had the baby. She patted the seat cushion next to her, indicating he should come sit beside her. Before he could get there, however, another person took the spot. He shrugged, indicating it didn't matter, and leaned up against the wall.

The dull murmur changed to silence when Rob Lerner introduced the segment called, "Fourteen Ways to Show Your Sweetheart You Love Her This Valentine's Day." Everybody cheered upon seeing Leonie, then quieted to hear what she had to say.

When asked what made love last a lifetime, his mother spoke easily and with a confidence that gave credibility to what she said. Dylan listened carefully, but it wasn't until the last point she made that he realized everything she said applied to him and Maddie. *Everything* except the last statement.

"You need to have the same goals, to want the same things from a relationship."

Again he sought Maddie's face in the crowd, and she looked at him and smiled. He smiled back, unsure whether she was pleased because his mother had done so well on TV or if she was trying to send him the message that they did share the same goals.

When the program was over and everyone was once again talking, she got up and came toward him. "This is Benjamin. Isn't he cute?" she said, looking up at him with a glow on her face. "Want to hold him?"

"No, that's okay," He tempered his refusal with a smile, but she saw through it.

"You look as if you'd rather walk across hot coals. Don't you like kids?"

"Sure, if they're somebody else's."

That had her frowning. "You don't ever want to be a father someday?"

"It's not something I've given much thought," he lied.

"Have you met Tom and Judy?" she asked, gently rocking Benjamin to and fro.

"Not yet."

"Come on. I'll introduce you. They're a really nice couple. You're going to like them." She led him over to the man and woman who appeared to be in their late twenties.

Dylan made all the appropriate comments, listening

as Maddie encouraged them to tell the funny story of how they'd met. Then they launched into new-parent anecdotes. As they stood talking, all Dylan could think about was that he and Maddie could be Tom and Judy, married, new parents who spent all of their time at a party talking about how they met and how wonderful it was to be parents.

He loosened the button on his collar, feeling as if in the past half hour it had shrunk. Never was he more grateful for his mother's appearance than he was at that moment.

She came up to him and said, "Thank you for coming tonight. I know you and Maddie had plans." She kissed him on the cheek.

It was the perfect opportunity for him to give Maddie the look that said it was time to leave. To his relief, she didn't protest, but gave the baby back to Judy, then pushed her arm through his and allowed him to take her to get her coat.

The rest of the evening went just as he'd planned. They ate a late dinner in the hotel's elegant dining room, danced to the small jazz ensemble playing in the lounge, then went back to the suite where red roses and heart-shaped balloons made it feel like Valentine's Day.

Only something wasn't right. Maddie noticed it, too. As he struggled to uncork the champagne that room service had sent, she asked, "What's wrong, Dylan?"

"What makes you think anything's wrong?"

She wore a shimmering red dress with tiny straps that emphasized her perfectly shaped figure. On any other night, his hands would have been working the dress free of her body instead of wrestling with the cork on the champagne bottle. But this wasn't any other night.

He kept thinking about what his mother had said about sharing the same goals. Maddie had told him she was content to have the same kind of relationship he wanted. She'd never mentioned a marriage or babies or even a commitment, yet in that little bit of time at Shane's her body language had said more than words had ever told him.

"Dylan, something's wrong," she repeated. "After everything we've shared these past four weeks, I think I know when something's not right between us." She didn't step any closer to him, but stood several feet away, as still as a store mannequin. "You're only going through the motions. Even when we danced I noticed it."

He set the champagne bottle down so he could loosen the tie around his neck. "It's warm in here." He walked over to the thermostat on the wall and adjusted the gauge. He could feel her eyes on him.

"You're uncomfortable with me. Why?"

He didn't answer but went back to trying to open the champagne. The cork finally popped, sending a shower of champagne into the air and all over his suit coat. "It figures," he muttered, reaching for the linen napkin on the room service cart.

"Dylan, you didn't answer me. You're making me nervous."

He glanced at her and saw fear in her eyes. The last thing he wanted to do was to cause her to be afraid of anything.

"I'm sorry, Maddie. This isn't going to work." He tossed the linen napkin back onto the cart.

"Here. Let me try." She reached for the champagne bottle but his hands stopped her.

"I don't mean that."

It was then that she realized how serious he was. "You mean us, don't you?" The words were barely above a whisper, as if she couldn't believe what he was saying.

"I don't think this long-distance thing is going to work out. I'm sorry."

She didn't speak. By the way her throat moved, he could see that she was struggling to hold back tears, which made it more difficult for him to tell her what he needed to. He couldn't have felt any worse had someone kicked him in the gut.

He searched for the right words, but knew there was no way to soften what he had to say. "When I saw you with that baby tonight, I realized that you need someone who can give you what you deserve in life," he began.

"Stop right there. Don't even tell me you're breaking up with me for *my* sake." She clicked her tongue in disgust. "That is so lame."

"It's true," he said quietly.

"You don't even know if I want a baby. I never said a word about children," she cried out in frustration.

"You didn't have to. I saw it in your face."

She made a sound of disbelief, then looked around at the room at the heart-shaped balloons and flowers.

"You planned this whole evening—" she flailed her arms about her "—so you could break up with me?"

"No, I wanted to make tonight special. I didn't know we were going to be having this conversation."

"We're not having this conversation. I'm leaving." She reached for her coat and began pulling it on.

"I don't want you to go."

"You think I want to spend the night here with you to celebrate getting dumped?"

"I'm not dumping you," he denied. "If you'd just give me a chance to explain..."

"Explain what? That you *love* me but you need to do what's *best* for me?" She grabbed her small overnight bag from the closet. "No thank you. That's not my idea of a romantic Valentine."

He tried to stop her from opening the door, but she was too fast for him. "Maddie, wait!"

"For what?" she called over her shoulder. "So you can tell me why you don't want me? No thanks."

"I do want you."

She turned and faced him. "Which one is it, Dylan? Either you do or you don't?"

"It's not that simple. You were there. You heard what my mother said—"

Again she cut him off. "You're telling me you're ending our relationship because of something your mother said about romance?" She looked heavenward in frustration. "I can't believe it. You tell me to ignore the advice your mother gives me because she's not qualified to be a romance coach and I break up with Jeffrey. Now all of a sudden she's an expert and you're breaking up with me because of something she said?''

''It's not fair of me to expect you to be in a long-distance relationship,'' he said.

''It doesn't have to be long distance and you know it. But that's what's really bothering you, isn't it? This isn't about babies or your mother. It's about commitment. You're afraid that what we have could turn out to be more than a casual, make-no-demands-just-have-a-good-time affair.''

He pointed a finger at her. ''You told me you wanted the same things as I did.''

She pointed right back at him. ''And you agreed with me when I said we had something more than either one of us expected.''

''It's not enough to...''

''To what?'' she challenged him. ''Make a *commitment* to each other?''

''I'm not ready to do that.''

''No, and you're never going to be, are you? Because you're afraid of turning out like your father.''

''I'm not my father,'' he reminded her in a steely tone.

''No? Well, we'll never know, will we—because you're too scared to find out.'' When he didn't answer, she started for the elevator. ''Goodbye, Dylan.''

He went after her. ''Wait. I'll take you home.''

She ignored him and hurried onto a waiting elevator. ''I know my way home'' were the last words he heard.

Dylan could only stand and stare as the doors closed.

"MADDIE, OPEN UP. I know you're in there. I saw your light."

"Please go away, Krystal. I'm not feeling well."

Her friend didn't do as she requested. "I'm not going away until you let me in. Come on, Maddie. Talk to me."

Wearily Maddie padded to the door, turned the lock and said, "It's open."

When Krystal entered, Maddie had her back to her as she trudged back to the bed, where she plopped down and pulled her pillow over her head. She felt Krystal's weight on the bed beside her.

"Tell me what happened," her friend pleaded.

"Nothing happened," she mumbled through the pillow.

"You're supposed to be at the hotel having your Valentine celebration with Dylan and you're here in your oldest, rattiest pajamas with your pillow over your head. What do you mean nothing happened?"

Maddie knew that sooner or later everyone was going to know she wasn't seeing Dylan anymore. You couldn't keep this kind of news a big secret, not when you lived with the guy's mother. "We broke up."

"I don't believe it. You two are perfect together."

Maddie held up a hand. "Please."

"For crying out loud, Maddie, will you take that pillow off your head? You've got nothing to be ashamed about."

She pushed the pillow aside. "It's over, Krystal," she said, then burst into tears.

Krystal gathered her into her arms and comforted

her as only a friend could do, saying all the things a friend was supposed to say at such a time.

None of them eased her pain, but it was comforting to have Krystal there to listen to her pour her heart out. And to bring her a pint of chocolate chocolate-chip ice cream, which they devoured together.

"You know, Maddie, you should talk to Leonie about this," Krystal said as she gathered their empty bowls and spoons together.

"I can't." Nor could she tell Krystal the true reason for Dylan's reluctance to commit to a serious relationship. Not without revealing his secret. "She's Dylan's mother. I can't put her in the middle."

Krystal sighed. "I suppose you're right."

Maddie knew she was, but she also knew that if there was one person she'd want to give her advice, it would be Leonie. As soon as Krystal was gone, Maddie got out of bed and went to her computer. She couldn't talk to Leonie, but she could send her a letter...an anonymous letter.

DYLAN WOKE THE FOLLOWING MORNING feeling as if someone had used his tongue as a street cleaner. As he tried to sit up, a sharp pain circled his head, intensifying until he thought he must be sleeping on a pillow made of nails.

He staggered to the bathroom, where he discovered his stomach was in worse shape than his tongue or his head. After being sick, he collapsed in a heap on the floor, which is where he felt he deserved to be. He couldn't believe he had a hangover. After Maddie had left, he'd gone to the bar across the street for a few drinks, but not enough to warrant this.

A few minutes later, he managed to shower and get himself together. He discovered just how *not together* he was when he saw his reflection in the mirror.

This should have been a morning on which he'd awakened next to Maddie, made love with her, made plans for the next time they'd be together. Should have been. He wasn't with her. She was gone. Out of his life.

He didn't think his day could get off to any worse start. Then he went home. He knew his mom would be upset that he and Maddie had split, but he hadn't expected the silent treatment from his own mother. She didn't say one word about Maddie. She didn't need to. Her silence was more deadly than any words she could have cast at him.

It had always been that way. When he and his brothers were kids and had done something wrong, she'd never yelled or criticized or even punished them. That had been their father's duty. She'd simply given them a look that said, *I thought you were better than that. You disappointed me.*

Today the look said, *You ought to be throttled and hung out to dry.* Then, as he rummaged through the cabinets looking for something to settle his stomach, she said, "You don't look so good. Are you feeling all right?"

"No, I have an upset stomach," he told her, then made a dash for the bathroom.

Concern had replaced the disappointment on her

face when he saw her again. "Are you going to be able to travel this afternoon?" she asked.

He wasn't sure of anything at the moment except that he felt awful. "I'm going to lie down until it's time to go to the airport," he told her, then staggered into Jason's room, where he crawled onto the bed.

He slept until there was a knock on his door. Expecting it to be his mother, he was surprised to see Garret.

"You look awful. Didn't you shave this morning?" he asked as he approached the bed.

"It wasn't high on my priority list. What are you doing here?"

"Mom's worried about you."

"Me? Don't you mean she's worried about Maddie?"

"Maddie's not the one who looks like something the cat dragged in. Mom says you've been throwing up all morning."

"It was the Scotch I drank last night."

"Drowning your sorrows, were you?" He pulled the chair away from the desk and set it next to the bed. "You have any pain?" he asked, sitting down.

"No, I'm always doubled up like this. Of course I have pain!"

Garret clicked his tongue. "The abuse a brother has to take. Now be a good boy and let the doctor check you over and we'll see if we can't make you feel better."

"HE'S WHAT?" Maddie asked in horror.

"He's not leaving until Valentine's Day," Krystal

told her. "After you left Dylan last night, he went to some ratty little hole-in-the-wall bar to drown his sorrows and ate some wings that weren't cooked properly or something. Ended up with food poisoning."

"Serves him right," Maddie said smugly, although she had to fight the urge to run downstairs and see him.

"Garret says he's pretty miserable."

"Good."

"You don't mean that."

"You're right. I don't."

Krystal sat down next to her on the love seat. "Why don't you go downstairs and talk to him? Maybe you two can work things out."

She shook her head. "I'm not going to do that. I can't."

Krystal spread her hands. "Okay. You want me to keep you posted?"

"Would you?"

"Of course."

"Nothing's going to change between us, Krystal."

Unfortunately, her friend didn't disagree.

SHANE ENDED UP taking Dylan to the airport, because Leonie had a Valentine's Day luncheon she couldn't miss. Noticing that his brother was still pale, he carried both of his suitcases for him, saying, "You sure you don't want to wait another day or two before you leave?"

Dylan didn't want to wait. Having to spend the extra days at his mother's knowing that Maddie was in the same house had been an additional source of pain for him. He'd get on the plane and suffer if need be.

"I'm a little weak, but it'll do me good to get back to the sunshine," he told his brother as they headed for the departure gate.

To Dylan's relief, Shane didn't say a word about Maddie. No one had—except Garret, who hadn't been able to resist saying, "I warned you not to get any ideas about Maddie."

"I'm glad you came home, Dylan," Shane said as they said their goodbyes. "It was good to see you."

"I feel the same way," he told his brother.

"I hope that means we don't have to wait another two years before we see you."

"I don't think so," he said, but he knew that since Maddie and he had broken up, he wouldn't be coming back to Saint Paul as often as he'd planned.

When the boarding call for his flight was announced, Dylan gave his brother a wave, gathered his laptop and his carry-on and headed for the gate. It felt strange to be leaving—almost as strange as it had felt when he'd come home. In a little over a month he'd once again started to think of Saint Paul as home.

A perky, young flight attendant helped him with his carry-on bag, then saw that he was comfortably seated in the first-class section. "Would you like something to read? Magazine, newspaper?" she asked, with a smile that told him she'd be open to other things if he wanted to inquire what they were. He didn't.

"No, thanks," he told her. "I have the paper." It was the last thing his mother had shoved at him this morning when they'd said their goodbyes. He'd tucked it into his laptop briefcase and pulled it out now.

It wasn't the daily news, but a smaller local paper. On the front page was a story about Valentine's Day. Next to it was a Post-it note from his mother. It was heart shaped and said, "Just in case you want to see your mother's work."

He found the page she'd indicated and began reading, smiling at the words his mother had chosen to use in her responses.

Then he got to the last letter. It said,

Dear Leonie: I'm in love with a wonderful man who says he loves me. The problem? He carries around the burden of being the only one who knows that his father cheated on his mother. It's a secret he's kept from his mother and the rest of his family. Now I'm afraid this destructive secret has destroyed our love.

It was signed "Sad in Saint Paul," but Dylan knew who'd written it. Maddie. He anxiously read his mother's reply.

Dear Sad in St. Paul: The secret of infidelity is a terrible burden for any child to bear. Is your boyfriend sure it *is* a secret? It could be that his mother knows about the affair but has never discussed it with him because she doesn't realize he carries this burden. No matter what the reason, he needs to understand that infidelity is a choice, not a matter of genetics.

It only took a moment for Dylan to move into action. He unbuckled his seat belt and reached in the overhead compartment for his carry-on.

"Sir, are you all right?" the stewardess asked as he pushed his way past passengers continuing to board.

"I will be once I get off the plane," he said as he strode toward the exit.

DYLAN COULDN'T BELIEVE what he'd done. He rarely acted on impulse, yet here he was sitting in his mother's kitchen instead of flying back to Saint Martin.

The sound of the front door opening had his heartbeat increasing. He knew his mother would see his jacket hanging on the coat tree, notice his carry-on sitting next to the door.

As he expected, she burst into the kitchen with a look of surprise on her face. "Did you miss your plane?"

"Did you want me to? Is that why you gave me the paper to read this morning?"

She approached the table cautiously. "I always told myself I wouldn't stick my nose in my kids' love lives, but I knew we needed to talk, Dylan."

"You know, don't you."

"That Maddie is 'Sad in Saint Paul'? Yes. I know that food poisoning was nasty, but lucky for you it delayed your leaving and I could get her letter and my response into the paper before you left."

He stood then and took her in his arms, holding her close. "I'm sorry, Mom."

"No, I'm the one who's sorry, Dylan." She gently

eased away from him. "I didn't realize you knew about your father."

"Dad didn't tell you?"

She shook her head and gestured for him to sit down beside her.

"But you knew about the affair? Didn't you realize that it was the reason Dad and I had so much trouble that summer?"

"I didn't learn about the affair until years after it was over. He never told me you knew and I never connected the two incidents. I thought the anger you always had toward your father was because the two of you were simply destined not to get along. You were so much alike," she said, shaking her head reflectively. "It never occurred to me that you could have known."

"He should have told you...or me," he said soberly.

She nodded in agreement. "But I didn't want to know the details. It was enough that he'd been unfaithful."

"You forgave him."

She nodded soberly. "But I never forgot."

He gave her a puzzled look. "Then how can you act as if you had this wonderful, happy marriage?"

"Because it was wonderful and happy. Dylan, just because your father made one mistake doesn't erase all the good things we shared. Don't get me wrong. It hurt something awful to think that he went to another woman to get something I thought only I could give him."

"Yet you stayed married to him."

"Because I loved him and he was a good man. And I wasn't willing to throw away twenty years of marriage because of one mistake he regretted immensely." She studied his face. "You don't understand, do you."

"I want to, Mom, but..."

She reached for his hand. "There is no perfect love. We all want to think there is, but there isn't. Love can be such an incredible high it often makes us believe we've got the best thing in the world."

"Is this what you tell your clients?"

"I tell them to be honest. Honesty is the single most important ingredient in a relationship."

"Then how could you forgive Dad?"

She sighed. "There is no easy answer, Dylan. I could have carried around the bitterness the rest of my life, but it wouldn't have made me happy. What made me happy was surviving an incident that could have very well ended my life with your father. You may not realize this, but he paid dearly for his mistake. If I can let go of the pain, you should be able to."

He wanted to.

"Why did you get off that plane, Dylan? For me...or for Maddie?"

When he didn't reply, she leaned closer to him, "She thinks you won't commit to her because of what you know about your father."

"Is that what you think, too?"

She paused, as if debating whether to tell him what she thought. "I don't think this is about your father."

He leaned back in the chair, tipping back on two legs. "You don't."

"No, I think it's about you. Ever since you were little you needed to be the one in control. You needed to be in charge. Love isn't something you can control, Dylan. You put your heart at risk. You have to let someone else take care of something you've always guarded closely."

Maddie hadn't said those exact words, but the message had been implied that night when she'd stormed out of the hotel room. "I thought I was doing the right thing for Maddie...letting her go."

"Maybe she doesn't need for you to tell her what's best." She stood, smoothing the wrinkles from her skirt. "I've said more than a mother should say and I need to change my clothes. I have a speaking engagement."

Dylan stood, too. "You said what needed to be said, Mom. Thanks." He kissed her cheek.

"So what are you going to do now? You're off the plane. It's Valentine's Day for another eight hours."

"I think I'll find a way to celebrate," he said with a slow grin.

MADDIE THOUGHT that the only good thing about Valentine's Day was that the stores were filled with chocolate. One could go into any candy shop and buy as much of the deepest, darkest, richest chocolate as one pleased without anyone knowing they weren't a gift for a Valentine, but a salve for a broken heart.

It's what Maddie had done. As soon as she'd broken up with Dylan, she'd gone and bought the most expensive box of dark chocolates she could find and consoled herself by eating them one by one. As wonderful as they'd been, they hadn't taken away the ache in her heart.

She wondered if anything would do that.

Certainly being alone on Valentine's Day didn't help. She'd come home from work to an empty house, knowing that Krystal had a date and Leonie had gone to speak at a special Valentine's dinner for residents of a convalescent home.

It's what Maddie should have done—volunteered to help at any one of the charitable events happening across the city. It would have been better than sitting home stuffing her mouth with the treats she'd received at the dance studio that day.

She smiled as she looked at the assortment of paper Valentines and candies she'd dumped on the table. It was definitely one of the perks to her job—someone always remembered her on the holidays. Today her students had greeted her with cards and candies and even a flower or two. She picked up the wilting red rose and sniffed it, then sighed.

''You look the way I feel,'' she mumbled to the flower, then set it aside so she could sort the treats she'd received. Chocolate kisses in one pile, candy hearts in another. But she kept seeing that wilting rose and finally, when she could no longer stand it, got up to put it in some water.

As she reached for a bud vase in the cupboard, she noticed an envelope on the counter. On the outside were the words, ''To Sad in Saint Paul.''

Maddie's heart leaped into her throat. Leonie had figured out that she was the one who'd written the letter.

Gingerly she lifted the flap and pulled open the sheet of paper. It was a typed response to her letter.

Dear Sad in Saint Paul: You are right. Your boyfriend is afraid to commit but not for the reason you think. This isn't about his father, it's about his feelings for you. He's been using what happened with his father as an excuse not to face the real issue—which is, his inability to give up control of his heart to another person. Love has made him vulnerable. It's also made him feel as if he could climb Mount Everest if it meant being with the woman of his dreams. You are that woman. If you're willing to take the risk of being in love with such a guy, he could make this Valentine's Day one you'll never forget.

There was no signature.

Maddie's heart pounded in her chest. She swallowed with great difficulty and tried to move, but her legs refused to take her anywhere. Cautiously she moved slowly out of the kitchen, down the hallway. She peeked into the living room, but it was empty. Then she walked toward Leonie's office. The door was closed.

She paused before entering, her hand on the doorknob, her heart pounding. Finally she pushed open the door. As she expected, it wasn't Leonie sitting behind the desk, but Dylan.

"Happy Valentine's Day, Maddie," he said in a voice that had her rushing to meet him as he rose to his feet.

She nearly knocked him down as she threw herself

into his arms and kissed him with an urgency that had both of them clinging to each other for support.

"You didn't leave," she said as tears trickled down her cheeks.

"I didn't leave," he said, holding on to her as if he were worried she'd disappear.

"How did you know about my letter to Leonie?"

"Didn't you see the paper?"

"She published it?"

"And a response...that had me jumping off the plane at the last minute. My mom is a wise woman, Maddie."

"Yes, she is, and I will be forever grateful to her," she said, staring up at his face. As long as she lived she didn't think she'd ever get tired of looking at his face.

"I will forever be grateful that I found you," he told her. "I love you, Maddie, and I don't want to think of a future without you in it."

"What are you asking me, Dylan?"

"To be mine." He pulled a small box from his pocket and handed it to her. "Happy Valentine's Day."

She opened it and inside was gold locket in the shape of a heart, bearing the inscription ML Be Mine DD. "It's beautiful."

"Will you be mine? And I'm not talking about a long-distance relationship, Maddie. I want us to be together. Every day. Not just on weekends."

For an answer she kissed him tenderly, then said, "Then we'll work it out. I have no roots here, Dylan. I love your mother as if she were my own, but my sisters don't live here. I'd follow you wherever your work takes you."

He kissed her back. "I don't know if I deserve you. I hurt you that night at the hotel. I'm sorry, Maddie."

"What happened, Dylan? We were so happy together when that evening started. Then we went to Shane's, and the next thing I knew you were pulling away from me."

"I was scared of what I saw when you held Tom and Judy's baby."

"And you started worrying that I would get pregnant?"

He shook his head. "No, the panic set in when I started fantasizing about what it would be like if you had my baby. You looked so natural, so right holding that little baby..."

"I never said I wanted to have children, Dylan."

"Do you?"

She knew this was where the risky part came in. She needed to be honest. "Someday."

He smiled then. "Good, because I want them, too. Spending these past six weeks here, I've realized that as great as it is to live on an island where the weather is always warm and the only responsibility I have in life is my work, I've missed being a part of this family."

"So we can have kids someday?"

"Someday. But first, I need you to be mine and only mine." From behind him on the desk, he reached for a box and handed it to her. Inside were the letters *I LUV U* in chocolate. "I promise to always be true."

"That's all I need...and a little chocolate now and then."

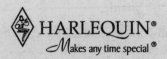

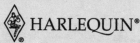

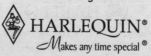

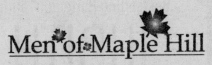

COLLECTIO

Jean Diwo

LES DAMES DU FAUBOURG

**

Le lit d'acajou

Denoël

Pour écrire cette saga dont la première partie commence à la fin du XVe siècle et s'achève à la veille de la Révolution, Jean Diwo a abandonné une longue carrière de journaliste. Formé à l'école des grands quotidiens puis de *Paris-Match* où il fut grand reporter avant de fonder et de diriger pendant vingt ans *Télé 7 jours*, il vous présente aujourd'hui ses *Dames du Faubourg*. Que celles-ci soient abbesses, bourgeoises ou femmes d'ébénistes, elles réservent bien des surprises au lecteur, qui trouvera plaisir à les fréquenter tout au long de ces pages denses et passionnantes.

Jean Diwo a donné une suite aux *Dames du Faubourg* avec son ouvrage *Le lit d'Acajou* paru aux Éditions Denoël en 1986.

A Irène

Chapitre 1.

LE THÉÂTRE DE LA RÉVOLUTION

Qui avait désigné comme « suspect » Bertrand de Valfroy? Quel être abject avait inscrit son nom sur le registre des dénonciations ouvert au greffe de la Commission de sûreté? Antoinette, le visage pâle et amaigri, décoiffée, se posait une fois encore la question en rédigeant la supplique qu'elle se faisait un devoir d'adresser chaque jour aux hommes politiques censés avoir quelque influence sur la marche de ce que personne n'osait plus appeler la Justice.

Bertrand Perrin, ci-devant de Valfroy, avait été arrêté une semaine auparavant alors qu'il sortait du bureau de bienfaisance de la section des Enfants-Trouvés où il exerçait les fonctions bénévoles de commissaire-trésorier. Cette arrestation avait plongé le quartier du Faubourg dans la désolation. Il se faisait une règle, chacun le savait, de demeurer étranger aux agissements des factions qui s'entre-déchiraient à la Convention, aux Jacobins et même au sein du Comité de salut public. Libéral, favorable aux idées généreuses semées par la Révolution, Valfroy fuyait comme la peste les Enragés, les Montagnards et les royalistes extrémistes. Les massacres de « blancs » et de « bleus » dans les départements et la Terreur qui saignait le pays lui étaient également intolérables. A son modeste poste, l'ancien lieutenant de Necker n'entendait servir que son pays et le peuple malheureux.

Antoinette ne pleurait plus. Consciente de l'issue, quasi certaine, de la détention de son mari, elle voulait conserver ses forces intactes pour lutter, malgré tout, contre l'infernale machine terroriste. Elle s'était juré de se battre, jusqu'au pied de l'échafaud s'il le fallait. Pour l'instant elle écrivait une nouvelle lettre à son beau-frère, Charles Delacroix, élu dans son département député à la Convention. Deux fois déjà, elle avait pressé l'avocat d'intervenir. Il n'avait pas répondu. Sa sœur Victoire lui avait seulement fait tenir une lettre dans laquelle elle expliquait que son mari ne pouvait pas faire grand-chose, inquiet qu'il était lui-même d'être arrêté. Antoinette avait déchiré la lettre et maudit sa sœur encore plus que son beau-frère, puis elle s'était calmée. Tout le monde vivait dans l'angoisse et ces phrases sans chaleur dictées par la peur n'excluaient pas tout espoir. Il fallait tenir, insister, laisser de côté les réactions d'amour-propre, frapper sans cesse aux portes qui refusaient de s'ouvrir, chercher de nouveaux appuis.

Riesener [1] se démenait dans les sections. Il aurait voulu voir Santerre qu'il connaissait de longue date mais Santerre, l'homme qui avait fait battre tambour à l'exécution du roi, venait d'être nommé général et chassait les blancs en Vendée. Réveillon [2] lui aussi faisait le tour de ses relations mais, en ce printemps de 94, la peur paralysait les plus audacieux. Restait Ethis, populaire de la Bastille à la « place du Trône-renversé ». Sa qualité de plus jeune « vainqueur de la Bastille » le rendait intouchable, et la joyeuse insolence qu'il affichait ne gênait personne parce que tout le monde en faisait les frais. Il était, en fait, le vrai soutien d'Antoinette. Lui seul savait la réconforter :

– M. de Valfroy m'a sauvé, je le sauverai, lui répétait-il. C'est un serment que je vous fais. Ayez confiance, Antoinette! Ethis est malin, il trouvera le moyen de rendre son père à la petite Lucie.

1. Célèbre ébéniste, beau-père d'Antoinette.
2. Parrain d'Antoinette. (Voir *Les Dames du Faubourg.)*

Lucie avait maintenant plus de quatre ans; elle comprenait tout du drame épouvantable qui se jouait dans la maison. Elle se taisait, ne pleurait que lorsqu'elle était seule et embrassait sa mère un peu plus fort. Ce jour-là, elle sauta au cou du jeune homme en lui disant, gravement : « Oui, Ethis, c'est toi qui peux sauver mon papa, je sais bien! »

Ému, Ethis embrassa Lucie et ravala un sanglot en annonçant maladroitement :

– Ce soir, je rentrerai tard, ne vous inquiétez pas, il faut que je passe au théâtre de la rue Antoine.

Depuis que l'abbaye était fermée après avoir été vidée des statues et des tableaux qui avaient échappé au vandalisme des premiers jours, le saint qui lui avait donné son nom était lui-même chassé du vocabulaire. Le faubourg Saint-Antoine était devenu « faubourg Antoine », la porte et la vieille rue qui menait à la Grève avaient elles aussi perdu leur saint. On avait d'abord ri de cette censure de voirie mais, chacun préférant ne pas se faire remarquer – on était pour moins que cela étiqueté ennemi de la Nation –, l'habitude avait été prise : le « faubourg Antoine » reliait maintenant la « place de la Bastille-démolie » à la « place du Trône-renversé ».

Antoinette avait sursauté en entendant Ethis dire qu'il allait au théâtre.

– Comment? Tu as envie d'aller voir jouer la comédie dans un moment pareil?

– Rassurez-vous, je ne vais pas au théâtre pour applaudir les acteurs dont je me moque mais pour y rencontrer quelqu'un. Peut-être celui qui sauvera M. Bertrand, mais n'en parlez à personne, c'est un secret.

Vers sept heures, alors qu'une brise venue des hauteurs de Montreuil et de la Pissote apportait enfin un peu de fraîcheur, Ethis se couvrit de son bonnet rouge à cocarde tricolore et remonta à grandes enjambées le Faubourg en direction de la Bastille. Son genou, blessé au cours de l'émeute chez Réveillon, ne le faisait plus souffrir et il s'accommodait de la légère claudication qui lui valait dans le quartier le sobriquet de « Traîne-sabot ».

Ethis traversa le terrain vague chaotique où se dressait naguère la forteresse de la Bastille, s'engagea dans la rue Saint-Antoine et s'arrêta devant le numéro 46. Surmontant le porche d'entrée, une pancarte tricolore décorée de piques et de drapeaux indiquait : *Théâtre de la Révolution.* C'était là une appellation bien ronflante pour la petite salle garnie de bancs de bois dont la scène, fermée d'un rideau rouge, occupait toute la largeur. Le propriétaire en était le citoyen Mareux qui accueillait chez lui aussi bien les troupes d'amateurs que les comédiens vacants des salles plus renommées du boulevard du Temple.

L'affiche du jour, accrochée à l'entrée, annonçait *Le Misanthrope* mais Molière n'intéressait pas Ethis. Escaladant les bancs, il traversa la salle encore vide parcimonieusement éclairée par une lanterne fumante et poussa une porte étroite qui s'ouvrait sur le côté de la scène. Dans les coulisses, installé devant une table de bois blanc, se tenait un jeune homme dont le visage rasé paraissait aussi gris que ses habits et la cravate qu'il portait sous le col de sa redingote. Penché sur un livre, il écrivait à la plume entre les lignes imprimées. Il leva la tête à l'entrée d'Ethis, sourit et déclara à la manière de Talma :

– Comment va mon frère Traîne-sabot? Quel vent d'autan le conduit chez Melpomène?

Ethis ignorait qui était Melpomène mais il serra chaleureusement les mains tendues de son hôte et s'assit sans façon sur un coffre. Il avait rencontré Charles-Hippolyte Delpeuch, plus connu dans le milieu du théâtre sous le nom de La Bussière, à la section des Quinze-Vingts. Comédien de son état, La Bussière était présentement secrétaire du propriétaire des lieux nommé « commissaire de la bienfaisance » de sa section. En l'absence du maître, souvent occupé par ses fonctions, La Bussière faisait office de secrétaire-régisseur-acteur. D'un tempérament discret et effacé, il se donnait de l'assurance en discourant dans la vie comme s'il avait été sur une scène :

– Sais-tu ce que les censeurs obtus exigent de moi, zélé serviteur de notre art admirable? Ces monstres de sottise qui ont interdit *Le Mariage de Figaro* m'obligent à corriger le sublime Molière. Tu ne me crois pas citoyen? Tiens, quand Célimène parle de Géralde à Acaste, elle le juge ainsi :

O l'ennuyeux conteur!
Jamais on ne le voit sortir du grand seigneur,
Dans le brillant commerce il se mêle sans cesse,
Il ne cite jamais que duc, prince ou princesse;

Eh bien! ce soir ces vers sans doute attentatoires à la sécurité de la République deviendront :

O l'ennuyeux conteur!
Jamais on ne le voit sortir de sa splendeur,
Dans le brillant commerce il se mêle sans cesse
Jamais on ne l'entend citer que sa richesse.

Qu'en dis-tu, Traîne-sabot?

Ethis n'en pensait rien. Il songeait à autre chose, au but de sa visite. Mais, comme si sa proclamation, qui eût pu lui valoir la guillotine, ne suffisait pas, La Bussière déchaîné se précipita et jeta à terre les bustes en plâtre de Le Pelletier et de Marat placés à chaque extrémité de la scène.

– Heureusement que nous sommes seuls, monsieur La Bussière! s'écria Ethis stupéfait.

– Bien sûr, mon frère, bien sûr, mais cela m'a fait du bien. Il y a longtemps que je ne supportais plus la tête de ces deux-là!

Sur scène, La Bussière jouait assez médiocrement la comédie. Le rôle de sa vie, il l'interprétait ailleurs, dans un théâtre où on ne l'attendait pas : le redoutable Comité de sûreté générale! Ethis était l'un des rares à connaître la double personnalité de l'acteur. La Bussière lui avait confié, un soir où ils étaient de garde à la section, comment l'un de ses amis, le critique Fabien Pilet, chef du service de la correspondance au bureau des détenus, lui avait procuré – le théâtre ne nourrissant pas son homme – un emploi de secrétaire dans son service.

En pleine Terreur, c'était un poste répugnant. Enregistreur des pièces accusatrices, il était chargé de mettre en ordre et de transmettre au Tribunal révolutionnaire les dossiers des prisonniers destinés pour la plupart à la guillotine. La Bussière était cependant le contraire d'un sanguinaire. Engagé dès le début dans la Révolution il en réprouvait aujourd'hui les excès :

– Je sais que ce métier est horrible mais il me permet de rendre des services. Ne m'en demande pas plus.

C'est à cause de cette confidence d'un soir qu'Ethis était là. « Si La Bussière rend des services, pensa-t-il, peut-être pourra-t-il sauver Valfroy. » Le comédien écouta en silence Ethis lui raconter comment Bertrand avait été arrêté, lui dire le désespoir de sa femme, le sien propre devant la terrible menace qui guettait son bienfaiteur :

– C'est un honnête citoyen, plein de générosité, qui a toujours défendu les libertés au côté de Necker. Trésorier de sa section, il n'a cessé de servir la cause du peuple. Si la Révolution doit le condamner à l'échafaud, moi, Ethis, le plus jeune des « vainqueurs de la Bastille », je tourne le dos à la Révolution !

La Bussière sourit :

– Je ferai tout ce que je pourrai, dit-il. Il faut attendre que le dossier passe entre mes mains. De toute façon, il me sera impossible de faire sortir M. de Valfroy du cachot, mais si je réussis à éviter le pire, ce ne sera pas si mal. Je vais essayer de faire en sorte qu'il ne soit pas jugé. Enfin, quand je dis jugé... Bref il faut tenter de lui sauver la vie. Mais, attention : jure-moi que tu ne parleras de cela à personne, pas même à sa femme pour la rassurer. La moindre imprudence nous conduirait tous à la guillotine !

Ethis rentra place d'Aligre le cœur plus léger. A Antoinette qui l'attendait, impatiente, il dit simplement qu'un ami s'occupait du sort de Bertrand et qu'il fallait garder courage. A son ton, elle sentit que tout espoir n'était pas perdu. Pour la première fois depuis l'arrestation de

Bertrand, elle s'endormit sitôt couchée, serrée contre la petite Lucie.

Le même soir, le comédien La Bussière n'avait pas été très applaudi sur les planches du théâtre de la Révolution ; le citoyen Delpeuch en gardait un peu d'amertume tandis qu'il gagnait le pavillon de Flore, siège du Comité de salut public et du Comité de sûreté générale. Son bureau était au deuxième étage. Sur le palier du premier, il salua un homme sanglé dans un habit bleu ciel, poudré, portant la perruque à l'ancienne mode. Maximilien Robespierre répondit d'un glacial : « Bonjour citoyen », et entra, l'air préoccupé, dans la salle des délibérations.

Delpeuch sourit intérieurement en imaginant ce que penserait l'« Incorruptible » s'il apprenait qu'il croisait chaque matin, en la personne de l'humble secrétaire du bureau des détenus, l'homme-grain de sable qui avait réussi à détraquer l'impitoyable mécanique du Tribunal révolutionnaire. En attendant, il fallait trier la pile imposante de dossiers qu'un garde venait de déposer sur la table. C'était un moment pénible. Delpeuch savait que neuf sur dix des noms calligraphiés, dont chacun étalait devant ses yeux l'entité d'une famille, d'un bonheur, d'un amour, seraient bientôt flanqués d'une croix qui signifierait leur radiation du monde des vivants. Il savait aussi que grâce à lui un ou deux de ces malheureux ne seraient pas traduits devant le tribunal et ignoreraient toujours pourquoi ils n'avaient pas été guillotinés avec leurs compagnons de geôle. Ces sauvetages d'inconnus, pour lesquels il risquait sa propre vie, lui permettaient de vaincre les répugnances qu'il éprouvait à exercer sa charge. Dix fois il avait voulu démissionner mais, toujours, sa conscience lui avait commandé de rester. Delpeuch s'était même ouvert de ses scrupules à un prêtre réfractaire bien connu des comédiens, l'abbé Carrichon qui se cachait dans Paris et accompagnait secrètement au supplice, en suivant les charrettes, les condamnés qu'il connaissait et à qui il avait promis de donner l'absolution en cas de malheur. Sans hésiter, l'abbé lui avait dit de continuer une tâche que Dieu, dans sa miséricorde, ne pouvait qu'approuver.

Delpeuch feuilleta rapidement les dossiers pour s'assurer que celui du ci-devant Valfroy n'était pas dans la pile Ce jour-là, la moitié des cartons concernaient les comédiens-français du théâtre de la Nation que le Comité avait fait arrêter en qualité d'ex-comédiens du roi et donc ennemis de la Révolution. Delpeuch blêmit en relevant parmi les noms des prochains guillotinés ceux de plusieurs camarades avec qui il avait joué naguère la comédie.

– Ce n'est pas possible, ce n'est pas possible! murmura-t-il. Qu'ont fait ces malheureux pour mériter la mort. Aussitôt il pensa : je vais essayer de les sauver. Si je suis pris, nous mourrons tous ensemble. Puis comme il ne manquait pas d'esprit, il sourit en songeant : c'est ma seule chance de faire partie des comédiens-français!

C'était jouer gros jeu. Soustraire un dossier est une chose, en détruire quinze en est une autre. Et pas n'importe quels dossiers : ceux-ci étaient transmis directement par Fouquier-Tinville, l'accusateur public, et portaient tous la vigoureuse apostille de Collot d'Herbois, ancien comédien lui-même et ancien royaliste qui ordonnait le jugement pour le 13 messidor. On était le 9. C'est dire qu'il n'y avait pas une seconde à perdre. Delpeuch-La Bussière réfléchit un instant et décida d'agir le jour même. Pour l'instant, il para au plus pressé : du carton marqué « comédiens-français » qui regroupait tous les actes d'accusation il retira un rapport du Conseil général de la commune, un virulent réquisitoire de Chaumette, la note de Collot d'Herbois à Fouquier-Tinville et plusieurs dénonciations de particuliers. Sans ces pièces, le procès, bien qu'on en connût déjà l'issue, ne pouvait s'ouvrir. Les agents de la Terreur, en effet, prenaient soin d'accommoder leurs actes les plus arbitraires d'un certain formalisme. Il ouvrit donc son tiroir et y glissa les feuilles accusatrices. C'est tout ce qu'il pouvait faire dans la journée, son bureau étant sans cesse traversé par des gens à l'air affairé qui n'auraient pas hésité à dénoncer le comédien-secrétaire s'ils avaient remarqué le moindre signe anormal dans son comportement.

A six heures, il expédia les autres dossiers – au moins deux charrettes évalua-t-il avec dégoût – et gagna tranquillement le théâtre du citoyen Mareux. *Le Misanthrope* était encore à l'affiche. Il tint avec un certain bonheur le rôle de Philinte et les applaudissements du tomber de rideau le mirent de bonne humeur. En sifflotant il regagna d'un bon pas le pavillon de Flore : il lui fallait parachever son œuvre de sauvetage des comédiens-français. Il s'arrêta un moment place de Grève où des cuisines publiques offraient à ceux qui n'avaient trouvé ni pain ni viande dans les boutiques vidées par la disette un modeste repas pour un billet de quinze sols.

La Bussière choisit deux harengs séchés parmi ceux qui pendaient en cordons au-dessus de la porte d'une échoppe. La cuisinière en plein air, la mère Marie, connue de tous les modestes serviteurs du théâtre, les jeta sur le gril. Une épaisse fumée empesta le quartier jusqu'au pont au Change. Quand l'odeur commença à se dissiper, Marie décréta que les harengs étaient bons à servir. Elle les plaça dans une assiette qui n'avait rien à faire dans ce décor de misère; c'était une fine porcelaine décorée aux armes de la maison de Duras. « La duchesse me doit bien cela », pensa La Bussière en souriant. L'ex-maréchale de Ségur ignorait dans sa prison des Carmes pourquoi elle ne passait pas en jugement... Seul le comédien eût pû lui répondre, qui avait escamoté son dossier, comme ça, sans intérêt ni profit, et qui mangeait ses harengs aux lentilles dans la vaisselle armoriée provenant du pillage de son hôtel.

Quand il fut rassasié – il avait la chance d'avoir un petit appétit – il reprit sa marche vers les Tuileries. Son itinéraire était minuté : il devait arriver au pavillon de Flore à une heure du matin, moment où les membres du Comité de salut public venaient d'entrer en délibération. L'escalier n'était pas éclairé mais La Bussière connaissait la largeur des marches de marbre et la longueur des paliers. Il savait se guider dans l'obscurité et trouver la porte de son bureau qui ne grinçait plus depuis qu'il en avait graissé les gonds. Une fois dans la place, il était tranquille, sûr que personne ne viendrait le déranger. Alors il pouvait commencer son étrange besogne.

A tâtons, il cherchait les pièces accusatrices dans le tiroir de sa table et les plongeait dans un seau d'eau qu'il avait rempli à moitié avant de partir. Méthodiquement, lentement, il malaxait le papier détrempé jusqu'à ce qu'il puisse en faire des boules qu'il mettait dans ses poches. Le plus dur du travail n'était pas achevé. Il lui fallait maintenant ressortir, descendre un étage au jugé, vérifier si la porte du premier qui menait à la salle des séances du Comité n'était pas gardée, dépasser très vite cette porte derrière laquelle on percevait presque toujours des éclats de voix ou des bruits de dispute, enfin gagner la sortie sans se faire remarquer. Seulement lorsqu'il avait franchi l'enceinte des Tuileries il pouvait se dire qu'il avait encore une fois réussi. C'est alors qu'il avait peur et se mettait à trembler. Le trac qui l'abandonnait dès qu'il entrait dans l'action de sa périlleuse mission reparaissait un moment, comme au théâtre, dès que le danger était passé. Ce jour-là, l'opération avait été particulièrement longue et la fatigue qui le submergea lui fit vite retrouver son calme. Trois quarts d'heure exactement après avoir quitté le Comité, il était couché dans sa chambre de la rue Saint-Nicolas, dans le Faubourg, et s'endormait. Le reste, à son réveil, n'était qu'un jeu d'enfant. Vers sept heures, avant de retrouver son bureau et de reprendre sa silhouette d'employé effacé, il se rendait aux bains Vigier du pont Royal. Tandis que la femme de charge remplissait la baignoire il regardait un instant couler la Seine par la fenêtre de sa cabine puis il se plongeait avec délices dans l'eau bien chaude où il avait précédemment jeté ses pelotes de papier. Trempées et pétries une nouvelle fois, il les divisait en petites boulettes qu'il lançait une à une, avec adresse, dans le courant.

Quand il ne restait plus trace des actes d'accusation du

Comité, il se séchait puis, détendu, content, regagnait le pavillon de Flore où l'attendait le bonjour distrait du citoyen Robespierre. Un salut qui, ce matin-là, lui causa un indicible plaisir.

Le dossier de Bertrand de Valfroy n'arriva sur le bureau de Delpeuch-La Bussière que la semaine suivante. Cela tombait mal. La veille, Fouquier-Tinville, scandalisé de constater que ses ordres étaient demeurés sans effet et que les comédiens-français n'avaient pas encore été jugés, avait saisi le Comité de salut public et écrit une lettre sévère aux citoyens, membres représentants du peuple, chargés de la police générale : *Votre bureau des détenus n'est composé que de royalistes et de contre-révolutionnaires qui entravent la marche des affaires. Depuis deux mois, il y a un désordre total dans les pièces du Comité : sur trente individus qui me sont désignés pour être jugés, il en manque presque toujours la moitié. Hier encore, tout Paris s'attendait à la mise en jugement des comédiens-français et il semble que les pièces principales du dossier ont été égarées!*

Une enquête avait évidemment été lancée mais, par miracle, La Bussière n'avait pas été suspecté. A vrai dire, le peuple était las de voir couler tant de sang et ses représentants ne mettaient pas beaucoup de zèle à servir la fureur de Fouquier-Tinville.

Le comédien-secrétaire ne s'en montrait pas moins prudent. Il n'avait tous ces jours subtilisé aucun dossier. Tapi dans son bureau, jamais il ne s'était fait une silhouette si discrète. Et voilà que survenait l'affaire Valfroy et, avec elle, un nouveau cas de conscience. Le dossier gris était là, devant lui. Il le regarda un moment, pensif, indécis. Allait-il le placer à sa droite, avec les autres comme la prudence le lui commandait? Ce simple geste équivalait à celui du bourreau. Et il avait promis à Ethis qu'il ferait l'impossible... Allons! il avait sauvé assez d'inconnus pour essayer d'étouffer le procès de

Valfroy. Puisqu'il avait commencé de jouer la pièce dramatique à laquelle il prêtait le titre d'*Illusion comique,* il n'allait pas quitter la scène au milieu d'un acte. Il ouvrit le dossier dont la minceur aurait dû entraîner un classement sans suite par le premier citoyen-fonctionnaire qui en avait eu connaissance. Au lieu de cela, il avait suivi la filière ordinaire, inexorable, qui menait à l'échafaud.

La Bussière sortit les trois uniques feuilles du carton : la première était une dénonciation d'un nommé Lavril qui affirmait que le ci-devant Valfroy avait été un conseiller de Capet et de la reine, même en dehors des périodes où Necker était au pouvoir. Il avait en outre, paraît-il, intrigué pour occuper une fonction à responsabilité dans une section afin de mieux servir le parti de l'étranger. Cela puait la haine. La décision de La Bussière ne tarda pas : cette feuille réduite en impalpables particules allait se diluer dans les remous du fleuve, et la bassesse, une fois encore, céder au pouvoir purificateur de l'eau. Il plaça la dénonciation, calligraphiée avec un soin extrême, comme si les pleins et les déliés bien formés devaient donner du poids au mensonge, dans le fond de son tiroir. La seconde pièce du dossier était une déposition favorable à Valfroy. Elle était signée par le président de la section des Enfants-Trouvés mais n'avait servi à rien. La Bussière la laissa en place avec le double de l'enregistrement d'écrou.

Et puis, le risque n'étant pas plus grand, le comédien décida de soustraire les pièces dangereuses d'un second dossier, celui d'une certaine vicomtesse Joséphine de Beauharnais; simplement parce qu'elle était jeune et qu'elle portait un joli nom.

La Bussière revint donc à une heure de la nuit, comme il l'avait fait si souvent, dans son bureau du pavillon de Flore. Sa besogne terminée, il descendait silencieusement l'escalier quand il entendit une porte s'ouvrir au premier étage, à cinq pas de l'endroit où il se trouvait. Cette fois il était pris au piège : impossible de remonter ni de poursuivre sa descente. Il demeura pétrifié l'espace de quelques secondes. Sa présence à une heure aussi tardive était inexplicable et la loi des suspects le vouait à une arrestation immédiate, sans compter qu'on découvrirait dans sa poche la preuve de ses agissements. Heureusement, les députés, qui échangeaient des propos très vifs, ne poussèrent pas tout de suite plus avant le battant de la porte et La Bussière, se rappelant l'agilité de Scapin, eut juste le temps de se précipiter dans un coffre à bois et de s'y tapir en retenant sa respiration. Trop occupés par leur dispute qu'ils poursuivaient sur le palier, à deux pas du coffre, les députés ne firent pas attention à la pointe de bonnet qui dépassait. Le malheureux régisseur du théâtre de la Révolution savait que sa vie ne tenait qu'au hasard d'un regard ou au moindre mouvement de sa part. Enfin, la discussion s'apaisa, les voix, parmi lesquelles il crut reconnaître celle de Billaud-Varenne, se firent moins violentes. Bientôt il entendit les derniers pas résonner sur les marches de marbre. Quand le silence fut rétabli, il attendit encore de longues minutes avant de sortir de sa cachette. Contrairement aux jours où son expédition nocturne se déroulait sans encombre, il n'avait pas peur et avait gardé, durant tout le temps du danger, une présence d'esprit et un calme qui l'étonnaient lui-même. Il regagna son domicile sans difficulté, en se demandant quelle tête pouvait bien avoir cette Joséphine qu'il venait de sauver. Trop jolie en tout cas pour la « petite fenêtre » du bourreau Sanson.

Il était plus de deux heures lorsque La Bussière s'allongea sur son lit, harassé par la longue marche du soir et nerveusement épuisé par le rôle, hors répertoire, qu'il venait d'interpréter magistralement. Il était fatigué mais content. Une fois encore il avait tenté le Diable et Dieu lui avait permis de sauver deux têtes. En songeant à Joséphine qu'il ne rencontrerait sans doute jamais si elle survivait à la Terreur, il eut une pensée pour une autre jeune femme, belle et fragile, qu'il avait plusieurs fois croisée dans les couloirs du Comité : c'était Lucile, la femme de Camille Desmoulins, qui avait été guillotinée la veille.

Le jeune homme était trop excité pour dormir. Son

esprit vagabondait, il se voyait au pied de l'échafaud et regardait Sanson exercer ses terribles fonctions avec l'impassibilité d'un bon artisan habitué à répéter les mêmes gestes professionnels. Le bourreau n'avait jamais fait qu'un avec son sinistre couperet. Qu'elle soit celle d'un roi, d'une jeune princesse, d'un savant, d'un législateur républicain ou d'un plébéien, il abattait la tête qu'on lui présentait, avec sérénité.

La Bussière, dont le métier consistait à se mettre dans la peau des autres, était fasciné par le personnage de Sanson, grand massacreur de l'espèce humaine. Il aurait voulu se glisser dans son âme pour quelques heures, savoir ce qui se passait dans sa tête... Enfin, il s'endormit en se disant que Valfroy ne passerait pas de sitôt en jugement et que « Traîne-sabot » serait content de lui.

A la même heure de ce jour de prairial 94, dans son cachot de la Petite-Force, Bertrand de Valfroy, recroquevillé sur son lit de paille pouilleuse, essayait de lutter contre le froid qui l'envahissait en s'enroulant dans une méchante couverture. La température était clémente en ce début d'été mais le froid venait de l'intérieur. Les prisonniers l'appelaient « le sang de glace » et disaient qu'il était un mélange d'angoisse, de faim et de solitude. Depuis son arrestation, Valfroy ne réussissait pas à trouver le sommeil. Il ne s'endormait que le matin, lorsqu'il avait avalé sa ration de fèves et de pain noir. Son emprisonnement brutal ne l'avait pas trop surpris. Il était un « suspect » tout désigné pour l'appareil policier mis en place par Robespierre, l'illuminé que l'exécution de Danton venait de sacrer roi. Bertrand connaissait trop bien le fonctionnement terroriste pour ne pas savoir qu'il vivait ses derniers instants dans cette antichambre de la mort où, chaque matin, les bonnets rouges venaient chercher leur contingent de condamnés. Condamné, on l'était dès lors qu'un garde vous poussait d'un coup de crosse entre ces murs sales, couverts de noms, d'initiales, de messages d'adieu gravés dans le plâtre avec l'ongle, une dent de peigne ou la pointe d'une épingle. Le jugement du tribunal n'était qu'une formalité que les derniers décrets contre les suspects rendaient plus dérisoire encore.

Valfroy savait tout cela. Robespierre était le maître d'une Assemblée terrorisée et d'une Commune à sa botte depuis l'exécution d'Hébert. Rien ni personne ne pouvait désormais le sauver. Il ne lui restait plus qu'à attendre la mort, à accepter courageusement l'inéluctable.

Seul avec ses souvenirs, il pensait interminablement à Antoinette et à la petite Lucie. Qu'allaient-elles devenir dans ce Paris affamé, déchiré, sanglant? Parfois, il s'accusait, se persuadait qu'il avait commis une faute inexpiable en entraînant Antoinette dans une liaison et un mariage voués au désastre. A d'autres moments, calme, résigné, presque libéré, il revivait sans tristesse, sans accablement, les cinq dernières années de son existence, le travail ingrat mais passionnant auprès de Necker, la découverte d'un grand amour à un âge où il ne l'espérait plus, la naissance de sa petite fille... Rompu par son métier à la rigueur de l'esprit, il s'appliquait alors à ne rien laisser dans l'oubli, à se remémorer chaque chapitre, chaque paragraphe d'une histoire marquée par le bonheur et qu'interromprait avant peu le couperet de la guillotine.

Antoinette lui faisait presque chaque soir, depuis qu'ils vivaient ensemble, le récit détaillé de sa journée. Maintenant, dans son cachot, ces bouquets de souvenirs lui revenaient en mémoire avec une prodigieuse netteté. C'était comme si sa femme avait été à ses côtés, nichée dans le creux de son épaule, non pas sur cette paille immonde mais dans le lit aux panneaux de marqueterie que Riesener leur avait offert. Valfroy ne sentait plus l'odeur fétide de la prison. Par une fenêtre imaginaire, ouverte sur les marronniers de la place d'Aligre, entrait la fraîcheur des jardins de l'abbaye toute proche. Retour en arrière miraculeux, Antoinette était là qui revivait avec lui, pour lui, ses journées, ses attentes, ses joies... Elle racontait bien Antoinette, surtout lorsqu'elle évoquait leur enfant, la petite Lucie...

Chapitre 2.

L'ÉTÉ 89

Perdu dans son rêve éveillé, insensible au bruit que faisaient les autres détenus, Bertrand avait l'impression de relire, avec Antoinette, les pages d'un livre plein d'images et de couleurs qui était le livre de leur vie.

.. La chaleur de juillet tombait comme un couvercle sur l'enclave provinciale de la place d'Aligre calée au cœur du vieux Faubourg entre le marché Beauvau et l'arc de cercle des maisons nouvellement construites. Ses bras blancs posés sur les roses d'amboine et de citronnier de sa table à écrire, Antoinette regardait, pensive, par la fenêtre grande ouverte, les frondaisons immobiles.

La jeune femme n'était pas descendue depuis le matin, lorsqu'elle avait été faire quelques provisions. Tout à son bonheur d'être bientôt mère, elle ne s'était pas inquiétée des bruits d'une brève canonnade parvenus assourdis dans son paysage serein. Pour l'heure, elle reprenait en écrivant la date « 14 juillet 1789 » une longue lettre à sa sœur Victoire. Celle-ci avait suivi son mari, l'avocat et fonctionnaire royal Charles Delacroix, ancien premier commis de Turgot au contrôle général des finances, installé maintenant à Givry-en-Argonne son pays natal. La lettre d'Antoinette était une sorte de journal dont la tenue l'obligeait chaque jour à rassembler et fixer ses idées, un peu désorientées depuis qu'une balle perdue avait failli la tuer durant le sac de la maison Réveillon, trois mois auparavant.

Lorsqu'elle eut rempli une page où il était question de « douce chaleur », de « branches nonchalantes » et de « percées de lumière », elle posa sa plume pour relire ce qu'elle avait écrit les jours précédents :

« ... Il y a des gens auxquels il n'arrive jamais rien, dont l'existence, un peu à l'image de la tienne, ma chère sœur, s'écoule lente et paisible comme la rivière proche de ta demeure. Ma vie, au contraire est un torrent qui m'emporte, me chavire, m'enivre à certains moments et, à d'autres, me précipite contre de méchants rochers qui blessent mon âme et mon corps. Ainsi, ma liaison avec cet irrésistible fou de Pilâtre de Rozier a été un fabuleux orage bariolé de rêves comme le ballon qui l'a tué alors qu'il essayait de franchir la Manche. Avec lui est morte ma jeunesse. A peine avais-je retrouvé un peu de sérénité auprès de M. de Valfroy, dont je t'ai dit la prévenance et la tendresse, qu'un coup fâcheux du hasard me plongeait au cœur de l'émeute qui a ravagé, rue de Montreuil, la demeure de notre ami Réveillon. Je me cachais dans le parc de la Folie Titon, attendant une accalmie des combats pour m'enfuir lorsqu'un coup de feu, parti d'on ne sait où, m'arracha la moitié du cuir chevelu. Si je ne m'étais pas agenouillée, la seconde d'avant, pour soigner un jeune garçon, presque un enfant, qui perdait son sang, je ne serais pas en train, aujourd'hui, de te décrire mes états d'âme; la balle m'eût traversé la tête. Ce petit insurgé de quinze ans, égaré dans une foule haineuse et surexcitée composée en grande partie d'éléments troubles venus de partout, m'a sauvé la vie. Je l'ai recueilli, les médecins ont soigné sa jambe, notre beau-père Riesener vient de le placer comme apprenti chez le maître menuisier Nadal [1] et Bertrand de Valfroy qui l'a pris en amitié s'est promis de l'aider. Voilà, tu connais Ethis. Oui, il s'appelle Ethis! Je l'attends, il ne va pas tarder à rentrer de l'atelier et me donnera les nouvelles du Faubourg

1. Jean-Henri Riesener, le plus célèbre ébéniste de son temps, avait épousé la veuve de son patron et ami, le maître Œben, père d'Antoinette et de Victoire. Voir le premier tome des *Dames du Faubourg*.

puisque le médecin m'interdit encore de me promener seule. Il ne manquera pas de me dire ce que signifient les coups de feu que j'ai vaguement entendus dans l'après-midi. Un peu plus tard, Bertrand arrivera de la Trésorerie ou de Versailles. Je ne sais pas si je t'ai déjà dit qu'il travaillait avec Necker, ce ministre honnête et compétent que le roi passe son temps à congédier et à rappeler.

« J'aurai donc le bonheur d'avoir Valfroy près de moi toute la soirée, peut-être la nuit. Il me dira des choses douces mais nous parlerons surtout de la grande nouvelle, de la divine surprise, du miracle... Ça tu ne le sais pas encore : j'attends un enfant avant la fin de l'année. Ce petit a survécu, dans mon ventre, aux affres de l'insurrection chez Réveillon et à ma blessure. C'est te dire qu'il s'accroche à la vie ! En voilà un, ou une, qui semble bien décidé à voir ce qui se passe sur notre pauvre Terre. Prie avec moi, ma petite Victoire, pour qu'il n'ouvre pas les yeux sur l'épouvante... »

Vers six heures, Ethis escalada les deux étages et se précipita comme une bourrasque dans la chambre d'Antoinette qui lâcha sa plume de saisissement.

– La Bastille est prise ! s'écria-t-il. Nous avons pris la Bastille !

Antoinette le regarda :

– Que racontes-tu ? Tu es fou ! Regarde, tout est calme et la Bastille est tout de suite là, derrière ces maisons. Ce ne sont tout de même pas les trois ou quatre malheureux coups de canon que j'ai à peine entendus, qui ont suffi à faire tomber cette forteresse bourrée de poudre et de fusils !

– Il y a eu plus de trois coups de canon ! proteste Ethis. On s'est battu... C'est tout de même extraordinaire que vous ne vous soyez aperçue de rien !

– Y a-t-il eu autant de morts que chez Réveillon ? questionna Antoinette qui avait bien du mal à croire ce que lui racontait Ethis.

– Sûrement moins. On parlait tout à l'heure d'une centaine de victimes chez les assaillants et d'une dizaine d'officiers et de gardes suisses chez les assiégés. Ce que je sais, c'est que Launay, le gouverneur, a été massacré et qu'on promène en ce moment sa tête au bout d'une pique dans les rues de Paris.

– Quelle horreur! Et tu me racontes cela, tranquillement, comme s'il s'agissait d'une procession de Vendredi saint! Mais, au fait, si ce que tu me dis est vrai, que faisais-tu à la Bastille? Cela ne t'a pas suffi de revenir boiteux de chez Réveillon? Et encore, par miracle! Tu m'avais juré que tu ne participerais plus jamais à ces émeutes où l'on compte plus de racaille que d'honnêtes gens. Je vois que je ne peux pas te faire confiance et c'est dommage!

– Laissez-moi vous raconter, Antoinette. J'étais chez mon patron, M. Nadal, quand un groupe armé de piques et de quelques vieux fusils est venu nous débaucher en hurlant que la Bastille était assiégée par le peuple et que tout le Faubourg était mobilisé pour abattre les canons dirigés contre nos ateliers.

– Et bien sûr, tu as été le premier à te précipiter!

– Non! C'est Nadal qui s'est écrié tout de suite: «Allez, on y va!» L'atelier tout entier a suivi et j'aurais eu honte de les laisser partir sans moi...

– Sans compter que cela te plaisait bien de te mêler à la bataille! Alors, mon pauvre petit oiseau à la patte cassée, raconte-moi ce qui est arrivé. Au moins, tu n'es pas blessé?

– Non, j'ai pensé à vous et j'ai été prudent. D'ailleurs, quand nous sommes arrivés tout était à peu près terminé. Les portes avaient cédé, les derniers assiégeants s'engouffraient dans le château.

– Et tu as suivi, brigand! Sans penser que tu pouvais très bien être tué à l'intérieur par les gardes qui n'ont tout de même pas dû vous laisser faire ce que vous vouliez!

– Presque. En tout cas quand je suis entré ils s'étaient tous rendus. Mais je n'ai pas été là-bas pour rien. Tenez,

Antoinette, je vous ai rapporté un souvenir de la Bastille!

Le garçon fouilla dans sa poche et sortit une grosse clé qu'il tendit à la jeune femme :

– C'est une chance d'avoir pu m'en emparer. Tout le monde voulait emporter quelque chose et les clés étaient très recherchées. J'ai trouvé celle-ci sur la porte d'un couloir que personne n'avait encore remarquée. Tenez Antoinette, prenez-la, elle est à vous. C'est le premier cadeau que je peux vous faire.

Antoinette ne savait pas si elle devait rire ou pleurer. Émue plus qu'elle ne le laissait paraître, elle prit la clé et embrassa Ethis :

– Merci mon garçon. Ce soir on la montrera à M. de Valfroy puis nous la rangerons précieusement pour Lucien... ou Lucie quand tu lui raconteras tes exploits.

– C'est donc bien vrai, Antoinette, vous allez...

– Oui, monsieur le héros. J'attends un enfant qui s'appellera Lucien ou Lucie. Tiens, tu seras son parrain!

– Moi? Vous ne vous moquez pas? Vous voulez que je sois le parrain de votre enfant?

– Oui, c'est un peu grâce à toi qu'il n'est pas mort avec moi dans le parc de Réveillon, et cela me fera plaisir que tu sois son ange gardien dans ce monde. Enfin, quand je dis ange...

– Vous ne pouvez pas savoir comme je suis fier! Alors, vous m'aimez vraiment? Pardon si je pleure, Antoinette. C'est la première fois, vous savez...

Ethis renifla, essuya deux grosses larmes avec le mouchoir que lui tendait la jeune femme et continua :

– C'est la première fois que quelqu'un de bien fait attention à moi. Je vous remercie du fond du cœur.

Antoinette prit les mains du jeune garçon et fixa avec affection ses yeux embués :

– Écoute, Ethis, tu es aussi quelqu'un de bien! C'est pour cela qu'on t'aime. Ce que je viens de te dire est sérieux. Il va falloir maintenant te mettre dans la tête que tu n'es plus seul, que tu es intelligent et que rien ne t'empêche de devenir un garçon, puis un homme heureux. Seulement, de grâce, ne cours pas te jeter dans la mêlée chaque fois qu'il y a des coups à recevoir. Dis-toi plutôt que M. de Valfroy n'est pas souvent là et que j'ai besoin de toi pour nous protéger, l'enfant et moi. Ton rôle de parrain commence maintenant. Est-ce que je peux compter sur toi?

– Je jure, mademoiselle Antoinette, que tant que je serai près de vous il ne vous arrivera rien. Dites à M. de Valfroy que je me ferais tuer pour vous défendre.

Elle sourit et se rendit compte que cette demande de protection lancée au gamin, sans réfléchir, pour lui donner confiance, n'était pas si gratuite. L'idée qu'Ethis allait veiller sur elle la rassurait. Elle alla préparer le souper en chantonnant, se disant qu'elle avait de la chance d'échapper aux privations qui commençaient à éprouver une grande partie de la population du Faubourg. L'inclémence du temps, ajoutée à l'anarchie économique et financière dans laquelle se débattait le royaume depuis de longues années, rendait en effet la vie de plus en plus difficile aux classes laborieuses. Le manque de pain, en particulier, exaspérait les gens du Faubourg. L'âge d'or de la commode était fini où, débordés de commandes, les ateliers des cours et des passages n'arrivaient pas à satisfaire tous les amateurs de meubles raffinés devenus presque des œuvres d'art. Fini le temps béni où les maîtres se disputaient les meilleurs compagnons ébénistes et marqueteurs venus de Hollande ou d'Allemagne. La pauvreté du royaume gagnait de proche en proche les classes aisées et obligeait les artisans du Faubourg à se séparer d'une partie de leurs ouvriers. Certes, quelques ateliers qui pouvaient s'enorgueillir d'une estampille prestigieuse comme celle de Bernard Molitor, de Georges Jacob ou de l'Allemand David Roentgen continuaient de meubler les demeures des grandes familles où l'on ne sentait pas arriver le souffle du boulet révolutionnaire qui emporterait titres, châteaux et têtes bien nées.

Jean-Henri Riesener, au royaume du bois, demeurait le plus grand, le plus riche, le plus respecté mais, perturbé par des soucis conjugaux et une brouille avec l'administration du Garde-meuble royal, il avait lui-même réduit sa production de chefs-d'œuvre. Il ne travaillait plus guère que pour la reine qui lui avait conservé ses faveurs.

C'est ainsi qu'au moment même où les insurgés prenaient la Bastille, Riesener mettait la dernière main à l'une des deux magnifiques commodes que Marie-Antoinette lui avait commandées pour le château de Saint-Cloud [1]. Il n'apprit la nouvelle qui devait bouleverser le monde qu'en quittant un peu plus tard son atelier de l'Arsenal. Il n'attacha d'ailleurs pas autrement d'importance à l'événement jusqu'à ce qu'il eût constaté, en rentrant au Faubourg, l'énorme concours de foule qui se pressait devant le portail béant de la prison. Le calme d'ailleurs était revenu autour de la porte Saint-Antoine que les insurgés les plus excités avaient quittée depuis longtemps pour aller promener la tête de Launay du côté de l'Hôtel de Ville et du Palais-Royal.

Riesener pressa le pas pour rejoindre son logement de la place d'Aligre qui était situé juste au-dessous de celui de sa belle-fille Antoinette. Il trouva celle-ci en compagnie de Valfroy qui venait d'arriver et se joignit à eux pour souper. Cela lui arrivait souvent depuis que sa trop jeune femme, Marie-Anne, était retournée habiter chez ses parents. Ce soir-là, justement, chacun avait envie de parler et d'échanger des nouvelles, à commencer par Valfroy qui appréciait la conversation de l'ébéniste dont le jugement lui était précieux pour connaître l'état d'esprit des ouvriers.

Riesener dut avouer qu'il était pris de court. Comme Bertrand de Valfroy, venu directement de la Trésorerie générale, il ne savait pas grand-chose et c'est Ethis qui raconta au collaborateur de Necker, de sa manière imagée mais fidèle, comment l'inconcevable s'était produit. La soirée intime dont Antoinette avait rêvé prit vite un tour politique. On en oublia l'enfant à naître pour débattre des

1. La seconde sera terminée et livrée en 1792!

difficultés du royaume et Valfroy ne cacha pas son inquiétude :

– Il est probable que demain le roi va une nouvelle fois rappeler Necker mais je ne vois pas comment celui-ci pourra sortir le pays de l'anarchie politique et financière où l'ont plongé la faiblesse du roi, les erreurs répétées des ministres, des courtisans et la grande peur que causent les bandes qui prolifèrent autour de Paris. Le pouvoir est tellement impuissant que tout est à craindre. J'ignore les répercussions qu'aura la prise de la Bastille. Peut-être aucune, peut-être la chute de la royauté. On peut s'attendre à tout...

– Notre pauvre enfant va naître à un bien mauvais moment, dit Antoinette. Cet après-midi encore, j'essayais de me persuader en écrivant à ma sœur que tout allait rentrer dans l'ordre, que les pauvres auraient du pain et que nous retrouverions le climat d'insouciance des débuts du règne... Je sais maintenant qu'il va falloir se battre pour notre petit !

– Nous nous battrons s'il le faut ! reprit Valfroy, mais ne dramatisons pas. Si Necker revient, je serai proche du pouvoir, en mesure de te protéger et de te faire quitter Paris.

– Moi aussi je suis là ! affirma Riesener. Tu sais que je ne te laisserai manquer de rien.

– Et moi, dit avec force Ethis, je vous ai juré tout à l'heure de mourir pour vous s'il le faut. Je vous protégerai jusqu'au bout avec l'enfant puisque je suis son parrain !

Antoinette raconta aux deux hommes étonnés par la sortie d'Ethis comment ce dernier était devenu dans l'après-midi le parrain de son enfant.

– C'est un gamin, ajouta-t-elle, mais je sais que je peux compter sur lui. N'oubliez pas que tout à l'heure il a pris la Bastille ! Tenez, il m'a même rapporté une clé, sans doute celle d'un cachot ?

– Seulement la clé d'une cuisine..., soupira le garçon. Les cachots étaient tous vides. On a paraît-il eu bien du mal à découvrir sept prisonniers épouvantés par le vacarme. Je crois qu'ils n'ont pas encore compris comment ils avaient été libérés [1].

– C'est bien Ethis, dit Valfroy. Maintenant tu vas oublier toutes ces folies pour te montrer digne de notre confiance. Moi aussi je compte sur toi! Puis, se tournant vers Antoinette, il ajouta : A propos, si Necker est rappelé comme je le pense, il va falloir que je parte à sa rencontre pour le mettre au courant de ce qui s'est passé à Paris. Il ne peut se fier au récit que lui fera l'émissaire du roi.

– Où est Necker? demanda Antoinette que la perspective de voir partir Bertrand n'enchantait pas.

– A Bruxelles où Mme Necker et Mme de Staël ont dû rejoindre le ministre. Mais toute la famille doit repartir pour la Suisse par les bords du Rhin. Je partirai donc vraisemblablement avec M. Dufresne de Saint-Léon pour les rattraper à Francfort ou à Bâle. Songez que Necker ignore tout de la situation et ne sait même pas encore qu'il va être rappelé!

Un peu plus tard Bertrand et Antoinette se retrouvèrent seuls, enfin, dans la chambre de la jeune femme. Avec une grande tendresse, il la prit dans ses bras et défit d'un geste adroit le nœud qui retenait ses longs cheveux.

– C'est comme ça que je t'aime, dit-il en perdant son visage dans les vagues blondes. Viens, ajouta-t-il au bout d'un moment, déshabillons-nous, j'ai une folle envie de te caresser, de sentir sous ma paume ton ventre qui s'arrondit, de laisser glisser la pulpe de mes doigts sur tes épaules, sur tes bras, sur tes cuisses, là où tu es plus douce que la soie. Nous ne parlerons pas, nos peaux échangeront leur secret et leur fluide, nous nous apaiserons l'un l'autre dans un plaisir bien plus subtil que celui que nous éprouverons peut-être tout à l'heure si nous en avons envie. Tu vois, l'acte brutal de la possession est banal, animal, à la portée de n'importe quel barbare, tandis que

1. Parmi ces sept « victimes de l'arbitraire royal », il y avait quatre escrocs-faussaires dont on instruisait le procès, le jeune comte de Solages coupable de crimes monstrueux et deux fous qu'on dut transférer à Charenton.

les caresses sont l'aboutissement d'une expérience, un art véritable, une musique dont on n'a jamais fini d'égrener les arpèges...

Antoinette l'écoutait, ravie. Avec Pilâtre de Rozier, elle avait connu l'amour fou. Valfroy, lui, l'avait initiée au solfège des caresses, un solfège qui leur permettait de composer, en jouant de leurs seuls corps, les chants d'un univers sensuel dont ils reculaient sans cesse les limites.

– Tu me donnes le vrai bonheur, mon amour. Personne d'autre que toi ne pouvait me faire ce présent, dit-elle en laissant ses doigts fins errer sur le corps de Bertrand.

Tandis que Valfroy courait les routes vers l'Allemagne à la rencontre de Necker, le Faubourg, après l'explosion du 14, retrouvait son calme. Les excès sauvages et inutiles qui avaient révolté la grande majorité des Parisiens étaient déjà escamotés sous les cocardes de la légende naissante. Oubliés les brigands contre lesquels le bon peuple des districts s'était armé le 13! Les bandits de Paris et de la forêt de Bondy qui terrorisaient depuis des mois la population sortaient blanchis des massacres auxquels ils avaient pris part après la prise de la Bastille. Puisque l'émeute avait triomphé, l'inconscient collectif éprouvait le désir de la magnifier. La chute de la forteresse dont la démolition avait d'ailleurs été décidée depuis plusieurs mois, était en soi un fait mineur. Qui pouvait imaginer que les vieux murs de Charles V dissimulaient une puissance mythique formidable?

L'événement avait en tout cas sorti Antoinette de l'état de langueur qui l'avait envahie depuis qu'à peine remise de sa blessure elle avait constaté qu'elle allait être mère. Elle avait été voir la brèche ouverte dans le mur d'enceinte de la Bastille et aperçu à l'intérieur une foule de gens affairés à enfoncer des portes et à piller ce qui pouvait être encore pillé. Elle avait aussi acheté *Le*

Journal de Paris qui, après avoir rendu compte de l'émeute, publiait le récit de la visite à l'Hôtel de Ville d'une députation de quatre-vingts membres de l'Assemblée présidée par le marquis de La Fayette. Antoinette apprit ainsi que « le roi comptant sur l'amour et la fidélité de ses sujets, avait donné l'ordre aux troupes de s'éloigner de Paris et de Versailles. Un peuple immense criant « Vive la Nation! Vive le Roi! » avait salué la députation à son arrivée. En vertu de la seule légalité de sa force nouvelle, le comité de la ville grossi des quatre-vingts députés venus de Versailles, avaient proclamé Bailly maire de Paris et La Fayette commandant général de la milice parisienne.

Inquiète de savoir Valfroy sur les chemins, Antoinette fut rassurée par ces nouvelles officielles qui semblaient inscrire la prise de la Bastille dans l'évolution libérale tant souhaitée par elle et les siens. De son côté, Ethis, prenait son rôle au sérieux. Il couchait sur une paillasse devant la chambre d'Antoinette et évitait de se mêler aux groupes qui se rassemblaient en permanence autour de la Bastille et à la porte des ateliers. « Je vais simplement aux nouvelles pour vous les rapporter toutes fraîches », disait-il à la jeune femme qui apprit ainsi, avec stupéfaction, qu'Ethis avait été inscrit sur la liste des « vainqueurs de la Bastille », ce qui le hissait quasiment au rang de héros national!

– Je croyais, dit-elle au garçon, que tu n'avais fait qu'entrer et chiper une clé. Ne trouves-tu pas que tu as bien facilement gagné tes lauriers?

– La plupart des huit cents « vainqueurs » – et la liste n'est pas close – n'en ont pas fait plus que moi. C'est mon patron qui a certifié sous serment que j'y étais avec les ébénistes du Faubourg, Jean Bauch, Molitor, Gegenbach et Jean-Baptiste Mazarin, l'artiste libre que vous connaissez et qui tient magasin à l'enseigne du *Nom de Jésus.*

– Tu auras peut-être une médaille. Reste à savoir si les héros d'aujourd'hui ne seront pas les accusés de demain! Enfin, mon petit « vainqueur », pense à ce que tu m'as promis et contente-toi de ces lauriers. Ne va pas exposer ta frimousse aux mauvais coups de la révolution, puisqu'il paraît qu'il s'agit d'une révolution!

Il s'agissait bien d'une révolution. La décision du roi de venir à Paris le 17 pour y être reçu à l'Hôtel de Ville devenu symbole de la résistance au pouvoir de Versailles montrait bien que les esprits avaient changé, comme les rapports entre les Français. Un énorme mouvement d'engrenages s'était mis en marche que personne ne semblait être en mesure de contrôler.

Touchée par l'espoir populaire surgi des portes enfoncées de la Bastille et par le jeune enthousiasme d'Ethis, Antoinette, comme tous les gens du Faubourg, attendait les bienfaits de l'imprévu et de la nouveauté. Elle regardait avec une attention bienveillante son petit monde bouger. « Allons, pensait-elle, je redeviens un peu intelligente, je sens mes forces revenir et mon cerveau s'alléger! »

Parfois, elle songeait à Pilâtre de Rozier [1]. Qu'aurait pensé son fou du ciel des événements qui bouleversaient toutes les règles de la société? Il ne serait sûrement pas demeuré indifférent à cette secousse née sur les lieux de la Folie Titon, chez Réveillon, théâtre de ses premières envolées dans la nacelle du ballon des frères Montgolfier. Elle le voyait très bien sanglé dans l'uniforme de la garde, la plume tricolore au chapeau, caracolant aux côtés du marquis de La Fayette qui n'eût pu qu'être conquis par ce risque-tout intelligent et brillant. L'Assemblée nationale eût déjà vibré cent fois à ses discours enflammés, brûlants d'idées originales toutes propres à engendrer des lois nouvelles. Hélas! Pilâtre était mort et Bertrand courait après M. Necker quelque part entre Colmar et Bâle.

Antoinette revoyait beaucoup plus souvent son beau-père, Jean-Henri Riesener. L'ébéniste continuait, en dépit des événements, à travailler pour Versailles. Le 14 au

1. Pilâtre de Rozier avait été, en 1783, le premier homme à s'élever dans les airs. Il était mort deux ans plus tard en tentant de franchir la Manche à bord d'un aéronef.

matin, une troupe d'émeutiers avait quelque peu pillé le Garde-meuble du roi. Aucun meuble n'avait été emporté mais plusieurs chefs-d'œuvre dont un bureau de Boulle et des commodes d'Œben avaient été stupidement endommagés. Riesener, pour sa part, ne décolérait pas depuis qu'il avait appris qu'un de ses cabinets-secrétaires, en placage d'acajou satiné, avait subi des déprédations. Il s'en prenait ouvertement aux fauteurs de troubles et Antoinette devait calmer ses propos vengeurs qui menaçaient pêle-mêle le duc d'Orléans, les émeutiers de la Bastille, Necker et ce « grippe-sols de Mirabeau qui commençait à faire trop parler de lui... ».

Le 17, Antoinette, accompagnée d'Ethis qui ne la lâchait pas d'une semelle, alla jeter un coup d'œil sur l'arrivée du roi à l'Hôtel de Ville. La foule était si dense qu'elle n'aperçut que de très loin le carrosse royal d'où Louis XVI semblait regarder avec étonnement le spectacle tout nouveau pour lui d'une troupe composée de soldats-citoyens. Sans doute s'étonnait-il aussi d'entendre les cris de « Vive la nation » supplanter ceux de « Vive le roi ». Antoinette n'apprit que le lendemain, dans *Le Moniteur patriote*, les détails de la cérémonie :

« ... Le nouveau maire de Paris, écrivait le journal, présenta au roi les clés de la ville sur un bassin de vermeil. " Sire, lui dit-il, j'apporte à Votre Majesté les clés de sa bonne ville de Paris. Ce sont les mêmes que celles qui ont été présentées à Henri IV : il avait reconquis son peuple, ici c'est le peuple qui a reconquis son roi. " Le roi sembla apprécier cette adresse. Il fut encore surpris de voir se former, entre l'endroit où son carrosse s'était arrêté et l'entrée de l'Hôtel de Ville une véritable « voûte d'acier » constituée de plusieurs centaines d'épées, tenues à bout de bras à la manière des francs-maçons par des gardes nationaux. Le roi s'avança tranquillement sous ce rideau de lames croisées et prit place sur le trône installé dans la grand-salle. Là il écouta la lecture de procès-verbaux de travaux de la Commune et donna l'approbation du silence à des décisions qui eussent paru inconcevables quelques jours auparavant : la formation de la milice bourgeoise, l'ordre de démolition de la Bastille, la nomination de La Fayette et de Bailly. Le roi ne manifesta aucune impatience durant tout le temps de cette lecture mais parut soulagé d'entendre Moreau de Saint-Rémy lui dire dans un discours flatteur : “ Sire, vous deviez votre couronne à la naissance, vous ne la devez plus maintenant qu'à vos vertus. ” Le moment le plus émouvant, parce que le plus chargé de symboles, suivit aussitôt. Bailly vint présenter au roi qui ne s'y attendait pas la cocarde tricolore. Louis XVI, embarrassé, regarda un instant l'insigne sans le prendre ni le refuser. “ Prenez-la, Sire ”, insista le maire de Paris. Le roi prit alors la cocarde et la joignit à son chapeau. »

Après s'être longtemps exclue de la vie sociale, Antoinette se passionnait pour les nouvelles politiques. Elle apprenait chaque jour dans les gazettes, dont le nombre se multipliait, que le peuple s'emparait un peu partout en province de petites bastilles. Cette excitation ne lui faisait pas oublier Valfroy dont l'absence commençait à lui peser. Elle s'apercevait sans déplaisir que le gentilhomme, rencontré dans le salon de Germaine de Staël, avait pris une place importante dans sa vie, et pas seulement parce qu'elle attendait un enfant de lui. Antoinette savait que les bras solides, les cheveux grisonnants et le visage marqué de Bertrand comptaient pour elle autant que sa bonté et l'élégance de ses manières. Elle était heureuse de ressentir combien lui manquait l'étreinte de celui près de qui elle n'avait d'abord cherché qu'une tendre protection.

Enfin, on apprit à Paris que les Necker et les Staël étaient sur la route du retour. Partout où ils passaient, disait *Les Révolutions de France et de Brabant*, journal de Camille Desmoulins, ils étaient accueillis comme des sauveurs. Les plus petites bourgades pavoisaient en l'honneur du financier genevois qui personnifiait l'évolution tranquille de la royauté vers le libéralisme. Antoinette imaginait la jubilation de Mme de Staël et était heureuse de savoir que l'homme de sa vie profitait un peu de la popularité délirante dont jouissait le grand homme.

Le 30 juillet, Necker arriva donc dans un Paris en fête et tandis que La Fayette l'accueillait à l'Hôtel de Ville, Valfroy faisait forcer les chevaux de sa voiture vers la place d'Aligre. Avec l'aide d'Ethis, Antoinette avait préparé un bain chaud à son vaillant diplomate.

– Viens mon chéri, lui dit-elle après les premières effusions, nous allons ajouter un seau d'eau bouillante dans la baignoire et je vais te laver, te masser, te parfumer comme aucune servante d'auberge ne l'a fait, j'espère, durant le voyage.

Il éclata de rire.

– Vois dans quel état je suis, regarde la poussière qui a pénétré tous mes vêtements et tu constateras que je n'ai pas bénéficié depuis longtemps de soins aussi délicats. D'abord, comment va notre garçon? ajouta-t-il en caressant le ventre rond d'Antoinette.

– Notre fille va très bien, répondit-elle avec une jolie révérence.

Ils rirent, Bertrand se laissa déshabiller, asperger, frotter, savonner en poussant les petits cris de plaisir que tout autre homme sensible et raffiné eût poussés à sa place. Le bonheur était revenu, dans les fourgons de Necker. Allait-il en être de même chez les gens de Saint-Antoine, chez les indigents des autres faubourgs, chez les sans-travail de Saint-Marceau, dans les familles d'immigrés récents entassés au fond des cours de la rue de Montreuil? Valfroy dit qu'il ne croyait pas au miracle et que Necker n'arrivait pas avec des sacs de farine dans ses bagages.

– Comme tu es pessimiste! Et l'enfant dans tout cela? Comment va-t-il naître? Et où? Devons-nous rester à Paris? Ne serait-il pas plus sage de se réfugier en province? Chez toi, dans ton château?

– Nous verrons. Pour le moment il n'y a aucune raison de quitter Paris. Nulle part tu ne serais plus en sécurité que dans ton Faubourg. Ici, tout le monde te connaît. Et puis, tu es sous la protection d'un « vainqueur de la

Bastille »... Non, ne ris pas, il se peut qu'un jour ce titre dérisoire, décroché par Ethis en allant chaparder une clé rouillée, nous sauve la vie! Enfin, nous n'en sommes pas là. En ces temps il faut vivre au jour le jour et ce soir est un soir magnifique puisque nous sommes réunis. Je me sens pourtant encore un peu tendu. Viens te serrer contre moi dans notre lit retrouvé.

Une nouvelle fois, M. Necker revint prendre sa place auprès du roi dès que le peuple lui eut témoigné sa satisfaction de le savoir rentré en grâce. Après une réception officielle à l'Hôtel de Ville, les Parisiens assemblés sur la place de Grève l'avaient réclamé à grands cris et le « Sully moderne », comme on l'appelait, dut paraître plusieurs fois à une fenêtre.

– Tout va donc bien, commenta Antoinette, lorsque le soir du 30 juillet Bertrand lui raconta cet accueil triomphal.

– Dis plutôt que tout va un peu moins mal, répondit Valfroy en hochant la tête.

Les événements, il est vrai, allaient vite, dont l'importance n'apparaissait pas toujours au bon peuple du Faubourg. Ainsi la nuit du 4 août, au cours de laquelle les deux ordres de la noblesse et du clergé avaient volontairement consenti à l'abolition du servage, à la réforme des jurandes et surtout à la suppression de tous les privilèges, ne parvint que deux jours après aux oreilles d'Antoinette.

– Crois-tu, demanda-t-elle à Valfroy, que ces dispositions, auxquelles on ne peut qu'applaudir, vont changer quelque chose à la vie de plus en plus difficile des gens?

– Dans l'immédiat, rien, répondit Bertrand, mais dans l'avenir sûrement beaucoup de choses. Et pour tout le monde.

Antoinette essayait de comprendre les dessous de cette politique nouvelle, fluctuante et brutale dont la confusion empoisonnait les rapports sociaux et familiaux. Elle parlait aux voisins, aux amis de son père et de son beau-père, aux maîtres ébénistes du Faubourg dont certains exerçaient maintenant une fonction officielle, tels Louis-François Devergille, marchand mercier, nommé commissaire et trésorier de section, ou Santerre, le brasseur de la rue de Reuilly, élu, lui, officier de la garde nationale. Malheureusement, ces nouveaux notables ne semblaient d'accord sur rien et leurs propos laissaient Antoinette perplexe. La seule chose évidente, c'est que Valfroy, hélas! avait vu juste : la fameuse nuit du 4 août n'avait pas rempli le pétrin du boulanger. En revanche, la suppression des corporations et la mise en sommeil des jurandes causaient quelques perturbations chez les gens du bois. La liberté donnée aux compagnons de s'installer à leur compte au moment où le travail se raréfiait dans les ateliers n'avait d'autre effet que de multiplier les faillites.

Le mariage lui-même n'avait pas modifié l'existence ouatée d'Antoinette que Valfroy avait décidée à devenir officiellement son épouse. Ils s'étaient mariés discrètement, à cause de l'enfant à naître, mais avaient gardé le secret.

– Je ne suis pas sûr que devenir baronne en un pareil moment soit un bienfait, avait dit Bertrand. Demeure donc Mlle Œben jusqu'à nouvel ordre.

Souvent Antoinette demandait à Bertrand des nouvelles de Germaine de Staël qu'elle ne voyait plus depuis le début de sa grossesse.

– Active comme dix, ma belle. Une tirelire à idées. La Révolution et la popularité de son père lui tournent un peu la tête. Son intelligence lui permet de comprendre, d'analyser toutes les situations que crée l'effervescence générale mais pour aboutir, hélas! à des considérations bien peu réalistes. Quant à Necker, mon pauvre maître, il paie bien cher les derniers effets de sa célébrité. Il se débat toujours dans ses comptes et tente de s'opposer à l'émission d'assignats, cette monnaie de papier qui ne pourra qu'accélérer, il en est sûr, la déroute financière de la France.

Valfroy veillait à ne pas inquiéter sa femme et minimisait le plus possible les événements qui entraînaient inéluctablement la Révolution vers des solutions extrêmes. Ce n'étaient pas les décisions de l'Assemblée qui le tourmentaient mais les luttes d'influence qui commençaient à fausser le généreux élan démocratique qui avait balayé le pays en quelques semaines.

– La vanité commence à s'emparer des hommes qui, portés au pouvoir par la volonté populaire, prennent goût à cette griserie, expliquait Bertrand.

– Ces hommes ont cependant établi la liberté religieuse, la liberté de la presse et adopté ce texte magnifique, la Déclaration des droits de l'homme et du citoyen dont tu te plais à reconnaître la grandeur, remarquait Antoinette.

– Sans doute, sans doute. Ces textes, ces décrets respirent la générosité, la justice, la liberté, et tu sais que j'y souscris de grand cœur. Mais ce ne sont encore que des principes. L'important, c'est ce qu'en feront demain ceux qui détiendront l'autorité.

Un soir de la fin août, alors que la chaleur faisait s'exhaler du vieux quartier du bois, en sommeil depuis le 14 juillet, l'odeur si particulière de la colle et de la sciure dont il était imprégné, Valfroy ramena avec lui place d'Aligre un homme d'un certain âge mais alerte, au teint rouge et à l'élégance un peu désuète.

– J'ai pensé, dit-il en embrassant Antoinette, que tu aurais plaisir à connaître M. Sébastien Mercier, un remarquable écrivain que les Necker apprécient. Il a écrit *Le Tableau de Paris*, un irremplaçable chef-d'œuvre pour qui aime cette ville. Grâce à lui, les Français des siècles futurs sauront comment nous vivions avant la Révolution.

L'homme s'inclina en souriant :

– Votre mari est trop bon, madame. Je ne suis qu'un vieux monsieur que mes amis disent un peu maniaque, finalement plus peintre qu'écrivain car je ne fais que saisir sur le vif les mille et un tableaux de notre vie quotidienne. Ce livre, je l'ai surtout écrit avec mes jambes tellement j'ai couru pour tout voir de cet affolant grouillement qu'est la vie parisienne.

– C'est le Bon Dieu qui vous envoie, monsieur Mercier, s'exclama Antoinette en lui tendant ses mains qu'il baisa avec une grâce qu'on ne lui aurait pas soupçonnée. Je m'ennuie dans ce quartier où il se passe paraît-il tant de choses. Allez-vous aussi écrire sur tous ces événements?

– J'écrirai plus tard ce que je vois aujourd'hui. Et Dieu sait s'il y a des choses à voir! Quelle chance nous avons chère madame de vivre une révolution! Je ne donnerais pas ma place pour une fortune, dont je n'aurais d'ailleurs que faire.

– Ce que vous appelez la chance ne me sourit qu'à moitié, s'exclama Antoinette en éclatant de rire. Comme vous l'avez peut-être remarqué, j'attends un enfant et, s'il m'était permis de choisir, j'opterais sans doute pour une période de calme et de prospérité!

– Votre enfant, madame, naîtra pourvu des droits naturels, inaliénables et sacrés de l'Homme. Une vie nouvelle va s'offrir à lui. Cela vaut bien quelques dérangements...

– J'entends bien ces rêves et tous ces beaux sentiments. J'ai heureusement les moyens de manger à ma faim et, si les choses ne changent pas, je pourrai acheter du lait et du pain pour mon petit. Mais songez à la misère de toutes ces femmes et de tous ces hommes qui, à deux pas d'ici, dans ce Faubourg naguère si prospère, ne vivent que de la charité. Plus de travail à l'atelier, plus de pain chez le boulanger, je doute qu'ils trouvent, eux, l'époque intéressante...

– C'est parce que cette misère existe depuis des années que la Révolution a éclaté. Je ne sais pas ce que demain nous réserve mais hier n'était pas tellement beau...

– Parlez-moi donc de cette Révolution, monsieur Mercier. Vous qui regardez si bien, faites-moi entendre un autre son de cloche que celui des commères ou les propos politiques un peu désabusés de mon cher mari.

– Cette Révolution, j'y crois, madame, puisqu'elle a

lieu. J'y crois comme je crois à la fraternité, à la liberté et à toutes les idées généreuses. Mme de Staël qui partage mes convictions me trouve pourtant trop idéaliste. Je crois que je suis surtout un original. Mais les originaux sont indispensables dans les révoltes car le peuple, lui, est conformiste et le conformisme allié à la violence ne peut que déboucher sur l'horreur.

– Monsieur, votre discours me plaît. Il aurait enchanté un ami tragiquement disparu, Pilâtre de Rozier, dont vous avez sans doute entendu parler. Comme vous c'était un original, un esprit original s'entend. Et je pense qu'il n'aurait pas eu non plus les yeux de tout le monde pour regarder notre époque.

– Si vous voulez frémir, ma douce Antoinette, coupa Valfroy, écoutez Sébastien Mercier vous exposer ses idées politiques. Tenez, la Bastille...

– La Bastille, mon ami, j'y aurais été enfermé si je ne m'étais pas réfugié à Genève après la parution d'écrits jugés séditieux. Cela dit, la prise de cette citadelle abandonnée quasiment sans résistance à la Révolution, ne me transporte pas. Ne serait-ce le symbole – et les révolutions les plus justes sont faites de symboles autant que de sacrifices – je regretterais peut-être la démolition de ce témoignage de l'architecture défensive du XIVe siècle. Si l'on cherchait un symbole, ce n'est pas la Bastille qu'il fallait détruire, c'est... Un éclair de malice passa dans ses yeux et il termina, sûr de l'effet qu'il allait produire : c'est Versailles!

– Versailles? Le château du grand roi? questionna Antoinette suffoquée.

– Parfaitement madame. Je suis constitutionnel et ne souhaite pas la chute de notre roi. Je dis au contraire que pour le sauver de la cour, de tous ces esclaves à perruque, de ces factions imbéciles qui ont empêché M. Necker de gouverner, pour mettre fin aussi à l'influence néfaste de la reine dans une période aussi difficile, il fallait tout de suite détruire Versailles! Ce château sublime avait été le vêtement d'un grand roi, d'un roi superbe et puissant. Puisqu'il ne devait plus y avoir de grand roi il y avait évidemment danger à laisser debout ce palais, centre de toutes les machinations politiques et relais des cours étrangères. Les peuples tiennent aux signes et aux signes apparents. La destruction prévoyante de Versailles eût frappé le peuple. Le monarque indécis et sa cour perfide auraient tout de suite compris que l'insurrection était sérieuse, décisive. Ils en auraient pris leur parti, à commencer par Louis XVI qui avait déjà attaché la cocarde tricolore à son chapeau et qui était passé sous la voûte d'acier des trente mille piques et épées croisées devant l'Hôtel de Ville sur une longueur de huit cents pas. Il serait resté à Paris au milieu de son peuple et croyez-moi, madame, la Révolution aurait aujourd'hui une autre tournure!

La visite de Mercier avait fort diverti Antoinette. Dès qu'il fut parti, elle éclata de rire et se tourna vers Valfroy :

– Eh bien! mon ami, voilà un curieux personnage. Vous avez bien fait de nous l'amener. Ses idées paraissent folles mais, à y bien réfléchir, il y a du vrai dans ce qu'il dit. Quand on écoute les gens du Faubourg, on s'aperçoit vite que le maintien d'une cour à Versailles, avec tout ce qu'elle comporte de luxe, de gâchis et d'étiquette hors saison, met en rage ceux qui n'ont ni travail ni pain.

Comme Valfroy rentrait maintenant presque tous les soirs place d'Aligre, la mission protectrice d'Ethis ne se justifiait plus guère mais le jeune garçon tenait à son serment. Il s'absentait pourtant souvent, le soir, « pour faire le tour des districts », disait-il. En fait tout était trouble et confusion à Paris où la nouvelle garde nationale, dont l'uniforme bleu de roi et la culotte blanche faisaient rêver Ethis, avait bien eu du mal à imposer dans les rues un ordre relatif. Les sentinelles des districts se disputaient le pavé aux portes mêmes des églises où l'on avait pris l'habitude d'aller faire bénir les drapeaux pour un oui ou pour un non. Ce désordre qui n'avait pour origine profonde que l'inimitié des chefs faisait l'objet d'articles réprobateurs dans la presse. Un soir, Antoinette découvrit dans *Révolutions de Paris*, l'un des journaux que rapportait Bertrand[1] cette mise en garde qui, de nouveau, la fit trembler pour Ethis, trop curieux pour demeurer longtemps tranquille :

« La mésintelligence qui règne dans les districts, la contradiction de leurs principes, de leurs arrêtés et de leur police, leur désunion avec le corps municipal, offrent depuis que le premier danger est passé le spectacle d'une épouvantable anarchie. »

Dans cette arnarchie, Ethis, fort de son jeune âge, de sa claudication et de son ruban de « vainqueur de la Bastille », évoluait comme un poisson dans l'eau. Un jour, il rentra à la maison en portant deux gros lièvres en bandoulière. C'était un spectacle inhabituel dans le Faubourg où l'on voyait plus souvent les apprentis marcher avec une chaise ou un fauteuil sur les épaules que chargés d'un trophée de chasse.

– D'où sors-tu ? demanda Antoinette éberluée.

– Depuis le 10 août, la chasse est ouverte à tout le monde. J'y suis allé avec un compagnon de l'atelier qui possède un fusil. Dans la plaine de Vincennes, il y avait tellement de chasseurs que la garde citoyenne a dû intervenir pour arrêter le carnage des lapins, des lièvres et des perdreaux. Moi, ils m'ont laissé passer car je suis un « vainqueur », et voilà ma chasse !

– Es-tu sûr d'avoir tiré toi-même ces pauvres bêtes ?

– Non, mais le principal est que ce soit nous qui les mangions !

Les événements donnaient au quartier, voué naguère en semaine au seul labeur, un caractère de fête permanente qui faisait un peu oublier les privations. Ainsi, pendant que les chasseurs s'éparpillaient dans la plaine, les dames du marché d'Aligre et de celui de la boucherie se rassemblaient devant la Bastille, aux mains des démolisseurs, pour se rendre à l'abbaye Saint-Antoine. Tam-

1. Trente-cinq journaux paraissaient alors à Paris.

bours et musique en tête, accompagnée d'un détachement de la garde citoyenne dont les piques et les fusils étaient garnis de fleurs, l'armée des marchandes à laquelle se joignaient beaucoup de femmes de compagnons, suivait deux jeunes filles entourant une enfant de huit ans couronnée de fleurs. Ensuite venaient deux groupes de dames, l'un portant un bouquet destiné à saint Antoine, l'autre à la Sainte Vierge. Pour la circonstance, l'abbesse qui tentait avant tout de maintenir la cohésion de son petit peuple, avait ouvert toutes grandes les portes de l'abbatiale et les dames du Faubourg assistèrent au *Te Deum* chanté en action de grâces de la Révolution, une révolution bon enfant.

– Ce côté fête de village plaît aux bonnes gens du Faubourg, dit Valfroy à qui Antoinette racontait le déroulement de ce pieux défilé. Mais la vraie révolution n'a pas encore commencé.

– Alors, notre petit?

– Notre enfant vivra comme vivront tous ceux qui naîtront en même temps que lui. Ce sera un enfant de 89. Nous improviserons autour de son berceau, selon les circonstances. Peut-être sera-t-il très heureux!

L'hiver commençait mal pour les pauvres gens. Dès novembre, une vague de froid comme on n'en avait pas connu depuis longtemps déferla sur la France déjà éprouvée par le manque de farine et de pain. L'installation aux Tuileries de la famille royale que les femmes de Paris, emmenées par la fameuse Théroigne de Méricourt, avaient été chercher à Versailles, n'avait pas rempli les fours des boulangers. Alors, comme de toute éternité en période de disette, le peuple, fût-il en révolution, se tournait vers Dieu et ses saints. Personne ne sut qui, au Faubourg, avait eu l'idée de cette singulière cérémonie mais le fait est qu'Ethis, un beau jour, annonça qu'il partait le lendemain en procession avec les gardes nationaux des districts du quartier et, naturellement, les « vainqueurs de la Bastille ». Valfroy lui fit remarquer qu'il n'y avait dans cette sainte promenade rien de très révolutionnaire.

– Si monsieur, répondit Ethis. Car il ne s'agit pas d'une procession ordinaire. Les gardes nationaux des districts du quartier et nous, les « vainqueurs », marcherons derrière les jeunes vierges représentant ces cantons. Et ce n'est pas tout ! Nous irons en chantant à Sainte-Geneviève mettre sous la protection de la patronne de Paris « un modèle de la Bastille ».

Comme Ethis n'avait pu fournir de détails sur ce « modèle », Antoinette et Bertrand se promirent d'aller le lendemain assister au départ de cette étrange procession qui, en pleine révolution, ramenait les Parisiens au XVe siècle, lorsque Louis XI promenait la Sainte Ampoule de Saint-Antoine-des-Champs à Notre-Dame pour faire cesser « le vent de bise qui l'incommodait ».

Antoinette reconnut quelques-unes des filles du Faubourg qui ouvraient le cortège et elle glissa en riant à Valfroy qu'elle ne se porterait garante en aucun cas de la virginité de certaines d'entre elles. Derrière, venait le fameux « modèle » tenu comme le Saint Sacrement par les quatre plus jeunes « vainqueurs », dont Ethis qui portait haut le front tellement il était fier. Le fameux « modèle de la Bastille » était une sorte de grande plaque de bois et de plâtre peints qui représentait, en relief, la forteresse au moment où elle était assiégée par le peuple.

Le cri des vierges du Faubourg ne dut pas toucher sainte Geneviève car le lendemain matin les boulangers manquaient toujours de farine et ne purent satisfaire la foule de femmes qui avaient fait la queue depuis l'aube à la porte de leur boutique.

Les événements révolutionnaires, la grossesse d'Antoinette et son mariage avaient bouleversé les habitudes de la fille du maître Œben. Réveillon, l'ami de sa mère, celui chez qui la Révolution avait commencé, ne donnait plus signe de vie. Le rôle de bouc émissaire qu'on lui avait fait jouer semblait l'avoir profondément marqué. Il avait en tout cas perdu son enthousiasme et le génie créateur qui l'avait si longtemps habité, le hissant d'une pauvre chambre de la rue Saint-Nicolas jusqu'aux nuages où les

Montgolfier et Pilâtre de Rozier avaient porté son nom, et aussi jusqu'à cette Folie Titon qui devait faire son malheur après avoir symbolisé sa fortune. Riesener lui-même, le grand Riesener, avait déserté le Faubourg. Il logeait maintenant près de son atelier de l'Arsenal.

Un jour, Antoinette se dit qu'il était navrant de se priver de la présence des gens qu'on aime. Elle résolut d'aller voir Réveillon dans son appartement de la rue des Bons-Enfants où il vivait discrètement avec sa femme. Elle avait envie d'entendre quelqu'un d'autre que Valfroy lui parler de cette Révolution qui avançait ses pions avec une lente constance sur l'échiquier des passions. Depuis qu'elle était une jeune fille, Réveillon lui avait expliqué avec simplicité et précision les événements politiques qui avaient marqué la fin du règne de Louis XV. Saurait-il, aujourd'hui, rassurer et conseiller la femme de trente-cinq ans que son état et l'agitation des esprits rendaient infiniment vulnérable?

Contrairement à ce qu'elle pensait, elle ne trouva pas un Réveillon aigri et abattu. Celui qui avait tapissé de papier peint la moitié des logements de Paris avait gardé le goût de l'élégance, autant pour son appartement flamboyant de scènes en trompe-l'œil que pour son discours fleuri où perçait toujours une nuance d'ironie.

– Mais dis donc, mon Antoinette, te voilà engrossée de belle manière. Quel bel enfant tu vas nous faire! Félicite ce bon Valfroy et surtout ne va pas te promener là où l'on tire au fusil sur tout ce qui dépasse et rompt ainsi la très sainte égalité des citoyens.

– Vous êtes contre cette révolution, oncle Réveillon? Je comprends, remarquez bien, que vous ne portiez pas dans votre cœur ceux qui vous ont ruiné!

– Mais non, Antoinette, je ne suis pas contre. D'abord, cette Révolution ne m'a pas ruiné. Regarde : je vis bien. Ensuite il ne serait pas raisonnable d'être opposé par principe à une machine qu'on a peut-être mise en route imprudemment mais que personne ne semble capable d'arrêter. Il est plus sage d'essayer de la surveiller et de faire en sorte qu'un de ses engrenages ne vous saisisse par la manche de votre chemise. Ils ont démoli la Folie Titon, ces imbéciles, sans savoir qu'il s'agissait d'un trésor d'art et de beauté. On leur a fait croire que ce chef-d'œuvre m'appartenait parce que j'avais gagné assez d'argent pour l'acheter. En fait il appartenait à tout le monde. Je l'ai fait visiter à tous ceux qui en avaient envie et je l'aurais volontiers offert à la Nation cocardière qui est en train de voir le jour. Je n'ai à me plaindre des vandales que pour trois raisons : la première, c'est que tu as failli mourir, toi l'innocente, dans ce soulèvement où les factions du duc d'Orléans, je l'ai su depuis, ont joué un rôle provocateur. La deuxième, c'est que j'ai bien failli moi aussi y laisser la peau. Enfin, je reproche moins à ces malheureux inconscients d'avoir brûlé les tableaux, détruit les meubles et brisé les statues que de m'avoir volé un objet auquel je tenais.

– Quel est donc cet objet, plus cher à vos yeux que le palais et ses richesses? questionna Antoinette, ravie d'avoir retrouvé le virtuose du paradoxe qui avait charmé sa jeunesse.

– Ils m'ont volé, les bandits, la médaille que le roi m'avait décernée en 1786. C'était un prix d'industrie pour services rendus à la papeterie française. Eh bien, cette médaille, je me battrai pour que la Nation, en la personne de l'Assemblée, me la restitue. Voilà une saine occupation pour quelqu'un qui n'a plus rien à prouver ni à désirer!

Antoinette éclata de rire :

– Mon oncle, je vous retrouve. On vous pille une maison bourrée d'œuvres d'art et vous réclamez une médaille! Je vous adore. Mais dites-moi franchement ce que vous pensez des événements. Je suis inquiète pour mon enfant.

– Je pense ce que doit penser Valfroy qui est un homme de bon sens : rien pour l'instant, sinon que l'accumulation des erreurs depuis un demi-siècle et la coupable faiblesse de deux rois ont rendu inévitable la transformation du mouvement d'idées créé par les philosophes en embrasement révolutionnaire. Quant à savoir comment ces turbulences vont évoluer c'est absolument impossible. Il nous reste à regarder. C'est passionnant. Cela me rappelle la fantastique envolée libre de Pilâtre et du marquis d'Arlandes à bord du ballon des frères Montgolfier, qui portait, tu t'en souviens, le nom de « Réveillon ». Le ballon était monté droit dans le ciel puis était parti, porté par le vent. Personne ne pouvait dire où il redescendrait sur terre. La Révolution, c'est pareil. On a fait un grand feu de paille et elle s'est envolée, livrée à beaucoup de vents contraires. Jusqu'où ira-t-elle? C'est sans doute ton enfant, ma petite Antoinette, qui le saura. Tu vois il a de la chance!

Antoinette revint toute ragaillardie au Faubourg. Maintenant, il fallait qu'elle revoie Riesener. Elle avait besoin de renouer avec l'univers du bois qui avait été si longtemps le sien. Riesener constituait l'indispensable chaînon qui la reliait à sa mère, vraie dame du Faubourg née près de l'abbaye et épouse de son père, le grand Œben, dont l'ombre, avec celle d'André-Charles Boulle, planait encore sur les cours à bois, les ateliers chargés de vapeur de colle et les passages mystérieux qui unissaient entre eux depuis plus de trois siècles les compagnons du ciseau et de la varlope. Elle avait perdu peu à peu le contact avec les gens du meuble et cela l'ennuyait de ne pas bien pénétrer les subtilités d'un changement qui affectait les formes et les décorations depuis déjà plusieurs années. Riesener n'était pas à la pointe du style qui était en train d'éclore mais il ne pouvait qu'être au courant de la vague du retour à l'antique qui emportait avec elle, dans les gouffres du démodé, les courbes arbitraires, les rocailles abusives, les moulures trop chantournées.

Comme elle portait bien sa grossesse et qu'elle n'avait, disait-elle, été depuis longtemps en aussi bonne santé, Antoinette résolut de rendre visite à Riesener dans son atelier de l'Arsenal. Le temps était frais, elle ajusta un fichu sur sa tête et jeta une ample pèlerine de drap noir sur la robe blanche à rayures rouges que la plupart des femmes portaient depuis les événements de juillet. Elle prit la rue de Cotte, l'une des voies nouvelles ouvertes par l'abbesse Gabrielle-Charlotte de Beauvau-Craon en même temps que la place d'Aligre, et se retrouva dans la grand-rue du Faubourg, tranquille comme aux plus beaux jours de « l'ère de la commode ». Antoinette répondit au salut de quelques vieux compagnons dont certains avaient travaillé pour son père, s'arrêta un instant devant la cour des Mousquetaires pour échanger quelques mots avec Adam Weisweiler, l'un des ébénistes favoris de la reine, dont Riesener appréciait fort le talent [1] et arriva devant la Bastille où grouillait une foule de démolisseurs. La barrière de la Râpée était toute proche; bientôt, elle franchit la voûte de pierre de l'Arsenal, ce temple du meuble d'où étaient sortis d'innombrables chefs-d'œuvre dont beaucoup portaient le poinçon du savoir-faire familial, celui d'Œben ou de Riesener.

Le maître, qui ne sacrifiait pas à la mode révolutionnaire considérée par lui comme un impardonnable laisser-aller, portait la culotte de soie et l'habit de velours à boutons d'argent. Il ouvrit ses bras à Antoinette.

– Tu ne m'as pas oubliée, ma petite fille, et cela me fait chaud au cœur. Sais-tu que la maternité te va bien? Tu es superbe. Viens dans le magasin que nous bavardions un peu.

Il installa la jeune femme dans un grand fauteuil d'acajou garni de soie bleue fleurdelisée et s'assit à ses côtés.

– Tu vois, le magasin est plein et j'ignore quand ceux qui ont commandé ces meubles viendront les chercher. Qui a l'envie, le courage et l'argent de meubler aujourd'hui une pièce de château? Je continue de travailler un petit peu pour garder la main mais le cœur n'y est plus...

– Je ne vois chez toi aucun meuble de ce genre antique dont on a tant parlé depuis quelques années.

– Tu n'en verras jamais. Non pas que je sois contre un renouvellement qui sans doute s'imposait mais, à mon

1. Un ravissant bureau à pupitre portant sa marque, mis à l'encan par la Révolution, retrouvé dans la succession du prince de Beauvau et racheté par Napoléon III, est aujourd'hui au Louvre.

âge, je préfère demeurer fidèle au passé d'artiste de ton père et au mien. On dit pis que pendre de la rocaille dont certains ont abusé. Ce n'est pas mon cas et je ne vois pas pourquoi j'irais chercher aujourd'hui mes motifs décoratifs et mes formes dans le répertoire gréco-romain. Si Dieu le veut, mes meubles demeureront plus tard, comme ceux de Boulle, étrangers aux normes d'une mode par nature capricieuse.

– Cela me fait du bien de t'entendre parler. Les hasards de la vie m'ont coupée de mes racines mais je demeure une fille du bois. Viens donc me voir de temps en temps dans cette maison de la place d'Aligre qui a été si longtemps la tienne. Bientôt l'hiver va venir et je ne pourrai plus beaucoup sortir de chez moi : je ne tiens pas à mettre mon enfant au monde dans un lit de copeaux de l'Arsenal !

Riesener sourit et embrassa Antoinette.

– Bon, je reviendrai au Faubourg. Pour toi. Et pour tous les beaux souvenirs que j'y ai laissés. Au fait, as-tu des nouvelles de ta sœur Victoire?

– Pas très récentes puisqu'elles datent de deux bons mois. Elle vit toujours à Givry-en-Argonne avec son mari qui s'étiole en plaidant de petites causes à Rethel ou à Sedan. Il ne s'est jamais consolé de la disgrâce de Turgot dont il était l'homme de confiance. Dans sa dernière lettre, Victoire me disait qu'il comptait se remettre en selle sur le cheval emballé de la Révolution. On peut lui faire confiance pour saisir l'occasion de revenir sur la scène politique dès qu'elle se présentera.

– Tu n'as pas l'air de le porter dans ton cœur?

– C'est un intrigant et je n'ai jamais compris ma sœur d'avoir épousé cet avocat sans charme. Elle n'a jamais eu, il est vrai, les mêmes idées que moi sur l'amour et sur le mariage.

Depuis que l'Assemblée nationale avait quitté Versailles à la suite du roi et s'était installée dans une salle de l'archevêché, les nouvelles des débats filtraient plus aisément. Valfroy y assistait souvent pour rendre compte à Necker des décisions les plus importantes prises par les députés. Un soir, il rentra plus tôt qu'à l'accoutumée et Antoinette étouffa un cri en voyant la manche de son habit déchirée et son visage tuméfié :

– Que t'est-il arrivé? On s'est battu à l'Assemblée? Tu es blessé?

– Ce n'est rien. Ne t'inquiète pas mais va tout de même me chercher de l'eau et un linge propre car je suis un peu meurtri. Encore heureux que cette sacrée rambarde ne m'ait pas éborgné!

– Vas-tu t'expliquer à la fin! Qui t'a mis dans cet état?

– La voix de Mirabeau peut-être. Figure-toi que le citoyen Honoré Riquetti, c'est son vrai nom, tenait la tribune depuis près d'une heure. Tu connais son éloquence. Ses phrases fulgurantes résonnaient dans la salle pleine à craquer comme chaque fois qu'il prend la parole. Soudain, au terme d'une envolée pathétique qui fit trembler le grand lustre de la salle, on entendit en guise d'applaudissements un bruit formidable suivi de cris angoissés. C'était la tribune du public, où je me trouvais, qui s'effondrait sur les députés. La mêlée qui suivit fut indescriptible, des blessés criaient et je me retrouvai accroupi sur la bedaine de Cazalès tandis que le talon du soulier du vicomte de Noailles me labourait le visage. Tu vois, termina-t-il en riant, que les révolutions ne sont pas sans danger!

– Et de quoi discutait-on aujourd'hui? demanda Antoinette en tamponnant doucement l'œil de son mari avec un mouchoir mouillé d'eau d'arnica.

– Des biens ecclésiastiques. Les débats sur cette grosse affaire durent depuis deux semaines et l'Assemblée est partagée sur la façon de mettre au service de la nation les richesses du clergé.

– Tu crois qu'ils oseront confisquer tous les biens de l'Église?

– Grâce, c'est le comble, à un évêque! M. de Talleyrand, soutenu par quelques effets de crinière de Mirabeau, a le 10 octobre réglé en quatre phrases la ruine de l'Église. Avant un mois celle-ci aura retrouvé l'état de pauvreté de ses origines. Le tout est de savoir où iront ces richesses et comment on les dispersera au bénéfice de l'État.

Le clergé français perdit ses biens et ses dernières illusions le 2 novembre, jour où Antoinette, elle, faillit bien perdre son enfant. Elle était sortie le matin, comme à l'accoutumée, faire ses courses au marché Beauvau qui se trouvait à deux pas de chez elle. Les commères qu'elle y avait rencontrées, presque toutes femmes de maîtres ou de compagnons du Faubourg, l'avaient complimentée sur sa mine avant de commenter le fait marquant du jour : il y avait du pain à volonté chez tous les boulangers du Faubourg. Quinze chariots de farine étaient arrivés à Paris dans la nuit et les fournils avaient pu être approvisionnés.

Assez lourdement chargée – elle avait acheté trois livres de pommes de terre, ce tubercule dont l'immense majorité des Français ne voulaient pas entendre parler malgré la campagne inlassable du pharmacien Parmentier –, Antoinette avait remonté avec peine ses deux étages. Sans même prendre le temps de retirer de son cabas le morceau de morue séchée qu'elle avait eu la chance de trouver au marché, elle s'allongea sur son lit et appela Marie, la petite servante que Valfroy l'avait obligée à prendre près d'elle depuis qu'elle était enceinte. C'était là une sage précaution : de violentes douleurs la secouaient à en crier. Elle porta la main à son ventre pour contenir les spasmes et s'aperçut que sa robe était tachée de sang.

– Marie, parvint-elle à articuler, je perds mon enfant, va vite rue Beauvau, dans la cour des Cinq-Frères, et dis à Blanche, la sage-femme, de venir tout de suite. Cours et dis-lui que c'est pressé, je me meurs...

Blanche Mantel, l'une des deux cents sages-femmes officiant à Paris, était connue dans le quartier pour son habileté et son énergie. Elle arriva peu après et calma l'angoisse d'Antoinette en lui caressant le front :

– Ne vous inquiétez pas, mademoiselle Œben. A deux mois de la délivrance, une petite hémorragie n'est pas forcément grave. Je vais vous soigner, vous faire boire une décoction de prêle et de potentille pour arrêter le sang et prévenir Bélois, le chirurgien de l'Hôtel-Dieu. C'est lui qui m'a instruite sage-femme et vous ne pouvez pas être mieux traitée que par lui.

Antoinette perdit encore beaucoup de sang mais elle ne souffrait presque plus quand Bélois arriva vers la fin de l'après-midi. C'était un brave homme dont la simplicité s'opposait aux discours prétentieux et à la fatuité ridicule des gens de la Faculté. Après avoir examiné Antoinette, il lui prit les mains et lui dit d'une voix douce et rassurante :

– Je ne veux pas vous bercer d'illusions, mademoiselle Œben. Franchement, vous avez une chance sur deux de garder votre enfant si vous êtes raisonnable, c'est-à-dire si vous ne bougez pratiquement pas de votre lit durant les six à huit semaines qui viennent. Si vous êtes sage, Blanche vous accouchera d'un bel enfant.

Quand Bertrand rentra, Antoinette dormait, pâle dans son grand lit. Ethis, en larmes, était accroupi à son chevet. Quand on lui eut expliqué ce qui s'était passé, il sentit sa gorge se nouer. L'idée qu'il s'en était fallu de si peu pour qu'Antoinette ne périsse avec son enfant le glaçait d'horreur. Il se pencha sur le visage exsangue de sa femme et lui embrassa le front avec une tendresse venue du tréfonds de lui-même.

– Il faut que tu vives, il faut que notre enfant vive! lui murmura-t-il à l'oreille. Courage, je suis sûr que tout va bien se passer...

Il avait parlé doucement, pour ne pas la réveiller mais elle l'entendit et ouvrit les yeux : Tu es là, alors la vie continue. Oui mon doux mari. Nous l'aurons cet enfant de la Révolution! »

Antoinette se remit rapidement. Nourrie au lait de poule, à la viande de bœuf et au pain blanc que Valfroy faisait chercher par un courrier spécial à la ferme du château de sa sœur, Mme d'Artigny, à vingt lieues de

Paris, elle retrouva aussi le teint rose dont on la félicitait si souvent. Comme elle ne pouvait pas bouger, elle devait se contenter des récits d'Ethis et de Valfroy pour savoir comment avançait cette Révolution dont elle devinait les rumeurs, à deux pas de chez elle.

La grande affaire était évidemment la confiscation des biens du clergé. Les liens entre l'abbaye et la communauté du bois n'étaient certes plus ce qu'ils avaient été au cours des siècles passés. Il n'en demeurait pas moins que le monastère, avec sa monumentale abbatiale, sa chapelle Saint-Pierre où tant de compagnons s'étaient mariés, son vieux pigeonnier qui datait de la fondation même de Saint-Antoine-des-Champs et que les religieuses conservaient comme une relique depuis le XIIe siècle, faisait partie intégrante du quartier. De très nombreuses familles étaient établies au Faubourg depuis des générations et les fils de 89 avaient tous en mémoire les récits des aïeux où l'abbaye et ses légendes tenaient tant de place. Comment ces gens simples et pieux qui, quelques semaines auparavant, avaient participé à la procession de la Bastille, auraient-ils pu ne pas se poser de questions à propos de leur abbaye? A qui allait-on vendre ces terres qui avaient souvent sauvé la communauté du bois de la disette? Allait-on démolir ces murs derrière lesquels les protestants du Faubourg, dont les noms étaient encore portés rue de Montreuil, avaient trouvé refuge le soir de la Saint-Barthélemy? Et puis, qu'allait devenir l'abbesse, Gabrielle-Charlotte de Beauvau-Craon qui, il y a quinze ans, avait rénové tout un quartier du Faubourg et qui de ce fait était très populaire?

Ces questions, Antoinette se les posait comme beaucoup de faubouriens, mais personne ne pouvait y répondre.

C'est dans cette atmosphère de guerre civile dans le peuple et de luttes d'influence chez les politiques de tous horizons qu'Antoinette arriva au terme de sa grossesse dans les premiers jours de 1790. Tout le nord de la France subissait les rigueurs d'un hiver terrible. La neige et le froid succédant aux pluies torrentielles qui avaient dévasté les récoltes de l'été entraînaient une disette mortelle à Paris et dans les grandes villes où le pain, quand on en trouvait, avait la teinte noirâtre de la farine révolutionnaire.

Antoinette nidifiait dans son confortable logement de la place d'Aligre, s'apercevant à peine de la misère des pauvres gens du quartier. Valfroy avait encore assez de moyens pour lui assurer le nécessaire, Riesener, le maître aux redingotes de soie, charriait lui-même, avec un apprenti, les tombées de bois et les sacs de copeaux jusqu'aux feux de la maison. Quant à Réveillon, le bon génie d'Antoinette, il s'occupait du superflu et gâtait la future maman comme il avait gâté la petite fille du Faubourg. Il ne se passait pas de semaine sans qu'il rendît visite à sa protégée, les bras chargés de friandises ou, ce qui était encore plus apprécié, d'un pain blanc, d'une douzaine d'œufs frais, d'un paquet de beurre. Un jour, il arriva triomphant au chevet d'Antoinette dont on attendait la délivrance d'un moment à l'autre.

– J'ai une nouvelle pour toi, s'écria-t-il : je viens d'acheter l'une des plus vieilles maisons du Faubourg. Ce sera son premier cadeau, au petit ou à la petite Valfroy!

– Une maison? En ce moment? Mais tu es fou, mon parrain. Et qu'a-t-elle de particulier cette maison? D'abord où se trouve-t-elle?

– Oh! ce n'est pas un palais. Rien de commun avec la Folie Titon. A propos je vais vendre ce qu'il en reste et la manufacture avec! La maison que je viens d'acheter se trouve juste en face du grand portail de l'abbaye. On l'appelle encore la « maison Thirion » du nom du premier ébéniste qui s'y est installé. Cela remonte à trois cents ans. Depuis, des générations de compagnons et de maîtres s'y sont succédé. Il ne reste sans doute pas grand-chose de la construction d'origine car elle a été restaurée, consolidée, agrandie je ne sais combien de fois mais la charpente était en bon chêne. Les arbalétriers et les pannes tiendront bien encore un siècle.

– Et qu'allons-nous faire de cette maison? Est-elle occupée?

– Les deux ateliers seulement par les frères Lorion, de bons ébénistes. Quand tu pourras bouger, nous irons la visiter. Et je suis sûr que lorsque tu auras respiré l'odeur de ces vieilles pierres, tu me comprendras. Elles sont culottées comme le fourneau d'une vieille pipe. Je crois que si l'on se penchait assez longtemps sur la stratification de ces murs couverts et recouverts de peinture, de buée, de colle et d'innombrables inscriptions dont certaines doivent remonter aux débuts, on pourrait retracer toute l'histoire de la maison. Ma mère, qui était pauvre, me parlait souvent de la « maison Thirion » où son père avait longtemps travaillé. C'est tout cela qui m'a fait acheter ce vestige du vieux Faubourg.

Antoinette l'attira vers elle et l'embrassa.

– Je t'aime, mon parrain. Mieux que quand tu dirigeais tes trois cents ouvriers dont beaucoup étaient de jeunes enfants...

– Tu me prends pour un négrier? Tu as peut-être raison mais j'en ai fait vivre, des familles du Faubourg! Et j'ai veillé à ce que les enfants ne soient pas malheureux chez moi. Heureusement, j'ai toujours été un peu poète, j'ai aidé Pilâtre de Rozier, l'amour de ta vie, à réaliser son rêve, à s'envoler de cette terre de misère; aujourd'hui, je tombe amoureux de cette vieille bicoque et je l'achète parce que je ne veux pas qu'elle soit démolie... Quelque chose me dit que ces murs ridés comme un vieux visage me livreront un peu de leurs secrets. Comme j'aimerais remonter le temps et connaître tous ces gens qui ont travaillé, créé, peiné et dont on ne se souvient même plus du nom...

– J'irai avec toi visiter la « maison Thirion ». Et tu verras, nous y ferons des découvertes!

Le lendemain, Réveillon entra comme un boulet dans la chambre d'Antoinette mollement allongée sur l'ottomane que Riesener avait fait installer.

– Eh bien, mon parrain, voilà une curieuse façon de venir distraire une malheureuse promise aux prochaines douleurs de l'accouchement. Vous m'avez fait grand-peur et vous savez que cela peut être grave dans mon état.

Enfin, je vous pardonne! Que me contez-vous aujourd'hui?

– Une bien jolie fable, madame, qui démontre qu'il ne faut pas toujours résister à ses caprices les plus fous. Figure-toi que sans t'attendre, j'ai été fouiner dans la maison de l'abbaye. Je passe sur le logement occupé encore il y a quelques mois et qui ne présente aucune particularité sinon d'être très sale. Au risque de me rompre les os, j'ai grimpé au grenier. Quel fouillis, mes amis! Il faudra des semaines pour trier tout cela, si on en a envie. Ma trouvaille de ce matin me laisse à penser que nous en aurons envie.

– Qu'as-tu donc découvert? Vite, je veux savoir.

– Attends une seconde, j'ai laissé cette surprise un peu encombrante dans le couloir.

Il revint en poussant devant lui un superbe berceau, finement sculpté auquel la garniture aux couleurs passées donnait un aspect attendrissant. En vraie fille d'ébéniste, Antoinette fut séduite, d'un seul coup d'œil, par la qualité du meuble et sa patine qui faisait ressortir les fleurs et les entrelacs admirablement dessinés dans le noyer. Sans hésiter une seconde, elle s'écria :

– Ce sera le berceau de mon enfant!

Réveillon jubilait. Sa filleule avait réagi comme il l'espérait. Il fit pivoter le corps mobile pour découvrir à l'intérieur de l'avant-pied deux lignes très fines gravées à la gougette.

– Regarde, Antoinette, je savais bien que cette vieille maison parlerait!

Il chaussa ses lunettes d'or et lut l'inscription que le temps n'avait pas effacée :

– « Berceau dessiné par Jean Marot et sculpté par le maître Louis Sommer pour Rosine Habermann, fille de Jeanne Racey et de Jacques Habermann, ouvrier du roi, en l'an 1641 [1]. »

– Et ce n'est pas tout, continua Réveillon. J'ai été feuilleter les vieux registres de la paroisse Sainte-Margue-

1. Voir *Les Dames du Faubourg*, t. I.

rite et j'ai découvert que cette Rosine est l'arrière-grand-mère de ta mère. Françoise-Marguerite était bien une Habermann, l'une des grandes familles qui ont fait le Faubourg! Tu te rends compte: tu vas endormir ton enfant dans le berceau de son aïeule! Cela arrive peut-être dans les nobles et anciennes familles mais dans notre monde, c'est plutôt rare. Cela dit, attends encore quelques jours pour accoucher, il faut me laisser le temps de faire regarnir le berceau par Loustet, le tapissier de la rue Saint-Nicolas qui a les plus belles soies de Lyon. Je ne suis pas mécontent de ma trouvaille et je vais continuer d'explorer le grenier. Je suis sûr que toute l'histoire de notre Faubourg, à travers un objet ou un autre, est présente dans ce paradis des araignées!

Pendant qu'Antoinette évoquait avec Réveillon le passé du vieux Faubourg, Ethis qui était allé traîner ses guêtres, ou plutôt son pantalon de toile à rayures rouges du côté de la Bastille, paraissait fort intéressé par ce qui se passait devant le fossé de l'ancienne forteresse, à deux pas du portail d'entrée. Il se fraya un passage, sans trop prendre garde aux gens qu'il bousculait. La foule entourait une sorte de comptoir installé devant un tas de pierres soigneusement rangées. Il demanda au compagnon ébéniste, Pierre Hurey, un autre jeune « vainqueur » qui se trouvait là, ce que signifiait ce rassemblement:

– C'est le maçon Palloy, chargé de la démolition de la Bastille, qui fait fortune en vendant pierre par pierre les restes du sinistre bâtiment. Tiens, regarde pour en tirer le meilleur bénéfice, Palloy a fait transformer sa pierraille en objets de tout genre: petits châteaux, dalles gravées, encriers, statuettes... J'espère tout de même que ce n'est pas uniquement pour enrichir ce malin que nous avons pris la Bastille, toi et moi...

Un peu gêné par le réflexe de vanité qui à ce propos, lui avait fait redresser la tête, Ethis ne put s'empêcher de penser qu'il n'avait tout de même pas fait grand-chose pour abattre le symbole du despotisme royal. Mais, après tout, il ne l'avait pas demandé, ce titre qui devenait chaque jour un peu plus prestigieux. Il était tout de même là le 14 juillet! Et l'un des premiers à entrer dans la brèche! Cela suffisait peut-être pour être un héros... Hurey qui parlait bien haut afin que personne n'ignorât qui ils étaient, n'en avait sûrement pas fait plus que lui. En tout cas, il était bien renseigné sur l'exploitation patriotique des ruines de la vieille citadelle :

– Cette vente n'est qu'une petite partie du trafic. De lourds convois chargés de caisses sont lancés chaque semaine sur les routes de France. En province aussi chacun veut avoir son petit souvenir de la Bastille! Il paraît que les bijoutiers du Palais-Royal enchâssent dans des montures d'or des cailloux garantis d'origine pour en faire des bagues et des pendentifs.

– Tout cela me dégoûte! s'exclama Ethis.

– Et moi donc, renchérit Hurey. Tiens, si je ne me retenais pas, j'irais flanquer en l'air tout cet étalage de pierrailles au nom des « vainqueurs de la Bastille »!

Ethis ne connaissait pas beaucoup Hurey, de trois ou quatre ans plus âgé que lui, qui travaillait chez le maître Leleu, l'ancien rival de Riesener, à deux pas de là rue Neuve-Saint-Antoine. Il savait cependant qu'il passait pour avoir la tête près du bonnet et il n'avait pas été étonné de le retrouver parmi les assaillants de la Bastille. Pour l'instant, il regardait le jeune homme s'échauffer, prendre à témoin les voisins et brandir la cocarde tricolore de son chapeau de coton vers Palloy et ses aides qui continuaient à débiter leurs pierres sans se douter qu'un orage menaçait.

Devant eux, une dame de la Halle, reconnaissable à son accoutrement et à son verbe haut, s'écria : « Il a raison le petit, ce qui se passe ici est honteux! » Ce à quoi un homme en bas arborant un foulard rouge sur sa redingote claire, un des nobles ou de ces grands bourgeois qui jouaient, tout au moins par la façon de s'habiller, aux révolutionnaires, répondit : « Eh bien, qu'il aille le renverser cet étal de pierres au lieu de crier si fort! »

Il n'en fallait pas plus pour libérer la colère d'Hurey. Brusquement, celui-ci s'empara du bras d'Ethis et l'entraîna en hurlant :

– Suivez tous les vainqueurs de la Bastille. Ensemble, arrêtons ce scandale! En avant!

Ces cris ne déclenchèrent pas un soulèvement général mais produisirent un violent remous dans la foule. De tranquilles passants se trouvèrent ainsi propulsés dans le sillage d'Hurey et d'Ethis vers l'estrade d'où le bonimenteur de service sauta juste à temps pour ne pas être emporté avec les pierres, la caisse et le trop malin Palloy qui hurlait au voleur en tentant de récupérer les pièces et les assignats qu'Hurey venait de faire voltiger d'un revers de main.

Le « vainqueur » exultait. Aidé par Ethis qui, évidemment, l'avait soutenu dans cette opération patriotique, il distribuait à qui en voulait les bastilles miniatures, les pierres plates ornées d'images tricolores, les bustes du roi et d'autres pièces plus rares.

L'arrivée de quelques gardes mit fin à la fête et les deux compères se retrouvèrent sans tarder, hilares, dans la grand-rue du Faubourg :

– Tu vois, conclut l'aîné en brandissant un caillou, il faut savoir se faire respecter. S'ils se figurent que la révolution est terminée, ils se trompent!

Le lendemain, le *Journal de Paris* et *Le Père Duchesne* faisaient état de l'incident, le second, par la plume d'Hébert, applaudissant les nombreux « vainqueurs de la Bastille » qui s'étaient opposés par la force au marchandage de leur sacrifice.

Dans la nuit du 2 janvier, alors qu'il gelait à pierre fendre et qu'on grelottait dans les maisons malgré tous les feux qu'on pouvait y entretenir, Antoinette ressentit les premières douleurs. Elle réveilla Valfroy.

– Mon ami, je crois que notre petit va naître cette nuit; je commence à avoir très mal. Va secouer Ethis qui dort comme une pierre et dis-lui d'aller tout de suite chercher Mme Mantel. Il sait où elle habite.

Bertrand, encore à moitié endormi, se leva et bredouilla quelques mots incompréhensibles qui firent tout de même sourire Antoinette. Inquiet, ému, il tournait en rond dans la chambre, cherchant ses habits, se cognant aux meubles et venant toutes les minutes essuyer le front de sa femme où commençaient de perler des gouttes de sueur. Antoinette finit par s'énerver :

– Vas-tu cessser ce manège? Calme-toi! C'est moi qui vais accoucher' Réveille vite Ethis et qu'il file tout de suite.

Une demi-heure plus tard, la sage-femme était là. Elle trouva Antoinette bien disposée.

– Tout va très bien se passer ma petite. N'ayez aucune crainte. Votre enfant sera au moins le millième que je mets au monde. Alors, vous pensez...

Antoinette ne savait pas ce qu'elle devait penser mais l'assurance de la bonne Blanche lui donnait confiance.

– D'abord, dit celle-ci, il faut pousser le feu de la cheminée et celui du poêle. C'est le travail des hommes. Après ils iront chercher tout le nécessaire, les bassines, le chaudron de cuivre et les linges. Tout cela est prêt depuis deux semaines mais l'enfant s'est fait attendre.

– Dois-je sortir? demanda Bertrand quand sa mission fut accomplie.

– Pour l'instant, vous pouvez rester. Au contraire, asseyez-vous auprès de votre femme et parlez-lui. Vous pouvez même mouiller un mouchoir dans du vinaigre et lui rafraîchir le front et les mains....

Heureusement les choses allèrent vite. L'eau avait à peine commencé de bouillir dans le chaudron qu'il fallut aider Antoinette. Secondée par Marie, la voisine qui avait eu cinq enfants, la sage-femme fit naître avec beaucoup d'adresse une petite fille toute dodue qu'Antoinette serra contre elle avant de sombrer dans un sommeil réparateur.

Une demi-heure plus tard, Lucie, lavée, emmaillotée de la tête aux pieds, était déposée précautionneusement dans son beau berceau.

Ainsi naquit le 2 janvier 1790 Lucie, fille de la Révolution, enfant de Bertrand Perrin, ci-devant baron de Valfroy et d'Antoinette Perrin, née Œben, dame du Faubourg comme sa mère et sa grand-mère. Contrairement à ce que l'on craignait, l'accouchement s'était déroulé sans incident et la nouvelle maman ne tarda pas à reprendre ses occupations de maîtresse de maison. Elle s'était récriée quand la sage-femme lui avait proposé d'engager une nourrice : « J'allaiterai mon enfant, avait-elle déclaré. D'abord parce que je l'ai toujours désiré, ensuite parce que, comme ça, je serai sûre que ma fille sera nourrie. »

Lucie devint immédiatement le centre de la famille. Ethis était fou de sa filleule qu'il appelait sa petite sœur et Riesener ne quittait plus la maison de la place d'Aligre. Il avait apporté une planchette à dessin, du papier, des crayons et recommençait sans se lasser le portrait d'Antoinette en train d'allaiter sa fille. La main du maître n'avait rien perdu de sa sûreté ni le trait sa précision. Tout en dessinant il parlait de sa vie étrange, de sa jeunesse dans le petit bourg de Glabeck, près d'Essen, de son apprentissage chez un vieux menuisier qui lui avait fait aimer le bois et lui avait appris à le travailler. Le métier était alors devenu pour lui une véritable passion. Il rêvait de meubles sublimes, de marqueteries si fines qu'on les prendrait pour des peintures, de bronzes ciselés et dorés dont il dessinait les détails, le soir, à la lueur d'une chandelle. Hélas, personne dans le bourg n'était assez riche pour s'offrir des meubles aussi coûteux.

Et puis, un jour, un ébéniste d'Essen lui avait dit que son cousin était parti chercher du travail à Paris, dans un quartier fantastique où, depuis des siècles, une sorte de communauté rassemblait les gens du bois, ébénistes, menuisiers, sculpteurs, serruriers et ciseleurs venus de toutes les régions d'Europe. Alors, sans s'arrêter aux conseils de sagesse de son père, huissier auprès du tribunal, il avait mis ses outils les plus précieux dans son balluchon et était parti rejoindre les immigrés du faubourg Saint-Antoine...

– Après, je dois tout à ton père. C'est Œben qui a fait de moi ce que je suis.

– Et à maman, tu ne lui dois rien?

– Bien sûr, je lui dois d'avoir pu continuer l'œuvre d'Œben, de lui avoir succédé alors que j'étais encore un simple compagnon. Mais je lui dois bien plus : je lui dois le bonheur de ma vie. Je l'ai beaucoup aimée Marguerite tu sais!...

La naissance de Lucie avait comme gommé la Révolution du cercle familial, tout au moins pour Antoinette qui vivait au rythme des tétées de sa fille dans un univers clos et serein sur lequel veillaient les hommes de la maison. Enfin, peu à peu, les nécessités quotidiennes eurent raison de l'état de grâce maternel. Antoinette songea à reprendre sa vie normale.

Chapitre 3.

LE BAPTÊME DU SANG

Le jour de ses relevailles, Antoinette décida de se rendre à l'abbaye afin d'y rencontrer Mme de Beauvau. Jamais, jusqu'à présent, elle n'avait éprouvé le besoin de fréquenter le monastère. Aujourd'hui, pourtant, une force plus instinctive que religieuse la poussait à tirer la clochette d'entrée de la vieille maison qui, déjà, n'appartenait plus à Dieu. Elle connaissait à peine la princesse en coule blanche mais il lui semblait soudain essentiel de se rapprocher de celle qui était, pour quelques heures encore, la « Dame du Faubourg ».

L'abbesse la reçut avec bonté et simplicité.

– Je vous connais peu, madame, lui dit-elle en la priant de s'asseoir dans le grand parloir où, depuis plus de trois siècles, treize mères abbesses s'étaient succédé, où des rois et des ministres avaient réfléchi au sort du pays, où des générations de maîtres et de compagnons du bois avaient fait alliance avec Dieu pour que vive et prospère leur communauté libre.

– Je vous connais peu mais je sais de quelle race vous êtes. Que vous veniez me voir à un moment où tant de gens jugent prudent d'ignorer l'abbaye me touche profondément. Demain, on va me chasser de ces lieux que le Bon Dieu a protégés depuis le roi Saint Louis et où j'ai régné durant trente ans. Je suis vieille, mon existence terrestre n'a plus d'intérêt. J'aurais pourtant aimé savoir qu'après moi une autre « Dame du Faubourg » poursuivrait la tâche entreprise...

– Une tâche à laquelle, ma mère, votre nom restera attaché. Vous avez créé un quartier, celui où j'habite, fondé un marché, permis de percer trois rues. Aucun des vieux habitants du Faubourg ne l'oubliera!

– Tout cela n'a pas d'importance. Le temps n'est plus aux petites vanités. Ce que j'ai fait, une autre abbesse l'aurait fait à ma place. Puisque la ville et le gouvernement étaient incapables de s'intéresser au bien-être des habitants du Faubourg, il fallait bien que le Bon Dieu s'en occupe!

L'abbesse éclata d'un grand rire :

– Allons, Antoinette, vous n'êtes pas venue pour m'entendre vous parler de ce marché Beauvau où vous faites chaque jour vos emplettes. Racontez-moi plutôt votre vie, distrayez-moi de toutes les infortunes qui accablent notre maison. De tout temps, les gens du Faubourg sont venus dans ce parloir, meublé par eux au long des siècles, nous apporter l'air frais de la vie et le sens des réalités. D'abord, comment traversez-vous la période difficile qui est la nôtre? Je sais que le nombre des indigents augmente chaque jour. Hélas! je ne peux rien faire pour aider ces malheureux. Tout acte de charité est considéré par les plus actifs des révolutionnaires comme la preuve que nous cachons des vivres. Hier encore une bande est venue fouiller l'abbaye de fond en comble pour y chercher de la farine. Je ne sais même pas si on nous laissera moissonner... Mais voilà que je repars sur mes malheurs. Allez, je ne dis plus un mot, je vous écoute!

Antoinette parla. Longtemps. De sa jeunesse, de son père le grand Œben, de sa mère morte tragiquement, de sa vie orageuse avec Pilâtre de Rozier, de Riesener son beau-père, de son mari, le délicat Valfroy, de sa petite Lucie... Il y avait des années qu'elle ne s'était pas confiée ainsi, pleinement. Cela lui faisait du bien d'enchaîner les souvenirs qui affluaient et que Mme de Beauvau-Craon écoutait en souriant, la tête légèrement inclinée sur la têtière de son fauteuil. C'est elle qui interrompit Antoinette en lui prenant la main :

– Savez-vous mon enfant que cela fait plus d'une heure

que vous êtes assise en face de moi et que vous me racontez la vie, votre vie! Entre ces murs, on ne sent pas passer le temps. Vous m'avez fait un plaisir extrême. Revenez, je vous prie avant qu'on m'ait chassée de la maison de Dieu

– Je vous promets de revenir, mère, mais on ne vous chassera pas. Ce serait trop injuste et la Justice est l'un des premiers mots qui figurent dans la Déclaration des droits de l'homme!

– Qu'est-ce qui est juste, Antoinette? On reproche aux ordres religieux d'être insolemment riches alors que le peuple et l'État sont démunis. Il y a du vrai là-dedans. Je me suis souvent demandé s'il était raisonnable et en tout cas conforme à la pensée du Christ de posséder autant de biens, des fermes, des maisons jusqu'à plus de quinze lieues, biens dont je ne peux contrôler l'exploitation et que M. de Plainville, l'avocat-archiviste, a mis plus de six mois à inventorier... Mais il y a sûrement un moyen d'accéder à plus de justice sans offenser Dieu...

Le soir venu, Antoinette fit à Bertrand le récit de sa visite à l'abbaye, elle lui rapporta les propos sereins mais désabusés de l'abbesse :

– Cette femme est une sainte. Elle semble se préparer à un sacrifice qu'elle juge, on le sent, inéluctable. Crois-tu vraiment que le Faubourg va chasser et peut-être même emprisonner les religieuses qui lui ont permis d'exister?

– Ma chère, ce qui était impossible il y a encore un an devient exécutable aujourd'hui. La roue de la révolution, je te l'ai dit, ne s'arrêtera que lorsque les Français en auront assez de se faire écraser. Nous n'en sommes pas là : l'engrenage fatal n'est pas encore lancé, il va même en ce moment si lentement qu'on le croirait bloqué. Mais ce n'est pas parce que la révolution fait la pause qu'il faut l'imaginer sans ressort.

La grand-rue du Faubourg et le quartier avaient il est vrai retrouvé un certain calme. Quelques maîtres et ouvriers libres essayaient même, comme pour forcer le destin, de rendre aux ateliers un semblant d'activité. Il restait du bon bois dans les cours et beaucoup préféraient l'utiliser plutôt que de rester les bras croisés. La commode finement marquetée, la table à écrire en placage de bois de rose, trouveraient bien un jour preneurs! Le Faubourg laborieux entamait l'année nouvelle avec un vague optimisme. Antoinette disait à tout le monde que c'était Lucie qui avait apporté la paix en naissant.

Valfroy était maintenant plus souvent libre. Sa charge auprès de Necker s'allégeait en même temps que celle de son maître dont l'autorité et l'influence se diluaient dans la confusion des pouvoirs. Bertrand ne se faisait guère d'illusions sur l'avenir du ministre qui annonçait chaque jour son prochain retour en Suisse. « Je resterai, disait-il, tant qu'il me sera permis d'influer tant soit peu sur la politique du roi. Je fais cela pour Louis XVI malgré ses fautes et ses faiblesses; et je fais cela pour le pays de France que j'aime tant! »

Valfroy rapportait ces propos désabusés à Antoinette qui, elle, ne voyait plus le monde qu'à travers les yeux de sa fille. De temps à autre, une décision de l'Assemblée nationale secouait la léthargie qui semblait avoir gagné le Faubourg : la division de la France en 83 départements par exemple, la suppression de vœux monastiques ou le décret ordonnant la vente des biens nationaux. Que va-t-on vendre et qui va acheter? Cette question revenait dans toutes les conversations. Les pauvres, eux, savaient bien qui profiterait de l'aubaine et qui s'enrichirait un peu plus dans cette foire fantastique et patriotique où la moitié de la France devait être mise à l'encan.

Questionné par Antoinette, Réveillon avait déclaré qu'il n'achèterait pas un acre des terres confisquées et que, d'ailleurs, les affaires ne l'intéressaient plus. La seule chose qui méritait son attention était, en dehors de la petite Lucie, la restitution de la médaille qu'on lui avait volée. Il accablait de lettres les députés et le bureau de l'Hôtel de Ville. Cela faisait sourire Valfroy. Antoinette qui connaissait bien son parrain disait que dans une période aussi grave, c'était l'insignifiance de l'enjeu qui excitait l'incorrigible joueur.

Le froid cessa heureusement avec le printemps. Quand les premières feuilles vertes apparurent sur les marronniers de la place d'Aligre, Lucie était déjà une petite fille éveillée. Elle ne comprit tout de même pas Valfroy qui lui annonça, le soir du 14 juin, qu'elle avait perdu dans l'après-midi tout droit de s'enorgueillir un jour d'un titre de noblesse.

L'arrivée avancée des beaux jours y était peut-être pour quelque chose mais la Révolution continuait de garder un visage bon enfant, presque rassurant. Les décrets instituant les départements et le principe de l'unité des poids et mesures furent en général bien accueillis. Puisque le roi lui-même venait de déclarer à l'Assemblée qu'il trouvait cela très bien, pourquoi, après tout, n'être pas révolutionnaire ?

Depuis qu'il avait juré de maintenir la constitution, Louis XVI avait conquis une grande popularité ; aussi l'annonce de sa visite à la manufacture de glaces de la rue de Reuilly fut-elle accueillie avec joie par tout le Faubourg. « Venez, je vous emmène, avait dit Ethis à Antoinette, il n'est pas question de manquer un pareil spectacle ! » Trop contente de revoir vivre son vieux quartier, Antoinette avait accepté. Lucie confiée aux soins d'une voisine, elle était partie, le cœur joyeux, « voir passer le roi », comme d'innombrables femmes du Faubourg l'avaient fait avant elle. L'époque, certes, était austère et la cérémonie n'avait rien à voir avec les défilés empanachés de François Ier ou la parade de noces de Louis XIV. Pourtant, elle ressentit un petit pincement au cœur quand le roi, la reine et Madame Élisabeth, conduits par La Fayette, s'arrêtèrent à l'entrée du Faubourg pour recevoir l'hommage du maire de Paris et des présidents de sections.

Le carrosse royal reprit ensuite sa marche vers l'abbaye et la vieille rue de Reuilly où se dressait l'imposante manufacture royale devenue rivale de Murano. A l'entrée de la rue, le roi montra une bâtisse surmontée de cheminées.

– Non, sire, dit La Fayette, la verrerie est un petit peu

plus loin. Ici c'est la brasserie de Santerre, l'homme qui dit-on a entraîné le peuple à l'assaut de la Bastille.

– Ah bon! dit le roi, sans se douter que les tambours du même Santerre, dont le nom apparaissait en grosses lettres sur l'enseigne, le conduiraient trois ans plus tard au supplice.

Lucie allait sur ses six mois, il faisait beau, Antoinette était heureuse. Valfroy, devenu tout simplement M. Perrin, ce qui ne le chagrinait pas, travaillait encore auprès de Necker. Il rapportait le soir des nouvelles plutôt alarmantes : les pouvoirs de son maître s'amenuisaient un peu plus chaque jour, il ne faisait aucun doute que celui qui avait été si souvent renvoyé par le roi allait sans tarder l'être encore une fois par ceux qui avaient exigé son retour!

– Tout est prêt à Coppet pour recevoir les Necker, disait Bertrand. Si sa fille, Mme de Staël, n'était sur le point d'accoucher, il serait déjà parti.

– Et toi, que vas-tu faire?

– Dieu merci je ne suis pas ministre, je ne suis qu'un homme de chiffres, un gérant de l'argent des autres. Les nouveaux maîtres de la France auront besoin de gens comme moi. Je travaillerai donc de mon mieux en attendant des jours meilleurs. Pour l'instant, le monde politique ne pense qu'à réussir la fête de la Fédération qui aura lieu comme tu le sais le 14 juillet. On a choisi l'emplacement du Champ-de-Mars et la date anniversaire de la prise de la Bastille. Tiens, Ethis va être une nouvelle fois à l'honneur!

Avant d'être à l'honneur, Ethis fut bientôt à la peine. Une peine douce et exaltante partagée avec deux cent mille volontaires. Ce qui se produisit à Paris au cours de cet été de 1790 relève de la magie. Ce fut comme si un dieu bienveillant avait fait couler des fleuves de miel au creux des fossés qui séparaient jusque-là les classes de la société. Dans la crainte que les travaux d'aménagement ne fussent pas terminés à temps, Paris tout entier s'était fait terrassier, maçon, charretier dans un élan qui relevait de la plus pure abnégation. Sur le chantier du Champ-de-Mars grouillant d'une foule empressée, on s'embrassait, on fraternisait, on fêtait en riant et en chantant l'annonce d'un nouvel âge d'or : « Nous sommes les enfants d'un même dieu, les fils d'une même patrie, nous sommes frères ! » criait un bourgeois juché sur un tas de sable tandis que, plus loin, un prêtre à cheveux blancs tirait une brouette. Des boutiquiers remuaient la terre et des dames du monde portaient des pierres dans les plis noués de leurs robes.

Réveillon avait voulu se rendre compte par lui-même de cet élan quasi surnaturel d'enthousiasme et de confiance. Le vieux sceptique était revenu ébloui, prêt à entraîner tous ceux qu'il connaissait dans cette mêlée fraternelle.

– Tu me connais, dit-il à Antoinette, je ne suis pas un tendre, je ne suis pas non plus un révolutionnaire farouche, moi à qui la révolution a tant pris. Eh bien ! ma fille, j'ai eu les larmes aux yeux en voyant une vieille femme porter de la terre dans son tablier et les pensionnaires de Mlle Montansier manier la pelle et la pioche. Bref, j'ai mis moi-même la main à la pâte : tiens regarde ces ampoules !

– C'est vrai que c'est merveilleux, parrain, j'irai moi aussi un de ces jours prêter la main à tous ces braves gens. Mais j'y pense : si les nobles, les prêtres, les bourgeois, les artisans et les gens du peuple sont d'accord et s'embrassent, ce n'est plus la peine de poursuivre la révolution... Elle est faite !

– Tu as raison ma chérie mais en regardant ce tableau aux couleurs si riantes, je ne pouvais croire qu'un orage, ou une main malfaisante, ne viendrait pas un jour le détruire. L'homme ne peut être bon bien longtemps. Des monstres vont se réveiller. Enfin, un petit coup d'air frais est toujours bon à prendre !

La fête de la Fédération tint les promesses de tous les inconnus qui avaient participé à sa réussite. Le roi vint, dans la voiture du sacre, prendre place au centre du fantastique cirque artificiel élevé en quelques semaines sur le Champ-de-Mars. La reine qui portait les couleurs de la nation était entourée du dauphin, des frères du roi et de la cour. Louis XVI prêta serment de fidélité à la constitution, serment repris par six cent mille hommes venus de la France entière... Il se mit à pleuvoir.

En cette fin d'année 91, Paris était tout blanc. La neige n'avait cessé de tomber deux jours durant et l'on avait dû déblayer à la pelle des chemins étroits autour de la place d'Aligre afin de permettre aux habitants de sortir de leurs maisons et de faire le tour des boutiques du Faubourg pour y acheter quelques subsistances : une livre de pain, des harengs salés ou, avec un peu de chance, quelques-uns de ces fameux tubercules dont personne n'avait voulu entendre parler, deux ans auparavant, lorsque Antoine-Augustin Parmentier avait publié son *Traité sur la culture et les usages de la pomme de terre.* Après des années d'incompréhension, la disette avait tout de même réussi à imposer la plante qui nourrit quand le pain vient à manquer.

Nonchalamment allongée sur le canapé que lui avait offert Riesener au moment de sa grossesse, Antoinette regardait en souriant sa petite fille essayer de faire remonter sur son fil l'émigrette de citronnier offerte par Réveillon.

– Viens, dit-elle, je vais te montrer. Mais parrain est incorrigible, tu es bien trop petite, à deux ans, pour jouer à l'émigrette.

Elle rembobina soigneusement le fil sur la roulette de bois, glissa son index dans la boucle et, du simple mouvement de la main, fit descendre et remonter le jouet qu'on appelait « le Coblentz » ou « l'émigrette » pour se moquer des nobles et des riches qui avaient préféré l'exil à une révolution qu'ils prévoyaient douloureuse. Paris était fou de ce jeu. Le menuisier-tabletier Rochet, installé rue de Lappe à l'enseigne du *Singe vert* en avait fabriqué vingt-cinq mille et avait fait fortune en quelques mois.

Lucie battit des mains en admirant sa mère et se jeta dans ses bras.

Antoinette caressa les boucles blondes de sa fille et soupira : « Tu n'as pas trop souffert jusqu'ici des malheurs du temps, prions pour que nous puissions continuer à t'élever convenablement. Et faire de toi une belle jeune fille... »

A côté d'elle sur sa table à écrire, des feuilles de papier couvertes de sa fine écriture brillaient sous la lueur d'un rayon de soleil dont on se demandait comment il avait réussi à braver l'hiver et à percer les branches des arbres poudrés à frimas. C'était le brouillon des lettres qu'elle avait écrites à sa sœur depuis le début des événements. Au hasard, elle jeta un coup d'œil sur un passage, puis sur un autre : « Toute la récente histoire de notre pauvre Faubourg est consignée là, pensa-t-elle. Il faut que je garde précieusement ces lettres pour Lucie. Elle verra dans quelle époque troublée elle est née et elle a grandi ! Il s'est passé tellement de choses depuis le jour où Ethis est venu m'annoncer tout à trac qu'il venait de prendre la Bastille ! La constitution civile du clergé, la mort et l'enterrement de Mirabeau, la loi interdisant les grèves, les associations ouvrières et supprimant du même coup les corporations et les jurandes, ce qui avait un temps mis le Faubourg en émoi. Il y avait encore eu la fuite du roi et l'arrestation de Varenne, la chasse aux prêtres réfractaires, l'élection de la nouvelle assemblée... »

Un voile de profonde tristesse assombrit alors son regard : elle allait oublier l'événement qui l'avait le plus touchée : un matin, les occupants de quarante couvents d'hommes et de soixante couvents de femmes avaient été en moins d'une heure jetés à la rue. Dès qu'elle avait appris la nouvelle, Antoinette s'était précipitée à l'abbaye dont les portes closes étaient gardées par un détachement du bataillon de Sainte-Marguerite en habit bleu, collet rouge et culotte blanche. Elle avait tenté de questionner l'un des gardes qui l'avait grossièrement rembarrée : « Tu t'intéresses donc à ces bêtes qu'on a chassées de leur repaire? Allez circule! » Antoinette n'avait rien répondu au butor, elle était rentrée chez elle en pleurant.

Jamais l'abbesse de Beauvau-Craon n'avait voulu lui dire ce qu'elle ferait le jour où on la chasserait de l'abbaye. Et ce fut comme si la dernière « Dame du Faubourg » avait été miraculeusement rappelée au ciel, à l'exemple de *L'Enlèvement de la Vierge par les anges,* le grand tableau de l'Italien Vivarini accroché au-dessus du maître-autel de l'abbatiale...

Personne, au Faubourg et ailleurs, n'entendit plus parler de la vingt-sixième et dernière abbesse de Saint-Antoine-des-Champs [1].

Le départ forcé des religieuses et la disparition quasi surnaturelle de l'abbesse de Beauvau-Craon avaient plongé les vieux faubouriens dans le désarroi. La Révolution cessait d'être cette gigantesque kermesse qui rompait la monotonie des jours et promettait des lendemains meilleurs. Pour la première fois, une loi votée par l'Assemblée bouleversait les structures du quartier et touchait le Faubourg en son point le plus sensible : l'abbaye, la cellule mère autour de laquelle s'était formée, au cours des siècles, la communauté des compagnons du bois. L'abbatiale, un des joyaux de l'art gothique, n'avait certes pas été abattue, on l'avait transformée en église paroissiale après qu'elle eut été vidée d'une grande partie de ses trésors. Mais pour combien de temps? Le vieux sanctuaire, desservi comme Sainte-Marguerite par un clergé constitutionnel, allait-il résister aux explosions révolutionnaires? Le peuple du Faubourg, les femmes surtout, se posaient la question. Elles regardaient, non sans émoi, de grands chariots franchir le portail, chargés à ras bord de sculptures, de meubles, de livres. La très riche

1. Mes recherches en bibliothèque et aux Archives de France ont été vaines. La famille de Beauvau-Craon elle-même ne possède aucun document concernant la fin de l'abbesse Gabrielle-Charlotte. (*N.d.A.*)

bibliothèque de Saint-Antoine-des-Champs, avec ses rangées entières de manuscrits enluminés et ses rayons d'incunables, devait être vendue comme toutes celles des maisons monacales. Une affiche collée sur le portail précisa un jour que la vente publique aurait lieu à l'hôtel Bullion où avaient été déjà dispersés les livres provenant de l'ordre de Cluny et des bénédictins. Au cours d'une promenade, Antoinette avait remarqué cette annonce et elle avait décidé d'assister à la vente. Le démembrement spirituel et matériel de l'abbaye la révoltait. Souvent, elle songeait à l'abbesse, évanouie dans Paris quelques instants après que les gardes, auxquels s'étaient joints quelques éléments de la populace, eurent chassé les religieuses de leur monastère. Assister à la vente, c'était une manière de s'unir une fois encore au passé du vieux Faubourg dont on vendait l'esprit. C'était aussi, pour Antoinette, une certaine façon d'honorer Mme de Beauvau-Craon et, qui sait, de lui faire signe là où elle se trouvait.

L'assistance était peu nombreuse dans le grand salon de l'hôtel que Claude de Bullion, président à mortier du Parlement et garde des Sceaux des ordres de Louis XIII, avait fait construire au siècle précédent, non loin de la place Royale, à deux pas de la Bastille. Antoinette admira un instant les immenses peintures de Blanchard et Vouet qui couvraient les murs. A part, dans le coin d'un tableau, une armoirie royale qui avait été lacérée à coups de pique, les toiles n'avaient pas souffert. Les meubles avaient presque tous été enlevés, il ne restait que quelques chaises et un grand bureau plat où Antoinette crut reconnaître la patte de son père. Les charges de commissaires-priseurs étaient supprimées depuis 1790 et c'est un des miliciens nommés par l'Assemblée qui officiait. Les livres étaient empilés sur le parquet et vendus par lots. Seuls quelques libraires, dont Guiffier qui avait acheté la veille, pour 10 000 livres, la bibliothèque de Saint-Maur, s'intéressaient à la vente, en prenant bien soin de ne pas enchérir les uns sur les autres.

Antoinette regardait distraitement les in-quarto et les in-octavo changer de pile au fur et à mesure que les adjudications étaient prononcées. Le spectacle lui semblait moins intéressant qu'elle ne l'avait imaginé; elle s'apprêtait à partir quand un homme d'une trentaine d'années, à l'élégance discrète, vint prendre place à côté. Elle répondit à son salut par un sourire et l'homme engagea sans embarras la conversation :

– Permettez, madame, que je me présente. Je suis Alexandre Lenoir. Artiste peintre de mon état, je me suis promis de tout faire pour sauver de la fureur des temps certains chefs-d'œuvre irremplaçables. Il existe bien une commission temporaire des arts chargée de ce travail mais ses membres sont incapables de discerner la valeur des immenses richesses abandonnées au pillage. Moi, je n'ai pas de mandat public mais je suis compétent. Alors, on me laisse faire, on me paye même un petit peu pour rassembler dans le vieux cloître des Petits-Augustins les plus belles pièces et les statues que je réussis à arracher aux casseurs des églises et des couvents. Plus tard, j'ouvrirai un musée... Mais vous, madame, que faites-vous dans ce marchandage à regarder les grimaces de l'huissier-crieur? Vous intéressez-vous aux livres anciens?

– Pas précisément, mais ceux-ci proviennent d'une abbaye qui m'est chère.

– Saint-Antoine-des-Champs? L'un des plus beaux chevets de l'art gothique... J'aurais aimé sauver les deux superbes statues en marbre blanc des petites princesses Jeanne et Bonne de France, filles de Charles V, mais je suis arrivé trop tard. Les vandales étaient passés avant moi!

– Et tous ces livres rares vendus à l'encan? C'est lamentable.

– Pas tellement. Ceux-là au moins, sont achetés par des libraires. Ces marchands font des affaires d'or mais je suis sûr que les livres qu'ils achètent seront bien conservés. J'ai vu, madame, tellement de scènes épouvantables que je ne peux que me féliciter de savoir ces ouvrages en bonnes mains. Je me suis brûlé l'autre jour en tentant d'arracher aux débris fumants de la bibliothèque Saint-

Germain-des-Prés un Homère en grec et en latin dédié à Henri IV. Et combien ai-je vu de magnifiques reliures lacérées à coups de baïonnette parce que estampées aux armes d'un prince ou d'un noble! Tenez, regardez ce monsieur vêtu de drap vert pomme : c'est Thomas Moore Slade de Londres, qui achète pour ses riches clients anglais. Quand le duc d'Orléans qu'on n'appelle plus que Philippe Égalité, décida de vendre ses collections, Slade a raflé toutes les plus belles pièces qui ont pris aussitôt le chemin de Londres. C'est regrettable mais que faire? Avec mes pauvres moyens je ne peux protéger comme je le voudrais notre patrimoine!

– Ce que vous faites est bien, monsieur, dit Antoinette qui écoutait son voisin avec intérêt. J'aimerais un jour vous présenter mon beau-père que les destructions d'œuvres d'art rendent littéralement fou. Vous le connaissez peut-être de nom, c'est Jean-Henri Riesener le maître ébéniste...

– Oh! Mais alors, vous êtes la fille du grand Œben. Comme je suis heureux d'avoir fait votre connaissance. Pour les besoins de ma mission, je dispose d'une vieille voiture qui, par miracle, n'est pas remplie aujourd'hui de morceaux de marbre ou de bronze arrachés à la destruction. Puis-je vous raccompagner?

Antoinette accepta sans façon et prit place dans un carrosse aux garnitures râpées couvertes d'une fine poussière, celle des chefs-d'œuvre. Entre deux cahots elle regardait à la dérobée le visage d'Alexandre Lenoir et ne pouvait s'empêcher de lui trouver une ressemblance avec Pilâtre de Rozier : même nez un peu pointu, bouche sensuelle et regard moqueur. Ce trajet en voiture lui rappelait, en tout cas, le premier soir où le séduisant pharmacien, qui ne s'était pas encore découvert une vocation d'aéronaute, l'avait raccompagnée jusqu'à la place d'Aligre. Un frisson la parcourut. Honteuse, elle s'arrangea pour que son regard ne croise plus celui de Lenoir.

Encore un peu troublée, elle s'appuya sur le bras qui se tendait pour l'aider à descendre et remercia le rédempteur de beauté. Celui-ci prit congé avec courtoisie :

– Comme vous me l'avez aimablement proposé, j'aimerais faire la connaissance de M. Riesener. Je vous ferai signe un jour prochain afin que vous veniez prendre une tasse de cacao – il m'en reste heureusement quelques grammes – avec votre beau-père. Vous verrez un logement modeste et sûrement en désordre : je suis célibataire...

– Non, monsieur Lenoir, c'est vous qui nous ferez le plaisir de venir dans notre maison. Moi je suis mariée, ajouta-t-elle avec un sourire, et vous aurez sûrement plaisir à connaître mon mari.

« Eh, oui ! Antoinette, tu es mariée et même mère de famille », se dit-elle en poussant la porte derrière laquelle on percevait le babillage de la petite Lucie.

Necker finalement retourné en Suisse, Valfroy était demeuré à la direction générale des Finances où l'on avait plus que jamais besoin de techniciens. Les commissaires nommés par l'Assemblée étaient souvent incompétents et il fallait tout de même surveiller les inquiétants mouvements d'assignats, gérer une situation toujours tendue et proche de la banqueroute que le ministre genevois redoutait tant. Bertrand n'était pas un ennemi de la Révolution, il ne gênait personne et personne ne songeait à se séparer d'un aide aussi précieux. Il accomplissait donc sa tâche avec conscience, sinon avec passion, et retrouvait chaque soir la douceur du foyer où Antoinette savait faire régner, malgré les difficultés et les privations, un certain bonheur de vivre. Par lui, les nouvelles fraîches, rarement apaisantes, arrivaient jusqu'à l'îlot de calme enfoui sous les frondaisons des marronniers de la place.

Ce soir-là, Antoinette avait retenu Riesener à souper et quand tout le monde fut installé autour de la vieille table de famille où avait jadis régné Marguerite Œben, Bertrand annonça :

– J'ai quelque chose de stupéfiant à vous apprendre

Pour que le calme et pondéré Valfroy manifestât une telle émotion, il fallait que la nouvelle fût d'importance.

Il avait annoncé la déclaration de guerre et la mise à sac des Tuileries avec plus de simplicité! Plus impatient qu'Antoinette et Riesener, Ethis posa sa cuillère et questionna :

– Vite, monsieur de Valfroy. De quoi s'agit-il?

– Eh bien, mon garçon, on a volé les joyaux de la Couronne!

Malgré sa gravité, le fait était sans commune mesure avec l'envahissement du pays ou l'emprisonnement de la famille royale. En ce mois d'août 92 où se jouait le sort de la Révolution, c'est pourtant lui qui allait retenir l'attention générale. Symbolisme du trésor royal ou pesée sur la conscience collective de mots magiques comme « le Régent », lourd de ses 136 carats, ou « le Sancy », estimé un million de livres l'année précédente dans l'inventaire des diamants de la Couronne, Paris et la France entière allaient réagir comme Ethis face à un événement aussi incroyable.

Et pourtant... Le vol, comme le raconta Valfroy et comme on put en apprendre les détails dans les gazettes, était bel et bien authentique.

Il faut dire qu'au lendemain de la prise des Tuileries, la rue appartenait aux nombreuses bandes armées qui attaquaient et pillaient tout ce qu'il y avait à attaquer ou à piller. La décomposition de la police commandée par Santerre, le brasseur du Faubourg promu général de la garde par la Commune, assurait l'impunité à tous les brigands, assassins et écumeurs de rues qui ne manquaient pas, d'ailleurs, de revendiquer une participation décisive à l'attaque du palais des Tuileries. Tout de même, il fallait de l'audace pour s'attaquer au Garde-meuble royal, cet énorme édifice bâti par Gabriel en pleine place Louis XV devenue place de la Révolution! C'était en principe le palais le mieux gardé de Paris puisque, chacun le savait, il renfermait les joyaux de la Couronne. Or, la garde n'existait que sur le papier. Les lourdes portes de la façade étaient bien entendu verrouillées mais aucune sentinelle ne les surveillait, pas plus que les entrées de derrière. A l'intérieur, pas le moindre gardien non plus devant l'armoire de fer renfermant le Régent et les autres joyaux : des voleurs audacieux pouvaient opérer en paix.

– C'est seulement aujourd'hui, expliqua Valfroy, que l'Assemblée a été mise au courant de cette fabuleuse maraude. En fait, les voleurs sont revenus trois nuits de suite afin de vider consciencieusement toutes les salles d'exposition et de conservation. Quel vacarme sur les travées quand Roland est venu annoncer que « des trente millions de diamants et objets précieux que contenait le palais, il n'en restait pas plus de cinquante mille livres »!

– A-t-on arrêté les voleurs? demanda Ethis.

– Deux seulement mais il y en aura d'autres. En attendant, chacun à l'Assemblée voit dans cette affaire insensée une conspiration fomentée par ses adversaires politiques. Certains accusent les amis de la reine soucieux de récupérer les richesses confisquées au trône. Fabre d'Églantine charge les Girondins, Roland et sa femme accusent Danton et Fabre. Marat, lui, s'en tient aux aristocrates. Les gens sincères et sensés, eux, pensent tout bonnement qu'il s'agit de bandits audacieux agissant pour leur compte personnel.

Le lendemain matin, Ethis sortit de bonne heure pour aller acheter *Le Moniteur* au marchand de gazettes installé en plein air, près de la fontaine Trogneux. Le jeune homme lisait maintenant parfaitement grâce aux leçons d'Antoinette. C'est lui qui déchiffra à voix haute l'article qui occupait la première page :

« La nuit a favorisé un grand attentat à la propriété nationale. Des brigands armés, au nombre d'une quarantaine, ont volé le Garde-meuble de la Couronne. Ils sont montés au moyen de cordes par les potences des réverbères qui donnent sur la place de la Révolution et sont entrés par les fenêtres de la colonnade qu'ils ont brisées.

« Deux de ces voleurs ont été pris par des gardes nationaux qui patrouillaient rue Saint-Florentin alors qu'ils se précipitaient de la galerie sur la place, accrochés à des cordes. Ils subissent un interrogatoire et par eux on espère pouvoir arrêter leurs complices. On a trouvé une grande quantité de diamants dans leurs poches ainsi que le riche hochet du dauphin. Hélas, presque tous les bijoux et les pierres précieuses ont été emportés par les fuyards qui se sont dispersés dans toutes les directions à l'arrivée de la garde. Ils en avaient semé sur leur route car un domestique a ramassé au petit matin une superbe émeraude au milieu de la rue Saint-Florentin. Il l'a rapportée au Garde-meuble.

« Le ministre de l'Intérieur Roland, le maire et le commandant général ont pris dès deux heures du matin des dispositions pour garder les issues de Paris. »

Cette affaire survenait dans un Paris encore traumatisé par les épouvantables massacres du début du mois au cours desquels un millier de gens enfermés dans les prisons avaient été égorgés par une horde de quatre ou cinq cents tueurs ivres d'une rage sanguinaire qui n'avait rien de révolutionnaire. Germaine de Staël, arrêtée au cours de la journée terrible du 2 septembre, avait été sauvée de justesse par Manuel, le procureur de la Commune. Derrière ce rideau d'horreurs, flottait heureusement le drapeau déployé par les volontaires qui s'engageaient pour se porter, les armes à la main, à la rencontre de l'envahisseur. Cet élan patriotique des Parisiens était le seul souffle rafraîchissant dans le climat de misère qui empoisonnait la capitale en proie, par ailleurs, aux discordes politiques.

Tout travail était suspendu dans les ateliers du Faubourg. L'inaction et les privations poussaient les jeunes à s'engager. Ethis avait voulu suivre Joseph Arné, le menuisier de la rue de Montreuil, « vainqueur » glorieux puisqu'il avait pénétré le premier dans la cour de la Bastille et s'enrôler dans la 35e division de gendarmerie, créée pour rassembler les braves de la première heure. Les objurgations d'Antoinette et celles de Valfroy n'auraient pas réussi à le dissuader de céder à son penchant pour le combat et l'aventure. Seulement, le garçon boitait depuis qu'il avait été blessé chez Réveillon et il n'avait pas été accepté.

Faute de pouvoir marcher aux frontières, Ethis s'était joint plusieurs fois à la foule qui s'était portée en masse à la Conciergerie pour demander la tête de deux voleurs des joyaux de la Couronne. La surexcitation du peuple était grande. Il exigeait une justice expéditive pour tous les bandits impliqués dans l'affaire. Le crime de lèse-majesté, devenu crime de lèse-Révolution, apparaissait d'autant plus impardonnable que la vente des trésors de la Couronne venait d'être décidée pour payer la levée de nouveaux régiments. Chaque fois qu'à la suite d'une dénonciation de bandits arrêtés par les commissaires, les gardes se rendaient au domicile d'un nouveau complice démasqué, la foule suivait en vociférant et en brandissant des piques et la police avait toutes les peines du monde à protéger les individus arrêtés. Enfin, les esprits se calmèrent et Ethis dut se contenter de suivre le fabuleux feuilleton du trésor de la Couronne dans les journaux.

La moitié des voleurs arrêtés, jugés et condamnés, les autres ayant réussi à s'enfuir, l'intérêt se porta sur les objets dérobés qu'on retrouvait parfois dans des conditions très curieuses. Le « Régent », le plus célèbre des diamants de la Couronne fut ainsi découvert dans un trou de charpente d'une maison de l'allée des Veuves [1]. On eut moins de chance pour le « Sancy » dont les 53 carats prirent le chemin de l'Espagne avant de poursuivre un destin aventureux aux Indes et en Angleterre et de rejoindre simplement le Louvre en 1976.

Quiconque serait passé brutalement des premières journées révolutionnaires de 89, empreintes d'idéalisme bon enfant, à la confusion extrême qui régnait en 1792 dans les rues, les esprits et les cercles politiques, n'aurait certes pas reconnu le Faubourg dont on avait déniché les saints. La transformation s'était opérée progressivement, au gré d'événements le plus souvent inattendus, et la citoyenne

1. L'avenue Montaigne aujourd'hui.

Antoinette Œben avait comme tout le monde, sans s'en apercevoir, changé sa façon de vivre et de voir les choses.

Que restait-il du Faubourg d'antan alors que quatre ateliers sur cinq étaient fermés et que ceux qui avaient résisté à l'endormissement progressif du quartier, travaillaient au ralenti ? L'amour du métier, la passion du bois qui avaient enfanté tant de chefs-d'œuvre, s'étaient dilués dans l'inaction. Emprisonnée, émigrée ou simplement anxieuse du lendemain, la clientèle s'était évanouie aux notes de *La Carmagnole*. Seuls quelques maîtres et compagnons fabriquaient encore des meubles usuels où la sculpture et la marqueterie n'avaient plus leur place, du moins dans la forme précieuse et élaborée qui avait fait la gloire du Faubourg. Sur le bois banal d'un mobilier modeste et utilitaire, les artistes d'hier sculptaient, quand ils en avaient l'occasion, des motifs révolutionnaires naïfs : faisceaux de licteur, bonnets phrygiens, piques et drapeaux. Oubliés les bois rares dans lesquels les Riesener et les Molitor fignolaient de prodigieuses marqueteries. Aujourd'hui, pour survivre, les anciens fournisseurs des princes fabriquaient des crosses de fusil tandis que les serruriers et les ciseleurs de bronzes affûtaient des sabres et forgeaient des canons de fusils.

Dans ce désordre où la foi révolutionnaire côtoyait la compromission, où l'amour de l'art était dévoré par la pauvreté, Jean-Henri Riesener ne pouvait qu'être malheureux. Il avait cessé de travailler à des chefs-d'œuvre invendables et traînait ses regrets d'atelier en atelier. Il n'y rencontrait que des confrères appauvris, découragés et allait finalement chercher quelque réconfort chez sa belle-fille Antoinette. Elle était la seule à s'intéresser à lui, la seule avec qui il pouvait parler de son métier et du Faubourg. Son fils Henri-François ne venait le voir que rarement. Bon peintre sans génie, il vivait en faisant le portrait des nouveaux hommes politiques, députés ou commissaires, qu'il peignait avantageusement coiffés de leur bicorne à cocarde. Il ne s'était jamais intéressé aux meubles ni à l'art de son père, et le temps ne faisait qu'accroître le fossé qui les séparait. Antoinette, au contraire, aimait écouter Riesener lui parler du bois, des meubles extraordinaires qu'il avait inventés et en particulier de ce fameux bureau du roi, commencé par Œben et achevé par lui comme un devoir sacré.

Ce soir-là, Réveillon était venu se joindre à eux. Antoinette était contente d'avoir auprès d'elle ses « deux pères » comme elle les appelait. Tous deux en effet, après la mort d'Œben, avaient joué auprès de la jeune fille le rôle de tuteurs affectueux et généreux. Elle leur en était reconnaissante. Son plaisir était d'autant plus grand qu'elle attendait Valfroy et surtout Alexandre Lenoir qui, tenant sa promesse, avait annoncé sa visite. Dire qu'Antoinette tenait salon serait exagéré mais elle aimait, le soir, réunir ses amis et les écouter raconter les dernières péripéties de la politique ou, plus simplement, les mille faits qui bouleversaient chaque jour l'horizon.

Lenoir conquit tout de suite les trois hommes par sa gentillesse et sa liberté de ton. Riesener qui tremblait pour les meubles qu'il avait construits, qui souffrait chaque fois qu'une de ses commodes avait subi des déprédations, ne pouvait qu'être passionné par la mission salvatrice de ce jeune homme à l'air bien tranquille qui vous disait, comme s'il s'agissait de la chose la plus banale du monde, qu'il avait dans l'après-midi badigeonné de blanc les statues de bronze provenant du tombeau des Condé et les avait fait passer pour du marbre afin qu'elles échappent à la fonte.

– Ne négligez pas les meubles, monsieur Lenoir. Il y a des merveilles qu'il faut aussi sauver. J'espère que les voleurs des bijoux de la Couronne n'ont pas endommagé les œuvres de Boulle, par exemple. Quant à moi, j'ai pris une décision : je vais racheter à l'administration du Garde-meuble les pièces qui portent mon estampille et que je trouve les mieux réussies. Je sais bien que mon genre n'est plus à la mode et que le peu de meubles qu'on fabrique encore doivent être conformes aux nouvelles règles de David sur le retour à l'antique. Mais cela ne durera pas et vous verrez que dans quelques années, peut-être quelques mois, je revendrai mes bureaux et mes commodes trois fois le prix que je les aurai payés.

– Crois-tu vraiment que cette opération soit raisonnable? demanda Antoinette.

– Je ne sais qu'une chose, c'est que je vais payer en assignats un bon bois verni et poli comme un ventre de femme, marqueté d'essences précieuses et garni de bronzes sublimes... Et puis, si ce n'est pas moi qui les revends, ce sera plus tard ta petite Lucie. Tiens, je lui en fais cadeau, de mes meubles. A une condition, pourtant, c'est qu'elle en conserve quelques-uns pour penser de temps en temps à ce vieux fou de Riesener qui, finalement, n'aura vécu que pour son bois et ses bronzes.

– C'est gentil pour nous ce que tu dis là. C'est gentil pour ma pauvre mère qui t'a tellement aimé et dont la mort a failli te rendre fou.

– Allons, ma bonne Antoinette, ne me fais pas dire ce que je n'ai pas voulu dire. Tu vois, j'aime encore mieux passer mon temps à racheter mes meubles et à attendre des jours meilleurs que de flatter David, comme le fait Georges Jacob, pour obtenir des commandes officielles.

– Ne sois pas injuste pour Jacob. Il est comme toi un grand créateur et sûrement le meilleur menuisier de sièges de notre époque.

Cette passe d'armes amusait Alexandre Lenoir, ravi d'entrer dans l'intimité de ces gens du bois, de ces citoyens du Faubourg dont il ne connaissait que les chefs-d'œuvre et la légende.

– Vos meubles, heureusement, craignent moins aujourd'hui que les statues et les livres mais soyez sûr que s'ils sont un jour en danger, nous les sauverons. Quant au fauteuil-trône qu'a construit Jacob pour le président de l'Assemblée vous refuseriez de le signer, pas plus que le bureau supporté par deux chimères assez ridicules. Si Jacob s'est abaissé pour obtenir cette commande, il a eu bien tort.

Antoinette guettait du coin de l'œil son parrain Réveillon. Il n'avait encore rien dit mais prenait l'air goguenard qu'elle lui connaissait bien : il attendait son heure pour annoncer quelque chose d'important. Comme elle était curieuse, elle résolut de faire avancer les choses :

– Parrain, vous nous cachez quelque chose. Qu'allez-vous nous apprendre? Fabriquez-vous une nouvelle montgolfière, installez-vous une autre fabrique de papier peint?

– Riesener achète, moi je vends. Je viens de céder ma manufacture de la Folie Titon aux citoyens Jacquemard et Bénard. J'ai fait une bonne affaire, eux aussi. Je ne souhaite qu'une chose : c'est qu'ils soutiennent la réputation de la maison et qu'ils continuent de faire travailler et vivre les trois cents ouvriers qui me restent.

– Ainsi Réveillon n'est plus au Faubourg! dit Valfroy. Voilà une page tournée. Et une page qui comptera dans l'histoire de ce vieux quartier que je regrette bien de n'avoir connu que dans les troubles de la Révolution. Je n'ai même pas pu admirer votre Folie que les émeutiers ont saccagée stupidement...

– Moi, je ne regrette rien. Un peu comme M. Lenoir, j'ai sauvé une première fois sous l'Ancien Régime, ce splendide petit palais de la pioche des démolisseurs. Je l'ai restauré et j'y ai mis les plus belles choses que j'ai pu trouver. Le destin, aidé par quelques fous manipulés, a eu raison de ces pierres innocentes. Tant pis, on construira à la place des ateliers... C'est tout de même dommage pour le quartier et pour Paris! Mais vous savez que je n'avais jamais pardonné une chose, une seule aux imbéciles d'avril 89 : m'avoir volé la médaille d'or que le roi m'avait décernée en 1785...

– On l'a retrouvée? coupa Antoinette en riant.

– Non, ma belle. On ne l'a pas retrouvée mais l'Assemblée m'en donne une autre en remplacement!

– L'Assemblée? demanda Valfroy. Auriez-vous réussi ce tour de force?

– Tenez mon ami. Lisez vous-même cette copie apostillée d'un décret daté du 14 mai. Il retira de sa poche une feuille de papier et la tendit à Bertrand qui lut, tout haut :

« Le 14 mai de l'an deuxième de la Liberté, l'Assemblée nationale a décrété que cette médaille serait donnée à

Jean-Baptiste Réveillon en remplacement du prix d'encouragement aux arts utiles, qu'il avait reçu du roi en 1786 pour services par lui rendus à l'art de la papeterie et qui lui fut enlevé au pillage de sa maison le 28 avril 1789. »

– Ainsi vous avez réussi ! dit Antoinette. Nous avons bien ri de vos démarches que nous pensions vouées à l'échec... Et aujourd'hui, la Révolution vous rend ce qu'elle vous avait pris ! Mais, maintenant que vous avez récupéré votre bien, dites-nous pour quelle raison vous vous êtes acharné à réclamer cette médaille ? En aviez-vous tellement envie ? D'un homme comme vous, c'est difficilement croyable.

– C'est justement d'un homme comme moi qu'une chose aussi saugrenue pouvait arriver. Au lendemain du pillage où nous avons bien failli laisser notre vie, Antoinette et moi, j'ai senti que nous allions traverser une période de troubles et de folie. J'ai alors décidé que je me retirais du jeu des affaires. J'ai loué ma fabrique en attendant de la vendre et j'ai refusé un peu plus tard de me mêler aux juteuses opérations sur l'achat et la vente des biens nationaux où l'on voulait m'entraîner. Seulement, je suis un joueur. Comme les tripots du Palais-Royal m'écœuraient, il fallait que je me trouve un jeu ou plutôt un pari difficile à tenter. Quel adversaire à la fois plus imprévu et plus difficile à battre que le pouvoir révolutionnaire ? J'ai donc pensé à me faire rendre ma médaille, une médaille qui, vous n'en doutez pas, m'est indifférente. « Allons, me disais-je, si tu gagnes c'est que tu n'as rien perdu de cet esprit combatif qui t'a permis de sortir de la pauvreté et de mener une vie agréable ! » Comme vous le voyez, cette médaille est bien plus qu'un petit bout de métal doré, c'est la preuve que je peux encore avoir confiance en moi. Elle me réconforte !

Antoinette était aux anges, heureuse d'avoir retrouvé son Réveillon fantasque et imprévisible. Lenoir, de son côté, découvrait avec un intérêt non dissimulé cet homme original dont l'existence n'avait été qu'une permanente aventure.

– Votre histoire de médaille m'enchante, monsieur Réveillon, mais ne trouvez-vous pas qu'il est dommage de mettre en veilleuse votre énergie, votre imagination, votre esprit d'entreprise?

– Je vous l'ai dit, cher monsieur, je me suis mis en congé révolutionnaire. Comme je ne veux pas me mêler de politique, que je me vois mal en orateur d'assemblée et que je refuse de gagner facilement de l'argent en trafiquant, il ne me reste qu'à regarder mes contemporains s'entre-déchirer. Cela m'attriste mais il faut avouer que nous vivons une époque passionnante et qu'il pourrait tout de même bien sortir du bon de ce désordre sanglant...

– Et pourquoi ne viendriez-vous pas travailler avec moi? Votre goût et votre connaissance de l'art sont unanimement reconnus. Vous pourriez m'aider à sauver maints chefs-d'œuvre de la destruction.

– Cela me plairait beaucoup mais je me suis juré de ne jamais accepter un poste ou une occupation officiels. Je refuse d'être acteur dans la pièce qui se joue actuellement. Je ne veux être qu'un spectateur!

– J'y pense, coupa Antoinette, n'avez-vous pas besoin d'un aide fort et dévoué qui transporterait vos livres, vos tableaux et peindrait vos statues? Je songe à notre protégé Ethis dont l'atelier vient de fermer faute de travail et dont l'inactivité me soucie. Je m'inquiète de ce qu'il traîne son oisiveté et son ruban de « vainqueur de la Bastille » dans toutes les manifestations de rues. Il est inculte et ne saura pas choisir l'œuvre qu'il faut sauver, mais si vous la lui désignez, il la sauvera! Faites cela pour nous et aussi pour vous, M. Lenoir.

– Pourquoi pas? J'ai besoin de bras solides. Où est-il, ce garçon?

– Il ne va sûrement pas tarder, nous vous le présenterons.

– N'y manquez pas. Je vais ces jours-ci visiter quelques brocanteurs du tour de Paris qui ont paraît-il récupéré des statues. Je vais les leur racheter ou les échanger contre des dalles de marbre que j'ai trouvées dans les décombres de l'église des Célestins. Votre Ethis me sera bien utile.

Voilà comment Ethis, l'enfant trouvé de chez Réveillon, « vainqueur de la Bastille » et parrain de Lucie, devint l'aide fidèle et bientôt indispensable d'Alexandre Lenoir, conservateur sans titre du dépôt des Petits-Augustins, asile des saints de pierre, des monarques de bronze et des princesses de Carrare.

Valfroy, lui, dut abandonner son poste au ministère. Personne n'avait mis en cause sa compétence mais son état de « ci-devant » et son passé au service des finances du roi, devenaient, avec les événements, des tares de moins en moins supportables pour les nouveaux maîtres du Trésor public. Il était inimaginable que Bertrand demeurât inactif. Un moment, il songea à entrer dans les affaires, à prendre une part dans l'une des nombreuses officines commerciales ouvertes depuis la vente des biens nationaux. Il rentra horrifié d'un court séjour dans un bureau spécialisé où l'on traitait l'achat et la vente des terres et immeubles confisqués. Commis de l'État, rompu à la rigueur de Necker, il n'avait pu supporter plus de quelques heures les malversations qui marquaient chaque marché ni les nombreux pots-de-vin distribués dans et autour de l'Assemblée :

– Si tous ceux qui se battent pour repousser l'ennemi hors des frontières ou qui défendent les idées de la Révolution contre les royalistes des provinces, savaient ce que l'on fait des biens de la France, je crois qu'ils planteraient leur baïonnette en terre et reviendraient mettre de l'ordre à Paris !

Antoinette, peu habituée à voir son mari tenir des propos aussi violents, le calma de son mieux :

– Mais tu savais tout cela, mon ami, Réveillon en a souvent parlé ici. Il est plus facile d'honorer la vertu que de la pratiquer. Il y a tout de même beaucoup de gens honnêtes parmi les ministres et les députés, et la Révolution saura bien un jour faire le ménage dans ses communs et ses palais. Ce travail n'est pas fait pour toi. Oublie tout ça et cherche une occupation qui te permettra de servir l'État et non de le voler.

– Tu as raison, mais il fallait que je me soulage. Tu vois, en face d'une telle scélératesse, je finis par comprendre Robespierre, l'Incorruptible, dont j'exècre pourtant la politique cruelle et dogmatique.

C'est finalement Riesener qui trouva une place à Bertrand de Valfroy. Le secrétaire-trésorier de la section des Enfants-Trouvés venait d'être nommé commissaire aux subsistances et l'on cherchait un remplaçant. La candidature du citoyen Perrin, dont personne n'ignorait la vraie personnalité, fut l'objet de longues discussions mais en fin de compte, les plus enragés des sans-culottes acceptèrent l'homme honnête et compétent, le mari d'Antoinette Œben, fille du Faubourg. La situation aurait pu être inconfortable mais Valfroy eut l'intelligence d'en retenir d'abord l'aspect enrichissant. Passer d'un ministère royal, où son poste auprès de Necker lui avait longtemps assuré une flatteuse considération, à la section sans-culottes la plus agitée de Paris n'était pas un itinéraire banal. A la cour, il avait vécu de très loin les débuts de la Révolution. A la place d'Aligre, chez Antoinette, il s'était rapproché des réalités. Maintenant, il se trouvait en plein cœur de cette mouvance, en perpétuelle mutation, dont le double visage, comme celui de Janus, reflétait tantôt le passé, tantôt l'avenir et pouvait passer de l'idéalisme touchant et doux à la violence la plus féroce. Pour la première fois, Valfroy se trouvait au contact direct de ceux qui représentaient la vraie force révolutionnaire. Il trouvait cela passionnant et observait en entomologiste cette fourmilière dont les issues semblaient bouchées. Comme personne n'enviait sa fonction et qu'il savait parler aux hommes avec adresse, il était respecté : « Bien plus qu'à la cour ! » disait-il en riant.

Si la section a été présente aux Tuileries le 10 août, elle n'avait guère fait parler d'elle durant les jours terribles des massacres de septembre. Les égorgeurs de l'abbaye, de la Force et de Bicêtre n'avaient pas été recrutés au Faubourg. Valfroy raconta en rentrant, le soir du 3 septembre, que ceux du district avaient même dans leur grande majorité été horrifiés par la sauvagerie avec laquelle cent cinquante ou deux cents tueurs avaient en quelques heures liquidé les suspects, les prisonniers de droit commun et même les pensionnaires de la Salpêtrière. Deux semaines plus tard, il rapportait heureusement une nouvelle plus glorieuse : le recul des Prussiens à Valmy.

Le pouls du Faubourg continuait à battre dans un corps affaibli, vidé d'une grande partie de son sang par les levées de volontaires dont beaucoup rentraient estropiés ou blessés quand ils n'étaient pas morts quelque part dans l'Est ou dans le Nord, la tête emportée par un boulet. Valmy, Jemmapes... les victoires redonnaient courage à ceux qui traînaient leur misère dans les rues et les passages déserts. Seuls quelques ateliers de menuisiers et d'ébénistes travaillaient pour meubler les ministères et les bureaux administratifs. Ceux qui abritaient des chaudronniers, des forgerons ou des cloutiers avaient été déclarés ateliers publics réservés à la fabrication des armes. C'est ainsi que, petit à petit, l'atelier de quincaillerie de Dauffe, qui fournissait depuis des générations les ébénistes du Faubourg, voyait son activité augmenter. Le nombre des ouvriers, 62 au début, atteignait au bout de quatre mois le chiffre de 264. L'atelier des platines occupait 182 ouvriers répartis par groupes de dix. A l'atelier des forges travaillaient 18 forgerons et 18 « tire-soufflets ».

L'atelier le plus spectaculaire, celui autour duquel s'agglutinaient les gosses était celui de l'émoulerie de baïonnettes. Un manège de 8 chevaux tournait inlassablement dans le claquement des fouets et l'odeur du crottin pour entraîner 12 meules qui crachaient des étincelles chaque fois qu'un ouvrier y appuyait de toute sa force la baïonnette qu'il voulait affûter [1].

C'est là qu'aurait sans doute travaillé Ethis s'il n'était

1. A la fin de l'an II l'émoulerie du Faubourg façonnait 9 000 baïonnettes par mois.

pas devenu le factotum d'Alexandre Lenoir. Le garçon était intelligent et il ne lui avait pas fallu longtemps pour apprendre à connaître dans les amas de pierres et de marbre les belles pièces qu'il fallait sauver. Cet instinct du beau étonnait Lenoir qui s'était pris d'affection pour Ethis à qui il s'efforçait d'enseigner les rudiments d'une science qui n'avait pas de nom et qu'il appelait la philosophie des formes.

Chaque journée était une aventure. Lenoir ne savait jamais ce qu'il allait trouver là où les vandales étaient passés ni s'il lui faudrait chicaner ou même se battre – cela lui était arrivé à la Sorbonne – pour préserver de la destruction ou de la fonte quelque chef-d'œuvre authentique. Rien ne pouvait plaire davantage à Ethis que cette vie hors du commun, pleine de surprises et qui lui donnait l'impression d'être quelqu'un. Le soir, il avait hâte de raconter à Antoinette comment s'était passée la journée. Aussi intéressée qu'amusée, elle l'écoutait décrire les pièces qu'ils avaient réussi à mettre en lieu sûr. Ethis parlait de Germain Pilon ou de Jean Goujon comme il parlait hier du brasseur Santerre. Valfroy partageait le soulagement d'Antoinette de savoir le garçon occupé intelligemment et soustrait aux dangers de la rue révolutionnaire.

Alexandre Lenoir était naturellement devenu un familier du deuxième étage de la place d'Aligre. Souvent, il reconduisait Ethis dans son carrosse déglingué et Antoinette lui offrait de partager le souper familial. C'étaient alors, autour de la soupière d'où s'échappait rarement un fumet de poule ou de cochon, d'interminables histoires dans lesquelles la gentille Lucie ne manquait pas de mettre son grain de sel.

Le petit choc au cœur qu'avait ressenti Antoinette le jour où elle avait rencontré Alexandre n'avait pas laissé de trace, en apparence, dans son esprit. Elle entretenait avec lui des relations amicales que, pour rien au monde, ni l'un ni l'autre n'aurait osé modifier. Tous deux savaient bien, sans se l'être jamais avoué, qu'un sentiment tout autre que l'amitié éclaterait le jour où l'équilibre précaire de leurs rapports viendrait à se rompre. « Quand on vit sur une poudrière, on ne bat pas le briquet! » se répétait Antoinette qui n'ignorait pas que la moindre étincelle imprudente causerait la fin de leurs relations. Or elle voulait continuer de voir Alexandre, il lui semblait même que son absence prolongée lui serait insupportable. Malgré le danger qu'il pouvait présenter, ce jeu inavoué et discrètement pervers ne lui déplaisait pas. Elle y retrouvait le parfum de ses premières rencontres avec Pilâtre de Rozier et se disait que ces frémissements émotifs n'étaient pas bien méchants, qu'ils ne faisaient de mal à personne, surtout pas à Bertrand qu'elle aimait tendrement et qu'elle ne tromperait jamais.

Le remplacement de l'Assemblée législative par la Convention n'aurait pas apporté de changement notable dans la vie familiale à laquelle la Révolution imprimait une sorte d'alanguissement, de platitude et de pauvreté, sans l'élection de Charles Delacroix. Le mari de Victoire Œben avait enfin réussi à sortir de l'ombre où l'avaient plongé les événements de 89. Choisi comme député par ses concitoyens de la Marne, il était revenu avec femme et enfants à Paris, ou plutôt à Charenton-Saint-Maurice.

Antoinette ne portait pas son beau-frère dans son cœur. Son ralliement aux Montagnards sur les bancs de la Convention n'avait pas arrangé les choses; mais elle était contente d'avoir retrouvé sa sœur. Victoire venait aussi souvent que possible place d'Aligre, heureuse de se replonger dans le quartier de sa jeunesse et de reprendre avec « Toinette », comme elle l'avait toujours appelée, une conversation interrompue depuis tant d'années.

Au temps de leur jeunesse, les deux sœurs avaient été voltairiennes et libérales tout en restant attachées au roi, comme Œben et Riesener. L'attitude opportuniste de son mari déplaisait à Victoire qui confiait ses désillusions à Antoinette :

– Je crois bien, ma petite sœur, que je n'ai pas fait le bon choix. J'ai été subjuguée par l'intelligence et la culture de Charles. Tu te rappelles combien de fois nous

nous sommes juré de n'épouser que des hommes intelligents? L'ambition, hélas! lui fausse complètement l'esprit. Il pense qu'il est bien, en ce moment, de hurler avec les loups et je crois qu'il est prêt à toutes les compromissions...

– Bref, tu ne l'aimes plus guère...

– Non, mais que veux-tu, il y a les enfants, il y a les intérêts communs, il y a aussi le fait qu'il m'aime et qu'il est gentil avec moi... Je me fais tout de même mal à l'idée d'avoir un mari jacobin. Et un Jacobin excité de surcroît! A propos, sais-tu qu'on va juger Louis Capet? La Convention doit en décider aujourd'hui et, bien qu'il n'ait pas osé me le dire, je suis sûr que l'ancien commis de M. Turgot va enfoncer ce roi qu'il était si fier de servir!

Non seulement Charles Delacroix appuya par un discours violent la diatribe de Saint-Just: « On ne peut régner innocemment, la folie en est trop évidente. Tout roi est un usurpateur », mais il se rangea le 16 janvier aux côtés des partisans de Robespierre. Quand, vers 20 h 15, son nom fut appelé de la tribune présidentielle, le député de la Marne se leva de son banc et déclara d'une voix blanche qu'il votait la mort du roi sans sursis.

– Nous avons un régicide dans la famille! annonça un peu plus tard Valfroy qui était demeuré à la section jusqu'à ce que le résultat du vote fût connu.

– 384 députés ont voté la mort, ajouta-t-il. 334 l'ont refusée. L'avenir dira si Delacroix a servi sa carrière en envoyant Louis XVI à l'échafaud. Pour ma part, je l'aurais laissé enfermé au Temple...

Ethis essaya de dire qu'une révolution qui ne tue pas les rois n'est pas une vraie révolution. Cet avis sans nuance lui valut une sévère admonestation d'Antoinette.

– Comment peux-tu parler ainsi? Tu es trop jeune pour émettre des opinions aussi graves. Attends d'avoir un peu plus de plomb dans la tête!

Antoinette, pour une fois, ne goûta pas le sens du paradoxe qui constituait pour elle l'un des charmes d'Alexandre Lenoir quand celui-ci, avec son sourire en coin qui avait le pouvoir de séduire comme celui d'agacer, lui coupa la parole :

– Pourquoi vous en prendre à Ethis, ma chère Antoinette ? D'abord il a gagné en prenant la Bastille la liberté de penser ce qu'il lui plaît. Ensuite l'opinion qu'il exprime, pour n'être pas la vôtre, ni la mienne, relève d'un sens politique certain. Il a dit en trois mots exemplaires ce dont discourent depuis des jours les orateurs les plus illustres de la Convention. Tenez, lisez, ajouta-t-il en tirant de sa poche *Le Moniteur* : « Les peuples ne rendent pas de sentences, ils lancent la foudre. Ils ne condamnent pas les rois, ils les replongent dans le néant ! » Je trouve la phrase d'Ethis bien supérieure à ce galimatias prétentieux de Robespierre. La place d'Ethis, je vous le dis, est à la Convention !

– Alexandre, vous êtes ridicule ! s'exclama Antoinette rouge de colère. Vous êtes aussi un être dangereux. Pour faire des mots, vous risquez de tourner la tête de ce garçon. Vous me décevez !

Ethis qui décidément se révélait fine mouche et qui détestait voir s'affronter à son sujet deux êtres qui lui étaient chers, eut le mot de la fin :

– Ne craignez rien Antoinette. J'ai la tête solide. Elle pense peut-être comme Robespierre mais elle restera sûrement plus longtemps que la sienne sur les épaules.

On rit mais Lenoir, comme Antoinette et Valfroy, se montra intraitable quand Ethis dit qu'il voulait assister à l'exécution du roi.

– Même dans une révolution c'est un spectacle horrible et malsain. Tiens, ton modèle Maximilien Robespierre, avec son œil froid et ses cheveux poudrés, se gardera bien d'aller voir tuer celui qu'il a condamné. Et puis, le 21, j'ai besoin de toi pour transporter une tête colossale de Minerve que j'ai repérée dans les décombres du cabinet de Montfaucon, à Saint-Germain-des-Prés. Tête pour tête nous préférons que tu t'intéresses à celle d'Athéna, déesse de l'intelligence, plutôt qu'à celle de ce pauvre Capet.

Le lendemain, Victoire profita de la voiture qui conduisait son mari à la Convention pour aller passer un moment près de sa sœur. Le vote de la veille l'avait bouleversée.

– Le nom de mes enfants restera attaché à cette condamnation. Que Charles soit mêlé à toutes ces basses besognes de la Révolution ne me plaît pas et je crois que nous ne sommes pas au bout des violences et des luttes intestines. Quand je lui parle de mon aversion et de mes craintes, il me répond que je n'ai pas de soucis à me faire et qu'il sera assez malin pour échapper à tous les pièges de la politique. Le pire c'est que c'est sans doute vrai et cela me fait encore plus horreur. Avec notre père et Riesener nous n'avons pas été habituées à toutes ces manœuvres, à ces intrigues, à cette haine qui oppose ceux qui sont censés travailler pour la même cause. Eux marchaient dans le droit fil du bois, ils ne construisaient pas leur œuvre avec des discours mais avec leurs mains. Tiens, j'aurais dû épouser le fils de Georges Jacob qui était amoureux de moi et ne pas me laisser prendre aux belles paroles de Delacroix, premier commis de Turgot au contrôle général des finances. Je me voyais déjà à la cour, affublée d'un « de Contaut » que mon soupirant comptait ajouter à son nom. Finalement j'ai passé presque toute mon existence dans des bourgs perdus, loin de toi, loin de tout ce que j'aimais. Et aujourd'hui, si mon avocat de campagne retrouve quelque notoriété, c'est en se mettant au service de nos nouveaux rois, ceux de la Révolution!

– Calme-toi ma chérie. Ton mari n'est tout de même pas un monstre. Être la femme d'un député de la Convention n'est pas non plus une position négligeable. Regarde Mme Roland, elle a autant de pouvoir que son mari le ministre, peut-être même plus.

– Tu me vois en égérie du député de la Marne? Enfin, tu as peut-être raison, il faut vivre et attendre. Tiens, à propos de vivre, mon conventionnel de mari aurait très bien pu se faire embrocher hier soir au Palais-Royal.

– Comment cela?

– Il dînait chez le restaurateur Février avec Le Pelletier de Saint-Fargeau et Maure un autre député. Soudain six particuliers sortirent d'un cabinet voisin et apostrophèrent Saint-Fargeau : « Le voilà ce coquin, ce scélérat de Saint-Fargeau qui vient de voter la mort du roi ! – Oui, je suis Saint-Fargeau et j'ai voté comme ma conscience me l'ordonnait ! » A ces mots, l'un des hommes, on sut plus tard que c'était un ancien garde du corps du roi, sortit de sous son habit un petit sabre nu qu'on appelle « briquet » et l'enfonça dans le ventre de Saint-Fargeau.

– Il n'en voulait qu'à Saint-Fargeau? Il ne s'est pas attaqué à l'autre député ni à ton mari?

– Non. Il avait hâte de se sauver, protégé par ses amis. Tu vois, s'il avait aussi embroché mon mari, tu aurais devant toi la veuve d'un martyr de la Révolution...

– Ne plaisante pas avec des événements aussi terribles. Viens plutôt un de ces jours partager notre maigre souper avec ton mari. Je le connais à peine. Sans doute aura-t-il beaucoup de choses à nous raconter. Tiens, j'inviterai aussi un ami que j'aime bien, Alexandre Lenoir qui tire des décombres, non pas les marrons du feu comme beaucoup, mais les chefs-d'œuvre qu'il sauve de la destruction.

– Dis donc, tu parles de ce monsieur avec beaucoup d'emballement ! Y aurait-il anguille sous roche? Serais-tu infidèle à ce bon M. de Valfroy?

– Tu es folle, coupa Antoinette en rougissant. Je n'ai nulle envie de tromper mon mari. Si tu veux mon avis, c'est ton député qui sera cocu le premier.

– Allons, ma Toinette, ne te défends pas comme ça. Après tout, s'il te plaît, je ne vois pas pourquoi tu te priverais. N'oublie pas que nous sommes en révolution et que les têtes commencent à tomber un peu partout en France. Moi, je t'assure que si je rencontrais quelqu'un d'aimable, qui sache me parler d'autre chose que d'argent et de citations en justice, je n'hésiterais pas une seconde.

– Que te voilà changée, ma sœur ! Je me rappelle le temps pas si lointain où tu me reprochais de vivre avec

Pilâtre alors que nous n'étions pas mariés. Aujourd'hui, tu es prête à tromper ton mari et tu m'encourages à tromper le mien!

La petite Lucie dormait dans le lit de princesse que Riesener lui avait fabriqué avec amour lorsque le berceau de Jean Marot était devenu trop petit. Le temps ne manquait pas à l'ancien ébéniste du roi qui refusait de transformer son atelier en fabrique de crosses de fusils: «Il y a bien assez de compagnons au Faubourg qui ont besoin de travailler pour manger, disait-il, ajoutant: et puis, si je faisais des crosses de fusils, je ne pourrais pas m'empêcher de les fignoler, de les poncer, et même de les sculpter, pourquoi pas? Une crosse taillée dans un bon bois, cela peut être un petit objet d'art. Mais ce n'est pas ce que l'armée demande, alors je préfère m'abstenir!»

En revanche, le lit de Lucie avait bénéficié de ses soins et de son talent en jachère. Pas de bronzes, pas de surcharges, tout tenait dans les formes et la pureté des courbes. Seul un petit fronton sculpté dans du noyer au grain fin représentant un ange décorait la partie supérieure du fond de lit et semblait veiller sur le repos de la petite fille. A Lenoir qui, pour le taquiner, lui avait dit qu'il aurait dû sculpter de préférence des attributs révolutionnaires, il avait répondu qu'il ne laisserait jamais personne lui choisir un dieu, même pas Robespierre, et qu'il restait fidèle à Jésus auquel croyait sa mère, sa grand-mère et tous ceux qui avaient porté son nom.

Ce soir-là, Ethis allait et venait dans la chambre, regardait dormir Lucie, remontait la couverture sur son menton et regardait Antoinette à la dérobée. Celle-ci, qui connaissait bien son «vainqueur» s'amusait du manège, voyant bien que le garçon cherchait comment il pourrait bien lui dire ce qu'elle croyait avoir deviné.

Enfin il s'approcha de celle qu'il considérait comme sa mère et se lança:

– Antoinette, j'ai un secret que je veux vous faire

partager mais promettez-moi de ne pas le raconter à d'autres. Voilà : je crois que j'aime une jeune fille. Mais de vrai amour, vous savez!

– Mais c'est merveilleux, s'exclama-t-elle. Aimer est la dernière chose dont il faut avoir honte. Est-ce que tu veux me dire quelle jeune fille, née sous une bonne étoile, a su retenir ton regard de « vainqueur »? Est-ce que je la connais?

– Je crois que oui. D'ailleurs vous connaissez tout le monde dans le quartier. C'est la fille d'Eugène Bénard, le commissaire civil de Popincourt.

Antoinette le regarda, étonnée.

– Une fille Bénard? Mais tu sais que c'est son père qui a racheté avec Jacquemard la fabrique de Réveillon?

– Oui. Et il est commissaire civil.

– D'abord, j'espère que tu as choisi l'une des deux jolies sœurs. Car je crois me souvenir que, sur les quatre filles, il y en a deux qui ne sont pas très belles.

– C'est la plus jeune et la plus jolie, celle qui s'appelle Marie.

– Et elle, est-ce qu'elle t'aime? Est-ce que tu lui as parlé?

– Oui, un peu.

– Comment cela un peu! Quand on aime quelqu'un on ne lui parle pas « un peu », on se jette à l'eau, on lui crie, on lui chante qu'on l'aime!...

– Je crois vraiment qu'elle a compris. Elle accepte de se promener avec moi.

– Alors c'est bien. Mais ne te monte pas trop la tête. Vous êtes très jeunes tous les deux et son père est riche...

– Cela n'a pas tellement d'importance aujourd'hui. La Révolution est passée par là, tous les hommes sont égaux!

– Ah! Tu crois cela? Ce n'est pas, hélas, parce qu'on a coupé la tête du roi qu'il n'existe plus ni pauvres ni riches. Même en pleine révolution il y a des pauvres gens qui souffrent de la faim et d'autres qui vivent dans le luxe et dînent dans les grands restaurants du « camp des

Tartares [1] ». Je te dis cela mon petit Ethis parce que je ne veux pas que tu sois un jour désespéré et que tu souffres. Tu comprends?

Ethis ne cherchait pas tellement à comprendre. Il découvrait l'amour et était fier de se promener le soir, avec Marie accrochée à son bras, dans les passages de la Boule-blanche ou de la Main-d'or où les planches empilées formaient des labyrinthes connus depuis toujours par les amoureux du Faubourg. Il y flottait une odeur de sève et de résine qui rappelait la forêt, un parfum enivrant qui avait fait bien des fois tourner la tête aux filles du quartier.

Marie était sage et Ethis timide. Leurs rendez-vous se traduisaient par quelques baisers échangés entre chêne et sapin. Ils n'en étaient pas moins heureux. Comme les horreurs du temps étaient loin quand le garçon pressait contre lui le corps fragile de la jeune fille et embrassait son cou enserré dans une corolle de linon à petites lignes tricolores. Le soir, pourtant, Ethis qui était un tendre dans sa carapace de sans-culotte, frémissait à la pensée que des jeunes filles à peine plus âgées que Marie et dont le cou était aussi blanc et doux que le sien étaient parfois conduites à la guillotine...

Par Valfroy on apprit un jour chez Antoinette que la Convention venait de créer le tribunal révolutionnaire malgré l'opposition de quelques Girondins, en particulier de Vergniaud qui s'était écrié à la tribune : « C'est une inquisition mille fois plus redoutable que celle de Venise que vous nous demandez d'instituer! »

Ce tribunal-guillotine jugeait sans appel tous ceux qui étaient soupçonnés de comploter contre la liberté, l'égalité, l'unité, l'indivisibilité de la République. C'était le début d'une période sanglante durant laquelle la Révolution, comme Saturne, allait dévorer ses propres enfants. Cette fureur de mort inquiétait Valfroy, qui en notait les

1. On appelait ainsi la partie du Palais-Royal qui abritait les restaurants célèbres et était devenue un étonnant carrefour de la prostitution.

échos dans la section où il œuvrait bénévolement pour le bien public.

– Tout le monde m'estime, disait-il, pourtant je sens qu'un jour je ne serai plus en sécurité parmi ces gens qui apprécient les services que je rends; mais quitter mon poste me rendrait encore plus vulnérable. Attendons des temps meilleurs.

A ces discours pessimistes, le mari de Victoire qu'on voyait maintenant de temps en temps place d'Aligre répondait par des tirades patriotiques empruntées aux chefs jacobins. Charles Delacroix n'était pas aimé chez Antoinette mais celle-ci disait qu'elle ne pouvait pas interdire sa porte à son beau-frère et qu'une attitude trop hostile envers le député risquait un jour d'être dangereuse. C'était la sagesse. Lenoir, encore plus réaliste, s'était dit qu'il fallait utiliser cette relation et obtenir grâce à Delacroix de nouveaux moyens pour accomplir sa besogne de brancardier des statues.

Trop heureux de se montrer sous un jour flatteur et de faire valoir son pouvoir, Delacroix avait obtenu de la Convention un décret augmentant sensiblement les ressources de Lenoir et mettant à sa disposition une deuxième voiture provenant d'une saisie chez Mme de Genlis qui avait joué un rôle parmi les précieuses de la Révolution avant d'émigrer opportunément. Ethis fut du même coup promu cocher-secrétaire d'Alexandre Lenoir et se vit attribuer un salaire de 36 livres, ce qui, compte tenu de l'inflation des assignats, ne lui permettait pas d'inviter Marie au *Café Hardy* qu'une cuisinière finaude venait d'ouvrir aux Tuileries et où les députés venaient entre deux séances manger une saucisse grillée ou des rognons à la broche.

La jeune Marie, d'ailleurs, n'attendait pas les invitations d'Ethis pour apprendre à bien manger. Sa mère était une remarquable cuisinière. Elle lui avait inculqué les principes de bons rôtisseurs et la jeune fille était capable de préparer comme le célèbre Grateau une soupe d'huîtres ou un chapon farci. Ces dispositions culinaires familiales avaient donné une idée à son père, le papetiercommissaire civil Eugène Balthazar Crescent Bénard. Homme d'affaires ingénieux, il s'était dit que sa femme et sa fille pourraient rédiger un livre de recettes adapté aux circonstances. Ce premier livre de cuisine édité sous le nouveau régime ne pouvait avoir qu'un titre : *La Cuisinière républicaine.* C'est sous cette appellation que parut au printemps de l'an II l'ouvrage des dames Bénard, dont Ethis rapporta triomphalement un exemplaire place d'Aligre. Antoinette qui voyait sans plaisir son Ethis lui échapper examina le livre avec une curiosité exempte de complaisance. Elle dut s'avouer que la mère et la fille savaient de quoi elles parlaient. Manger républicain, c'était avant tout manger des pommes de terre, aussi les recettes étaient presque toutes à base des tubercules chères à M. Parmentier, accommodés aux champignons, à la « sauce Convention » ou tout simplement au lard. Antoinette qui n'avait jamais eu de goût particulier pour la cuisine trouva ces assaisonnements fort savants. Elle en fit compliment à Ethis qui rougit de plaisir.

– Je te promets d'essayer ces recettes, ajouta-t-elle en souriant. Nous verrons comme cela si ta dulcinée est vraiment bonne cuisinière et si tu peux l'épouser plus tard [1].

Sans l'aide de Riesener et de Réveillon la misère eût régné place d'Aligre comme dans tant d'autres familles. L'héritage d'Antoinette avait fondu depuis longtemps et le travail de Valfroy à la section était bénévole. Heureusement l'ébéniste était très aisé et le papetier riche de la vente de ses fabriques. Grâce à leur générosité, la petite Lucie ne manquait de rien et la famille supportait la pénurie qui accablait Paris. La Révolution avait un moment piétiné mais elle éclatait maintenant avec fréné-

1. *La Cuisinière républicaine* n'eut hélas pas le succès escompté : la pénurie devenant générale il fut bientôt impossible de trouver dans les villes les ingrédients indispensables. Les pommes de terre non plus d'ailleurs.

sie, entraînant dans ses engrenages affolés tous ceux qui tentaient de lui résister. Suspecté par la Convention, le général Dumouriez, héros de Valmy et de Jemmapes s'était réfugié dans le camp autrichien et les nouvelles de Vendée n'étaient pas bonnes. Autant de prétextes pour durcir la répression et éliminer les tièdes de la Révolution. La création d'un Comité de salut public, approuvée par toutes les sections de Paris, présageait la chute des Girondins et plongeait dans l'anxiété tous ceux qui avaient cru à une révolution sans excès. C'était le cas chez Antoinette où même le jeune Ethis, sous l'influence d'Alexandre Lenoir, avait perdu beaucoup de sa fougue. Pris au jeu de sa nouvelle fonction, il accablait d'opprobre les vandales et il n'était pas rare de l'entendre dire le soir qu'il avait sauvé trois anges venant de Sainte-Opportune. Ce qui faisait sourire Antoinette et Valfroy qui ne reconnaissaient plus leur petit sans-culotte du Faubourg. C'est pourtant lui qui découvrit dans *L'Ami du Peuple* de Marat que parmi les vingt-cinq membres du Comité de salut public, figurait le nom de Charles Delacroix.

– C'est peut-être notre salut, dit Antoinette à Valfroy. Mon beau-frère te défendra si tu es menacé. C'est sans doute un arriviste mais il n'est pas méchant homme!

– Comment dire aujourd'hui qui est méchant et qui ne l'est pas? Enfin, je ne crois pas que notre beau-frère me fasse guillotiner!

– Tais-toi, ne dis pas des choses pareilles! s'écria Antoinette en se jetant dans les bras de son mari.

Lenoir les regardait sans rien dire. Il hocha la tête, et Antoinette qui surprit son air las et désabusé commença d'avoir peur. Le releveur de statues, comme l'appelait Bertrand, venait de plus en plus souvent place d'Aligre. Il arrivait le soir sans crier gare, attachait la bride de son cheval à un arbre, tirait de son carrosse délabré un objet sauvé qu'il voulait montrer à Riesener et presque toujours un pain blanc enveloppé dans une toile. Le pain noir à la fécule de pomme de terre était le lot de chacun et une flûte de bon froment était un luxe que seuls les gens très aisés pouvaient s'offrir. Encore fallait-il trouver le boulanger qui cuisait à ses risques et périls ce pain défendu.

– Je trompe tous les boulangers de Paris, disait-il en riant quand on lui demandait comment il réussissait à multiplier les petits pains blancs. C'est leurs femmes qui me ravitaillent!

Allez savoir pourquoi, cette explication évidemment fausse ne faisait pas plaisir à Antoinette. Elle ne pouvait s'empêcher de penser qu'il y avait peut-être du vrai dans la boutade de Lenoir et que toutes les boulangères de Paris ne faisaient qu'une, jolie avec ses bras ronds enfarinés, prompte à retrouver Alexandre quand son mari était au pétrin. « Ma parole, serais-je jalouse? s'était-elle demandé plusieurs fois. Et pourquoi donc? Lenoir ne m'est rien, je ne suis pas sa maîtresse et j'aime mon mari... » Toutes ces bonnes raisons, elle le savait bien, n'effaçaient pas l'attirance qu'exerçait sur elle le séduisant Alexandre toujours prêt à raconter un nouvel exploit et à se montrer un ami attentionné. Jamais il ne s'était permis la moindre privauté, sa correction était un exemple de bonne éducation mais la manière dont il la regardait n'en était que plus dangereuse. Antoinette aurait su ruiner une espérance déclarée mais elle restait sans arme devant cette ferveur muette qui la mettait mal à l'aise et la ravissait à la fois.

Un jour, Lenoir arriva frémissant :

– Ça y est, ils vont détruire Saint-Denis! Sur proposition de Barère, la Convention a décidé que « les tombeaux et mausolées des ci-devant rois, élevés en l'église de Franciade [1], dans les temples et autres lieux seraient détruits ».

– Cela va nous donner du travail! s'exclama Ethis d'un air gourmand.

Comme un pompier peut être secrètement alléché par un bel incendie, Ethis n'était pas mécontent d'apprendre qu'un nouvel acte de vandalisme allait donner à Lenoir et

1. La localité de Saint-Denis était maintenant nommée Franciade.

à lui-même l'occasion d'exercer leur compétence. Le jeune homme réussissait d'ailleurs fort bien dans l'infortune artistique et Lenoir ne manquait jamais de le complimenter en public. Laissé longtemps en jachère, son goût se développait en même temps que ses connaissances et il se trompait rarement sur la qualité d'une sculpture découverte au milieu de nombreux débris.

– La destruction des « traces de féodalité qui rappelaient des rois, jusque dans leurs tombeaux, l'effrayant souvenir » – je cite Barras – va se présenter sous un aspect tout à fait nouveau pour nous, dit Lenoir. Pour la première fois, en effet, je vais assister, à la tête de la commission des monuments, à une démolition officiellement décidée et organisée. A charge pour moi de choisir et de conserver les œuvres dignes de figurer dans les richesses artistiques de la France. Autrement dit, je vais me battre avec les piocheurs et essayer de limiter les dégâts. Je compte sur toi pour m'aider, Ethis. N'oublie surtout pas de porter bien visible ton ruban de « vainqueur de la Bastille ». Il impressionnera ceux à qui tu vas retirer sous le pic le buste de Louis XIV et le sceptre de Charles VII.

Les démolisseurs ne chômèrent pas. En trois jours, 51 tombeaux furent renversés, mutilés ou brisés. On avait creusé dans le cimetière deux fosses de trois mètres de profondeur pour y jeter les corps exhumés. Lenoir qui ne s'occupait pas de cette opération macabre nota cependant pour la postérité que dans la première fosse réservée aux Valois on avait précipité 63 corps : 10 rois depuis Dagobert jusqu'à Henri IV, 10 reines, 24 princes et 11 grands personnages dont Suger et Duguesclin. Pour la deuxième fosse, il compta 7 rois, 7 reines et 47 princes et princesses de la maison de Bourbon.

– Le spectacle est affreux, raconta-t-il tandis qu'Antoinette horrifiée se bouchait les oreilles. Pourtant ce matin, le premier cercueil ouvert, celui de Turenne, contenait un corps miraculeusement conservé. Le grand capitaine, en état de momie sèche, avait même conservé sur son visage les traits du buste de marbre qu'Ethis réussit à soustraire à la masse d'un démolisseur.

– L'ont-ils jeté aussi dans la chaux vive? demanda Riesener.

– Non. Les profanateurs, après avoir hésité, ont remis le corps de Turenne au gardien de la cathédrale. Il paraît qu'on l'enverra au jardin des Plantes en qualité de phénomène anatomique [1].

– Les tombeaux devaient être pleins d'objets précieux et de reliques. En avez-vous sauvé quelques-uns?

– Vous voulez le détail, chère Antoinette? Voilà le fruit de nos efforts. Il sortit un carnet de sa poche et lut :

– La couronne de Charles V, l'anneau de Jeanne de Bourbon, les couronnes de Louis XII et d'Anne de Bretagne, le suaire de soie qui enveloppait dans le même coffre de bois le roi Dagobert et la reine Nanthilde, la main de justice de Charles IV... Cela vous suffit? Il y en a encore deux pages... Ah! on a aussi retrouvé dans un reliquaire venant de la Sainte-Chapelle la couronne d'épines du Christ que Saint Louis avait acquise à Constantinople.

– Grâce à vous, en somme, presque toutes les statues de valeur ont pu être sauvées? dit Riesener.

– Ne croyez pas cela! Tenez, le superbe mausolée d'Henri II dû aux talents conjugués de Germain Pilon et de Philibert Delorme a été réduit en morceaux, broyé par la masse d'une bigue. Il a fallu neuf charrettes pour emporter les fragments de marbre.

– Et vous n'avez rien pu faire pour empêchei ce vandalisme?

– Hélas non! Il fallait occuper tous ces bougres qui étaient venus pour démolir et qui entendaient bien jouer de la masse et de la pioche. Pendant qu'ils massacraient Henri II, nous sauvions *Les Trois Grâces* du même Germain Pilon et les mettions en lieu sûr dans mon musée des Petits-Augustins.

– Brisent-ils aussi les meubles? demanda encore Riesener qui aurait donné les plus belles statues de Paris pour

1. Napoléon fera transférer Turenne du jardin des Plantes aux Invalides.

sauver le « bureau du roi », l'œuvre d'Œben qu'il avait achevée après la mort de celui-ci.

– A Paris, non. Certains meubles ont certes été détériorés mais je n'ai pas connaissance qu'on en ait brûlé ou brisé. D'ailleurs ministres, commissaires et secrétaires en ont besoin pour leurs bureaux. Comme il n'est pas question qu'un symbole de l'Ancien Régime figure dans un local officiel, c'est votre ami Beneman qui est chargé de faire disparaître les couronnes et les blasons.

– Je sais, je suis passé hier dans son atelier du passage de la Boule-blanche. Il était en train d'épurer un bureau de six pieds de long, peut-être une œuvre de Gaudreaux, destiné au Comité de salut public. Il substituait des bonnets phrygiens et des faisceaux de piques aux chiffres royaux. Voilà où en est réduit un maître comme Beneman !

Riesener qui avait de quoi vivre s'était refusé à exécuter ce genre de travaux qu'il jugeait dégradants. Pas plus de caisses à munitions que de crosses de fusils, le beau-père d'Antoinette préférait passer son temps à Versailles où la Convention vendait par centaines, chaque jour, les meubles, effets précieux et objets d'art provenant du « ci-devant château royal ». Par un curieux hasard, c'est Charles Delacroix qui, au nom du « Comité d'aliénation » de l'Assemblée signait les affiches annonçant ces ventes par extinction des feux.

– Voilà le mari de ta sœur qui vend Versailles, maintenant! avait tonné Riesener, comme si la pauvre Antoinette avait eu quelque chose à voir dans les missions de plus en plus importantes qu'on confiait à Delacroix. Et puis, calmé, il prenait la patache de Versailles pour assister aux ventes et racheter ses meubles lorsque ceux-ci figuraient sur le catalogue.

– Comme ça je suis sûr qu'ils ne seront pas détruits et je fais une bonne affaire. La Révolution ne va pas durer encore dix ans. La vie bientôt reprendra ses droits et tout le monde aura besoin de meubles. Je revendrai alors les miens!

Ainsi les secrétaires des appartements de la reine, les

bureaux à cylindre du cabinet royal et les bonheurs-du-jour de Madame Élisabeth reprenaient le chemin de l'atelier où ils avaient été conçus. Ces déménagements qui coûtaient presque aussi cher à Riesener que les meubles eux-mêmes avaient quelque chose de dérisoire et de touchant. L'acharnement du vieil ébéniste du roi à sauver son œuvre imposait le respect, personne à l'Arsenal ou au Faubourg ne se serait permis la moindre critique. Seulement, Riesener était en train de se ruiner, sans se rendre compte que l'époque où l'on criait la France à l'encan n'était pas celle où il convenait de miser sur l'art et la beauté [1].

Il est vrai que la Révolution marchait à pas de géant, balayant tous ceux qui trouvaient l'allure trop vive. Les événements se succédaient maintenant à un rythme aussi précipité que celui de la « sainte guillotine ». L'assassinat de Marat par Charlotte Corday, Toulon aux mains des Anglais, la levée en masse, la Terreur « mise à l'ordre du jour » par la Convention : autant de faits tragiques qui laissaient loin derrière eux l'agonie du Faubourg qui, après avoir meublé les rois, n'avait plus de commandes que de l'armée. Le rabot s'était émoussé sur les piques des sans-culottes, la paume des sculpteurs avait perdu son cal, la joie de vivre des compagnons de l'ébène et du bois de rose s'était en même temps évanouie dans l'odeur fade qui montait de la place de la Révolution où trônait la sinistre machine.

Place d'Aligre, comme partout à Paris la tension montait chaque jour davantage. La peur commençait à ravager les visages et les esprits. Valfroy dissimulait ses craintes pour ne pas effrayer Antoinette mais on le sentait nerveusement à bout. Il travaillait toujours à la section.

– Ce n'est pas de là que viendra le danger, avait-il dit un jour à Riesener : c'est de l'extérieur. Une simple lettre

1. Les procès-verbaux des ventes de Versailles existent. On y relève par exemple sous le numéro 2340 : une table à écrire en bois de palissandre, mosaïque richement ornée de bronze doré d'or moulu, au citoyen Riesener, de Paris : 3 210 livres.

adressée au Comité de salut public peut suffire pour faire arrêter n'importe qui, un hébertiste comme un royaliste ou même un Jacobin trop tiède. Si je suis arrêté, c'est ainsi que cela se passera. Mais il ne faut pas désespérer. Surtout ne dites rien à Antoinette.

Antoinette n'avait pas besoin d'une telle confidence pour deviner les sombres pensées qui couvaient sous les cheveux gris de son mari. En six mois, ceux-ci avaient changé de couleur, des rides profondes marquaient maintenant le visage de Bertrand de Valfroy. L'ancien officier du régiment des gardes n'était pas un poltron. Il avait vu la mort de près et n'avait peur que pour sa femme et sa fille. Que deviendraient-elles s'il était arrêté ? Réveillon et Riesener ne vivraient pas éternellement et qui pouvait dire ce qu'il resterait de son modeste domaine bourguignon quand la tornade révolutionnaire se serait apaisée ?

Ethis, lui, vivait à la température de ses amours. Quand Marie avait été gentille et lui avait permis de l'embrasser entre les murs de planches de la cour des mousquetaires, il rentrait joyeux et racontait ses exploits de la journée au côté de Lenoir. Si la jeune fille n'avait pu fausser compagnie à sa mère ou si elle s'était montrée quelque peu indifférente, Antoinette reconnaissait tout de suite le visage des mauvais jours : yeux à demi fermés, bouche serrée et traits agités. Ces signes de nervosité et de violence contenue l'inquiétaient, elle savait que le petit sauvage du sac de la Folie Titon était toujours prêt à se réveiller, à rejeter le manteau douillet dont elle l'avait enveloppé : Elle n'ignorait pas que son Ethis, qu'elle chérissait à la fois comme un fils et comme un petit frère, était, lorsqu'il avait cet air buté, capable de commettre les pires sottises.

Heureusement, Alexandre Lenoir apportait un peu de fraîcheur et de fantaisie dans l'atmosphère lourde qui régnait place d'Aligre. D'un naturel enjoué, passionné par son travail sans crainte pour sa tête car il était l'alibi des hommes politiques, incapables d'empêcher les excès des démolisseurs. Il était devenu en quelques mois indispensable à l'équilibre de la famille. Antoinette lui en savait gré qui n'avait pas oublié les circonstances de leur rencontre ni les sentiments ambigus qui l'avaient marquée. Elle se rendait compte qu'elle serait très malheureuse s'il cessait ses visites et sentait que lui-même était irrésistiblement attiré au Faubourg. Cette situation n'aurait pu évoluer qu'à la faveur d'un encouragement de sa part, encouragement qu'elle prenait bien garde de donner! Elle aimait son mari.

Sans un caprice du sort, ce hasard qui tient une si grande place dans l'éternelle comédie de l'amour, les choses en seraient sans doute restées là. Prudence d'Antoinette, extrême correction de Lenoir, ils se voyaient rarement seuls. Alexandre n'arrivait place d'Aligre que le soir, lorsque la maison était déjà pleine. Un jour pourtant, en mettant une bûche dans la cheminée, il avait frôlé un genou d'Antoinette qui avait tressailli et tourné les yeux.

– Vous êtes une vraie feuille de sensitive, Antoinette! lui avait-il chuchoté... Vous connaissez les expériences de M. Sigaud de Lafont qui fait jaillir des étincelles en rapprochant deux boules électrisées. Nous sommes dans le même cas, mieux vaut nous écarter l'un de l'autre!

– Mais je ne vous fuis pas Alexandre! Si j'ai frissonné c'est parce que j'ai froid. Tenez, donnez-moi la couverture qui est sur le fauteuil...

En lui couvrant les épaules il ne put s'empêcher d'appuyer doucement la main sur son bras. Cette fois, elle ne trembla pas mais ferma les yeux. Les premiers contacts de l'amour causent des émotions d'une intensité indépendante de leur durée. Il suffit d'une seconde pour bouleverser l'existence de deux êtres parfaitement maîtres d'eux-mêmes: Antoinette et Alexandre surent, à cet instant, qu'il se passerait un jour quelque chose entre eux.

Pourtant la vie continuait. Pas gaie mais pas non plus dramatique. Curieusement, le Faubourg qui avait joué un grand rôle en 89 et durant les journées des Tuileries se trouvait comme protégé du vent de folie qui soufflait sur la France. La « sainte guillotine », devenue pour certains Parisiens l'objet d'un véritable culte, était installée loin, place de la Révolution, le sang ne coulait pas dans les caniveaux du quartier. On suivait bien sûr dans la presse les événements qui, pour être formidables, avaient de moins en moins de prise sur les sensibilités émoussées par tant d'horreurs. Seule l'exécution de Marie-Antoinette émut les cœurs les plus tendres. Et Lenoir fut triste le jour où André Chénier monta sur l'échafaud : c'était un compagnon de jeunesse. Personne, en revanche, ne pleura Danton qui avait attendu sa condamnation pour regretter d'avoir fait instituer le Tribunal révolutionnaire. L'écho des harangues sanguinaires lancées du haut de la tribune ne parvenait pas jusqu'aux cours, passages et impasses du Faubourg. La réaction des femmes obligées chaque jour de courir les boutiques pour trouver de quoi mal nourrir leurs enfants ne prêtait pas à confusion : « Qu'ils se massacrent entre eux puisqu'ils ne sont pas capables de nous donner du pain ! »

Un jour de prairial, pourtant, les plus indifférents eurent froid dans le dos. Le rapport de Couthon sur la réforme du Tribunal révolutionnaire jugé trop débonnaire portait la cruauté à son paroxysme. La loi votée le 22 spécifiait qu'une seule peine serait désormais prononcée : la mort. L'article 8 précisait que pour condamner les ennemis du peuple les preuves morales suffisaient, et l'article 9 ordonnait à tout citoyen de dénoncer les conspirateurs et les contre-révolutionnaires.

– Il ne nous restait pas beaucoup de liberté, cette fois, ce mot sacré qui a soulevé tout un peuple est rayé de nos lois. Même si l'on en use encore pour justifier des atrocités !

C'est Bertrand de Valfroy qui venait de prononcer ces paroles terribles. Chacun se tut autour de la table, abandonnant sa ration de harengs séchés dans les assiettes.

– Tout à l'heure, continua Valfroy, j'ai rencontré Tavernier à la section. C'est l'un des commis-greffiers du tribunal. Il m'a rapporté avoir entendu Fouquier-Tinville dire à la buvette en brandissant le papier qu'il tenait à la main : « La dernière décade n'a pas mal rendu, il faut que celle-ci aille à quatre cents, quatre cent cinquante. » Il parlait des mises en jugement.

– Comment ces hommes qui ont vécu courageusement et souvent généreusement les premières années de la Révolution en sont-ils arrivés là? demanda Riesener. Est-il vrai que ce Fouquier a annoncé en pleine Convention : « Les têtes tombent comme des ardoises »?

– Oui, et il paraît que cette constatation le comblait d'aise, répondit Lenoir. Voyez-vous monsieur Riesener, le fanatisme, quelle qu'en soit la couleur, est le pire des fléaux qui puissent s'abattre sur un pays. Aujourd'hui il est jacobin. Les Jacobins règnent en tyrans sans qu'aucun frein moral ou simplement humanitaire vienne arrêter leur fureur sanguinaire. Pourquoi ont-ils remplacé les grands principes de 89 par le couperet permanent? Parce qu'ils ont peur. Ils ont commencé de tuer ceux qui ne pensaient pas comme eux, puis ceux qui étaient supposés ne pas penser comme eux. Aujourd'hui, ils guillotinent n'importe qui. Si ce qu'ils nomment eux-mêmes la Terreur s'arrêtait, ce sont eux qui seraient condamnés. Alors, comme il faut continuer à juger et qu'il ne leur reste plus guère d'ennemis, ils s'assassinent entre eux. Les Jacobins les plus forts guillotinent les plus faibles. Tout cela au nom de la Patrie et de la République en danger. En fait, ils tuent parce qu'ils ne peuvent pas s'arrêter de tuer.

– La peur, coupa Valfroy, vous avez dit le mot juste! Un peu plus tard, quand cette barbarie aura fait place à des temps plus cléments, il sera intéressant d'analyser le rôle qu'a joué la peur dans le comportement révolutionnaire.

– Je crois même qu'aujourd'hui la peur est dépassée, reprit Lenoir. La doctrine terroriste des Jacobins est devenue une fin en soi, une suite de cruautés inutiles qui éclipsent totalement les idées de liberté, d'égalité et de fraternité. Ces gens sont devenus fous. Pourquoi ne pas convenir qu'ils sont atteints de névrose, pour employer un mot nouveau. De névrose révolutionnaire!

Antoinette écoutait Alexandre Lenoir avec une sorte de curiosité admirative. Elle ne l'avait jusqu'à présent entendu parler que de ses missions de sauvetage. C'était il est vrai un sujet passionnant où il excellait. Ce soir, elle découvrait un autre homme, plus profond, capable de comprendre et d'expliquer, aussi bien que Valfroy, les sentiments complexes qui animaient les maîtres de la Révolution. Elle se dit qu'elle avait beaucoup de chance d'avoir parmi ses proches deux hommes aussi intelligents.

Vers huit heures, Ethis rentra joyeux et avala de bon appétit les restes de poisson séché demeurés dans les assiettes. S'il n'était pas capable d'analyser comme Lenoir les menées secrètes de la politique, il avait conscience du dévoiement des idées et souffrait de voir « sa » révolution transformée en bain de sang. Il était aussi un collecteur de nouvelles incomparable, un informateur précieux, souvent au courant avant tout le monde de ce qui se passait à la Commune, à la Convention et dans les sections éloignées de Paris. Du faubourg Marcel à la place des Victoires tout le monde connaissait son bonnet rouge et son ruban bleu de « vainqueur ».

Quand il fut rassasié, il se tourna vers Antoinette, sa confidente privilégiée, et annonça qu'il venait d'apprendre une nouvelle extraordinaire. Cabotin rompu aux effets du théâtre de la rue, il attendit d'avoir capté l'attention et piqué la curiosité de chacun avant de lancer sa bombe :

– La guillotine va déménager : Sanson l'installe demain à la Bastille !

– A deux pas de chez nous ? lança Antoinette furieuse. Quelle horreur ! Tu me feras le plaisir, Ethis, de ne pas te mêler aux brutes qui sortent de leur fange pour aller assister aux exécutions !

– Non, non, je n'irai pas... Mais j'ai déjà vu des têtes tomber, tu sais...

– Je ne sais rien du tout et ne veux rien savoir, mais si j'apprends que tu te mêles aux monstres qui viennent insulter les condamnés jusque sur l'échafaud, je cesserai de t'aimer et même je te mettrai à la porte de chez moi!

Ethis éclata de rire et s'écria: « J'ai quelque chose à vous montrer! » Content de son effet, il sortit un jeu de cartes de sa poche et l'étala sur la table.

– C'est Marie qui me l'a donné. Son père a acheté le brevet aux deux inventeurs du nouveau jeu et compte gagner beaucoup d'argent en les imprimant.

Les cartes passèrent de main en main.

– On ne reconnaît plus rien, dit Riesener. Comment voulez-vous jouer au piquet avec ces machins-là. Tiens! qu'est-ce que c'est que ce personnage assis sur un siège romain? Vraiment! Il n'y avait pas de choses plus urgentes à changer que les cartes à jouer!

– Vous ne vouliez tout de même pas, dit Valfroy, que les bons patriotes tuent le temps en jouant avec des figurines qui rappellent sans cesse le despotisme et l'inégalité. Je trouve pour ma part cette initiative fort louable. Imaginez-vous les aides de M. Sanson, se reposant de leurs œuvres le jour où ils ont guillotiné Louis XVI, annoncer un « quatorze de rois gagnant »? Ces estimables citoyens ne risquent plus pareille mésaventure. Ils annonceront, j'ai lu ça dans *Le Journal de Paris*, un quatorze de Génies...

– Celui qui a décidé d'appeler les anciens rois des génies devrait normalement être guillotiné dans les vingt-quatre heures, lança Antoinette en riant. Mais comment s'appellent maintenant les valets?

– Les Égalités. Et les dames les Libertés. Et la Loi remplace l'as.

– Allons, tout cela est très bien, conclut Lenoir. Que des gens s'intéressent encore aux jeux de cartes en ces temps où les têtes tombent comme des ardoises, pour reprendre la charmante expression de M. Fouquier-Tinville, me paraît tout à fait réconfortant.

Les Libertés et les Égalités de carton avaient fait oublier l'installation de la guillotine à la porte du Faubourg. On se sépara plus gaiement que d'habitude. Avant de partir, Lenoir donna ses instructions à Ethis pour la mission du lendemain:

– Mon cher Ethis, je vous attends à neuf heures tapantes sur le parvis de Notre-Dame. Nous aurons du travail car l'entrepreneur chargé de la toilette jacobine de la cathédrale, un nommé Varin, ne travaille pas dans la délicatesse. Enfin, nous essaierons tout de même de sauver quelques statues.

Très naturellement, il se tourna vers Antoinette :

– Au fait, mon amie, pourquoi ne viendriez-vous pas avec Ethis ? Notre-Dame n'est pas loin et vous assisterez à quelques belles démonstrations de vandalisme. Il faut avoir vu cela une fois dans sa vie de contemporain de la Révolution. Et puis, vous apprendrez aussi comment votre cher Ethis arrache la tête d'un saint des mains d'une brute avinée prête à la broyer. Comment il sait dire au bon moment à un vandale-chef : « Citoyen, j'ai le devoir de conserver ce morceau de marbre car j'ai pris la Bastille ! » en lui montrant son ruban bleu de « vainqueur ». La relation entre les deux événements n'est pas évidente mais ça marche presque toujours. On peut dire que le patrimoine artistique de la France doit beaucoup au ruban d'Ethis... Alors, vous viendrez ?

Il avait lancé cette invitation sans trop espérer. Depuis l'incident de la cheminée, elle prenait garde en effet d'éviter toute intimité et il s'attendait à un refus poli. A son grand étonnement, Antoinette accepta en souriant :

– Mais oui ! Il y a longtemps que je souhaitais vous accompagner et votre offre me comble de plaisir, s'il peut toutefois y avoir quelque plaisir à voir détruire une cathédrale !

– J'ai vu Varin abattre la flèche de la Sainte-Chapelle et j'ai retenu mes larmes quand cette dentelle de pierre s'est écrasée à vingt pas de nous. Rassurez-vous, demain les tours de Notre-Dame resteront debout. Les marteaux jacobins ne s'en prendront qu'aux saints. Ah ! ne mettez pas votre jolie robe à rayures roses ni une perruque. Habillez-vous comme une femme de la halle car vous serez complètement couverte de poussière. Prenez aussi un châle pour vous couvrir la tête et le visage.

Antoinette alla vite se coucher. Elle dit bonsoir à

Valfroy, souffla la chandelle et se tourna sur le côté droit, la tête à demi enfouie sous le drap. Elle avait hâte d'être seule, de pouvoir réfléchir à la réponse qu'elle venait de faire. Elle avait dit oui spontanément, sans penser que son attitude réduisait à néant toutes ses résolutions. Elle était contente cependant : pour une fois que la vie lui proposait autre chose que la solitude et la banalité ! Et puis, tout de même, il ne fallait pas exagérer, elle n'avait pas accepté un rendez-vous galant mais simplement d'accompagner Ethis sur son lieu de travail. « Je suis idiote », se dit-elle, en se retournant vers son mari déjà à moitié endormi et qu'elle réveilla tout à fait en l'embrassant.

Le lendemain, il faisait beau. Antoinette se leva heureuse et fit chauffer en chantant sur les braises rallumées le lait de la petite Lucie. Les grandes personnes se contenteraient, comme chaque matin, d'une infusion de chicorée grillée et d'un morceau de pain gris. Antoinette s'ingénia ensuite, en fouillant dans sa garde-robe appauvrie, à s'habiller en respectant les consignes de Lenoir mais sans pourtant sacrifier la coquetterie. Bertrand l'embrassa, lui souhaita une bonne journée et partit pour la section.

– Si tu savais comme j'ai assez de ce travail dont l'inutilité m'accable. La Convention crée chaque jour de nouveaux bureaux, la Commune aussi. Cela entraîne une prolifération de papiers... Enfin, ce poste me sauve peut-être la vie, il faut être patient.

Lucie laissée à la garde de la voisine, il ne restait plus qu'à rejoindre Lenoir. Antoinette prit le bras d'Ethis, fier comme un général aux armées. En traversant le terre-plein encore encombré de pierraille où se dressait naguère la tour de la Bertaudière, ils aperçurent sur la droite, presque en face de la porte Saint-Antoine, un attroupement que la garde essayait de contenir. Ils découvrirent en approchant des hommes qui déchargeaient des pièces de bois de deux gros chariots : c'était la guillotine qu'on installait à l'emplacement de la forteresse. « Triste symbole, pensa Antoinette. Combien de têtes innocentes aura coûté cette liberté dont on entend tellement le nom et dont on goûte si peu les effets. » Elle entraîna Ethis qui, lui, se serait bien approché pour voir comment ces hommes affairés et consciencieux assemblaient, comme s'il s'était agi d'un travail de voirie ordinaire, la sinistre machine à raccourcir les Français.

La porte franchie, la rue Saint-Antoine offrait un spectacle plus désolant que le Faubourg où l'on percevait encore, malgré la misère, une ambiance ouvrière et chaleureuse. Ici, les beaux hôtels du Marais, vidés pour la plupart de leurs habitants et de leurs richesses, laissaient aux passants l'impression débilitante d'une rue désertée. Des gens s'agitaient pourtant devant l'hôtel de Boisgelin. Grimpés sur des échelles, ils démolissaient à coups de marteau les armoiries et les blasons de la famille Sully et des Turgot de Saint-Clair qui avaient jadis habité cette belle maison bâtie par Androuet du Cerceau. Enfin les tours de Notre-Dame apparurent au sud. Devant le parvis, faisant les cent pas autour de son vieux carrosse, Alexandre Lenoir attendait.

Il s'inclina devant Antoinette et lui fit compliment de sa toilette de travail :

– Surtout enveloppez-vous bien la tête dans votre fichu, sinon vous allez retrouver vos cheveux poudrés comme pour un bal à Versailles!

A ce moment un bruit formidable retentit et un nuage de poussière blanche s'éleva, voilant presque toute la façade de la cathédrale.

– C'est une bombe à poudre? demanda Antoinette que ce bruit de tonnerre avait fait sursauter.

– Non, c'est saint François ou saint Anastase qui vient de se fracasser sur le parvis. Tenez, regardez là-haut les démolisseurs de M. Varin. Ils mettent du cœur à l'ouvrage, les bougres. Normalement, ils devraient seulement trancher la tête des statues mais il arrive qu'elles soient emprisonnées entre des colonnes, alors tout passe pardessus bord.

– Mais vous ne pouvez rien récupérer des statues de ces malheureux saints?

– Non, il faudrait un miracle pour qu'une tête ou deux aient résisté à la toilette révolutionnaire. Nous verrons cela tout à l'heure. C'est à l'intérieur que nous pouvons espérer sauver certains morceaux de marbre. Venez, nous allons entrer.

Ils se frayèrent un passage à travers les gravats et pénétrèrent dans la nef. Une fade odeur de plâtre, de poussière et d'humidité y remplaçait celle de l'encens.

– Je vais vous présenter mon ennemi, ce Varin, capitaine des vandales. Avec lui je fais patte de velours, quoiqu'il m'en coûte, car c'est le seul moyen de conserver quelque chose. Tenez, je vais essayer de négocier le sauvetage de ces anges en argent qui ont miraculeusement résisté, dans leur chapelle, à une première dévastation.

Intéressée par le marchandage dont Lenoir semblait avoir une grande habitude, elle le regardait de loin discuter avec l'entrepreneur. Tous deux faisaient de grands gestes, se montraient tour à tour les pauvres angelots suspendus au-dessus d'un autel à moitié détruit. On aurait cru deux maquignons se disputant une vache sur le foirail. Finalement ils se dirigèrent, toujours en parlant, vers Antoinette à qui Ethis expliquait comment son patron arrivait quelquefois à fléchir les casseurs les plus obtus.

– Antoinette, je vous présente M. Varin qui assume la rude tâche d'appliquer la loi républicaine en supprimant des ci-devant édifices royaux toute trace de féodalité. Il veut bien parfois m'aider à accomplir ma mission, elle aussi couverte par la loi républicaine, qui consiste à sauver les plus belles œuvres du patrimoine de la France. Hélas! aujourd'hui il ne veut rien savoir pour épargner ces angelots promis à la fonte.

Antoinette souriait comme elle savait le faire quand elle voulait séduire. Elle regardait dans les yeux le bonhomme qui se dandinait sur ses courtes jambes. S'étant soudain juré de le circonvenir, d'obtenir la grâce des deux anges, elle attaqua:

– M. Lenoir m'a dit combien il vous en coûtait de détruire ou d'envoyer à la fonte certaines œuvres irremplaçables. Alors, je vous en prie, monsieur, puisque je suis là aujourd'hui, accordez-moi le privilège de laisser M. le Président de la commission mettre ces deux angelots en lieu sûr. Ils ne pèsent pas bien lourd et leur valeur ne peut guère influer sur les ressources de la République. Laissez-nous, je vous en prie, ces chérubins...

Le sourire de plus en plus appuyé d'Antoinette mettait le gros entrepreneur dans tous ses états. Il ne savait plus où il en était, M. Varin! Il bafouillait :

– C'est que, madame, ils ne sont pas en bois, ces anges, ni en pierre. C'est du bel et bon argent et tout ce qui est en métal précieux est impérativement confisqué. Tenez, si vous voulez je vous abandonne un saint... Il en reste 70 à déloger, vous n'avez qu'à choisir.

Antoinette s'amusait. De temps en temps, elle lançait un regard vers Alexandre et Ethis qui avaient du mal à retenir leur rire. Elle sentait que le poisson était sur le point de mordre, il ne fallait surtout pas le ferrer trop tôt :

– Un saint! s'exclama-t-elle. Mais il y en a trop, des saints, et M. Lenoir ne sait plus où les mettre. Tandis que des anges...

– Mais ils sont en argent, madame!

– C'est justement parce qu'ils sont en argent que M. Lenoir veut les conserver. Allez, un bon mouvement, laissez-les-moi!

– Non, ce n'est pas possible. Je ne serais pas un bon patriote si je n'appliquais pas la loi.

L'affaire semblait fichue et Antoinette s'apprêtait à effacer de ses lèvres un sourire inutile quand Ethis eut une idée. Il était comme ça, Ethis. Il se taisait longtemps, semblant se désintéresser de tout et puis, soudain, il s'exprimait avec volubilité, le plus souvent pour faire une remarque originale, avancer un jugement intéressant. Brusquement, il s'adressa à Varin :

– Et si vous ne saviez pas qu'ils sont en argent, ces

anges, ils ne vous intéresseraient pas, vous les laisseriez à M. Lenoir...

– Oui, sûrement, mais ils sont en argent!

– Laissez-moi faire et dans cinq minutes vous n'en serez plus sûr.

Avec une agilité de chat, il dressa une échelle qui se trouvait là et monta décrocher les statuettes. Sans un regard pour Varin qui le fixait médusé, ni pour Antoinette et Lenoir qui se demandaient ce qu'il manigançait, Ethis se dirigea vers un seau dans lequel trempait un pinceau et badigeonna les angelots de peinture blanche. Il revint alors, tout souriant, un ange dans chaque main.

– Monsieur Varin, dit-il, avec le plus grand sérieux, permettez-vous à mon maître, M. Lenoir, de conserver ces deux statuettes en bois peint?

Varin lui-même ne put s'empêcher de sourire. Il mâchouilla quelques mots incompréhensibles puis finalement se tourna vers Antoinette:

– Puisqu'ils sont en bois, je permets, madame, à M. Lenoir de les emporter.

Antoinette ravie embrassa Ethis. Pour un peu elle aurait aussi sauté au cou de Varin mais elle avait jugé au dernier moment qu'il était trop laid. Il se contenta donc de remerciements. Pour être tout à fait aimable, elle lui posa quelques questions sur la mise au goût jacobin de Notre-Dame:

– Que font donc ces gens, monsieur, juchés sur des échafaudages?

– Il y a, madame, 6 250 fleurs de lis et autres signes de féodalité qui gâtent les vitraux. Mes hommes sont en train de les recouvrir d'une couche de peinture à l'huile grasse [1].

Tandis qu'Ethis allait ranger les anges dans la voiture, Lenoir décida d'aller fouiller le tas de débris qui bouchait presque l'entrée de la cathédrale. Antoinette s'était assise

1. Varin a expliqué lui-même comment il avait guillotiné 80 statues sur la façade de Notre-Dame et comment il avait « épuré les vitraux à la peinture grasse ».

à l'écart sur une pierre et le regardait, avec une certaine tendresse, remuer les morceaux de marbre, les examiner avec attention avant de les rejeter. Elle le trouvait séduisant dans sa longue redingote qui avait longtemps perdu ses couleurs sur les chantiers mais avait gardé l'allure du bon faiseur. Son grand foulard de soie blanche volait au vent et s'accrochait au ruban d'un chapeau noir à larges bords. « Quelle destinée, pensa-t-elle, que celle de cet homme qui a été amené à abandonner son métier de peintre pour se muer en justicier du beau. »

Enfin, il retira une tête des décombres. De loin elle avait l'air intacte et Antoinette poussa un cri de joie. Brusquement, elle eut conscience qu'elle réagissait exactement comme au temps de Pilâtre de Rozier, quand son fou du ciel avait réalisé quelque exploit. Cela lui fit un petit coup au cœur et elle regarda Alexandre avec d'autres yeux, sans être sûre encore que c'étaient ceux de l'amour.

Elle allait se précipiter vers lui pour voir la tête de pierre qu'il tenait à bout de bras quand survint l'un de ces incidents imprévisibles qui peuvent aussi bien être sans importance que faire dérailler la vie. Les hommes de Varin travaillaient toujours au-dessus des portails mais suffisamment loin de Lenoir pour que celui-ci ne risquât pas d'être touché par les saintes têtes qui tombaient du ciel de temps à autre comme des pommes mûres. Et, pourtant, c'est l'une de ces têtes – on sut plus tard que c'était celle de Donatien – qui joua le rôle du petit grain de sable.

Au lieu de choir sur l'oreiller mou des gravats, la tête tomba sur une dalle de marbre et éclata comme si elle eût été chargée de mitraille. Elle se désintégra en cinquante ou cent petits morceaux et l'un d'eux, coupant comme un rasoir, rencontra dans sa trajectoire le visage de Lenoir. Celui-ci poussa un cri et s'appuya sur les épaules d'Antoinette et d'Ethis aussitôt accourus. Il avait le visage en sang. La pierre semblait l'avoir touché à la tempe, tout près de l'œil droit. Antoinette fit un tampon d'un morceau de son écharpe et le pressa sur la blessure pour tenter d'arrêter l'hémorragie. Sa décision fut vite prise. Plutôt que d'aller chercher l'un des introuvables médecins qui demeuraient encore à Paris – la plupart étaient aux armées –, elle résolut de transporter le blessé chez lui. Heureusement, Lenoir n'habitait pas loin, rue des Lions, dans un petit appartement que lui prêtait son ami Hilaire Rouillé du Coudray. Celui-ci avait émigré dès le début de la Révolution mais Lenoir avait obtenu de la Commune le droit de continuer à occuper les trois pièces situées au-dessus du porche d'entrée.

– Ethis, s'écria-t-elle, va vite chercher la voiture. Tu sais où loge M. Lenoir, nous allons le conduire chez lui.

Elle aida le blessé à s'asseoir sur les coussins défoncés du carrosse et s'installa à côté, en continuant d'éponger le sang qui coulait d'une large estafilade tandis qu'Ethis faisait s'envoler la voiture d'un violent coup de fouet.

– Cela saigne beaucoup, murmura Lenoir, mais je ne pense pas que je sois gravement touché. Si l'œil n'est pas atteint tout ira bien. Il esquissa un pauvre sourire et ajouta : Heureusement, vous êtes là!

Antoinette était là, trop absorbée à s'occuper d'Alexandre pour avoir le temps de s'inquiéter. Elle lui tenait une main qu'elle trouvait glacée tout en maintenant serré le tampon de linge contre son œil. Enfin, Ethis dans un grand fracas, arrêta le carrosse devant le numéro 11. Il fallut conduire Lenoir, à moitié aveuglé par son sang, jusqu'au petit escalier situé à la gauche de l'entrée. Enfin, après avoir cherché la clé dans une cachette ménagée sous la rampe de fer forgé, Ethis et Antoinette purent allonger le blessé sur son lit :

– Ethis, pendant que je lave la plaie, cours vite chez l'apothicaire de la rue du Petit-Musc, c'est tout près, achète des pansements ainsi que de l'huile de millepertuis et, s'il en a, des emplâtres de pâquerettes. Prends de l'argent dans ma bourse, moi je m'occupe d'Alexandre.

Antoinette était une bonne soigneuse. Toute jeune, sa mère lui avait appris les plantes qui guérissent. Elle connaissait les simples et savait par exemple qu'une compresse d'huile de millepertuis arrêterait l'hémorragie, désinfecterait la plaie et calmerait la douleur. En attendant, avec une douceur extrême, elle nettoyait le visage du blessé. Elle s'en voulait un peu de constater qu'elle prenait un certain plaisir à s'occuper d'Alexandre, à lui tenir la main ou à laisser sa paume un moment sur son front. Si l'estafilade, large de deux bons pouces, n'avait pas frôlé l'œil de si près, elle se serait presque réjouie d'un accident qui lui permettait sans rien avoir fait pour cela d'entrer dans l'intimité de celui qui, elle s'en rendait compte, lui était de moins en moins indifférent. Son malade semblait d'ailleurs apprécier ses soins :

– Quelle chance que vous soyez venue, Antoinette! Vous êtes ma bonne fée, vous m'avez protégé. Sans vous je suis sûr que ce maudit éclat m'aurait crevé l'œil. Et, sans vous, qui m'aurait soigné? Votre main sur mon front m'a déjà guéri et je n'ai que faire des drogues qu'Ethis est allé chercher. Antoinette, venez plus près, regardez-moi. Je vais vous dire quelque chose que je n'aurais jamais osé vous avouer sans ce stupide accident...

– Chut! Chut! Monsieur Lenoir. Ne dites rien qui puisse compromettre la douceur du moment que nous vivons. Laissez-vous soigner et dites-vous qu'il y a des choses possibles et d'autres qui ne le sont pas. Tiens, voilà Ethis. Vous allez voir qu'un cataplasme de millepertuis est bien plus agréable que la paume de ma main...

Elle éclata de rire et s'en fut préparer sa médecine. En fait, Antoinette était désorientée. La tête de saint Donatien avait en tombant, détruit les défenses qu'elle avait eu tant de mal à établir entre elle et Alexandre. C'était un peu comme si elle se retrouvait nue devant celui dont elle devait fuir l'amour. Elle venait d'éviter qu'un mot grave, lourd de conséquences ne fût prononcé mais pourrait-elle encore longtemps couper le chemin à un feu dont le hasard ranimait sans cesse les braises.

Ethis était parti ranger la voiture aux Petits-Augustins. Antoinette lui avait demandé de rentrer tout de suite après place d'Aligre afin de reprendre la petite Lucie chez Marie, la voisine, et lui faire manger sa soupe au lait. Elle pouvait avoir confiance : Ethis adorait la petite fille qu'il considérait comme sa sœur.

Antoinette se rendit compte alors qu'elle était seule avec Lenoir, chez lui, et qu'elle le soignait avec l'attention et la dévotion d'une épouse ou d'une amante. La lotion de millepertuis avait fait des miracles et il ne subsistait de l'émotion de la matinée qu'une longue balafre sur la joue d'Alexandre. Celui-ci parlait déjà de repartir sur le chantier de Notre-Dame mais Antoinette l'obligea au contraire à se déshabiller et à se coucher pendant qu'elle allait essayer de trouver quelques provisions dans les boutiques du quartier.

– Mon cher, une blessure à la tête ne se traite pas par-dessus la jambe. La vôtre a l'air bénigne parce qu'elle ne vous fait plus souffrir mais regardez-vous dans une glace : vous allez promener jusqu'à la fin de vos jours une superbe cicatrice qui vous fera passer pour un bretteur ou un rescapé de Valmy. Ce côté esthétique mis à part, vous pouvez très bien vous retrouver, si vous ne vous reposez pas, avec un échauffement du cerveau qui risque de vous laisser idiot. Alors, de grâce, pensez aux statues qui, elles, ne veulent pas mourir!

Quand Antoinette revint, chargée en tout et pour tout d'un chou, de quelques pommes de terre et d'un minuscule morceau de lard, Lenoir était allongé sur son lit. Il avait changé ses vêtements tachés de sang contre une chemise à col de dentelle qui paraissait d'un autre âge et une robe de chambre dont la soie bleue montrait de beaux restes.

– Bravo! Vous êtes, Alexandre, d'une élégance qui illustre les voluptés du nonchaloir! C'est bien dit, non? Comme vous avez été raisonnable, je vais essayer de vous préparer des pommes de terre où le lard sera rare mais ma bonne volonté abondante. Autant vous dire que je n'ai jamais été une très bonne cuisinière, alors attendez-vous à tout. Dites-moi tout de même si dans une maison de célibataire on peut trouver du petit bois, des bûches et un briquet.

Ils dînèrent gaiement au bord du lit. Lenoir était un agréable conteur mais Antoinette connaissait, pour les avoir entendues plusieurs fois, les meilleures histoires de sa chasse aux trésors. Alors, il lui raconta l'histoire de la maison où il habitait :

– Avant d'émigrer, mon ami ci-devant du Coudray a eu la bonne idée de me confier les archives de cet hôtel qui a connu bien des propriétaires avant d'échoir à son grand-père Le Féron, seigneur du Plessis, grand maître des Eaux et Forêts. Sa locataire la plus illustre fut jadis la marquise de Sévigné. Dans ces pierres aujourd'hui bien vieilles elle perdit son mari, blessé à mort au cours d'un duel et gagna une fille à qui elle écrivit plus tard de si jolies lettres... Mais tout cela a peu d'intérêt, parlez-moi plutôt de vous, belle Antoinette. On dit de votre vie qu'elle a été une extraordinaire aventure et je n'en connais que les têtes de chapitre : Œben, Riesener, Pilâtre de Rozier... Ah! celui-là! comme je l'envie! Rendez-vous compte, il a été le premier à s'envoler dans les airs et le premier à être aimé de vous. Après ces deux exploits, il n'avait plus rien à espérer sur cette terre. C'est pourquoi peut-être il est mort si jeune...

– Monsieur Lenoir vous dites des sottises, s'exclama Antoinette furieuse. Il lui restait beaucoup de bonheur à espérer.

– Et quoi donc?

– Mais à continuer de m'aimer et à être aimé! C'est pourquoi, encore aujourd'hui, je ne lui pardonne pas de s'être tué stupidement en tentant l'impossible.

– Vous avez raison. Si vous le voulez, parlez-moi de lui. Et de vous...

Longtemps, Antoinette raconta sa vie, le succès fulgurant de son père, arrivé d'Allemagne à vingt ans et ouvrier privilégié du roi à vingt-cinq; la mort tragique de sa mère après qu'elle eut épousé Riesener, l'élève d'Œben; la fantastique réussite sociale de Réveillon, l'enfant du Faubourg; la vie tumultueuse et grisante au côté de Pilâtre; le sac de la Folie Titon et sa blessure; Valfroy et la Révolution...

Tandis qu'elle parlait, Alexandre lui avait pris la main et elle ne l'avait pas retirée. Elle ne savait plus où elle était. Ce flot de souvenirs, cette maison qu'elle ne connaissait pas et, tout près, le beau visage balafré de Lenoir qui ne la quittait pas des yeux, qui buvait ses paroles et lui caressait doucement le poignet. Soudain, elle se sentit envahie par un irrésistible besoin de tendresse. Il lui sembla que son sang coulait plus chaud dans ses veines. Elle n'était plus la forte Antoinette que la vie avait endurcie, elle se retrouvait, petite fille fragile, découvrant les premiers émois de l'amour. Plus rien n'existait au monde qu'elle et Alexandre. Et ce fut elle, cette fois, qui chercha son regard. Elle se souleva du coussin où elle était accroupie, prit doucement sa tête dans ses deux mains et lui dit : « Maintenant embrassez-moi. Il y a peu d'instants comme celui-ci dans la vie. Nous allons le partager. »

C'était comme si le temps avait été arrêté par quelque main complice. Tout ce qui avait été jusqu'alors leur existence était gommé, perdu dans un passé aussi lointain que celui de la « Mécanique céleste » de M. Laplace. Antoinette et Alexandre s'étreignirent, confondant leurs âmes et leurs corps.

La nuit tombait lorsqu'ils sortirent ensemble de l'état de grâce où les avait plongés l'acte d'amour et les minutes d'éternité qui l'avaient suivi. C'est Antoinette qui renoua la première avec la réalité. Elle embrassa longuement Alexandre et murmura :

– Je ne sais pas, après ce qui vient de se passer, ce qu'il adviendra de nous, des sentiments qui nous ont irrésistiblement poussés l'un vers l'autre, mais je ne regrette rien. Il m'est difficile de dire cela mais je n'ai pas de remords, je n'ai même pas la sensation d'avoir trompé Bertrand. Ce qui nous est arrivé est autre chose. Il va nous falloir un peu de temps pour comprendre...

Alexandre se taisait. Il voulait reculer le moment où il faudrait tourner le dos au bonheur. Il savait bien qu'il n'était pas le maître du jeu. C'est Antoinette qui déciderait et Antoinette, pour l'instant, se rhabillait. Pour elle, le rideau magique qui les avait protégés était déjà levé, un autre rôle l'attendait sur une autre scène, de l'autre côté de la porte Saint-Antoine, dans le logement de la place d'Aligre où Lucie devait depuis longtemps réclamer sa maman.

Elle avait refusé l'offre de Lenoir de la raccompagner. Il n'y avait guère qu'un quart d'heure de trajet entre la rue des Lions et le Faubourg; l'air frais du soir lui ferait du bien et, surtout, elle avait besoin d'être seule pour réfléchir. Il s'était passé tellement de choses durant cette journée où le hasard s'était joué de sa vie et de ses résolutions!

La marche solitaire et le bruit sec de ses pas sur les vieux pavés de la rue Saint-Antoine lui rappelaient un autre cheminement qui l'avait conduite à un carrefour de sa vie, le soir où elle était partie seule annoncer à Riesener, dans son atelier de l'Arsenal, que sa femme Marguerite, sa maman à elle, venait d'être écrasée par un carrosse.

Comme ce jour-là, il lui semblait avancer dans un épais brouillard. Dans son esprit le passé, le présent et l'avenir se mélangeaient curieusement. L'avenir? Qu'allait-il arriver lorsqu'elle aurait poussé la porte de son logement de la place d'Aligre? Allait-elle mentir à Bertrand ou, au contraire, lui avouer qu'elle l'avait trompé? Dans ce cas, elle connaissait d'avance sa réaction : il enfouirait sa peine profonde sous une superbe dignité, souffrirait en silence, se replierait dans sa coquille et lui rendrait sa liberté. Et Lucie dans tout cela? A la férocité d'une époque qui, malgré tous les efforts, ternissait son enfance, fallait-il ajouter le gâchis d'une vie familiale éclatée? Et puis elle aimait profondément Valfroy, l'idée de le perdre lui était intolérable...

Elle remuait toutes ces idées quand au bout de la rue elle aperçut le haut des frondaisons de la place, de « sa » place. Une éclaircie se fit alors dans son esprit : elle devait cacher la vérité à Valfroy et signifier à Alexandre que leur aventure serait sans lendemain. Soulagée d'avoir pris une décision qui mettait en veilleuse son conflit intérieur, elle grimpa très vite les deux étages, pressée soudain d'embrasser les siens. Arrivée sur le palier, elle fut surprise de trouver la porte ouverte et d'entendre un bruit de voix confus qui venait de la grand-salle. Elle comprit tout de suite qu'il s'était passé quelque chose de grave. Un accident? Lucie? Dieu merci la fillette accourait et se jetait dans les bras de sa mère.

Antoinette ouvrait la bouche pour demander ce qui se passait quand elle se retrouva entourée de visages amis, tous marqués de tristesse. Un regard lui suffit pour savoir qui manquait dans ce concert de désolation :

– Bertrand! s'écria-t-elle. Il est arrivé quelque chose à Bertrand!

Le silence qui suivit lui montra qu'elle avait vu juste.

– Mais parlez donc bon sang! Dites-moi la vérité. Bertrand est mort?

Riesener ne répondit pas, il était là immobile, comme paralysé. Les voisins eux non plus ne disaient rien. Ils étaient bien une dizaine, accourus des autres logements et des maisons proches. Comme dans l'un de ces rêves où les profils défilent très vite, Antoinette reconnut Léon Delanois, le vieux maître de Georges Jacob dont l'atelier périclitait, Pafrat qui avait pris part à l'assaut de la Bastille et qui venait de s'engager aux Volontaires du Faubourg, Pabst, l'un des grands ébénistes de son temps qui survivait en restaurant les meubles des émigrés destinés aux bureaux officiels... Tous étaient des amis de Riesener et connaissaient Antoinette depuis toujours. Ils semblaient effondrés.

Ce fut Ethis qui rompit le silence. Il s'approcha d'Antoinette et la regarda en lui tenant les deux mains :

– C'est terrible Antoinette. M. de Valfroy vient d'être arrêté alors qu'il quittait son bureau. On pense qu'il a été enfermé à la Petite-Force. Tous les sans-culottes de la section ont protesté. Certains se sont même battus contre les gardes mais rien n'y a fait. L'ordre venait du Comité de salut public.

Tout le monde alors se mit à parler, qui pour dire des paroles d'espoir, qui pour jeter l'anathème sur les Jacobins, Fouquier-Tinville et Robespierre. Antoinette, elle, demeurait comme assommée par la nouvelle. Elle était livide. Sans Ethis qui la soutenait, elle se serait écroulée. Finalement on l'assit sur l'ottomane, face aux portraits de ses parents qui trônaient toujours sur les tapisseries de Réveillon, là où Œben les avait un jour accrochés.

Un peu calmée par l'eau de mélisse qu'une voisine venait de lui faire boire, Antoinette essayait de remettre de l'ordre dans son esprit. Ses préoccupations sentimentales lui paraissaient soudain d'une insignifiance ridicule à côté de l'arrestation de Bertrand. Elle avait pensé des dizaines de fois à cette menace qui pesait sur la famille. Bertrand n'en parlait pas mais il savait qu'il était à la merci d'une quelconque dénonciation depuis que cette odieuse pratique avait été proclamée vertu patriotique. Il savait aussi que s'il n'avait rien à craindre des membres les plus excités de sa section, où il était respecté, rien ne pourrait arrêter le processus d'une accusation lancée par le Tribunal révolutionnaire, accusation qu'une simple lettre anonyme pouvait déclencher. Sous la Terreur, on n'était pas impunément baron et ancien commis du roi !

Les yeux fermés, serrant toujours le poignet d'Ethis qu'elle devinait prêt à fondre en larmes, Antoinette pensait à tout cela. L'issue d'une telle arrestation, hélas ! semblait fatale : un citoyen déclaré « suspect », même sans raison et sans preuve, n'avait pas plus d'une chance sur dix d'échapper au couperet. Un moment, le remords la saisit. Et si ce malheur n'était que la conséquence d'une trahison qui, soudain, lui paraissait monstrueuse ? Si la Némésis, Dieu ou ses saints réglaient leurs comptes et faisaient payer à l'innocent Bertrand sa propre faiblesse ? Et puis elle se raisonna, se dit que le ciel ne pactisait pas avec la Terreur pour distribuer ses punitions et qu'il était stupide de mêler des événements qui n'avaient rien à voir entre eux.

– On verra plus tard pour les regrets et la morale! s'écria-t-elle soudain devant Ethis étonné. Ce qu'il faut maintenant c'est se battre, remuer ciel et terre, alerter le monde entier pour arracher Bertrand aux griffes des êtres sanguinaires qui gouvernent aujourd'hui.

Chapitre 4.

LES SURVIVANTS

Bertrand de Valfroy avait été transféré à l'Abbaye, prison encore plus sinistre que la Petite-Force, où les traces de sang des massacres de septembre étaient encore visibles sur les murs. Il partageait son cachot avec un jeune homme de vingt-sept ans, fonctionnaire au ministère de la Guerre, qui ignorait les causes exactes de son arrestation et dont le visage émacié et la nervosité trahissaient l'angoisse. Ardent révolutionnaire, membre des Cordeliers, ami de Saint-Just, il ne se faisait guère d'illusions sur le sort qui l'attendait. Non seulement sa présence n'était pas un réconfort pour Valfroy mais ses crises de désespoir affectaient le courage de Bertrand. Celui-ci n'était toujours pas jugé et il se demandait chaque jour les raisons d'un sursis dont il semblait le seul à bénéficier. Il avait vu disparaître un à un tous ses compagnons. Vincent, à son tour, allait être transféré à la Conciergerie, dernière étape avant le procès et la guillotine. Lui en était toujours à attendre sa comparution. Certains jours, il pensait que c'était bon de se sentir en vie et reprenait espoir, mais le plus souvent, il ressentait cette attente comme un supplice ajouté à la certitude de la mort prochaine. Comment aurait-il pu deviner qu'il devait à Ethis et à un comédien obscur la faveur de respirer encore l'air empesté de son cachot?

Antoinette, de son côté, continuait ses démarches désespérées, écrivait des lettres aux députés et remuait ciel et terre pour sauver son mari. Ses relations avec Alexandre Lenoir étaient devenues ce qu'elle avait souhaité. Elle avait eu une explication franche avec le jeune homme : « J'ai dix ans de plus que vous, j'éprouve de l'amour et de la tendresse pour mon mari et vous comprendrez qu'après le drame qui vient de me séparer de lui, il ne peut être question de poursuivre notre courte histoire. Remarquez, Alexandre, que je ne regrette rien. Je garderai toute ma vie le souvenir d'un après-midi hors du temps qui restera pour nous deux le plus doux des secrets. »

Lenoir avait répondu comme elle l'espérait à ses propos et se conduisait en parfait gentilhomme. Il lui avait simplement demandé la permission de demeurer auprès d'elle et la petite Lucie l'ami affectionné et vigilant toujours disponible et prêt à les aider. Depuis Notre-Dame, rien n'était venu mettre en péril une amitié qui ne pourrait plus jamais, ils en étaient sûrs, redevenir de l'amour.

Ethis, lui, prenait une place de plus en plus importante dans la famille dont il se sentait responsable depuis l'incarcération de Valfroy. Son sérieux et son attitude protectrice faisaient sourire Antoinette, tout à fait consciente par ailleurs du secours que lui apportait le garçon. Souvent elle lui disait, et ce n'étaient pas des paroles de circonstance : « Mon petit Ethis, si tu n'étais pas là, je ne sais pas comment je pourrais vivre. J'ai beaucoup de chance de t'avoir près de moi en ce moment ! »

Le commis de M. Alexandre Lenoir rougissait de plaisir et redoublait d'attentions. Une crainte pourtant le poursuivait. Il voyait avec inquiétude Antoinette s'agiter à propos du sort de son mari. Un jour, elle lui dit qu'elle allait se rendre à la Convention pour rencontrer son beau-frère et le sommer d'intervenir. Ethis que les événements avaient mûri et dont l'intelligence longtemps laissée en friche, se développait chaque jour davantage, sentit tout de suite le danger : si Charles Delacroix allait mettre son nez dans l'affaire Valfroy et déclencher une enquête qui risquait fort de faire découvrir le manège de

La Bussière? Le danger lui parut assez grand pour qu'il se décide à mettre Antoinette dans le secret. Un soir où ils étaient tous les deux frileusement installés devant l'âtre, il lui conta par le menu comment le comédien du théâtre de la Révolution avait jusque-là réussi à empêcher le jugement de Bertrand en même temps que celui d'une centaine d'autres détenus.

Antoinette n'en croyait pas ses oreilles. Elle regarda Ethis un moment, l'attira contre elle et éclata en sanglots :

– Ainsi tu as réussi à faire cela, toi? Sans l'aide de ton ami, il est certain que notre pauvre Bertrand serait exécuté depuis longtemps. Tu m'avais un jour redonné de l'espoir en me parlant d'un mystérieux secours. Pourquoi m'as-tu laissée dans l'ignorance? Je sens mon sang qui se réchauffe et qui bat plus vite. Si M. de Valfroy est sauvé, ce sera grâce à toi!

– J'ai juré, Antoinette, de ne révéler à personne, pas même à vous, le secret de La Bussière. Si je vous ai parlé aujourd'hui c'est uniquement parce que je craignais qu'une intervention auprès de votre beau-frère Delacroix ne fasse découvrir les raisons pour lesquelles votre mari ne passe pas en jugement.

– Sois tranquille, mon petit Ethis. Le secret sera bien gardé et je n'irai pas voir mon beau-frère. Je sais d'ailleurs par ma sœur qu'il n'a pas levé le petit doigt pour sauver Bertrand. Elle dit que c'est par peur. Peut-être est-ce la vérité. Je sais, moi, que si les rôles avaient été inversés, M. de Valfroy n'aurait pas agi ainsi. Vois-tu, Ethis, ce qui différencie ces deux hommes qui ont à peu près le même âge : l'un a du cœur, de la vertu, c'est un être de qualité; l'autre est un arriviste, un égoïste qui ne voit que son intérêt. Ethis, je te le dis avec toute ma tendresse : c'est M. de Valfroy qu'il faut prendre pour modèle. Tu n'y gagneras pas forcément la richesse mais sûrement du bonheur.

Ainsi allait la vie place d'Aligre où comme dans toutes les familles du Faubourg chacun essayait de tenir, de surmonter les difficultés sans cesse accrues du ravitaillement et, surtout, de vaincre l'angoisse que la Grande Terreur, officiellement décrétée, distillait comme un poison jusque dans les foyers qui n'avaient guère à craindre ses excès les plus sanglants.

Ces excès, personne ne pouvait plus les ignorer dans le vieux quartier de l'Abbaye. La guillotine qui avait été déplacée du Carrousel à la place de la Révolution [1] puis à la Bastille venait d'être finalement installée à la barrière du Trône-renversé. Les charrettes où l'on avait naguère entassé quinze condamnés et qui en transportaient maintenant de trente à cinquante empruntaient toutes la grand-rue du Faubourg après avoir fait leur plein dans les trente prisons de la capitale. Quelquefois les curieux – il y en avait de moins en moins parmi les vieux habitants du quartier – reconnaissaient des visages connus dans le cortège brinquebalant des suppliciés. Ethis rapporta un jour que dans la fournée du matin on avait aperçu les époux Toison, bien connus de tout le vieux Faubourg. Ils tenaient un petit théâtre de marionnettes sur le cours Saint-Antoine derrière la Bastille. On sut le lendemain de quel crime on les avait punis de mort : ils avaient habillé l'une de leurs poupées en Charlotte Corday et lui avaient fait crier « A bas Marat ».

Rien de tel qu'un martyr pour ressouder les énergies révolutionnaires qui tendaient à se diluer dans le flot de sang de la Terreur. Le meurtre de Marat était arrivé à point : on lui élevait des temples, des arcs de triomphe et Ethis, toujours lui, revint un soir de son travail avec une feuille vendue un sou sur les marches de l'Hôtel de Ville. C'était une prière composée par un nommé Brochet, où Jésus se confondait avec Marat. Antoinette ne put s'empêcher d'éclater de rire en en déchiffrant la fin : « Cœur de Jésus, cœur de Marat. O sacré cœur de Jésus, ô sacré cœur de Marat. »

– Il leur reste encore Hébert! dit Lenoir qui conservait dans une poche de sa redingote l'article du *Père Duchesne* écrit au lendemain de l'exécution de Marie-Antoinette. Il

1. Place de la Concorde.

lut : « J'ai vu tomber dans le sac la tête du Veto femelle. Je voudrais, foutre, pouvoir vous exprimer la satisfaction des sans-culottes quand l'architigresse a traversé Paris dans la voiture à trente-six portières... »

Alexandre Lenoir conservait ce monstrueux chef-d'œuvre d'Hébert comme le témoignage le plus significatif de la folie révolutionnaire.

– Après de tels propos signés par l'inspirateur du culte de la déesse Raison, comment en vouloir à ceux auxquels les événements ont tourné la tête et qui se contentent d'assassiner les statues!

Réveillon demeurait un fidèle de la place d'Aligre. Depuis qu'il avait décidé d'abandonner les affaires, il s'ennuyait dans son bel appartement de la rue des Bons-Enfants que sa femme – « la plus triste figure que je connaisse », disait Antoinette – entretenait avec un soin maladif. Chez sa filleule, à deux pas de la rue Saint-Nicolas où il était né, il retrouvait l'atmosphère chaleureuse du Faubourg, le seul lieu de Paris où il était bien. Les deux ébénistes qui occupaient la maison Thirion quand il l'avait achetée quelques années auparavant étaient partis faute de travail et il s'était mis dans la tête de la restaurer.

– Quand Lucie sera en âge de se marier, disait-il, elle n'aura qu'à s'installer. A moins que je ne vienne habiter moi-même le Faubourg pour y finir mes vieux jours.

Deux de ses anciens ouvriers travaillaient donc depuis quelques semaines à gratter les parquets, les poutres, à lessiver les murs sous la surveillance attentive de Réveillon qui, à l'exemple des fouilles conduites par les Italiens à Pompéi depuis trente ans, prétendait pouvoir retrouver sous les couches de peinture des murs les plus anciens des traces, des témoignages de la vie des premiers habitants de la maison, en particulier de ces Cottion et de ces Thirion dont il avait réussi à déchiffrer les noms sur les registres de Sainte-Marguerite échappés par miracle aux autodafés qui avaient suivi la réforme religieuse. Au fond de l'atelier du rez-de-chaussée, la pièce la plus ancienne, il avait ainsi découvert gravée dans la chaux, sous des strates de suie, de poussière et de colle, une sorte de toise qui avait permis jadis d'enregistrer la croissance des enfants de la famille. Ce jour-là il était allé tout de suite chercher Antoinette qui se moquait volontiers de ses recherches.

Ensemble avec mille précautions, en approfondissant avec un stylet les traces de lettres, ils avaient ainsi mis au jour des vestiges de la plus vieille famille du Faubourg. Sur une grande feuille de papier, Antoinette avait reproduit ces signes et ces dates qui avaient sans doute été les jalons d'un bonheur. Au-dessus de chaque trait vertical elle put reconstituer un prénom et puis, jusqu'à une certaine hauteur, des dates correspondant à des encoches : Perrine dont on pouvait retrouver la taille et l'âge : « 2 ans, 2 pieds 8 pouces » et une date : 1527. A côté, la marque de Denis, avec un patronyme : Thirion. A 2 ans, lui mesurait 2 centimètres de plus, c'était en 1526. Une troisième toise concernait peut-être le fils des précédents : il s'appelait Christophe Habermann, était né en 1550, « au Louvre » précisait l'inscription. A 6 ans ce gaillard mesurait 3 pieds 5 pouces et l'on pouvait suivre sa croissance jusqu'à l'âge de neuf ans.

Antoinette comme Réveillon était émue :

– Vous aviez déjà remarqué ce nom d'Habermann sur le berceau découvert dans le grenier. L'un de mes ancêtres aurait donc été l'un des premiers ébénistes installés dans le Faubourg? C'est passionnant et émouvant. Je vais conserver tous ces souvenirs pour Lucie.

– Tu vois que ce n'était pas une si mauvaise idée de racheter cette vieille maison. Je savais que ses murs nous raconteraient des histoires! N'oublie pas qu'il nous reste tout le grenier à fouiller. Nous ferons cela un jour avec Ethis. Tu ne peux pas savoir combien ces trouvailles me font plaisir! Et puis, c'est sain, en ces temps de fureur où la mort rôde devant chaque porte, de pouvoir se plonger dans la mémoire des âges. Ils ont dû en subir eux aussi des malheurs, tous ces gens dont la trace est demeurée jusqu'à nous. Et le monde continue d'exister. Aujourd'hui le Faubourg semble mort, abandonné, mais il renaîtra un jour. De nouveau on entendra dans les cours le bruit de la scie et le chuintement de la varlope...

– Merci, mon parrain, de me parler ainsi! dit Antoinette sans chercher à dissimuler l'émotion qui l'étreignait. Vous avez raison. Il faut se souvenir du passé pour supporter le présent. Cette visite à la vieille maison m'a fait oublier un instant le calvaire de Bertrand mais, vous le savez, je pense sans cesse à lui. Comme nous serons heureux le jour où il reviendra! Car il reviendra, j'en suis sûre!

– Ton beau-frère n'a rien fait. Cela ne m'étonne pas trop. Mais peut-être est-ce mieux ainsi...

– C'est mon sentiment. Valfroy aurait dû passer dix fois en jugement et...

Elle essuya une larme et continua:

– Si on l'a oublié au fond de son cachot, mieux vaut sans doute ne pas réveiller les bourreaux!

Le soir, en rentrant, elle montra à Lucie les signes qu'elle avait déchiffrés sur les murs de la maison Thirion. Elle lui raconta ce qu'elle savait ou plutôt ce qu'elle imaginait de la vie des ancêtres du Faubourg. La petite fille l'écouta, grave et passionnée, aussi attentive que lorsqu'elle écoutait un conte de M. Charles Perrault.

– Je veux, dit-elle, aller voir cette maison et chercher avec toi. C'est mon père chéri qui sera content quand il reviendra et que nous lui raconterons nos trouvailles!

Les semaines s'ajoutèrent aux semaines. Chaque jour qui passait faisait renaître l'espoir et Antoinette commençait à croire vraiment l'extravagante histoire du comédien-secrétaire qui veillait dans les bureaux du Comité de sûreté sur la vie de son mari. Pourtant les heures étaient longues. La tristesse et la peur qui flottaient sur Paris n'épargnaient pas la place d'Aligre hier encore bruissante des cris et des conversations des marchands de légumes. Chacun restait terré dans son logement, Antoinette attendait le soir avec impatience. C'était pour elle le moment où Ethis faisait circuler un peu d'air frais dans la salle assombrie par un printemps pluvieux. Souvent, Alexandre Lenoir l'accompagnait. Il apportait alors sa part de provisions achetées au hasard de ses pérégrinations et partageait le souper familial auquel Riesener se joignait fréquemment. Le spectre de la guillotine qui la poursuivait tout le jour disparaissait alors de la pensée d'Antoinette. En parlant, elle cessait de considérer Bertrand comme un mort en sursis...

Les nouvelles que rapportaient les hommes n'étaient pourtant pas rassurantes. Plus de mille condamnations à mort avaient été prononcées depuis le début de l'année et les charrettes continuaient de défiler matin et soir dans le Faubourg. Seule la situation aux frontières était encourageante. La République et son armée de va-nu-pieds avait tenu bon et résisté aux efforts de l'Europe conjugués. Ce succès permettait à Lenoir des analyses brillantes, sévères et souvent paradoxales.

– Le génie infernal de Robespierre, disait-il, a peut-être sauvé la France. L'Histoire trouvera bien des thuriféraires pour tresser des lauriers à ce fanatique aux veines glacées!

– Ainsi, vous êtes prêt à justifier l'assassinat d'innombrables innocents? coupait Antoinette toutes griffes dehors.

– Mais non. Le danger ne justifie pas la Terreur. La France a connu des moments aussi graves et repoussé bien des invasions sans recourir à un tel mépris des individus. C'était il est vrai au temps des rois et non sous le despotisme d'un gouvernement issu de la Déclaration des droits de l'homme!

– Vous blasphémez mon ami. Vous semblez faire bien peu de cas du culte de l'Être suprême! dit Antoinette moqueuse.

Cédant à la force du mythe et à une volonté de puissance qu'il prenait pour de la vertu, Maximilien

Robespierre avait en effet fait voter par la Convention, au terme d'une envolée oratoire aberrante, un décret qui plongeait les citoyens ayant conservé quelque esprit critique dans une profonde perplexité : « Le peuple français reconnaît l'existence de l'Être suprême et l'immortalité de l'âme, et il sera institué des fêtes pour rappeler l'homme à la pensée de la divinité et à la dignité de son être. »

– A propos de l'Être suprême, interrompit Riesener, savez-vous que David m'a fait demander par le fils Jacob si je voulais aider la commission chargée d'organiser la cérémonie du 20 prairial aux Tuileries?

– Vous avez accepté? demanda Antoinette, déjà prête à fustiger son beau-père.

– Non. J'ai refusé, figure-toi! Et quelle raison j'ai invoquée? J'ai dit que j'avais trop de commandes en retard!

Tout le monde éclata de rire et la conversation s'attarda sur David. Le peintre qui au temps de la royauté avait un atelier au Louvre était un vieil ami de Riesener. Henry, le fils de ce dernier avait été son élève. Les artistes, tous deux appréciés de la cour, s'estimaient. Depuis 89, David essayait d'amener l'ébéniste à entrer dans le cercle des artistes dévoués à la Révolution. Riesener se serait peut-être finalement laissé circonvenir si le peintre ne s'était pas fait élire député, siégeant à la Convention dans les rangs de la Montagne. « Qu'est-ce qu'un artiste a à faire avec la politique! » avait dit Riesener. Les rapports entre les deux hommes s'étaient encore distendus quand David avait voté la mort du roi et accepté de faire partie du Comité de sûreté.

– Ce David n'est pas un méchant homme, commenta Riesener. S'il était ce soir au milieu de nous, il vous étonnerait par ses connaissances en art et en peinture, il vous parlerait de l'assimilation de l'art antique par l'art révolutionnaire et du nouveau style qui va en advenir. Si seulement il s'était borné au rôle d'artiste qui est le sien! Je l'aurais bien aidé à organiser la fête de la Fédération et toutes les cavalcades patriotiques. Mais, franchement, cet être de tous les talents m'est insupportable. Il ne peut résister au moindre hochet officiel. Avec un chapeau à plumes et une écharpe tricolore on en fait un serviteur zélé du pouvoir. Je suis sûr que si un roi remonte un jour sur le trône, David sera le premier sur les rangs pour faire son portrait!

Sans Riesener mais avec une armée de terrassiers et de menuisiers, David préparait donc aux Tuileries le triomphe d'un Être suprême qui, aux yeux de la plupart des gens, n'était autre que Robespierre lui-même. Selon une habitude qui remontait à la première fête du Champ-de-Mars, David avait dressé une montagne artificielle avec ses pics et ses précipices, au pied de laquelle devait prendre place la Convention. Les ouvriers montaient des estrades pour les délégations des sections, les enfants, les vieillards, les jeunes filles et les mères de famille. Entre les fenêtres du château, des peintres inscrivaient des maximes où il n'était question que de fraternité, de liberté et de probité. Leur peinture n'était pas encore sèche quand on apprit que Condorcet s'était empoisonné dans sa prison pour échapper à la guillotine, qu'André Chénier avait été exécuté et que le grand chimiste Lavoisier avait à son tour mis sa tête dans la lucarne après que l'un de ses juges, l'immortel Coffinhal, lui eut signifié, au cours de son procès, que « la République n'avait pas besoin de savants »!

Enfin arriva le grand jour. Une fête est une fête, et comme les Parisiens n'avaient guère d'occasions de se réjouir, les Tuileries étaient bondées d'une foule joyeuse et colorée quand Antoinette y pénétra, tenant par la main la petite Lucie qui n'avait jamais vu autant de monde. Personne ne savait quel était cet Être suprême qu'on célébrait avec tant de faste. Un citoyen qui tentait d'expliquer qu'il s'agissait du nouveau Bon Dieu révolutionnaire suscita un grand mouvement d'hilarité dans le public, ce même public qui acclama quelques minutes plus tard Robespierre lorsqu'il apparut marchant seul à la tête de la Convention. Applaudissait-il un dieu vivant ou un bourreau? Peut-être tout simplement le costume très

Ancien Régime du grand prêtre poudré à blanc, sa cravate de mousseline artistement nouée sur un linge et un gilet de piqué d'une blancheur irréprochable. Un habit bleu barbeau, une culotte courte, des bas de soie et des souliers à boucle d'or complétaient ce costume qui n'avait vraiment rien de la couleur mythologique que David avait voulu donner à la fête.

Installée dans les bras de sa mère, Lucie ne perdait rien de ce spectacle extraordinaire ponctué par les accords de l'orchestre de la République.

– Qui c'est, ce monsieur? demanda-t-elle soudain en désignant le personnage qui prenait place sur l'autel dressé devant le palais et s'asseyait dans un fauteuil qui avait bien l'air d'un trône.

– C'est lui, c'est Robespierre, ma chérie, le président de la Convention.

Antoinette avait répondu sans réfléchir, ne se doutant pas de la réaction de la petite fille qui s'écria :

– Celui qui a mis en prison mon père chéri?

La phrase était tombée des jolies lèvres de Lucie alors que la musique venait de s'arrêter si bien que tout le monde autour l'entendit. Antoinette qui serra sa fille contre elle en lui chuchotant de se taire perçut quelques paroles désobligeantes mais surtout des rires. Une femme à côté d'elle essaya même d'entrer en conversation en plaignant la pauvre petite fille privée de père mais Antoinette ne répondit pas et s'éloigna : ce n'était pas parce que l'échafaud faisait pause, en ce jour de liesse religieuse, qu'il ne fallait pas être prudent.

Un œil averti se serait peut-être aperçu que cette fête, en dépit de son succès populaire, distillait une curieuse impression de fin de règne. Robespierre, certes, avait été applaudi par une grande partie de la foule mais beaucoup avaient remarqué les murmures des députés qui s'enflaient lorsqu'il passait devant eux. On percevait dans les rangs de la Convention des remarques qui ne pouvaient prêter à confusion telles que « mascarade », « orgueil fou ». Bourdon de l'Oise, commentant le côté romain de la cérémonie, s'était même écrié pour être entendu de tous ses collègues : « Si nous sommes revenus aux temps antiques, alors il y a encore des Brutus ! »

Le métaphysique et très long discours du doge des Tuileries n'arrangea pas les choses. La fête de l'Être suprême marquait sans doute l'apogée de son hégémonie mais Robespierre déjà n'était plus le maître du jeu. Longtemps accoutumés, comme à une sorte de drogue, aux exécutions banalisées, aux tueries qui après avoir ensanglanté la place de la Révolution rendaient irrespirable l'air de la barrière du Trône renversé, les Parisiens commençaient à être saisis de nausée devant ces têtes qui tombaient à un rythme infernal. Le temps venait pour Robespierre de « boire la ciguë », comme il l'avait prophétisé naguère dans un discours. C'est au sein de la Convention qu'il allait trouver ses bourreaux : l'Assemblée qu'il avait si longtemps dominée et terrorisée ne le reconnaîtrait bientôt plus pour maître.

En attendant, les exécutions interrompues pour la fête de l'Être suprême reprenaient : vingt-six le 14 juin, dix-huit le 15 et quarante-deux le 16. Le 17 soixante et une personnes étaient conduites à l'échafaud et cinquante-quatre le lendemain dont six femmes et deux jeunes filles de dix-sept et dix-neuf ans. Chaque jour la liste des exécutions s'allongeait. Le 17 juillet une fournée de quarante-deux condamnés avaient encore eu la tête tranchée et, parmi eux, les seize carmélites de Compiègne [1].

Dans la journée du 20 prairial, la nouvelle se répandit dans le Faubourg que le fils de Louis XVI et de Marie-Antoinette, celui que les royalistes saluaient du titre de Louis XVII et que les révolutionnaires appelaient Capet, venait de mourir au Temple par suite des mauvais traitements de ses geôliers et que son corps avait été inhumé discrètement dans le cimetière de Sainte-Marguerite durant la nuit. Le vieux quartier du meuble n'accueillit pas la nouvelle sans tristesse et commisération. La

1. Ce n'est là qu'un court extrait du *Journal intime d'un bourgeois de Paris,* tenu par Nicolas Célestin Guittard. Dans un registre spécial, cet homme précis et scrupuleux a consigné chaque jour l'effarante liste des exécutions en 1794.

mort d'un enfant de dix ans dont rien n'avait justifié l'effrayante captivité, éclairait l'atroce réalité d'une terreur qui s'éternisait dans le sang.

C'est Ethis, toujours à l'affût des nouvelles, qui rapporta la confirmation de la mort de l'enfant et son enterrement dans le petit cimetière du Faubourg.

– Je sais tout, annonça-t-il. Par Marie, ma fiancée...

– Hein? coupa Antoinette. Tu es fiancé? Je croyais que tu ne voyais plus la petite Bénard, que vous étiez fâchés...

– Oui, mais nous sommes réconciliés. Quand la Révolution sera finie nous nous marierons.

– Ah bon! Et alors que t'a-t-elle dit?

– Son père qui est commissaire civil a assisté le commissaire de police Dusser qui était chargé par le Comité de sûreté générale de l'inhumation du petit Capet. Dusser a ordonné, d'accord avec le père Bénard, d'inhumer l'enfant dans une fosse séparée et non dans la fosse commune du cimetière Sainte-Marguerite. Dénoncé comme royaliste, M. Bénard a bien failli pour cela être traduit devant le Tribunal révolutionnaire[1]!

– Que cette jeune et innocente victime repose en paix! murmura Antoinette en se signant.

Déjà Ethis était lancé dans l'explication d'un autre mystère auquel les commères du quartier ne trouvaient pas de réponse: où étaient enterrés les suppliciés de la place du Trône renversé? Les tombereaux où l'on avait mis les corps prenaient le chemin de la proche campagne, entourés de gendarmes, et personne n'avait osé les suivre.

1. Malgré l'acte de décès officiel rédigé au Temple le 24 prairial de l'an III et certifié par le commissaire Dusser, « la question Louis XVII » continue de passionner de nombreux historiens. L'enfant du Temple et de Sainte-Marguerite ne serait pas le dauphin mais un autre enfant mort dans la prison et dont on aurait fait passer le corps pour celui du fils de Louis XVI. A l'appui de cette thèse aventureuse, les exhumations de 1846 et 1894 qui auraient montré que les ossements trouvés dans la bière étaient ceux d'un jeune homme de quinze à dix-huit ans. Des travaux entrepris en 1832 lors de l'élargissement de la rue Saint-Bernard ayant sensiblement modifié l'état des lieux, rien ne prouve que le cercueil ouvert fût celui du petit roi.

La proximité de la guillotine, installée au bout du Faubourg, rendait d'actualité ces considérations macabres. Même ceux qui n'allaient jamais assister aux exécutions savaient que l'architecte de la commune, Poyet, avait fait pratiquer dans la chaussée, un trou destiné à recevoir le sang des décapités et que ce procédé n'empêchait pas les odeurs méphitiques de se répandre dans le quartier; on savait aussi que le citoyen Coffinet, connu comme inventeur à tout faire, avait proposé, sans être encore entendu, d'établir sur une brouette un coffre doublé de feuilles de plomb dans lequel tomberait le sang qui serait ensuite versé dans la fosse commune [1].

– Je sais où se trouve la fosse commune des guillotinés! annonça donc Ethis avec un air de satisfaction qui lui valut aussitôt les reproches d'Antoinette. Celle-ci supportait mal qu'on fît allusion devant elle à la guillotine:

– Tu n'as pas d'autres sujets d'intérêt! s'écria-t-elle. Vous me dégoûtez tous à vous repaître de sang et de cadavres. As-tu seulement songé que Bertrand, que tu considères comme ton père, pourrait un jour être l'un de ces suppliciés qui intéressent tes pensées morbides?

Un silence se fit. Ethis, désemparé, la regardait les larmes aux yeux:

– Pardonne-moi, murmura-t-il en embrassant Antoinette. Je ne voulais pas te faire du mal. Tu sais combien j'aime M. de Valfroy et comme je serais perdu s'il lui arrivait malheur...

– Que voulez-vous Antoinette, dit Lenoir, ces enfants vivent depuis des années au cœur d'un drame effrayant où la mort est présente à tous les instants. En parler comme d'une banalité est pour beaucoup de gens une façon de la nier, d'échapper à son destin. Je crois qu'on peut comprendre les réactions d'Ethis...

– Je sais tout cela mon ami mais je voudrais tellement qu'Ethis ne sorte pas abîmé et insensible de toute cette barbarie! Va mon Ethis. Puisque tu as commencé,

1. Souvenirs de l'architecte Poyet.

dis-nous où l'on enterre les victimes de la Terreur.

– C'est parce que c'est dans le quartier, sinon je n'en aurais pas parlé, s'excusa Ethis d'un air malheureux.

– Alors? dit Lenoir. Raconte!

– C'est au bout de la rue de Picpus, dans l'ancienne propriété des Augustins. Il y a paraît-il une ancienne carrière de sable où l'on a creusé des fosses communes de quinze mètres.

Il n'en dit pas plus pour ne pas peiner Antoinette et se mit à parler de ses promenades avec Mlle Marie Bénard, ce qui détendit l'atmosphère; mais ce fut Réveillon qui apporta sur le coup de sept heures la grande nouvelle: Robespierre venait d'être désavoué pour la première fois par la Convention dont les forces divisées cherchaient maintenant ouvertement à se détruire.

– Robespierre, raconta Réveillon, vient de faire un long discours qui n'est que la justification de son passé révolutionnaire, celui d'un homme qui se retrouve seul après avoir fait le vide de la mort autour de lui. Il a attaqué tellement de gens sans les nommer que les neuf dixièmes des conventionnels ont pris peur et jugé que leur salut n'était plus de son côté. La décision d'imprimer son discours a été renvoyée aux comités. Pire qu'un désaveu, il s'agit là d'un camouflet. C'est la première défaite de l'Incorruptible qui, en ce moment, parle aux Jacobins. On n'ose pas l'espérer mais c'est peut-être un grand tournant qui s'annonce, la fin de la Terreur et celle de son inspirateur.

– Mais alors, dit Antoinette timidement, comme si elle craignait qu'une joie trop prompte ne fasse obstacle à la délivrance qui perçait, Bertrand pourrait peut-être échapper pour de bon à la mort, et même être libéré...

– Disons qu'une lueur d'espoir se fait jour, répondit Réveillon, mais ne nous réjouissons pas trop vite. Robespierre a encore la parole et nous savons quelle arme redoutable il en fait!

– Êtes-vous sûr de vos informations? demanda Lenoir.

– Oui. Je m'intéresse peu à la politique vous le savez

mais j'ai quelques amis à la Convention qui sont anxieux autant que nous et qui, comme nous, espèrent la fin de ce carnage dont l'inutilité apparaît chaque jour davantage.

Antoinette ne put fermer l'œil de la nuit. Le lendemain matin, elle demanda à Ethis de ne pas rejoindre Lenoir sur le chantier de l'église Saint-Louis des jésuites, rue Saint-Antoine, où il se passait de drôles de choses. Alexandre Lenoir n'avait pas réussi à sauver les deux reliquaires qui se trouvaient de chaque côté de l'autel et qui contenaient l'un le cœur de Louis XIII, l'autre celui de Louis XIV. Les châsses d'argent richement ciselées avaient été envoyées à la fonte à l'hôtel des Monnaies. Quant aux viscères royaux, ils étaient devenus la propriété de celui qui les avait achetés, le peintre Saint-Martin, afin de les transformer en « mummie ». On appelait ainsi la couleur brune obtenue en broyant du cœur humain dans de l'huile. Ce mélange évidemment très rare et très recherché par les artistes donnait un glacis parfait, irréalisable à l'aide de peinture minérale ou végétale. Inutile de dire qu'Ethis suivait cette affaire prodigieuse avec beaucoup d'intérêt. Mais, ce matin-là, ce n'était pas ce genre d'histoire qu'Antoinette attendait d'Ethis [1].

– Ce que nous a raconté hier soir Réveillon m'a bouleversée, lui dit-elle. Songe que c'est peut-être le retour prochain de M. de Valfroy qu'il nous a annoncé! Alors je ne tiens plus en place. Je sors de ma coquille et nous allons tous les deux aller faire le tour du Faubourg pour essayer d'en savoir davantage. La nouvelle est tellement importante qu'on ne doit parler que de cela à la porte de tous les ateliers.

– Faites-moi confiance, Antoinette. Nous saurons tout ce qui s'est passé hier et ce qui se trame aujourd'hui à la Convention et dans les sections.

Le Faubourg en effet était en ébullition. Pour la

1. Saint-Martin utilisa en partie le cœur de Louis XIV qui paraît-il était le plus gros et restitua, lors de la Restauration, celui de Louis XIII ainsi que le reste du cœur du Roi-Soleil. Selon Jacques Hillairet, Louis XVIII lui offrit en contrepartie une tabatière en or.

première fois depuis longtemps, les anciens Girondins, les modérés et même les partisans de Barère, de Billaud-Varenne, de Tallien et de Barras osaient élever la voix; mais Robespierre avait encore des fidèles dans les sections de Popincourt et des Quinze-Vingts : les plus exaltés des sans-culottes, ceux que les discours inspirés et terrifiants de Robespierre entraînaient depuis quatre ans dans les voies les plus sanglantes. Étonnés de trouver des contestataires parmi ceux qui s'étaient tus jusque-là pour sauver leur tête, ils répliquaient violemment en menaçant de les dénoncer au Comité de sûreté.

– L'atmosphère a changé, murmura Antoinette à l'oreille d'Ethis, on sent qu'il s'est passé quelque chose.

– Laissez-moi un moment me mêler aux groupes qui se forment un peu partout et je vous promets de vous rapporter les dernières nouvelles. On ne se méfie pas de « Traîne-sabot » et j'ai des oreilles pour entendre.

Antoinette sourit et le laissa aller. Elle rejoignit de son côté une petite assemblée de femmes qui paraissaient fort excitées elles aussi. Sans attendre, elles rapprochaient la nouvelle de l'échec des robespierristes du ravitaillement défaillant :

– Nous avons besoin de pain, disait l'une, et on ne nous offre que des têtes coupées!

– Nous avons assez de tout ce sang répandu! disait une autre.

– Et pourquoi Robespierre n'irait-il pas essayer à son tour le couteau de Sanson?

La phrase était dite, celle que beaucoup de gens avaient sur les lèvres. C'était Louise Devergille qui l'avait prononcée. Antoinette qui connaissait depuis longtemps cette famille bourgeoise de marchands merciers du Faubourg prit la main de la femme, la serra et murmura : « Taisez-vous. Soyez prudente, on ne sait pas comment les choses vont tourner... » Louise Devergille sourit :

– Merci ma bonne Antoinette mais je me moque de ce qui peut arriver. Mon mari Louis-François dont vous connaissez l'activité à la section de Sainte-Marguerite [1] a été arrêté il y a trois jours par les suppôts de Robespierre. S'il devait être guillotiné je deviendrais une tigresse, une nouvelle Charlotte Corday.

Ethis hors d'haleine, revint à ce moment et annonça en hachant ses mots :

– Robespierre a parlé, interrompu tout de suite par Tallien et Billaud-Varenne. Il a paraît-il été arrêté par décret en compagnie de son frère, de Couthon, de Lebas et de Saint-Just. Pour le sauver, la Commune vient de décider une insurrection. Henriot déjeune au Faubourg pour soulever le peuple...

On ne connut que le soir par Lenoir les détails de cette journée du 9 thermidor : la libération par la Commune des cinq prisonniers ramenés à l'Hôtel de Ville, leur mise hors la loi par la Convention et finalement l'échec de l'insurrection : Lebas s'était tiré un coup de pistolet et était tombé mort dans les bras du frère de Robespierre qui s'était lui-même cassé une jambe en se jetant par une fenêtre. Quant à Maximilien, le demi-dieu du Champ-de-Mars, un gendarme lui avait fracassé la mâchoire d'un coup de feu [2].

Le dernier acte était pour le lendemain. Robespierre gisait maintenant la tête enveloppée d'une sorte de toile à sac. Le sang coulait de sa mâchoire pendante et inondait son habit bleu de ciel. On l'avait transporté dans la salle d'audience du Tribunal révolutionnaire qui, pour la première fois depuis longtemps, ne tenait pas séance. Allongé sur le grand bureau plat où les juges posaient d'habitude les dossiers [3], cet homme de trente-six ans,

1. Commissaire et trésorier du district et de la Commission des secours de Sainte-Marguerite dès juillet 1789, élu commissaire de la section en 1790 et 1792, emprisonné sous la Terreur, libéré après Thermidor, Louis-François Devergille sera de nouveau désigné comme électeur en l'an V.

2. Cette thèse du gendarme Merda est controversée par ceux qui prétendent que Robespierre s'est tiré lui-même un coup de pistolet dans la tête et s'est manqué.

3. Il faudra attendre une vente du XIXe siècle pour apprendre que ce bureau, récupéré par le Comité de salut public dans les réserves du Mobilier royal, portait l'estampille de Riesener !

figure de proue de la Révolution et de la Terreur, maître durant deux années de la France, attendait son exécution.

C'est à dix-huit heures que la charrette le conduisit au pied de cette guillotine inconnue : les condamnations n'étaient pour lui que des signatures, il n'avait encore jamais vu le sinistre couperet qui avait tranché la tête de tant de ses amis.

L'annonce de l'exécution de Robespierre éclata à Paris comme un coup de canon. Antoinette était en train de faire manger un bol de soupe à Lucie avant de la coucher quand Ethis, que Lenoir appelait le « Mercure du Faubourg », fit irruption dans le logement de la place d'Aligre :

– Robespierre est mort ! Robespierre est mort ! La Terreur est finie ! Je vais rassembler des amis pour aller libérer M. de Valfroy !

Tout essoufflé, il se jeta dans les bras d'Antoinette qui riait et sanglotait à la fois. Enfin, l'engrenage infernal semblait pouvoir s'arrêter. Pour la première fois, l'espoir faisait place à une réalité libératrice. Antoinette refrénait pourtant l'envie de crier son bonheur. Robespierre n'était pas le seul pourvoyeur de l'échafaud. Tant que Bertrand demeurerait en prison, il serait à la merci d'un déferlement populaire et sauvage. Le souvenir des massacres de septembre était encore présent dans toutes les mémoires !

Bientôt le carrosse déglingué de Lenoir s'arrêta devant la porte. Réveillon qui avait rencontré Riesener devant l'hospice des Enfants-Trouvés arriva à son tour en compagnie de l'ébéniste. Le petit groupe qui avait soutenu Antoinette durant les mois terribles de la Terreur se retrouvait autour d'elle à l'heure où le ciel s'éclaircissait.

– Vous êtes tous là, vous êtes tous là ! répétait-elle. Et puis, la réalité des choses reprenant le dessus, elle demandait : Et maintenant ? Que va-t-il arriver ? Va-t-on libérer les détenus ?

Ethis qui préférait l'action aux supputations annonça à

nouveau qu'il allait constituer une petite troupe pour aller enfoncer les portes des prisons. Tous l'en dissuadèrent.

– Pas question! s'exclama Lenoir. Il faut laisser les événements évoluer, savoir ce que vont faire les sections et la Commune. Bertrand n'est pas le seul détenu et des mesures générales seront sûrement prises demain ou dans les jours qui viennent. Ce n'est vraiment pas le moment d'aller risquer un mauvais coup.

Ethis n'obtint que la permission d'aller traîner ses sabots dans le Faubourg afin de sentir le vent et de connaître les réactions des sans-culottes des sections de Sainte-Marguerite et des Quinze-Vingts. Il n'était évidemment pas question de dormir un soir pareil. Les fenêtres grandes ouvertes sur les marronniers de la place laissaient entrer de l'air frais. Pour la première fois on s'apercevait que c'était l'été, on avait envie de sourire à la vie. Antoinette ajouta dans la marmite de soupe qui cuisait doucement dans l'âtre un morceau de lard qu'elle conservait depuis longtemps dans le saloir.

– Nous souperons gras ce soir, dit-elle. Comme si nous étions certains que la Terreur est bien finie!

Réveillon annonça que, dans ce cas, il allait tout de suite rendre visite à un vieil ami de jeunesse qui tenait un cabaret dans le passage de la Main-d'or.

– Je suis sûr, ajouta-t-il, qu'il va trouver pour moi dans sa cave une bouteille de vin de Champagne oubliée sous un tas de bois.

Ainsi expira la Terreur qui avait bien failli faire mourir la France. Le soulagement fut immédiat. On avait craint une réaction violente de la Commune, mais la Commune usée qui n'avait rien pu faire pour sauver Robespierre et sa politique avait sombré avec lui. La légitimité avait triomphé, la Convention libérée de ceux qui l'avaient asservie allait pouvoir s'efforcer d'éteindre les derniers feux d'une révolution dont beaucoup pensaient qu'elle avait consumé les derniers enthousiasmes.

Les sections elles-mêmes, fiefs des sans-culottes, venaient, comme Antoinette le lut dans *Le Moniteur*, « déposer au sein de la Convention nationale leur profession de foi et apporter leurs félicitations ». La section « Bon Conseil » avait même réclamé l'honneur d'avoir arrêté « ce scélérat d'Henriot, satellite forcené de Catalina-Robespierre ». Dans le même numéro du 11 thermidor, Barras, le tombeur de « l'Incorruptible » avec Tallien et Billaud-Varenne, qui venait d'être nommé commandant provisoire de la Force publique de Paris, constatait la situation satisfaisante de la ville : « La joie se peint sur tous les visages, les conspirateurs sont maudits et voués à l'exécration publique. »

Ethis, lui, ne quittait pas le portail d'entrée de l'Abbaye. Les détenus politiques devaient être libérés d'un instant à l'autre et il voulait être là quand Valfroy sortirait afin de le ramener tout de suite place d'Aligre. Le vieux carrosse aux chefs-d'œuvre attendait un peu plus loin. Ethis en avait même brossé avec soin les coussins déchirés.

Le cauchemar prit fin le matin du 12 quand, lentement, comme hébétés, les rescapés de la guillotine franchirent la porte de la prison en cherchant dans la foule un visage connu. Antoinette, épuisée par les émotions de ces derniers jours, avait accepté, sur les conseils de Lenoir et de Riesener, de demeurer à la maison. Ses nerfs n'auraient pas supporté l'attente dont on ne pouvait prévoir la durée. Ethis reconnut tout de suite la haute silhouette de Valfroy dans la cohue qui entourait maintenant l'entrée. Sans s'occuper des protestations qui fusaient, il se fraya un passage dans la foule, bousculant tout le monde et criant : « Monsieur de Valfroy ! Monsieur de Valfroy ! »

Bertrand enfin l'entendit et s'avança en lui ouvrant ses bras. Tandis qu'ils s'étreignaient, Ethis constata combien la détention l'avait changé. Il portait une barbe grise mal taillée sur ses joues creuses. Son teint était blafard, ses cheveux tout blancs. Ses épaules naguère droites et larges tombaient sous un vêtement qui n'était plus que haillons. Enfin, Bertrand réussit à dominer son émotion et à prononcer quelques paroles qui avaient bien du mal à sortir de sa gorge sèche :

– Merci Ethis. Et Antoinette? Comment a-t-elle supporté ce cauchemar? La petite Lucie va-t-elle bien? Mon Dieu, comme j'ai hâte de les retrouver!

– C'est vous, monsieur de Valfroy qui avez vécu un calvaire! Elles vont bien toutes les deux et tout le monde vous attend là-bas. N'avez-vous pas trop souffert?

– Cela aurait été supportable s'il n'y avait pas eu, du premier jour au dernier, l'angoisse de cette mort qui pouvait arriver à chaque instant. Je ne sais pas par quel miracle j'ai échappé à la guillotine. Presque chaque matin j'entendais appeler le nom d'un ou plusieurs de mes malheureux compagnons. Transfert à la Conciergerie! On savait ce que cela voulait dire : le Tribunal révolutionnaire, votre cas expédié en quelques minutes et l'échafaud. Je n'ai jamais figuré sur la liste fatale. Peut-être un jour saurai-je pourquoi. Il se peut que mon beau-frère Delacroix soit intervenu...

Ethis l'écoutait en souriant :

– Votre beau-frère n'a rien fait du tout. Celui qui vous a sauvé ne vous connaît pas et vous ne le connaissez pas. C'est un comédien... Je vous raconterai comment cela s'est passé. J'avais juré à Antoinette de vous sauver la vie. Quel bonheur d'avoir réussi!

– Je ne comprends rien à ton histoire, Ethis, mais tu me raconteras tout à l'heure en détail comment tu m'as évité de faire la connaissance de Sanson. Cela m'intéresse!

– En attendant, monsieur le Baron, voulez-vous monter dans mon carrosse? Hier, à votre place, se prélassaient trois dames superbes. *Les Trois Grâces* de Germain Pilon, que M. Lenoir a réussi à faire transférer dans son musée des Monuments français. Vous pesez moins lourd que cette statue de marbre. Mais vous ne pesez même plus rien du tout! Il va falloir qu'on se débrouille pour vous trouver à manger. En tout cas, pour le souper de ce soir il y a de quoi fêter votre retour. Tout le monde s'y est mis : Riesener, Réveillon et mon maître bien-aimé Lenoir qui est aussi habile à découvrir un jambon dans une arrière-boutique de Paris qu'un chef-d'œuvre dans les ruines d'une abbaye.

Bertrand écoutait sans l'entendre le bavardage ininterrompu d'Ethis. Il était trop fatigué pour suivre son discours pittoresque mais un peu décousu. Et puis, il avait perdu l'habitude de parler... Tandis que le jeune garçon encourageait de la voix et du claquement de son fouet le vieux cheval du Comité de sauvetage des œuvres d'art, il ne pensait qu'aux deux êtres qu'il allait retrouver, sa femme et sa fille, se demandant si elles le reconnaîtraient dans le fantôme déguenillé qu'il était devenu.

A la fin, alors qu'ils arrivaient devant le passage de la Bonne-Graine, à quelques tours de roue de la place d'Aligre, il demanda à Ethis :

– Tu m'as trouvé changé, hein? Je sais que j'ai vieilli d'au moins dix ans entre les murs de mon cachot et, vois-tu, j'ai peur de ce moment tant attendu. Que vont penser Antoinette et Lucie?

Ethis ne savait pas grand-chose. Antoinette avait bien réussi à dégourdir cet esprit en friche que le sort lui avait confié, cependant la base manquait et le jeune garçon enregistrait sans ordre ni méthode mais avec une soif d'apprendre incroyable toutes les connaissances mises à sa portée. Surtout, il avait l'intelligence du cœur et se trompait rarement lorsqu'il s'agissait d'exprimer sa sensibilité, de prendre sa part des malheurs de ceux qu'il aimait. Valfroy lui avait parlé moins pour chercher un interlocuteur que pour se libérer de son angoisse. Il n'attendait pas de réponse à sa question et pourtant Ethis, par quelques mots simples, lui rendit son courage :

– Ce que vont penser Antoinette et Lucie en vous retrouvant? Comment, monsieur de Valfroy, pouvez-vous vous poser une telle question? Depuis votre arrestation, nous vivons tous dans l'attente de votre retour! Avez-vous oublié que nous vous aimons? Quand je dis « nous » c'est d'abord, bien sûr, Antoinette et la petite fille. Vos cheveux blancs et vos rides, loin de vous faire aimer moins, vont vous ouvrir leur cœur encore plus grand! Tenez, nous arrivons, regardez qui est à la fenêtre...

Profondément ému, Bertrand n'essayait pas de retenir les larmes qui coulaient sur ses joues creuses. C'est à travers elles qu'en levant la tête il aperçut Antoinette qui le guettait en soutenant dans ses bras, sur le rebord de la croisée, une jolie petite fille coiffée d'un bonnet de dentelle bleue. Déjà elles étaient en bas et le ci-devant de Valfroy, le miraculé de Thermidor, les étreignit en même temps.

Le village d'Aligre comme on appelait maintenant couramment le quartier créé par l'abbesse de Beauvau-Craon, n'était pas très étendu. Tout le monde s'y connaissait et la Terreur qui avait divisé tant de familles n'avait pas ébranlé l'esprit de solidarité qui liait ces gens depuis souvent plusieurs générations. Les nouvelles s'y répandaient comme traînée de poudre et l'escalier d'Antoinette se trouva bientôt assiégé. Tout le monde voulait voir le revenant de la guillotine pour le féliciter et partager un rare instant de bonheur arraché au tragique de l'époque.

Réveillon, prévenu alors qu'il traînait ses guêtres du côté de la fontaine Trogneux où la queue s'allongeait depuis qu'un accident, survenu à la pompe Notre-Dame, avait ralenti considérablement le débit d'eau potable, arriva presque en même temps que Riesener. Celui-ci alerté dans l'atelier du maître Beneman qu'il aidait à restaurer un secrétaire estampillé à son nom, livré en 80 à Versailles « pour le service de la reine » et que Tallien avait choisi pour meubler un coin de son bureau, ne fit qu'un bond jusqu'à la place.

Tous deux eurent du mal à se frayer un passage dans les rangs des voisins et à pénétrer dans le logement où tout le monde riait et pleurait à la fois. C'est seulement une heure plus tard qu'Antoinette réussit à renvoyer le petit monde fraternel du Faubourg. Réveillon, Riesener et Lenoir, arrivé lui aussi, furent priés de revenir le lendemain pour fêter l'événement :

– Ce soir mes amis, je veux être seule avec Bertrand.

On a tellement de choses à se dire, Ethis déjà s'occupe du bain de son père...

– De son père? demanda Lenoir surpris.

– Oui, de son père. Quand Bertrand a su qu'Ethis l'avait sauvé il m'a demandé tout de suite si j'acceptais qu'il adopte le garçon. « Je comptais te le proposer », ai-je répondu mais j'aime mieux que ce soit toi qui en aies parlé le premier! Me voilà donc mère d'un jeune homme de dix-neuf ans! Et j'en suis heureuse!

– Et Ethis? Comment a-t-il pris cela?

– Votre fidèle commis, vaillant sans-culotte et vainqueur de la Bastille, pleure de joie dans le gilet de son nouveau père en lui racontant comment un acteur inconnu l'a arraché aux douceurs de M. Sanson!

– Demain sera pour nous tous, un jour de fête. Je sais où me procurer un chapon qui rendra à M. de Valfroy le goût de vivre.

– Merci pour le chapon, Alexandre, mais pour le goût de vivre, je m'en charge, répondit en riant Antoinette.

– Je vous fais confiance sur ce sujet, douce Antoinette. Et il ajouta: Permettez-moi de vous embrasser sur les deux joues et de vous souhaiter beaucoup de bonheur!

C'était comme si la chape de plomb qui pesait sur Paris avait sauté, entraînant avec elle l'immense chagrin qui accablait le peuple traumatisé par cinq années de révolution et l'effrayante Terreur dont on venait d'apprendre qu'elle avait ordonné, en quarante-sept jours, 1 376 condamnations à mort. Au soulagement général s'ajoutait pour la famille Valfroy la joie d'avoir retrouvé un mari et un père.

Après un moment d'abattement, Bertrand reprenait des forces et des couleurs. Le ravitaillement de la capitale était toujours aussi déplorable mais chacun s'ingéniait à apporter au rescapé de quoi se refaire une santé. Ethis, en particulier, mettait ses dons de débrouillardise au service de celui qui était devenu son père. Avec l'argent qu'aurait dépensé Antoinette pour acheter un morceau de lard et quelques misérables légumes, il se procurait des œufs, du lait, des pommes de terre. Quand on lui demandait comment il s'y prenait, il répondait que c'était son secret. Le fait est que lorsqu'il rentrait le soir il fallait décharger le carrosse de colis mystérieux dont il disait que c'étaient des statuettes et autres sculptures qu'on ne pouvait abandonner dans la voiture. Antoinette apprit bien plus tard le rôle discret joué dans cet approvisionnement par Alexandre Lenoir qui ajoutait souvent le poids de sa propre bourse dans la balance du marchand. En contrepartie, il partageait presque chaque soir le souper familial qui retrouvait insensiblement la gaieté d'autrefois.

Les nouvelles ne manquaient pas dans cette période thermidorienne où les décisions politiques allaient presque toujours dans le sens de l'allégement des contraintes et de la libération de la peur. La guillotine avait cessé de fonctionner avec sa régularité sinistre et journalière. La Convention avait aussi très vite réorganisé le Tribunal révolutionnaire, en entourant ceux qui devaient y comparaître de garanties qui leur permettaient de se disculper et de se défendre. La Déclaration des droits de l'homme et du citoyen, longtemps confisquée par les Jacobins et les robespierristes, redevenait le fondement d'une République à visage humain.

La sécurité personnelle retrouvée en même temps que les grands principes qui avaient soulevé la France en 89 étaient d'une telle importance que cet affranchissement de la Terreur faisait passer beaucoup de choses. Peu importait finalement que les « insectes », les « impurs », les « corrompus » que Robespierre avait dénoncés avec rage fussent maintenant au pouvoir. D'abord étaient-ils tous si méprisables? Ensuite valaient-ils qu'on leur sacrifiât la vie d'innocents et l'esprit même de la Révolution? La lutte contre l'ennemi extérieur qui avait servi de prétexte à tous les excès se poursuivait avec succès sans Robespierre et ses fanatiques. Place d'Aligre on respirait : Valfroy parlait de retrouver une occupation au service du pays, Antoinette avait ressorti les toilettes légères depuis longtemps rangées au grenier, Lenoir était officiellement nommé conservateur du musée des Monuments français qu'il avait créé et défendu avec une indomptable ténacité. Ethis enfin, qui avait abandonné son uniforme de sans-culotte depuis qu'il avait un père aristocrate, était de plus en plus amoureux.

Antoinette avait pensé que ses promenades au bras de Marie n'auraient pas de lendemain et que leur bluette ne durerait pas plus d'une saison. Mais les passages du Faubourg avec leurs cachettes, leur odeur de bois séché et leurs gros pavés creusés au long des siècles par le poids des charrettes, possédaient une influence magique. Depuis des générations, les jeunes gens se répétaient un vieux proverbe d'atelier : « Qui traverse un passage du Faubourg, de sa belle est amoureux toujours. » La Révolution avait peut-être eu raison de la religion mais pas des sortilèges du bois! Marie semblait éprouver un amour grandissant pour Ethis à mesure que cet arbuste sauvage, soigné par Antoinette et Lenoir, prenait de la branche. C'est vrai que le petit sans-culotte du passage de la Bonne-Graine devenait un beau garçon. Sa claudication avait à peu près disparu depuis qu'il ne se chaussait plus de sabots, et ses cheveux blonds qu'il laissait pousser sur le conseil de sa mère adoptive donnaient à son visage un peu rugueux une élégance naturelle que remarquaient les jeunes filles du quartier. Il les dédaignait n'ayant d'yeux que pour Marie.

Les parents de la jeune fille n'avaient pas vu d'un bon œil cet amour naissant. Les Bénard étaient des petits-bourgeois assez fortunés à qui la Révolution ouvrait les portes d'une promotion sociale inespérée. Eugène Bénard avait su jouer habilement des événements et se plier aux contraintes révolutionnaires, se retrouvant toujours, avec son titre flatteur de commissaire civil, du côté où penchait la balance politique. La fin de la Terreur, qu'il avait vue arriver avec soulagement, le voyait donc pourvu d'un solide brevet patriotique et d'un titre de propriété de l'ancienne manufacture de papier peint Réveillon. La médaille de « vainqueur » d'Ethis ne pesait évidemment pas lourd en face de cette notoriété. Seul son rattachement à la famille Valfroy lui valait quelque considération avec la caution de Réveillon et son poste de commis d'Alexandre Lenoir. Un mariage n'était cependant pas envisageable. Les nouveaux moutardiers du pape n'entendaient pas se mêler au fretin révolutionnaire. Ethis n'était après tout qu'un enfant trouvé!

Fine mouche, Marie évitait de provoquer ses parents et continuait de s'arranger pour rencontrer son amoureux le plus souvent possible. Ethis l'avait d'abord amusée, maintenant elle admirait la façon dont il s'était adapté et se passionnait pour son travail au côté d'Alexandre. Il faut dire qu'il avait un don étonnant de conteur et qu'il n'hésitait pas à enjoliver ses récits d'exploits épiques auprès desquels la victoire de Jourdan à Fleurus n'était qu'une dispute d'enfants. Le sauvetage de la *Diane au cerf*, arrachée dans le parc d'Anet aux vandales qui voulaient la détruire sous prétexte que la chasse était un droit féodal, était devenu une nouvelle bataille de Poitiers au cours de laquelle le nouveau Charles Martel avait assommé trois Sarrasins à la file. Bref, Marie voulait Ethis et attendait sagement le moment où elle pourrait tenter de convaincre ses parents. « Un jour, disait-elle au jeune homme, il y aura un grand coup de tonnerre et le ciel s'éclairera. Soyons patients... »

Le tonnerre survint le soir où Ethis lui apprit que Bertrand de Valfroy avait décidé de l'adopter :

– Alors, s'était-elle écriée, tu t'appelleras de Valfroy et tu seras un jour baron?

– Je n'avais pas pensé à cela! dit Ethis en riant. Mais je te ferai remarquer que si j'ai pris la Bastille – avec chacun des huit cent soixante-deux « vainqueurs » – c'est pour qu'il n'y ait plus de noblesse.

– Laisse faire le temps et tu verras que les « ci » reprendront le devant! Mais je me moque bien que tu deviennes un jour baron. J'ai dit cela en pensant à mon père. Cela m'étonnerait que ce farouche révolutionnaire ne change pas d'opinion à ton égard lorsqu'il apprendra que l'enfant trouvé du Faubourg est maintenant le fils d'un aristocrate!

– Tu crois que...

– Je crois que j'aimerais bien t'épouser un jour et que ton adoption facilitera les choses!

Ethis qui tenait Marie serrée contre lui dans le recoin de la cour des Trois-Frères où ils avaient l'habitude de se rencontrer, la lâcha de saisissement et s'écria :

– Quoi? Tu songes sérieusement que nous pourrions un jour nous marier? Le seul fait que tu puisses imaginer cela est extraordinaire!

Il la reprit dans ses bras, l'embrassa et continua :

– Mais qu'est-ce qui m'arrive! Moi qui ai toujours pris des coups sur la tête depuis que je suis né, voilà que je n'ai plus que des bonheurs! Je n'y crois pas encore : répète-moi que tu voudrais m'épouser!

– Que croyais-tu donc petit sot? Que je m'amusais avec toi en attendant de trouver quelqu'un d'autre? Mais je t'aime! Et si toi tu m'aimes nous nous marierons avant l'année prochaine. J'aurai dix-neuf ans et il faudra bien que mon commissaire de père comprenne que depuis la Révolution les femmes ne sont plus des objets appartenant à un père ou à un mari!

– Bien dit, ma chérie!

Et il l'entraîna dans une sorte de folle sarabande, la faisant tourner sur les pavés ronds au risque de la faire glisser. Il sifflait, il chantait et elle le regardait en riant aux éclats. La veuve du maître ébéniste Pafrat, volontaire du Faubourg, ancien de la Bastille et capitaine-canonnier mort à Lille en 93, qui sortait de chez elle, les regarda en murmurant : « Allons! En voilà deux qui se moquent pas mal de cette foutue Révolution! Qu'ils en sortent vivants et qu'ils soient heureux! »

Antoinette n'avait jamais cessé de voir sa sœur mais, durant la Terreur, leurs relations étaient devenues plus lointaines. La mauvaise volonté ou l'impuissance de Charles Delacroix qui n'était pas intervenu pour sauver Bertrand avait créé un fossé entre les deux familles, fossé qu'Antoinette n'était pas pressée de combler. Victoire, malgré ses griefs contre son mari, s'était finalement accommodée de son rôle de femme de député jacobin régicide. Ami de Tallien, Charles Delacroix avait été comme ce dernier un terroriste consentant et l'avait suivi encore lorsque, sentant l'opinion publique virer, il s'était posé en tombeur de Robespierre. Il faisait partie de ces conventionnels habiles qui après avoir soutenu la Terreur profitaient de la réaction thermidorienne. L'épuration ayant libéré des places au Comité de salut public, Delacroix avait failli être nommé. Il attendait maintenant un poste de chargé de mission dans les départements. Cela faisait beaucoup de raisons pour que l'invitation à dîner lancée par Victoire et son mari aux Valfroy fût fraîchement reçue place d'Aligre.

– Je voudrais bien me réconcilier avec ma sœur, déclara Antoinette, mais je refuse de voir celui qui ne t'a pas porté secours.

Valfroy fut plus conciliant :

– Ce monsieur ne m'intéresse pas mais pense à Victoire. Ils font tout de même le premier pas. Nous n'avons pas tellement d'amis...

Le mot était malheureux et Antoinette éclata :

– Heureusement qu'il y a les femmes pour tenir un peu à la fierté ! Vous, les hommes, vous n'êtes que des valets complaisants. Quant aux amis, si nous en avons peu c'est parce que nous les choisissons !

Lenoir qui assistait à l'algarade et qui se gardait bien d'intervenir fut prié de donner son avis. Visiblement embarrassé, il toussa trois fois avant de répondre :

– Il est évident qu'Antoinette a raison sur le fond. Pourtant, il faut bien considérer les choses. J'ai pris ces derniers temps l'habitude d'être pratique et efficace, souvent au détriment d'honorables scrupules. En agissant ainsi j'ai réussi quelques sauvetages impressionnants. Je pourrais vous donner la liste des chefs-d'œuvre que j'ai échangés contre une blessure d'amour-propre. En regardant Antoinette s'enflammer – vous étiez très belle en colère, ma chère ! – j'ai pensé que M. Delacroix qui n'a pas voulu ou qui n'a pu tirer Bertrand de son cachot est aujourd'hui votre débiteur. Pourquoi refuser l'aide qu'il ne peut pas vous refuser? Laissez-le payer sa dette!

– Mais quelle dette? Nous n'avons rien à lui demander? dit Antoinette sèchement.

– Et pourquoi pas une place dans l'un de ces innombrables comités qui sont censés régler les affaires de la République? Le pays a besoin d'hommes comme Bertrand de Valfroy et seul l'appui d'un personnage important peut le faire engager là où il sera utile. Je vous assure que Delacroix sera ravi de soulager sa conscience et surtout de démontrer à sa femme – et à vous – qu'il n'est pas aussi méprisable qu'elle le croit. Croyez-moi, acceptez ce dîner qui permettra à Valfroy, je tiens le pari, de gagner de quoi nourrir sa famille et de cesser de se morfondre dans ce logement certes plus agréable que la prison mais qui lui deviendra vite insupportable s'il ne trouve pas une occupation.

– Vous êtes le diable, dit Antoinette calmée, mais un diable qui ne manque pas de bon sens et puisque les scrupules n'ont plus cours aujourd'hui, allons dîner avec le représentant du peuple!

Voilà comment, un jour de la fin novembre 1794, les deux filles du maître Œben se retrouvèrent à la table du député Delacroix, chez *Véry,* au Palais-Royal. Pour Antoinette et Bertrand, c'était malgré tout la fête, la première depuis bien longtemps. Elle avait mis une robe qui datait des premiers mois de la Révolution et qui ne la dénudait pas assez pour être à la nouvelle mode des robes tuniques en voile qu'on commençait à voir apparaître dans les endroits chics. Antoinette était tout de même très belle et son beau-frère, en bon avocat, sut le lui dire en des termes qu'elle ne put s'empêcher de trouver aimablement choisis.

Delacroix n'était pas antipathique. Charpenté, solide, le geste large, le front haut couronnant un visage aux traits réguliers, il était le type même du député de province qui avait acquis une aisance parisienne tout en conservant l'empreinte du pays. On l'imaginait énergique, prêt à foncer sur l'obstacle, comme le sanglier de son Argonne natale. La réserve des Valfroy à son égard ne lui avait pas échappé, sans doute même l'avait-il prévue. Intelligemment il mit lui-même la conversation sur le sujet sensible : la détention de Bertrand.

– Je sais que vous attendiez de moi une intervention, un geste. Je n'ai rien fait et vous avez le droit de m'en vouloir. Comme ma femme m'en veut pour la même raison. Alors je vais vous expliquer, franchement, pourquoi j'ai agi ainsi. Il n'est pas vrai qu'une action de ma part m'eût fait courir un risque quelconque mais je savais qu'il ne serait d'aucune utilité en pleine Terreur. Peut-être même aurait-il pu être dangereux. A l'époque, Fouquier-Tinville vouait à la guillotine les contre-révolutionnaires. C'est ainsi qu'il désignait ceux qui, paraît-il, entravaient au bureau des détenus la marche des affaires. Il est vrai que certains dossiers disparaissaient mystérieusement et n'étaient jamais transmis au Tribunal révolutionnaire. L'accusateur public était alors si furieux que toutes les interventions en faveur de suspects arrêtés déclenchaient immédiatement, sur son ordre, le passage en jugement des malheureux.

– Alors merci, mon cher beau-frère, de vous être abstenu, dit Valfroy d'un ton poli mais sec. Dans un climat aussi tragique...

– J'espère que vous me croyez. Je pense sincèrement que si j'avais levé seulement le petit doigt vous ne seriez pas ce soir en train de dîner avec nous.

On en resta là et la suite du repas se déroula dans une atmosphère plus sereine où la Terreur ne manqua pas d'être mise en accusation. Avec le rôti on dévora Saint-Just. Au dessert on mangea Robespierre et Henriot. De bonne foi peut-être, Charles Delacroix brûlait ceux qu'il avait soutenus. « Bah ! dans une révolution les vainqueurs sont ceux qui en sortent vivants ! » dit le soir Valfroy à sa femme. Et Antoinette lui répondit en caressant ses cheveux blanchis : « Tu es donc vainqueur mon amour. Pour notre bonheur ! »

La meilleure nouvelle arriva trois jours plus tard sous

forme d'un pli porté par un messager et scellé de la marque du Comité des sciences de la Convention : « A compter du 15 fructidor, le citoyen Perrin-Valfroy est nommé trésorier de la nouvelle administration des Communications par la télégraphie aérienne avec les appointements de lieutenant du génie. »

La prédiction de Lenoir s'était réalisée : Delacroix avait tenu parole et fait désigner son beau-frère à une place dont le moins que l'on puisse dire est qu'elle ne manquait pas de hauteur. Le télégraphe de M. Chappe annonça donc la réconciliation des Valfroy et des Delacroix. L'été était radieux place d'Aligre malgré les pluies qui noyaient Paris et un approvisionnement de plus en plus difficile. Les Autrichiens causaient bien quelques soucis du côté italien mais Paris tout entier semblait vivre en état d'apesanteur depuis qu'il ne traînait plus au pied le boulet de la Terreur et que la guillotine n'ensanglantait plus ses pavés. La brusque délivrance entraînait une sorte de folie collective, une explosion de plaisirs qui se situaient aux antipodes de la république spartiate que Maximilien Robespierre rêvait d'imposer aux Français. Le cyclone de la banqueroute enveloppait dans son cornet ce qui restait d'une société marquée par tant d'épreuves et de changements qu'elle n'était souvent plus reconnaissable.

Dans cette grande parade de l'après-Thermidor, les femmes tenaient le haut de l'estrade. Elles se vengeaient d'avoir été contraintes d'être admirables en devenant les symboles d'une vie où la facilité et la liberté des mœurs côtoyaient le désespoir. Mieux qu'un décret, le danger, l'imprévu, l'incertitude du lendemain, avaient libéré les femmes. Pour montrer qu'elles survivaient et qu'il fallait compter avec elles, elles se déshabillèrent !

Les plus audacieuses, les plus belles aussi peut-être, arborèrent pour aller au bal à l'Élysée ou à Tivoli des toilettes de gaze et de mousseline drapées à la grecque sur leurs corps nus. Cothurnes lacés sur le mollet, cheveux coiffés en berger d'Arcadie, elles suscitèrent d'abord une curiosité amusée. Mais on était au mois d'août, les étoffes étaient rares et chères. Pourquoi ne pas oser ?

La mode de chez Frascati n'était évidemment pas celle du Faubourg où la nudité emmousselinée n'était pas de mise. Les gens les plus pauvres et les plus simples sont aussi les plus rigoristes. Pourtant Antoinette était tentée d'essayer un jour de plein soleil l'une de ces tuniques nouvelles qui n'avaient rien à voir avec celle qu'elle avait portée au Palais-Royal pour dîner avec Delacroix. Sans doute avait-elle passé l'âge des folies. Mais elle était encore belle et les formes de son corps, comme celles de nombreuses femmes, avaient en fin de compte bénéficié du régime imposé par les privations : elles avaient gardé la minceur de la jeunesse. L'Antoinette de thermidor promenait une silhouette guère différente de celle de la jeune fille qui, sept ans auparavant, avait conquis le cœur de Pilâtre de Rozier au bal de la Folie Titon.

Un jour où sa sœur Victoire s'était fait déposer chez elle par la voiture du député, elle l'emmena *à Pygmalion* [1], un nouveau magasin ouvert rue Saint-Denis où l'on vendait des aunes de ces étoffes arachnéennes aux couleurs pastel qui faisaient de si jolies tuniques à l'ancienne. Après avoir longuement hésité, elles rentrèrent au Faubourg avec chacune deux mesures de voile blanc.

– Nous doublerons le drapé, avait dit Antoinette. Ce sera tout de même plus convenable.

Les deux sœurs reprenaient les vieilles habitudes de leur jeunesse, d'interminables confidences entrecoupées de fous rires.

– Tu ne crois pas que Delacroix va trouver cette tenue trop osée. La femme d'un député influent..., avait demandé Antoinette.

– Ma chère, si tu voyais comment s'habille la belle Thérésia, la maîtresse de Tallien, depuis qu'il l'a fait sortir de prison ! Remarque, elle peut tout se permettre, c'est une femme superbe. Tallien au pouvoir, tous les espoirs lui sont permis !

Changeant de conversation, Victoire continua :

1. Le magasin *A Pygmalion* fondé en 1793 existait encore en 1930 à l'emplacement du n° 100 actuel de la rue de Rivoli.

– Tu n'as rien remarqué l'autre soir chez *Véry*? Mon mari le cache du mieux qu'il peut mais il lui arrive une chose affreuse.

– Non. Nous n'avons rien vu. Qu'a-t-il donc?

– A l'endroit où les hommes situent leur virilité, tu vois ce que je veux dire, il lui pousse une grosseur dont le volume semble augmenter. Tant que cela ne se verra pas, cela ira, mais après...

– Il n'a pas vu de médecin?

– Si bien sûr, plusieurs même. Ou ils ne savent pas ce que c'est, ou ils conseillent d'opérer, d'enlever cette boule graisseuse. Mais il faut attendre qu'elle ait encore grossi...

– Évidemment, il... vous..., hasarda Antoinette.

– De moins en moins souvent. Je n'ai pas très envie, tu sais!

– Ma pauvre Vic. C'est peut-être le moment de prendre l'amant auquel tu songes depuis si longtemps.

– J'y pense, figure-toi. Mais ce ne sera pas n'importe qui. J'attendrai de trouver l'oiseau rare pour tromper mon député de mari.

Chapitre 5.

L'ENFANT A L'OISEAU

Une certaine forme de vie qui n'était pas celle de la fin de l'Ancien Régime et encore moins celle de la Terreur rendait au Faubourg un léger souffle d'activité. Comme chaque fois qu'une crise grave avait, au cours des siècles, entraîné la fermeture des ateliers et la misère, un besoin de renouvellement du mobilier se faisait sentir une fois le calme revenu. Hélas! Les Parisiens étaient trop pauvres pour donner du travail à tous les menuisiers et ébénistes dont l'entreprise avait résisté à l'ouragan de la Révolution. Seuls pouvaient acheter des meubles neufs ceux qu'on appelait les agioteurs et qui continuaient de s'enrichir dans le trafic des biens nationaux ou par le rachat à un prix de misère des dépouilles de familles ruinées.

Devant le Vieux Louvre se tenait une sorte de grand déballage où l'on pouvait acquérir meubles, tableaux, argenterie. Il fallait vendre ce qui vous restait pour survivre! Le Faubourg n'avait pas grand-chose à voir dans cette immense braderie, encore que c'était dans les vieilles cours et les passages étroits que demeuraient les derniers virtuoses du bois, capables de restaurer les meubles que le grand déménagement de l'Histoire avait détériorés. On ne fabriquait pas encore mais on rafistolait : des pièces magnifiques estampillées de noms illustres ou des meubles d'usage courant achetés devant la porte d'un ci-devant confisqué. Cela suffisait pour gagner quelques livres et, surtout, pour se donner l'illusion que la vie reprenait. L'odeur revenue de la colle forte, âcre et pénétrante, aidait à entretenir ce mirage teinté d'espérance.

C'est ainsi qu'un soir où toute la famille se trouvait réunie autour d'une potée dont Antoinette avait eu un mal fou à rassembler les ingrédients, Lenoir s'adressa en souriant à Riesener :

– Savez-vous, maître, qu'une de vos plus belles commodes vient d'échapper aux grandes ventes de Versailles et qu'elle va orner le salon d'apparat du Petit Luxembourg où s'installent nos nouveaux Directeurs? Au moins restera-t-elle en France et ne prendra-t-elle pas le chemin de l'Angleterre comme une grande partie de notre patrimoine.

– Comment est-elle, cette commode? demanda Riesener intéressé.

– D'après le bordereau d'enlèvement, il s'agit d'une commode que vous auriez exécutée en 1776 pour la chambre du roi à Versailles.

– Je vois. C'est une de mes œuvres les plus réussies. Des bronzes superbes enrichissent des panneaux de marqueterie très travaillés. A l'époque, je n'étais pas tellement connu mais Louis XVI m'avait témoigné sa satisfaction. Je suis vraiment heureux que ce meuble ait été choisi par le Directoire exécutif. Est-il en bon état au moins [1]?

– Il a subi quelques détériorations et je voulais justement vous demander si vous accepteriez de le restaurer. Je sais que vous avez toujours refusé de vous livrer à ce genre de travail mais les temps ont changé. Cette commode n'ira pas décorer la salle d'audience du Tribunal révolutionnaire! Et puis, il serait navrant qu'un de vos confrères manquât cette réparation délicate.

Pour le principe, Riesener émit quelques objections

1. Cette commode, tirée du Garde-meuble pour le service du Directoire exécutif, sera retrouvée plus tard au château d'Eu. Elle se trouve aujourd'hui au musée Condé à Chantilly.

mais il était flatté de savoir qu'il n'était pas oublié et trop content de retravailler sur une de ses œuvres.

– C'est bon, j'accepte. Quand pourrai-je me mettre au travail?

– Tout de suite. D'autant que vous aurez aussi à réparer un bureau mécanique que vous a commandé jadis M. de Fontanieu, l'intendant général de la Couronne.

– Comment? On a retrouvé cette machine qui m'a donné tant de mal?

– Oui, mon cher, mais ses rouages ne fonctionnent plus très bien et la marqueterie se décolle par endroits.

– Ça ne fait rien. C'est une sacrée bonne nouvelle que vous m'apprenez là! Ce bureau, je l'aurais racheté à n'importe quel prix. Le grand panneau marqueté représente les figures de l'Astronomie et de la Géométrie. Je suis sûr qu'Antoinette n'a pas oublié cette pièce. Je la revois, un jour où elle était venue avec sa mère, à l'Arsenal, en train de tourner les manivelles et de faire jouer des mécanismes que personne ne pourrait imaginer aujourd'hui. Il n'y a que le père Libongoutte – tu sais bien, Antoinette, le vieux Joseph de la rue de Charenton – qui puisse m'aider à remettre en marche ces ressorts et ces roues dentées.

L'idée de retrouver ses meubles avait d'un coup transformé Riesener. Lui, toujours abattu et prêt à se plaindre, était redevenu gai et bavard :

– Ainsi, me voilà donc rembarqué dans le métier! Je me demande si je vais encore savoir découper un placage de bois de rose et caler un panneau sur l'établi!

– Mais oui! dit Antoinette en éclatant de rire. Ne nous embête pas avec tes états d'âme! Tout le monde sait que tu jubiles en pensant à tes outils!

Le souper fut donc gai et il fallut qu'Antoinette se fâche pour que Lucie consente à aller se coucher. La fillette venait de fêter son sixième anniversaire et Ethis avait fait à sa filleule un cadeau extraordinaire. Il avait trouvé dans une vente de l'hôtel Bullion, rue Jean-Jacques Rousseau, là où Lenoir et Antoinette s'étaient rencontrés, une poupée automate absolument merveilleuse. On ne savait à quelle princesse ce jouet avait appartenu mais son mécanisme recelait bien plus de surprises que le bureau de M. de Fontanieu. Elle chantait grâce à une boîte à musique dissimulée sous sa jupe ou bien passait et repassait un fil de laine dans un tambour à tapisserie. En appuyant sur un petit bouton, Margot, c'est ainsi que Lucie l'avait baptisée, posait son aiguille et se coiffait à l'aide d'un peigne minuscule.

– Je veux bien aller me coucher, dit la petite fille, mais à condition que Margot m'endorme en chantant!

On rit et Valfroy raconta avec son talent habituel l'une des innombrables histoires qu'engendrait le fameux télégraphe optique de M. Chappe dont il était devenu l'ardent avocat et l'administrateur diligent. Le système qui avait fait sourire au début fonctionnait assez bien et Bertrand, promu « ingénieur-télégraphe », trouvait finalement plus amusant de développer le réseau Chappe que de se pencher à longueur de journées sur les finances désastreuses de la nation.

– Nous venons d'installer la ligne de Brest après celles de Paris-Lille, de Paris-Strasbourg et de Paris-Lyon. Cette dernière ira bientôt jusqu'en Italie.

– Combien y a-t-il de relais pour atteindre Brest? demanda Lenoir.

– Quatre-vingts! Les dépêches arrivent en huit minutes depuis le télégraphe central établi sur les bâtiments de l'administration centrale, rue de l'Université [1]. Ce n'est pas mal, non? Malheureusement, le télégraphe doit se reposer la nuit et les jours de brouillard. Mais tout cela, je vous l'ai raconté dix fois. Ce que vous ignorez, c'est que M. Chappe vit en ce moment des heures douloureuses. Un curieux, entiché de physique, vient de découvrir que son système se trouve décrit tout au long dans un livre de Porta, publié en 1563, *La Magie nouvelle,* et qu'un nommé Amontons avait imaginé deux ans plus tard un télégraphe adapté aux ailes des moulins! Cette révélation

1. Cet hôtel a été détruit en 1845 par le percement de la rue des Prés-aux-Clercs.

touche beaucoup le pauvre homme qui prétend, mais personne ne le croit, qu'il n'a jamais eu connaissance du livre de Porta.

Ces soirées de la place d'Aligre où chacun rapportait les nouvelles dont il avait eu connaissance comblaient de joie Antoinette qui avait ainsi l'impression de vivre plus intensément une époque passionnante. Réveillon, tombé assez gravement malade, avait déserté un moment le cénacle mais il revenait maintenant souvent l'après-midi voir Antoinette et Lucie. Il reparlait de la vieille maison du Faubourg et pensait sérieusement à en faire un inventaire complet, à commencer par le fameux grenier qui, disait-il, devait receler des trésors. Une expédition prochaine avait même été décidée à laquelle Ethis devait apporter le secours de ses bras solides, développés par le transport des statues de marbre au musée des Monuments français.

Lenoir n'était ni un archéologue ni un expert. Il n'avait pour lui que le goût des œuvres d'art et une volonté de fer pour mener à bien la tâche gigantesque qu'il s'était lui-même assignée : sauver du désastre l'essentiel du patrimoine artistique de la France. Critiqué depuis le début, il l'était encore lorsqu'il fut officiellement reconnu directeur du musée des Monuments français, l'ancien dépôt des Petits-Augustins qu'il avait rempli de pièces prestigieuses. Son efficacité l'avait toujours mis à l'abri des attaques de la nonchalante Commission temporaire des Arts composée d'artistes sans talent. Aujourd'hui, les choses allaient mieux avec le Conservatoire du Muséum que David avait enfin réussi à mettre en place, aidé par quelques amis dont Fragonard et Le Sueur. En fait, les deux organismes se complétaient très bien : le Conservatoire pour les tableaux et le musée de Lenoir pour les statues et monuments.

L'installation des Directeurs n'avait, hélas! pas mis fin au saccage des établissements religieux, églises et couvents. Les murs, devenus biens nationaux, étaient vendus à des prix dérisoires pour servir d'écuries ou de magasins à fourrage. Lenoir qui suivait avec consternation ce démantèlement rapporta un jour cette nouvelle stupéfiante :

– Mes amis, vous ne me croirez pas! Notre-Dame de Paris vient d'être adjugée 45 000 francs à un marchand de biens! Il a le droit de la détruire, de démonter les vitraux et de casser la façade déjà privée de ses statues [1].

– J'ai moi une autre nouvelle à vous apprendre, dit Antoinette : l'abbaye Saint-Antoine va être démolie. On ne conservera que les bâtiments les plus récents pour y installer un hôpital! Je tiens cela de la femme du gardien.

– Personnellement, je ne m'insurge pas contre une telle décision, coupa Valfroy. Puisque ce couvent n'abrite plus de religieuses, autant qu'il serve à quelque chose. Quant aux vieux bâtiments, ils s'effondreront tout seuls si on ne les démolit pas. Du moment qu'on ne touche pas à l'abbatiale...

– Justement, l'abbatiale va aussi disparaître!

– Mais c'est idiot! s'insurgea Lenoir. Le chevet est une pure merveille de sculpture gothique. Et cette modeste église ne gêne absolument pas l'installation d'un hôpital! Quant à l'abbaye elle-même...

– Vous n'êtes pas né dans ce quartier, dit Antoinette, vous ne pouvez pas comprendre ce que signifie pour nous la disparition de l'abbaye qui a tenu tant de place dans l'histoire du Faubourg. Privé du clocher de l'abbatiale, celui-ci va perdre ses racines et son âme... Je me revois assise pour la dernière fois en face de l'abbesse de Beauvau-Craon déjà résignée à l'inévitable...

– Au fait, demanda Lenoir, a-t-on su finalement ce qu'elle était devenue?

– Non. Personne ici n'a jamais eu de ses nouvelles. Elle est sortie la dernière, le jour de l'évacuation et on ne l'a pas revue. Peut-être a-t-elle réussi à regagner la Lorraine, berceau de sa famille. Peut-être a-t-elle été arrêtée et guillotinée...

1. L'acquéreur se montrant insolvable, Notre-Dame demeurera heureusement propriété de la ville de Paris.

La soirée qui avait commencé gaiement sombrait dans la mélancolie. Antoinette s'en rendit compte :

– Enfin ! ne pleurons pas sur ce que nous ne pouvons empêcher. La vie continue que diable ! Tiens, Ethis, on ne t'a pas beaucoup entendu ce soir. Aurais-tu perdu ton bagout ? Tes amours te donneraient-elles quelque raison d'être morose ? Comment va Marie ?

– Elle va bien mais son père refuse toujours qu'elle se marie avec moi. Il lui réserve paraît-il pour époux un cousin de Barras qui a fait fortune en agiotant au Palais-Royal.

– Quelle horreur ! s'écria Antoinette. Il va falloir qu'on s'occupe sérieusement de vous deux. Cela fait déjà trop longtemps que vous vous retrouvez en cachette au fond des passages. Je vais aller voir ces gens-là et leur dire qu'il faut vous marier !

– Merci Antoinette. Mais je ne suis pas sûr que cela serve à quelque chose. M. Bénard ne voit que l'argent, et de l'argent, je n'en ai pas. Vous voyez, cette Révolution n'a servi à rien. La liberté ? On a failli couper la tête de M. de Valfroy. L'égalité ? Je suis trop pauvre pour épouser Marie. La fraternité ? Mes compagnons de la Bastille ne me regardent plus parce que je vis chez des aristocrates !

– Mon pauvre « Traîne-sabot », dit Antoinette en lui prenant la main, comme te voilà désabusé ! Mais chasse ces idées noires : la vie ne fait que changer et recommencer. Aujourd'hui tout n'est que désillusion mais demain le soleil reviendra dans ton cœur. Regarde, l'existence était ici un calvaire quand M. de Valfroy était en prison. Il en est sorti vivant et les rires sont revenus. Alors, fais-moi confiance, je ne sais pas encore comment je vais m'y prendre mais vous vous marierez avant la fin du printemps, je te le promets !

Riesener était donc revenu devant son établi de l'Arsenal. L'atelier du maître, naguère bruyant d'activité, où les chansons des compagnons se mêlaient dans une drôle de musique au sifflement de la varlope et au crissement de la scie, était désert et silencieux. Jean-Henri était seul face à ses chefs-d'œuvre; la commode de la chambre du roi et la table de l'intendant général que le Garde-meuble lui avait fait livrer et, plus loin, au fond de l'atelier, une vingtaine de meubles, plus beaux les uns que les autres, qu'il avait rachetés lors des ventes de Versailles dans l'espoir de les revendre un jour à leur vrai prix. Il avait là, devant lui, toute sa vie en raccourci. Chaque reflet surgi de l'amboine ou de l'acajou sous l'effet d'un rayon de soleil venu de la verrière ravivait sa mémoire, lui rappelait les traits fins d'une princesse, le visage compassé d'un duc, clients d'hier disparus dans la tourmente. Il revoyait aussi la silhouette du compagnon qui l'avait aidé à construire ce délicat bureau de dame commandé par la reine et ce cabinet majestueux destiné au comte d'Artois. Lui aussi était mort. Engagé dans l'armée du Nord, un boulet lui avait labouré la poitrine.

– Allons, se dit Riesener. Restaurons les meubles de nos nouveaux maîtres plutôt que de pleurer sur le passé. Et remercions-les d'avoir préféré mon estampille à celle de Jacob ou d'un autre sujet du « roi David » pour orner leurs salons.

Il en était là de ses réflexions quand il sentit une présence derrière lui. Il se retourna et ouvrit les bras à la petite Lucie qui précédait sa mère.

– Vous êtes venues voir le vieux capitaine au milieu de sa flotte désarmée! dit-il souriant. Eh bien, voilà, ces navires d'apparat n'ont plus rien à faire dans l'océan de pauvreté qui nous noie. Il faut se faire une raison, mes meubles vaudront peut-être un jour des fortunes, mais aujourd'hui ils ne valent rien!

– Pourquoi es-tu si pessimiste? interrompit Antoinette. Tu sais bien qu'on n'a jamais fait de plus beaux meubles que les tiens.

– Peut-être mais le goût d'aujourd'hui s'oppose à toutes mes idées. David réussit à imposer la sobriété des formes et des décorations. L'art classique romain et le style étrusque ne sont pas pour moi...

– C'est vrai mais ne sois pas amer. Il est normal que le goût change. Ton art a été un art royal fait pour des rois. Celui de David, avec son retour aux sources antiques, est un choix politique. Des meubles simples et moins chers, voilà ce qui convient sans doute aux temps actuels. Pourtant nos Directeurs préfèrent tes meubles! Au plus haut niveau, la démocratie comme la royauté a besoin de bois somptueux, d'or et de bronze pour illustrer sa légitimité. Mais nous ennuyons Lucie avec nos discours. Elle a absolument voulu venir te voir travailler. Montre-lui donc tes chefs-d'œuvre, tes outils et ton atelier. Tiens sculpte-lui donc un petit bonhomme ou une poupée!...

Pendant des jours on parla place d'Aligre du style nouveau, de David qui avait réussi une fois encore à peindre sa veste aux couleurs du plus fort et qui, après avoir été peintre du roi, ami des Girondins puis conventionnel robespierriste se retrouvait artiste officiel du Directoire; on parla beaucoup aussi de Jacob et de son incomparable talent de menuisier en sièges.

– J'ai vu, dit Riesener, un fauteuil d'acajou néo-antique qu'il a fait d'après l'esquisse d'un siège romain en bronze. C'est superbe mais ça ne se vend pas. Trop cher! Jacob m'a dit que son fils le poussait à créer des sièges légers en bois ordinaire. Je suis sûr qu'ils vont réussir. Hélas, ce qui est possible pour les sièges et les canapés ne l'est pas pour l'ébénisterie telle que je la conçois. Je crois que je vais abandonner l'établi une fois pour toutes et accepter la place d'arbitre-expert au tribunal de commerce que m'a proposée Delacroix.

Charles Delacroix poursuivait sans tapage sa carrière politique. La Constitution de l'an III l'avait hissé un peu plus haut dans la hiérarchie. Élu au Conseil des Anciens, il voyait s'ouvrir devant lui les portes dorées du Luxembourg où le Directoire exécutif avait besoin d'hommes sûrs et habiles. Très lié avec deux des cinq directeurs, Rewbell et Carnot, il l'était moins avec Barras, le plus puissant. N'importe, il avait ses entrées dans le grand salon de réception où trônait Mme Tallien devenue la maîtresse de Barras et qu'on appelait « Notre-Dame de

Thermidor» en raison du rôle de dame d'œuvres qu'elle avait joué après la destitution de Robespierre.

Sans Charles, Antoinette et Valfroy n'auraient jamais eu connaissance de l'atmosphère étrange qui régnait au Luxembourg. Un curieux amalgame de l'ancienne étiquette royale et du laisser-aller révolutionnaire présidait au remplacement, *de facto,* de la monarchie par l'aristocratie nouvelle. Delacroix n'eut aucune peine à faire inviter sa belle-sœur et son beau-frère à une réception donnée par le Directoire à l'occasion de l'anniversaire du 9 thermidor. Il ne déplaisait pas à Delacroix de montrer à la famille les preuves de son ascension et l'occasion de la célébration de la chute de l'Incorruptible ne pouvait mieux tomber : il avait été nommé la veille ministre des Relations extérieures. C'était une promotion inespérée. Victoire n'y croyait pas elle-même quand elle vint l'annoncer à sa sœur :

– Je me suis sûrement trompée sur les vertus de mon mari. Le voilà ministre ! Tu te rends compte ? Je sais qu'il est rusé comme le paysan d'Argonne qu'était son père mais, tout de même, j'ai peine à imaginer que je vais être, que je suis déjà, la femme du ministre des Relations extérieures. Je suis heureuse que vous veniez demain au Luxembourg car je ne connais pas grand monde dans cette nouvelle cour où les Directeurs chamarrés d'or et coiffés de plumes entourent de leurs soins des femmes vêtues d'une simple tunique en mousseline des Indes. Quand je dis simple d'ailleurs... En y regardant de plus près, on s'aperçoit que les drapés sont retenus aux épaules et à la ceinture par des camées antiques et que le ruban qui retient leurs cheveux est orné d'un saphir monumental ! Je n'ai rien de tout cela à me mettre et en attendant que mon mari m'offre une tenue convenable, je porterai demain ma robe de chez *Pygmalion.* Et toi ?

– Je ferai comme toi et mettrai sur mes épaules mon châle de cachemire. C'est tout ce qui me reste de ma splendeur passée... Elle rit et ajouta : C'est un cadeau de Pilâtre, tu te rends compte ! Il l'avait payé une fortune. C'était pour se faire pardonner je ne sais quelle folie...

– Ne te fais pas de soucis, tu seras belle, comme toujours. Même si tu es moins élégante que la Tallien ou Mme Château-Regnault, on te remarquera au bras de M. de Valfroy qui, entre nous, a retrouvé toute sa séduction. Le télégraphe de M. Chappe lui réussit mieux que la Force. Tu as de la chance d'avoir un homme comme lui, garde-le!

– Mais je n'ai pas l'intention de m'en séparer! Et même si on voulait me le prendre, je t'assure que je défendrais mon bien! Et toi au fait où en es-tu avec ton député, pardon avec ton ministre?

– Toujours pareil. Le mal dont je t'ai parlé ne va pas mieux... Franchement, crois-tu qu'un poste de ministre puisse remplacer ce que tu penses?

Elles éclatèrent de rire et se donnèrent rendez-vous pour le lendemain.

– J'aurai une voiture pour moi toute seule, nouvelle noblesse exige! Et je passerai vous chercher tous les deux à cinq heures.

Antoinette se préparait depuis le matin pour cette réception qui l'intéressait finalement beaucoup. D'abord, il n'était pas désagréable d'être invitée dans ce palais du Luxembourg rafraîchi et redoré après qu'il eut servi de prison durant la Terreur. C'est là qu'avaient abouti en fin de compte tous les fils qui, au long de sept années interminables, s'étaient enchevêtrés, usés, rompus. Leur écheveau, fruit amer de la Révolution, était maintenant entre les mains des rescapés qui n'étaient ni les plus brillants ni les plus honnêtes et essayaient de le démêler pour tisser un nouvel habit à la République hésitante. Voir de près ces survivants dans le beau costume que leur avait dessiné David excitait Antoinette, heureuse de sortir pour un soir du Faubourg qui, après avoir été l'antichambre glorieuse et bariolée de la Révolution, n'en était plus que l'office, abandonné à sa misère.

Elle avait sorti du vieux coffre qui la suivait depuis son

enfance la robe-chemise de *Pygmalion* et son écharpe indienne pour les repasser. Lucie suivait tous ses gestes et l'assaillait de questions. Les « pourquoi » et les « qu'est-ce que c'est » appelaient des réponses qu'Antoinette s'efforçait de donner. Cela l'amusait, lui faisait penser que sa fille n'était pas sotte et que, dans quelques années, elle pourrait en faire une amie et une confidente. A sa demande elle dut essayer la robe et se déshabilla derrière le paravent qui cachait sa table de toilette. Une grande glace dont Œben avait jadis sculpté le cadre était posée dans le coin, elle s'y aperçut par hasard en se retournant. Il y avait longtemps qu'elle ne s'était regardée nue dans un miroir. Brusquement, son corps auquel elle ne prêtait guère attention l'intéressa. Elle dégagea une chaise qui lui cachait ses jambes et redécouvrit sa silhouette longue et mince avec une complaisance qui la fit sourire.

– Allons, se dit-elle, pour une femme de quarante-trois ans tu n'es pas si mal. Tes seins qui n'ont jamais été volumineux se tiennent encore bien droits et si quelques rides vieillissent ton visage, la peau de ton ventre et de tes bras reste lisse. Bertrand ne ment pas trop quand il te dit que tu as un corps de jeune fille...

Les appels impatients de Lucie qui avait hâte de voir sa mère vêtue comme les dames qu'on rencontrait aux Tuileries ou rue des Veuves, au cours des promenades du dimanche, la rappelèrent à la réalité. Elle enfila sa robe en prenant bien soin de draper la mousseline comme il était indiqué dans *Le Journal des dames* qu'elle avait acheté pour la circonstance. Avec mille précautions, elle mit les bas de soie qu'elle conservait soigneusement depuis des années, roulés dans un papier fin, et passa les chaussures vertes en organsin, rangées elles aussi depuis 93. Restait les cheveux mais, là, il s'agissait d'une opération longue et délicate à n'entreprendre qu'au dernier moment. Pour paraître devant Lucie dont elle appréhendait un peu le jugement, elle se coiffa à la diable, enserrant ses longues mèches blondes où le gris ne se voyait presque pas, dans un carré d'étamine verte tiré lui aussi de son « coffre des jours heureux » comme elle l'appelait. Un dernier coup d'œil au miroir complice et elle se montra, redressant la tête comme une actrice qui entre en scène.

Elle attendait des cris qu'elle espérait admiratifs mais la petite fille restait muette, sa petite bouche ouverte, les yeux fixés sur elle.

– Eh bien, Lucie, tu ne dis rien. Tu ne me trouves pas belle?

– Oh! si alors, je te trouve belle. Tellement belle que je ne peux rien dire.

– Mais tu pleures ma parole! s'exclama Antoinette en l'attirant vers elle et en essuyant deux grosses larmes qui coulaient sur les joues roses. Qu'est-ce qui t'arrive?

– Je ne sais pas. C'est des larmes de bonheur. Quand je t'ai vue magnifique, toute blanche. J'ai été tellement fière que j'ai senti une grande chaleur et des larmes qui venaient. Tu n'es pas fâchée?

– Non ma chérie, je ne suis pas fâchée. Je suis même heureuse. Cela me fait tout de même un peu peur de te savoir aussi sensible... Mais je suis bête, il faut au contraire se réjouir de voir que ces années terribles qui ont marqué toute ton enfance n'ont pas terni ta fraîcheur.

– C'est quoi « terni », maman?

Cette dernière question qui venait alors qu'elle ne l'attendait pas eu raison de l'émotion qui étreignait Antoinette et qu'elle essayait de retenir. C'est elle qui éclata en sanglots. Lucie qui avait déjà oublié son émoi lui essuya les yeux à son tour et l'embrassa :

– Il ne faut pas pleurer. Cela va te rendre toute laide!

– Tu as raison, je suis idiote. Tu vois, c'est fini. Merci chérie...

– Oh! tu sais! Entre femmes!

Ce mot de Lucie fit beaucoup rire Victoire lorsqu'elle vint prendre les Valfroy sur le coup de cinq heures dans l'un des carrosses du ministère. La voiture n'était pas aussi dorée que du temps de la maison royale mais à côté du chariot à statues de Lenoir elle paraissait d'un luxe inouï.

– Mon mari est ministre depuis vingt-quatre heures, il a à peine mis les pieds dans son bureau mais il a déjà deux voitures. J'en profite, bien sûr, mais je trouve cela assez scandaleux!

Assis en face des deux femmes, Valfroy souriait en les regardant. Il pensait que la vie est vraiment une drôle de chose qui permet quelquefois dans les moments les plus désespérés des retournements de situation prodigieux. Il n'y avait pas si longtemps, il attendait dans une prison infecte l'heure d'être guillotiné. Aujourd'hui, il se rendait dans un carrosse ministériel à l'une des réceptions les plus brillantes de l'année! Il souriait en regardant ces deux femmes belles et élégantes dont l'une, la sienne, éclatait de bonheur en échangeant avec lui des petits signes complices. Tout paraissait dérisoire au sceptique voltairien dans cette situation à la mesure du désordre de l'État. Il allait sans savoir pourquoi – pour faire plaisir à sa femme sans doute – s'incliner devant des dignitaires emplumés et complimenter des idiotes à demi nues dans leur tunique romaine, sous les cristaux d'un lustre de Bohême qui ferait miroiter les ors républicains. Il savait qu'en se penchant un peu à la portière de la voiture ses yeux croiseraient ceux de quelque affamé ou d'une pauvre femme portant dans ses bras l'enfant qu'elle ne pouvait plus nourrir...

– Allons, pensa-t-il, pas de regrets hypocrites. Va boire le vin du Rhin et manger les brioches de la Révolution triomphante et cesse de penser. Hier, c'était mauvais de trop penser dans le cachot, ça l'est autant en liberté!

– A quoi songes-tu? demanda Antoinette.

– Je me disais que vous étiez très jolies toutes les deux et que nous avons beaucoup de chance de faire partie de ceux qui peuvent encore sourire.

Valfroy tapota pour la faire gonfler la cravate de dentelle qu'Antoinette lui avait amidonnée avant de partir et lissa les rabats de son habit de velours miel, acquis à grands frais pour remplacer celui de la prison. Il allait dire quelque chose mais Antoinette ouvrit la bouche avant lui :

– Peut-être allons-nous rencontrer Germaine de Staël. Je crois qu'elle vient de rentrer de Suisse. J'aimerais bien la revoir mais sans doute ne se souvient-elle pas de moi.

– Cela me fait penser à son père. Mon maître, l'honnête Necker, doit avoir bien de la peine à Coppet lorsqu'il reçoit les nouvelles d'une France qu'il aime autant que son propre pays. Trente milliards d'assignats en circulation ! Lui qui a tout tenté, même l'impossible, pour éviter la banqueroute !

Déjà la voiture entrait dans la rue de Vaugirard en direction de la rue des Fossés-Monsieur-le-Prince, encombrée de toutes sortes de voitures qui attendaient leur tour pour déposer les occupants devant le portail de l'ancien hôtel de Brosse. Un moment, le carrosse dut s'arrêter devant le couvent des Carmes et Valfroy eut un petit frisson en se rappelant qu'il avait passé là les plus terribles moments de son incarcération. Il se demanda si les traces du sang des victimes des massacres de septembre demeuraient encore visibles, comme lorsqu'il y était, sur les marches du couloir d'entrée. Heureusement, la voix de Victoire le tira de ses sombres souvenirs :

– Nous y voilà, dit-elle. Je vais vous dire, j'ai le trac. Comme à notre premier bal. Tu te souviens, Antoinette...

– Ne vous tracassez pas, ma sœur, vous n'avez qu'à suivre et à faire comme tout le monde. Vous allez rencontrer ici plus d'anciennes lavandières que d'habituées des salons. Remarquez que s'il n'y avait que des « dames ci-devant », vous seriez tout de même parmi les plus belles. Je les connais.

Tout se passa effectivement le mieux du monde. Chaperonnées par Valfroy qui naviguait comme un bon capitaine dans le flot des invités où son assurance ouvrait des passes comme par enchantement, les deux sœurs arrivèrent dans le grand salon qui avait été autrefois la chambre de Marie de Médicis et où se tenaient les dignitaires entourés, ce n'était pas un hasard, des femmes les plus belles et les plus élégantes de l'assistance.

Elles reconnurent à sa haute stature Charles Delacroix chamarré comme un papegai de Guyane qui parlait à un autre bel oiseau : « Je crois que c'est Barras », souffla Valfroy. C'était lui, l'homme fort du Directoire, qui salua avec beaucoup d'aisance la femme de son nouveau ministre et ne manqua pas de regarder Antoinette d'un regard que Bertrand jugea un peu trop appuyé :

– Le vicomte rouge – de moins en moins rouge d'ailleurs – a remarqué ma femme, glissa-t-il moqueur à l'oreille d'Antoinette.

Ce n'était pas Barras qui intéressait Antoinette. Avec sa sœur elle cherchait la reine de la République, « Notre-Dame de Thermidor », la belle Thérésia, la femme de Tallien qui venait de passer des bras du petit général sans le sou Buonaparte dans ceux de Barras tandis que son amie Joséphine de Beauharnais quittait ce dernier pour le « général Vendémiaire », surnommé ainsi depuis qu'il avait réprimé l'émeute royaliste dans les rues de Paris.

Cette chronique de l'échange amoureux ajoutée à la réputation d'élégance et de beauté qu'elle traînait dans les franges de son péplum ne pouvait que captiver les deux sœurs heureuses de découvrir les dessous du libertinage politique. Une fois encore, Valfroy qui s'amusait en constatant que les mœurs de la nouvelle cour ne se différenciaient guère de celles de Versailles, dirigea les regards de Victoire et d'Antoinette dans la bonne direction :

– Regardez là-bas, au pied de la colonne, sous les bébés joufflus de Rubens. Mme Tallien est celle qui rit en écoutant la personne enroulée dans un voile bleu pâle qui n'est autre que la respectable Mme d'Aiguillon. Comment trouvez-vous l'Aphrodite de la République?

– Superbe! répondirent en chœur les deux sœurs.

C'est vrai qu'elle était belle, Thérésia, dans les ailes de papillon de sa tunique de mousseline, ses cheveux noirs courts et bouclés comme ceux d'une déesse antique. Barras qui en avait fini avec Delacroix s'approcha et passa son bras autour de sa taille quasi nue. Elle lui sourit et posa sa belle main sur le bras du Directeur.

– Quand je pense que Tallien est sûrement à deux pas! dit Antoinette.

– Tallien, enchaîna Valfroy, n'est pas mécontent de la puissance que représente la favorite du nouveau roi son ami. Il se moque bien de ce que les autres peuvent penser. Quant à elle, je crois qu'elle n'a d'amour que pour ses charmes dont elle sait jouer diaboliquement afin d'allumer les convoitises.

Delacroix qui goûtait dans son beau costume les premières griseries du pouvoir vint rejoindre sa famille :

– Belle soirée n'est-ce pas? Je suis heureux, mon cher Valfroy, que vous soyez venu. J'aurai plaisir à vous présenter à quelques personnalités. Venez avec moi, et vous aussi mesdames!

Content de lui à n'en pas douter, le ministre fit les honneurs du Luxembourg aux deux sœurs et à un Valfroy cérémonieux, un peu goguenard. Il leur présenta quelques membres du Conseil des Anciens venus avec leurs femmes dont aucune ne pouvait songer à rivaliser avec Victoire et Antoinette qui glissa à l'oreille de sa sœur : « Valfroy avait raison, nous sommes parmi les plus belles! » Ils firent aussi la connaissance de Lazare Carnot qui avait conservé la distinction de l'officier du génie qu'il était en 1789, ainsi que celle de deux autres directeurs Rewbell et Letourneur pas très à l'aise dans leur uniforme galonné. Enfin, la voiture reprit le chemin de l'Arsenal et de la Bastille pour déposer les Valfroy place d'Aligre avant de rejoindre Charenton-Saint-Maurice où logeaient encore Victoire et son mari en attendant de prendre possession de leur appartement officiel.

– Ouf! s'exclama Antoinette en se jetant tout habillée sur le lit. Je suis contente d'avoir vu ça mais je plains ma pauvre sœur qui va devoir recommencer souvent cette exhibition de plumes et de mousseline. Et toi, mon amour de mari, que penses-tu de la soirée?

– J'espère que cela ne s'est pas trop vu mais je me suis follement amusé. Quand je pense que ces nouveaux messieurs qui se flattent d'avoir eu raison de la Terreur m'auraient, il y a deux ans, envoyé sans hésitation à la guillotine! A part La Revellière-Lépeaux qui s'était mis à l'abri, tous faisaient partie du Comité de sûreté ou du Comité de salut public. Avant de l'abattre ils étaient tous des suppôts de Robespierre!

– La cour républicaine est-elle mieux que ne le fut la cour de Versailles?

– Elle est sûrement plus drôle mais si tu veux mon avis aussi ridicule!

Valfroy qui avait déjà ôté son vêtement de velours et ses bas de soie n'eut pas grand-peine à dénuder Antoinette : il n'y avait qu'une ceinture à dénouer pour que s'ouvre le grand pétale de voile blanc. Bien vite, ils se blottirent sous la courtepointe et Bertrand glissa dans le creux de l'oreille de sa femme qu'il allait inventer « la caresse Directoire » pour célébrer cette journée historico-familiale.

C'est le lendemain qu'Antoinette décida de s'occuper sérieusement des amours d'Ethis. Elle avait longuement réfléchi et dressé la liste de tous les arguments susceptibles de vaincre l'opposition des parents de Marie. A vrai dire, elle comptait surtout sur son adresse pour flatter la vanité de ces bourgeois révolutionnaires. Elle avait demandé à Lenoir d'établir une pièce certifiant qu'Ethis Perrin de Valfroy était employé dans les services du musée des Monuments français. « N'hésitez surtout pas sur les cachets, lui avait-elle recommandé. Il faut impressionner ces gens! »

Alexandre lui avait apporté une véritable citation à l'ordre du jour de l'armée du patrimoine national, signée de Lenoir et de David lui-même. Ethis était devenu « commis expert en œuvres d'art » sur ce papier officiel chargé de cire rouge à la marque du « Directoire exécutif, direction du musée et du conservatoire des Arts ». Pour avoir l'air officiel, cela avait l'air officiel et Antoinette dit qu'avec une proclamation aussi ronflante, il n'était pas possible au cogérant des papeteries Réveillon de refuser un tel gendre. Elle plaça le précieux vélin au fond de son cabas, mit sa plus belle robe de lainage décorée à la façon indienne et partit vers la rue de Montreuil d'un pas décidé.

L'ancien palais de la Folie Titon avait été complètement détruit durant l'émeute du printemps 89 et les Bénard habitaient dans l'un des bâtiments de la fabrique. Le portail de la rue de Montreuil était encore debout, il permettait d'accéder à ce qui avait été autrefois un superbe jardin et n'était plus qu'un terrain vague.

Depuis l'après-midi terrible du 21 avril, Antoinette n'était jamais revenue en ces lieux qui avaient tellement marqué sa vie. Elle ressentit un coup au cœur en apercevant les débris de la Folie déjà recouverts d'herbe. Presque tous les arbres du parc avaient été abattus pour faire du bois à brûler. Seuls deux grands chênes étaient encore debout. Antoinette les reconnut, c'est dans leurs branchages que la montgolfière de Pilâtre de Rozier s'était abîmée lors d'un des premiers essais du ballon construit dans les ateliers Réveillon. L'arbre au pied duquel elle avait été relevée blessée avec Ethis avait, lui, été abattu.

Elle sourit tristement en regardant un moment ces pauvres vestiges et reprit sa marche vers la fabrique dont on voyait la cheminée fumer au fond de la propriété. La manufacture, malgré les événements, occupait encore une centaine d'ouvriers qui fabriquaient des papiers peints à motifs révolutionnaires. Sur le côté, une porte à panneaux d'ébénisterie permettait d'accéder à l'appartement des Bénard. Elle avait choisi l'heure de l'avant-dîner afin d'être certaine de les trouver tous les deux. Ils étaient effectivement dans la grande salle d'entrée, prêts à s'asseoir à table avec leurs trois filles parmi lesquelles Antoinette reconnut tout de suite Marie, la plus jolie. « Allons, Ethis a bon goût », pensa-t-elle en saluant l'ancien commissaire civil et sa femme, une blondasse sans âge mais peut-être pas sans énergie. La vivacité de son regard frappa Antoinette. Lui était le bourgeois important, trop gros, sûr de lui qu'elle connaissait de vue. Quant à Marie, la seule avec ses parents à avoir compris la raison de la visite de « la fille Œben » – comme quatre sur cinq des habitants du Faubourg appelaient encore Antoinette – un éclair de ses yeux verts avait suffi à cette dernière pour imaginer les pensées qui devaient défiler derrière son beau front lisse.

Sans être désagréable – Antoinette était tout de même une « dame du Faubourg » à qui l'on devait des égards – l'accueil manquait de chaleur. La jeune femme décida d'écourter les préliminaires :

– Merci de me recevoir. J'ai beaucoup entendu parler de vous par mon parrain Réveillon qui apprécie la manière dont vous lui succédez et je suis heureuse de vous connaître. Ce que j'ai à vous dire est important et j'aimerais vous voir en particulier. Vos charmantes jeunes filles ne m'en voudront pas...

– Venez madame nous allons nous mettre dans mon cabinet.

Antoinette sourit intérieurement en pensant que M. Bénard parlait comme feu le roi et le suivit avec son épouse dans une petite pièce encombrée par un grand bureau plat chargé d'échantillons, de modèles, d'essais de motifs tricolores chargés des emblèmes de la Révolution : faisceaux, piques, drapeaux et feuilles de chêne.

– Tenez, madame, dit Bénard tandis qu'ils s'asseyaient autour de la table, voici un papier qui vous touchera.

Il tendit à Antoinette une suite de motifs représentant des montgolfières où les dédicaces et les initiales royales avaient été remplacées par des cocardes et des bonnets phrygiens. Elle remercia et dit : « Mon cher Pilâtre serait bien étonné de voir son ballon habillé à la mode du jour. »

On parla encore un petit moment de choses sans importance et Antoinette attaqua :

– Vous vous doutez du but de ma visite. Votre fille Marie et mon fils Ethis s'aiment depuis longtemps et vous n'ignorez pas qu'ils se rencontrent. Je crois que le moment est venu de songer à les marier.

– Votre fils..., lança Mme Bénard.

Le ton sur lequel elle avait prononcé ces deux mots valait tous les discours. Il mit d'un coup Antoinette en état de riposte offensive. Blême, elle lança :

– Oui, madame, mon fils! Et pas seulement depuis que M. de Valfroy l'a adopté mais depuis le jour où il m'a sauvé la vie et où je l'ai aidé moi aussi à survivre. Vous pouvez lui refuser votre fille mais vous ne pouvez pas dire qu'il n'est pas mon fils. Et je ne suis pas sûre, s'il était sorti de moi, qu'il aurait les qualités de ce garçon dont je viens défendre le bonheur.

La réplique avait fait mouche et la bonne dame se mordillait la lèvre tandis que son mari essayait de temporiser :

– Ma femme ne voulait pas vous être désagréable, madame Œben, mais nous ne savions pas que...

– Mais si, vous saviez. Tout le Faubourg est au courant. Car Ethis y est plus connu et plus populaire que tous les hauts personnages de la République. Qu'il soit aussi l'un des plus jeunes « vainqueurs de la Bastille » ne peut pas vous être indifférent, monsieur le Commissaire civil. D'autre part...

– D'autre part, madame, il y a un point qu'on ne peut négliger. Il est brave, certes, et paré de nombreuses qualités mais la différence de situation familiale rend, avouez-le, le mariage impossible. A moins que vous ne nous apportiez des garanties ignorées de nous jusqu'à maintenant...

Voilà, ça y est, pensa Antoinette, nous plongeons dans le sordide. Calme-toi ma fille. Je sais bien que tu paierais cher pour envoyer tous ces papiers, et le pot de colle avec, à la tête de cet imbécile. Mais cela n'arrangerait pas l'affaire de nos deux tourtereaux.

Elle avait envie de mordre, elle sourit :

– Oublieriez-vous, monsieur le Commissaire civil, qu'il y a eu la Révolution? Les choses ne sont plus tout à fait les mêmes qu'au temps de la royauté. Les fortunes se font et se défont aujourd'hui avec une incroyable rapidité...

Antoinette parlait posément, piquait ses banderilles une à une et sentait qu'elle marquait des points. On s'était cantonné jusqu'à maintenant dans les généralités, elle jugea qu'il était temps d'en venir aux questions personnelles et de mettre en valeur la nature originale d'Ethis. « Pas question, pensa-t-elle, de toucher à la psychologie, ces gens obtus ne seront sensibles qu'aux arguments ficelés de grosses cordes. Il faut les étonner. » Elle sortit le certificat dûment estampillé de Lenoir et le tendit à Mme Bénard :

– Voyez vous-même, madame. Vous croyez avoir affaire à un enfant trouvé, pauvre et inculte. En réalité, Ethis notre fils, a bien changé. Je préfère ne pas vous parler de cela moi-même. Je laisse le soin à MM. David et Lenoir de vous dire qui il est aujourd'hui.

Léontine Bénard jeta un coup d'œil vers son mari avant de lire l'attestation et la lui passa.

Antoinette vit tout de suite que le papier faisait son effet.

– S'agit-il du célèbre Louis David? demanda le père.

– Naturellement. Et de notre grand ami Alexandre Lenoir, directeur du musée des Monuments français.

– Évidemment, ce sont des gens de qualité..., commenta Mme Bénard.

– Madame, s'amusa Antoinette, ne dites pas ce mot-là! Ils sont d'ardents soutiens de la Révolution.

– Mais bien sûr, Mme Œben a raison, lança Bénard en jetant un regard courroucé vers sa femme. Ne dis pas de sottises!

– Je voulais seulement dire que c'était des gens tout à fait distingués, s'excusa la pauvre dame.

– Eh oui! Vous ne le saviez pas mais Ethis et ma famille sommes bien entourés. Je ne vous parle pas de Riesener mon beau-père, ni de Réveillon mon parrain, mais d'une nomination qui ne peut que grandir nos familles, puisque nous devons nous allier : mon beau-frère, le mari de ma sœur Victoire vient d'être promu ministre des Relations extérieures par le Directoire exécutif!

Un silence s'établit dans le petit bureau. Antoinette en profita pour feuilleter distraitement un album de dessins destinés à être imprimés. Du coin de l'œil, elle surveillait les parents de Marie en proie à une profonde réflexion. Il était sûr qu'elle avait frappé juste, qu'ils commençaient à entrevoir que la considération est une monnaie comme une autre qui leur manquait aujourd'hui comme elle leur avait manqué au temps de la royauté. Tous ces noms qu'Antoinette avait lâchés comme par hasard au cours de la conversation chantaient à leurs oreilles. Ils ne savaient que dire, se frottaient les mains ou se grattaient le nez en exhalant des petits soupirs qui faisaient penser à Antoinette qu'elle était sur le point de gagner la partie. Elle aurait pu brusquer les événements, emporter sans doute un acquiescement mais elle préféra les laisser dans un trouble qui devait les amener, si elle ne s'était pas trompée, à venir eux-mêmes proposer d'échanger leur fille contre quelques miettes de prestige. Elle prit donc congé par quelques phrases aimables et ajouta avant de pousser la porte :

– Votre charmante Marie n'aura, croyez-moi, pas à rougir de son mari ni de sa belle-famille. Et si par-dessus le marché ces deux-là sont heureux, je ne vois pas quelle raison vous ferait empêcher leur mariage. L'argent ? Nous n'avons pas, c'est vrai, des charrettes d'assignats ni d'actes de propriété de biens nationaux mais nous avons un nom, un nom qui durera peut-être plus longtemps que ces fausses richesses.

Antoinette était fort contente d'elle et se prit à chantonner en remontant le Faubourg. Au coin de la rue Traversière, elle se trouva nez à nez avec Martin Ohnenberg, un vieux maître, ami de Riesener, qui portait dans le Faubourg le titre de « roi de la commode », ce qui n'était pas rien. Elle le trouva bien vieilli, comme pliant sous le poids d'une charge invisible. Son visage gris et triste s'éclaira en reconnaissant Antoinette qui l'embrassa trois fois à la mode de Saint-Antoine.

– Comment allez-vous, monsieur Martin ? Trouvez-vous encore un peu de travail ? Faites-vous toujours ces commodes au caisson droit orné de vos fameux trophées d'instruments de musique?

L'ébéniste rejeta en arrière une longue mèche de cheveux blancs et découvrit deux yeux étrangement pâles, presque blancs, comme délavés.

– Hélas, non! Antoinette, je ne fais plus rien. Mon atelier est vide, désespérément vide. Si vide que je le quitte. Je ne peux plus le chauffer l'hiver. Cela me fait mal au cœur mais que veux-tu, les marchands, les décorateurs et les merciers qui me faisaient travailler ne vendent plus rien. Caplain lui-même, le tapissier, a fermé sa boutique. Je vais m'installer dans la cour de la Juiverie en attendant des temps meilleurs, ou simplement la mort.

– Allons, qu'est-ce que c'est que ce désespoir? Tous les maîtres et les compagnons sont comme vous, mais cela ne durera pas. Bientôt vous reprendrez vos outils et vous retrouverez votre fierté d'artiste.

– Tu as raison, il est sûr qu'on refera des meubles au Faubourg. Mais quand? Je crois bien que pour moi c'est fini! Je vais aller vivre avec ma sœur et mon beau-frère, Gleitz, un bon compagnon lui aussi. Riesener l'a beaucoup fait travailler. Au fait, comment va ton beau-père?

– Mal lui aussi! Il dit qu'il avait encore des centaines de chefs-d'œuvre à enfanter et qu'on a châtré son talent. Il est malheureux comme vous, mon pauvre Martin...

Brusquement, il la quitta et s'enfonça dans la rue Traversière. Elle le vit essuyer furtivement des larmes, comme s'il en avait honte. Il tourna tout de suite à gauche dans la petite cour du numéro 4, celle où s'ouvrait son atelier où il entrait peut-être pour la dernière fois [1].

Cette renconte avait un peu assombri Antoinette qui ressentait viscéralement tous les drames que vivait son Faubourg. Heureusement, Ethis était devant la porte de la place d'Aligre en train de bavarder avec un voisin qui

1. Martin Ohnenberg, l'un des nombreux ébénistes venus d'Allemagne au milieu du XVIIIe siècle pour s'installer au Faubourg, est mort vers 1800, rue de la Juiverie. Son estampille n'a pas de prix aujourd'hui.

venait de rentrer des Armées avec le grade de capitaine et un moignon en guise de main droite.

– Monte, dit-elle en passant, j'ai une nouvelle pour toi.

Elle n'avait pas dit à Ethis qu'elle allait voir les parents de Marie. La surprise du garçon fut donc grande quand elle lui raconta son entrevue.

– Mais c'est extraordinaire ce que vous avez fait, Antoinette! Je recommence à croire que j'épouserai Marie! Vous pensez vraiment que ses parents vont changer d'idée et m'accepter, moi, l'enfant trouvé?

– Cesse donc de raconter que tu es un enfant trouvé! Tu es notre fils et c'est bien assez pour pouvoir épouser Marie.

– Comment avez-vous pu seulement vous faire écouter?

– Mon cher Ethis, j'ai mis en jeu toutes les ressources de ma rouerie féminine. J'ai flatté leur vanité, je leur ai fait comprendre que l'argent sans la considération était peu de chose dans les temps que nous vivons. Ils avaient l'air ébranlés. Si, de son côté, ta bonne amie est assez adroite, je crois que nous irons bientôt à la noce!

Ethis embrassa Antoinette, fit une cabriole qui faillit renverser la table à écrire et alla chercher la petite Lucie qu'il entraîna dans une danse effrénée à travers la pièce.

Antoinette les regardait, heureuse et émue: « Mon Dieu, murmura-t-elle, faites que j'aie gagné aujourd'hui le droit au bonheur pour Ethis! »

La France du Directoire s'était installée dans une sorte de relâchement où la grande misère côtoyait la richesse insolente. Entre les deux, les moins pauvres arrivaient à mener une existence acceptable à condition d'être assez débrouillards. C'était le cas de « la Famille », comme Antoinette appelait son petit monde. Grâce à son ingéniosité de maîtresse de maison, à l'efficacité dégourdie d'Ethis et à la générosité de Lenoir, on ne souffrait pas vraiment de la faim place d'Aligre. On ne se régalait certes pas à chaque repas. Certains soirs on pouvait même s'amuser à compter les yeux du gras dans son assiette de soupe au pain mais, à côté des jours sombres de la Terreur, c'était presque la belle vie.

Les Bénard avaient finalement donné leur consentement et le mariage devait être célébré à l'automne. Il n'était pas question de faire une grande fête. D'abord les temps ne s'y prêtaient pas, surtout au Faubourg. Ensuite l'éventualité d'un mariage religieux avait finalement été abandonnée; personne ne tenait vraiment à la bénédiction du vicaire de Sainte-Marguerite, l'un des premiers prêtres à s'être mariés en 92, et qui prêtait son église aux théophilanthropes [1]. Le mariage devait donc se résumer à un passage vite expédié devant le maire du VIIIe arrondissement qui réunissait depuis peu les quartiers du Marais, du faubourg Saint-Antoine, de Popincourt et des Quinze-Vingts. Un repas réunirait les proches et les témoins chez les parents de la mariée.

Il restait à trouver un logement pour abriter les amoureux. Les locaux vides ne manquaient pas. Il y avait même deux petites chambres à louer dans la maison d'Antoinette qui aurait bien aimé garder Ethis auprès d'elle mais Léontine Bénard voyait d'un mauvais œil cette quasi-cohabitation. Elle avait aussitôt proposé d'accueillir le jeune couple chez elle à la manufacture. Finalement, Réveillon sauva la situation en offrant sa maison du Faubourg que les ouvriers de Bénard remettraient en état.

Ainsi, une fois de plus, la vieille maison des Thirion et des Cottion retrouvait un petit air de jeunesse. Consolidée, restaurée, repeinte, elle gardait son charme d'antan et même ce seuil de pierre aux reflets verts qui promettait le bonheur aux amoureux qui la franchissaient. Ethis et Marie ignoraient ce pouvoir légendaire mais remarquè-

1. Secte nouvelle et religieuse réunissant « les amis de Dieu et des hommes ». Elle prêchait une morale simpliste et les vertus sociales. Sera interdite par le gouvernement consulaire en 1801.

rent un « T » joliment gravé dans la pierre le jour où ils vinrent visiter leur future demeure.

– Ce « T » veut dire quelque chose, annonça Ethis en grattant avec son ongle le sable qui s'était déposé dans le creux de la lettre. Peut-être le nom d'un des premiers occupants. Nous demanderons à Antoinette.

– Non, il veut dire « trésor »... ou encore mieux « talisman », soutint Marie. Tiens, nous choisirons pour notre premier enfant un nom qui commence par un « T »!

– Thérèse?

– Ou Théodore!

Ils éclatèrent de rire et s'embrassèrent, les pieds posés sur la marche miraculeuse.

Les travaux allaient bon train. Réveillon, trop heureux de voir sa maison utilisée et de pouvoir occuper son temps surveillait tout. Quand Bénard omettait d'envoyer un nombre suffisant d'ouvriers, il allait lui-même à la manufacture faire son choix parmi ses anciens employés. Mais il restait toujours à explorer le fameux grenier. Un jour il décida qu'il fallait en finir avec ce voyage dans le passé :

– Si cela continue, je mourrai avant que la maison ait livré tous ses secrets. Alors, vous, les jeunes, vous allez monter, explorer les combles jusque dans les plus petits coins, ouvrir tous les paquets et me descendre ce qui vous paraît intéressant. J'examinerai cela avec Antoinette. Allez! Ouste! Au travail!

Après avoir enfilé de vieux vêtements pour arracher sans crainte leurs trésors aux araignées, Ethis et Marie commencèrent à déblayer les vieux chiffons, les paquets enveloppés dans des toiles à demi mangées par les rats, à se frayer un passage dans la poussière et le terril désagrégé, à trier d'innombrables objets échoués depuis un siècle, deux peut-être, dans ce dépotoir des ans.

De temps en temps, Réveillon, posté sous la trappe, entendait un grand bruit, celui d'un meuble qui s'effondrait sans doute, des cris, des rires, des bruits de pas étouffés par la poussière. Sans cette sacrée crise de goutte qui l'avait empêché de sortir pendant plus d'un mois, il serait bien monté rejoindre les jeunes gens. « Est-ce qu'ils ne vont pas laisser passer quelque chose de précieux ? » se demandait-il.

Enfin, après une bonne heure de fouille, les deux fiancés réapparurent en haut de l'échelle, sales, noirs, couverts de toiles d'araignée :

– On en a pour des jours à explorer tout le grenier, dit Ethis. Mais nous descendons pour boire et nous reposer. Tenez monsieur Réveillon attrapez toujours cela !

Il tendit un paquet long, ficelé par une corde de chanvre tressée à la main et couvert d'une épaisse couche de poussière. Intrigué, Réveillon avança les deux mains et reçut le ballot qui laissa de longues traînées grisâtres sur les revers de son bel habit de laine maïs.

– Ce sont des cannes ! cria Ethis. Et tenez, attrapez encore ce panneau de marqueterie. Il représente une tête de femme. C'est bizarre !

Déjà Réveillon ouvrait le paquet avec son couteau et une dizaine de cannes, certaines fines et garnies de pommeaux d'ébène ou de métal, d'autres plus grossières visiblement taillées dans la forêt. Et puis, ne ressemblant à aucune autre, un long bois d'un seul jet enrobé dans une double guirlande de sculptures dont on devinait la finesse sous la poudre du temps.

– Cela n'a pas l'air mal, dit Réveillon. Descendez, nous allons tout essuyer et y regarder de plus près. A commencer par ce bâton de pèlerin qui n'a sûrement pas été sculpté avec un couteau.

A l'aide d'un chiffon, ils réussirent à enlever presque toute la poussière qui recouvrait les cannes, laissant de côté celle dont les sculptures nécessitaient l'emploi d'une brosse. Il s'agissait d'objets assez banals.

– Je ne crois pas que nous ayons fait une découverte extraordinaire, dit Ethis. Cela ne valait pas la peine de se salir autant. Aucun de nos « incroyables » ne voudrait de ces bâtons.

– Mon cher Ethis, vous n'avez encore exploré qu'une petite partie du grenier ! souligna Réveillon, un peu piqué.

Et puis il nous reste cette canne qui nous réserve peut-être une surprise agréable. Avec ses rubans qui tombent en poussière, cela m'a l'air d'être une canne de compagnon du tour de France. Et qui ne date pas d'hier!

Marie alla emprunter une brosse aux ouvriers qui collaient dans sa future chambre des tentures représentant des montgolfières. C'étaient des coupes d'un papier imprimé avant la Révolution et les ballons, copiés sur celui de Pilâtre de Rozier et du marquis d'Arlandes, étaient décorés du monogramme du roi et de la reine. Elle avait choisi ce papier pour faire plaisir à Antoinette. Après avoir jeté un coup d'œil sur la pièce et calculé la place qu'occuperait le lit, face à la fenêtre ouvrant sur la grand-rue du faubourg, elle revint nettoyer la canne qui, à chaque coup de brosse, révélait de nouveaux motifs, de nouvelles inscriptions.

– Ce n'est pas une canne, s'écria Réveillon, c'est un vrai livre qui raconte des histoires. Tenez, je vois une suite de noms. Je suis sûr que nous allons y retrouver les Cottion, les Thirion, les Habermann qui sont à n'en pas douter les ancêtres d'Antoinette. Quel flair j'ai eu d'acheter cette maison! C'est une maison magique, vous y serez heureux!

– Je suis déjà heureuse, monsieur Réveillon, s'exclama Marie. Si je n'étais pas si sale je vous embrasserais!

– Alors, va vite te débarbouiller, ma belle!

Réveillon avait raison. A une dizaine de pouces du pommeau, entre les deux guirlandes d'angelots qui à eux seuls étaient tout un roman, des noms finement gravés apparaissaient suivis de dates.

– Tiens, lis Ethis, toi qui as de bons yeux, dit Réveillon.

– Je vois « Jean Cottion 1449-1515 » et puis encore « 1470-1471 ». Cette canne aurait donc plus de trois cents ans, ce n'est pas possible!

– Pourquoi? Le bois, quand il n'est pas dans l'eau ou dans la terre, se conserve très bien. Tu as en main, mon garçon, la canne d'un compagnon qui a dû en parcourir des kilomètres, comme on dit aujourd'hui! Il faudra demander à Lenoir qu'il recherche dans ses livres ce qui se passait à Paris à cette époque. Et dessous? Quels autres noms sont inscrits?

– « Denis Thirion 15 juin 1545-été 1546. »

– Et encore? demanda Réveillon, impatient.

– Encore un nom. Mais il a dû être gravé moins profondément car il est difficile à lire.

C'est Marie qui déchiffra : « Christophe Habermann 1575-1577. » Après, plus rien. Les angelots continuaient leurs volutes mais aucune autre inscription n'était discernable.

– Cela voudrait dire que la canne de Jean Cottion n'a plus servi depuis le voyage de ce Christophe Habermann.

– Eh oui! Et qu'elle est peut-être dans ce grenier depuis sa mort. La date de celle-ci ne figure pas sur la canne mais elle doit se situer autour de 1610-1620. C'est probablement peu après qu'on a relégué la canne là-haut. Les autres sont bien plus récentes, elles n'ont pas plus d'une cinquantaine d'années. Au cours d'un rangement ou après un décès, quelqu'un de soigneux les a montées au grenier et a joint au paquet la canne de compagnon qui devait traîner dans un coin.

Les deux jeunes gens qui n'avaient entrepris l'exploration du grenier que pour faire plaisir à Réveillon semblaient maintenant fascinés par cet objet, témoin des existences terrestres de plusieurs générations de maîtres, de compagnons, d'artisans venus des provinces et de l'étranger pour fonder la communauté du bois au faubourg Saint-Antoine. Marie caressait de son index les angelots de Jean Cottion comme l'avaient fait avant elle Élisabeth la petite couventine, Anne et bien d'autres [1]. Elle ressentait au contact du bois le léger frisson voluptueux qu'avaient connu les amoureuses du temps passé. Comme Élisabeth avait regardé Jean, comme Anne avait caressé Denis du regard, Marie leva les yeux vers Ethis. Celui-ci souriait en la contemplant et le vieux Réveillon,

1. Voir *Les Dames du Faubourg,* tome I.

plus ému qu'il ne le laissait paraître, murmura simplement :

– Cette maison va trop bien à votre amour. Je vous la donne en cadeau de mariage. A une condition pourtant. C'est que la canne de compagnon sorte de son purgatoire et accède à votre paradis. Mettez-là en bonne place dans votre logement, elle vous portera bonheur.

– Merci, monsieur Réveillon, s'exclamèrent en chœur les jeunes gens. Et Ethis ajouta : Est-ce qu'il y a encore des compagnons qui partent faire leur tour de France?

– La Révolution a dû arrêter le cours de ces merveilleux voyages qui procuraient la sagesse et le talent. Maintenant les jeunes partent aux Armées et ils reviennent mutilés, ce qui les empêche au retour d'exercer un métier. Mais le temps du compagnonnage reviendra...

Ethis écoutait, l'œil rêveur. Il prit la main de Marie et dit :

– J'aimerais bien que mon fils soit ébéniste, comme M. Riesener. Et qu'il fasse son tour de France comme Jean Cottion...

– Et il emporterait la canne! murmura Marie en souriant.

Il restait le panneau de marqueterie que Réveillon avait essuyé et qu'il examinait avec attention, ses lunettes suspendues au bout du nez sans doute pour y voir mieux. Il tournait et retournait l'étrange tableau composé aurait-on dit de tous les bois de la création. Cela allait du frêne, presque blanc, à l'ébène en passant par l'amarante, le rouge sang Sainte-Lucie, le sapan et le citrin. Chaque parcelle de bois précieux, finement découpée dans le fil ou dans le bout pour varier les effets, était comparable à une touche de couleur. Le tout, tenu dans un cadre de bois de fer comme dans un étau, représentait une figure de jeune fille, belle et souriante.

Réveillon semblait fasciné. Pour répondre à l'interrogation muette des deux jeunes gens visiblement intrigués, il finit par murmurer :

– Ce n'est pas Dieu possible! Boulle, le grand Boulle

aurait donc habité cette maison! Tenez, regardez ce qu'il y a d'écrit au dos du panneau.

Une fois encore le bois, miraculeusement conservé dans le grenier, révélait un secret, gravé à la gougette comme sur la canne. Serrés l'un contre l'autre et penchés sur l'envers du panneau, Ethis et Marie lurent en même temps :

« André-Charles Boulle à Rosine Habermann pour son mariage avec Frédéric Andrieu. Au faubourg Saint-Antoine, 1655. »

– C'est le grand ébéniste du roi dont parle souvent M. Riesener? demanda Ethis.

– Sans aucun doute. Il va falloir qu'Antoinette rassemble les dates et les noms, ceux de la canne, ceux trouvés sur le mur de l'atelier et ceux que vous allez encore découvrir mes enfants, car il n'est pas question de s'arrêter en si bon chemin. Mais regardez bien ce tableau. C'est prodigieux! Il fallait vraiment que ce Boulle soit un fameux artiste pour réussir un pareil portrait! Riesener et Lenoir n'ont pas fini d'être étonnés...

Un peu partout dans Paris on démolissait les couvents, les chapelles et beaucoup d'églises qui n'avaient pas été reconverties à la religion nouvelle. L'abbaye Saint-Antoine avait jusque-là survécu à la casse. En partie transformée en hôpital depuis 1795, elle paraissait devoir être épargnée, en particulier l'abbatiale et la petite chapelle Saint-Pierre. Et puis, un matin, Ethis qui travaillait à l'installation de sa maison aperçut, depuis la fenêtre ouverte sur l'abbaye, un groupe d'ouvriers qui attaquaient à la masse et à la pioche les fines sculptures du chevet avant d'abattre les colonnes considérées comme des joyaux de l'art gothique. Qui avait donné cet ordre absurde? A la demande d'Antoinette, Delacroix était pourtant intervenu et avait reçu l'assurance que les deux églises resteraient en état; de son côté, Lenoir avait fait agir David. Et voilà que l'irréparable était en train de se produire.

Ethis dévala aussitôt le Faubourg pour aller prévenir Antoinette. Il savait combien sa mère adoptive était attachée à son quartier et craignait sa réaction. Depuis longtemps, heureusement, les événements l'avaient rendue fataliste. Elle avait appris qu'il existait une échelle des malheurs et que la sagesse commandait d'en tenir compte en ne confondant pas le regret et le désespoir :

– Je m'y attendais, dit-elle. Le Faubourg a été, tu en sais quelque chose, le berceau de la Révolution. C'est normal qu'il y fermente encore la vieille révolte des sans-culottes. Ici on tient aux symboles. La Folie Titon en était un, la Bastille n'en parlons pas... Il ne restait que la vieille abbaye et le clocher de l'abbatiale qui agaçait les derniers admirateurs de Marat et de Hébert. La misère dans laquelle se débattent la plupart des gens du quartier a dû encore une fois servir de détonateur.

Antoinette soupira et continua :

– Tu vois, Ethis. Tu seras le premier habitant de la maison Thirion qui ne verra pas l'abbatiale en ouvrant sa fenêtre. Finalement, tout cela n'est pas très grave. Nous avons connu pis tous les deux, n'est-ce pas?

Lenoir prévenu dit que personne ne prendrait le risque d'arrêter une destruction tout de même préférable à un soulèvement populaire.

– Vous voyez, dit-il le soir au souper, je ne crois pas à grand-chose mais il me plaît de penser que si Dieu existe il a dans sa miséricorde sacrifié sa vieille église du Faubourg à la folie de quelques-uns de ses enfants égarés.

Ainsi disparut l'abbatiale qui durant des siècles avait symbolisé l'unité d'une communauté née de l'art et de l'amour du bois. Dans le même élan destructeur la petite chapelle Saint-Pierre où s'étaient unies des générations de compagnons avait été rasée avec la bibliothèque et l'antique parloir des abbesses où Henri IV avait négocié en secret son entrée dans Paris.

Lenoir n'avait rien pu sauver des ruines qui puisse prétendre à une place dans son musée. Seul Ethis avait extrait d'un tas de gravats un morceau de chapiteau représentant un visage de sainte dont les traits ressemblaient, disait-il, à ceux de Marie : « Je le ferai sceller, avait-il décidé, au-dessus de la porte d'entrée de notre maison. Ainsi il restera tout de même une pierre de l'abbatiale dans le Faubourg ! »

Le chapiteau était effectivement en place lorsque le 15 avril 1797, le soir des noces, il fit entrer Marie dans leur nouvelle maison. Le mariage s'était déroulé comme prévu dans la plus grande simplicité. Le maire du VIIIe arrondissement, décoré de son écharpe tricolore et de la cocarde, leur avait rappelé en bafouillant un peu les droits et les devoirs des époux républicains, ils avaient signé le registre frappé sur sa couverture des emblèmes du Directoire, imités par les témoins qui étaient Réveillon et Lenoir pour le marié, sa sœur aînée Marthe et Jacquemart l'associé de son père pour la mariée. Alexandre Lenoir avait fait faire pour Ethis, en guise de cadeau, un superbe habit en velours champagne rehaussé d'un galonnage et de boutons argentés. « Qui reconnaîtrait mon petit oiseau blessé de 89 dans ce jeune homme élégant et bien fait ? » avait dit Antoinette en l'embrassant. Riesener et les Valfroy avaient fait bourse commune pour offrir aux jeunes mariés le lit de leurs amours. Ce lit avait été l'objet de bien des discussions. Riesener aurait volontiers choisi de faire construire un « lit à la reine » sculpté, orné de quelques beaux bronzes et garni de satin de Lyon. Mais Antoinette qui connaissait les goûts des enfants s'était récriée :

– Un lit de cour dans cette petite chambre, tu n'y penses pas ! Les jeunes préféreront mille fois un lit comme les font maintenant les frères Jacob, en plus simple naturellement. Tu sais une sorte de nacelle en bois d'acajou sobrement décorée de filets d'ébène. La petite pourra s'amuser par la suite de lui adjoindre un baldaquin.

Valfroy et Lenoir s'étant rangés à son côté, Riesener rendit les armes de bonne grâce :

– Vous avez raison. Il faut aux jeunes un mobilier jeune. Je vais demander cela à François Pabst qui sera trop heureux de travailler dans le neuf. Depuis qu'il restaure les meubles des émigrés saisis par le gouvernement...

Le repas servi dans une salle de la manufacture Titon fut excellent, gai et sans histoire. Le menu n'était pas celui que les Tallien servaient à *La Chaumière* ou dans leurs appartements de la rue de la Victoire mais tout de même exceptionnel comparé aux repas de tous les jours où le son mélangé à un peu de farine épaississait souvent un maigre potage.

Les Bénard gagnaient à être connus et Antoinette s'en voulait un peu de les avoir traités en petits-bourgeois enrichis. Eugène était loin d'être sot, il l'avait montré dans ses affaires et surtout au Comité civil, pendant la Terreur où, s'occupant de tâches administratives, il s'était tenu prudemment à l'écart des luttes politiques. C'était un brave homme, un peu avare, qui, comme il le disait, avait eu de la chance. Il s'était rendu compte qu'Ethis, en dépit des apparences, n'était pas un mauvais parti et voir Marie heureuse lui enlevait ses derniers préjugés. Valfroy, avec ses manières de seigneur obligeant et délicat qui avait connu le roi et Necker, l'impressionnait; Riesener, le grand maître du siècle d'or du Faubourg était un homme célèbre; Lenoir était presque l'égal de David dans la hiérarchie de l'art officiel et Réveillon, fondateur de la manufacture, constituait à lui seul une garantie de bon aloi. Restait Antoinette qui visiblement le fascinait. Elle aussi avait connu et connaissait encore une foule de gens célèbres mais, surtout, elle possédait tous les dons qui manquaient à sa femme Léontine. Elle était belle, Léontine manquait de charme; elle parlait bien et elle avait de l'aisance, sa malheureuse épouse était empruntée dans ses manières comme dans ses propos. Enfin, Antoinette était douée d'une finesse et d'une intelligence dont il découvrait un peu plus la séduction à chaque rencontre.

– Tu pourrais faire ce que tu voudrais de Bénard, lui disait en riant son mari. Il te mange des yeux et semble toujours stupéfait de voir qu'une femme peut être à la fois belle et intelligente. Moi je savais que cela existait mais, avant toi, je n'avais jamais rencontré quelqu'un qui réponde aux deux qualités.

– Tu es sot. Si tu espères me faire rougir par tes compliments tu te trompes.

– Pourquoi? Parce que tu es consciente de tes avantages?

– Peut-être, monsieur le Baron, peut-être...

Bref, l'union d'Ethis et de Marie qu'on avait crue impossible s'ouvrait officiellement sous les meilleurs auspices. Un seul problème compliquait l'avenir de leur vie à deux : quel métier allait exercer Ethis pour faire vivre sa famille? Sa mission au côté d'Alexandre Lenoir ne pouvait s'éterniser. Elle lui avait permis d'échapper aux tentations de la rue et sans doute à un engagement politique ou militaire aux conséquences imprévisibles. Surtout, il avait beaucoup appris au contact quotidien de Lenoir qui avait su éveiller l'intelligence de l'enfant sauvage, canaliser son énergie débordante, en faire un jeune homme ouvert à la vie.

Questionné par Antoinette et son mari, Ethis avait pris un air grave qui les avait fait sourire.

– Je me pose cette question depuis longtemps! La solution la plus simple serait évidemment d'entrer à la manufacture. Mon beau-père me l'a offert. Mais cela ne me plaît pas. Je voudrais être libre et réussir par moi-même. Et pourquoi ne deviendrais-je pas ébéniste ou menuisier? C'est un métier qui redeviendra bon, et je n'étais pas maladroit chez le maître Nadal. Quel dommage que j'aie dû interrompre mon apprentissage!

– C'est la maison Thirion qui t'a donné cette idée? demanda Antoinette. Il est vrai que tous ceux qui l'ont habitée étaient des maîtres ou des compagnons du bois. Mais, vois-tu, je crois que malheureusement la période est mal choisie pour apprendre ce métier difficile. Et puis, tu n'as plus l'âge d'un apprenti! Pourquoi ne chercherais-tu pas à utiliser les connaissances que notre ami Lenoir t'a permis d'acquérir? Tu connais bien les styles, les objets d'art en pierre ou en bronze, les meubles aussi depuis que tu en entends parler. Lenoir te trouvera bien une place chez un marchand ou un grand mercier. Et plus tard, si tu deviens propriétaire d'un magasin, tu gagneras beaucoup plus d'argent à vendre les meubles qu'à les fabriquer.

– Voilà une bonne idée! s'exclamèrent en même temps Valfroy et Ethis dont l'œil s'alluma.

– Mais le magasin est tout trouvé! L'atelier du rez-de-chaussée ne nous sert pas et peut facilement être aménagé. Je n'ai pas tellement envie de travailler pour les autres, je pourrai très bien m'installer directement à mon compte!

– Tu ne crois pas que tu vas vite en besogne? dit Valfroy. Penses-tu vraiment être capable de trouver des marchandises, de les acheter et de les revendre?

– Je me crois capable de me débrouiller. Je connais par M. Lenoir tous les brocanteurs et tous les marchands qui me prêteront des objets à vendre. Et puis, une idée me vient : pourquoi ne vendrais-je pas les papiers peints que fabrique mon beau-père? Avec Marie qui a beaucoup de goût on pourrait installer des logements, fournir les meubles, les tapisseries, tout quoi...

Antoinette et Bertrand étaient tout de même étonnés de la maturité de leur fils adoptif. Quand ils furent seuls elle laissa éclater sa surprise :

– Dis donc, j'ai l'impression que notre petit Ethis va en surprendre plus d'un! Quel aplomb! Nous en parlerons à Lenoir. Le plus fort c'est qu'il est capable de réussir son coup!

Mme Delacroix était venue au mariage d'Ethis et avait excusé son mari retenu par la réception d'un ambassadeur. Elle avait retrouvé sa sœur qu'elle voyait plus rarement depuis qu'elle devait tenir salon. Victoire avait invité cent fois Antoinette aux bals et aux réceptions officielles qu'elle donnait dans l'Hôtel de la rue du Bac où était installé le ministère mais les Valfroy n'aimaient guère se mêler aux invités de ces réunions où tel agioteur connu côtoyait un robespierriste repenti ou un ancien membre du Comité dont on disait qu'il avait des dizaines de guillotinés à son actif.

– C'est à ceux qui sont au faîte des honneurs de venir voir leurs frères et leurs amis demeurés à un rang modeste! disait-elle à sa sœur qui se rebiffait en l'accusant d'être méchante et injuste.

– Tu crois que cela m'amuse de voir tous ces gens? Combien de soirs j'aimerais mieux souper avec vous d'un méchant pot de bouillon que partager les banquets officiels qui sont de honteux gâchis. Et puis d'abord, je viens te voir puisque je suis là!

Elle pleurait un peu et les deux sœurs s'embrassaient en riant après qu'Antoinette eut promis de venir au prochain dîner du ministre. Ce jour-là Victoire ajouta :

– Vous faites bien de venir car je pense que ce sera l'une des dernières réceptions de Son Excellence!

– Pourquoi? Charles va quitter son poste?

– Il y a de grandes chances ou plutôt de grands risques. Figure-toi que ton ancienne amie Germaine de Staël s'est mis dans la tête de mettre un revenant, Talleyrand, l'ancien évêque d'Autun, à la place de Delacroix!

– Talleyrand est revenu d'Amérique?

– Oui. Mme de Staël a même réussi à le faire rayer de la liste des émigrés. Maintenant elle veut en faire un ministre et assiège Barras jour et nuit – tu vois ce que je veux dire – pour en faire un ministre. Barras n'aime pas Talleyrand mais elle finira par avoir gain de cause car mon mari ne peut presque plus se montrer en public!

– La grosseur dont tu m'avais parlé?

– Oui. C'est affreux. La tumeur a pris des proportions effrayantes et l'on parle d'une opération. Talleyrand n'aura pas de mal à chasser cet infirme et à prendre sa place. J'ai vu l'autre jour cet homme à qui paraît-il rien ne résiste, ni l'argent ni les femmes. Eh bien, il est très séduisant. Son intelligence fait un peu peur quand on sait qu'il l'emploie d'abord à s'enrichir mais on s'y laisserait prendre facilement.

– Eh bien, dit Antoinette en riant, laisse partir le

ministre et reste avec son successeur qui a l'air de tellement te plaire!

– Ne dis pas de bêtises. Enfin, si l'occasion se présentait... Cela dit je vais rentrer pour soigner mon pauvre gros mari que j'aime bien.

Deux semaines plus tard, Antoinette se demandait si cette conversation avait été de la prescience ou si Victoire en savait alors plus qu'elle ne disait : le 17 juillet Charles Delacroix était nommé ministre plénipotentiaire auprès de la République batave et envoyé à La Haye tandis que Talleyrand s'installait rue du Bac.

Victoire était venue place d'Aligre annoncer la nouvelle et Antoinette, à son grand étonnement, la trouva heureuse, pleine d'allant :

– Tu ne sembles pas trop regretter tes salons dorés, dis donc! Remarque, c'est mieux ainsi...

– Mais figure-toi que je n'ai pas encore quitté mes salons dorés. Avec beaucoup d'élégance M. de Talleyrand m'a prié de conserver mes appartements le temps que je le souhaiterais. Cela me permet de m'organiser avant de revenir habiter la maison de Charenton-Saint-Maurice.

– M. d'Autun est-il toujours aussi prévenant? Et toi, le trouves-tu aussi séduisant? Tu ne comptes pas aller retrouver ton mari à La Haye?

– Non, c'est lui qui reviendra pour se faire enlever sa monstruosité. Moi, je reste à Paris!

– Avec Talleyrand?

– Oui! Maintenant tu as tout deviné. Je te raconterai plus tard. Figure-toi que je suis heureuse pour la première fois depuis bien longtemps!

Antoinette aurait bien voulu en savoir davantage mais Victoire se refusa à tout autre commentaire. Ce n'était pas son genre d'avoir des secrets pour sa sœur et celle-ci se dit qu'on avait dû lui recommander le silence avec beaucoup d'insistance. Qui? Talleyrand sans doute... « Que voilà ma pauvre sœur embarquée dans une drôle d'affaire. Enfin, elle semble heureuse. Depuis le temps qu'elle avait envie de tromper son mari, elle n'a pas choisi n'importe qui! »

Cette révélation avait beaucoup frappé Antoinette. A la date du 1er avril 1797, elle la consigna dans son journal dont elle avait repris la rédaction depuis le retour de Valfroy. « Talleyrand, écrivit-elle, n'est pas un homme à s'embarrasser longtemps d'une femme mariée. Je souhaite de tout mon cœur que cette liaison ne fasse pas trop souffrir ma pauvre sœur peu habituée à mener une existence tourmentée ! »

Son inquiétude était bien vaine. Quinze jours plus tard, c'est une Victoire radieuse qui descendait place d'Aligre d'un carrosse tout neuf, discrètement décoré à la mode de l'époque et qui portait l'insigne du gouvernement directorial sur les portières. Lucie, qui regardait à la fenêtre, aperçut la première le brillant équipage et cria de joie en voyant qui en descendait :

– C'est tante Victoire, c'est tante Victoire !

Elle se précipita à sa rencontre dans l'escalier tandis qu'Antoinette occupée à dépouiller laborieusement un lapin qu'Ethis avait rapporté d'une de ses « tournées », comme il disait, expéditions sur lesquelles il ne donnait jamais de détails, se passait vite les mains à l'eau.

– Félicitations ma chère, tu es resplendissante. Est-ce l'amour ? lui glissa-t-elle à l'oreille tandis qu'on accordait sans conditions à Lucie la permission d'aller voir la voiture de plus près.

– Si ce n'est pas l'amour, cela lui ressemble. Je vis un moment exaltant. Charles-Maurice avec sa fougue, son entrain et sa façon de montrer partout et toujours qu'il est le maître des événements, me change de ce pauvre Delacroix. J'ai vécu jusqu'à maintenant avec un bonnet de nuit, je passe aujourd'hui avec un homme dont la conversation est étincelante et les manières aimables, tous les moments qu'il lui est possible de m'accorder.

– Tu ne crains pas une déception qui te fera très mal ?

– Non, ma grande et raisonnable sœur. C'est drôle, hein, comme les rôles ont changé ? Je prends ce qui m'est donné et si désillusion il y a j'en prendrai mon parti. Je ne suis plus, tu sais, à l'âge des passions folles, tout ce que je fais est sagement raisonné. En profitant enfin de ma vie comme je l'entends, j'emmagasine de la chaleur pour l'avenir...

– Quelle surprise de t'entendre! Il semble que d'un coup la sagesse des épicuriens ait pris en charge ton esprit de petite-bourgeoise bien comme il faut. Tiens, j'ai l'impression de lire Ninon de Lenclos, dans le recueil de lettres rassemblées au siècle dernier par un certain Damour. Lenoir vient de m'offrir ce livre qui m'enchante.

– Je t'étonne, hein?

– Beaucoup. Mais pour parler sérieusement, cela va t'amener où? Tu as tout de même deux enfants en pension et un mari chez les Bataves!

– Cela va me mener, attention, tiens-toi bien : à un troisième enfant!

– Tu ne vas pas me dire que tu es grosse?

– Si ma belle. Germaine de Staël a assez clamé partout que le pauvre Delacroix n'était plus un ministre mais une vieille femme enceinte! C'est tout de même plutôt mon rôle... Non?

– Mais ton mari...

– Il y a bien longtemps que mon mari ne peut prétendre faire un enfant. C'est là le point délicat de l'affaire. Il va falloir que je me montre extrêmement diplomate avec l'ambassadeur. Quant au monde, il sera difficile de l'empêcher de jaser. Enfin, on verra. Tu vois j'ai été incapable de laisser passer l'occasion d'avoir un enfant d'un être intelligent Pourquoi ne serait-ce pas un petit génie?

Antoinette, abasourdie, ne disait rien. Elle contemplait sa sœur qui brusquement était devenue une autre.

– Je ne voulais rien te cacher, surtout pas te mentir, ma Toinette. Maintenant tu vas me promettre de garder tout cela pour toi. Je ne te demande pas de ne rien dire à Valfroy, tu ne pourrais pas t'en empêcher mais je sais qu'il n'y a pas de crainte avec lui. Si tu lui demandes de se taire, il se taira.

C'est ainsi que Charles Delacroix apprit un soir dans

son ambassade de La Haye qu'il allait être père d'un enfant qu'il ne pouvait avoir conçu. La longue lettre de Victoire devait être tendre et persuasive puisqu'il y répondit très affectueusement en faisant mille recommandations à sa femme pour qu'elle ne commette pas d'imprudence, ni en se fatiguant inutilement, ni en faisant le voyage de Hollande comme elle se le proposait.

Charles était tout de même un sacré bonhomme. On peut imaginer qu'après avoir lu la lettre de Victoire, il réfléchit, se regarda dans une glace, se dit qu'il aimait la mère de ses deux autres enfants, laquelle avait eu jusqu'alors une conduite irréprochable. Sans doute se dit-il aussi qu'il ne voulait pas perdre une femme qui l'aimait encore, il en était sûr et il avait raison. On peut aussi penser qu'il prit la lettre, l'approcha des chandelles qui éclairaient son bureau et la brûla en se disant qu'après tout il souhaitait depuis longtemps un troisième enfant et qu'il se lamentait de ne pouvoir l'engendrer. Cet enfant serait donc le sien. Il porterait son nom. Et il l'aimerait comme les deux autres.

Ethis continuait de travailler avec Lenoir, mais les temps avaient changé. Fini les expéditions aventureuses dans les chantiers de démolition et les bagarres avec les casseurs excités. La guerre des statues était terminée et le directeur du musée rangeait, étiquetait, tentait de grouper par époque et par auteur les œuvres qu'il avait récupérées. Ethis l'aidait dans ce travail mais n'y trouvait guère de satisfaction. A vrai dire il ne songeait qu'à son idée de boutique de meubles et d'objets anciens. Sans cesse il questionnait Lenoir, lui demandait où il pourrait trouver à bon prix ces petits bronzes qui avaient échappé à la fonte et que commençaient à rechercher les amateurs et les prospecteurs pour l'Angleterre. Lui-même partait visiter, pour se rendre compte, les magasins d'antiquités qui s'étaient ouverts les uns à côté des autres sur la partie du quai Malaquais qu'on avait détachée pour lui donner le nom de Voltaire, mort dans l'une de ces maisons.

Il entrait, regardait, discutait avec les acheteurs éventuels et s'apercevait avec fierté que son goût joint à sa science toute neuve le mettait au niveau de la plupart des amateurs. Mêlé grâce à Lenoir au marchandage et au troc des pièces d'art remises en circulation lors de la dispersion des biens des émigrés, il lui arrivait de mettre la main sur tel objet recherché par un marchand et de toucher sa part de la transaction. Bref, avec une opiniâtreté qui faisait l'admiration de Lenoir et de la famille, il apprenait petit à petit son futur métier. Il commençait même à se constituer une réserve, entassant dans l'atelier de la maison Thirion les meubles et les objets les plus hétéroclites parmi lesquels Lenoir affirmait non sans fierté qu'on ne décelait aucune trace de mauvais goût.

Le projet d'Ethis était naturellement la grande affaire de la famille. Riesener et Réveillon s'en mêlaient, le premier offrant en dépôt quelques-uns des meubles qu'il avait rachetés et l'autre certains souvenirs des premiers essais des montgolfières, telles la lorgnette du marquis d'Arlandes ou la veste brûlée de Pilâtre de Rozier au cours du premier survol de Paris en ballon libre.

Le départ d'Ethis avait un peu bouleversé les habitudes de la communauté aligroise mais celle-ci se retrouvait au moins deux fois par semaine avec un convive nouveau, la jeune Marie. C'est elle qui rapporta un soir une nouvelle stupéfiante venant d'un client de son père : un rapport de l'administration du Garde-meuble proposait au ministre de l'Intérieur de brûler un certain nombre de tapisseries anciennes pour en tirer la valeur métallique qu'elle contenait.

– Il paraît, ajouta Marie, que beaucoup de ces vieilles tapisseries, tissées presque toutes à Bruxelles, sont de véritables chefs-d'œuvre!

– Ethis, nous allons voir cela dès demain. Il faut absolument que nous en sauvions quelques-unes!

Leur récit fut accablant :

– Le 18 avril, on a brûlé à la Monnaie soixante pièces dont *La Fable de psyché,* dessin de Raphaël au chiffre de

François Ier et les autres fabriquées à Bruxelles d'après les dessins de Jules Romain, de Lucas et de Dürer. Tout cela parce qu'elles étaient rehaussées d'or et d'argent. L'administration se flatte d'avoir ainsi récupéré en lingots une cinquantaine de milliers de livres ! Le plus extraordinaire, c'est que ces imbéciles sont persuadés d'avoir servi la République ! J'ai tout de même réussi à sauver l'une des deux tapisseries d'après les cartons de Raphaël *Actes des apôtres*. Elle sera vendue aux enchères [1]. L'autre œuvre similaire a été brûlée !

– Et moi, j'ai récupéré pour ma boutique une portière de char fabriquée aux Gobelins d'après Le Brun. Il y a au Garde-meuble un désordre si grand que j'ai pu l'emporter dans la voiture sans que personne ne me demande rien !

– Bravo ! s'exclama Antoinette. Continue comme cela, tu monteras ta boutique à bon compte, mais tu te retrouveras en prison ! N'oublie pas, Ethis, que tu portes un nom auquel tu te dois de faire honneur !

Le garçon rougit, s'excusa et sortit honteux.

– Ce n'est pas grave, dit Lenoir. C'était pour sauver cette pièce des fourneaux de la Monnaie. Et puis, Ethis a pris de mauvaises habitudes avec moi. Depuis deux ans nous passons notre temps à soustraire des objets de valeur à la destruction.

– Ne le défendez pas. Vous savez très bien que cela n'a rien de commun. Ce n'est pas parce qu'on tue à la guerre qu'on peut devenir assassin une fois la paix revenue. Ethis n'est plus un gamin perdu, il est temps qu'il s'en rende compte.

Un nom nouveau commençait à être connu dans le Faubourg, celui de Buonaparte. Depuis longtemps ce jeune général sorti des rangs de la République était un familier des cercles directoriaux, mais il avait fallu l'insurrection de Vendémiaire et surtout son mariage avec Joséphine Tascher de la Pagerie, veuve du général de

1. Cette tapisserie, échappée aux flammes, a finalement trouvé une place au Victoria and Albert Museum à Londres.

Beauharnais, guillotiné sous la Terreur, pour que ce drôle de patronyme corse, « Buonaparte », franchisse le pas des vieilles cours et des passages du Faubourg.

Victoire, elle, le connaissait et aussi Joséphine, la créole, qu'elle avait souvent rencontrée dans les salons du Luxembourg où elle était l'invitée quasi permanente de Barras et de la belle Thérésia Tallien. Questionnée un jour où elle était venue voir sa sœur, elle raconta comment Buonaparte avait pris d'assaut le cœur d'une Joséphine hésitante et l'avait épousée le soir du 9 mars 96, huit jours après avoir été nommé général en chef de l'armée d'Italie.

– C'est Charles Leclerc, un obligé de son mari, secrétaire du comité d'état civil de la section de la Butte-des-Moulins qui a procédé au mariage. M. Bénard doit le connaître puisqu'il est aussi fabricant de papier peint. C'est un petit homme gentil et timide qui a bien cru ce jour-là perdre la raison. Le général est arrivé à dix heures du soir avec deux heures de retard. Barras et Tallien, les témoins de Mme de Beauharnais, attendaient avec la mariée qui se demandait si le Corse n'avait pas changé d'avis au dernier moment. Elle était paraît-il très élégante dans une robe de mousseline blanche parsemée de fleurs bleues et rouges et serrée à la ceinture par une écharpe tricolore. « Je n'ai plus d'autre opinion que celle de mon mari », avait-elle répondu à Barras qui s'étonnait de la voir parée aux couleurs de la République. Enfin Buonaparte apparut essoufflé avec Lemarrois son secrétaire d'état-major.

– Mariez-nous vite, monsieur le Maire!

Le brave Leclercq obtempéra et lut l'acte de mariage qui comportait une bonne demi-douzaine d'erreurs ou de faux témoignages : Joséphine s'était rajeunie de quatre ans et Buonaparte vieilli de deux par galanterie. Pour simplifier, le marié était déclaré né à Paris et le capitaine Lemarrois avait dû lui aussi se vieillir car il n'avait pas les vingt et un ans réglementaires pour servir de témoin. Tout fut cependant expédié en quelques minutes, militairement, et Napolione Buonaparte passa au doigt de

Joséphine un mince anneau d'or gravé à l'intérieur de ces deux mots: « Au Destin. » Joséphine signa de son vrai nom: Marie-Joseph Detascher, et Napolione du sien ce curieux acte de mariage [1]. Aujourd'hui le général se couvre de gloire en Italie!...

– Comme tu racontes bien, ma Victoire! J'adore tes chroniques du grand monde. Dommage que tu l'abandonnes pour te livrer encore une fois aux joies de la maternité!

– La dernière, sois-en sûre, mais il est vrai comme je te l'ai déjà dit que j'attends beaucoup de cet enfant dont la venue semble charmer... Delacroix.

– Hein? Ton mari est content?

– Mais oui. Il veut un fils. J'espère que je lui ferai un fils. Je lui dois bien ça non? Surtout pas un mot de ce que je t'ai dit. A personne. Les gens s'étonneront bien assez tôt. Ils jaseront un moment. Ceux qui connaissent l'état de Charles... Et puis on oubliera... Moi-même je ne penserai sans doute plus à Talleyrand!

– Ma chérie, tu as mis le temps, mais tu es vraiment devenue une femme de ton époque. C'est moi, la « fille sans morale » de 83, qui fais maintenant figure de duègne.

– Attends. Rien ne dit que la vie ne te réserve pas encore quelque surprise. Je n'ai pas oublié la lettre où tu m'écrivais: « Toi à qui il n'arrive jamais rien... »

– Raconte-moi tout de même. Ton mari? Comment a-t-il réagi quand tu lui as écrit que tu attendais un enfant?

– Rien, je t'ai dit. Il a compris et il a accepté. Je vais d'ailleurs le revoir bientôt car il revient à Paris pour se faire enlever sa tumeur. C'est une opération terriblement douloureuse et je me demande comment il va la supporter. Mais il est physiquement très courageux, un vrai

1. La mairie du IIe arrondissement était alors établie dans l'hôtel Mondragon confisqué. La salle où s'est déroulé le mariage existe toujours, au premier étage du n° 3, rue d'Antin. Elle est classée et sert aujourd'hui de bureau au président de la Banque de Paris et des Pays-Bas qui a acheté l'hôtel en 1869.

sanglier d'Argonne. Je vais m'occuper de lui et le soigner. Je l'aime bien, tu sais...

Et le temps passait. Le Directoire s'usait à gouverner entre la richesse usurpée et la misère de ceux que la Révolution n'avait pas enrichis. Le Faubourg qui avait fourni les premières troupes en 89 stagnait dans sa pauvreté originelle. De temps à autre un maître qui avait reçu une petite commande ou la sous-traitance d'un marchand rouvrait son atelier et replaçait le pot de colle sur les braises. A l'odeur, le quartier savait que Caspar-Schneider, l'ancien fournisseur de la reine, ou Guillaume Beneman [1] qui mourait de faim après avoir eu son heure de gloire à la fin du règne, travaillaient. Ce n'était hélas qu'un parfum illusoire. Bien vite la torpeur revenait.

Seuls les frères Jacob, mais ils n'étaient pas établis au Faubourg, continuaient d'employer régulièrement quelques compagnons. Leur père Georges, figure de proue du « style fin de règne » l'un des successeurs de Riesener à la cour et chez les princes, qui avait régné jusqu'à la Révolution sur ses quinze ateliers de la rue Meslée et n'avait dû qu'à la protection de David de survivre à la grande tourmente, avait accumulé dans ses magasins des sièges inspirés de l'antique, surtout ses fameux fauteuils « curules » en acajou d'un prix si élevé qu'ils ne trouvaient pas preneur. Retiré en 1796, il avait légué les ateliers somnolents à ses deux fils, François-Honoré et Georges qui tout de suite avaient su se plier au goût de l'époque. Sans renoncer à la mode de l'antique, ils l'infléchissaient vers une interprétation plus légère, produisant presque exclusivement des sièges, des tabourets faciles à loger et à bouger dans les salons huppés du Directoire. Mlle Mars, la célèbre actrice, était devenue

1. Lors d'une vente à Monaco, le 11 novembre 1984, Mes Picard et Tajan ont adjugé pour la somme record de 15 000 0000 francs un médailler estampillé Beneman qui avait figuré à Versailles dans la salle des bijoux.

l'une de leurs clientes fidèles. Plus menuisiers en sièges qu'ébénistes, les deux frères profitaient avec opportunisme du fait que les chaises et les fauteuils s'étaient détériorés plus vite que les autres meubles. Pour asseoir leur prestige, les nouveaux notables avaient d'abord besoin de sièges : les frères Jacob étaient prêts à assumer cette charge.

Le petit monde de la place d'Aligre s'était lui aussi installé dans une vie dont chacun ressentait la fragilité. Le salaire de Valfroy au télégraphe Chappe n'était pas très important mais il permettait à sa famille de vivre mieux que l'immense majorité des gens du Faubourg. Réveillon, Riesener et Lenoir, « ma trinité » comme disait Antoinette, versaient leur écot dans la marmite familiale chaque fois qu'ils s'invitaient à souper. C'était une poule, une tranche de lard ou un morceau de viande qu'ils avaient réussi à dénicher dans une boutique où ils étaient connus.

Le départ d'Ethis avait affecté Antoinette. Depuis plus de sept ans qu'il vivait à ses côtés, la protégeant avec sa petite fille de ses jeunes épaules, sauvant son mari de la guillotine, apportant dans les moments les plus sombres le réconfort de sa tendresse gouailleuse, le garçon de la Folie Titon était devenu pour elle un fils, un frère, un compagnon sur lequel elle avait pris l'habitude de compter. Son absence laissait un vide auquel elle avait du mal à s'habituer. Heureusement Ethis n'habitait pas loin et il n'était guère de jour où il ne fasse un saut, place d'Aligre, le temps d'embrasser Antoinette et de s'assurer « que tout allait bien ». Et puis il venait souvent avec sa femme partager le souper. Marie avait conquis tout le monde par sa bonne humeur et sa gentillesse. Elle secondait de son mieux le bouillant Ethis dans l'installation de la boutique qui commençait à prendre de l'allure. Le père Bénard avait d'abord vu d'un œil méfiant le projet de son gendre dont le caractère fantasque, l'aplomb et la jeunesse lui faisaient peur, mais il commençait à se prendre au jeu et à croire à ce qu'il n'appelait plus que pour la forme une folie. Lui aussi, dans ses visites aux clients et dans ses déplacements, cherchait des objets ou des petits meubles susceptibles d'être exposés et vendus.

Bref, le magasin de la vieille maison Thirion était devenu l'affaire de tous. Rarement en public mais souvent lorsqu'il était seul avec lui, Lenoir conseillait habilement Ethis qui prenait ces remarques à son compte et jouissait ainsi d'un prestige accru auprès de son entourage. Seule, la fine Antoinette devinait qui avait eu l'idée des projets que son garçon exposait avec autorité... N'empêche qu'Ethis avançait. Avec la complicité de son maître et l'argent que lui prêtaient Réveillon et son beau-père, il ratissait les brocanteurs, les ventes publiques et les déballages que les particuliers ruinés exposaient au coin de certaines rues. Il était rare qu'il ne revînt pas avec une statuette, un tableau intéressant ou une petite table à ouvrage dont la marqueterie se décollait et qui était tout de suite confiée à Riesener. Le vieux maître bougonnait :

– Quand je pense que j'ai refusé beaucoup d'argent pour ne pas restaurer les meubles confisqués en disant que ce n'était pas digne de ma réputation !

Naturellement il s'exécutait. Lui, le grand Riesener, recollait les meubles d'un obscur compagnon. Comme il n'avait personne pour l'aider, il prenait même le vieux tampon de chiffons à vernis et accordait au rafistolage de la petite table le même soin qu'il prenait naguère à « donner le fini » aux chefs-d'œuvre destinés à la chambre du roi. Il le faisait pour Ethis qu'il aimait et à qui il ne pouvait rien refuser. Il le faisait aussi, sans l'avouer, parce que cela lui faisait du bien de retrouver son atelier, de sentir l'odeur sucrée du vernis et de constater que le manche de ses outils avait gardé cette forme et ce poli subtils qui ne faisaient qu'un avec sa main quand il les tenait, serrés à poigne pour certains travaux ou souplement épousés pour d'autres tâches plus délicates.

Un jour, le tableau de chasse de Lenoir et d'Ethis approcha du miracle. Ils revinrent alors que la famille au complet était déjà installée autour de la table de noyer construite par Œben lorsqu'il avait emménagé place d'Aligre. Enveloppé dans une vieille couverture, le garçon portait comme le Saint-Sacrement un objet mystérieux. « La trouvaille de ma vie ! » s'écria-t-il.

– C'est Ethis le premier qui l'a aperçue au milieu d'un tas de vieilleries sans importance ! précisa Lenoir.

– Qu'est-ce que c'est? demanda la première Lucie, bientôt reprise par tout le monde.

– Vous êtes bien curieux. Devinez donc, répondit Ethis radieux en montrant son paquet dont la forme bizarre ne permettait pas d'imaginer ce qu'il pouvait contenir.

– C'est une statue ! cria Lucie.

– Je ne crois pas. Cela n'a pas l'air de peser aussi lourd, constata Antoinette. Allez, tu nous as assez fait marcher. Dis donc ce que tu as déniché.

Lentement Ethis défit la couverture qui enveloppait un second paquet, emballé cette fois dans de vieux exemplaires du *Mercure français*. Une tête apparut, puis des bras menus et tout le corps de poussière d'un petit enfant qui semblait être sculpté dans le bois ou fondu dans le bronze peut-être. Comme aurait fait une sage-femme mettant un enfant au monde, Ethis tint un moment la statuette à bout de bras et la tendit à Antoinette :

– Tenez, en attendant que Marie vous en fasse un vrai ! Lucie avait deviné, c'est une petite statue de bronze. Elle était tellement sale que personne ne la distinguait dans les débris qu'un bonhomme vendait pour trois fois rien au coin de la rue du Pas-de-la-Mule.

– C'est un très bel objet, dit Antoinette. Il faut le nettoyer et le faire briller !

– Pas trop, Antoinette, pas trop, affirma Riesener qui regardait en connaisseur le modelé très fouillé de la statuette. C'est un bronze patiné qu'il ne faut surtout pas décaper à l'acide ni avec tout autre produit à récurer. De l'eau, du savon et un peu de cire, voilà ce qu'il faut à ce petit garçon qui est une vraie merveille. Tu as eu vraiment le coup d'œil mon garçon. Je te félicite.

– Eh oui, enchaîna Lenoir, mon élève a le coup d'œil. Il sait très bien distinguer le beau du moins beau et ne risque pas de passer à côté d'un chef-d'œuvre sans le voir.

Car c'est un chef-d'œuvre qu'il a découvert tout à l'heure et acheté pour moins d'une livre. Tenez, regardez, Riesener, le nom qui est gravé sur le bronze du socle. Mettez vos lunettes car on le voit à peine sous la crasse.

L'ébéniste mouilla son doigt, frotta à l'endroit que lui indiquait Lenoir et déchiffra à haute voix : « Pigalle Fecit 1768 » et « Bronze par Thomire ».

– Pigalle! Tu as trouvé un Pigalle? s'écrièrent ensemble Valfroy et Réveillon.

– Parfaitement, dit Ethis tout fier de voir que sa trouvaille était appréciée. Et regardez, l'enfant tient un oiseau dans ses deux petites mains ouvertes comme un nid.

– J'ai une idée! interrompit Marie qui avait pris à son tour la statuette et qui l'admirait en la faisant pivoter. Mais ce qu'elle est lourde!

– Alors, cette idée? demanda Ethis.

– Nous ouvrirons la boutique à l'enseigne de *L'Enfant à l'oiseau.* Ta statue va nous porter bonheur. Si tu es d'accord, nous essaierons même de ne pas la vendre. En tout cas de la garder le plus longtemps possible. Maintenant je voudrais bien que M. Lenoir m'explique qui est ce Pigalle dont on a l'air de faire si grand cas. J'avoue mon ignorance.

– Je me souviens, coupa Ethis. C'est cet artiste qui avait sculpté le portail de la chapelle des Enfants-Trouvés, au Faubourg, et ce Christ en croix du couvent de la Madeleine de Traisnel rue de Charonne. Je vous vois encore blanc de colère en apprenant que tout cela avait été démoli avant notre arrivée.

– Bravo, bravissimo, Ethis! Tu as de la mémoire et dans le métier c'est la moitié de la réussite. Mais tu connais aussi le buste de Voltaire en marbre que j'ai récupéré au musée. Il est de Pigalle, mort il y a une dizaine d'années couvert de gloire et d'argent après avoir été l'un des plus grands sculpteurs de son siècle. Il habitait un très bel hôtel bâti sur les terrains qu'il possédait au pied de la butte Montmartre. Tu as mis la main sur un petit chef-d'œuvre et ta femme a raison, si vous le pouvez, gardez cette statuette qui vaudra cher dans quelques années.

– Parlez-nous donc un peu plus de ce Pigalle, demanda Réveillon que la découverte d'Ethis avait excité et qui, du coup, retrouvait la passion des belles choses qui l'avait abandonné depuis le sac de la Folie Titon.

– Il était de la taille des Caffieri, Lemoyne, Falconnet, peut-être meilleur. C'est lui qui a conseillé Houdon à ses débuts. Ses deux plus belles œuvres doivent être à Berlin. Le roi Louis XV avait fait cadeau de ses statues de Vénus et de Mercure au roi de Prusse. C'est lui aussi qui avait terminé la statue de Louis XV qui ornait il n'y a pas si longtemps la place Royale et qui a été détruite. Ah! j'oubliais : Pigalle que le roi avait anobli à la fin de sa vie était le fils d'un menuisier de la rue Neuve-Saint-Martin, au coin de la rue Meslée où les Jacob ont leur atelier... Riesener l'a peut-être connu... Mais non, c'était bien avant...

Sans attendre, Antoinette et Marie avaient fait la toilette de l'enfant et de son oiseau. Une solide friction au chiffon de laine leur avait rendu un poli légèrement brillant qui mettait en valeur leurs formes adorables. La statuette trônait maintenant au milieu de la table et, ce soir-là, jamais potée au chou n'avait paru meilleure à la « famille d'Aligre », comme on appelait souvent dans le quartier les Valfroy et leurs amis.

Dès le lendemain, le ferronnier-maréchal Despert à qui Antoinette avait confié le précieux trésor d'Ethis commençait dans son atelier du cul-de-sac de la Forge-royale, devenu cul-de-sac de la Forge-républicaine, à façonner la future enseigne de la vieille maison Thirion.

Curieux homme que ce Despert dont le torse d'athlète se découpait dans le rougeoiement de la forge. Son arrière-grand-père battait déjà le fer sur la grande enclume accroupie à l'entrée comme le gardien fantastique de l'antre d'Héphaïstos. Son enseigne, *La Forge royale* avait donné son nom à l'impasse ouverte sur le Faubourg et où les ateliers d'ébénistes se succédaient de porte en porte. Aubin Despert ou le fils Despert, successeur de son père qui avait fabriqué pour Œben et Riesener des mécaniques de tables et de fauteuils, n'avait pas vingt-cinq ans mais sa force extraordinaire en avait fait l'une des gloires du Faubourg. Il était capable disait-on d'immobiliser un cheval de gros trait et de le ferrer en même temps. Mais sa renommée datait de plus loin : il n'était encore qu'un gamin de quinze ans quand, le 14 juillet 89, il était allé décrocher le drapeau blanc de la tour de la Bazinière et l'avait promené en vainqueur sur le haut des remparts de la Bastille. Après cet exploit, à la mort de son père, il s'était mis en marge des mouvements révolutionnaires et s'était retiré dans sa forge où le travail n'avait jamais manqué. Il s'y était fait des muscles et une solide réputation de tête de pioche. Il avait durant la Terreur été à deux doigts d'être arrêté comme suspect pour un motif assez surprenant : il avait catégoriquement refusé de réparer le couperet de la guillotine, alors installée place du Trône-renversé, en disant que « seul le bourreau pouvait toucher un tel outil sans se salir les mains ».

Pour son ami Ethis, Aubin avait abandonné une commande de l'intendance, des palonniers de fourgons d'artillerie : « Cela va me redonner un peu d'habileté, avait-il dit. Mes mains et mes bras n'en peuvent plus de faire toujours la même chose ! »

L'enseigne flambant neuf et peinte par le meilleur artiste de la manufacture de papier avait déjà attiré bien des clients dans le « magasin », comme il devenait de bon ton d'appeler une boutique. On pouvait lire sur la façade, au-dessus de la porte et des deux larges ouvertures percées dans le mur : « Marchand-mercier antiquaire ». C'était un peu pompeux mais finalement proche de la réalité : l'amateur trouvait sur les rayons et sur les vieux établis convertis en comptoirs du papier peint en rouleaux, ce qui était nouveau, de la peinture, du vernis, de la colle en plaques. D'un autre côté six petits meubles de Riesener – des tables de chevet et des guéridons – étaient mis en valeur par de beaux et chauds tissus que Marie avait drapés sur les murs. Enfin, c'était le rayon d'Ethis, tout un lot d'objets, de bibelots, de petits tableaux et de statuettes qui ne prétendaient pas rivaliser avec les pièces rares exposées chez les antiquaires du quai Malaquais mais qui étaient tous de bon goût. Et puis, bien sûr, *L'Enfant à l'oiseau* qui trônait dans une niche fourrée de velours et que, chaque soir, Ethis ou Marie remontaient dans leur chambre de peur qu'il ne tentât un voleur. Plusieurs clients avaient voulu acheter le bronze de Pigalle mais un refus courtois leur avait été opposé. D'ailleurs, les nouveaux marchands n'avaient pas besoin de se défaire de leur statue fétiche : les affaires, sans être extraordinaires, leur permettaient déjà de vivre mieux que les artisans du Faubourg.

La boutique qui avait été durant des mois le grand souci du clan allait donc plutôt bien quand une autre affaire plus grave et plus intime vint inquiéter Antoinette. Charles Delacroix était toujours à La Haye et Victoire à Saint-Maurice qui attendait que son ventre s'arrondisse sans, semble-t-il, se faire trop d'embarras.

– Tu es inconsciente! lui disait sa sœur. Si ton enfant doit naître comme tu me l'as confié vers la fin avril, personne parmi les gens qui vous connaissent ne pourra croire que Charles a pu t'engrosser neuf mois avant, c'est-à-dire en juillet. C'est lui le malheureux qui avait l'air d'une femme enceinte avec son énorme tumeur qui à l'évidence le rendait incapable d'avoir des rapports avec toi. Que comptes-tu faire?

– Rien du tout. M. de Talleyrand n'a fait que passer dans ma vie, le temps de me faire l'enfant que je souhaitais dans des conditions très agréables. Les gens feront s'ils le veulent des calculs mais le nouveau-né sera le fils ou la fille de Charles Delacroix qui l'aimera comme il aime ses autres enfants. Figure-toi que cet accident conjugal est en train de consolider notre ménage qui, tu le sais, était sur le point d'éclater! Je vois maintenant mon mari d'un autre regard, je le trouve bon et courageux. Tu ne me croiras pas mais nous échangeons des lettres d'amoureux. Il m'écrit presque à chaque courrier et je lui réponds. Si seulement l'opération qu'on va lui faire pouvait le guérir! Je souhaiterais tellement le rendre heureux!

– Quand aura lieu cette opération? Cela va être terrible!

– Il va abandonner son poste chez les Bataves ces jours-ci et le chirurgien décidera... Pourvu que tout se passe bien!

Le soir du 6 septembre la berline du courrier étranger déposa devant sa maison de Saint-Maurice un Delacroix exténué qu'il fallut aider à descendre. Victoire qui courait à sa rencontre étouffa un cri en voyant que le mal qui le tenaillait depuis des années avait fait les dernières semaines des progrès foudroyants. La masse énorme qui pesait sur son bas-ventre avait encore grossi.

– Mon pauvre ami, dit-elle en l'embrassant, il faut vite te soigner, sinon il sera trop tard. Dès demain tu verras le chirurgien.

– Ne t'inquiète pas, je suis décidé à tout faire pour que cesse ce martyre. Et toi? Comment vas-tu? J'espère que tu ne te fatigues pas trop. Songe à l'enfant qui va naître. Je te rappelle ce que je t'ai écrit : si tu acceptes de ne plus jamais voir le père et de ne jamais dire à l'enfant qu'il n'est pas de moi, je le considérerai comme mon fils ou ma fille et il ne sera plus question de cette affaire qui ne concerne que nous deux.

– Je ne vois plus depuis longtemps la personne dont tu parles et si tu le veux bien il en sera fait comme tu dis. Tu peux être sûr de l'amour que je te porte.

Le lendemain, ce n'est pas un chirurgien mais huit qui se retrouvèrent autour du lit de Charles Delacroix. Imbert-Delonnes avait tenu à prendre l'avis de ses confrères avant de se lancer dans une opération aussi risquée.

– Messieurs, dit-il en montrant la masse graisseuse, je crois qu'il est grand temps d'intervenir. Qu'en pensez-vous?

– Je pense qu'il n'est pas temps, je dis qu'il est trop tard, dit le premier médecin.

– Le malade ne résistera pas à un tel choc, prédit le second. Il mourra sous votre scalpel!

– Une telle opération n'a jamais été tentée. Les chances

de succès sont nulles. Je suis contre! annonça le troisième d'une voix sépulcrale.

Tous les chirurgiens sauf un se montrèrent hostiles à l'ablation de la tumeur. Imbert-Delonnes les remercia et dit qu'il allait conférer avec le patient.

– Monsieur le Ministre, vous avez entendu mes confrères. Je ne suis pas sûr qu'ils aient tort. Mais je suis sûr que si l'on ne fait rien vous allez mourir bientôt dans de grandes souffrances. Il se peut que votre mal appartienne à la catégorie des *noli me tangere* comme nous disons. Il se peut aussi que je réussisse et que vous soyez sauvé. Je ne puis ajouter qu'une chose : j'ai confiance! Maintenant c'est à vous de décider. Tout de suite parce que demain il sera peut-être trop tard.

– Merci. Voulez-vous je vous prie appeler ma femme qui doit attendre à côté et me laisser seul avec elle. Dans deux minutes vous aurez votre réponse.

En quelques mots, Delacroix résuma la situation à Victoire qui retenait ses larmes.

– Avant de prendre ma décision, je veux ton avis ou plutôt ton autorisation car je sais bien ce que je veux répondre à Imbert.

– Mon désir le plus cher est de te retrouver vaillant et fort. Pour t'aimer comme aux premiers temps de notre mariage. Tu ne peux plus vivre avec cette infirmité. Je vais prier le dieu de mes parents, n'en déplaise à tes amis, pour que l'opération réussisse. Si tu le veux, je te tiendrai la main...

L'opération eut lieu le 13 septembre 1797. Sans autres témoins que trois aides. En guise de coupe-douleur, on fit prendre à Delacroix une légère croûte de pain et un verre de vin d'Espagne et l'intervention commença. Le malade se livra au scalpel avec un courage extraordinaire. Quand la souffrance était trop forte il s'écriait : « C'est ma seule chance de survivre, c'est ma seule chance de survivre... »

Le supplice dura deux heures trente et se termina par l'ablation d'une boule graisseuse de vingt-huit livres! Le sanglier d'Argonne était encore vivant. Quand on lui eut serré un large pansement de toile autour du ventre, Victoire fut admise auprès de son mari.

Le malheureux était évidemment sorti très affaibli de cette opération épouvantable au cours de laquelle il avait perdu la moitié de son sang. Imbert-Delonncs n'aurait gagné son pari qu'au moment où les plaies cicatrisées ne risqueraient plus de s'infecter. Et le miracle eut lieu. Heureuse conjonction du talent du médecin, du courage du patient et pourquoi pas des prières de Victoire, la guérison se fit jour après deux semaines d'angoisse. Peu à peu la cicatrisation s'avançait, Delacroix reprenait des forces et sa femme qui le soignait avec dévouement pouvait commencer à espérer retrouver un mari.

On n'aurait pas su grand-chose de cette extraordinaire réussite si le chirurgien Imbert-Delonnes, fier à juste titre de son succès, n'avait pas publié sept mois plus tard le compte rendu détaillé de l'intervention dans un opuscule destiné aux médecins et si l'essentiel de ce rapport n'avait pas été reproduit en bonne place dans *Le Moniteur* du 13 avril 1798, « par ordre et aux frais du gouvernement pour servir les amis de l'humanité ».

Il n'était pas dans les usages de rendre publiques de telles informations médicales. Aussi, cette parution fit-elle grand bruit. Nul n'ignora comment Imbert-Delonnes avait extrait un « sarcocèle de 28 livres, tumeur monstrueuse dans laquelle se trouvaient confondus les organes les plus délicats de l'homme ». On apprit aussi, ce qui était réconfortant, comment le convalescent avait pu se lever au bout d'un mois, marcher le quarantième jour et se trouver guéri au début du deuxième mois. *Le Moniteur* ajoutait que « le patient qui avait perdu depuis des années les avantages de la virilité les avait retrouvés aujourd'hui en même temps qu'une santé parfaite ».

La lecture du journal plongea Antoinette dans l'inquiétude et la colère : comment après de telles révélations publiques allait-on accepter la naissance de l'enfant de Victoire ? Celle-ci dont la détermination et l'optimisme ne se démentaient pas, la rassura : « Si Delacroix était encore ministre cela aurait pu être gênant mais je ne sors plus dans le monde, on ne me voit pas dans les salons, qui donc aurait l'idée de venir me chercher ici, à Charenton, pour s'occuper de notre vie privée qui, d'ailleurs, n'intéresse personne. »

Les deux sœurs n'eurent d'ailleurs guère le temps de s'interroger plus avant : cinq jours après la parution de l'article, Victoire mit au monde un garçon qui fut déclaré, en bon républicain, à la mairie de Charenton-Saint-Maurice sous le nom de Ferdinand-Victor-Eugène Delacroix.

– Eugène Delacroix... cela sonne bien! avait dit Antoinette lorsque sa sœur lui avait montré son poupon. Et elle avait ajouté : j'espère que ce garçon aux traits fins sera plus tard le petit génie que tu souhaites.

Antoinette et Valfroy n'avaient rien dit aux autres membres du clan des confidences de Victoire. Eugène était le fils de Charles Delacroix et cela ne prêtait à aucun commentaire. Alexandre Lenoir, cependant, était trop fin pour ne pas remarquer que cette naissance cachait quelque mystère. Avec cette liberté de propos dont il avait l'habitude, il engagea un soir la conversation sur ce sujet sensible :

– Dites donc, Antoinette, il y a quelque chose que je ne comprends pas dans la venue au monde de votre neveu. Si je sais compter, il est né le 26 avril et a donc été conçu neuf mois auparavant, c'est-à-dire en juillet ou à la rigueur au début d'août 97. Or chacun sait qu'à cette époque, Charles Delacroix qui n'avait pas encore été opéré était incapable de procréer. Notre jolie Victoire aurait-elle été visitée par l'ange Gabriel? Il y a un précédent mais cela n'est pas passé inaperçu!

– C'est curieux, je n'y avais pas songé, mentit effrontément Antoinette qui ajouta : Je me refuse pour ma part à discuter de ce sujet qui ne regarde que ma sœur et son mari!

– Hum! fit simplement Lenoir.

Antoinette le regarda à la dérobée et sentit qu'elle devait se montrer un peu plus convaincante :

– Et pourquoi le petit Eugène n'aurait-il pas été conçu

après la guérison de Charles? Celle-ci, vous l'avez lu dans *Le Moniteur*, a été incroyablement rapide et l'enfant a pu naître avant terme... [1].

– Cela fait, ne trouvez-vous pas, beaucoup de suppositions! Mais après tout cette affaire nc me regarde pas. Eugène a un père qui l'a reconnu, le reste n'a aucun intérêt!

– Alors, mon cher Alexandre, nous nous en tiendrons là si vous le voulez bien!

Seuls quelques initiés marquèrent leur étonnement dans les semaines qui suivirent l'accouchement. Chacun, dans cette période difficile, avait d'autres chats à fouetter que de s'intéresser au bébé fragile dont les traits enfantins ressemblaient déjà à ceux de Talleyrand, comme le confiait Victoire à Antoinette, sa seule confidente.

– Regarde, le profil est le même. Je me demande comment Charles va le trouver quand il reviendra des Pays-Bas. Il s'est beaucoup inquiété de ma santé et de celle du nouveau-né. Tiens, regarde la lettre qu'il a envoyée à Laurette [2] pour lui demander de veiller sur moi. Elle est arrivée par la dernière poste.

Antoinette prit la lettre écrite avec élégance sur un vélin à la marque de l'ambassade et lut :

La Haye, 13 floréal an VI

J'apprends avec bien de la satisfaction, ma chère Laurette que ma femme se trouve dans la meilleure condition. Engagez-la à se bien ménager et à se conserver pour ses enfants, pour son mari dont elle connaît toute la tendresse.

Je vous prie de l'embrasser pour moi. Je remercie

1. Cette hypothèse hardie sur la naissance d'Eugène Delacroix a été retenue par quelques auteurs, garants intransigeants de la fidélité de Victoire Œben. Je lui ai préféré la thèse autrement romanesque qui attribue à Talleyrand la paternité du futur géant de la peinture. Ce choix est aussi défendu par de nombreux historiens dont Jean Orieux qui souligne que certains faits ne s'expliqueraient pas dans la carrière d'Eugène Delacroix sans cette étonnante filiation. (*N.d.A.*)
2. Parente qui aidait Victoire après ses couches.

Guillemardès et Adèle de ce qu'ils ont bien voulu initier le nouveau-né dans le monde républicain.

Je vais ce soir à Amsterdam pour trois jours. Je ne répondrai pas que ma femme reçoive régulièrement une lettre à chaque poste. Recommandez-lui de ne pas s'inquiéter. Le commandant Enkenbrock est porteur de cette lettre que je vous adresse à Charenton pour qu'elle ait promptement de mes nouvelles. Je vous embrasse de tout mon cœur.

Delacroix Charles.

– C'est gentil, non? dit Victoire quand sa sœur eut terminé sa lecture. Charles ne s'étend pas sur l'enfant mais il y fait paternellement allusion. Il faut dire qu'il ne l'a pas encore vu!

Delacroix fit plus tôt que prévu la connaissance d'Eugène. Un mois après sa naissance, une révolution chassait le gouvernement batave en place et l'ambassadeur était rappelé à Paris, Paris où l'ancien ministre était déjà bien oublié. L'activité, l'intelligence et l'entregent de Talleyrand avaient fait du simple bureau d'exécution qu'était le ministère des Relations extérieures l'un des centres importants du gouvernement où Delacroix n'avait plus sa place. Aucun poste ne fut proposé au mari de Victoire, chassée du cercle mouvant des amours de l'ancien évêque.

Après s'être présenté vainement trois fois au Directoire, Charles Delacroix tira les leçons de son étrange vie publique qui l'avait mené plusieurs fois aux frontières des plus hautes responsabilités mais ne lui avait jamais permis d'y accéder. Encore très fatigué par son opération, il décida de faire retraite, de disparaître de la scène politique en attendant des temps meilleurs.

Ce fut l'époque des retrouvailles familiales, des soupers place d'Aligre et des dimanches à Charenton sur les bords de la Seine. Les deux sœurs étaient ravies de se voir presque chaque semaine et d'échanger des clins d'yeux complices en regardant pousser le citoyen Eugène Delacroix. Charles n'était pas désagréable. Les hommes du clan, longtemps réticents à son égard, l'admettaient maintenant à part entière dans leurs discussions. Il savait il est vrai être passionnant lorsqu'il racontait les séances historiques de la Convention, les réunions houleuses du Comité de salut public où il avait siégé plusicurs mois ou encore son ambassade mouvementée à La Haye.

Chez les Valfroy, comme maintenant dans toutes les familles, les faits et gestes du général Vendémiaire constituaient un sujet fréquent de conversation. Buonaparte avait brûlé les étapes en Italie comme en France. Chaque ville prise de l'autre côté des Alpes augmentait son prestige dans les pays où le Directoire n'en finissait pas de durer, renaissant de ses cendres à chaque nouvelle élection. Gagnante aux urnes, l'opposition était étouffée et ses représentants souvent déportés. Ne pouvant pas se mettre d'accord sur le politique on se réconciliait sur l'image que Buonapartc coloriait de lui-même sur les champs de bataille, une image qui aidait les Français à croire qu'ils n'avaient pas tout à fait perdu la Révolution.

Un jour, Ethis intrigua tout le monde en demandant ce qu'il y aurait à manger le lendemain.

– Ce que vous apporterez mes enfants! dit Antoinette. Ce n'est pas avec ce que je trouverai au marché que vous ferez bonne chère. Si vous voulez faire la fête, découvrez une poule ou un rôti de cochon chez l'un de vos traiteurs, je vous les ferai cuire. Mais pourquoi cette question? Et pourquoi mettre les petits plats dans les grands un jour de semaine?

– Parce que demain je vous amène un invité!

– Qui? Qui? s'exclama Lucie.

– Je ne vous le dis pas, c'est une surprise.

– On le connaît? demanda Antoinette.

– Vous ne l'avez jamais rencontré mais vous le connaissez. Je ne vous en dis pas plus sinon vous devineriez.

Le lendemain matin, la poule, bien dodue pour une fois, était sur la table d'Antoinette où Ethis venait de la déposer avec un sourire triomphal.

– Elle est belle, dit Antoinette. Où l'as-tu trouvée?

– Chez un vainqueur de la Bastille bien sûr! Mon ami Aubin Despert, le forgeron, élève des poules derrière son atelier du cul-de-sac de la Forge-royale. Je lui procure du grain que me repasse un autre « vainqueur » et il me donne une poule de temps en temps. A ce soir! Je viendrai sur le coup de six heures avec l'invité.

– Dis-moi qui c'est ou je ne fais pas cuire la poule!

– Pas de marchandage. Tu n'en sauras pas plus que les autres!

La poule était grasse mais elle était dure. Antoinette se félicitait de l'avoir plongée assez tôt dans le bouillon de légumes qui chauffait dans l'âtre depuis le matin. Avec deux pommes achetées au marché et un reste de farine de froment elle avait fait une tarte qui embaumait. Pour peu que Valfroy, qui entretenait de bonnes relations avec les relais télégraphiques de la proche campagne, rapporte un morceau de roue de Brie ou un fromage à la feuille de Dreux, le souper serait réussi et le mystérieux invité bien traité.

Personne ce soir-là n'était en retard.

– Ma parole, dit Antoinette, l'odeur de la poule doit se sentir aux quatre coins de Paris!

Seul Ethis manquait. Le bougre avait bien manigancé son affaire. Il voulait que tout le monde soit là lorsqu'il arriverait. Lucie ne tenait plus en place. A chaque minute elle criait qu'elle avait trouvé et lançait un nom inattendu qui faisait rire.

Elle annonçait triomphalement son dernier invité imaginaire : « le général Buonaparte » quand la porte s'ouvrit laissant entrer Ethis qu'accompagnait un grand diable vêtu d'une houppelande vert pomme qui laissait apercevoir le bout de bottes rouges. Il était coiffé d'un chapeau très haut à bords rigides et son visage maigre s'accommodait mal d'un sourire contraint. Mais comment n'être pas intimidé en arrivant dans une maison inconnue pleine de gens qui vous regardent bouche bée comme une bête curieuse?

Enfin Ethis rompit le silence qui devenait gênant :

– Cela fait des années que je prie mon ami à souper en

lui disant que vous seriez ravis de faire sa connaissance mais ce n'est qu'aujourd'hui qu'il a accepté. Je vous présente Charles de La Bussière, comédien des théâtres parisiens.

Le nom de La Bussière avait fait l'effet d'une bombe. Chacun s'exclama, Antoinette murmura un « Ah ! c'est vous monsieur ! » à peine audible, Riesener répéta au moins dix fois : « Merci monsieur, merci !... » Réveillon retrouva sa voix de manufacturier plus forte que le bruit des machines pour crier : « Vous êtes un héros ! » Quant à Valfroy, visiblement très ému, il s'était précipité sur l'acteur et l'embrassait comme au théâtre en disant : « Je vous dois la vie. Je resterai, monsieur, votre obligé jusqu'à mon dernier souffle. »

Seul, Lenoir avait gardé son calme et regardait tout le monde s'agiter avec ce sourire narquois qui agaçait Antoinette après l'avoir séduite. Il se tenait un peu à l'écart avec Marie qui, n'ayant pas vécu la Terreur place d'Aligre, se sentait quelque peu étrangère à l'excitation familiale.

– Ma chère Marie, lui murmura-t-il à l'oreille, j'ai l'impression d'assister à une très bonne pièce de théâtre. Aucun de nos auteurs à succès n'aurait pu imaginer cette scène inattendue et émouvante. Chacun sans s'en rendre compte joue son rôle à merveille. L'acteur le moins bon est sans conteste le comédien. Il a l'air contrit et embarrassé de la doublure qui n'a pas appris son rôle. Cela dit, c'est un foutu personnage que cet être timide qui a sauvé plus de deux cents personnes promises à la guillotine ! Je lui tire mon chapeau et le lui dirai tout à l'heure.

– Ethis m'a souvent parlé de cet être étrange qui après avoir sauvé tous ces gens a repris ses rôles sans gloire au théâtre Mareux, rue Saint-Antoine. Il n'a jamais voulu tirer profit de ses actes de courage et vit paraît-il difficilement de ses pauvres cachets...

Dès le début du souper, La Bussière retrouva heureusement ses moyens et, le métier aidant, se révéla un convive agréable et captivant. Valfroy se fit expliquer par le détail comment l'homme aux bottes rouges avait réussi à le sauver. Lenoir, lui, voulut savoir quels autres personnages il avait arrachés pour ainsi dire des mains du bourreau.

– Je n'en ai pas dressé la liste, c'eût été trop dangereux et j'avais autre chose à faire, mais je me rappelle quelques noms : d'abord bien sûr ceux de mes camarades comédiens dont la plupart ignoraient mon existence, j'étais trop petit pour eux qui étaient célèbres. Je pense à Mlle Montansier, à Mlle Chabert, au grand tragédien La Rive et à bien d'autres comédiens-français...

– Mme Buonaparte ne vous doit-elle pas aussi la vie? demanda Marie.

– Ah! madame, ce fut ma plus belle nuit! Trente-huit personnes ont cette fois-là été sauvées du Tribunal révolutionnaire. Outre les comédiens, je sais que j'ai fait disparaître les dossiers de la vicomtesse de Beauharnais qui sans cela eût été guillotinée comme son mari, de M. de Florian dont j'avais joué les pièces et qui est mort dans son lit en 94, plusieurs dames dont les noms m'étaient connus ont la même nuit aussi bénéficié de mon industrie : Mmes de Buffon, de Bouillon, La Fayette, d'Aiguillon...

– Vous saviez que vous risquiez vous-même votre vie mais cela ne vous arrêtait pas, ajouta Antoinette en servant à l'acteur le dernier morceau de poule. Et pour rien, sans aucun autre avantage que d'avoir fait le bien... Je vous admire, monsieur, et ne sais comment vous remercier d'avoir sauvé mon mari.

Dès qu'il cessait de raconter son incroyable exploit – avec simplicité et modestie – il retrouvait la grandiloquence et la voix trop modulée de l'acteur sans génie : Vous me remerciez déjà trop, madame, en me permettant de partager votre souper! répondit-il. Mais si vous tenez encore à m'obliger, venez me voir jouer André de *L'Heureux Quiproquo,* la pièce de Patrat, au théâtre Mareux.

– Nous viendrons tous! dit Valfroy. Ce sera une joie de vous applaudir!

A huit heures, l'invité au haut chapeau s'excusa : il

passait dans le dernier acte de l'*Hamlet* de Ducis. D'un geste large il s'enroula les épaules de sa houppelande et disparut dans la nuit en direction de la porte de la Bastille.

– Quel homme bizarre! dit Valfroy, mais s'il n'avait pas été bizarre je ne serais pas aujourd'hui avec vous. Aucune personne normale n'aurait accompli un acte aussi insensé. A quoi tient la vie tout de même!...

– Qu'est-ce qui peut pousser un être quelconque à devenir un héros? Je me pose souvent la question..., murmura Lenoir pensif.

– Pour La Bussière, je crois le savoir...

Tous les regards se tournèrent vers Ethis.

– Je crois le savoir car il m'a souvent parlé, à la taverne *Les Amis de la Patrie* ou dans les coulisses du théâtre. Eh bien, je peux vous dire que les moments de danger extrême qu'il vivait volontairement ont été les meilleurs de sa vie. Si c'était à recommencer, je suis sûr qu'il jouerait de nouveau son existence. Pour sauver des innocents sûrement mais aussi pour le plaisir. Il m'a décrit celui qu'il ressentait quand il croisait Robespierre dans l'escalier du pavillon de Flore et le saluait, les poches pleines des dossiers qu'il venait de subtiliser au Tribunal de salut public. « Ce plaisir, m'a-t-il répété souvent, aucun rôle ni aucune pièce ne pourra jamais le procurer à un acteur, fût-il le plus grand! »

Chapitre 6.

LA RÉPUBLIQUE CHANGE DE DÉCOR

Les journaux étaient pleins des exploits du général Buonaparte. Menée avec une rapidité foudroyante, la campagne d'Italie avait fait du petit officier sans le sou un héros que la légende populaire enroulait déjà dans sa dragonne tricolore. Le bon peuple avait même francisé son nom et l'appelait Bonaparte.

La France du Directoire avait il est vrai bien besoin de héros. Les géants de la Révolution s'étaient entre-guillotinés et il fallait bien reconnaître que les Directeurs-fonctionnaires, malgré leurs chapeaux à plumes et leurs soutaches dorées, ne faisaient pas le poids. Auréolé de pauvreté et de victoires, Bonaparte arrivait à point pour consoler un peuple chagrin.

On parlait beaucoup du général au Faubourg et chez les Valfroy. Bertrand rapportait de l'administration du télégraphe la copie des dépêches échangées par le Directoire et le général en chef de l'armée d'Italie, dépêches qui révélaient des dissentiments profonds en même temps que l'irrésistible ascension de Bonaparte, trop populaire pour être officiellement désavoué.

Lenoir, de son côté, interprétait pour ses amis les conversations qu'il avait avec le directeur du Muséum.

– Il est certain que Bonaparte est promis aux plus hautes destinées. David en effet penche de plus en plus vers lui et vous savez qu'il ne s'est jamais trompé de direction dans ses choix successifs. Son flair est infaillible pour deviner où va souffler le vent.

– Je vous trouve bien sévère, dit Riesener. David a des défauts mais il a tellement de talent ! Et puis son opportunisme lui a souvent permis de rendre des services.

– C'est pourquoi je ne le juge pas. Je trouve même très bien qu'il survive officiellement à tous les naufrages. Imaginez qu'il ait été antirobespierriste et guillotiné : nous aurions perdu tous les chefs-d'œuvre qu'il a peints depuis 94 et tous ceux qu'il peindra encore. Il a été le peintre du roi, le peintre des Jacobins, le peintre du Directoire. Il sera celui de Bonaparte si Bonaparte arrive au pouvoir.

Ethis qui avait besoin de renouveler ses enthousiasmes ne jurait que par le Corse. Il allait même très loin en prédisant que Bonaparte sauverait le Faubourg :

– C'est un homme de la Révolution et il sait ce que le faubourg Antoine a fait pour elle. S'il le veut et s'il réussit à ranimer les ateliers moribonds, il aura derrière lui tous les anciens sans-culottes !

Les femmes du quartier n'étaient pas en reste. Elles le trouvaient séduisant, ce général aux longs cheveux dont on vendait des estampes coloriées à tous les coins de rues. Son mariage avec Joséphine dont on disait qu'il n'était pas sans nuages, avait passionné les foules. Et puisqu'il n'y avait plus de Dieu, plus de prêtres et qu'on démolissait les églises, elles reportaient leur foi sur l'homme qui avait vaincu les Autrichiens et déjà gagné tant de villes à la République.

Cette popularité grandissante n'était pas sans inquiéter le Directoire qui préférait savoir Bonaparte aux armées que dans sa maison de la rue de la Victoire, l'ancien hôtel Concordet devenu propriété de Joséphine. Convaincus qu'il est toujours dangereux de laisser un général encensé s'ennuyer dans Paris, les Directeurs se laissèrent docilement convaincre que l'Égypte était une proie facile et que la France devait y précéder l'Angleterre. Aussi vit-on avec un certain plaisir Bonaparte s'embarquer à Toulon avec 32 000 hommes pour Malte et Alexandrie, les uns parce que l'expédition d'Égypte « éloignait le sabre », les autres parce que l'Orient chantait aux oreilles du peuple.

Bonaparte trépignait à Paris mais il savait aussi qu'il n'est pas bon de s'y laisser oublier. Le jour même de cette fin de juillet 98 où sur fond de pyramides, son armée massacrait les mamelouks, un extraordinaire cortège ordonnancé par lui trois mois auparavant, depuis l'Italie, traversait la capitale.

Lenoir avait annoncé depuis longtemps à ses amis de la place d'Aligre cet événement considérable.

– J'aide David à organiser pour le 9 Thermidor l'entrée triomphale à Paris des œuvres d'art envoyées d'Italie par Bonaparte. Je ne sais pas si cette razzia de chefs-d'œuvre est conforme aux lois morales internationales mais je peux vous dire qu'elle n'a porté que sur des pièces extraordinaires. Un cortège comme on n'en a pas vu depuis les victoires antiques se formera au Muséum et gagnera le Champ-de-Mars. Ne manquez pas ce spectacle et dites bien à Ethis qu'il n'y a rien pour lui dans ces trophées!

Toute la famille était naturellement devant le Muséum quand les trompettes d'un détachement de cavalerie ouvrirent la marche dans un tonnerre d'applaudissements. Les cinquante chars, alignés dans le boulevard sud, étaient partagés en trois divisions. La première suivait la musique, précédée d'une grande bannière tenue par des jeunes filles et qui annonçait en lettres bleues: « Histoire naturelle. » Derrière venaient les professeurs du Muséum et dix chars portant exposés des minéraux, des pétrifications, les naturalisations d'un lion d'Afrique et d'un ours de Berne...

La deuxième division, précédée d'une autre musique militaire, était annoncée par l'inscription : « Livres, manuscrits, médailles, musique, caractères d'imprimerie des langues orientales. » Une députation d'artistes dramatiques, de typographes, de musiciens et de bibliothécaires ouvrait la marche à six chars lourdement chargés.

L'événement, c'était cependant la troisième division nommée simplement « Beaux-Arts », soutenue par la délégation la plus nombreuse, celle des artistes peintres, sculpteurs, graveurs, architectes... Six chars lourds suivaient, annoncés par une seconde bannière : « Monuments de la sculpture antique. » Le premier éclipsait les huit autres chargés pourtant de magnifiques statues : solidement arrimés sur la plate-forme, les quatre chevaux de bronze doré arrachés à la basilique Saint-Marc symbolisaient l'art antique et la gloire guerrière.

– C'est l'une des plus belles choses du monde ! dit Lenoir qui avait rejoint un instant ses amis. Leur origine demeure mystérieuse. Tout ce qu'on sait, c'est que les Vénitiens les rapportèrent en 1204 de Constantinople et qu'ils ornèrent la façade de Saint-Marc jusqu'à ce que Bonaparte les fît descendre de leur niche byzantine pour les ramener au galop à Paris.

– Et quelles sont ces autres statues ? demanda Ethis en désignant les autres chars qui venaient de s'ébranler.

– Tu as là sous les yeux les Muses, Apollon, la Vénus du Capitole, l'Antinoüs égyptien, l'Apollon du Belvédère... Il faut que tu apprennes à connaître la sculpture antique. Je te prêterai un livre...

Déjà d'autres voitures se mettaient en route, réservées celles-là aux tableaux dont on pouvait voir les plus importants. Lenoir cita au passage : Le Titien, Véronèse, Jules Romain...

Enfin, précédant un nombreux détachement de troupes qui fermait la marche, on contempla un instant le buste de Brutus porté par quatre soldats.

– Curieux choix ! dit Valfroy. Le triomphe de Bonaparte s'achevant sur le profil de Brutus ! J'espère pour David que personne n'y verra malice...

Depuis le jour où le roi Louis XI avait appelé le peuple de Paris à se rassembler autour de « la Croix de la Trahison », érigée devant l'abbaye Saint-Antoine-des-Champs pour stigmatiser l'attitude de son vieil ennemi Charles le Téméraire, les princes, les rois comme les tenants du pouvoir révolutionnaire n'avaient jamais manqué de convier les Parisiens à se réunir pour communier dans la fête ou la protestation opportuniste. Le Directoire, à son tour, trouvait bon de rassembler et divertir le peuple, ne serait-ce que pour lui faire oublier le prix exorbitant de la livre de pain. Toute proposition allant en ce sens – même émanant de Bonaparte – bénéficiait de la bienveillance officielle.

C'est ainsi qu'Ethis proposa un jour d'emmener Lucie admirer le spectacle dont la renommée s'étendait jusqu'au village Saint-Antoine pourtant bien replié sur lui-même. Il s'agissait des panoramas dont Lenoir avait déjà vanté la nouveauté spectaculaire. Un de ses amis, le peintre des paysages Pierre Prévost, avait été mêlé par hasard à cette entreprise que le succès rendait fort lucrative. L'ingénieur américain Robert Fulton avait pensé qu'un spectacle qui faisait courir ses compatriotes pouvait intéresser les Parisiens. Il avait obtenu sans peine de l'administration un brevet d'importation qu'il avait cédé à un certain Mr. James, Américain lui aussi. Cet estimable businessman parti à la recherche d'un associé artiste avait rencontré Lenoir qui lui avait fait connaître Prévost. Abandonnant les vues de Paris à l'huile et à l'aquarelle, celui-ci s'était voué aux panoramas et s'en trouvait heureux. Tandis que Fulton proposait au Directoire d'autres inventions mirobolantes : une sorte de bombe sous-marine qu'il appelait « torpédo » et un bateau pouvant naviguer en profondeur nommé « nautilus », les Parisiens se pressaient en foule pour admirer les gigantesques toiles peintes qui donnaient, grâce à un éclairage spécial et à un jeu de perspective savant, l'impression du relief.

Lucie allait sur ses dix ans. C'était une grande fille blonde gracieuse et futée que les privations n'avaient pas affectée. Les leçons de sa mère, de son père et surtout le contact de tous les gens d'esprit qui fréquentaient la place d'Aligre avaient heureusement pallié l'enseignement défaillant de la période révolutionnaire. Elle savait écrire, avait lu tous les livres de ses parents et dévorait maintenant ceux que Lenoir lui prêtait. Elle adorait Ethis et sa jolie belle-sœur. Sortir en leur compagnie était une fête, la visite aux « panoramas » ajoutait au plaisir de la promenade celui de la nouveauté. Un mot de Lenoir devait leur servir de sésame pour connaître la magie panoramique sans « faire la queue », comme on disait depuis la pénurie de 1794.

Ils furent en effet très bien reçus par Prévost dans le royaume du trompe-l'œil qui dressait ses deux tours sur le boulevard Montmartre [1]. Il s'agissait de deux énormes rotondes dont la courbure intérieure était calculée pour accroître l'illusion du voyage autour du monde auquel invitaient les affiches de l'entrée.

Paris et la Seine, Rome et ses ruines, le Nouveau Monde avec ses Indiens, l'Inde et ses tigres faisaient rêver les petits et les grands enfants de la Révolution. Un panorama attirait particulièrement la foule. C'était celui, tout nouveau, que Prévost venait de terminer : Bonaparte monté sur un cheval blanc haranguait ses troupes alignées entre le sphinx et la première pyramide. En légende, le peintre avait écrit la phrase reproduite dans tous les journaux sans que personne sache comment elle était parvenue à Paris ni si Bonaparte l'avait réellement prononcée : « Soldats, du haut de ces pyramides quarante siècles vous contemplent. »

Lucie rentra émerveillée. C'était justement un jour où le clan se réunissait et elle eut un auditoire attentif pour écouter le récit de son voyage autour du monde. Antoinette dut cependant la faire taire car Riesener avait invité ce soir-là son vieil ami Georges Jacob. Les deux ébénistes s'étaient connus au temps de leur jeunesse. Riesener arrivé depuis peu d'Allemagne était le compagnon d'Œben à l'Arsenal, Georges Jacob celui du maître Delanois, rue de Charenton. Ils étaient tous deux parvenus au sommet de leur profession, le premier se spécialisant dans les meubles importants, bureaux et commodes, Jacob dans les sièges où excellait le grand Delanois. Tous deux avaient servi le roi et cette gloire avait failli être fatale à Jacob durant la Terreur : comme Valfroy il avait été victime d'un dénonciateur.

– Je m'en suis mieux tiré que vous grâce à l'appui de

1. Nom dû au voisinage de la porte Montmartre, remplacé pendant la Révolution par celui de Mont-Marat.

David, dit-il à Bertrand, mais cela n'aurait pas suffi. J'ai dû dire à mes accusateurs que j'offrais 500 bois de fusils à la nation. Après, David m'a demandé de meubler la tribune de la Convention et j'ai réussi à vivoter. Aujourd'hui les commandes reviennent. Les enrichis de la Révolution ont besoin de chaises, de fauteuils, de lits mais je suis las. Mes deux fils reprennent le fonds de la rue Meslée. Ils ont du talent, plus que moi sans doute mais réussiront-ils à faire revivre mes cinq ateliers et à réembaucher près de trois cents compagnons ébénistes, menuisiers, sculpteurs, fondeurs, ciseleurs, doreurs... C'est que les temps ont bien changé!

Riesener qui n'avait jamais eu l'esprit d'entreprise de Jacob et avait préféré la quiétude de l'artiste aux soucis de l'industriel, admirait son ami qui joignait à ses qualités de créateur celles de l'homme d'affaires.

– Tu vois, dit-il à Ethis, j'ai fait des meubles royaux et suis resté fidèle à ma conception du beau. Je ne pense pas que j'aie eu raison. Aujourd'hui j'envie Jacob d'avoir su évoluer. Cette fin de siècle demeurera marquée par son estampille. Ensemble nous avons exploité la rocaille Louis XV et le style apaisé qu'on appellera peut-être Louis XVI. Après, il m'a lâché pour inventer dans les dernières années de la monarchie ces meubles inspirés de l'antique, convenant aux idées philosophiques et républicaines qui étaient dans l'air.

Ethis écoutait bouche bée la leçon des maîtres. Leurs propos passionnés lui faisaient regretter de n'avoir pas persévéré dans le métier du bois et, puisqu'il était marchand, il se disait qu'il avait de la chance de pouvoir ainsi s'instruire au contact des meilleurs ébénistes du monde. Il avait mille questions à leur poser mais il n'osait pas les interrompre. Enfin il s'enhardit :

– Me permettriez-vous, monsieur Jacob, d'aller vous voir dans vos ateliers de la rue Meslée? Je viens d'ouvrir une petite boutique dans le Faubourg et voudrais devenir un grand marchand de meubles, un expert...

Le mot fit sourire mais le garçon était si touchant que Jacob l'invita tout de suite :

– J'ai vu ton magasin l'autre jour en passant. Tu as quelques jolies choses mais si tu veux être mieux qu'un marchand de vieilleries, il te faut tout savoir sur les meubles, le bois, les arts antiques. Viens quand tu voudras. J'ai cédé mes ateliers aux enfants mais suis là presque tous les jours. Il paraît qu'on a besoin de moi. Mais tu as Riesener qui peut t'en montrer et t'en raconter autant que moi...

– Oui mais ce sont vos sièges qui m'intéressent! Ici au Faubourg on n'en construit presque pas et tout le monde sait que vous êtes le meilleur menuisier. Je voudrais que vous me montriez comment les chaises, les fauteuils et les canapés ont évolué grâce à vous. Pour moi c'est très important!

Tout le monde se regarda. On savait dans la famille qu'Ethis était un garçon intéressant, réfléchi et intelligent mais on n'arrivait pas, Antoinette la première, à croire qu'il avait pu évoluer jusqu'à devenir un homme à l'esprit aussi clairvoyant.

– Tu iras loin mon garçon, affirma Jacob avec gentillesse. Tu es comme moi quand j'ai quitté la ferme de mes parents pour venir travailler à Paris. Je voulais réussir et j'ai réussi mais, bon Dieu! ce que j'ai dû travailler pendant quarante ans! Et pas seulement avec mes mains! Mais il n'y a pas de soucis à se faire de ce côté-là : la tête fonctionne bien, et vite. Alors viens voir mes sièges. Je te montrerai que s'il n'y a qu'une façon de s'asseoir il y en a cent et mille de présenter au cul des bonnes gens un petit coin rembourré. Maintenant, si tu veux que je te donne un conseil, apprends à dessiner. Peut-être qu'un jour tu imagineras pour les ébénistes et les menuisiers des meubles nouveaux, comme ces diables de Percier et de Fontaine. Je te montrerai comment, d'après leurs dessins, j'ai meublé la Convention car David n'avait donné que l'esquisse du fauteuil présidentiel. Et aussi, plus près de nous, l'hôtel du général Bonaparte.

– Mais je connais bien MM. Percier et Fontaine. Ce sont des amis de M. Lenoir. Ils viennent souvent au musée pour dessiner les statues et les monuments que nous avons sauvés!

– ... Que M. Lenoir a sauvés, rectifia Antoinette. Sois un peu plus modeste s'il te plaît.

– Pourquoi? interrompit Lenoir. Ethis peut très bien dire « nous » car sans son aide je n'aurais pas réussi la moitié de ce que j'ai fait.

– Ah! vous! coupa Antoinette, Ethis peut dire ou faire n'importe quoi, vous trouvez toujours que c'est merveilleux!

– Mais non, chère Antoinette, quand je dis qu'Ethis est étonnant ou merveilleux, encore que j'emploie rarement ce qualificatif, c'est tout simplement parce qu'il l'est. Et vous en êtes fort heureuse!

On rit et la conversation revint sur les expertises que Jacob et Riesener devaient effectuer le lendemain en compagnie de deux autres notables de la scie et du rabot, les ébénistes Magnien et Molitor.

– Nous sommes tous un peu « à la retraite »! constata Riesener. Enfin notre désignation montre qu'on ne nous a pas tout à fait oubliés.

– Comment va Magnien? demanda Antoinette, il y a bien longtemps que je l'ai rencontré. A-t-il encore un peu de travail?

– Très peu. Il a lui aussi beaucoup travaillé pour la cour, et ses anciens clients ont disparu. Il n'a jamais digéré qu'on lui ait fait décrocher son enseigne *Au nom de Jésus* qui se balançait depuis des lustres au vent du Faubourg. Sans renier la Révolution, il attend avec impatience le moment où il pourra rendre Jésus à sa maison.

On se quitta tard, non sans que Jacob ait exprimé à Antoinette sa gratitude de lui avoir permis de retrouver un soir l'atmosphère du vieux Faubourg. Le maître répéta à Ethis qu'il l'attendait mais qu'il devait étudier le dessin. La rue Meslée où il habitait au-dessus de ses ateliers était à une demi-lieue de la place d'Aligre : « C'est encore à la portée de mes jambes », dit-il en s'engageant d'un pas alerte vers l'ancienne Bastille.

L'arrivée à Fréjus de Bonaparte, retour d'Égypte, fut annoncée par les journaux de Paris, deux jours seulement après le débarquement du général. Le télégraphe de M. Chappe avait joué son rôle d'estafette optique. La nouvelle fit grand bruit au Faubourg où le peuple reportait sur le vainqueur d'Arcole et de Rivoli ses espoirs déçus. D'abord, avec Bonaparte, c'était l'esprit de la Révolution qui continuait de gagner. Ensuite, on pensait depuis déjà longtemps qu'il était le seul à pouvoir mettre de l'ordre dans la république des Directeurs. Tout cela, naturellement, pour se convaincre que le petit homme providentiel allait s'intéresser aux artisans et rendre la prospérité au Faubourg.

C'est dire que la prise du pouvoir par Bonaparte et Sieyès, le 18 brumaire, un mois tout juste après le retour d'Égypte, fut accueillie avec enthousiasme de la place du Trône à la Bastille. Le clan suivait avec plus de réalisme le succès de celui qu'on considérait déjà comme l'homme fort du consulat provisoire. Une fois encore les nouvelles vinrent de Lenoir ou plus précisément de ses amis Percier et Fontaine qui se trouvaient placés, un peu par hasard et beaucoup par David, près du nouveau soleil promu Premier consul depuis le jour de Noël 1799.

– L'histoire est cocasse, raconta Lenoir. Figurez-vous que les deux compères avaient été chargés par l'ancien ambassadeur Chauvelin de restaurer sa résidence de la rue Chantereine [1]. La maison voisine appartenait à Joséphine qui l'habita jusqu'au retour de son bouillant époux. Elle vit donc s'avancer les travaux et admira le travail de Percier et Fontaine. Comme l'idée lui était venue de remettre en état l'autre maison qu'elle possédait du côté de Rueil, la Malmaison, elle pria David de lui faire connaître ces jeunes gens qui savaient rajeunir l'ancien en lui gardant son panache.

– David est donc bien devenu bonapartiste? demanda Marie.

1. Bien qu'elle ait été débaptisée en 1797, personne n'appelait cette rue par son nouveau nom : rue de la Victoire.

– Depuis la chute du Directoire, naturellement. Mais vous connaissez mon avis sur la question : je trouve parfaitement raisonnable la souplesse d'échine de David, sauf son ascension de la Montagne en 93. Il n'existe qu'un David qui n'a qu'une vie ; et la France, depuis la mort du roi – qu'il a votée, ne l'oublions tout de même pas – n'a cessé de changer de maîtres. Comme les maîtres ne plient pas devant les artistes, David s'est fait aux maîtres. Pour l'heure, il va peindre Napoléon Bonaparte avec la même bonne conscience et le même talent qu'il peint Louis XVI. Bonaparte y gagnera et l'art encore plus !

– Alexandre, vous êtes un cynique, coupa Antoinette. Même si votre raisonnement se tient, j'ai du mal à l'admettre.

– Parce que vous refusez d'être lucide. Je suis sûr que M. Riesener qui connaît et apprécie David partage mes sentiments.

– La postérité pardonnera tout à David, répondit le maître. Un artiste ne se survit que par son œuvre. Qu'importe si pour le réaliser il a préféré la flatterie à la dignité. Qui se souviendra dans un ou deux siècles, en admirant un tableau de David, que le peintre de génie qui l'a signé avait courtisé Robespierre ?

– Et la maison de Mme Bonaparte ? demanda Marie que ces digressions n'intéressaient pas.

– Eh bien, l'autre jour, David et le peintre Isabey, qui fait en ce moment le portrait « Mme Premier consul », sont venus chercher Percier et Fontaine pour les conduire au Luxembourg où ils furent reçus par Joséphine. « Le Premier consul, leur dit-elle, ne tient pas à habiter ici. Moi non plus. Nous avons donc décidé de convertir la vieille demeure de Rueil en un palais digne d'un chef d'État. L'architecte Vautier, chargé des travaux ne me donne pas satisfaction. Eh bien, j'ai vu ce que vous avez fait rue Chantereine et je vous confie le soin de transformer la Malmaison en une résidence confortable qu'il faudra meubler à la mode de l'époque. Je crois savoir que vous avez déjà travaillé avec le maître Georges Jacob et ses fils... »

A ce moment, Bonaparte fit irruption dans le salon, comme il en avait l'habitude et s'adressa à David : « Où sont donc, monsieur David, les chefs-d'œuvre envoyés d'Italie après le traité de Tolentino? Je sais qu'on les a promenés dans Paris, mais maintenant? Il faut montrer toutes ces merveilles au peuple.

– Je crois, monsieur le Premier consul, qu'ils sont au Louvre.

– Et pourquoi ne mettrait-on pas ces belles choses sous le dôme des Invalides? Ce serait un hommage rendu à l'armée qui en a permis la prise. » L'idée était assez saugrenue, continua Lenoir, mais Bonaparte n'a pas l'habitude d'être contredit. Son ascendant, son autorité, sont tels qu'il faut beaucoup d'audace pour exprimer un avis différent du sien. David à qui l'étrangeté de la proposition n'avait pas échappé s'en tira en disant que le monument serait sans doute trop exigu. Sans doute pour s'amuser et pour voir comment les jeunes Percier et Fontaine se tireraient d'une situation aussi délicate, il ajouta : « Mais voilà deux architectes qui connaissent sûrement les dimensions du dôme. Leur avis peut être intéressant. » Bonaparte se tourna vers les jeunes gens, les toisa et demanda : « Alors, messieurs, que pensez-vous de ma suggestion? »

Percier, timide de nature, laissait d'ordinaire à Fontaine le soin de discuter avec les clients importants. Il bredouilla quelques mots et Fontaine vint à son secours. Il avait déjà pris la décision d'être franc : « Pour intéressante que soit votre idée, monsieur le Premier consul, je me sens obligé de vous dire que je ne l'approuve pas complètement. Je pense que les drapeaux que vous avez pris à l'ennemi seront plus à leur place aux Invalides que des œuvres d'art. »

Un silence glacial accueillit cette réplique. Seule Joséphine regarda d'un œil curieux et amusé cet inconnu qui osait s'opposer au Premier consul. Celui-ci fut bref : « Nous allons voir cela. Attendez-moi! »

Ils attendirent trois heures. Joséphine avait depuis longtemps épuisé la conversation sur la Malmaison. Elle était sortie quand Bonaparte revint avec le général Murat : « Venez, David, et vous aussi messieurs. Nous allons au Louvre ! »

Le Premier consul monta avec Murat dans une première voiture et les artistes dans une autre. Au Louvre, l'arrivée inopinée de Bonaparte causa quelque émoi. Le directeur chargé des dépôts eut toutes les peines du monde à trouver la clé des salles où dormaient les chefs-d'œuvre d'Italie. Enfin, le général put faire ouvrir quelques caisses et contempler certains marbres. Il s'arrêta un moment devant les chevaux de Saint-Marc qu'on avait alignés dans une salle particulière, comme à la parade, puis s'éloigna sans mot dire en entraînant Murat...

Jusque-là, Lenoir avait été écouté avec un intérêt passionné. Lucie elle-même n'avait pas dit un mot. Soudain tout le monde se mit à poser des questions, à discuter de l'attitude de Fontaine. Antoinette qui aimait bien montrer qu'elle était chez elle maîtresse des débats fit taire l'assemblée et dit :

– Il est sûr que ce Bonaparte va apporter de l'animation et des changements. Sa façon d'être, si cavalière qu'elle soit, ne manque pas de charme. Quant à vos amis Fontaine et Percier, on a envie de les connaître après tout ce que vous nous avez raconté. Amenez-les donc un soir...

– Mais au fait, coupa Marie, où va-t-on mettre les trésors italiens ?

– Je n'en sais encore rien mais les drapeaux, eux, vont aller dans l'église des Invalides !

– Bonaparte a donné raison à Fontaine ?

– Eh oui ! Cela montre que les grands ne détestent pas forcément être critiqués. Mais c'est tout de même une attitude hasardeuse dont il faut savoir mesurer les conséquences. Revenons à nos drapeaux, sinon la jolie Marie va me rappeler à l'ordre. Trois jours après la rencontre, David annonça à Fontaine que le Premier consul avait adopté son idée et que la translation des emblèmes aux Invalides devrait avoir l'éclat d'une fête nationale.

– Je crois bien, dit Riesener, qu'on ne va manquer ni de fêtes ni de défilés. C'est un moyen qui a fait ses preuves pour entretenir une popularité!

Le lendemain était un dimanche, jour où Ethis n'ouvrait pas son magasin, où le télégraphe était fermé et où Lenoir laissait dormir ses statues. Cette perspective dominicale fit penser à Antoinette que floréal arrivait, le joli mois de mai dont les gens du Faubourg, même dans les moments les plus sombres, ne manquaient jamais de célébrer la venue.

– Et si demain nous faisions une folie pour fêter le printemps? Il ne fait pas encore assez beau pour aller manger une friture sur les bords de la Marne mais je propose de casser la cagnotte et d'aller déjeuner chez les *Frères provençaux.*

La proposition fut accueillie par des cris de joie. Il y avait presque six mois que les perdants, lorsqu'on jouait à la bouillotte, glissaient du bel et du bon argent dans une tirelire de faïence peinte représentant un cochon rose.

– Si la cagnotte n'est pas suffisante, dit Réveillon, j'ajouterai le complément. Ce sera d'ailleurs justice car j'ai joué moins souvent que vous.

Des trésors de guerre et des drapeaux conquis la conversation tourna vers ces fameux frères qui avaient ouvert deux ans plus tôt un restaurant rustique au Palais-Royal et dont la renommée allait grandissant. D'abord fréquenté par les soldats de Bonaparte en transit à Paris, l'établissement attirait maintenant les gens de plume et les acteurs qui avaient les moyens de s'offrir un dîner dont le prix, sans être considérable, dépassait largement la moyenne.

– Il ne s'agit pas de frères, précisa Alexandre Lenoir mais de beaux-frères qui se sont mis dans la tête de faire aimer aux Parisiens les spécialités marseillaises. Leur poisson est paraît-il le plus frais qu'on puisse manger à Paris et ils l'accommodent d'une façon très particulière. Mais attention! Nous allons être au moins sept et il faut aller retenir des places demain matin de bonne heure. Qui va se charger de cette mission importante?

Comme son regard se portait avec une insistance souriante du côté d'Ethis et de Marie, ceux-ci répondirent en même temps :

– Nous irons tous les deux et ferons une promenade d'amoureux en vous attendant.

– C'était mon rêve depuis longtemps d'aller dîner ou souper dans l'un des restaurants célèbres du Palais-Royal. Je suis bien contente ! ajouta Marie.

– Nous sommes tous ravis ! enchaîna Antoinette. Ce n'est pas tous les jours qu'on peut s'offrir une fête pareille. Mais ce n'est pas non plus tous les jours le printemps !

Le clan Valfroy se retrouva donc le lendemain, à midi tapant, installé sur des bancs de bois, de chaque côté d'une table où les assiettes vernissées comme autant de soleils égayaient une nappe blanche sur laquelle trônait déjà un panier de légumes aux couleurs d'un marché de Provence.

– Ils appellent ça « l'anchoïade », précisa Lenoir qui seul était déjà venu chez les frères. On mange les tomates, les oignons, les céleris, les artichauts et même les œufs, car il y a aussi des œufs durs, regardez, avec une sauce à l'huile d'olive dans laquelle on a écrasé des anchois.

Il fallut expliquer à Lucie ce qu'étaient les olives, les anchois et les petites asperges fines comme des crayons qu'envoyait d'Aubagne par la malle-poste le troisième frère ou beau-frère, on ne savait plus, qui restait au pays pour assurer le ravitaillement.

Ensuite, il fallut choisir parmi les plats que proposait avec son accent chantant et sa drôle de façon de mettre des « e » partout, l'un des maîtres du lieu. L'autre était à côté, dans la cuisine d'où sortait un étrange parfum.

– Je vous offre aujourd'hui la véritable bouillabaisse marseillaise. Goûtez-la car c'est un miracle de pouvoir mettre dans une marmite parisienne une rascasse pêchée la veille, ou presque, dans les calanques. Vous avez aussi la brandade de morue. Encore un plat marseillais comme les rougets à la provençale. Vendredi il y aura l'aïoli... Quel régal mes amis !

Chacun écoutait avec ravissement ce Méridional au verbe haut et au teint coloré qui faisait de sa cuisine une source intarissable de tableaux parlés. On décida finalement de commander de tous les plats afin de pouvoir les goûter en partageant. La « rouille » de la bouillabaisse fit faire la grimace à Lucie qui préféra tremper généreusement son pain dans la brandade. Valfroy avait choisi un vin des coteaux de Provence pour arroser ce festin ensoleillé et apaiser dans les gorges le feu sournois des piments et du safran. Quand le dessert arriva, une superbe corbeille de fruits, la gaieté régnait chez les Valfroy comme d'ailleurs aux autres tables. C'est à ce moment qu'Ethis prit la parole :

– Grâce à vous tous notre magasin d'antiquités et de décoration à l'enseigne de *L'Enfant à l'oiseau* fait de bonnes affaires. Nous songeons même, Marie et moi, à louer la boutique voisine, celle du doreur Lajolais, afin de nous agrandir. Alors, en ce jour de fête, notre « enfant » vous offre une bouteille de vin de Champagne.

Un tonnerre d'applaudissements salua cette décision qui allait faire pétiller un peu plus la fin du repas. Mais déjà Ethis redemandait le silence :

– Je n'ai pas terminé. Nous avons encore quelque chose à vous dire ! C'est une grande surprise.

– J'ai deviné, s'écria Lucie en se levant.

– Tu serais bien maligne, petite sœur. Qu'as-tu deviné ?

– Marie va avoir un enfant !

La phrase tomba dans le silence. Chacun se regardait comme si ce que venait de dire Lucie était l'évidente vérité. Que pouvaient annoncer d'autre les deux jeunes gens à ce moment du repas ? L'étonnant, c'est que c'était la petite fille qui avait trouvé.

– Comment as-tu deviné ? demanda Marie. Personne n'est au courant. Ma mère elle-même ne sait encore rien !

– Je ne sais pas. Quand Ethis a parlé, ma petite mécanique a fonctionné et j'étais sûre que je ne me trompais pas.

– Que cet intermède ne fasse pas oublier l'essentiel, dit Valfroy. C'est une nouvelle qui nous procure à tous la plus grande joie possible en ce premier jour du printemps. Nous savons maintenant ce que sera notre prochain rendez-vous avec le bonheur!

En disant ces mots il avait pris la main d'Antoinette qui, tout en riant, essuyait deux larmes.

Cette journée mémorable devait faire, durant des semaines, le centre d'intérêt des réunions de la place d'Aligre. Elle le serait restée encore longtemps si une autre nouvelle n'était venue surprendre l'ensemble de la famille. Un matin, alors qu'Antoinette était seule, un homme frappa à la porte et demanda à lui parler. A sa vareuse d'artilleur délavée et fripée qu'il portait sur un pantalon de grosse toile beige, elle vit qu'il s'agissait d'un soldat, sans doute l'un de ces blessés rescapés du maudit siège de Saint-Jean-d'Acre, qu'on rencontrait maintenant dans les rues autour des Invalides.

Il souleva la calotte de feutre rouge qui couvrait quelques rares cheveux blonds décolorés par le soleil et se présenta :

– Je suis le sergent canonnier Dubuisson, j'arrive d'Alexandrie par le dernier bateau et je viens vous donner des nouvelles de votre frère.

– Mon frère Henri-François! Est-il vivant? s'écria Antoinette devenue toute pâle. Cela fait presque dix ans que nous n'avons pas de ses nouvelles. Où est-il?

– A Paris, madame, à l'hôpital de santé militaire du Val-de-Grâce. Il m'a demandé, à moi qui peux marcher, de venir vous dire qu'il ne vous a pas oubliée, ni son père qu'il regrette d'avoir quitté sur un coup de colère. Il voudrait savoir si vous acceptez de le revoir...

– Mon Dieu! Mon petit François...

Antoinette, chancelante, s'était assise et pleurait. Devant elle, l'homme hochait la tête et triturait sa calotte. Il se sentait désemparé, lui qui venait de vivre les pires atrocités, devant cette femme qu'il sentait aussi faible que les éclopés du désert d'Égypte. Maladroit, il s'agenouilla et prit la main d'Antoinette comme il l'avait fait si souvent avec ses camarades blessés ou moralement effondrés :

– Allons, madame, remettez-vous. Je ne vous apporte pas de mauvaises nouvelles. C'est un vrai miracle qu'il soit revenu vivant de l'enfer d'Orient. Vous allez le retrouver...

– Pardonnez ma défaillance, monsieur. J'ai honte de n'avoir pas su maîtriser mon émotion devant vous qui venez de subir tant de souffrances. Voyez, cela va mieux. Asseyez-vous et racontez-moi ce qui est arrivé à mon petit frère.

– Ses aventures, il vous les contera lui-même. J'ai fait sa connaissance sur le bateau le premier parti de Toulon qui transportait une grande partie de l'artillerie vers Alexandrie. Nous avons fait toute la campagne d'Égypte ensemble puis celle de Syrie sous les ordres du général Bonaparte et de Kléber. Blessé au cours de la bataille d'Aboukir, il doit la vie au chirurgien Larrey qui l'a soigné dans des circonstances épouvantables.

– Dites-moi tout de suite dans quel état il se trouve, coupa Antoinette.

– Il va vivre, madame, et c'est l'essentiel, mais il a eu la peste.

– Quelle horreur! Presque tous ceux qui ont été atteints sont morts, dit-on?

– Hélas! La plupart des pestiférés n'ont pu être sauvés et rapatriés.

– J'espère qu'il pourra continuer à peindre et dessiner...

– Oui... Vous savez, c'est le dessin qui lui a sauvé la vie. Pendant tout le début de la campagne il n'a cessé de remplir des cahiers, saisissant sur le vif Bonaparte, les officiers, les soldats au bivouac. Il venait de dessiner le chirurgien Larrey et ses aides en train de soigner des blessés quand la maladie l'a surpris. Les chirurgiens étaient alors dans l'impossibilité de secourir tous les blessés et encore moins les pestiférés. Sans doute aurait-il été abandonné sur le champ de bataille, comme beaucoup d'autres, si M. Larrey ne l'avait pas reconnu et désigné aux brancardiers en disant : « Conduisez-le à l'infirmerie, je vais m'occuper de lui tout de suite. »

– Peut-on aller le voir?

– Naturellement. Je crois que si vous ne veniez pas vous et son père, il se laisserait mourir... Il a tant souffert!

– Je préviens le maître Riesener et nous allons nous rendre tout de suite à l'hôpital. Si vous y retournez attendez-nous. Je vais louer une voiture et vous n'aurez pas à refaire le chemin à pied. C'est que vous ne semblez pas non plus remis de vos épreuves.

– Nous sommes vivants, François et moi, madame. N'est-ce pas ce qui compte?

– Vous avez raison. Venez avec moi. Nous trouverons une voiture à la porte Saint-Antoine et passerons chercher mon beau-père.

Henri-François Riesener, le fils de Marguerite et du maître ébéniste, n'avait, on le sait, jamais été tenté par le bois. Tout jeune, il voulait peindre des portraits et avait étudié le dessin chez des artistes amis de son père. Mme Vigée-Lebrun lui avait ainsi enseigné les rudiments d'un art difficile où le jeune homme, sans se révéler un génie, semblait devoir jouer un rôle honorable. Riesener lui-même qui avait d'abord regretté que son fils ne reprenne pas les outils qui l'avaient rendu célèbre, admettait que la peinture était un beau métier : « Tu gagneras plus d'argent en faisant le portrait de tes contemporains qu'en meublant leur salon. Seulement il faut travailler et je veillerai à ce que tu ne t'endormes pas sur tes pinceaux. »

Il y avait tellement veillé que le garçon, après avoir longtemps accepté l'autorité pesante de son père, s'était muré dans une résistance passive puis avait rejeté ce qu'il appelait la « tyrannie paternelle ». Longtemps, Antoinette avait réussi à éviter des éclats trop violents et à maintenir une certaine harmonie dans la famille mais, un soir, il y avait neuf ans de cela une scène violente avait éclaté entre le père et le fils qui avait quitté la maison en claquant la porte et en annonçant qu'il allait s'établir en province, loin d'un vieil ébéniste aigri qui avait eu son heure de gloire mais qui n'avait plus de clients et qui, de plus, ne comprenait rien à la peinture.

Les remous de la Révolution n'étaient pas faits pour apaiser les querelles mais plutôt pour causer la dispersion des familles. Antoinette apprit seulement par hasard, en 95, que son frère vivait à Lyon puis, plus tard, qu'il s'était engagé dans l'armée d'Italie. Et voilà qu'il revenait d'Orient avec pour seule auréole de gloire bonapartiste les stigmates de la peste. D'un coup Antoinette retrouvait le petit qu'elle avait élevé après la mort de leur mère et que le vieux Riesener allait accueillir les bras grands ouverts, elle en était sûre.

C'est bien ainsi que les choses se passèrent. A sa sortie de l'hôpital, Henri-François revint habiter place d'Aligre et fit souffler sur les réunions du clan un vent d'épopée où l'odeur de la poudre le disputait à la pestilence. Au Faubourg, comme dans la plupart des familles parisiennes, on n'avait qu'une idée lointaine et bien fragmentaire des batailles engagées au-delà des Alpes et maintenant au-delà des mers. L'accumulation des victoires, le nombre des drapeaux pris à l'ennemi et la richesse des trophées artistiques donnaient à la guerre de flatteuses senteurs méditerranéennes que rehaussaient les couleurs que lui prêtait M. Pellerin dans ses ateliers d'Épinal. C'était, hélas! un panorama moins brillant que le jeune Riesener déroulait au cours de ses récits. Son œil de peintre lui avait permis d'enregistrer des scènes entières de batailles qu'il racontait comme s'il eût eu un pinceau à la main.

Un soir, Lenoir, répondant au désir d'Antoinette, avait invité Percier et Fontaine à venir partager la potée familiale. Antoinette aimait l'idée d'être l'animatrice d'une réunion de gens d'esprit et de bon goût. De leur côté, les deux architectes étaient curieux d'approcher Riesener et Réveillon, géants faubouriens d'un monde révolu. C'est pourtant Henri-François qui les passionna. Ce témoin de l'Histoire, arrivé directement des champs de bataille, leur faisait découvrir une nouvelle planète, un monde inconnu où le rouge n'était pas « la poudre pourpre de Cassius » que broient les peintres pour garnir leur palette mais le sang des hommes déchiquetés par la mitraille.

Afin de ne pas impressionner Lucie, François Riesener s'était jusqu'alors abstenu de décrire les scènes sanglantes auxquelles il avait assisté. Pressé de questions et aussi pour rendre hommage à Dominique Larrey, son sauveur, il se laissa entraîner dans la description hallucinante d'une opération qui avait permis à l'un de ses camarades de survivre à une épouvantable blessure :

– Le siège de Saint-Jean-d'Acre avait fait au moins deux mille blessés qu'il fallait pour la plupart opérer. Certains étaient atteints de la peste et la chaleur était telle que les plaies s'envenimaient en quelques heures. C'est là que j'ai vu faire des prodiges au chirurgien Larrey. Celui-ci avait établi un hôpital de fortune dans une maison abandonnée par ses habitants. Il opérait sur la table de la cuisine et c'était presque une chance de pouvoir en disposer : j'ai vu ailleurs Larrey et ses aides chirurgiens installer leurs patients contre un volet posé sur des tonneaux ou même assis sur un tambour. C'est là, dans cette cuisine, que des soldats traînèrent par les pieds le général Lannes touché une nouvelle fois à la face. Ils le croyaient mort et n'avaient pas voulu laisser son corps aux Turcs. Larrey remarqua pourtant que le pouls du blessé battait encore. Avec une dextérité extraordinaire il enleva la balle qui s'était logée entre les deux yeux. La plaie guérit très vite et le général put rejoindre son état-major. Peu de temps après, c'est Arrighi, le cousin de Bonaparte [1] qu'on releva la carotide externe coupée. Un canonnier eut la présence d'esprit d'enfoncer ses doigts dans la plaie et de comprimer l'artère le temps que Larrey

1. Futur duc de Padoue. *Cf. Le Baron Larrey, chirurgien de Napoléon,* par André Soubiran.

accoure et lui fasse en hâte un pansement compressif. Pendant l'opération, une boîte de mitraille éclata au milieu du groupe. Personne heureusement ne fut touché. Larrey regarda une seconde son chapeau criblé d'éclats et, impassible, continua son travail.

– Comment un être humain peut-il supporter des opérations aussi terribles? demanda Marie.

– Le choix est réduit, sais-tu : c'est souffrir ou mourir! Toujours à Saint-Jean-d'Acre il fut fait soixante-dix amputations. C'est je crois le plus terrible.

– On ne fait rien pour diminuer la douleur? questionna Antoinette à son tour.

– Que faire? Une rasade d'alcool réussit parfois à abrutir le malheureux qui assiste conscient à la boucherie qui le mutile d'un bras ou d'une jambe. Il sent le couteau lui couper les chairs, la scie pénétrer ses os. Et tout cela le plus souvent à quelques centaines de mètres de la ligne de bataille dans le vacarme des fusillades et des batteries!

– Comment imaginer ces horreurs quand on passe, comme nous, notre temps à décorer de soie les appartements de la Malmaison! soupira Fontaine qui ajouta : Ce soir, avec vous, nous représentons les deux faces, ô combien opposées! de la réalité politique, la douceur de vivre d'un côté, la terreur de mourir de l'autre...

– Ne croyez-vous pas, mes amis, coupa Antoinette, qu'il serait temps de revenir à des propos plus gais? Mon petit frère doit maintenant oublier le sang et les canons pour envisager une existence plus sereine. Il m'a dit qu'il ne pensait qu'à se refaire une palette et à peindre les femmes exquises qui hantent les salons consulaires. Peut-être, messieurs, pourriez-vous le présenter à David?

– J'y pensais justement, dit Percier. Nous avons besoin de bons peintres et le Premier consul aime retrouver dans des cadres dorés la représentation de ses victoires. Pour le moment nous essayons de rendre habitable le palais des Tuileries où il compte s'installer. Venez, monsieur, nous y retrouver demain...

La conversation s'attarda ensuite sur les meubles :

– Monsieur Riesener, questionna Fontaine, pourquoi vous, le meilleur ébéniste de notre époque, avez-vous abandonné votre atelier? Le métier ne vous manque pas?

– C'est le métier qui m'a abandonné, monsieur. Avant même la fin du règne j'ai subi une sorte de disgrâce. Pas de la reine qui m'avait gardé sa confiance et qui savait que j'étais le seul à pouvoir fabriquer certains meubles, mais je n'avais pas l'échine assez souple pour les gens du Mobilier national qui m'oublièrent bien vite dans leurs commandes. Les grands ébénistes, il est vrai, ne manquaient pas et l'on m'a préféré Molitor, Guillaume Beneman et même mon rival vigilant Jean-François Leleu qui avait si bien imité ma première commode à coins arrondis.

– Mais vous avez tout de même eu du travail jusqu'à la Révolution?

– Bien assez il est vrai, mais 89 est arrivé. Petit à petit le commerce des meubles s'est engourdi faute de clients, et les ébénistes ont dû abandonner leurs outils.

– Georges Jacob, lui, a pu continuer de travailler...

– Bien modestement, il a dû se séparer de la plupart de ses compagnons. David l'a soutenu par quelques commandes officielles. Moi pas : toujours cette échine... Mais il faut être franc : le retour à l'antique ne m'a jamais inspiré. Fuyant la mode nouvelle, je suis resté fidèle aux grands principes que m'avait inculqués mon maître Œben, le père de notre Antoinette. J'ai sans doute eu tort mais il est difficile à un artiste d'aller contre ses goûts profonds. Georges Jacob, lui, a toujours été un inventeur, un créateur, et c'est bien normal qu'on s'adresse aujourd'hui à lui pour meubler les nouveaux palais. Et puis, il avait ses fils qui l'ont entraîné. Enfin, Jacob était dès l'origine un spécialiste des sièges plus qu'un ébéniste. C'est par les chaises, les fauteuils et les lits qu'il a survécu et lancé, c'est tout à sa gloire, le style nouveau librement inspiré de la ligne des meubles romains. Je n'ai plus rien à faire dans ce métier qui a changé et va continuer de changer.

– Et vos meubles? On nous a dit que vous en aviez racheté quelques-uns aux ventes de Versailles?

– Ils sont invendables aujourd'hui. J'ai ainsi un petit musée à l'Arsenal. Venez les voir un jour... Il y a encore une chose que je ne vous ai pas dite : je suis vieux et je n'ai plus qu'un désir : reprendre la sculpture que j'ai abandonnée il y a bien longtemps, par exemple faire les cadres des tableaux que mon fils va peindre. Dès demain je vais ressortir mes gouges et les affûter!

Alexandre Lenoir n'avait guère été bavard jusque-là. Il avait laissé parler François dont les récits de guerre l'avaient passionné et les invités qui semblaient apprécier la chaude atmosphère de la place d'Aligre, cette pièce simple et accueillante meublée tout de même, ils le soulignèrent en souriant, par le maître Jean-François Œben ébéniste du roi, ce qui n'était pas si courant. Le maître trônait toujours dans son cadre doré, à côté de Marguerite, au-dessus d'un bureau qui visiblement semblait beaucoup intéresser les deux architectes. Ce fut finalement Percier qui demanda :

– Ce bureau splendide est aussi l'œuvre de votre père, madame?

Antoinette sourit :

– Non, c'est un cadeau de Jean-Henri, mon beau-père. Il est beau, n'est-ce pas?

Riesener buvait du miel en écoutant ces compliments et en regardant son œuvre comme si c'était un autre qui l'avait signée.

– Ce meuble a une histoire, dit-il. Il fut durant six ans la pièce principale du boudoir de la reine Marie-Antoinette à Fontainebleau. Je l'ai racheté en 92 pour qu'il ne soit ni endommagé ni vendu en Angleterre. Il était mieux à sa place dans les lambris argentés en plein et décorés d'arabesques des appartements royaux mais j'aime le voir ici, j'aime savoir qu'Antoinette y range ses lettres et ses papiers. Et puis j'aime bien aussi qu'elle l'ait placé sous le portrait d'Œben qui, s'il avait vu ce bureau, aurait été content de son compagnon.

Il s'agissait d'un bureau-secrétaire à cylindre, une sorte

de modèle réduit du fameux bureau du roi commencé par Œben et achevé par Riesener mais dont aucun bronze ne venait alourdir les lignes fines et pures. Pas de marqueterie non plus : le devant des tiroirs, les côtés et le dessus mobile étaient entièrement recouverts de losanges de nacre [1].

– Quel travail! dit Fontaine. Il serait inimaginable de réaliser un tel meuble aujourd'hui. Le Premier consul s'effraie des dépenses proposées pour remettre en état la Malmaison, et les meubles commandés aux fils Jacob seront très simples. Ainsi le veulent la mode et l'état des finances. Je crois, monsieur Riesener, que vous aurez été l'un des derniers grands ébénistes à créer ce genre de chefs-d'œuvre. Les meubles du XVIIIe siècle, les vôtres en particulier, iront un jour dans les musées. Peut-être qu'on les copiera mais on ne fera jamais mieux!

Il était tard, au moins deux heures du matin, quand Percier, en regardant le feu qui s'éteignait doucement dans la cheminée, donna le signal du départ. Il proposa, avec Fontaine, de ramener Réveillon dans le cabriolet qui les attendait mais Lenoir avait l'habitude de déposer chez lui l'ancien fabricant de papier peint. Il avait changé son vieux carrosse, effondré un jour en plein embarras de voitures sous le poids d'un morceau du portique d'entrée du château d'Anet, contre un boguet qu'il trouvait tout à fait incommode pour transporter ses acquisitions. Réveillon comme Antoinette préféraient, on s'en doute, cette nouvelle voiture plus maniable et plus confortable.

Quand la cavalerie des invités eut quitté la place dans un bruit épouvantable de sabots et de jurons, Antoinette poussa un soupir de soulagement et s'effondra dans le grand fauteuil que Riesener lui avait apporté lorsqu'elle attendait Lucie.

1. A la suite de circonstances inconnues, le bureau en nacre de Riesener devint la propriété, à Londres, d'Alfred Rothschild puis de l'antiquaire Duveen et de F. Dinshaw à qui l'État français le racheta à New York pour le replacer dans son cadre d'origine, le boudoir de Marie-Antoinette à Fontainebleau.

Ouf! J'ai cru qu'ils ne partiraient jamais. Je suis harassée.

– C'est qu'on se trouve bien chez toi, ma bonne Antoinette! dit Valfroy. Si l'on savait, parmi les beaux esprits du Consulat comme tes dîners sont agréables, on ferait la queue pour être reçu dans ton « salon du Faubourg ».

– Et l'on s'ennuierait autant chez nous que chez les riches. Merci bien, nous continuerons à choisir nos invités. Je suis heureuse car la soirée a été très réussie. Percier et Fontaine sont passionnants. Et je crois bien qu'ils vont réussir, grâce à David, à rendre mon pauvre frère à la peinture. Allez, il est tard, allons nous coucher!

La vie n'était pas toujours rose au Faubourg mais elle devenait moins sombre. Certes les familles les plus pauvres souffraient toujours du chômage et des difficultés de ravitaillement mais on était loin des grandes disettes de la Révolution. Depuis longtemps les boulangeries vendaient du pain à discrétion et il n'y avait guère de viandes, de poissons, de fruits et de légumes qu'on ne puisse se procurer, à la condition évidemment d'avoir l'argent pour les payer.

Le travail lui-même devenait moins rare. Si la Révolution avait laminé la noblesse qui constituait l'essentiel de la clientèle du quartier, elle avait enrichi beaucoup de gens, les agioteurs, les trafiquants de biens nationaux et une partie de la bourgeoisie qui avait su faire fructifier son capital. Longtemps, ces nouveaux riches avaient préféré demeurer discrets et ne pas faire étalage de leurs biens. Cette époque était aujourd'hui révolue, comme si la désignation de Bonaparte au rang du Premier consul avait libéré les nantis de leur fausse honte. C'était d'ailleurs une bonne chose. Comme le disait Ethis avec son bon sens pratique : « Peu importe qui possède l'argent, il faut qu'il sorte des bas de laine pour remettre le commerce et l'industrie en marche. » C'est ce qui se produisait progressivement et le Faubourg profitait de la reprise.

Le nouveau style, plus simple dans ses formes, moins cher dans ses applications, convenait aux notables du Consulat trop contents, en épousant la mode, de se démarquer de l'Ancien Régime et de se considérer comme des héritiers fidèles de la Révolution. Pour le Faubourg voué depuis près de deux siècles aux prodiges de la marqueterie et aux cambrures gracieuses, il s'agissait d'une véritable conversion. On n'en était plus aux meubles copiés de l'antique que David avait dessinés pour Georges Jacob mais il fallait en conserver l'esprit tout en renonçant à sa sévérité. Jacob et ses fils avaient fait l'essentiel pour les sièges, le Faubourg allait une fois de plus s'adapter et varloper au goût du jour.

Si Riesener se désintéressait de la mode nouvelle, Ethis en suivait passionnément les conséquences dans les ateliers. Il se disait que cette évolution était peut-être sa chance. Il avait ainsi remarqué que l'engouement pour l'acajou qui avait, dès 1780, supplanté le bois de rose et de violette, reprenait de plus belle après avoir un temps laissé la place aux bois clairs durant la Révolution et le Directoire. Ethis, on s'en convainquit à cette occasion, avait une sorte de génie des affaires. Ayant appris qu'un chargement de bois d'acajou venait d'arriver à Bercy, il prit une option sur la moitié de cet arrivage. Le soir même, il proposait à son beau-père une association :

– Monsieur Bénard, les ateliers du Faubourg s'entrouvrent, on recommence à fabriquer des meubles et tous les maîtres et ouvriers libres qui reprennent la scie et le riflard [1] vont avoir besoin de bois. Pas de n'importe quel bois : de l'acajou! Et de l'acajou, il n'y en a plus dans les cours ni chez les marchands de bois qui ont d'ailleurs presque tous fermé. Or, je viens d'apprendre par un ami qu'un chargement vient d'arriver à Bercy. Il faut acheter tout de suite une partie de ce bois dont tout le monde va

1. Petite varlope à dégrossir.

avoir besoin et le revendre au détail. Je n'ai malheureusement pas l'argent pour réaliser cette opération, aussi je viens vous proposer de vous associer à moi.

Eugène Bénard, roublard, rompu aux affaires, avait écouté son gendre en silence. Sa stupéfaction était grande. Ce garçon à qui il avait donné sa fille de mauvais gré, cet enfant trouvé qui l'avait déjà passablement étonné en ouvrant une boutique d'antiquités, voilà qu'il venait aujourd'hui lui proposer une affaire en discutant avec lui d'égal à égal! Le plus fort était que l'idée qu'il avançait était loin d'être irréfléchie!

– Ainsi, mon garçon, vous me demandez de devenir votre associé mais vous n'avez pas un écu à mettre dans l'affaire que vous me proposez. Vous ne trouvez pas votre démarche un peu osée?

– Je vous apporte l'idée, une idée sans risque qui vous permettra de faire un bénéfice appréciable et qui nous rendra possible l'agrandissement de notre magasin. Je fais naturellement cette démarche en accord avec Marie. Songez que vous allez être grand-père et qu'il faut dès maintenant penser à l'avenir de l'enfant.

– Mon cher Ethis, les affaires n'ont rien à voir avec les liens familiaux. Je ne sais pas encore quelle sera ma réponse mais sachez qu'elle ne sera pas influencée par eux. D'abord, quelle somme attendez-vous de moi?

– Vingt mille francs environ.

– Hein? Vingt mille francs! Vous êtes fou mon garçon!

– L'acajou vaudra le double dans quelques mois. Il faut que vous veniez avec moi voir l'arrivage et que je vous explique dans quelles conditions l'affaire peut être conclue. Nous avons un grand avantage : les locaux dont vous disposez pour entreposer le bois et les voitures pour le transporter.

– Et si je refuse? Pensez-vous que j'aie besoin d'un garçon, certes audacieux mais ignorant tout du commerce pour traiter cette affaire? Votre idée, comme vous dites vaut une commission, rien de plus!

– Non je veux plus que cela, mettons le tiers des bénéfices encore que la moitié serait plus juste.

– Vous voulez rire mon gendre. Je vais peut-être en effet traiter cette affaire, mais seul, et vous vous contenterez de la commission que je vous abandonnerai.

– Cela n'est pas possible. Vous n'achèterez pas ce bois sans me considérer comme votre associé!

Eugène Bénard éclata de rire :

– Et pourquoi donc?

– Parce que c'est moi qui ai l'option et que si vous n'acceptez pas mon offre, M. Réveillon est prêt à traiter avec moi!

Cette dernière réplique laissa Bénard pantois. Il se rendait compte qu'il avait en face de lui un partenaire dont il fallait oublier l'âge et le passé tellement il était habile. Il n'en était pas au point de le considérer comme aussi fort que lui mais ne pouvait s'empêcher d'admirer la justesse de ses arguments et la fermeté de son caractère. Bref, le mari de sa fille commençait à l'intéresser et il se disait que Marie qu'il avait toujours considérée comme la plus intelligente de la famille, avait fait le bon choix en épousant le Traîne-sabot de la Bastille. Le vieux madré regarda un long moment le jeune loup et lui tendit la main :

– Tu es plus fort que je ne le pensais et cela me plaît. D'accord pour le tiers à condition que l'affaire soit saine. Nous irons demain matin à Bercy voir tout cela de près. J'y pense : ne peux-tu pas demander à Riesener de nous accompagner? J'aimerais qu'il nous donne son avis sur la qualité de l'acajou...

– Je lui demanderai de revenir... Vous pensez bien que c'est la première chose que j'ai faite de montrer le bois à M. Riesener. Il a dit qu'il est très bon!

– Sacré Ethis! Tu auras donc toujours le dernier mot!

Jean-Henri Riesener, s'il ne faisait plus de ces meubles divins qui avaient fait sa gloire, était constamment sollicité. Expert dans les litiges qui opposaient les gens du bois à leurs clients ou à leurs fournisseurs, conseiller des marchands et des collectionneurs dont la race qu'on croyait éteinte commençait à renaître, bon génie des confrères qu'une difficulté technique tourmentait, il ne refusait ses services qu'à ceux qui lui demandaient de restaurer des meubles portant ou non son estampille.

– Je ne suis pas un raccommodeur! disait-il. Tant pis s'il n'y a plus d'ébénistes capables de reprendre un panneau de marqueterie un peu élaboré!

C'est pourtant un travail que vint un soir lui proposer Percier :

– Je sais, maître, que vous rechignez à remettre vos meubles en état mais le message dont je viens vous faire part est un peu particulier.

– Ce sont toujours des gens très bien qui me demandent de faire une exception pour eux! Or cela m'ennuie de réparer des meubles splendides qu'on a laissé abîmer par sottise ou détériorer par hargne.

– Il s'agit d'une personne dont le goût est unanimement reconnu et dont l'esprit et la beauté font l'admiration de tout ce que Paris compte de gens raffinés.

– Dites-moi son nom, au moins. Mais cela ne me fera pas changer d'idée. Adressez-vous à Ignace Pabst qui a une famille à nourrir et qui accepte ce genre de travail!

– Cette dame s'appelle Mme Récamier.

– Juliette Récamier! s'écria Antoinette qui assistait à l'entretien. La femme la plus célèbre de son temps, celle dont le charme éclipse celui de Mme Bonaparte! Tu devrais accepter, ne serait-ce que pour approcher ce phénomène de beauté convoité par tous les mâles consulaires.

Tout le monde avait entendu parler de Mme Récamier, la femme du riche banquier dont le salon réunissait les hommes les plus en vue et les femmes dont l'indiscipline politique et le franc-parler faisaient froncer le sourcil à Bonaparte. La jolie Pauline, Laure Junot, la bruyante générale Lefèbvre et l'encombrante baronne de Staël étaient les habituées les plus fidèles de l'hôtel de la chaussée d'Antin considéré jusque dans les capitales étrangères comme l'un des mieux fréquentés et des plus luxueux de Paris. Aucune femme n'aurait repoussé l'occasion d'aller voir ce qui se passait derrière ce portail vert du n° 7 de la rue du Mont-Blanc qui semblait attirer toutes les voitures de Paris. Antoinette la première avait envie de savoir. C'est pourquoi elle poussait Riesener à accepter de faire pour la plus belle ce qu'il refusait à tout le monde :

– Il s'agit d'un de tes chefs-d'œuvre que tu dois sauver. Va chez Mme Récamier, ne serait-ce que pour me raconter...

Elle savait que le vieux maître, flatté quoi qu'il en dise, finirait par se laisser convaincre.

– D'abord, reprit-il, quel est ce meuble? Vaut-il au moins la peine d'être restauré?

– J'en suis sûr, dit Percier. C'est une admirable commode en loupe d'orme, je crois, aux coins arrondis et discrètement rehaussée de bronzes, l'une des dernières que vous avez dû construire en 1790.

– Avec un marbre blanc... Oui, je vois. Une belle forme... Bon! Emmenez-moi un jour chez cette personne, que je me rende compte si sa beauté est digne de ma commode!

Voilà comment le grand Riesener se retrouva la semaine suivante en face de « l'ange de la chaussée d'Antin ». Celle-ci, prévenue des réticences du maître, était bien décidée à jouer de tous ses charmes, ce qui ne lui était pas difficile, sa captivante beauté assurant naturellement un pouvoir de séduction auquel il était difficile de résister. Riesener n'échappa pas à la règle commune : il tomba amoureux de Juliette dès que celle-ci apparut dans l'antichambre où il venait lui-même de pénétrer.

– Monsieur Riesener, c'est un honneur et un plaisir pour moi de vous accueillir dans cette maison. Je ne vous dis pas cela parce que j'ai besoin de vos conseils et de votre aide mais parce que je vous admire d'avoir fabriqué les plus beaux meubles du monde.

Le maître n'en demandait pas tant. Il était conquis et était prêt, pour cette jeune femme de vingt-trois ans, à reprendre son fin ciseau de marqueteur.

– Madame, vous me comblez. Montrez-moi cette commode qui, paraît-il, a souffert de la Révolution comme un quelconque ci-devant.

Tout en la suivant dans le long couloir couvert de miroirs encadrés d'acajou, il admirait cette fine silhouette qui dégageait la grâce d'un autre temps. Elle lui rappelait Antoinette à vingt ans, l'époque où il ne pouvait empêcher son esprit, habité depuis toujours par la beauté, de vagabonder autour des formes exquises de sa belle-fille, apparences quasi divines auxquelles il pensait lorsqu'il recherchait la courbure idéale à donner au front d'une commode.

Juliette Récamier l'introduisit dans un petit salon visiblement en cours de décoration.

– Vos amis Percier et Fontaine n'ont pas terminé cette pièce où votre meuble doit resplendir sur un fond d'acajou.

– D'acajou? ne put s'empêcher de s'étonner Riesener. Cette commode dont les formes exaltent les veinures exceptionnelles de cette racine d'orme a été conçue pour être placée dans une pièce aux murs clairs ou pastel. Le ton sombre de l'acajou va lui manger ses formes...

– Vous croyez? J'ai voulu que cette demeure où je reçois beaucoup reflète la mode de notre époque et la crée au besoin. Percier rechigne un peu mais il fait finalement ce que je souhaite.

« Tiens donc, pensa Riesener, son mari paye et, si elle veut de l'acajou, ils lui donnent de l'acajou! » Il aurait préféré imaginer son meuble dans un salon tendu de soie bleu de ciel mais enfin...

Avant d'examiner de près les morceaux de placage qui se décollaient à l'avant et sur les côtés de la commode, il se recula pour en apprécier les proportions et l'élégance que donnait au meuble l'une de ses dernières trouvailles, l'arrondi des arêtes latérales. La moulure du marbre dont il avait dessiné lui-même le profil, et les poignées de tiroirs, discrètes comme des boutons d'habit, lui semblèrent parfaites.

– Peut-être penserez-vous que je ne suis pas modeste, madame, mais vous avez là un des meubles dont je suis fier. Il m'avait été commandé par la duchesse de Brancas et n'a été terminé qu'au début de la Révolution. M. Grimod de La Reynière doit posséder le pendant de cette commode.

– Je suis consciente de sa beauté, monsieur Riesener, et j'aimerais que vous la remettiez en état.

– C'est entendu. Faites-la porter à mon atelier et je ferai le nécessaire.

– Merci. Voulez-vous visiter ma maison? Je serais heureuse de savoir ce que vous en pensez.

Ce qu'il en pensait, il se garda bien de le dire à Juliette. C'est Antoinette qui eut quelques heures plus tard la primeur des impressions du maître.

– Alors, cette Mme Récamier? T'a-t-elle enjôlé comme tous les hommes qui l'aperçoivent? Est-elle vraiment belle? questionna-t-elle curieuse.

– La grâce parfaite, la séduction personnifiée, la beauté pensive! Voilà Mme Récamier. Je ne regrette pas d'avoir accepté de faire réchauffer mon pot de colle pour plaire à cet ange tombé du ciel dans la médiocrité de notre temps!

– Eh bien, mon cher! Voilà une opinion sans nuance! Il faudra tout de même que je m'arrange pour entrevoir cette déesse vivante. Et son fameux hôtel de la chaussée d'Antin, comment l'as-tu trouvé?

– Mon ange de lumière vit dans les ténèbres! La grâce s'abîme dans un décor pédant et gai comme un tombeau romain! Dieu me garde d'habiter jamais une maison pareille!

– Explique-toi. Je sais que tu n'aimes pas beaucoup les modes nouvelles mais je ne t'ai jamais entendu les juger aussi durement.

– Tiens, sa chambre! Elle vous la présente comme un sublimé de l'art nouveau. Moi je me serais cru dans un cercueil d'acajou. Qu'ai-je vu en entrant? Des pilastres en bois d'acajou, des chambranles et des portes en bois d'acajou. Du plafond, quatre rideaux en mailles d'or descendent sur un lit d'acajou joliment dessiné par Jacob. C'est la seule chose que je ne déteste pas dans ce gynécée d'acajou où flottent des rideaux de soie violette ornementée de noir. Je me demande comment cette femme qui est la raison de la mode et du goût peut dormir ainsi, entre une table de nuit en acajou sur laquelle des fleurs se meurent dans un vase en tôle et une autre table d'acajou supportant une lampe antique dorée. Que voit-elle en se réveillant le matin dans ce Pompéi cendré? Une grande statue de marbre à droite et un candélabre de bronze sur la gauche!

Antoinette avait écouté Riesener en riant. Il y avait longtemps qu'elle ne l'avait pas entendu vitupérer la mode avec tant de véhémence.

– Allons, dit-elle, calme-toi. Et dis-toi que ta commode va apporter quelque élégance dans cette maison sombre et froide.

En fait, elle était bien près de partager les idées de Riesener. Élevée dans le culte d'une création permanente, d'un raffinement exempt de toute afféterie et d'une élégance où se mariaient les bois rares, les marqueteries délicates et l'or des bronzes originaux, elle goûtait peu cette accumulation d'acajou qui alourdissait des lignes qu'on prétendait simplifier « à l'étrusque ».

– Je ne suis pas contre l'acajou, j'en ai utilisé beaucoup, mais quand la mode fait perdre toute raison à ceux qui achètent comme à ceux qui fabriquent, alors là, je ne suis plus d'accord!

La fièvre passée, Riesener ne tarissait pas d'éloges sur Mme Récamier. Il posait des questions à Lenoir, achetait les journaux où l'on parlait des réceptions de la rue du Mont-Blanc et recollait avec un soin jaloux les lamelles de loupe d'orme qui avaient tendance à quitter la fameuse commode à jupe arrondie. Cette passion du vieil artiste pour l'éclatante beauté de la jeunesse avait quelque chose d'émouvant. On s'en moquait place d'Aligre mais avec gentillesse; on comprenait le maître quand il affirmait que si Juliette voulait renoncer à son attirail discordant et offensant pour l'œil, il se remettrait volontiers à l'ouvrage pour meubler l'hôtel du banquier Récamier.

En attendant, l'Égypte était reine dans les rares sculptures qui avaient résisté au souffle du vent d'Étrurie et sur les motifs cuivrés des tiroirs et des sabots de sièges.

Comme autant de médailles décernées aux meubles de l'ère napoléonienne, l'acajou se voyait épinglé du sphinx égyptien, du lotus en éventail, de la palmette ou de la rosace pharaonesque. C'était un moyen facile de célébrer le retour d'Égypte mais qui ne pouvait suffire à des artistes comme les Jacob. Dans leurs ateliers, à nouveau pleins de compagnons de toutes spécialités, les deux frères fabriquaient des sièges par centaines mais en prenant le soin coûteux de renouveler constamment les modèles. Ils ne le savaient pas encore mais c'était sur leurs établis que commençait de s'élaborer le style du siècle nouveau dont le « 8 » se profilait sur l'horizon consulaire.

Tandis qu'Ethis aménageait le nouveau magasin qu'il avait réussi à acheter avec le bénéfice réalisé sur la vente de l'acajou, Marie s'arrondissait. Forte de ses vingt ans, elle portait sa grossesse avec élégance. La mode des tuniques larges effaçait son ventre et tout le monde s'accordait à dire qu'elle n'avait jamais été aussi jolie. Son visage rieur s'accordait bien à sa coiffure à la Titus. Comme beaucoup de jeunes femmes, elle s'était fait couper les cheveux dont elle laissait vagabonder les mèches à peine frisées. Cette manière de se coiffer qui ne seyait qu'à certaines jeunes femmes avait déclenché une violente campagne dans les gazettes où les écrits contre la coupe à la Titus ou à la Caracalla se révélaient parfois d'une rare violence. Durant toute une soirée on avait débattu chez Antoinette de ce grave problème. Riesener et Lenoir étaient contre mais Percier défendait le négligé étudié qui donnait aux jolies femmes une allure un peu masculine :

– Laissez donc les femmes arranger leurs cheveux comme elles veulent. C'est à elles de ne pas se tromper. Qui oserait affirmer que Mme Tallien et Joséphine ne sont pas charmantes en Titus ? En revanche, Pauline a eu tort de se couper les cheveux. Cette beauté parfaite n'a qu'un défaut : ses oreilles trop grandes et un peu décollées qui se trouvent maintenant à découvert.

– Et moi ? demanda Marie, coquette, en faisant bouffer de ses doigts écartées des petites mèches rebelles.

– Vous ma petite Marie répondit Percier en riant, vous êtes ravissante. Vous pouvez tout vous permettre. Tenez, Antoinette, donnez-moi un morceau de papier. Je ne suis pas coiffeur mais je vais inventer une coiffure pour la future maman.

Et Percier, qui avait dessiné toute la journée les meubles du salon de la Malmaison, se mit à tracer d'un crayon rapide le portrait de Marie en disposant frisettes et cheveux raides de la plus adorable des façons :

– Voilà, madame, comment votre coiffeur doit traiter votre charmante petite tête. Qu'en pensez-vous ? Je suis si content de moi que j'ai bien envie d'abandonner le Premier consul, ses palais et ses meubles pour me consacrer aux cheveux des dames. Je gagnerais sûrement plus d'argent !

On rit et l'on parla d'une autre mode qui commençait à percer dans la rue, celle du réticule – c'était le nom de la gibecière romaine – qu'on avait aussitôt appelé « ridicule ». Les frêles tissus dans lesquels les femmes s'habillaient ne pouvaient en effet supporter des poches, elles devaient tenir à la main ou fourrer dans leur corsage bourse, mouchoir et miroir. Nécessité fait loi, on avait donc inventé le réticule que les dames portaient au bras, suspendu à une chaîne.

– Voilà ce qu'il nous faut vendre ! s'écria soudain Ethis qui, décidément, se révélait remarquable en affaires. Comment n'y ai-je pas pensé plus tôt ! Je vais faire fabriquer de très jolies poches, ornées de perles et de broderies, et je suis sûr que nous aurons des clients.

– Sûrement moins que tu ne penses, remarqua Antoinette. Le Faubourg n'est pas riche, ce ne sont pas les femmes d'artisans qui pourront s'offrir tes ridicules.

– Heureusement, le Faubourg revit, dit Ethis. Un à un les ateliers rouvrent et certains maîtres embauchent. Les Jacob ne peuvent pas tout faire ! Et puis, je pourrai toujours mettre en vente mes ridicules par des amis qui ont des boutiques mieux placées. Le principal, c'est de bien fabriquer, la vente suivra!

On s'était habitué à entendre parler Ethis comme un vrai patron. Chaque fois pourtant les idées qu'il lançait, les réussites qu'il annonçait surprenaient Antoinette qui revoyait toujours en lui le garçon révolté tombé sur elle en perdant son sang à la Folie Titon. Il y avait déjà plus de dix ans de cela mais, pour elle, Ethis était toujours « Traîne-sabot », son frère, son fils, son petit. Elle regarda Valfroy et sourit :

– Il n'a pas fini de nous étonner, notre « vainqueur » !

Une fois encore, chacun rentra tard chez soi. Le temps n'était pas compté place d'Aligre et, comme on se sentait bien dans le vieux logement d'Œben dont Antoinette avait su faire, comme disait Lenoir, le refuge de l'amitié et de l'intelligence, les heures passaient sans qu'on s'en aperçoive. Après Alexandre Lenoir, Fontaine et Percier, les deux maîtres d'œuvre du Premier consul, s'étaient laissé prendre au charme du salon Saint-Antoine tout imprégné de l'art et de la vie du siècle finissant. Ils s'y trouvaient mieux que dans les demeures officielles et avouaient en riant qu'ils n'aimeraient pas vivre dans les décors pompéiens qu'ils dessinaient à longueur de journée.

Quelqu'un d'autre devenait une assidue de la place d'Aligre : Marie qui découvrait auprès d'Antoinette le plaisir de la conversation et le bonheur d'une existence calme et généreuse. Elle supportait de moins en moins sa famille à l'esprit étriqué où l'argent tenait lieu de tout. Depuis qu'elle était enceinte, elle venait presque chaque jour retrouver Antoinette qui, ravie, l'accueillait à bras ouverts. C'est à elle qu'elle confiait ses joies, ses craintes, ses espoirs, tout ce fardeau d'une jeunesse étouffée par la Révolution et dont elle n'avait jamais pu se décharger sur sa mère, bonne mais sotte, et encore moins sur son père, avare de sa tendresse comme de son argent.

Ce jour-là, Marie n'avait pas son sourire habituel quand elle arriva place d'Aligre. Elle paraissait préoccupée.

– Qu'est-ce qui ne va pas? demanda Antoinette. Tu parais bien soucieuse aujourd'hui. Est-ce déjà ton chenapan de bébé qui te fait des misères?

– Oh non! Il va bien et moi aussi, mais Ethis m'inquiète.

– Ethis? Que se passe-t-il? demanda aussitôt Antoinette toujours sur le qui-vive lorsqu'il s'agissait de son fils.

– Rien de grave mais son activité débordante, son désir de réussir, me font peur. Il n'est plus aussi attentif qu'avant à mon égard, il ne pense qu'à ses affaires, qu'à fabriquer un tas de choses, qu'à en acheter d'autres pour les revendre. J'ai peur, Antoinette, parce qu'il me fait penser certains jours à mon père. Je voudrais tellement qu'il ne devienne pas comme lui, uniquement préoccupé de gagner de l'argent...

Antoinette sourit, rassurée :

– C'est cela qui te tracasse? Rassure-toi. Je connais bien Ethis. C'est moi qui ai un peu fait ce qu'il est aujourd'hui. Je n'ai pourtant pas changé son caractère, il a toujours été comme ça : un cavalier qui ne sait que lancer son cheval au galop. Avec cela, sous un air faussement naïf, une volonté de fer. Mais Ethis est le contraire d'un égoïste. Il est la générosité même et tout ce qu'il fait en ce moment, c'est pour toi et pour l'enfant qui va venir. Cela dit, il vaut tout de même mieux le calmer, je lui parlerai, sans dire bien entendu que tu es venue me dire ton inquiétude. Ethis, vois-tu, a tellement besoin de se venger de sa jeunesse. Te rends-tu compte de ce que c'est que d'être un enfant trouvé? Sa chance a été d'être blessé en même temps que moi. Si nous ne l'avions pas recueilli, Dieu sait quelles sottises il était prêt à faire! Il n'aurait sûrement pas survécu aux tempêtes de la Révolution. Il aurait été se faire tuer aux Tuileries ou sur un champ de bataille lointain. Peut-être aurait-il été massacré avec les malheureux prisonniers de septembre... Alexandre Lenoir nous a aidés à faire un homme de ce gamin perdu. Ce fut assez facile car le fond était bon. Maintenant c'est à toi ma petite Marie de calmer ce torrent impétueux. Tu dois avoir sur lui une influence plus grande que la nôtre. Ethis est profondément intelligent mais tu es une femme, tu es plus fine, plus adroite. A toi d'utiliser ces armes. Je t'assure que ton fougueux et amoureux mari ne demande qu'à être influencé par une femme aussi belle, aussi douce et qui de plus lui fait un enfant.

– Merci Antoinette. Je savais bien un peu toutes ces choses mais je souhaitais que vous m'en parliez. J'ai compris qu'Ethis avait besoin d'une femme forte qui le comprenne et qui l'aide. Je crois que je peux être cette femme!

– Si ce n'est pas toi, ce ne sera personne! Alors, pas de pleurnicheries ni d'états d'âme. L'amour, le vrai, c'est rendre l'autre heureux mais aussi plus fort et plus intelligent! Eh bien, dis donc, il me semble que nous avons échangé des idées bien sérieuses aujourd'hui. Parle-moi maintenant de ton enfant. Où en es-tu?

– J'atteins le quatrième mois. Il va bientôt falloir qu'on me saigne!

– Je trouve personnellement cet usage absurde. Moi, j'ai refusé et j'ai mis au monde Lucie très normalement. Il est vrai qu'on était en plein début de la Révolution et que personne ne tenait plus compte des vieilles pratiques. A ta place, je verrais avant la sage-femme ou le médecin qui t'accouchera. Sais-tu au moins qui ce sera?

– Ma mère connaît Marthe Furet qui loge passage de la Main-d'or. Je crois que c'est elle qui a mis au monde ma plus jeune sœur.

Il y avait bien longtemps qu'Antoinette était sans nouvelles de sa sœur. Victoire, il est vrai, vivait tantôt à Charenton, tantôt dans le manoir que son mari avait acheté près de Givry-en-Argonne, qu'il appelait « le château » et qui lui avait permis un temps d'ajouter « de Contaut » à son nom. Charles Delacroix avait cessé toute activité politique depuis que Talleyrand lui avait pris sa place au ministère. Son opération l'avait fatigué et sans doute souhaitait-il faire oublier les rumeurs qui avaient couru au moment de la naissance de son fils Eugène. Et puis, un jour, Victoire débarqua à l'improviste, selon son habitude :

– Coucou, c'est moi ! Nous sommes rentrés avant-hier de Contaut et j'ai juré à Charles que je le quittais s'il ne me laissait pas la voiture aujourd'hui pour venir te voir.

Les deux sœurs s'embrassèrent longuement et Antoinette demanda :

– Pourquoi n'as-tu pas amené Eugène ? Il a maintenant deux ans et je n'ai fait qu'apercevoir mon neveu.

– Ce matin il tousse, il vomit, je l'ai laissé avec sa nourrice. Tu sais, c'est un enfant dont la santé est délicate. Cela m'inquiète un peu... Mais il a un si beau visage !

– Et comment va Charles ? Quelle force de la nature !

– Il étonne tout le monde, moi la première. Il s'est pratiquement remis de son épouvantable opération. Mais l'inactivité lui pèse. Il commence à regretter d'avoir critiqué Bonaparte au moment des campagnes d'Italie. Il n'aime pas le Premier consul mais il s'est rallié, faisant savoir qu'il approuvait le coup du 18-Brumaire. Tu vois, il n'a pas changé : toujours du côté du manche ! La récompense n'a pas tardé : il vient d'être nommé préfet à Marseille. Ta pauvre sœur va une nouvelle fois reprendre sa vie de romanichelle. Nous partons la semaine prochaine.

– Avoue que tu n'es pas si mécontente. Tu as toujours aimé les situations officielles. « Madame la Préfète »... cela t'ira bien !

– Tu es méchante. Donne-moi plutôt des nouvelles de tout le monde.

Les deux sœurs retrouvèrent durant quelques heures la complicité de leur jeunesse et Victoire promit de venir souper avec Charles un soir avant de partir.

Quand Antoinette raconta le soir à Valfroy la visite de Victoire et la nomination de son mari, il éclata de rire.

– Delacroix est le type parfait de l'homme politique. Quelle constance! Et quelle habileté! Songe qu'il a servi Louis XVI avant de voter sa mort, qu'il a été membre du Comité de salut public et partisan de Robespierre avant de se féliciter de sa chute, d'échapper aux rigueurs thermidoriennes et de devenir ministre du Directoire. Il déteste Bonaparte mais le voilà préfet. Vraiment, ces exploits politiques renouvelés me font béer d'admiration!

Antoinette rit aussi mais son regard s'assombrit en voyant le visage de son mari, éclairé en plein par le candélabre. Depuis quelque temps, elle trouvait Valfroy fatigué. Ses traits étaient tirés, elle constatait qu'il flottait de plus en plus dans ses vêtements. Aux questions qu'elle lui posait, il répondait qu'il ne s'était jamais mieux porté et qu'il est bon à partir d'un certain âge de n'être pas trop gros. Antoinette faisait mine de le croire mais elle savait qu'il ne lui disait pas la vérité.

Un jour, pourtant, elle réussit à le décider de consulter un médecin. Pris par la fièvre, il n'avait pu se rendre au centre du télégraphe et le Dr Lefèvre, que Lucie avait été prévenir, arriva dans la soirée en s'excusant:

– Je n'ai jamais eu autant de malades à soigner! C'est curieux, en pleine Révolution, au moment de la Terreur même, alors que la disette sévissait, très peu de gens étaient malades. Enfin... Examinons M. de Valfroy.

Lefèvre jouissait d'une grande popularité dans le Faubourg, où il habitait depuis de longues années un petit hôtel rue de Charonne, juste à côté de l'ancienne maison des Filles-de-la-Croix. Durant toute la Révolution il avait exercé avec une grande humanité, soignant gratuitement des indigents et se dépensant sans compter car si, comme il le disait, il y avait alors peu de malades, il y avait aussi très peu de médecins. Il conduisait lui-même son vieux coupé dont la capote rapiécée laissait passer la pluie, et son cheval, un oreillard noir, était célèbre dans tout le quartier. Surtout, le Dr Lefèvre était un bon médecin. De nombreux confrères avaient recours à son diagnostic dans les cas difficiles. Après avoir bavardé un moment avec son malade sur les derniers perfectionnements apportés récemment au télégraphe de M. Chappe, il commença de l'ausculter et de lui prendre le pouls. Ses belles mains blanches palpaient le torse amaigri de Valfroy à qui il demandait de temps en temps de respirer alors qu'il plaçait son oreille sur un point précis du dos ou de la poitrine.

– Voyez-vous, dit-il, sans doute pour dissiper l'angoisse qui s'installait, mes doigts et mes oreilles sont les seuls aides pour tenter de savoir ce qui se passe dans le corps de mes malades. Ce sont des auxiliaires précieux et plus sûrs qu'on ne pourrait le penser.

Antoinette ne le quittait pas des yeux mais son visage restait d'une impassibilité souriante. Maintenant, il questionnait Valfroy, lui posait des questions à la suite qui paraissaient n'avoir aucun rapport entre elles... Enfin il se releva et dit qu'il s'agissait d'une anémie, c'est-à-dire d'un manque de sang.

– Vous manquez de fer, monsieur de Valfroy. Je vais vous ordonner une potion qui vous rendra vos forces.

– Puis-je continuer de me rendre à mon travail? demanda Bertrand.

Lefèvre hésita une seconde – cela n'échappa pas à Antoinette – avant de répondre :

– Si vous vous en sentez la force, allez-y, sinon reposez-vous. N'importe comment il faut attendre que le traitement fasse de l'effet. Pour le moment je vous conseille de rester sagement chez vous où votre femme va vous dorloter.

Dès qu'il eut quitté la chambre, il fit signe à Antoinette qu'il voulait lui parler.

– Je vais lui donner quelques remèdes qui vont améliorer son état mais je dois vous le dire, madame, le mieux ne durera pas...

Antoinette se raidit, ferma les yeux un instant puis s'assit sur le bord de son canapé.

– J'ai compris tout de suite que c'était grave. Vous pouvez tout me dire, je suis forte. Va-t-il mourir?

– Je ne peux pas répondre à votre question. Je n'en sais

rien. Mais en conscience je crois que votre mari est atteint d'une grave maladie sanguine. Je reviendrai dans quelques jours et lui prendrai un peu de sang pour l'examiner. Si c'est ce que je crains il y a peu d'espoir de le sauver mais, souvent, la nature humaine est plus forte que les médecins. Elle réagit et permet des guérisons inespérées.

Antoinette ne put s'empêcher d'essuyer une larme. Elle se reprit aussitôt :

– Vous et moi, docteur, nous allons sauver mon mari. Il n'est pas possible qu'un homme si bon, si juste, si attentif aux autres quitte le monde sans qu'on fasse tout pour le sauver.

– Mais nous ferons tout, madame. Seulement, il faut que vous sachiez que les chances sont faibles, très faibles. Si vous le souhaitez, nous pourrons demander une consultation à un confrère...

– Pas maintenant, cela l'inquiéterait... J'ai confiance en vous. C'est vous qui déciderez si cela est utile.

Bertrand de Valfroy ne devait plus retourner dans son bureau de l'hôtel de Villeroy où était installé le télégraphe central et d'où il voyait, à travers les rideaux de la fenêtre, les bras du grand sémaphore s'agiter dans le ciel de Paris. Les remontants administrés par le Dr Lefèvre ne firent illusion que quelques jours. Sa pâleur et son affaiblissement plongeaient chaque jour un peu plus Antoinette dans le désespoir. Elle cachait pourtant son inquiétude et faisait en sorte que la vie de la maison ne soit pas modifiée. Les amis continuaient de venir chaque semaine et Valfroy, calé dans son fauteuil, prenait part aux discussions, posait des questions, s'intéressait aux histoires, aux bruits de Paris dont Percier, Fontaine et Lenoir se faisaient l'écho comme à l'accoutumée. Il demeurait d'une humeur égale et faisait taire gentiment ceux qui lui parlaient de sa santé :

– Je suis là avec vous, la tête fonctionne, que demander de plus ? Parlez-moi plutôt de ce qui se passe au gouvernement. Que va donner la division du territoire en préfectures et arrondissements ? Je trouve que c'est une bonne idée de permettre aux gens de s'administrer un peu eux-mêmes dans la région où ils vivent, même si l'on sait que les petites communautés sont plus faciles à surveiller que les grandes...

Un jour, Fontaine annonça que le Premier consul, sans attendre la fin des travaux, avait décidé de s'installer aux Tuileries.

– Vous ne trouvez pas, dit Valfroy en souriant, que cela a un petit air monarchiste? Ce diable de petit Corse n'a pas fini de vider son sac. Je suis sûr qu'il nous réserve encore bien des surprises! Et cette banque centrale?

– La Banque de France, vous voulez dire? souligna Lenoir. Eh bien, ça y est. Elle est formée par la fusion de plusieurs banques privées. Le gouvernement lui a confié son compte courant avec le cautionnement des receveurs généraux.

– C'était une vieille idée de Necker. Je vais lui envoyer une lettre pour l'informer. Sa fille est à Coppet et n'a pu le tenir au courant. Il est bien dommage, voyez-vous, que Bonaparte n'ait pas auprès de lui un homme comme Necker...

– Pour le moment, le Premier consul a, hélas! autre chose à faire que de s'occuper de finances, dit Percier. J'ai su qu'il partait demain rejoindre son armée pour essayer de délivrer Masséna enfermé dans Gênes et de battre les Autrichiens qui sont en train de reprendre toutes les places italiennes conquises par les Français. Les deux autres consuls, Cambacérès et Lebrun, doivent tenir l'ordre à Paris et dans le pays. Bonaparte va essayer de passer les Alpes, au col du Saint-Bernard, avec cinquante mille hommes, dix mille chevaux, sept cents mulets et toute l'artillerie. C'est de la folie... Et j'ai la conviction qu'il va réussir!

– Cette épreuve terrible qui attend tous ces hommes a dû me fatiguer, murmura Valfroy en souriant. Pardonnez-moi de vous laisser mais je vais aller me coucher.

Il ne devait plus se relever. Après une nuit à peu près paisible, Antoinette le retrouva le lendemain matin encore plus affaibli. Ses traits s'étaient comme incrustés dans son visage blême, seules ses pommettes saillaient et elle s'aperçut en lui saisissant le poignet que son pouls battait la mesure de la vie avec une lenteur déclinante.

Antoinette eut conscience que c'était la fin. Elle ne s'était jamais fait d'illusions sur l'issue de l'affection qui usait jour après jour le sang de son mari. Mais on s'habitue à la maladie qui accable un être cher, on triche d'abord pour ne pas l'inquiéter, puis on se laisse prendre à son pauvre jeu, on s'installe dans la pathologie sans se rendre compte de l'évolution du mal. Antoinette en était arrivée à croire que la mort allait se lasser. Et puis, d'un coup, elle se retrouvait devant l'atroce réalité : Bertrand allait les quitter, elle, la petite Lucie, Ethis et tous les amis...

Vers midi, Valfroy sortit de l'engourdissement qui l'avait, comme s'il s'était agi d'une ultime répétition, retranché un moment du monde des vivants. Il demanda à boire et fit signe à Antoinette de s'asseoir près de lui. Maintenant qu'elle sentait l'échéance proche, elle avait retrouvé son calme et se savait prête à affronter le tragique de la situation. Elle posa sa main fraîche sur son front et lui sourit.

D'un signe des yeux, Bertrand la remercia et murmura :

– Continue de sourire ma bien-aimée. Je ne veux pas quitter ce monde dans les larmes mais tout imprégné de ta grâce un peu moqueuse. Il aurait été atroce de mourir il y a six ans, loin de vous, jeté sous le couperet. Aujourd'hui, c'est tout différent. J'ai accompli mon temps sur terre et je vais m'en aller, sereinement, après vous avoir dit adieu. Je crois que j'ai envie de voir un prêtre : ce fameux pari sans doute... Après, je passerai un moment avec Lucie, Ethis et toi, naturellement. Enfin, je verrai une dernière fois nos amis, ceux qui nous ont aidés à supporter ces années terribles. Après, je serai très fatigué et je m'endormirai, ta douce main sur la mienne. Tu m'as donné dix ans de bonheur, Antoinette. C'est beaucoup! Promets-moi de ne rien perdre de ta vie en inutiles et douloureux regrets. Tu as je crois été heureuse avec moi, tu le seras sans moi. Si je suis sûr de cela, je vous quitterai en paix...

Antoinette avait gardé son sourire mais elle pleurait en même temps. Heureusement Bertrand avait refermé les yeux. Elle lui embrassa la tempe, sortit de la chambre et appela Lucie qui lisait *La Princesse de Clèves* et rougissait en même temps que l'héroïne de Mme de Lafayette quand M. de Nemours lui avouait qu'il l'aimait...

– Lucie, tu sais que ton père est très malade. Je ne t'ai jamais dit combien c'était grave, mais aujourd'hui il faut que tu saches : il est très mal...

– Ne me dis pas que mon père chéri va mourir !

– Hélas, ma petite fille ! C'est une question de jours, d'heures peut-être. Je te demande d'être forte. Il sait qu'il va nous quitter mais ne veut pas nous voir pleurer. Il va falloir dominer notre chagrin et lui sourire jusqu'au bout. C'est tout ce que nous pouvons faire pour lui...

Lucie jeta son livre et se serra contre sa mère :

– Je ne suis plus une petite fille, j'ai dix ans et je ne pleurerai pas devant lui. Tu ne m'avais rien dit mais je me doutais qu'il ne guérirait pas. Ethis, lui, est-il au courant ?

– Oui. Tu vas aller le chercher. En même temps, passe à Sainte-Marguerite. Dis au curé que le baron de Valfroy est très mal et qu'il a demandé le secours de la religion.

– Je ne savais pas que notre père était croyant. Il ne parlait jamais de Dieu et n'allait pas à la messe.

– S'il m'a demandé de faire venir un prêtre, c'est qu'il lui reste une part de religion. Celle de l'enfance sûrement, la plus pure... Va et ne me laisse pas trop longtemps seule.

Valfroy reçut l'extrême-onction et demanda à voir les enfants.

– Ne soyez pas trop tristes, dit-il. Je m'éteins sans souffrir après dix ans de bonheur passés avec vous comme je me suis endormi si souvent le soir après une journée de fatigue. J'ai rédigé mon testament. Tu sais, Antoinette, ce qu'il contient et où il se trouve : dans le tiroir de ta table à écrire. Il est aussi court que ma fortune puisque je laisse à ma sœur la jouissance, sa vie durant, du petit domaine de la famille. C'est elle qui l'a fait subsister, vaille que vaille, au prix de gros efforts. Tout ce que je possède en dehors revient à ma femme et à ma fille qu'il va falloir élever. Toi, Ethis, tu t'es tiré d'affaire tout seul. Non seulement tu n'as pas besoin d'aide mais tu es sûrement plus riche que moi. Alors, je te lègue seulement mon nom et un devoir sacré à accomplir. Tout à l'heure tu seras le chef de famille : je te confie ta mère et ta petite sœur. Tu les as déjà protégées jadis quand tu n'étais encore qu'un garçon sauvage dont le cœur battait la tendresse. Aujourd'hui que tu es un homme fort et respectable tu vas faire encore mieux. Prends soin d'elles, fais qu'elles ne manquent de rien. Tu vois, c'est à toi qui m'as déjà sauvé la vie que je demande le plus. C'est parce que j'ai confiance en toi et que je t'aime.

Ethis depuis longtemps s'était agenouillé auprès du lit. Il avait embrassé la belle main diaphane de Bertrand et il pleurait doucement.

– Mon père, dit-il, c'est vous qui m'avez fait ce que je suis et tout ce que je posséderai sera à Antoinette et à Lucie aussi bien qu'à ma femme et mes enfants. Vous pouvez compter sur moi comme si j'étais vraiment votre fils.

– Mais tu es vraiment mon fils, comme tu es le fils d'Antoinette! Allons, baron de Valfroy, relève-toi, sèche tes larmes et souris-moi!

Épuisé, Bertrand avait fermé les yeux et Antoinette qui ne le quittait pas du regard remarquait que son nez se pinçait et qu'il avait de plus en plus de mal à respirer.

– Mes enfants, allez tout de suite prévenir Riesener, Lenoir, et demandez à ce dernier d'alerter Fontaine et Percier. Passez aussi chez Réveillon. Je sais qu'il ne peut plus guère se déplacer mais il doit être averti. Ce soir, M. de Valfroy et nous trois avons besoin de tous nos amis!

– Viens! dit Ethis, nous allons louer une voiture cours Saint-Antoine pour aller plus vite.

A ce moment, Bertrand appela d'une voix faible : il voulait voir la petite Lucie. Ethis partit donc seul tandis que la mère et la fille revenaient au chevet du mourant.

– Venez, toutes les deux, je veux emporter l'image de vos visages avec moi. C'est l'image du bonheur. Lucie, tu es une grande fille, je te demande de prendre soin de ta mère. Embrassez-moi une dernière fois...

Il semblait que Valfroy qui avait toujours dirigé sa vie avec une régularité d'horloge, sans laisser de prise aux circonstances, avait réussi jusqu'au bout à contrôler le destin et à compter les dernières minutes qu'il lui restait à passer dans ce monde. Le moment était venu, il l'avait compris. Quand Lenoir franchit la porte de la chambre, essoufflé d'avoir cravaché son pauvre cheval, Bertrand de Valfroy venait de rendre, dans un mouvement des lèvres qu'on pouvait prendre pour un sourire, son dernier soupir d'honnête homme.

On l'inhuma dès le lendemain, car le temps s'étais mis au chaud, dans le petit cimetière de Sainte-Marguerite. Il rejoignait dans l'argile du vieux Faubourg les soldats de Condé et de Turenne tués dans les combats de juillet 1652, les 73 victimes de la Terreur décapitées sur la place de la Bastille les trois jours où la guillotine y avait été dressée et aussi l'« enfant mort au Temple » qui était peut-être le petit roi Louis XVII.

C'était le désir du baron de Valfroy de reposer au cœur du Faubourg, avec les gens du bois, dans ce quartier où la pauvreté tenait lieu de noblesse et où il avait trouvé le bonheur.

Dès le soir du décès, le cercle des amis s'était resserré autour d'Antoinette. Ethis, avec la bénédiction de Marie dont la délivrance approchait, venait coucher chaque nuit place d'Aligre afin de ne pas laisser seules les deux femmes. Lenoir arrivait tous les soirs à l'heure du souper, Fontaine et Percier, les « frères siamois », comme on les appelait, venaient chaque fois qu'ils pouvaient s'échapper des chantiers du Premier consul, Riesener ne quittait guère le logement et, souvent, Réveillon, malgré ses infirmités, frétait une voiture pour aller embrasser sa filleule et Lucie dont la jeune détermination faisait l'admiration de tous. « Mon père, disait-elle, serait malheureux, là où il est, s'il me voyait pleurer ! »

Et la vie reprit, sans Valfroy dont le fauteuil restait vide quand le clan se réunissait sous le portrait du maître Œben et de la douce Marguerite. Il ne serait venu à l'idée de personne de s'y asseoir. C'est bien plus tard qu'Antoinette annonça qu'elle ne voulait plus voir ce siège inoccupé :

– Chacun d'entre vous, mes amis, et Ethis naturellement, s'y assoira à tour de rôle. Loin de moi l'idée d'introduire ici une sorte de rite macabre. Bertrand était plutôt un silencieux, il avait horreur des mots inutiles mais il aimait rire et appréciait les gens d'esprit. Son plus grand désir était que nous pensions à lui dans la gaieté et que l'atmosphère de notre « salon du Faubourg » ne soit en rien attristée par sa disparition. Je compte sur vous tous pour respecter cette dernière volonté.

Marie avait vécu sa grossesse avec beaucoup de crânerie. Pourtant, à mesure que le terme approchait, elle était sujette à de nombreux malaises qui inquiétaient fort sa mère et surtout Antoinette qui avait pris en main l'accouchement de sa belle-fille. Consultée, la sage-femme Marthe Furet déclara que selon elle l'enfant se présentait mal. « Il vaudrait mieux, dit-elle, que la petite aille se faire accoucher à l'hôpital par un médecin. »

– Pas du tout ! coupa Antoinette. Nous allons trouver un très bon médecin qui viendra délivrer Marie chez elle. Je vais en parler à Fontaine ou à Percier, ils connaissent tout le monde !

Consultés le soir même, les deux architectes éclatèrent de rire :

– Marie ne peut tomber mieux. Nous avons, il y a plus de six mois, dessiné les plans de deux pièces que l'illustre Baudelocque veut remeubler dans son hôtel de la rue des

Tournelles. Malgré nos prières, nous n'arrivons pas à nous faire régler la juste rétribution de notre travail. Le vieux semble assez avare. Eh bien, si nous lui demandons d'accoucher Marie pour le prix de notre talent, il acceptera tout de suite.

Percier avait vu juste. C'est donc Baudelocque, le premier docteur de l'hôpital de la Charité, l'accoucheur des grandes dames, le spécialiste des césariennes, qui eut le privilège de venir mettre au monde, dans la vieille maison Thirion du Faubourg, l'enfant d'Ethis dit « Traîne-sabot » et de la jolie Marie. La vieille Marthe ne s'était pas trompée : l'enfant était mal placé et Baudelocque eut grand mal à l'amener à se présenter par les pieds et à procéder à l'extraction. Enfin, transpirant dans sa veste de soie couverte par un tablier, il déposa dans les bras de la mère Furet une boule sanguinolente en criant : « C'est je crois bien un garçon! » comme s'il n'en était pas sûr.

Baudelocque était un brave homme autant qu'un habile médecin. Il accepta sans façon le verre de vin de Champagne que lui offrit l'heureux père, comme il avait accepté naguère les rafraîchissements royaux après avoir mis au monde le troisième enfant de Marie-Antoinette. Il donna quelques ordres à la sage-femme, reprit le pouls de Marie qui somnolait et chargea Antoinette de faire mille compliments à MM. Percier et Fontaine.

– Me voilà donc grand-mère! s'exclama-t-elle quand le bonhomme fut reparti dans sa voiture curieusement peinte en vert pomme et conduite par un cocher vêtu de drap pourpre.

Antoinette était folle de joie : Ethis avait eu le temps de lui dire que le garçon s'appellerait Bertrand. Antoine fut choisi comme second prénom. Pour ne pas créer de conflit familial le nouveau-né fut encore nommé Eugène. C'était le nom du citoyen Bénard, le père de Marie. Bertrand était né le 12 messidor de l'an VIII, au moment où le Faubourg s'apprêtait à vivre l'un de ces événements populaires et patriotiques qui n'avaient cessé, au cours des siècles, de marquer l'histoire locale en même temps que celle du pays. Le lendemain, 1er juillet du nouveau siècle, Bonaparte rentrait à Paris. L'annonce de sa victoire à Marengo avait suscité un enthousiasme délirant. On s'était arraché *Le Moniteur* qui d'ailleurs parlait de « Maringo », et dès les premiers coups de canon tirés du parc des Tuileries, les ateliers du Faubourg s'étaient vidés. Les ouvriers du bois comme ceux de la verrerie et les papetiers de la rue de Montreuil s'étaient spontanément groupés autour de la fontaine Trogneux et sur le terrain vague qui avait pris la place de l'abbatiale démolie pour commenter le placard que le préfet de police avait fait afficher et crier « Vive la République! Vive Bonaparte! » avant d'aller dans les cabarets boire à la santé du Premier consul. Le vainqueur revenait, auréolé de lauriers et de légende. Il devait faire son entrée par la porte Saint-Antoine, dans ce Paris dont il venait d'achever la conquête à Milan et à Marengo. Dès le petit matin, la foule s'était rassemblée dans la grand-rue pour acclamer Bonaparte mais son attente fut vaine. La plupart des Parisiens avaient regagné leurs maisons quand la calèche verte encadrée par les cavaliers de la garde consulaire traversa la place du Trône et entra au milieu de la nuit dans la grand-rue du Faubourg. Seuls étaient encore là les gens du quartier qui avaient préparé des feux jusqu'à la Bastille. En quelques minutes le Faubourg s'embrasa mais ce n'était pas de colère. Le peuple qui avait renversé la royauté illuminait pour fêter son nouveau maître. Au premier étage de la maison Thirion, couché dans l'éternel berceau de Jean Marot, un nouveau-né prénommé Bertrand pouvait penser qu'on l'accueillait de bien bruyante façon.

Chapitre 7.

ANTOINETTE ET SON CLAN

Ce qui n'avait été qu'un frémissement durant le Directoire et la première partie du Consulat devenait réalité : le vieux Faubourg du meuble reprenait vie. Ce n'était certes pas l'activité fébrile des périodes glorieuses, celles de la Renaissance, du triomphe de Boulle ou du « siècle de la commode ». Pourtant, beaucoup d'ateliers fermés depuis 1792 renaissaient de la cendre des vieux copeaux ranimée sous les pots de colle forte. On entendait çà et là chanter la scie à refendre et frapper le maillet. A nouveau des voitures à bras roulaient dans les passages, charriant des planches épaisses et des carcasses de sièges.

Antoinette qui avait de la sève de noyer dans les veines, sentait le renouveau de son quartier comme un printemps. Elle aimait se promener avec Lucie dans les cours cachées où elle découvrait avec un plaisir sensuel quelque vieil artisan au travail ou, le plus souvent, un jeune compagnon plein d'ardeur qui tentait de faire revivre l'atelier d'un ancien. Les grands maîtres du temps de la royauté étaient morts ou avaient cessé de travailler. Ceux qui avaient réussi à conserver quelque activité durant la Révolution cédaient leurs ateliers aux enfants. Ainsi les trois fils de Simon Mansion, le vieil ébéniste de la rue de Charenton, succédaient à leur père; Pabst qui avait survécu en réparant les meubles confisqués par la République n'apparaissait presque plus dans son atelier du 195 de la grand-rue du Faubourg. Hélas! la maison autrefois prospère périclitait sous la direction de ses deux fils. Georges Jacob lui-même avait cédé son fonds de la rue Meslée à ses enfants. Ainsi que Riesener et Molitor, il se considérait comme retraité, se prêtant avec eux aux expertises commandées par le tribunal.

Ce jour-là Antoinette avait décidé de rendre visite à Emmanuel Caumont dans un atelier de la rue Traversière qu'elle connaissait depuis toujours. C'était, au temps de sa jeunesse, celui de Jean Caumont, un ami de Riesener qui, comme lui, était resté fidèle au style Louis XVI qui avait fait sa renommée. La Révolution n'avait pas laissé indifférent cet homme aimable et doux qui, dans sa section des Quinze-Vingts, avait toujours lutté contre les excès et les aventures. Il avait été l'un des premiers à tenter de s'opposer à l'arrestation de Valfroy et Antoinette lui en était reconnaissante. Elle venait d'apprendre sa mort, survenue quelques semaines auparavant, et voulait témoigner son amitié à Emmanuel.

Arrivée au numéro 4, elle reconnut le petit passage grossièrement pavé où la verdure encadrait les portes vitrées derrière lesquelles on distinguait des établis et des meubles finis, poncés prêts à être vernis, entassés les uns sur les autres.

– Tu vois, dit-elle à Lucie, quand j'étais petite, un peu plus vieille que toi tout de même, je venais jouer dans ce passage qui respire encore un peu la campagne. Au Faubourg, il y a partout, au fond des cours et dans des endroits bien cachés, des arbres, des lilas, des murs couverts de vigne qui, certaines années, produisent même quelques grappes de raisin. Viens, nous allons dire bonjour à Emmanuel qui a bien du chagrin. Comme toi il vient de perdre son père...

Elles poussèrent la porte qui raclait les carreaux du sol. Le grincement fit relever la tête à un grand jeune homme blond fort appliqué à décalquer sur une pièce de bois qui devait être un devant de fauteuil le contour d'un gabarit de carton. Un grand sourire éclaira son visage quand il aperçut Antoinette :

– Mademoiselle Œben... pardon, madame de Valfroy,

quelle bonne surprise de vous voir. J'ai appris votre malheur, sûrement connaissez-vous le nôtre. Ma pauvre mère ne se remet pas de la mort du père. Moi, j'ai le travail. Maintenant qu'il n'est plus là j'essaye de mettre à profit toutes les leçons qu'il m'a données. Je voudrais faire honneur à son poinçon que je place bien en vue sur mon établi.

Il prit le sceau d'acier forgé et passa son doigt sur les lettres en relief dont la gravure rustique, comme celle de toutes les estampilles, datait du jour de 1774 où son père avait gagné la maîtrise.

– C'est mon talisman. Malheureusement je ne pourrai guère l'utiliser sur des meubles d'un style dont personne ne veut plus. Je vais être obligé, si je veux gagner ma vie, d'abandonner les meubles de rois pour ceux que désirent les acheteurs. Le père était un fervent révolutionnaire, sauf pour les meubles. Comme votre beau-père il n'a jamais pu se résoudre à abandonner la grâce des formes et l'élégance des sculptures. Le résultat, vous le voyez : plusieurs milliers de francs de meubles invendables. Moi, je me mets aux lits antiques et aux sièges étrusques. Eugène Barreau de la rue de Charenton m'a prêté des dessins de modèles.

Lucie qui avait toujours entendu parler de bois et de styles par sa mère, Riesener et les amis de la place d'Aligre, ne perdait pas une parole de ce que disait le jeune homme. Claude avait une vingtaine d'années, guère plus. Les privations ne semblaient pas l'avoir affecté : il était beau et fort. Sa chemise ouverte, car il faisait chaud laissait deviner des muscles fins et solides. Antoinette reconnaissait en lui la silhouette racée des gens du bois et elle s'amusait à constater combien Lucie était fascinée par ce jeune dieu de l'ébène dont les gestes et les paroles relevaient d'un rituel né trois siècles auparavant avec les premiers compagnons de l'abbaye. « Allons, pensa-t-elle en souriant, voilà ma Lucie pour la première fois amoureuse ! »

– Vous avez tout à fait raison, Emmanuel, de suivre la mode nouvelle. Votre père et Riesener devaient trop à l'ancien style pour le trahir au profit de formes qu'ils jugeaient sans beauté. Vous, ce n'est pas pareil, il faut au contraire vous adapter et aller dans le sens de la vie. Un jour, je vous présenterai mes amis Fontaine et Percier qui sont avec David les grands prêtres de l'antique. Vous verrez qu'ils savent très bien parler du style qui se crée sans cesser d'admirer les chefs-d'œuvre d'hier.

Lucie, qu'on n'avait pas entendue jusqu'alors, enchaîna avec une véhémence et une sûreté qui laissèrent le jeune homme éberlué :

– Bien sûr, monsieur, qu'il faut faire des meubles nouveaux. Ce sont les jeunes compagnons qui doivent créer et non pas les anciens maîtres. Je suis sûre que vous réussirez et que nos amis vous aideront !

Antoinette était fière de sa fille.

– Lucie vous étonne ? C'est qu'elle a toujours partagé la vie des grandes personnes et que les grandes personnes que nous fréquentons sont plutôt intelligentes. Elle n'a pas onze ans et se délecte de la lecture de *La Princesse de Clèves.* Je ne sais si je dois m'en réjouir ou m'en inquiéter.

– Je sais très bien, maman, que tu es très contente d'avoir une fille qui n'est pas sotte.

Comme il faisait beau, on s'attarda dans le Faubourg. La moitié des personnes rencontrées étaient de vieilles connaissances pour qui Antoinette était restée à quarante-cinq ans « Mlle Œben ». C'était une manière élégante, pour les gens du bois de l'autre temps, de rendre hommage au plus grand d'entre eux. Elle en était heureuse et fière.

– Maintenant il est temps de rentrer, dit Antoinette. Ce soir nous avons notre clan qui vient souper et Percier a fait déposer par un courrier de la maison de Joséphine une poularde de l'élevage de la Malmaison où il finit d'installer les deux dernières chambres. Nous avons juste le temps de l'enfourner.

Cette longue promenade avec Lucie avait constitué pour Antoinette un bonheur dont elle goûtait encore le parfum en se déshabillant avant de se mettre à la cuisine.

Elle était prête à rire, à entraîner sa fille dans une de ces danses folles qui se terminaient dans un fou rire. Et puis d'un coup, le nuage de cendres, le regard qui se brouille et les larmes qui affluent. Depuis la mort de Bertrand, il lui arrivait d'être étreinte subitement par une douleur où elle ne discernait pas la part du physique de l'atteinte morale. Il suffisait d'un rien, d'une pensée surgie à l'improviste, d'un objet retrouvé ou d'une lettre oubliée pour la plonger dans le désespoir. Ce jour-là, en se rappelant l'observation de Lucie à propos des meubles et son assurance stupéfiante, elle avait pensé immédiatement: « Son père ne va pas en revenir!... » Et puis, tout de suite, le rappel à l'ordre, le signal du réel, l'avertissement du présent: « Impossible. Ton mari est mort; tu ne lui raconteras plus jamais rien! » Cette brutalité de la raison avait immédiatement déclenché la crise de larmes et cette douleur indescriptible qui vous serre le cœur, les poumons, le ventre comme dans l'étau d'un tourmenteur.

Peu après, Ethis qui venait lui aussi déposer quelques provisions pour le souper, la trouva sanglotante, étendue sur son lit, la tête dans ses deux bras repliés. Il ne dit rien, hésita un instant puis s'allongea près d'elle, la prit dans ses bras et lui caressa doucement les cheveux en murmurant: « Antoinette, ma mère chérie, ne pleurez pas. Vous n'êtes pas seule, on vous aime... »

La maladresse de ses phrases les rendait encore plus touchantes. Elles firent d'abord redoubler les sanglots puis leur douce musique commença à pénétrer Antoinette qui se laissa bercer et se calma peu à peu. Antoinette se releva, regarda Ethis, emprunté dans sa tendresse et sa sensibilité, et lui sourit:

– Merci, mon Ethis. Il n'y a que toi qui pouvais me guérir ce soir. Lucie aurait fondu avec moi. Mais tu es venu. Viens, je vais te raconter notre promenade comme je l'aurais fait à Bertrand s'il était encore là. Tu vois, il m'arrive encore de rêver qu'il va rentrer et nous apporter la primeur d'une nouvelle cueillie au télégraphe. Le réveil est brutal et terrible... Mais le jeune Bertrand de Valfroy est là! C'est à lui qu'il faut penser. Comment va-t-il?

– Il est superbe. Il est fort. Il a, dit sa mère, un cœur de forgeron qu'on entend de la pièce voisine. Marie a été, vous le savez, un peu souffrante ces derniers jours mais elle m'a dit qu'elle allait revenir vous voir chaque jour comme elle en a pris l'habitude. Vous l'avez conquise elle aussi. Je crois qu'elle ne peut pas se passer de vous. Quelle chance!

– Tâche de l'amener ce soir avec le petit Bertrand que nous coucherons dans ma chambre. Il faut maintenant qu'elle tienne sa place dans nos réunions. Elle y apprendra, comme tu l'as fait toi-même, toutes ces choses qui rendent la vie plus belle et plus intéressante et dont on ne prend conscience qu'au contact de gens d'esprit.

– Merci. Je crois que je n'aurai pas trop de mal à la décider.

La soirée fut opportunément réussie. Réveillon n'était pas là mais Riesener avait amené Georges Jacob qui s'ennuyait depuis qu'il avait laissé son atelier à ses fils. Quant à Alexandre Lenoir, il avait une grande nouvelle à annoncer :

– Depuis le sénatus-consulte qui l'a nommé Premier consul à vie, Bonaparte vit dans l'exaltation. La remise à l'armée française des trois places d'Ulm, Ingoldstadt et Philipsbourg a accru encore sa popularité et il veut que la célébration de l'anniversaire de la fondation de la République, le 22 septembre, soit éclatante.

– C'est drôle, remarqua Marie qui prenait la parole pour la première fois, les Parisiens sont dans l'enthousiasme parce qu'ils ont un nouveau roi qui va leur faire applaudir la République!

– Bravo Marie, dit Antoinette. Tu te mets vite au diapason de nos esprits persifleurs. Il est bien vrai que le peuple le plus révolutionnaire du monde est prêt à se prosterner devant un général qui le nourrit de victoires. Alors, Alexandre? Que va faire notre monarque républicain?

– Il a trouvé le moyen de rehausser l'éclat des cérémonies.

– Quoi donc?

– Bonaparte va appeler Turenne à la rescousse, comme on dit à l'armée.

Lenoir jouit un instant de l'étonnement de l'assemblée et poursuivit :

– Figurez-vous que j'ai été convoqué ce matin aux Tuileries et que le Premier consul m'a demandé ce qu'était devenu le corps du vaillant capitaine. Je lui ai dit comment il avait échappé, par miracle, à la profanation des tombeaux de la basilique de Saint-Denis et avait été transporté au jardin des Plantes avant que je le recueille dans un sarcophage de mon musée des Monuments français. Ethis qui a vécu avec moi cette aventure, ne l'a sûrement pas oubliée! Bonaparte qui avait écouté mon récit avec attention a réfléchi un moment en plaçant la main droite sous son menton, comme sur les gravures, et m'a dit : « Très bien, monsieur Lenoir. Puisque par bonheur vous détenez les restes de Turenne, nous allons les placer sous le dôme des Invalides dans un monument digne de ce grand Français. Ce sera l'événement majeur des fêtes du 22 septembre. Je vous remercie. » Voilà, mes amis. Préparez-vous à assister à un curieux cortège!

Trop heureuse d'avoir un soir le grand Jacob à sa table, Antoinette le questionna sur l'entreprise de la rue Meslée qui croulait sous les commandes :

– Comment se fait-il, monsieur, que vos ateliers refusent du travail alors que ceux de notre Faubourg ont tant de mal à revivre?

– La renommée sans doute. Mais elle vient de ce que notre nom s'est trouvé associé dès l'origine au nouveau style. David m'a engagé dans cette voie qu'il avait ouverte et que MM. Fontaine et Percier ont su empierrer de leur grand talent. Sans doute aussi dois-je mon succès au fait que mon maître Delanois m'a spécialisé dans la fabrication des sièges et que c'est par les sièges que tout a commencé...

– Jacob oublie de vous dire qu'il a un immense talent, coupa Riesener. Ce qu'il a fait personne d'autre ne pouvait même s'y essayer!

– Peut-être, peut-être..., soupira le maître, mais ce succès inespéré ne va pas sans inconvénients. Je n'aurais pas dû grandir autant, racheter sans cesse des ateliers, employer de plus en plus d'ouvriers. Aujourd'hui mes fils ont près de trois cents compagnons, ébénistes, menuisiers de sièges, fondeurs, ciseleurs, sculpteurs qui travaillent rue Meslée. C'est trop, nous ne sommes pas des financiers rompus aux affaires et l'équilibre des géants est toujours précaire. Les deux frères n'y arrivent plus et me demandent de revenir pour les aider. Je le fais un peu mais je commence à devenir vieux. Souvent je t'envie, mon vieux Riesener. Tu n'es pas riche mais tu n'as pas ces soucis. Et tes meubles retrouveront un jour leur vraie valeur alors que mes chaises et mes fauteuils moisiront, brisés, dans les greniers! Et au fait, que devient ton fils Henri-François le portraitiste? Il n'était pas maladroit...

– Il est à Lyon où il travaille pour David. Tu sais, c'est un saltimbanque. Il ne veut pas se fixer et préfère voyager. J'aimerais mieux, bien sûr, l'avoir près de moi, sa sœur aussi... Mais que veux-tu, chacun fait sa vie comme il l'entend. Enfin, j'ai Ethis qui est un peu notre fils à tous. Ce diable de garçon réussit très bien. Tu sais qu'il s'est établi marchand dans la vieille maison Thirion du Faubourg. En attendant de ne vendre que des meubles et des antiquités – c'est son rêve – il offre aux chalands un tas d'affaires utiles ou baroques qu'il déniche je ne sais où. Il a même acheté et revendu aux ébénistes un chargement de bois d'acajou!

– Un jour, je vendrai vos meubles, monsieur Jacob! dit Ethis en riant. Avec ceux de Riesener que je rachèterai dans les ventes. En attendant il faut bien vivre et j'ai en ce moment plusieurs pièces de soierie qui viennent de Lyon et qui sont superbes. N'en avez-vous pas besoin pour tapisser vos sièges? Si vous voulez, je viendrai vous les présenter rue Meslée?

– Pourquoi pas? répondit Georges Jacob en éclatant de rire. Tu me fais l'effet d'un fameux marchand. Et même d'un homme d'affaires bien entreprenant. Je ne me fais pas de souci pour toi. Tu deviendras riche!

– Il a été tellement pauvre! dit Antoinette en regardant son fils avec tendresse.

Ethis ne se souciait pas outre mesure qu'on parle de lui. Pour le moment il s'intéressait aux goûts de ce Bonaparte qu'il n'aimait tellement pas mais qui le fascinait :

– Messieurs Percier et Fontaine, vous qui avez le privilège de voir souvent le Premier consul, dites-nous ce qu'il pense de l'art, des meubles et des artistes? Les gens du bois voient en lui leur sauveur. Cet enthousiasme risque-t-il d'être déçu?

– Tu nous poses là deux questions, répondit Fontaine. Il est certain que Bonaparte fera ce qu'il pourra afin de maintenir les bonnes dispositions que montre à son égard le peuple turbulent des faubourgs, celui de Saint-Antoine en particulier. Je l'ai plusieurs fois entendu dire qu'il fallait donner du travail à ces braves gens qui ne cessent de lui témoigner leur attachement. Mais il doit s'occuper de tant de choses!... Quant à ses goûts, ils sont doubles et contradictoires. Rien n'est trop fastueux lorsqu'il s'agit de donner un décor imposant à sa puissance. Rien n'est assez simple quand il est question de ses appartements et de ses meubles personnels. Dans ce cas toute fantaisie est à proscrire.

Aucun meuble n'entre aux Tuileries sans que Bonaparte ait vu et le plus souvent corrigé le dessin qui lui est soumis avant la fabrication. Notre ami Jacob en sait quelque chose!

Une fois de plus la réunion des amis de la place d'Aligre avait été réussie. Antoinette avait retrouvé sa joie de vivre. Elle promit de ramener le lendemain de bonne heure le petit Bertrand qui dormait béatement et que sa mère n'eut pas le courage de réveiller.

La cérémonie et le défilé annoncés par Alexandre Lenoir avaient été fixés au dernier jour complémentaire de l'an VIII. Fidèle à la tradition républicaine, le Premier consul avait fait demander à tous les départements d'envoyer des représentants afin de donner à la manifestation un caractère national. C'est donc un cortège considérable qui se rendit le matin du 22 septembre au musée des Petits-Augustins pour aller chercher le char sur lequel reposait le corps de Turenne. David lui-même avait dirigé au côté de Lenoir l'ordonnance de la cérémonie. Grâce à Alexandre, Antoinette et Lucie avaient pu se faufiler dans la cour de l'ancien couvent et assister aux derniers préparatifs.

Le char était attelé de quatre chevaux blancs. Au dernier moment, Lenoir vint placer sur le cercueil l'épée de Turenne tandis qu'un dragon, le plus grand de toute l'armée sans doute, serré dans son uniforme blanc et bleu, amenait un cheval bai, semblable à celui que montait ordinairement le vaillant capitaine. C'est lui qui ouvrit la marche précédant le char dont les cordons étaient tenus par quatre vieux généraux de la République.

Lucie regardait avec émerveillement ce spectacle qui n'avait rien de mortuaire et qui avait amené autour du musée et sur le parcours une foule considérable où rares étaient sans doute ceux qui avaient entendu parler de Turenne avant ce jour de fête nationale. Derrière le char et devant la troupe bigarrée des autorités où tous les costumes civils et militaires semblaient être représentés, marchaient des invalides escortés par des soldats revenus d'Italie et d'Autriche.

Le curieux cortège gagna à petits pas les Invalides. Bonaparte, entouré des représentants des départements, attendait dans la cour d'honneur. Avant de reposer dans son mausolée, le corps de Turenne fut placé sous le dôme tandis qu'une musique funèbre emplissait la coupole. Au premier rang, Bonaparte écouta les deux discours prononcés l'un par son frère Lucien, l'autre par le ministre Carnot.

Le soir il y eut une représentation gratuite à la Comédie-Française. Le Premier consul et Joséphine y assistèrent. En applaudissant Molé, Fleury et Mlle Mars dans *Le Cid,* Bonaparte pensait qu'il avait eu raison d'être républicain puisque la République avait fait de lui un maître plus puissant que ne l'avait été le roi de France. Consul à vie, il ne lui restait plus qu'un échelon à monter pour arriver au rang suprême. Il sourit et ranima les bravos de la salle en reprenant ses applaudissements pour le vainqueur des Maures.

Durant des jours, Lucie raconta à tout le monde la grande journée du défilé. Turenne, son épée, son cheval bai, le cortège des invalides, le char dont elle disait qu'il n'avait rien de funèbre et ressemblait à celui du bœuf gras, tout y passait avec un luxe de détails qui faisaient rire Antoinette et Ethis. Celui-ci n'avait pu accompagner sa mère et sa sœur et il le regrettait. Ce jour-là il était occupé par une affaire importante. Il envisageait de louer d'abord, puis de racheter, un magasin qui se trouvait libre à la suite d'une faillite dans la première partie du Faubourg, non loin de la Bastille. Il savait que la situation de la maison Thirion n'était pas idéale. Le secteur de l'abbaye devenue hôpital était celui des ateliers, non du commerce. Les marchands importants tenaient boutique dans les premiers numéros de la grand-rue, autour du magasin de la veuve Héricourt, spécialisée depuis trois décennies dans le commerce des meubles. Sa boutique à l'enseigne de *La Providence* était la plus connue.

Ethis aimait traîner ses guêtres dans ce coin commercial du Faubourg et bavarder avec les autres marchands-merciers dont la situation n'était guère brillante. Le propriétaire de la boutique *La Levrette* désespérait de vendre les meubles emmagasinés durant les premières années de la Révolution.

– J'ai, disait-il à Ethis, des commodes superbes de Catherinet, de Guignard et de Wolff qui sont aujourd'hui invendables. Elles ne sont plus à la mode et je n'ai pas les moyens de passer des commandes de meubles nouveaux, genre Jacob, aux menuisiers et ébénistes qui, eux non plus, n'ont pas d'argent à avancer. Je ferai bientôt faillite, c'est sûr.

Le patron de *La Renommée* n'était pas mieux loti; celui du *Lion d'or* avait annoncé à Ethis qu'il ne pouvait pas payer ses fournisseurs et qu'il devait vendre son actif.

C'est cette boutique, qui jouxtait celle de la veuve Héricourt, que lorgnait le garçon. Il attendait que la faillite fût prononcée pour la louer au propriétaire, le maître carrossier René Boutin qui avait eu la sagesse d'acheter quelques boutiques et échoppes juste avant la Révolution. A dire vrai, Ethis ignorait comment il allait pouvoir réaliser cette opération. Il avait demandé à son beau-père Eugène Bénard de participer à l'affaire mais celui-ci avait refusé tout net, en prétextant que la manufacture de papier peint avait dû licencier deux cents de ses ouvriers. C'était vrai. La prospérité du temps de Réveillon était passée depuis longtemps et il ne restait plus rue de Montreuil qu'une centaine d'employés, dont de nombreux enfants, ce qui indignait Antoinette. Ce ralentissement des affaires n'avait pas écorné la fortune du bonhomme mais son avarice lui interdisait d'aider sa fille et son gendre.

Ce refus n'avait pas entamé l'enthousiasme d'Ethis qui débordait d'idées et annonçait chaque jour un nouveau projet.

– La maison Thirion à l'enseigne de *L'Enfant à l'oiseau* nous fait à peu près vivre, disait-il. Marie continuera d'abord de la tenir et moi je vendrai des meubles à l'entrée du Faubourg. J'ai déjà fait le tour des ateliers et plusieurs jeunes qui viennent de s'installer ou qui succèdent à leur père sont prêts à mettre leur fabrication en dépôt dans mon magasin. Je sais ce qu'il faut vendre : pas de pièces importantes mais des petits meubles à l'antique, des tabourets, des sièges tout simples. Les Jacob ne refuseront pas de me confier le dessin des guéridons [1] qu'ils fabriquent pour le Premier consul. Vous vous rappelez, Georges nous a dit l'autre soir que Bonaparte en voulait partout, à Malmaison, aux Tuileries et qu'il en emportait même plusieurs en campagne. Il mange paraît-il en un quart d'heure et prend ses repas sur ces guéridons simples et légers qu'il fait dresser là où il lui prend

1. Le guéridon de l'abdication, conservé à Fontainebleau, est l'un de ces petits meubles. Il avait été facturé 80 francs (Inventaire de la régie du Palais, 1809).

fantaisie de dîner ou de souper. Cela m'étonnerait fort que l'on n'achète pas « les petites tables de Bonaparte ». Surtout que je ne les vendrai pas cher !

– Tu n'auras même pas à demander un plan à Jacob, dit Percier, c'est moi qui ai dessiné le modèle ! Tu sais que je trouve bonne ton idée de vendre les tables de Bonaparte ! Mon petit Ethis, tu vas vite devenir plus riche que nous tous.

– Il n'aura pas de mal, coupa Fontaine. Le Garde-meuble ne nous a pas encore payé la moitié des travaux de Malmaison. Quant aux Tuileries...

– Tout cela est bien joli, remarqua Antoinette, mais installer une boutique coûte de l'argent et de l'argent nous n'en n'avons pas. Tu as une femme, un enfant, il ne faut tout de même pas faire des bêtises !

– Et la statue de Pigalle ? interrompit Ethis. Vous l'avez oubliée ?

– Quoi ? Tu veux vendre ton porte-bonheur ? Tu avais dit que jamais tu ne te séparerais de *L'Enfant à l'oiseau.*

– Les affaires ne vont pas avec la sensiblerie, annonça Ethis d'un ton si sérieux que tout le monde éclata de rire.

– Vous riez, reprit-il, mais je sais que j'ai raison. Bien sûr que j'aime ma statuette découverte par miracle dans un tas de brocante. Mais j'aimerai encore mieux le magasin que j'ouvrirai et qui nous fera vivre agréablement. Il faut savoir ce que l'on veut ! La difficulté, c'est que je ne vendrai jamais mon *Enfant* assez cher pour pouvoir payer ma boutique...

– Même pas cher, il faudrait déjà trouver un acheteur ! dit Lenoir. Tu sais, en ce moment, les gens ne se battent pas pour les œuvres d'art. Enfin, si tu es décidé, j'essaierai de te trouver un amateur.

Au début de prairial, mai 1800 selon le vieux calendrier qui retrouvait la préférence de beaucoup, Antoinette reçut une lettre de sa sœur Victoire datée de Marseille où son mari était nommé depuis maintenant trois mois.

– Tout de même! s'écria Antoinette en décachetant l'enveloppe après avoir payé le port au facteur de lettres.

Elle s'allongea tranquillement sur le canapé et commença à lire :

Ma Toinette,

Après des semaines de folies, je peux enfin trouver le temps de t'écrire. Me voilà donc préfète de ce département incroyable qu'on appelle les Bouches-du-Rhône. Il y a moins de voitures qu'à Paris mais tout le monde est dehors, et les embarras de la rue y sont encore plus nombreux. Ajoute à cela la langue provençale, la gaieté des gens, leur façon de gesticuler et le soleil, tu auras une vision éteinte d'un volcan dont il faut avoir vu les explosions, senti les vapeurs et entendu le vacarme pour se rendre compte de ce qu'est réellement la ville de Marseille.

Charles s'est à peu près remis de son opération. Il a au moins retrouvé une silhouette normale et s'il ne danse pas aux soirées de la préfecture, il peut se déplacer sans canne et accomplir facilement les devoirs de sa charge. Il lui a fallu beaucoup de courage, à moi aussi, pour s'adapter à ce nouveau poste. Les Marseillais ne sont pas méchants mais ils ne voient pas venir d'un bon œil un envoyé de Paris. Arrivant de si loin, nous pensions au moins que les nouveaux administrés de Delacroix ne connaîtraient rien de nous et que le passé serait par force absent dans l'établissement de nos relations. Eh bien, penses-tu, tout le monde était en quelques jours au courant de la carrière de Charles, de ses engagements successifs, de son infirmité et même des bruits qui ont couru à Paris au moment de la naissance d'Eugène.

Comme arrivée discrète, ce fut réussi! Les journaux satiriques qui foisonnent dans la ville s'en sont donné à cœur joie et les quolibets comme les chansons ont fleuri sur la Canebière. (Ce drôle de nom est celui de la rue principale de Marseille.) A titre d'exemple, voilà le genre d'épigrammes qui nous ont accueillis :

« Pauvres Marseillais! Vous avez été pendus
« Guillotinés, fusillés. Il ne vous manquait plus
« Que Lacroix pour être crucifiés. »

Au début, cela me touchait mais à voir comment les railleries et les insultes glissaient sur le cuir tanné par la politique de mon cher mari, je m'y suis habituée. Charles me répétait : « Ils se lasseront avant nous. Laissons dire et surtout ne répondons pas! » Il avait raison, maintenant nous sommes acceptés et personne ne nous agresse. Et puis, tu connais mon mari : il n'a pas survécu à la Révolution sans apprendre à flatter le citoyen. Il donne les récompenses qu'il faut aux vainqueurs du jeu de boule et tape dans le dos des représentants des pêcheurs. Remarque que Delacroix est un bon préfet. Sa puissance de travail impressionne beaucoup dans cette ville de soleil où la nonchalance a qualité de vertu. Il a une grande idée, c'est de faire installer des trottoirs dans les voies importantes de Marseille. Cela devrait lui valoir une bonne popularité.

Mais je m'aperçois que je ne te parle que de Delacroix. Tu vas te demander si je suis retombée amoureuse. La réponse est non mais il est vrai que son élégance au moment de la naissance d'Eugène m'a rapprochée de lui. Aujourd'hui je me demande pourtant s'il n'a pas adopté cette attitude chevaleresque parce que c'était celle du moindre mal pour sa carrière politique qu'un scandale eût irrémédiablement brisée. Ne me dis pas que je suis méchante, j'essaie simplement d'être lucide. Le principal c'est l'immense bonheur que me donne Eugène. Il n'a pas une santé de fer mais il est beau et intelligent. Charles, il faut en convenir, est pour lui un excellent père. Ils s'entendent parfaitement.

Les autres enfants vont bien. Ils se plaisent dans cette ville exubérante et gaie. Je crois qu'ils vont bientôt parler comme les Marseillais! Ta dernière lettre me montre que tu as pris le dessus et que tu t'habitues à vivre sans Bertrand. Valfroy était l'homme le plus droit, le meilleur et le plus beau que j'aie connu. Dis-toi que tu as eu beaucoup de chance de partager sa vie. Deux grandes passions dans une existence, c'est rare, tu sais! Comme je souhaiterais que ce soit vrai aussi pour moi! J'aimerais bien voir de près le petit garçon d'Ethis qui est sûrement la merveille que tu me dis. Donne-moi vite des nouvelles de tout le monde, en particulier de Riesener qui n'a pas la vieillesse que méritait son talent. Et Réveillon? Et tes habitués de la place d'Aligre? Tu vois, tu n'es pas préfète, tu n'as pas un mari galonné et emplumé, tu n'as pas de voiture ni de domestiques à ta disposition mais je t'envie!

Dieu te garde ma grande sœur chérie. Embrasse très fort Lucie et toute la sainte famille. Je t'aime.

Victoire.

Antoinette sourit et referma sa lettre. Allons, Victoire n'avait pas changé. La vie demeurait pour elle une pirouette toujours à recommencer. Et elle la recommençait pour s'étourdir et sans doute oublier qu'elle était passée à côté de la vie. Sous ses airs de franchise délurée elle avait toujours été sage. Sauf une fois, et par bonheur ce coup de folie avait donné un sens à son existence avec la naissance d'Eugène. Cette réflexion à propos de sa sœur lui fit soudain penser à sa propre destinée, ce qui n'était pas arrivé depuis longtemps. Elle avait été aimée, elle avait aimé, elle avait connu la passion et aussi l'amour sage, l'amour tendresse. Cela en n'ayant appartenu qu'à deux hommes... Elle passait sous silence son aventure d'un jour avec Alexandre Lenoir mais n'était-ce pas là un péché d'omission? N'éludait-elle pas volontairement le souvenir de cette liaison éphémère qui, elle s'en rendait bien compte, lui revenait plus souvent à l'esprit depuis la mort de Bertrand. Comme elle, Lenoir avait été d'une loyauté absolue depuis leur étreinte passionnée qui avait coïncidé avec l'arrestation de Valfroy. Aujourd'hui, Bertrand n'était plus là, hélas! Et elle savait qu'elle regardait Alexandre avec d'autres yeux bien qu'elle s'efforçât de n'y laisser rien paraître. Célibataire, Lenoir avait une vie personnelle dont il n'avait jamais parlé et qu'Antoinette n'avait pas essayé de surprendre. Et voilà que, soudain, le côté secret de son ami la tourmentait. Cela avait commencé par une curiosité amusée mais, maintenant, elle pensait aux amours d'Alexandre avec un sentiment qui ressemblait fort à de la jalousie. Voulait-elle vraiment reconquérir Lenoir? Elle s'en défendait en pleurant son bonheur perdu avec Valfroy.

Les choses en seraient peut-être restées là sans le hasard d'une conversation échangée un soir où Percier et Fontaine étaient venus partager un superbe pâté de veau de Pontoise que Lenoir avait rapporté de chez Chevet. Ce pâté doré que faisait réchauffer Antoinette et dont les effluves exquis se mêlaient au fumet d'une sauce aux truffes que Lucie avait pour mission de remuer dévotement, avait une histoire. Il était exclu qu'Antoinette et ses commensaux pussent acheter chez Chevet la plus petite terrine ou le moindre morceau de jambon. Les prix pratiqués par le célèbre traiteur de Paris n'étaient accessibles qu'aux enrichis des biens nationaux et à quelques dignitaires qui avaient su tirer de respectables revenus du feu de la Révolution.

Pour le bonheur du clan, Lenoir avait jadis rendu service à Germain Chevet alors qu'il était horticulteur à Bagnolet et qu'il fournissait en roses Marie-Antoinette. Le bonhomme avait été arrêté en 1793, relâché à cause de ses dix-sept enfants mais condamné à arracher ses rosiers dont les fleurs avaient été respirées par des aristocrates. Lenoir, à qui un ami avait présenté le malheureux fleuriste de la reine, avait aidé ce dernier à louer une échoppe au Palais-Royal où chaque mètre de trottoir était âprement convoité. C'est là, galerie Montpensier, qu'il avait commencé à faire fortune en fabriquant des petits pâtés de viande ou de volaille que ses fils et filles allaient vendre dans tout le quartier. Devenu l'un des rois de la gastronomie parisienne avec Corcellet et Labour, il gardait une vive reconnaissance au conservateur du musée des Monuments français et lui faisait porter chaque mois l'un des mets succulents dont Talleyrand, le comte d'Orsay ou Mme Tallien faisaient leur ordinaire. C'était une oie grasse, six perdrix rouges du Dauphiné, un jambon de Mayence ou un fromage de Chester... Le plus souvent cette bonne chère venue de la mémoire du cœur faisait les délices des amis de la place d'Aligre.

Percier et Fontaine n'avaient donc pas manqué ce rendez-vous où l'on partageait l'amitié en même temps qu'un souper savouveux. Ils avaient de leur côté apporté trois flacons de vin de Châteauneuf-du-Pape obtenus, eux aussi, grâce à l'une de ces astuces qui n'avaient jamais cessé de fleurir durant la Révolution.

La soirée était donc gaie. Percier laissait son ami Fontaine, qui racontait mieux que lui, décrire la mauvaise humeur de Joséphine en découvrant que la chambre bleu et blanc qui serait la sienne aux Tuileries était celle qu'avait occupée Marie-Antoinette. « Regardez, avait-elle soupiré, ce lit d'acajou et de bronze ! Il ne va pas du tout ici. Heureusement que j'ai Malmaison ! »

– Il faut bien avouer, dit Percier, que la décoration à l'antique ou « à la moderne » comme vous voudrez, fait un drôle d'effet sous les plafonds et boiseries de Louis XIV !

– C'est une faute, presque un sacrilège, souligna Riesener qui ne manquait jamais une occasion de dénigrer la mode actuelle. Il y a, ajouta-t-il, des mélanges qu'il ne faut pas faire. Si vous n'avez pas les moyens de placer vos acajous dans le cadre qui leur convient, gardez les anciens meubles !

Percier sourit et ne répondit pas. Il ne souhaitait pas entamer une discussion sur les anciens et les modernes avec le vieux maître aigri et désabusé qui prenait de plus en plus facilement la mouche lorsqu'on abordait ce sujet. Il se tourna vers Lenoir :

– Savez-vous que nous travaillons pour votre amie Élise ? Il ajouta aussitôt, moqueur : J'espère que vous aurez l'occasion de voir la chambre que nous lui préparons. Aimez-vous l'acajou ? Les Jacob fabriquent meubles, chambranles, portes, piédestaux... tout en acajou ! C'est à croire que Mlle Lange se livre à une compétition avec sa voisine Juliette Récamier !

L'allusion à Mlle Lange et à l'intimité qui la liait à Lenoir n'avait pas échappé à Antoinette. Si quelqu'un l'avait regardée à ce moment, il aurait remarqué sur son visage, à la commissure des lèvres, le léger tressaillement qui trahissait ses sentiments les plus secrets. Elle-même fut surprise de cette réaction incontrôlée, elle ferma les yeux un instant pour reprendre le contrôle d'un cœur qui s'était mis soudain à battre un peu trop vite.

Lenoir n'avait pas relevé le mot de Percier mais il ne laissa pas passer l'occasion de prendre l'architecte à son propre jeu. Avec ce sourire narquois qui avait mis tant de gens mal à l'aise lorsqu'il leur disputait une œuvre pour son musée, il renvoya la balle à son ami :

– Mon cher, laissez-moi m'étonner de vous entendre vous gausser de l'engouement des gens à la mode pour le bois d'acajou. J'ai même cru discerner dans vos propos une critique voilée de ce style monumental, j'allais dire sépulcral, qui semble devoir devenir celui de notre époque. Car ce style, cette sévérité empruntée aux Romains, c'est bien vous, avec Fontaine, qui les avez développés par vos dessins et vos créations après que David eut donné l'impulsion. L'excès de grâce vous fâchait, supportez maintenant le poids de la lourdeur !

– Voilà qui est bien parlé, monsieur Lenoir ! s'exclama Riesener.

C'est Antoinette qui, tout en mesurant l'indiscrétion de sa question, relança la conversation sur la dame de la chaussée d'Antin :

– Dites donc Percier, cette Mlle Lange dont vous parliez n'est-elle pas cette fille de musiciens ambulants qui fit naguère, alors qu'elle n'était qu'une enfant, les beaux soirs du théâtre de la Montansier et un peu plus tard ceux de la Comédie-Française ?

– Si fait, chère Antoinette. Son talent réel, sa beauté éclatante et sa... gentillesse en avaient fait à la veille de la Révolution la petite reine de Paris. Les chroniqueurs célébraient son charmant visage, sa bouche plus fraîche qu'une rose et son adorable taille.

– Ma parole, vous avez appris ces articles par cœur? coupa Antoinette en riant.

– Presque. J'étais amoureux d'elle mais n'avais aucune chance de gagner les faveurs de celle dont on écrivait aussi, bien perfidement : « Son cœur est une hostellerie... » En 1793, son train de vie ostentatoire et surtout son appartenance à la Comédie-Française la menèrent à Sainte-Pélagie. Je crois bien qu'elle s'est tirée de ce mauvais pas, comme votre mari, grâce aux agissements du bon La Bussière qui réduisit en une boule de papier mâché son acte d'accusation.

– Ah! Elle me devient sympathique, cette jeune personne malgré ses mœurs légères!

– Allons, Antoinette, murmura Lenoir en la fixant de ses yeux rieurs, vous n'allez tout de même pas devenir un parangon de vertu! Si vous commencez dans la fleur de l'âge à jouer les dames prudes, qu'est-ce que ça sera quand vous serez une vieille dévote courant après son salut! Mais puisque vous semblez vous intéresser à Mlle Lange qui est d'ailleurs aujourd'hui l'épouse d'un banquier honoré sinon honorable mais en tout cas fort habile, qui a gagné une fortune avec la fourniture générale de l'armée du Nord, je vais poursuivre le portrait qu'a esquissé Percier. J'adore les situations singulières : pendant que la jolie Elise se morfondait dans sa prison révolutionnaire, celui qui devait devenir son généreux protecteur et son époux s'enrichissait en équipant les soldats de l'an II! Sortie de Sainte-Pélagie et avant de retrouver des équipages somptueux et un lit d'acajou, Mlle Lange dut se contenter d'un séjour sans luxe mais sans danger, à deux pas d'ici, dans la fameuse maison de santé Belhomme de la rue de Charonne. C'est là qu'un premier banquier, hollandais celui-là, M. Hope, vint la chercher.

– Jolie dame en vérité, monsieur le Conservateur. Mais qu'allait-elle faire dans cette pension dont on a dit tant de choses?

– Qu'est-ce donc que cette maison Belhomme? questionna à son tour Lucie qui était maintenant admise à assister aux réunions du clan.

Antoinette pensait que sa fille, bien qu'un peu jeune, ne pouvait que profiter d'une conversation intelligente entre des grandes personnes liées par l'amitié, la culture et le souci du beau.

– Dommage, dit Riesener, que Réveillon ne soit pas là. Il a connu personnellement le Dr Belhomme et pourrait te raconter mille histoires sur ce médecin étonnant qui hébergea durant la Terreur les personnages les plus divers. Je connais tout de même beaucoup de choses sur la vie de monsieur et vais essayer de t'en faire le récit. C'est en 87 ou 88 qu'il acheta rue de Charonne, tout près du prieuré de la Madeleine-de-Traisnel, une maison qu'il transforma en une sorte de pension de famille très prospère. En 89 il devait avoir une cinquantaine de pensionnaires dont la plupart étaient fous. Peu après la prise de la Bastille, Belhomme se fit nommer capitaine de la section de Popincourt et offrit de loger dans son hôtel les suspects assez fortunés pour s'offrir une pension plus confortable que les prisons de Paris. Qualifiés de fous ou de contagieux, ces pensionnaires vivaient dans un luxe correspondant à leurs ressources. Certains avaient un salon à leur disposition et pouvaient recevoir. Ils jouissaient surtout d'un inappréciable avantage : ils ne couraient pas le risque, tant qu'ils payaient une pension très chère, 600 à 1 000 livres par mois, d'être traduits devant le Tribunal révolutionnaire. En fait, on achetait chez Belhomme l'assurance de garder sa tête sur les épaules.

– Mon père aurait donc pu y aller au lieu d'être enfermé à la Force ? demanda Lucie que l'histoire passionnait au plus haut point.

– Peut-être, dit Antoinette, mais nous n'avions pas assez d'argent.

– Mais qui allait donc chez ce docteur ?

– Des gens riches comme la duchesse d'Orléans, plusieurs membres de la famille de Talleyrand, Volney, un savant, député à la Convention et accusé de royalisme, d'autres députés moins connus, la veuve de Pétion l'ancien maire de Paris, Ramponneau le restaurateur.

– Et n'oublions pas la belle amie de M. Lenoir ! lança

Antoinette. J'espère que sa fortune lui permettait d'être bien traitée!

– Que devenaient les pensionnaires qui ne pouvaient plus payer le docteur? demanda encore Lucie qui, décidément, ne voulait rien laisser dans l'ombre.

– Eh bien, le bon docteur les renvoyait à la Conciergerie! Ils passaient alors très vite en jugement et beaucoup d'entre eux furent ainsi condamnés à la guillotine. Linguet, par exemple, un diplomate émigré qui avait commis l'imprudence de revenir à Paris en pleine Terreur. La duchesse de Choiseul qui ne parvenait plus à payer sa pension fut elle aussi envoyée à la Conciergerie et guillotinée.

– Mais c'est affreux tout cela! s'écria Lucie en éclatant en sanglots. J'espère, ajouta-t-elle en s'essuyant les yeux avec le mouchoir que lui tendait sa mère, que ce vilain monsieur qui a profité du malheur des autres a été lui aussi guillotiné?

– Pas du tout, continua Riesener. Sa pension n'étant plus assez grande pour recevoir tous les clients, il loua la maison contiguë, l'hôtel de Chabannais.

– Belhomme eut tout de même quelques ennuis, dit Lenoir. Je crois qu'il a été condamné...

– Oui, approuva Riesener. Je me rappelle très bien l'histoire. La section avait envoyé d'office à Belhomme deux détenus démunis d'argent. Le docteur qui ne plaisantait pas avec la gestion, organisa une collecte auprès des autres pensionnaires pour payer leur note. Devant le peu d'empressement des pseudo-malades déjà rançonnés, les prisonniers de la section se retrouvèrent sans feu, sur la paille, dans une pièce sans fenêtre. L'un des deux, un nommé Ducassoy, compagnon menuisier chez Brickle, rue Saint-Nicolas, fit parvenir une dénonciation à la section, accusant Belhomme d'exiger des sommes exorbitantes des gens riches et de traiter de façon inhumaine les pauvres sans-culottes. Cela fit un bruit du diable. Fouquier-Tinville que l'on croyait de connivence mais qui ne l'était sûrement pas puisqu'il mourut pauvre l'année suivante après avoir serré la main de Sanson qu'il connaissait bien, envoya un substitut enquêter rue de Charonne. Arrêté comme suspect de concussion et d'incivisme, Belhomme fut d'abord incarcéré aux « Écossais » puis dans une maison de santé de la rue Picpus semblable à la sienne avant d'être condamné à six ans de fers.

– C'est bien fait, conclut Lucie avec logique.

– Oui, mais Belhomme a été libéré il y a deux ou trois ans. Il a rouvert sa pension qui a maintenant pour directrice la jeune femme qu'il vient d'épouser. Si vous cherchez une bonne pension pour soigner vos rhumatismes ou vos écarts de raison, adressez-vous à la pension du Dr Belhomme. Elle est toujours ouverte rue de Charonne.

– C'est dégoûtant! dit encore Lucie.

– Oui et non. Cela peut se discuter, dit doucement Lenoir qui maniait avec art et délectation le paradoxe. Belhomme a tout de même été un bon révolutionnaire. Membre influent de sa section de sans-culottes, il a suppléé par son initiative au surpeuplement des prisons officielles. Peut-être a-t-il prélevé des droits de pension exagérés mais il ne prenait cet argent qu'à des individus qui n'avaient plus aucun droit à le posséder puisque ci-devant suspects ou royalistes. Là encore il palliait les déficiences du gouvernement révolutionnaire qui n'avait pas convenablement vidé les poches des ennemis de la République. Et puis, tout de même, si Belhomme n'avait pas existé, des dizaines de Français auraient été exécutés. Aujourd'hui, ils vivent librement, crient « Vive le Premier consul » et bénissent le bon docteur de la rue de Charonne. Ceux qui faute de moyens suffisants ont été guillotinés après avoir séjourné un certain temps dans la pension ont eu tout de même leur existence prolongée et ont pu vivre leurs derniers jours dans un certain confort. Je trouve que vous êtes injustes envers Belhomme. Ceux qu'il a sauvés devraient lui faire élever une statue!

Lucie manifesta son désaccord et tout le monde rit avant de s'apercevoir comme chaque semaine, qu'il était fort tard.

Lenoir qui était un noctambule fut selon son habitude le dernier à prendre congé. Il semblait de très bonne humeur, comme si les piques d'Antoinette à propos de Mlle Lange l'avaient mis en joie. Il rit une dernière fois quand Antoinette, sur le pas de la porte, lui glissa en confidence :

– L'heure me paraît bien tardive, mon pauvre Lenoir, pour rejoindre la chambre d'acajou de votre belle maîtresse. Pardonnez-moi de vous avoir retenu aussi longtemps et présentez-lui mes excuses pour le contretemps.

La porte refermée, Antoinette se regarda dans sa grande glace ovale et murmura : « Ma fille tu es en train de faire une bêtise. Tu te jettes au cou de Lenoir qui, après tout, a bien le droit de coucher avec qui il veut. Il est bien trop fin pour ne pas avoir saisi tout ce que cachaient tes propos aigres-doux. S'il fait semblant de ne pas comprendre tu vas souffrir, ma petite Antoinette. Enfin! sauf avec mon bon Valfroy, l'amour n'a jamais été pour moi une chose facile!

Paris et la France se remettaient lentement de la secousse révolutionnaire. Passé le fol entracte du Directoire durant lequel chacun s'était débarrassé, à sa manière et selon la classe sociale à laquelle il appartenait, de l'encombrant fardeau moral de la Terreur, venaient maintenant des temps plus calmes. On appréciait le ciel serein qui baignait le volcan éteint d'une révolution dont on ne pouvait oublier la violence. Le fantastique mouvement qui avait changé tant de choses en si peu de temps n'existait pratiquement plus que dans les mots, des mots qu'utilisait avec subtilité le Premier consul pour montrer qu'il tenait sa légitimité du peuple. Et puis la France, Paris et dans Paris le faubourg Saint-Antoine, ressentaient le soulagement d'être gouvernés. Comment Bonaparte qui imposait sa loi au-delà des frontières n'aurait-il pas été rassurant? Personne n'avait oublié les victoires des Pyramides et de Jaffa mais qui savait que le général Menou, successeur de Kléber assassiné, négociait avec les Anglais pour sauver en Égypte les débris de son armée?

Il se murmurait au Faubourg que Bonaparte aimait les artisans du bois et que le Mobilier national allait passer des commandes afin d'accélérer la reprise. Cela entretenait l'espoir des maîtres et des compagnons qui végétaient encore dans les cours et les passages. La nouvelle en tout cas avait ancré Ethis dans son idée que le commerce des meubles n'allait pas tarder à connaître de nouveau des beaux jours et qu'il fallait être prêt pour profiter de ce réveil. Le rachat de la boutique *Au Lion d'or* tardait malheureusement à se concrétiser. Son propriétaire avait réussi à vendre quelques pièces de sa réserve et hésitait à céder son fonds. Quant à Ethis, il continuait de chercher les capitaux qui lui manquaient encore pour faire repartir le lion sur la bonne patte.

C'est au cours d'une de ses pérégrinations autour de la place de l'ancienne Bastille qu'il rencontra dans le magasin de la veuve Héricourt que venait de reprendre son neveu Louis Menesson, un homme d'une trentaine d'années qui parlait de coton français, de basin anglais et des métiers qu'il se proposait d'installer dans ce quartier qu'il trouvait agréable et où il trouverait facilement de la main-d'œuvre. Quand Ethis lui eut dit qu'il connaissait le faubourg Saint-Antoine comme sa poche et qu'il pourrait peut-être lui être utile, il se présenta :

– Je m'appelle François Richard, je suis normand mais je vis entre Paris et Nemours où je possède une propriété. Je cherche un très grand local pour y établir une manufacture de tissu de coton. Si vous connaissez quelque chose susceptible de me convenir, vous me rendrez service. Et vous? A qui ai-je l'honneur?...

Comme chaque fois qu'il avait à prononcer le nom qui était maintenant le sien, Ethis hésita une seconde. Il avait toujours l'impression d'usurper un patronyme encore nouveau pour lui. Quant au titre de baron, pour rien au monde il ne l'aurait mis en avant. Enfin, il répondit :

– Valfroy. Mais appelez-moi Ethis, tout le monde me connaît ici sous ce nom. Il n'est pas impossible en effet que je puisse vous mettre sur la voie du local que vous souhaitez. Je cherche moi aussi à reprendre un fonds de mercier-marchand de meubles, la boutique à côté pour ne rien vous cacher. Actuellement je suis établi dans la grand-rue mais trop loin de la Bastille. Avez-vous un peu de temps? Si oui accompagnez-moi jusque chez moi. Je vous ferai découvrir en cours de route les endroits les plus secrets du quartier.

L'homme, un grand blond au teint rose, visage rasé et cheveux courts, élégant dans son habit à basques de drap fin et ses bottes à revers brillantes comme des miroirs, sourit largement :

– Ethis, c'est bien cela votre nom? Vous m'êtes sympathique. Montrez-moi votre vieux Faubourg. Il va bien falloir que je l'arpente pour y loger mes métiers! Un jour, quand nous aurons mieux fait connaissance, je vous raconterai ma vie. Vous verrez, c'est une histoire assez étonnante.

– La mienne n'est pas mal non plus. Je vous apprendrai comment un coup de mousquet chez Réveillon m'a fait baron!

– Vous m'intriguez. Allons, marchons et dites-moi d'où vient ce curieux nom d'Ethis et si vous le souhaitez ce beau patronyme de Valfroy.

Ethis aimait raconter son histoire. Non pas pour se montrer sous un jour intéressant mais parce que son récit lui permettait de parler des bienfaits dont il avait été l'objet et de rendre hommage à Antoinette et à son père adoptif. Il ne se fit donc pas prier pour se décrire tel qu'il était – enfant trouvé vêtu de vêtements donnés lorsqu'une balle abattit sur lui Antoinette qui soignait sa propre blessure dans le parc de la Folie Titon devenu en une flambée de colère le premier champ de bataille de la Révolution.

François Richard l'écoutait, intéressé par un récit où il retrouvait certains traits de sa propre existence. En regardant Ethis qui marchait à son côté et faisait de temps en temps de grands gestes pour désigner une cour où travaillait un ébéniste connu : Magnien qui s'était rendu célèbre en faisant distribuer des cartes à jouer révolutionnaires au dos desquelles il avait fait imprimer une publicité pour son magasin-atelier *Au nom de Jésus,* ou Pabst qui travaillait avec ses deux fils, Richard se revoyait dix ans plus tôt, arrivant à Paris sans argent mais avec des idées plein la tête.

– Ainsi, demanda-t-il, votre mère adoptive est la fille du grand Œben et la belle-fille de Riesener! Ces noms m'inspirent une admiration que vous ne pouvez pas imaginer. J'éprouve depuis mon enfance une sorte de fascination pour le bois. J'aurais voulu devenir ébéniste ou menuisier mais dans le petit village du Calvados où je suis né il n'y avait personne pour me prendre en apprentissage. Et puis mon père prétendait avoir besoin de moi pour exploiter une ferme pas plus grande qu'un jardin de curé. Finalement, à dix-sept ans, je me suis retrouvé garçon de magasin à Paris. Si encore j'avais vendu des meubles! Non, je mesurais des aunes de tissu à longueur de journée. C'est peut-être pour ça, remarquez, que je veux aujourd'hui monter à Paris une manufacture de tissage de coton aussi importante que celles de l'Angleterre! Vous voyez, je vous envie de vivre au milieu des gens du bois et de vendre bientôt des meubles...

– Vous avez envie de connaître des ébénistes? Cela vous plairait de rencontrer Riesener? Si vous êtes libre demain mercredi, je vous invite chez ma mère. Vous nous raconterez votre histoire et je vous dirai si j'ai déniché le local dont vous rêvez. En dehors de Riesener, de ma mère et de ma petite sœur, vous ferez la connaissance de gens intéressants qui seront sûrement passionnés par votre histoire de coton.

– J'accepte de grand cœur. A quelle adresse devrais-je me rendre?

– Venez me chercher ici sur le coup de six heures. Nous sommes arrivés chez moi, voici ma petite boutique, à l'enseigne de *L'Enfant à l'oiseau.* Venez, je vais vous présenter à ma femme. C'est la fille de Bénard, le propriétaire de la manufacture de papier peint de la rue de Montreuil. Ce n'est pas un mauvais bougre mais il est rat comme pas un. Tenez, il refuse de me prêter la petite somme qui me permettrait d'aménager le magasin que je suis en train d'acheter. Le beau-père a bien des locaux inoccupés à la Folie Titon mais vous n'y seriez pas tranquille. Je vous trouverai mieux!

Antoinette ne se montra pas tellement ravie d'avoir un invité de plus mais elle ne savait rien refuser à Ethis et celui-ci lui fit un portrait tellement flatteur de Francois Richard qu'elle finit par être contente d'accueillir un hôte nouveau.

– Ce qui m'ennuie, dit-elle, c'est que nous n'aurons pas ce soir un souper bien fameux. Pas de chapon ni de gigot mais simplement un ragoût de mouton aux haricots.

– Merveilleux, Antoinette. C'est ce que je préfère! Vous le réussissez si bien!

Antoinette était il est vrai devenue une excellente cuisinière. Sa mère Marguerite lui avait jadis appris les bonnes recettes du Paris des maraîchers, cette plaine de Reuilly et de Charonne qui s'étendait jusqu'aux confins de Montreuil et qui alimentait depuis des siècles les Parisiens en primeurs, en fruits et aussi en gibier car les lièvres et les lapins aimaient creuser leur terrier dans la terre meuble des champs de salades et des vergers. A cette cuisine de l'Ile-de-France, simple mais franche et vouée à la fraîcheur des produits cultivés sur place, Antoinette, comme sa mère, avait ajouté la vigueur des recettes que les Allemands, venus nombreux s'installer au Faubourg durant le XVIIIe siècle, avaient apportées de Franconie ou de Rhénanie. Œben et Riesener eux-mêmes aimaient bien retrouver dans leur assiette un bon morceau de *Pichelsteiner-fleisch* [1] ou un *Labskaus* [2] qui leur rappelaient la cuisine de leur mère. Il était aussi courant dans les familles du Faubourg d'ajouter au bouillon quelques

1. Échine de porc fumée servie souvent sur un lit de choucroute.
2. Viande de bœuf hachée et assaisonnée cuite dans la poêle et servie avec un œuf frit. C'est l'ancêtre du « hamburger » que les Américains feront découvrir au monde entier après l'avoir adopté.

Knödel, petites quenelles appréciées dans toute l'Allemagne.

Antoinette alla demander le mercredi matin à Marie de venir l'aider à préparer le souper.

– Ethis a invité ce soir un homme qui, paraît-il, veut s'installer au Faubourg pour y tisser du coton. Viens de bonne heure avec ton fils, tu me prêteras la main pour préparer un souper qui soit tout de même convenable. Nous verrons à trouver quelque plat un peu gourmand à ajouter à notre ragoût.

– Entendu. Vous savez, Antoinette, combien j'aime être avec vous. Si je ne viens pas plus souvent place d'Aligre, c'est parce que j'ai peur de vous déranger. J'adore faire la cuisine. Tiens, vous me montrerez comment vous préparez votre ragoût de mouton et de haricots. Je n'ai jamais rien mangé d'aussi bon! Quant au plat de relevé, je confectionnerais bien une omelette aux écrevisses, c'est un mets que je réussis très bien, mais...

– Mais tu n'as pas d'écrevisses! Comme nous n'avons pas les moyens d'aller en acheter chez Chevet, il faut qu'Ethis se débrouille. Il connaît tout le monde du côté de la Râpée et les enfants passent leur temps à pêcher des écrevisses dans les petits bras de la Seine. Et s'il n'y a pas d'écrevisses nous ferons une omelette aux herbes ou à la tomate. J'irai chercher des œufs frais chez la mère Ménars, près de Charonne. Allons, je n'avais pas très envie de faire ce souper et voilà que maintenant cela m'ennuierait s'il était supprimé. « La cuisine, disait ma mère, c'est comme l'amour : il suffit de s'y mettre! »

Ethis eut les écrevisses, Antoinette rapporta de Charonne deux kilos de beaux haricots blancs, meilleurs que les soissons de sa réserve. Quant à Marie, elle réussit le petit miracle de trouver pour un prix raisonnable cinq belles truffes grises venues se faire croquer à Paris dans la besace de Gédéon, personnage original et haut en couleur du passage de la Bonne-Graine qui faisait chaque mois le voyage à pied jusqu'en Bourgogne où il avait, disait-il, une bonne amie. Ce qui était sûr, c'est que le trimardier du Faubourg revenait chaque fois chargé de champignons, de truffes grises, de bouteilles de marc et de charcuteries délectables qu'il revendait à ses clients parisiens. Ses affaires, qui avaient prospéré pendant les périodes noires de la Révolution où Paris connaissait la disette, étaient plus difficiles maintenant que le ravitaillement était à peu près assuré. Il conservait pourtant une clientèle fidèle qui lui permettait de reprendre la route le 1er de chaque mois, une chanson aux lèvres et sa besace en bandoulière. Les deux femmes avaient décidé de s'habiller pour recevoir « l'homme du coton », comme elles l'appelaient. Sans posséder des armoires pleines de robes, de châles, de turbans, de mantelets et de spencers comme Mme Récamier, Mme Salvage ou Mme Tallien, Antoinette et Marie avaient une ou deux toilettes élégantes, coupées dans de fins tissus, qu'elles n'avaient pas souvent l'occasion de porter.

– Créons cette occasion ! avait dit Antoinette. Puisque nous avons un invité, faisons-lui honneur en nous faisant plaisir. Dis à Ethis de mettre sa redingote de velours vert, elle lui va bien ; moi je préviendrai Riesener. Quant aux autres, nous n'avons pas de souci à nous faire, Lenoir, coquet, a toujours la taille serrée dans son habit à basques pour faire croire qu'il est encore plus mince. Percier et Fontaine, eux sont toujours vêtus comme s'ils sortaient de chez le Premier consul. Le plus fort, c'est que c'est vrai, ils viennent souvent des Tuileries ou de Malmaison quand ils arrivent ici dans notre petit logement d'artisans.

– Logement d'artisans peut-être, mais c'est celui d'Œben et de Riesener ! Et puis, sûrement qu'on doit s'y trouver mieux que dans les grands salons dorés puisque vos amis ne manqueraient pour rien au monde l'un de vos soupers-causette !

– Tu as raison ma petite Marie. Le vent du Faubourg fait frissonner nos petites réunions et aide les pensées à s'envoler. Fêtons donc ce privilège. Dans le fond, cela m'amuse toujours d'étudier le comportement d'un nouveau venu, soudain isolé dans le clan comme un agneau au milieu des tigres. Ou il comprend tout de suite qui nous sommes, ce qu'est pour nous le bonheur et il a envie de revenir. Ou il n'assimile pas notre esprit et nous prend pour des originaux qu'il convient de fuir. Tiens, dix minutes après l'arrivée du cotonnier, je te ferai un signe, oui ou non, de la tête. Je saurai déjà si nous avons des chances de le revoir.

En fin de journée, il faisait déjà nuit quand Ethis arriva avec son nouvel ami. L'escalier était sombre mais une fois la porte poussée, l'appartement d'Antoinette apparaissait comme un rêve de lumière. Marie avait disposé des bougeoirs un peu partout et la flamme vacillante des chandelles faisait reluire de feux irréels la marqueterie des meubles et l'or de leurs bronzes. La table, agrandie par un grand plateau rond, avait été mise sous les portraits de Jean-François et de Marguerite Œben, entre une superbe commode blonde de Riesener qui n'avait jamais été livrée au Trianon et un chiffonnier qu'Œben avait construit jadis pour sa femme aux premiers temps de leur mariage. Ce décor royal, aussi splendide qu'inattendu dans ce lieu, surprit François Richard qui s'exclama avant même d'avoir salué Antoinette : « Dieu que c'est beau ! » Il se reprit bien vite et s'inclina :

– Pardonnez-moi, madame, je ne m'attendais pas à trouver un palais au cœur du Faubourg. Je vous remercie de me donner le plaisir d'être votre hôte ce soir. Je ne pouvais pas rêver une meilleure introduction dans votre quartier où je vais je pense m'installer bientôt.

– Pas mal, pensa Antoinette en répondant d'un sourire. Voilà un coton qui a la tenue de la soie.

Elle était belle dans sa robe-tunique de mousseline blanche dont la taille haute mettait en valeur des seins dont personne n'aurait pu croire qu'ils étaient ceux d'une femme de quarante-cinq ans. Un schall [1] rouge-orange couvrait ses épaules nues et elle avait enfermé ses cheveux comme le prescrivait *Le Costume des Dames parisiennes,* la dernière revue de mode vendue à Paris, dans un turban en casque qui laissait deviner quelques fils gris dans les mèches blondes.

1. Venu de l'Inde et de l'Angleterre, le châle s'écrivait alors ainsi.

Antoinette se laissa admirer quelques secondes pour jouir du plaisir de se sentir encore belle et désirable puis elle se tourna vers Marie :

– Je crois que vous vous connaissez déjà.

Richard, très à l'aise, dit avec peut-être un peu trop de manières qu'il avait ce plaisir. Il admira les meubles sans dire de sottises sur leur ligne et leur décor. C'était un bon point car Antoinette supportait mal qu'un béotien se permette de porter des jugements irréfléchis sur les œuvres des gens du bois. Enfin Riesener arriva et le vieux maître reçut avec une jubilation évidente les compliments d'un invité jugé d'emblée sympathique puisqu'il n'hésitait pas à affirmer que les meubles à l'antique n'étaient qu'objets sans intérêt à côté des purs chefs-d'œuvre qu'il avait le grand honneur d'admirer.

Lenoir fit peu après son entrée, regarda de son œil d'aigle le nouveau venu et s'enquit poliment de ses activités.

– Je tisse le coton, monsieur. Grâce à Ethis, je vais je crois m'installer bientôt tout près d'ici.

– Tu as déjà trouvé un local pour M. Richard? questionna Antoinette.

– Je l'espère. L'ancien couvent de Notre-Dame-du-Bon-Secours, rue de Charonne, qui avait été adjugé en même temps que l'abbatiale et une partie de l'abbaye, est à vendre. M. Richard ira voir demain si cette grande maison lui convient.

On en resta là pour l'instant. Marie qui avait noué un tablier sur sa jolie robe fourreau-caraco au vert attendri, apportait un plat où mijotait encore, dans sa croûte dorée, une omelette dont le fumet ne pouvait laisser aucune narine civilisée insensible.

– C'est un quartier de lune surprise! dit Lucie. Devinez ce qu'il y a dedans avant le partage. Moi, je ne joue pas car je sais. Allons... Dites ce que Marie a mélangé aux œufs, tout à l'heure, dans la terrine!

– Des foies de volailles, dit Lenoir.

– Non, il n'y en a pas un seul, annonça Lucie.

– Des champignons, lança Percier qui se flattait d'être un parfait gourmet.

– Il a failli y en avoir mais finalement on a trouvé quelque chose de meilleur.

– Humez! humez! précisa Marie. On ne sent que cela. Vraiment, vous n'avez pas de nez. Je me demande pourquoi on se donne tant de mal, messieurs, à cuisiner pour vous.

– Je crois que j'ai trouvé, dit à son tour Richard d'une voix qu'il essayait de rendre timide. J'ai reconnu un certain parfum. Mais il y a autre chose que je n'arrive pas à découvrir, quelque chose dont l'odeur est masquée par celle de la truffe.

– Vous avez gagné pour les truffes. Ce sont des truffes vertes. Et le reste?

Tout ou presque tout ce qui peut être fourré dans une omelette fut cité, des fines herbes aux crêtes de coqs en passant par les fonds d'artichauts, le poivron doux et les filets d'anchois. Personne ne pensa aux queues d'écrevisses et un grand cri s'éleva quand Antoinette coupa l'omelette en deux : on entendit alors des « J'ai failli le dire », « J'avais reconnu l'odeur! », « Je savais que c'était ça! »...

Marie fut complimentée comme elle le méritait. Chaque bouchée était commentée et donnait lieu à discussion. Ces gens qui vivaient au milieu d'œuvres d'art ou qui en fabriquaient considéraient qu'un plat réussi, pour être éphémère, n'en était pas moins digne d'éloge, au même titre qu'un beau meuble ou qu'un tableau.

– Quel est votre secret, Marie, pour obtenir un mélange aussi onctueux où les saveurs se marient si bien? M. David, s'il était là, vous ferait un joli discours où il comparerait la sapidité de la truffe aux lumières que laisse filtrer un vert de Véronèse. Je dirai pour ma part, puisque ma fortune vient du talent des Romains, qu'Appicius eût apprécié cette omelette mollette où les écrevisses se prélassent en attendant d'être croquées!

C'est Fontaine qui venait de parler. Il fut applaudi et François Richard qui avait choisi de jouer les violettes dans cette assemblée où il se sentait un peu dépaysé s'exclama :

– Que cela est bien dit ! Je fais bien modeste figure, moi le cotonnier, dans un milieu aussi brillant !

– Eh bien, monsieur le Cotonnier, dit Antoinette qui ne laissa pas passer l'occasion de faire valoir son invité, parlez-nous justement de ce coton que vous comptez anoblir au point d'en faire des robes élégantes et même, pourquoi pas, de l'utiliser dans la décoration et le garnissage des sièges ! Jusqu'à maintenant, seuls les Anglais savaient faire de belles étoffes avec ces mousses venues d'Égypte et de Libye. Il y a bien quelques métiers installés rue de la Roquette et du côté de Picpus mais il s'agit de productions artisanales sans importance. Dites-nous donc ce que vous allez faire ?

– Des pièces et des pièces de tissu. Comme les Anglais ! Mais il faudrait que je vous raconte ma vie et je crains de vous ennuyer.

Chacun se récria, sans souci de politesse d'ailleurs car l'homme était intéressant. On était curieux de savoir ce qu'avait derrière la tête ce jeune élégant fraîchement débarqué au Faubourg.

– Fils de fermiers normands peu fortunés, j'ai commencé ma carrière à Rouen où je comptais bien trouver le moyen de gagner ma vie autrement qu'en cultivant une pauvre pièce de terre trop petite pour subvenir aux besoins de la famille. A dix-sept ans j'étais garçon de magasin et, à vingt et un, serveur de café à Paris dans un grand établissement de la rue Saint-Denis. Une place rêvée pour écouter les conversations des gens d'affaires qui fréquentaient le café et me frotter à eux avec l'espoir de pouvoir un jour les imiter. L'idée de spéculer ne me quittait guère. Je pensais savoir comment faire fructifier un argent qu'hélas je n'avais pas. Pour posséder cette mise de fonds, je n'avais qu'un moyen : économiser. C'est ce que je fis, rassemblant ainsi un millier de francs, somme qui me permit de spéculer sur les basins anglais, alors marchandises de contrebande [1]. Cette opération réussit au-delà de toute espérance et je réalisai une petite

1. Étoffe dont la chaîne est de fil et la trame de coton.

fortune que je perdis en un jour sur la foi d'un renseignement mensonger. A la Force où je me retrouvai enfermé pour dettes, j'eus tout loisir de réfléchir aux risques des affaires et aux pièges qui guettent les néophytes. Je parvins à m'évader à la faveur du sac de la manufacture Réveillon, en 89, et pus reprendre mon négoce de basin et d'étoffe de coton à un moment où ces matières de première nécessité manquaient chez les fournisseurs de l'armée comme chez tous les citoyens. En moins d'un an je refis une partie de ma fortune et, plutôt que d'amasser des assignats, achetai en 92 un domaine à Fay, près de Nemours.

– Et vous avez réussi à passer à travers tous les périls de la Révolution? demanda Lenoir que le récit de Richard semblait passionner.

– Heureusement, la fougue de la jeunesse était passée et j'eus la sagesse de me réfugier à temps en Normandie. Je ne suis rentré à Paris qu'après la chute de Robespierre. Quelques métiers à tisser installés dans les dépendances d'une guinguette de la rue Bellefonds, près de Montmartre, puis à l'hôtel Thorigny au Marais m'ont permis de vivre convenablement et de développer mes affaires après avoir eu la chance de rencontrer un négociant aussi habile que franc en amitié, Lenoir-Dufresne, qui est devenu mon associé.

– Lenoir? questionna Marie, n'est-ce pas un parent de notre ami Alexandre?

– Un lointain cousin peut-être, dit Alexandre qui ne se connaissait pas de parent filateur. C'est donc avec ce M. Lenoir que vous allez vous installer rue de Charonne?

– Oui. Nos deux noms sont maintenant liés. C'est la marque « Richard-Lenoir » que nous inscrirons au-dessus du portail des sœurs de Notre-Dame-du-Bon-Secours si nous achetons leur ancienne maison.

– Et combien de métiers comptez-vous installer rue de Charonne? demanda Ethis qui était soulagé de voir son invité accueilli avec autant d'intérêt par le clan.

– On ne compte pas par métier mais par broche. Nous

aurons je pense au moins douze mille broches, je ne sais pas encore combien de mule-jennys...

– Qu'est-ce que c'est qu'une mule-jenny? demanda Antoinette.

– Un métier renvideur mécanique. Je ne peux pas vous expliquer, il faudra que vous veniez visiter la manufacture lorsqu'elle sera installée.

– Et tout ça fonctionnera comment? A la main?

– En partie hélas! Mais nous aurons un manège de chevaux pour entraîner les broches. Les projets ne manquent pas. C'est l'argent qui fera défaut pour créer une industrie de filature digne de la France. Les Anglais ont sur ce point une avance considérable sur nous. Enfin, peut-être serons-nous aidés par le gouvernement. Il paraît que le Premier consul attache beaucoup d'importance à la création de nouvelles manufactures.

– Le Premier consul attache de l'importance à un tas de choses, coupa Riesener, il a promis de s'intéresser au sort des gens du bois mais on ne voit rien venir.

– Je ne vous ai pas dit l'essentiel, continua Richard. Si nous nous lançons dans une pareille aventure, c'est parce que nous avons découvert Lenoir et moi un secret qui permet des développements considérables.

– Un secret? lança Lucie subitement émoustillée.

– Oui, le secret de la fabrication du basin anglais. Un voyage discret à Manchester nous a permis de trouver ce que je cherchais depuis que j'ai commencé à vendre cette fameuse étoffe venue d'Angleterre. Je me suis toujours dit qu'il n'y avait aucune raison de ne pas la fabriquer nous-mêmes. Maintenant je sais comment il faut modifier les broches. L'une des premières choses que nous ferons rue de Charonne sera d'installer un atelier de mécanique!

– Votre histoire de secret m'en rappelle une autre, dit Antoinette. Ma mère m'a souvent conté l'aventure d'une certaine Rosine Habermann dont elle était la descendante, qui était partie avec son mari et deux autres jeunes Strasbourgeois à Venise pour voler le secret bien gardé des verriers de Murano qui seuls savaient fabriquer des miroirs. C'était au temps du roi Louis XIV qui entendait voir la France produire ses propres glaces. Les jeunes gens ont réussi et le mari de Rosine est devenu le directeur de la Manufacture royale de glaces, celle qui existe encore rue de Reuilly, en plein Faubourg. Françoise-Marguerite, ma mère, était l'arrière-petite-fille de cette Rosine, une femme exceptionnelle paraît-il, amie des artistes de son temps, du grand Boulle et de Ninon de Lenclos [1]!

– Vous tenez beaucoup d'elle, dit Lenoir. Vous êtes aussi, chère Antoinette, une femme exceptionnelle! Plus tard vos petits-enfants raconteront les épisodes de votre existence, celle d'une vraie « dame du Faubourg »!

Sensible au compliment d'autant plus qu'il venait d'Alexandre, Antoinette rougit un peu, s'en rendit compte et, au lieu de cacher son trouble, le fit remarquer en riant avec la franchise qui était l'une des marques profondes de sa personnalité.

– Voilà que vous me faites rougir comme une petite fille! Réservez donc vos flatteries, monsieur Lenoir, à vos jeunes et belles amies, à Mlle Lange par exemple! Rougir à mon âge! Vous vous rendez compte!

– Mlle de Lenclos, à qui vous faisiez allusion tout à l'heure, avait presque le double de cet âge quand tous les beaux esprits et les séducteurs de Paris venaient dans sa ruelle lui faire une cour pressante.

C'était Percier qui venait de parler. Il fit un clin d'œil complice à Lenoir et poursuivit :

– Ne vous étonnez donc pas si notre ami Alexandre, homme d'esprit et séducteur impénitent, vous couvre de louanges. Le fait est que si vous n'existiez pas notre vie à tous serait bien différente. Comme nous nous ennuierions toute la semaine si nous ne pouvions penser au souper du mercredi!

– C'est vrai Antoinette, appuya Marie, vous êtes merveilleuse et je voudrais vous ressembler!

– Personne n'a plus de compliments à me faire? dit Antoinette en éclatant de rire. Alors rendez je vous prie la

1. Voir *Les Dames du Faubourg.*

parole à notre hôte. M. Richard n'a pas fini de nous parler de ses projets.

– Oh! Je n'ai plus grand-chose à vous raconter! Attendez que je devienne votre voisin. J'aimerais tout de même vous présenter mon associé Lenoir-Dufresne. C'est un homme agréable et intéressant. Voulez-vous tous venir souper un soir avec lui? Nous pourrions ainsi fêter mon entrée au Faubourg.

Personne n'était contre un projet aussi agréable. On se sépara dans la bonne humeur, non sans avoir un long moment débattu sur le pas de la porte, après avoir laissé partir l'invité, de ses qualités, de ses défauts éventuels. Il ressortit de cet examen que François Richard était quelqu'un de fréquentable, sans être pour autant admis aussi promptement membre à part entière du clan.

Chapitre 8.

LE SOUPER CHEZ *VÉRY*

La vie au Faubourg retrouvait un rythme à peu près normal. Il y avait toujours des pauvres mais les ateliers rouvraient les uns après les autres, le plus souvent repris par les fils des vieux maîtres de l'autre siècle. Les jeunes dont l'adolescence avait été tellement perturbée par la crise révolutionnaire étaient dépolitisés. Ils ne songeaient qu'à vivre le mieux possible et à reconstruire la communauté du Faubourg dont ils n'avaient connu que la misère mais dont les anciens leur parlaient avec nostalgie. Beaucoup d'entre eux épousaient les filles d'autres familles d'ébénistes et de ces mariages naissaient des réunions d'ateliers, légalisées dans la profession par l'accolage des deux noms sur un poinçon d'acier, comme le symbole du renouveau et de l'espoir.

Antoinette suivait ce réveil avec l'attention et la vigilance d'une mère. Le Faubourg était son royaume, elle le parcourait sans cesse, accompagnée le plus souvent par Lucie qui commençait elle aussi à s'y reconnaître dans le labyrinthe des cours et des passages où elle notait le nombre et la hauteur des piles de planches qui depuis des siècles constituaient l'indiscutable thermomètre de la santé du quartier. C'est ainsi que la mère et la fille s'aperçurent un jour qu'au numéro 150 de la grand-rue, les volets de bois qui obstruaient l'atelier de Jean-Marie Petit depuis des années avaient été enlevés et qu'une grande animation régnait derrière les vitres qu'une vieille femme s'efforçait de nettoyer. La famille Petit était l'une des plus connues du Faubourg. Alliée aux Schlichtig-Weber, originaires de Bavière, elle avait constitué jusqu'aux premières années de la Révolution un modèle de réussite. Sans jamais atteindre la renommée des grands maîtres, Petit et ses deux beaux-frères avaient fourni le Mobilier de la couronne et, surtout, les marchands en meubles courants de bonne qualité. Après 89, il avait été l'un des premiers à incruster ses chiffonniers et ses commodes de motifs révolutionnaires. C'était une bonne idée qui lui avait permis de survivre deux ans. Et puis, comme la plupart des ébénistes du Faubourg, il avait dû fermer et vivre sur le capital qu'il avait eu la sagesse de se constituer.

Antoinette, curieuse, poussa la porte et un grand gaillard d'une trentaine d'années aux traits rieurs et à la peau brunie par un soleil qui ne pouvait être celui qui éclairait la fontaine Trogneux toute proche, lui tomba dans les bras.

– Antoinette! Quel bonheur de vous revoir!

– Jean-Nicolas! Te voilà revenu?

– Eh oui! Et vivant! Et entier! C'est un miracle! J'ai eu la sagesse de ne pas continuer à tenter le sort. J'ai profité d'une blessure, aujourd'hui guérie, pour quitter l'armée. Capitaine des volontaires de la Bastille, sergent puis lieutenant au régiment d'Alsace, enfermé, je n'ai jamais su pourquoi, à la maison Mahey puis à Picpus sous la Terreur, sauvé par le 9-Thermidor, j'ai fait partie de la première armée d'Italie sous les ordres de Bonaparte. Je pense que c'est assez d'aventures pour un seul homme! Et puis, j'avais envie de retrouver le Faubourg et les parents.

– Et de reprendre tes outils! J'ai toujours entendu Riesener dire que tu étais un menuisier de sièges très habile. Tu reprends l'atelier de ton père? Je l'ai rencontré l'autre jour, il a l'air fatigué.

– Il ne va pas bien et ne pourra sûrement plus beaucoup travailler. J'espère qu'il pourra tout de même me donner un coup de main quand j'aurai trop de commandes!

Il éclata d'un grand rire.

– Pour l'instant je n'en ai pas une seule mais je pars courageusement à l'attaque! D'ailleurs, pour me donner du cœur à l'ouvrage, j'épouse samedi prochain Angélique Lambert, la fille du tapissier de la rue de Reuilly. Vous vous rendez compte, Antoinette, elle m'a attendu pendant tout ce temps où j'essayais de passer entre les boulets! C'est tout de même de l'amour ça!

– Je pense bien! Épouse, tu ne retrouveras jamais une autre femme aussi folle! Maintenant, si tu veux travailler, je te conseille d'aller voir les Jacob. Ton père connaît bien Georges, et leur atelier devenu une vraie manufacture ne suffit pas à fournir les clients. Il font souvent travailler les gens du Faubourg, surtout pour les sièges qui constituent l'essentiel de leur activité.

– J'y avais pensé.. Et que devient Ethis, notre petit «Traîne-sabot» de la Bastille? Toujours aussi fou et enthousiaste?

– Rangé, mon cher. Marié à une fille riche qui ne lui a pas apporté un sou de dot, et père d'un adorable garçon qui s'appelle Bertrand. Bertrand de Valfroy...

– Mais c'est votre nom, enfin celui de votre mari!

– Oui. Avant de mourir mon pauvre Bertrand a adopté Ethis qui lui avait sauvé la vie. Me voilà donc grand-mère. J'espère d'ailleurs que bientôt Ethis pourra t'acheter des meubles : il vient de louer une boutique près de la Bastille et va s'établir marchand-mercier. Il a déjà un petit magasin dans l'ancienne maison Thirion et se débrouille très bien. Mon avis c'est qu'il va faire un homme d'affaires redoutable!

– Eh bien, en voilà des nouvelles! Dites à Ethis que je voudrais bien le revoir. Quand je pense que nous avons pris la Bastille ensemble!

Encore une fois, il rit bruyamment et continua :

– Une bonne plaisanterie cette prise de la Bastille. Il faut avoir vécu une vraie bataille pour savoir ce qu'est le vrai danger!

Le soir, à son habitude, Ethis arriva en coup de vent place d'Aligre. Il embrassa Antoinette et Lucie avant d'annoncer triomphant :

– Ça y est, Richard achète Notre-Dame-du-Bon-Secours et lorgne même la Madeleine-de-Traisnell ! Et ce n'est pas tout. Pour me remercier, il m'avance l'argent destiné à l'aménagement du magasin et aux premiers achats ! Il m'a dit qu'il me faisait confiance, qu'il se retrouvait tout à fait en moi à ses débuts ! Ça, Antoinette, c'est à vous que je le dois, je ne l'oublierai jamais !

– C'est bien de le penser et de le dire, mais ta réussite tu ne la devras jamais qu'à toi et à toi seul. C'est ton courage, ta persévérance...

– Peut-être, mais avant cela il y a vous et M. de Valfroy qui m'avez sorti de la rue et m'avez fabriqué.

Était-ce la certitude d'avoir réussi à accomplir la première partie de son rêve, était-ce un trop-plein d'amour et de reconnaissance... Ethis se mit soudain à sangloter et se jeta dans les bras d'Antoinette, bien près, elle aussi, de succomber à l'émotion.

Seule Lucie gardait sa sérénité. Tout au plus était-elle étonnée.

– Pourquoi pleures-tu Ethis? Tu devrais au contraire être joyeux !

– Il arrive ma chérie qu'on pleure de bonheur. Je souhaite que tu connaisses souvent ces larmes-là !

Antoinette ne pleura pas de bonheur mais elle ressentit un délicieux picotement quand un peu plus tard Alexandre Lenoir fit une entrée inattendue. Depuis qu'Ethis ne travaillait plus pour lui, ses visites étaient rares en dehors des soupers du mercredi. La surprise d'Antoinette ne fut donc pas feinte.

– Que se passe-t-il, Alexandre? Vous vous êtes trompé de jour?

– Non, madame, je viens tout simplement vous chercher pour vous emmener souper. Allez donc mettre votre jolie robe, celle que vous portiez l'autre soir pour recevoir l'homme du coton, poudrez-vous et emprisonnez vos beaux cheveux dans un chou de dentelles. Ce n'est pas que je trouve cela très seyant mais il paraît que c'est la mode.

– Mais vous êtes devenu fou! Vous arrivez comme cela, sans prévenir et vous voulez m'emmener tout de go souper je ne sais où. Je n'ai plus l'âge de ces fantaisies! Un autre jour si vous voulez mais ce soir je suis fatiguée, nous avons traîné tout l'après-midi avec Lucie dans le Faubourg...

– Ah non! c'est ce soir ou jamais, venez, je vous enlève!

Lucie faillit bien à ce moment recevoir la plus belle gifle de sa vie. Elle n'était heureusement pas à portée de main lorsqu'elle lança d'un ton condescendant et apitoyé qui déplut à sa mère :

– Mais dis donc oui, maman! Tu en meurs d'envie...

Voyant poindre la colère d'Antoinette, Alexandre sourit et lui prit la main :

– N'en veuillez pas à Lucie. Elle n'a été insolente – et si peu! – que parce qu'elle vous aime. Elle veut que vous soyez contente. Alors c'est oui? Je descends prévenir que je garde la voiture.

– Et si je disais non?

– Je penserais que vous êtes un peu sotte de nous priver d'une agréable soirée. Depuis trop longtemps nous nous voyons à peine, presque toujours dans l'animation de conversations où chacun essaie de briller. Eh bien, je m'aperçois que j'ai beaucoup de choses à vous dire. Et vous?

– Monsieur Lenoir, votre fatuité m'agace. Il faut croire que je vous aime bien pour accepter vos fantaisies. Maintenant, si vous voulez m'emmener souper, laissez-moi me préparer. Intéressez-vous donc à Lucie, votre complice, qui a découvert au fond d'une armoire toute une liasse de dessins et de projets de son grand-père Œben. Elle trouve cela passionnant et va sûrement avoir mille questions à vous poser. Elle a trouvé les plans et les descriptifs du fameux bureau du roi. Avant d'interroger Riesener, elle veut savoir la part qui revient à ce dernier dans l'achèvement du meuble. Je crois que Lucie est prise par le doux démon du bois. Elle adore aller d'un atelier à l'autre, parler aux ébénistes qui pour elle sont des sortes de dieux, mettre son nez au-dessus de la sorbonne [1] pour respirer l'odeur de la colle. Si elle était un garçon, je crois qu'on aurait vite un homme du bois en plus dans la famille.

Antoinette s'enferma dans sa chambre et tourna un peu la grande glace ovale et où elle s'était si souvent regardée petite fille, puis adolescente et femme, afin de l'éclairer par un rayon de soleil qui traversait le feuillage des marronniers de la place. Elle approcha son visage, mit les deux paumes de ses mains sur ses joues et les tira doucement en arrière pour effacer les quelques rides qui commençaient à se frayer un passage aux commissures des lèvres. Ce geste machinal commun à toutes les femmes la rassura plutôt.

– Ainsi, se prit-elle à murmurer tout bas, me voici appréciée. Alexandre me prie à souper comme il l'aurait fait il y a cinq ans. Rien ne l'y forçait, c'est donc qu'il avait envie de me voir, de me sortir, de se montrer avec moi dans un endroit où il connaît du monde. Serais-je donc encore désirable? Je sais qu'il m'a aimée mais je croyais bien que j'étais depuis longtemps remplacée dans son cœur. Serait-il fâché avec cette Mlle Lange qu'il semblait si bien connaître?

Elle sourit en songeant que vingt-cinq ans auparavant, dans cette même chambre où le soleil pénétrait plus généreusement car les arbres étaient moins hauts, elle se préparait en se posant mille questions pour sortir avec Pilâtre de Rozier. L'avait-elle aimé celui-là avec ses fureurs de casse-cou et ses tendresses d'enfant gâté par la gloire! Quand elle pensait à lui, après avoir goûté un moment la douceur du souvenir, une vision d'épouvante la faisait tressaillir : elle revoyait le ballon d'argent suivre docilement le vent d'est vers l'Angleterre et puis, soudain, s'enflammer et tomber comme un brandon sur la plage,

1. Poêle rond, en fonte, nourri des tombées de bois de l'atelier et sur lequel chauffe en permanence un pot de colle.

derrière une dune... C'était chaque fois la même chose. Elle prenait alors dans sa main la petite médaille d'or qui pendait à son cou pour l'embrasser, cette médaille qu'elle lui avait offerte et qu'il portait le jour de son accident.

– Allons, Antoinette! Pas d'attendrissement exagéré. Tu n'es pas si vieille puisqu'on t'invite, tu es même encore assez belle. Alors profite du bonheur que te réserve peut-être ce soir d'été. Et ne te pose pas la question stupide de savoir si tu aimes Alexandre. Lucie a raison : si tu ne l'aimais pas tu ne serais pas en train de te parfumer comme une demoiselle le soir de son premier bal!

Elle avait remis sa tunique de mousseline dont Lenoir avait remarqué l'élégance l'autre soir mais, pour ne pas donner l'impression de porter toujours la même robe, Antoinette l'avait assortie d'un autre schall, celui venu du Cachemire, dont jadis Pilâtre lui avait fait cadeau. Elle avait hésité pour se coiffer entre un chapeau de dentelle dont s'était moqué Alexandre et une résille de fleurs qui laissait à ses cheveux une liberté de saison. Finalement elle avait choisi de libérer ses mèches blondes : « L'air guindé ne m'a jamais été, je ne vois pas pourquoi je changerais aujourd'hui. »

Alexandre avait été patient. Il avait laissé Antoinette prendre son temps, d'autant plus facilement que Lucie l'avait follement amusé par ses remarques sérieuses et ses questions pertinentes. Il avait fini par lui promettre de venir la chercher un jour elle aussi, de l'emmener déjeuner chez Frascati et lui faire visiter ensuite son musée. « Je te montrerai, avait-il dit, ma plus belle statue : la *Diane au cerf*, symbole des chasses royales, sauvée de la destruction au château d'Anet et que je viens de récupérer. Je pense sincèrement que cette œuvre sublime est de la main de Jean Goujon mais tout le monde n'est pas de cet avis. Les uns penchent pour Benvenuto Cellini, d'autres pour Germain Pilon. Mais cela n'a pas d'importance : ce qui compte, c'est d'avoir réussi à conserver la statue. » Lenoir avait dû expliquer qui étaient Goujon, Cellini et Pilon, et le temps avait passé aussi vite pour lui que pour Antoinette dont l'entrée fut saluée par les bravos de Lucie qui eut le bon goût de trouver sa mère très belle.

Dehors, il faisait doux. Les gens bavardaient sur le pas des portes et les enfants jouaient en se cachant derrière les arbres. Les voitures de Lenoir avaient toujours été si discrètes, sinon déglinguées, que jamais elles n'avaient suscité l'envie ou les remarques désagréables des habitants du quartier. Antoinette il est vrai était aimée, connue de tous par sa gentillesse et sa serviabilité. On savait qu'elle n'avait jamais été riche et l'on était plutôt fier de la voir recevoir au Faubourg des gens connus ou d'une situation sociale élevée. On admira donc sa toilette sans arrière-pensée quand elle sortit au bras d'Alexandre, et les enfants vinrent lui ouvrir la portière pour monter dans la voiture. La dernière acquisition du conservateur était un cabriolet qui avait dû déjà beaucoup rouler mais, comme son propriétaire n'y transportait plus de pierres, il était propre. Antoinette put s'asseoir sur un coussin taillé dans le reste dépareillé d'une tapisserie de Bruxelles qui avait dû être superbe. Ce luxe inattendu surprenait dans la cabine aux capitons râpés et aux serrures rouillées :

– J'ai fait des frais pour vous, dit Lenoir en souriant. Ce n'est pas encore un carrosse de ministre mais c'est mieux que la vieille guimbarde qui ramenait Ethis. Georges, nous allons chez *Véry*.

Le cocher fit claquer son fouet et la voiture démarra en projetant Antoinette contre Lenoir. Elle rit, et s'exclama : « Vous l'avez fait exprès ! » Mais elle ne retira pas la main qu'avait saisie son compagnon en profitant de la secousse.

– Je vous ai entendu dire que vous m'emmeniez chez *Véry* ? Vous êtes fou ! Vous allez vous ruiner !

– Mes moyens ne me permettent pas en effet de prendre pension dans cette estimable maison mais aujourd'hui n'est pas un jour comme les autres. Et puis, me ruiner pour vous, Antoinette, serait un délice sans nom.

– Cessez de dire des sottises. Vous m'avez surprise

avec votre enlèvement mais vous savez bien que les femmes qu'on enlève sont toujours consentantes. Cela me fait plaisir de vous retrouver. N'oubliez tout de même pas que c'est vous qui m'avez délaissée!

– Par discrétion. Vous ne m'imaginiez pas pendu à votre porte après la mort de Valfroy.

– Bertrand est mort depuis déjà longtemps et vous vous êtes facilement contenté de ne me voir qu'à nos soupers du mercredi! Enfin! je ne vais pas d'emblée vous accabler de reproches. Nous avons une soirée devant nous, autant dire l'éternité, essayons d'en profiter pour refaire connaissance.

Véry et son frère, deux Lorrains solides et entreprenants, avaient ouvert l'année d'avant un nouveau restaurant en bordure des Tuileries, sur la terrasse des Feuillants où se trouvait déjà une autre maison renommée tenue par un certain Legacque qui avait connu le succès grâce à un groupe de fins mangeurs, l'illustre « Société des mercredis » qui y tenait ses assises hebdomadaires sous la présidence de Balthazar de Grimod de La Reynière. Curieux personnage, cet écrivain gourmet et extravagant qui avait survécu à la guillotine et aux privations de la Révolution! Sa fortune lui avait permis jusque-là de satisfaire ses fantaisies les plus étonnantes, celle par exemple d'avoir chez lui, pour commensal favori, un cochon apprivoisé, astiqué et parfumé qui le suivait partout comme un caniche.

Les frères Véry avaient visé haut en prétendant offrir aux Parisiens le restaurant le plus luxueux et le meilleur de la capitale. Il était aussi le plus cher et surtout fréquenté, comme *Les Trois Frères* ou *Beauvilliers*, par les nouveaux riches du Consulat qui n'étaient autres que les anciens trafiquants des biens nationaux et les fournisseurs des armées.

Installés depuis dix ans sous les voûtes de bois du Palais-Royal, les Véry avaient abandonné les arcades pour bâtir aux Tuileries un établissement qui éclipsait tous les concurrents par le faste de ses marbres, le vernis de ses acajous et le nombre de ses miroirs. L'antique était à la mode, ils firent souper leurs clients dans des suites de salles décorées à la façon de Pompéi, dont les glaces multipliaient à l'infini la taille et le nombre.

Véry en personne vint accueillir Antoinette et Alexandre.

– Monsieur Lenoir, votre table est retenue dans le petit salon. J'ai pensé que vous y seriez plus tranquille. Installez-vous, je viendrai moi-même prendre votre commande.

Imperturbable, Lenoir gardait le petit sourire moqueur qui agaçait parfois Antoinette et guidait celle-ci à travers les tables occupées jusqu'à celle qui leur était réservée et sur laquelle une bouteille de vin de Champagne rafraîchissait déjà dans un seau d'argent.

Elle était médusée par l'accueil fait à Lenoir, incapable de comprendre comment celui-ci, dont elle connaissait les ressources, pouvait être l'habitué d'une maison aussi luxueuse. Elle s'assit sans rien dire puis, n'y tenant plus, demanda d'un air qu'elle ne voulait sûrement pas aussi agressif :

– Avez-vous fait soudain une fortune inavouable? Trafiquez-vous sur les équipements de guerre pour pouvoir faire de cet endroit votre salle à manger habituelle? Si c'est cela, j'aime mieux m'en aller tout de suite!

Cette fois, Alexandre éclata de rire :

– Mais non, je suis aussi pauvre que peut l'être un conservateur de chefs-d'œuvre inestimables, mais il se trouve que j'ai rendu service, par l'intermédiaire de nos amis Percier et Fontaine aux frères Véry qui en bons chrétiens lorrains n'oublient pas les bienfaits. Alors de temps en temps, ils me servent un menu princier pour le prix d'un dîner chez *Duron.* Avec mon autre obligé, le bon Chevet, je suis sûr de ne jamais avoir faim. Vous pouvez donc choisir ce soir ce qu'il vous plaît dans la carte que Véry va commenter pour vous. Ne craignez pas de me ruiner!

– J'aime mieux cela! Il m'aurait déplu que vous ayez fait fortune subitement en vous livrant à quelque agiotage. Mais quel service avez-vous pu donc rendre à Véry pour qu'il vous en soit si reconnaissant?

– Percier et Fontaine ne s'en vantent pas mais ils ont dessiné les plans de cette maison. Véry voulait de l'antique, ils lui en ont donné! Trop, à mon goût. Mais notre restaurateur souhaitait aussi une statue et c'est là que je suis intervenu en lui dénichant, à la demande de Fontaine, chez un brocanteur de Nogent le buste romain que vous apercevez là-bas à côté du jet d'eau. Il était un peu cassé de partout et je l'ai fait restaurer. L'homme est aussi fier de son marbre que de ses truffes au vin de Champagne et je trouve cela réconfortant. Ah! il voulait à tout prix savoir quel personnage illustre avait été sculpté dans cette pierre de Carrare veinée comme une escalope de levraut au sang. Je lui ai affirmé que c'était l'empereur Caracalla. C'est peut-être vrai. Dans ce cas vous dînez ce soir, ma chère Antoinette, en compagnie de celui qui rêvant d'être Achille tua un esclave pour avoir à pleurer un Patrocle. Il fit aussi empoisonner son favori Festus pour gémir comme Alexandre sur le sort d'Ephestion. Mais il serait malséant de parler de poison chez le bon Véry qui vient justement prendre notre commande.

L'aîné des frères Véry qui s'occupait des clients tandis que son frère surveillait l'armée des cuisiniers, n'avait ni la mine réjouie ni l'embonpoint de la plupart de ses confrères. Grand, sec, presque austère, il avait gardé la réserve des paysans forestiers des Vosges où il était né une cinquantaine d'années auparavant. Il n'en fut pas moins aimable avec Antoinette.

– C'est la première fois, madame, que vous venez manger chez moi. Je le sais parce que je n'oublie jamais la tête d'un client. Si vous revenez dans dix ans, je vous reconnaîtrai! Je peux ce soir comme chaque jour vous faire choisir entre vingt sortes de hors-d'œuvre froids et chauds. Il y a aussi neuf espèces de potages et si vous n'aimez pas la pâtisserie [1] vous pouvez préférer aux dix pâtés inscrits sur la carte une douzaine d'huîtres d'Ostende ouvertes sur-le-champ par les femmes préposées à cet effet dans l'une des antichambres. La base du repas est

1. La pâtisserie concernait alors les pâtés et non les desserts.

le bouilli, le vrai, celui du Valtin, mon village, que je sers avec vingt sauces différentes ou bien le filet de bœuf grillé au bois... Après il vous restera à choisir entre 31 entrées de volaille, 28 de veau ou de mouton, 28 sortes de poisson... Non, seulement 26, car la marée ne nous a pas apporté de turbot, aujourd'hui. Je passe sur les rôtis et les entremets. Vous en trouverez la liste sur la carte comme celle des légumes, des écrevisses et du macaroni. Comme boisson vous pourrez vous prononcer entre 22 espèces de vins rouges et 20 de blancs.

Antoinette ouvrait de grands yeux en écoutant Véry jouer sa scène, comme un comédien déclame avec naturel son rôle préféré. Quand il eut terminé et qu'il leur eut laissé une liste de mets longue comme un attendu de jugement, elle demanda en riant à Lenoir :

– Quelle mécanique! Il est toujours comme ça? Au début son discours m'a donné faim mais il a fini par me rassasier.

– Non. Il réserve sa grande tirade pour les nouvelles têtes ou les gens qu'il veut honorer. Maintenant, étudions la carte d'un peu plus près car cette accumulation pantagruélique fait partie du plaisir.

Il se rapprocha d'Antoinette afin de pouvoir découvrir en même temps qu'elle la cascade de plats offerte à l'appétit des soupeurs. Fut-ce le hasard ou une manœuvre légère bien amorcée, le genou d'Alexandre effleura celui de sa compagne. Un choc net ou une pression trop appuyée n'aurait pas produit l'effet de ce frôlement qu'Antoinette ressentit comme une caresse d'autant plus sensuelle qu'elle était imperceptible. Elle n'en laissa rien paraître et ne retira pas sa jambe. Lenoir de son côté continuait à détailler la carte comme s'il ne s'était rien passé :

– Suprême de poulet aux pois, 3 francs – aux concombres, 3 francs. Blanquette de poularde, 3 francs. Chapon au consommé, 10 francs – le quart 2,10 francs. Kariz ou pilon à l'égyptienne, 3 francs. Poulet à la tartare, 6 francs – moitié 3 francs. Pigeon de volière à la crapaudine ou aux pois, 2 francs. Caille à la financière, 3 francs. Perdrix au chou ou à la purée, 4 francs...

– Arrêtez, Alexandre, je vous en prie, supplia Antoinette. L'artichaut à la barigoule se mélange aux œufs brouillés et l'oreille de veau farcie à l'anguille à la tartare. Choisissez pour moi un menu léger qui ménage ma tendance à l'embonpoint et ne parlons plus de toutes ces sauces qui me donnent mal au cœur.

– Vous avez raison. Laissons la littérature et passons aux actes. Je vous propose de commencer par des huîtres d'Ostende ou d'Étretat, ces dernières sont plus petites, de suivre par un fricandeau de veau de Pontoise à la chicorée. Voulez-vous ensuite un poisson, une sole aux fines herbes par exemple ou une truite? Nous pourrions terminer par un dessert léger : des fraises et des framboises au sucre avec des macarons...

– Je dis oui à tout. Commandez... mais resservez-moi avant un peu de ce vin de Champagne qui ne va pas tarder, je le sens, à me faire dire des bêtises. Il y a si longtemps que je n'ai pas fait la fête! Vous me rajeunissez de vingt ans, Alexandre. Je me sens redevenir celle à qui Pilâtre faisait découvrir Paris et les ors du Palais-Royal. J'étais amoureuse pour la première fois de ma vie. Et de l'homme après qui couraient toutes les femmes...

– Et ce soir? N'êtes-vous pas aussi un peu amoureuse? Ah! comme j'envie ce Pilâtre de Rozier!...

– C'est vrai, à l'époque on nous a beaucoup enviés, moi surtout. Mais tout cela est bien vieux. Des drames, des larmes et des scènes, il ne reste rien. Tout a été gommé. Il ne demeure au-dessus de ma mémoire qu'un voile de douceur, de bonheur qui flotte comme une fumée... Mais qu'est-ce que je vous raconte, mon pauvre Alexandre. Nous ne sommes pas là pour disséquer mes états d'âme!

– Continuez si vous en avez envie, tout ce qui vous touche m'intéresse et je prends vos confidences pour une marque de confiance. Mais vous n'avez pas répondu à ma question, une question il est vrai à la limite de l'impolitesse : êtes-vous ce soir un peu amoureuse?

Antoinette sourit doucement et regarda Alexandre en serrant un peu plus fort sa jambe contre la sienne :

– Croyez-vous mon ami que je serais là si je n'étais pas amoureuse? Nous nous sommes aimés une fois, une seule parce qu'il était pas possible qu'il y ait une deuxième fois. J'ai tout fait pour oublier. J'y étais même je crois arrivée quand vous êtes revenu tout à l'heure éclater comme un boulet de canon dans ma petite vie tranquille de mère de famille. A un moment où rien ne nous interdit de nous rencontrer si nous en avons envie.

– Vous en avez envie?

– Oui! Et vous le savez depuis le jour où je n'ai pu maîtriser mon agacement quand Fontaine à fait allusion à Mlle Lange. Je crois bien que je la déteste, celle-là!

Ils sourirent en même temps et se seraient embrassés sur-le-champ si les serveurs n'étaient pas venus s'affairer autour de la table pour y poser un superbe plateau d'argent où brillaient les huîtres sur leur lit d'algues et de glace

– Fêtons donc ces « truffes de la mer » comme les chantait Horace. Septembre avec son « r » de rien nous les ramène. Et vidons une coupe de ce vin subtil. Je bois, Antoinette, à votre amour.

– Et moi au vôtre!

Cette fois leurs lèvres s'unirent. Il en fallait plus que ça pour choquer les soupeurs et les serveurs de chez *Véry*!

Antoinette était heureuse. Elle était gaie, elle riait, s'amusait du spectacle de la salle où, à chaque instant, un acte nouveau se jouait autour des tables garnies de mets sans cesse renouvelés et dont elle essayait de reconnaître la nature. Certains arrivaient portés à bout de bras dans une gerbe de flammes bleues embaumant l'alcool ou la liqueur. D'autres parvenaient jusqu'aux assiettes dans des cassolettes de porcelaine ou dans des petites marmites de cuivre polies comme des bijoux.

A la table voisine s'étaient installés deux hommes, visiblement des habitués, dont la seule préoccupation semblait être de manger et de parler de ce qu'ils mangeaient. Ils en parlaient d'ailleurs avec une sensibilité et une recherche qui amusèrent d'abord Antoinette puis qui l'intéressèrent vraiment. Le plus jeune surtout, il ne devait avoir guère plus de vingt-cinq ans, philosophait avec bonheur sans souci d'être entendu des autres convives.

– C'est M. de Borose, souffla Alexandre à Antoinette. Un jeune homme riche et cultivé qui entend appliquer avec tout le sérieux et la sagesse qu'elles supposent, lorsqu'elles sont bien comprises, les théories d'Épicure. Tenez, écoutez-le.

– L'homme, disait-il à son compagnon de table, commet un péché en dédaignant les dons de la nature. Devrait-il ne cueillir et ne manger sur terre que les fruits amers et laisser pourrir ceux dont la douceur charme le palais?

– Comme vous avez raison! Avons-nous offensé Dieu en demandant à Véry de nous préparer ce sauté de filets de perdreaux aux truffes? S'il existe des bonnes choses dans ce monde, c'est parce que Dieu l'a voulu ainsi et nous sommes dans le vrai en pensant que les bonnes choses sont pour les bonnes gens. Si nous pensions l'inverse, il faudrait nager dans l'absurdité et croire que le Bon Dieu a créé les bonnes choses pour les méchants...

La démonstration de M. de Borose ravissait Antoinette qui se serait bien mêlée à la conversation si les tables avaient été plus rapprochées.

– Ce monsieur est brillant, dit-elle à Lenoir. Pour un peu je l'inviterais à l'un de nos soupers. Mais il mangerait moins bien qu'ici...

– Ne mésestimez pas nos agapes. Je me rappelle des repas remarquables. Mais de grâce, laissons M. de Borose à ses commensaux habituels : il doit vite devenir insupportable! Un de mes amis a dîné une fois chez lui. Il paraît que tout était tellement parfait, des mets servis au choix des convives jusqu'à l'ordonnancement de la conversation qu'on en venait à souhaiter que le maître d'hôtel renversât la saucière pour apporter un peu d'imprévu à la réunion.

Avant de quitter ce lieu de délices, Antoinette dut aller admirer de près la statue de Caracalla sous la conduite du maître de maison qui remercia encore Lenoir de la lui avoir procurée pour un prix dérisoire.

– Les œuvres d'art, les vraies, n'ont pas de prix! conclut Alexandre d'un air docte qui fit rire Antoinette. Et d'ajouter : La preuve, c'est que je peux parfois grâce à vos bontés goûter à votre cuisine qui est un chef-d'œuvre renommé jusqu'à la cour de Russie. On gagne toujours à aimer les belles choses!

Dehors, l'air des Tuileries sentait la forêt. Main dans la main, « les doigts unis comme tenons et mortaises » – c'est Antoinette qui le fit remarquer –, ils firent un grand tour sous les arbres du jardin avant de regagner la voiture qui les attendait en bas de la terrasse des Feuillants [1]. Ils se taisaient, afin de ne pas troubler par des paroles banales un moment dont ils ressentaient la divine rareté. Ce n'est que lorsqu'ils distinguèrent les lanternes du cabriolet qu'Antoinette s'arrêta et murmura : « Serrez-moi fort et embrassez-moi Alexandre! »

Ils s'étreignirent longtemps, en silence. Cette fois, c'est Alexandre qui dit :

– Venez ma douce, il est temps que je vous ramène place d'Aligre. Nous avons la vie devant nous pour nous aimer et puisque je vous ai retrouvée, soyez sûre que je ne vais pas me laisser oublier!

Le souper chez *Véry* marquait un nouveau tournant dans la vie d'Antoinette. Elle n'avait certes rien changé des habitudes hospitalières de la place d'Aligre : elle continuait de recevoir ses amis chaque mercredi, elle s'occupait avec autant d'attention de sa fille Lucie et veillait avec tendresse sur Riesener dont la santé devenait précaire. Le vieux maître avait essayé de reprendre une activité réduite dans un atelier de la rue Traversière loué à son ami l'ébéniste Charles Richter. Il s'était mis sans enthousiasme à construire des petits meubles dans le goût du Consulat mais avait bien vite renoncé : « Faute d'ar-

1. Au niveau de l'actuelle place des Pyramides avant que la rue de Rivoli fût percée.

gent pour engager de bons compagnons et se procurer de beaux bronzes», disait-il. En fait parce que cela l'ennuyait.

– Ce n'est pas grâce à ces petites tables d'acajou que je redeviendrai célèbre, si je dois jamais le redevenir. Mieux vaut oublier cet essai, je ne suis décidément pas fait pour vivre à l'antique!

Désabusé mais lucide, il vivait chichement dans les deux pièces qu'il avait conservées à l'étage au-dessus d'Antoinette. Parfois, son fils Henri-François venait le voir lorsqu'il passait par Paris. Le peintre avait souvent proposé de l'accueillir dans la maison qu'il habitait à Lyon mais l'ébéniste du roi avait refusé :

– Quitter le Faubourg? A mon âge? Mais je mourrais dans la semaine si je devais me dépoter! C'est très gentil de ta part mais, ici, j'ai Antoinette, Lucie et tous mes compagnons. Maintenant que j'ai définitivement rangé mes outils, mon seul plaisir est d'aller rendre visite aux amis, de tourner comme une vieille bête dans les ateliers où, Dieu merci! on m'accueille avec amitié et respect. Souvent, même, un jeune me demande conseil pour trouver la courbure d'un col de cygne ou sculpter le dossier plein d'un cabriolet. Cela me permet d'approcher le bois, de sentir le copeau frais et de passer de temps en temps la paume de la main sur une pièce de tilleul bien poncée. Et puis il y a Ethis et sa boutique qui commence à prendre tournure. Lui aussi a besoin de conseils pour ses achats. Tu vois, Henri, que je ne peux pas quitter le Faubourg. Mais sais-tu ce qui me ferait plaisir? C'est qu'un jour tu peignes mon portrait, dans l'habit de velours vert brodé que je mettais pour aller chez la reine! Cela te paraît bête?

– Pas du tout père, rien ne peut me faire plus plaisir. La prochaine fois que je viens à Paris, je m'installe quelques jours place d'Aligre et je te fais le portrait. C'est juré!

Ce jour-là il embrassa son père plus longuement qu'à l'habitude et lui dit à l'oreille pour que Lucie n'entende pas : « Si tu as besoin d'argent ou de quoi que ce soit, dis-le-moi. Je vends très bien mes tableaux et je peux t'aider. »

Une larme coula sur la joue ridée du maître.

– Merci, fils. Cela me fait plaisir que tu y aies pensé mais je n'ai besoin de rien. Il me reste assez pour vivre et j'ai encore en réserve presque tous les meubles que j'ai rachetés dans les ventes de Versailles. Je sais bien qu'il n'y a plus guère d'amateurs pour ce genre de pièces mais, tout de même...

Henri ne fut pas dupe, il connaissait la fierté de son père, il remit avant de partir quelques louis à Antoinette pour qu'elle achète ce qui pouvait lui manquer.

Riesener allait souvent en effet chez Ethis dont l'activité ne connaissait plus de bornes. Grâce à l'association qu'il avait conclue avec Richard, il avait pu installer le magasin de meubles, de tissus et de papiers peints « le plus coquet du Faubourg et peut-être même de Paris », comme il disait avec fierté. Quel concurrent il est vrai aurait pu s'offrir les services d'un Percier? Celui-ci lui avait fait gentiment un plan à l'aquarelle du magasin. Deux étais de chêne qui avaient vieilli sans grâce dans l'ancien atelier étaient maintenant transformés en colonnes doriques grâce à un enduit de stuc. Le reste était à l'avenant, la boutique semblait garnie de marbre et quelques grotesques imités des ruines d'Herculanum, qu'un élève de Fontaine était venu peindre sur les murs, achevaient de donner le ton du jour à *L'Enfant à l'oiseau.* Marie en effet avait tenu à transférer l'enseigne et la statuette de Pigalle dans la nouvelle boutique : « Cet enfant est notre ange gardien, avait-elle déclaré, nous le conservons près de nous! »

Le magasin était à peine achevé qu'il était déjà célèbre dans tout le Faubourg. D'abord, parce qu'Ethis était connu comme le loup blanc. Qui n'avait, de la Bastille à la place du Trône, entendu parler de « Traîne-sabot », du « vainqueur », de l'enfant trouvé devenu « de Valfroy ». Et tous ces gens qui passaient et repassaient pour voir l'état des travaux puis pour juger de l'effet! Les clients, eux aussi, commençaient à fréquenter la boutique où

Marie et son sourire faisaient merveille. Mme Macheron, la veuve d'un ciseleur mort au Carrousel sur les marches du grand escalier avec la première vague des assaillants du 10 août, s'occupait du petit Bertrand et de la maison Thirion que les jeunes gens continuaient d'habiter. Ethis, lui, était finalement peu dans son magasin. Toujours à l'affût d'une affaire de bois ou d'un lot de meubles dont un ébéniste voulait se défaire, il courait du matin au soir, allait voir son ami Richard qui installait ses broches et ses deux manèges dans l'ancien couvent de la rue de Charonne, passait une heure ou deux dans les ateliers des Jacob pour se familiariser avec la fabrication des sièges nouveau style. Il rendait aussi souvent visite à son ancien patron Alexandre Lenoir. Depuis que Valfroy était mort, il considérait le directeur du musée des Monuments nationaux comme son père et ne faisait rien sans lui demander conseil.

Le garçon n'avait pas oublié la phrase de Georges Jacob : « Apprends à dessiner. » Deux ou trois jours par semaine, il allait retrouver Riesener place d'Aligre. Le maître l'initiait aux règles de la perspective, lui faisait copier des motifs de décoration et lui apprenait à croquer une commode ou un siège. « Tu dois pouvoir, lui disait l'ébéniste, montrer à un client en trois coups de crayon le meuble qui lui convient et que tu veux lui vendre. » Ethis s'appliquait comme dans tout ce qu'il faisait. Sans être particulièrement doué, il arrivait à dessiner correctement.

Depuis plus d'un mois, Antoinette remettait le moment d'écrire à sa sœur. Victoire lui avait pourtant adressé une longue lettre pour lui raconter sa vie à Marseille et lui donner des nouvelles de sa famille. Charles semblait réussir dans sa mission : « Contre toute attente, écrivait-elle, le paysan de l'Argonne a conquis la Canebière, cette grand-rue marseillaise qui se jette dans le port! Après l'avoir brocardé pour ses trottoirs, les gens trouvent que c'était une bonne idée... Quant à Eugène, il parle avec l'accent du pays! C'est un bon petit garçon qui nous inquiète souvent avec sa santé mais qui finalement pousse bien. Son visage est fin comme un crayon de Greuze, tu sais ce peintre dessinateur dont ton ami Lenoir fait si grand cas... »

Antoinette venait de relire la lettre et s'était finalement installée devant sa table à écrire. Elle s'aperçut encore une fois qu'elle avait mille fois plus de choses à raconter que sa sœur, prisonnière de ses obligations de préfète et d'une vie familiale monotone. « Elle n'a mis qu'une seule fois de la fantaisie dans sa vie, pensa Antoinette en souriant. Un coup de tonnerre! Mais l'orage aura été bref, la revoilà en train de faire des grâces, d'échanger des propos insignifiants avec des femmes qui ne le sont pas moins, de dire à l'épouse du notaire que ses filles sont ravissantes bien qu'elles soient laides comme des guenons scrofuleuses. »

Par où commencer? Antoinette décida d'aborder l'essentiel : sa vie personnelle. Elle raconta l'invitation inattendue de Lenoir, sa courte hésitation et le fabuleux souper chez *Véry*. « Une fois de plus Victoire va m'envier, se dit-elle, mais tant pis! Je lui dis tout! » Cela tint en quelques mots : « Il ne s'est rien passé le premier soir car il était tard mais nous nous sommes retrouvés le lendemain dans son logement de la rue des Lions. Depuis, la vie a pris pour moi d'autres couleurs. Je l'aime et je suis aimée. Je sais qu'il est plus jeune que moi mais seul le bonheur est comptable de notre âge! »

Elle parla ensuite d'Ethis, la mutation de « Traîne-sabot », sa revanche qu'il ne trouvait jamais complète et son activité d'insecte dans la termitière du Faubourg.

Il lui restait encore à raconter Paris, ses toilettes, ses officiers de passage en uniformes d'or et de pourpre et ses invalides aux culottes trouées. Paris et ses odeurs de monarchie rampante sous les sabots des chevaux de Bonaparte. Paris et sa manie de l'antique qui donnait un coup de vieux aux plus beaux meubles de leur père. Paris en acajou qui prenait des allures de café londonien. Enfin, Paris où les chansons remplaçaient les journaux interdits. A ce propos, Antoinette répondait au souhait de sa sœur qui lui demandait de lui décrire le climat politique de la capitale : « A Marseille nous ne savons pas grand-chose de ce qui se passe à Paris. Seules nous parviennent les nouvelles officielles. Doit-on croire la presse qui assure que Bonaparte y est adulé et que les révolutionnaires d'hier mettent en lui tous leurs espoirs ? Tiens-tu toujours salon le mercredi ? Dans ce cas tu dois être bien informée. Inutile de te dire que ce que tu m'apprendras demeurera entre nous. Je n'en parlerai même pas à Charles si tu le souhaites. »

Je n'ai pas, écrivit Antoinette, *de choses secrètes à te raconter. Il est vrai que le Premier consul jouit d'une grande popularité dans les milieux ouvriers qui ont mis leurs espoirs dans la fermeté avec laquelle il gouverne. Je crois que la plupart des gens ne s'aperçoivent pas qu'ils vivent sous le pouvoir absolu d'un seul homme. Et quel homme! En fait, ils sont fatigués d'agitation, ils ont soif de repos et sacrifient à cette quiétude les idées de la Révolution, qui, il faut bien le dire, n'ont jamais débouché sur des progrès tangibles. Ainsi l'ouverture de la session du sénat et du tribunat a plongé certains dans l'anxiété : allait-on assister de nouveau à des délibérations tapageuses et inutiles qui n'auraient pour effet que de semer la discorde entre les Français? On n'a tout de même pas encore pris son parti du retour aux habitudes monarchiques et religieuses. D'où un climat d'inconfort intellectuel et politique qui suscite l'opposition de certains républicains. Quant aux royalistes, il paraît que Bonaparte les craint plus que tout.*

Comme tu le sais, le gouvernement a supprimé la célébration du 21 janvier, jour anniversaire de la mort du roi. Ce n'était évidemment pas pour que les royalistes manifestassent à leur façon. Ainsi, la police a sévi contre ceux qui avaient placé un drap mortuaire de velours noir croisé de satin blanc sur le portail de l'église de la

Madeleine et affiché le testament de Louis XVI à la porte de l'église Saint-Jacques-de-la-Boucherie.

Je pense que vous êtes au courant à Marseille d'une contre-révolution coutumière qui a beaucoup fait parler dans le Faubourg, je veux parler de la rentrée en grâce du mot « madame » qui, politesse consulaire exige, doit désormais remplacer le terme de « citoyenne ». Celui de « citoyen » est évidemment aussi proscrit. Quant au tutoiement mis en usage par les sans-culottes, il y a beau temps qu'il est banni. La classe bourgeoise n'avait jamais pu s'y accoutumer et il n'y a plus guère que dans les ateliers qu'on se tutoie.

Bonaparte n'aime pas la presse. Pour éviter d'être critiqué il a procédé à des coupes claires et même blanches dans la forêt des journaux. Alexandre Lenoir m'a dit qu'on en imprimait près de deux cents à Paris et que, le 17 nivôse, Bonaparte a réduit ce nombre à treize! Heureusement les journaux consacrés aux sciences et à la littérature peuvent continuer de paraître.

Je ne ferai pas l'injure à la femme d'un préfet de l'informer de la création d'une nouvelle organisation judiciaire : tribunal de première instance, cour d'appel, cour d'assises, cour de cassation... Il faut dire que le Premier consul ne reste pas inactif! Chaque jour apporte une nouvelle loi, un nouveau décret. Tiens, par exemple, on peut maintenant se rendre à l'étranger sans être considéré comme émigré. Il faut bien avouer que c'est aussi ça la liberté!

Pour terminer mon panorama de la vie parisienne, je peux t'assurer que nous ne manquons ni de fêtes commémoratives, ni de défilés ni de Te Deum. *La dernière en date des manifestations publiques était une cérémonie organisée pour rendre hommage à Washington qui vient de mourir. On a mis des crêpes à tous les drapeaux.*

Je t'abandonne ma chère Victoire car j'ai rendez-vous avec Alexandre. Cela m'ennuie de laisser Lucie souvent seule, il est vrai qu'elle devient grande. Je ne lui ai pas fait de confidences mais je crois qu'elle a tout compris. Elle est contente de me voir heureuse et elle aime bien Lenoir qui, tu t'en doutes, est gentil avec elle. Mes amours avec Alexandre dureront ce qu'elles dureront mais j'ai appris depuis bien longtemps que, dans la vie, il n'y a jamais rien de définitif. Sauf la mort, mais je n'ai pas envie de mourir! Embrasse mes neveux et en particulier ton petit Eugène que je ne connais pas beaucoup. Dis à ton mari des choses aimables et fais une grimace aux bourgeoises que tu reçois sous tes lambris dorés. Mille baisers.

Ta sœur chérie.

Antoinette n'avait pas pu raconter à sa sœur la mémorable journée du 14-Juillet 1801 qui, deux semaines plus tard, devait marquer pour l'Histoire la fin des derniers vestiges concrets de la Révolution. Le Premier consul pensait que la grandeur et l'autorité, la sienne en l'occurrence, ne pouvaient se passer d'une assise religieuse légale. La célébration de la fête du 14-Juillet offrait une occasion de rendre au clergé le rôle qui lui avait été brusquement ôté par la Révolution.

Il s'agissait en fait de faire avaler au peuple la pilule du concordat signé deux semaines auparavant. Hercule Gonsalvi, cardinal de la Sainte Église romaine, et Joseph Spina, archevêque de Corinthe, étaient venus au nom du pape adopter la convention en dix-sept articles qui, « compte tenu du fait que la religion catholique, apostolique et romaine était celle de la majorité des Français et notamment celle des trois consuls », déclarait que le culte de la religion catholique serait public; que les évêques seraient à l'avenir nommés par le Premier consul et confirmés par le pape, et que le gouvernement ferait une nouvelle implantation des diocèses.

Les *Te Deum* ont toujours été pour les monarques un moyen pratique et économique d'accorder les réjouissances populaires aux vertus théologales. Sur la proposition de Joseph Bonaparte, le concile national, « considérant que la religion a toujours été dans l'usage de consacrer par des cérémonies saintes les grands événements qui influent sur le sort des peuples », décréta « qu'il serait chanté un *Te Deum* à Notre-Dame, en action de grâces de tous les bienfaits que le Seigneur a répandus sur le peuple français ».

Le Moniteur et tous les journaux avaient annoncé cette cérémonie en même temps que la multitude des distractions profanes qui seraient offertes aux Parisiens. Comme à l'habitude, David avait été chargé de veiller à l'ordonnancement de cette gigantesque kermesse et Fontaine prié de prêter son crayon et ses pinceaux aux projets de mise en scène des réjouissances publiques. C'est dire que le petit cercle de la place d'Aligre était au courant de tous ces préparatifs et que Lucie entendait bien participer aux fêtes annoncées.

Antoinette et Lenoir, qui paraissaient avoir une autre occupation en vue ce jour-là, abandonnèrent à Ethis et à Marie le soin d'accompagner la fillette. Pour Ethis, ce n'était pas un pensum. Badaud dans l'âme, il se plaisait au milieu de la foule parisienne. Quant à Marie, elle n'était pas mécontente de quitter la boutique du Faubourg et d'aller voir la fête aux Champs-Élysées. Fontaine leur avait obtenu des billets pour tous les spectacles et Lucie en avait profité pour dire qu'elle ne pouvait porter sa vieille robe devenue trop courte dans les tribunes et les enceintes réservées où il n'y aurait que des gens distingués et élégants. Réveillon dont la santé s'était améliorée et qui était présent ce jour-là, proclama que Lucie avait raison et qu'il lui offrait une robe neuve.

La petite lui sauta au cou et Antoinette dit à son parrain, toujours heureux de faire plaisir :

– Si tu lui offres autant de robes qu'à moi, Lucie sera la jeune fille la mieux habillée du quartier.

– C'est vrai que je t'ai habillée bien souvent ! Tu portais si merveilleusement la toilette !

– Tu portais, tu portais ! Voudrais-tu dire que je m'habille mal en vieillissant ? s'insurgea Antoinette, faussement en colère.

– Pas du tout mais je dois avouer que je préfère offrir des robes aux jeunes filles qu'aux dames mûres. Enfin, quand tu accompagneras Lucie, choisis-toi aussi une toilette. Tu sais que tu es toujours un peu ma fille ! As-tu de l'argent? Je te rembourserai. Sinon passe demain à la maison.

Toujours généreux, Réveillon! Il avait il est vrai vécu si près de la famille Œben qu'il la considérait comme sienne. N'avait-il pas été le compagnon de jeux de Marguerite, la mère d'Antoinette, alors qu'ils habitaient tous deux sur le même palier rue Saint-Nicolas? Il avait certes de l'affection pour sa femme mais celle-ci, constamment malade, ne sortait pas depuis des années de son bel appartement de la rue des Bons-Enfants où il s'ennuyait à mourir. S'il n'avait tenu qu'à lui, il serait revenu depuis longtemps habiter le Faubourg. Il y avait bien pensé en achetant naguère la maison Thirion qu'il avait ensuite donnée à Ethis. Justement, tiens, il y pensait, à la maison Thirion :

– Dis donc Ethis, as-tu continué les recherches que nous avions commencées au grenier? Je suis sûr qu'il y a encore un tas de découvertes à faire.

– Je dois vous avouer que non. Nous avons eu tellement de choses à faire pour ouvrir le magasin et le transférer près de la Bastille! Mais je vous promets de faire bientôt de nouvelles recherches. Antoinette, elle aussi, voudrait bien retrouver des traces de ses ancêtres. Il y a déjà la canne de compagnon du tour de France que je conserve précieusement. Je ne l'ai jamais descendue à la boutique car je suis sûr que j'aurais dû tous les jours en refuser la vente. Avec *L'Enfant* c'est notre porte-bonheur. Et puis, qui sait, peut-être qu'elle resservira un jour!

La canne de compagnon intéressait peu Lucie qui ne pensait qu'à sa robe :

– Où irons-nous acheter nos robes? demanda-t-elle.

– *A Pygmalion,* peut-être. Mais c'est bien loin. Pourquoi ne pas aller *A la Belle Fermière,* à côté du magasin d'Ethis? Il n'y a pas longtemps que c'est ouvert mais j'y ai vu en vitrine de jolies choses. Ethis connaît d'ailleurs peut-être le propriétaire...

Ethis naturellement connaissait :

– Oui, il s'appelle Parisot et ne s'endort pas aux affaires. Je suis un paresseux à côté de lui. Il m'a dit qu'il partirait ailleurs car, au Faubourg, il ne peut pas s'agrandir comme il le souhaiterait. Si vous allez le voir dites qui vous êtes, je lui aurai parlé et il vous fera sûrement une réduction.

Au 5 de la grand-rue du Faubourg battait en effet l'enseigne champêtre qui deux siècles auparavant aurait eu sa raison d'être mais qui surprenait, aujourd'hui, entre la boutique de l'épicier-marchand de couleurs Théodore Pépin et l'atelier de Martin Carlin qui, lui, travaillait à *L'Enseigne de la colombe.*

La façade de la boutique où Antoinette et Lucie venaient d'entrer n'était pas grande mais le magasin s'engageait profondément dans une suite d'anciens ateliers donnant sur le passage Balny [1] et qui avaient été réunis. Les murs qui avaient tous été repeints de couleur claire étaient garnis d'étagères que les pièces d'étoffes multicolores superposées transformaient en drapeaux. Entre chaque comptoir installé devant les piles de tissu se dressaient des mannequins habillés des pieds à la tête et qui fascinaient la petite Lucie.

Antoinette demanda à une employée d'aller chercher le propriétaire du magasin. Elle s'attendait à voir arriver l'un de ces marchands de tissus grincheux qui sentent le coutil et passent leur temps à admonester un personnel anémique. C'est un homme à peine plus vieux qu'Ethis qui surgit du fond de la boutique. Mince, élégamment vêtu d'un habit bleu serré et d'un pantalon clair, il s'inclina en souriant discrètement.

– Je suis sûr que vous êtes Mme de Valfroy. Votre fils Ethis m'a parlé de vous. Je suis heureux de faire votre connaissance. Ethis est un charmant voisin mais, ce qui est plus important, c'est un remarquable entrepreneur. Il réussit merveilleusement dans les affaires et gère très bien son magasin qui est en train de devenir le plus important du quartier. Il ne se passe pas de jour sans qu'il ait une nouvelle idée. Il est un peu comme moi, c'est pourquoi nous nous entendons bien.

1. Supprimé en 1910.

– Je vous remercie, monsieur. C'est vrai qu'Ethis est actif et intelligent mais je trouve parfois qu'il a un peu trop d'idées. J'ai peur qu'il ne se disperse et néglige sa vie de famille. Sa femme est très jeune...

– Elle travaille avec lui, je la connais. Rassurez-vous, ils s'entendent très bien. Ethis a une telle volonté de réussir! C'est pour vous aussi qu'il est ambitieux : il veut vous montrer que ce que vous avez fait pour lui n'a pas été vain. Il vous aime et vous admire tellement!

– Je le sais et je suis fière de lui. Mais je vois que vous connaissez très bien Ethis, plus que ne le laisseraient supposer des relations de bon voisinage. Tant mieux si vous êtes son ami. Essayez pourtant de freiner un peu ses enthousiasmes!

– Il pourrait aussi souvent freiner les miens! s'exclama Parisot en éclatant de rire. C'est votre fille? ajouta-t-il en regardant Lucie. Si c'est elle que vous voulez habiller, cela ne sera pas difficile : elle est mince et jolie.

– Si je comprends bien, cela sera plus difficile pour moi? souligna malicieusement Antoinette.

Le jeune homme joua la confusion :

– Comment? Je n'ai jamais dit une chose pareille. C'est que je ne pensais pas que vous me feriez l'honneur d'être ma cliente. Comptez sur moi pour vous habiller aussi bien que le ferait Mlle Larampe sur le Boulevard. Et cela vous coûtera dix fois moins cher. D'autant plus que je vous ferai des prix très doux...

– Vous êtes un flatteur, monsieur Parisot. Et un habile marchand. Voyons d'abord pour la petite. Elle est invitée le 14 et le 15 aux fêtes du Concordat. Sans vouloir rivaliser d'élégance avec les enfants des grandes dames du Consulat, il faut qu'elle fasse honneur à M. Fontaine qui nous a procuré des billets pour les tribunes officielles.

– Je sais ce que je vais proposer à Mademoiselle...

– Lucie, dit Antoinette.

– Un bien joli nom! Eh bien, je pense que ce modèle ira parfaitement à Mademoiselle Lucie.

Il ouvrit une grande boîte cartonnée d'où s'échappa un flot de mousseline bleu pâle et présenta en la tenant par les emmanchures une ravissante robe dont le tissu imitait par sa légèreté et ses marbrures diaphanes une aile de papillon.

– Cette robe, dit-il, n'est pas à vendre. Elle a été faite pour l'une des filles du maire de l'arrondissement. Mais si le modèle convient à Mademoiselle, je peux vous livrer la même, à sa taille, dans les vingt-quatre heures.

C'était la première fois que Lucie devait porter une autre toilette que celles que lui taillait sa mère, le plus souvent dans d'anciennes robes à elle. La petite était donc heureuse et émue plus qu'elle n'aurait voulu le laisser paraître. Pour un peu elle aurait pleuré en passant l'étui de toile si fine qu'on aurait dit de la soie et dont la taille haute soulignait les prémices de sa poitrine d'adolescente.

– Ne trouvez-vous pas votre jeune fille très élégante? demanda Parisot. Il faudra simplement confectionner la robe un peu plus longue et donner de l'ampleur aux épaules. J'ai plusieurs étoffes qui conviendraient mais celle-ci me semble tellement bien accordée au teint et aux cheveux de Lucie que je vous conseille de la retenir.

– Et à toi, Lucie? Est-ce qu'elle te plaît? questionna Antoinette, troublée elle aussi de voir sa petite devenir d'un coup une jeune fille.

– Je trouve qu'elle me va très bien! répondit Lucie avec le sérieux d'une dame habituée à fréquenter les salons de tailleurs et de couturières.

Antoinette sourit à Parisot et dit:

– Maintenant à moi. Je n'irai pas aux défilés du Concordat mais je vous avoue mon plaisir à me faire faire une robe. Depuis la Révolution j'ai été plutôt privée de cette satisfaction!

– Je vais vous montrer les derniers journaux de mode français et anglais. Je les reçois tous! dit avec fierté le «marchand de tissus-habilleur», comme il se faisait appeler. Cela va vous donner des idées. Voici le *Journal des Dames et des modes* avec ses figurines en couleur et *L'Arlequin* qui reprend beaucoup de modèles du premier, quelques almanachs de mode et, si l'élégance anglaise vous tente, *Records of Fashion, The Miroir de la Mode...* [1].

Antoinette mit longtemps avant de se décider. La sagesse la poussait à choisir un vêtement d'usage, facile à porter en toute circonstance. Pourquoi pas l'une de ces robes en laine fine que les Anglaises mettent pour marcher dans Hyde Park ou voyager hors de Londres, avec une sorte de gilet court ne descendant pas au-dessous de la taille? La voyant regarder une gravure de *The Elegances of Fashion,* Parisot montra qu'il connaissait son métier et qu'il avait fait un séjour à Londres:

– On commence à appeler cette petite veste à Paris comme à Londres un « spencer ». Tiens, son histoire va amuser Lucie. Un Anglais, lord Spencer, ayant trop bu à son dîner, s'endormit un jour le dos tourné à la cheminée. Quand on le réveilla, les pans de la redingote qu'il portait par-dessus son habit étaient brûlés. Au lieu de la retirer, il la fit rogner avec des ciseaux et sortit ainsi affublé. Les badauds de Londres crurent qu'il s'agissait d'une mode nouvelle et l'adoptèrent en même temps que les amis de lord Spencer. D'Angleterre, le spencer vint en France mais ce sont surtout les femmes qui l'ont adopté!

Antoinette réfléchissait. Elle se disait que durant ces dix dernières années elle avait payé son tribut à l'adversité et qu'elle pouvait s'offrir le luxe d'un agréable superflu. Elle avait envie d'une robe de soirée pour accompagner Alexandre Lenoir quand il l'emmenait souper ou au théâtre. Elle en avait assez de cacher sa misère sous le châle des Indes! Elle atteignait un âge où la toilette est importante pour une femme. Et puis, un vêtement de tous les jours, elle pouvait toujours se le tailler et le coudre elle-même... Elle hésita encore un moment et se décida:

– C'est une folie mais il faut savoir être folle de temps

1. Nombreux dans la seconde moitié du XVIIIe siècle, les journaux de mode cessèrent de paraître dès le début de la Révolution. En revanche, les publications anglaises proliférèrent sous le Consulat et l'Empire. Les Anglais influèrent beaucoup sur la toilette française en la rendant plus pratique et plus libre.

en temps : je voudrais la toilette blanche du *Journal des Dames,* celle aux manches bouffantes et dont le bas est orné d'une torsade cerise et d'une dentelle à plat.

– Oh ! oui ! Comme tu as raison, s'écria Lucie. Je veux que tu sois très belle quand tu sors avec Alexandre !

Antoinette sursauta mais ne releva pas la réflexion de sa fille. Il était évident que malgré toutes les précautions qu'ils prenaient, Lucie était au courant de ses relations avec Lenoir. « Après tout, c'est mieux ainsi », pensa-t-elle, et elle lui demanda de l'aider à choisir l'étoffe.

– Je ne vois que la percale des Indes pour une robe de ce style, dit Parisot. Ne vous souciez pas du prix, on s'arrangera toujours. Quant à la couturière capable de vous copier ce modèle, je vous indiquerai celle qui a l'habitude de travailler pour moi !

Un peu plus tard, Antoinette et Lucie sortaient de *La Belle Fermière* en chantonnant. « Maman, je suis heureuse ! » dit la fillette. « Moi aussi ma chérie ! » répondit la mère en serrant la petite main qu'elle tenait dans la sienne. Elles s'arrêtèrent naturellement un peu plus loin à la boutique d'Ethis qui venait de rentrer du marché du Temple où, disait-il, il avait fait une rencontre de la plus haute importance. « Je ne peux pas m'empêcher de sourire quand je l'entends parler ainsi mais je sais que c'est probablement vrai ! » pensa Antoinette.

Ethis fut heureux de savoir que sa mère et sa sœur avaient été bien reçues par son ami Parisot.

– C'est un garçon extraordinaire ! dit-il. Il n'avait pas trois sous quand il a commencé et tu sais ce dont il rêve maintenant ? Ouvrir un immense magasin sur plusieurs étages où il vendrait des vêtements très bon marché parce que fabriqués en grand nombre selon un procédé qu'il a inventé : ils seraient par exemple coupés dans plusieurs épaisseurs d'un même tissu. On n'a pas fini d'entendre parler de Pierre Parisot, croyez-moi.

– Tu sais qu'il pense aussi beaucoup de bien de toi ? C'est à croire que vous vous entendez pour vanter réciproquement vos mérites ! dit Antoinette en riant

– Si cela était vrai, avouez, ma mère, que ce serait rudement malin!

– Dis donc, Ethis, c'est demain dimanche, venez souper place d'Aligre. Je coucherai Bertrand. Si Marie veut venir m'aider, nous ferons des prodiges. C'est vrai, l'envie me prend de cuisiner. Chez moi c'est plutôt bon signe. J'enverrai Lucie prévenir Réveillon, il s'ennuie tellement chez lui!

– Bien entendu, nous viendrons mais je pense que tu seras surtout contente d'avoir Bertrand!

– Serais-tu jaloux?

– Et tu n'invites pas Lenoir?

Venant après la réflexion de Lucie, la question d'Ethis piqua Antoinette:

– Pourquoi me demandes-tu cela? Il s'agit d'un repas familial et non d'une de nos réunions du mercredi.

– Je te demande cela parce que je pense que la présence d'Alexandre te fera plaisir et que j'aime te savoir heureuse, tout simplement.

– Tu es gentil. Ce que tu dis est vrai, pourquoi le cacher? Je préviendrai Alexandre qui tient, tu l'as deviné, une place dans mon cœur.

Marie était une bonne cuisinière. Elle n'avait pas naguère écrit pour rien avec sa mère un recueil de « recettes révolutionnaires ». Faute de denrées disponibles, le livre n'avait guère eu de succès mais il lui en était resté de solides notions culinaires et un goût du mijotage qui ne demandait qu'à s'épanouir devant un four ou une cheminée. L'idée de passer une journée presque entière au fourneau avec Antoinette la comblait de joie et elle arriva, sitôt prévenue, pour prendre en compagnie de sa belle-mère les dispositions qui s'imposaient.

Il fallait d'abord choisir le menu. Après de longues discussions et une visite chez Parmain, le nouveau boucher installé depuis peu rue Traversière, les deux cuisinières optèrent pour une poitrine de veau farcie à la bourgeoise. C'était, pensaient-elles, un plat assez bon marché qui convenait parfaitement pour sept ou huit personnes et qui nécessitait une cuisine élaborée, ouverte à toutes leurs initiatives. Il fut convenu que Marie passerait en fin de matinée chez Parmain chercher la poitrine et qu'elle viendrait vers onze heures place d'Aligre. On se contenterait d'une collation, un peu de jambon et de pain, et l'on se mettrait aussitôt en cuisine. Réveillon et Lenoir furent instamment priés de ne pas arriver avant six heures et Ethis avait des comptes à vérifier. Quant à Lucie, elle garderait son neveu pendant que les femmes s'affaireraient autour de leurs casseroles.

Ainsi fut fait. En attendant la poitrine de veau, il fallait s'occuper de la farce, mélange savant qui allait requérir les talents les plus subtils. Antoinette était passée le matin chez la mère Deugros, la maraîchère dont les planches s'alignaient au bout de la rue Saint-Bernard de chaque côté du chemin qui menait jadis à la courtille du Temple. En passant devant l'église Sainte-Marguerite, elle avait eu une pensée pour l'enfant mort au Temple qui était enterré dans le petit cimetière et qu'on disait être le dauphin ou plutôt Louis XVII. Un peu plus loin elle avait souri en se rappelant que c'était par ce chemin que Réveillon s'était enfui devant les émeutiers qui saccageaient sa Folie Titon... Et elle avait sauté au cou de Thérèse Deugros dont le fils avait été l'apprenti de Riesener avant de tomber aux Tuileries. C'est un peu grâce à elle que la famille avait pu supporter les privations révolutionnaires. Antoinette alla elle-même avec la patronne choisir les salades et les légumes du souper. Méticuleusement elle cueillit toutes les herbes qui donneraient son goût à la farce.

– Ma belle, conseilla la vieille jardinière, si tu mets du cerfeuil, n'ajoute pas de persil, ils ne s'aiment pas tellement ces deux-là et se contrarient. En revanche, prends quelques feuilles d'épinards et un peu d'oseille pour verdir ta farce. Quelques côtes de poirée [1] qui une fois pilées et cuites lui donneront du moelleux et une bonne poignée d'estragon qui lui ne se laisse pas voler son parfum...

1. Variété de bette.

En rentrant, Antoinette s'aperçut qu'elle avait oublié de dire à Marie d'acheter chez le boucher la viande nécessaire à la farce. Elle décida d'y passer. Sa belle-fille était justement dans la boutique :

– Que je suis contente de te voir arriver ! J'ai pensé à la farce mais je ne savais pas quoi prendre...

– Il faut d'abord du veau, quatre ou cinq onces dans la noix, décida Antoinette ; quatre de lard, un peu de graisse de porc, deux onces de rognons, et deux ou trois onces de moelle de bœuf. Maintenant les fantaisies sont permises. J'ai toutes les herbes, tu ne vois pas quelque chose à ajouter ?

– Pourquoi ne pas incorporer à notre farce une oreille de veau que nous ferons cuire au blanc et que nous découperons en petits morceaux ? Ces dés un peu croquants sous la dent apporteront une surprise. Qu'en dis-tu ?

– Je trouve que c'est une bonne idée. Si M. Grimod de La Reynière t'entendait, il ferait aussitôt essayer cette trouvaille par son cuisinier.

Chargées de leurs paniers, les deux femmes rentrèrent en chantonnant place d'Aligre où Ethis qui avait amené le petit Bertrand les attendait.

– Tiens, coupe donc quelques tranches dans le jambon de Bayonne, nous allons faire un petit en-cas avant de nous mettre au travail. Tu pourras aussi allumer le feu dans la cheminée pour faire de la braise et préparer le tourne-broche. Après on ne veut plus te voir dans la maison avant six heures !

Un peu plus tard, tandis que Lucie jouait avec le petit Bertrand, les deux cuisinières s'affairaient devant la longue table de noyer, polie par l'usage depuis le temps qu'elle était sortie de l'atelier d'Œben. Le plus cocasse était que le maître qui, naturellement, ne fabriquait pas d'ordinaire ce genre de meubles, avait tenu à la marquer de son moindron comme s'il s'était agi d'un bureau de marqueterie destiné au roi.

– Un jour, avait dit sa femme Marguerite, cette table de cuisine vaudra peut-être très cher à cause de ta plaisanterie !

– Penses-tu, les gens ne sont pas si bêtes! avait répondu le maître.

Tout en racontant cette histoire à Marie, Antoinette avait sorti toutes les victuailles et s'amusait à les disposer sur la table.

– Dommage, dit-elle, que mon frère Henri-François ne soit pas là : regarde quelle belle nature morte il aurait pu peindre!

En attendant, il fallait éplucher les légumes de la farce ainsi que le chou et les laitues destinées à la garniture. Comme le jeune Bertrand de Valfroy avait daigné s'endormir, Lucie vint aider sa mère et Marie et décrivit pour celle-ci les beautés et l'élégance de la robe que M. Parisot était en train de lui confectionner.

Les légumes cuisaient déjà quand les femmes s'attaquèrent au gros du travail : hacher menu la viande de veau et le lard ainsi que les herbes.

– Et le mitonnage? demanda Marie.

– Je l'avais oublié! Remplis vite une terrine de lait, je découpe des tranches de pain blanc car il faut le mettre tout de suite à tremper.

Le hachage des morceaux de noix, du lard et des rognons fut long et pénible. Les deux femmes se relayaient pour manier le hachoir qui était aussi lourd qu'une masse de sculpteur.

– Je crois que nous avons dit trop vite à Ethis de s'en aller! dit Marie en riant. C'est un travail d'aide cuisinier qu'il aurait très bien pu faire!

Antoinette sortit du grand buffet une énorme terrine qui servait en principe à faire mariner les pièces de gibier et y jeta la viande déjà hachée, les herbes qu'on décida finalement de laisser toutes crues à part la poirée, la graisse, la moelle de bœuf. Poivré, salé, le mélange commençait à sentir bon.

– Qu'est-ce que ça va être quand elle cuira! dit Lucie avec une mine gourmande.

– Sublime! répondit sa mère en ajoutant : passe-moi donc le mitonnage et la grande spatule.

C'était un bel outil sorti d'un bloc de merisier et qui

avait été utilisé autrefois par Œben et Riesener pour faire des moulages en plâtre. Antoinette l'avait récupéré pour sa cuisine et la spatule servait à tout : à remuer la soupe dans le grand chaudron, à retourner les rôtis, à mélanger les ragoûts ou, comme aujourd'hui, à malaxer la farce à laquelle Marie venait d'ajouter trois jaunes d'œufs, deux tranches de jambon et une de lard coupées en dés ainsi que les petits morceaux d'oreille encore tout blancs qu'elle venait de sortir du bouillon.

– Je crois que nous y sommes bientôt. Je n'en peux plus de remuer! dit Antoinette en tendant la cuiller de bois à Marie.

Devant elle, la poitrine de veau attendait, généreuse et superbe. Sa poche, bien découpée par Parmain qui décidément était un bon boucher, contint presque toute la farce de la terrine : au moins quatre livres d'un mélange onctueux dont l'odeur à la fois délicate et subtilement corsée embaumait le thym et la sarriette. Dans l'âtre, la braise était rouge, Marie tenait déjà la broche, effilée comme la baïonnette d'un grenadier de la Garde, quand Antoinette eut une hésitation.

– Attends! Je me demande s'il n'y a pas mieux à faire que de rôtir notre poitrine. J'ai peur que la viande de veau, si fragile, ne sèche et ne durcisse exagérément, même si nous l'arrosons comme il faut. Je crois qu'elle mijotera mieux dans la braisière où la farce elle aussi cuira plus à son aise.

– Tu as raison. Prépare le trépied, il reste une mince tranche de couenne pour garnir la cocotte que je vais foncer au saindoux.

Ainsi fut fait et, quand le grésillement du cochon se mêla à celui du brasier, les deux femmes se regardèrent en riant, goûtant le plaisir simple de s'être données sans retenue à l'élaboration d'un chef-d'œuvre qui, pour être éphémère, n'en serait pas moins apprécié tout à l'heure par ceux qu'elles aimaient.

Le repas fut gai. Lenoir avait prévenu qu'il s'occupait de la boisson et les trois bouteilles de vin de Bourgogne qu'il apporta, cachetées de cire rouge comme des décrets, furent appréciées par tous les convives. Réveillon que les plaisirs de la table rendaient lyrique proclama que « l'élégance virile et fruitée de ce vin vieilli dans les caveaux bourguignons s'alliait merveilleusement à la saveur gourmande du rôti farci et de sa sauce moelleuse et veloutée comme les larmes d'un dévot ».

Lucie fit remarquer que les larmes étaient salées et pas du tout moelleuses, ce qui fit douter le bon Réveillon de ses dons poétiques.

– Tu peux bien te moquer ! dit-il. Mais lis L'*Almanach de la table* de M. Grimod de La Reynière et tu verras que ce gastronome-philosophe, quoique un peu fou, ne parle pas autrement des soupers mirifiques qu'il offre à ses amis. Un plat réussi, et Dieu sait si cette poitrine l'est, a besoin d'être assaisonné de paroles épicées comme de sel et de poivre !

Réveillon fut applaudi et Riesener annonça qu'il montait une seconde chez lui pour chercher le dessert. C'était une surprise car Antoinette et Marie avaient prévu des fruits. L'ébéniste de la reine revint bientôt en portant devant lui, sur ses deux mains, un plat où luisait, comme un disque d'or, un superbe gâteau.

– C'est un pithiviers ! dit-il. Mais attention, pas une de ces pâtes molles à la frangipane avare. J'ai demandé à Mme Dumaine qui est de là-bas, vous savez la femme du bronzier de la rue de Charonne, de me le faire comme elle seule à Paris sait le réussir. Tenez, elle a même gravé à la pointe du couteau sur le couvercle du gâteau doré à l'œuf la rosace qui est au vrai pithiviers ce que l'estampille de Jacob est à un fauteuil.

Lucie battit des mains et chacun y alla de son compliment.

– C'est aussi pour fêter une bonne chose qui m'est arrivée ce matin ! ajouta Riesener. Figurez-vous que j'ai vendu l'un de mes meubles rachetés aux ventes de Versailles. Ce n'est pas la plus belle pièce mais enfin cela montre qu'il y a encore des gens capables d'apprécier une œuvre d'Œben, de Molitor ou de Riesener.

Le 24 messidor, Lucie ne tenait plus en place. Elle refusa d'aller se coucher avant d'avoir entendu, à neuf heures du soir, la salve d'artillerie qui devait annoncer le début des festivités : des spectacles gratuits donnés dans les principaux théâtres de Paris.

Le lendemain, les canons retentirent de nouveau à six heures, donnant le branle aux réjouissances qui allaient marquer la journée. A sept heures, Ethis et Marie encadrant Lucie fraîche et jolie dans sa robe bleue, s'engageaient dans le Faubourg en direction de la Bastille. Déjà, de nombreux Parisiens se hâtaient vers les Champs-Élysées où la fête était organisée. Cela faisait un bon bout de chemin à parcourir depuis la place d'Aligre mais le cœur y était. Et le soleil aussi qui faisait briller le dôme de l'église Saint-Louis des jésuites, rue Saint-Antoine. Plus on avançait vers le carré Marigny et la place de l'Étoile, plus la foule était dense. Au Palais-Royal, Ethis annnonça qu'on allait s'arrêter dans une buvette pour se rafraîchir. Ces quelques instants de repos n'étaient pas inutiles car il commençait à faire très chaud. Marie et Lucie étaient vêtues légèrement mais Ethis pestait dans son habit de lainage et disait qu'il regrettait sa blouse de sans-culotte. Enfin, on arriva à hauteur de l'Élysée où était installé un théâtre en plein air et des guinguettes qui ressemblaient à des gros paquets ficelés de rubans tricolores.

Lucie ouvrait de grands yeux. C'était la première fois qu'elle assistait à une fête populaire et tout l'émerveillait, à commencer par une grande affiche peinte aux couleurs de la France qui annonçait pour l'après-midi et la soirée vingt-deux orchestres, entre le carré de la Laiterie et la place de l'Étoile. Au centre de celle-ci, un grand rocher – David avait un faible pour ces fausses montagnes depuis la fête de la Fédération – servait de piédestal à la Renommée, haute de trente pieds, qui célébrait les victoires républicaines. La place de l'Étoile, qu'on appelait aussi « l'Étoile de Chaillot » à cause des quelques allées qui s'y croisaient, était flanquée de deux lourds monuments édifiés par Ledoux pour les services de l'octroi. Des gens s'y affairaient, montés sur les toits pour préparer le feu d'artifice. Une foule gaie et bon enfant où l'on retrouvait quelques vieux costumes révolutionnaires mêlés à ceux de la mode du moment, parcourait en tous sens ce champ de manœuvres sans soldats où les responsables, reconnaissables à leur brassard tricolore, mettaient la dernière main aux préparatifs des jeux : mâts de cocagne et concours de bagues dans l'ancien Cours-la-Reine, salle de valse allemande et cirque pour les chevaux de Franconi au carré Marigny.

Les invitations offertes par Fontaine ne servirent pas à grand-chose : la foule était si nombreuse que les places réservées dans les trois théâtres où s'exhibaient danseurs de corde, escamoteurs et voltigeurs avaient été prises d'assaut dès le matin par des débrouillards qu'il n'était pas question de déloger. Malgré cette faille de l'organisation qui empêcha Lucie de faire admirer sa belle robe dans les tribunes officielles, la jeune fille s'amusa beaucoup. Ethis était généreux, il avait tout le temps la main à la poche pour offrir un sirop d'orgeat, une glace à la praline ou l'un de ces gros beignets qu'un bonhomme habillé en cuisinier faisait dorer dans une grande bassine de friture.

Le soir venu, Marie épuisée demandait grâce et Ethis aurait mérité son vieux surnom de « Traîne-sabot », la fatigue ranimant les douleurs de son ancienne blessure. Seule Lucie était encore vaillante et comme elle tenait absolument à voir le feu d'artifice, Ethis dit qu'il valait mieux s'attabler dans une guinguette et manger des saucisses en attendant que les aides des frères Ruggieri mettent le feu aux innombrables fusées installées à l'Étoile.

Un bouquet grandiose qui renaissait sans cesse de ses fumées retombantes et qui était censé symboliser des trophées à la gloire des armées marqua le point final de cette journée triomphale.

Il fallait maintenant revenir au Faubourg et le chemin parut beaucoup plus long qu'à l'aller. Heureusement, dans toutes les rues la fête continuait, des groupes formaient des farandoles, d'autres chantaient en chœur, un bal s'était même spontanément organisé devant l'Hôtel de Ville. Quand la famille arriva place d'Aligre, une bougie brillait encore à la fenêtre d'Antoinette qui n'avait pas voulu s'endormir avant le retour de sa fille. Ragaillardie, Lucie aurait bien passé le restant de la nuit à raconter à sa mère tous les événements extraordinaires auxquels elle avait assisté. Elle dut cependant aller se coucher sans attendre tandis que Marie et Ethis, enlacés, regagnaient la maison Thirion, où bien souvent au cours des siècles passés d'autres couples avaient terminé dans l'amour une longue journée de liesse populaire.

Le lendemain, il n'était question à Paris que de la « fête à Bonaparte ». Le Premier consul avait atteint son but : regrouper derrière sa personne et sa gloire le peuple de la capitale en le persuadant par des flonflons de résonance révolutionnaire que la République continuait sous l'autoritarisme consulaire. D'ailleurs, *Le Moniteur* n'avait pas attendu pour enfoncer le clou bonapartiste. A côté d'un compte rendu détaillé des réjouissances publiques, un article non signé mais dont on pouvait deviner qui l'avait inspiré, tirait enseignement de la journée :

« Un parallèle entre cette fête et celles qui l'ont précédée serait assurément ici déplacé ; on ne peut cependant s'empêcher de faire remarquer que celle-ci avait un caractère particulier, qu'elle était vraiment nationale, vraiment populaire et que chacune de ses parties avait pour objet d'offrir un amusement. Le plaisir y naissait de la variété ; elle n'avait pas un plan suivi ; l'espèce de désordre qui y régnait en faisait le charme ; son irrégularité la rendait piquante et cette irrégularité même, occupant à la fois le spectateur sur un grand nombre de points, avait cet avantage que les dangers ou du moins les inconvénients de la foule n'existaient nulle part. Cette fête n'était point consacrée à la fraternité, nul emblème ne la rappelait comme un devoir, et ce sentiment qui ne veut pas être commandé mais dont la communication est si rapide lorsqu'il naît sans contrainte, paraissait animer tous les cœurs. L'égalité s'était établie sans qu'on eût reçu l'ordre de l'admettre. Une liberté riante et douce régnait partout. L'air du bonheur et de la satisfaction animait toutes les physionomies. »

– Voilà, dit Lenoir après avoir lu l'article, une subtile nécrologie de la République dont on garde le nom parce qu'il est pratique et que ses quatre syllabes détiennent encore un pouvoir explosif à ne pas négliger. Qu'il est habile, de la part du gouvernement, de parler de bonheur, de douceur, de liberté riante... Il faut tout de même avouer que la Révolution n'a jamais réussi ou n'a pas eu le temps de faire que les mots deviennent autre chose que des abstractions. Les gens ont soif de vivre et la fête est une boisson dont le peuple aime se désaltérer!

– Vous voici donc devenu contre-révolutionnaire, presque antirépublicain! dit Antoinette. Le pouvoir d'un Bonaparte vous attire?

– Mais non, ma douce Antoinette. Je croyais que vous commenciez à me connaître mais vous ne comprenez rien à mes opinions qui je dois en convenir sont souvent déroutantes. Je m'y perds moi-même parfois...

– Alors expliquez-moi! coupa Antoinette en riant.

– Je vais essayer. Je ne suis ni un théoricien ni un homme d'action. Mettons que je suis un témoin capable de se transformer en garde-fou. Sous la Révolution, j'ai pensé qu'il était de la plus grande importance de sauver le patrimoine artistique que nous laissaient mille ans de royauté. Je suis prêt aujourd'hui à essayer de sauver ce qui mérite d'être sauvé de l'acquis républicain, en dehors de Bonaparte qui, lui, ne gardera que ce qui l'arrange : un drapeau et un vocabulaire.

– Je crois, Alexandre, que vous êtes surtout un original. Et c'est pour cela que je vous aime tant.

Le succès de la fête du 14-Juillet engagea naturellement le gouvernement à en organiser d'autres. Le 1er vendémiaire fut ainsi célébré l'anniversaire de la fondation de la République, mais les amusements publics parurent fades aux Parisiens. On se rattrapa le 9 novembre à l'occasion de la paix qui venait d'être signée avec l'Angleterre.

Cette paix générale qu'il s'agissait de célébrer avait pour corollaire le commerce, source inépuisable de richesses. On fêta donc le commerce. Heureusement, il faisait encore beau car David et ses amis Percier et Fontaine avaient imaginé, pour changer, de faire triompher le libre-échange sur les flots paisibles de la Seine. C'était moins loin que l'Étoile et, cette fois, Antoinette conduisit sa fille entre le pont Neuf et le pont Royal où se dressait une énorme pièce montée représentant le temple du Commerce. Une flottille de chaloupes et de barques, ornées et pavoisées aux couleurs des divers pays de l'Europe, remonta le fleuve, de Chaillot jusqu'au temple où une petite frégate lâcha sa bordée de huit canons. Les « peuples » s'y rassemblèrent et offrirent à la Paix l'hommage de leurs chants et de leurs danses.

Alors, on vit un superbe ballon monter majestueusement dans le ciel. Antoinette serra un peu plus fort la main de Lucie. Ces ascensions, de plus en plus courantes, ne relevaient plus de l'exploit comme au temps où elle regardait son Pilâtre attiser le feu au milieu de la nacelle pour faire monter la montgolfière de Réveillon. Antoinette ressentait pourtant chaque fois un pincement au cœur. Il lui semblait que c'était sa jeunesse qui s'envolait dans les nuages et, la nuit qui suivait, elle était en proie au même cauchemar : le ballon de Pilâtre s'enflammait et tombait sous ses yeux comme une boule de feu.

Cette fois le ballon était superbe avec les drapeaux de toutes les puissances qui flottaient et se mélangeaient autour de son enveloppe brillante comme de l'argent. Quand il fut assez haut dans le ciel, les aéronautes lâchèrent un parachute multicolore soutenant une effigie de Mercure.

Lucie regarda alors Antoinette et lui glissa à l'oreille :

– Ne regarde pas, maman, je sais que cela te fait mal...

Antoinette, troublée, retint ses larmes en embrassant sa petite fille qui semblait lire à livre ouvert dans ses pensées.

Et la vie continua dans le Faubourg renaissant. Ébénistes et menuisiers tenaient encore le haut du pavé avec les autres métiers du meuble, les bronziers, les marchands de bois, les serruriers et les vernisseurs-laqueurs, mais, à côté, l'activité industrielle se développait du Trône à la Bastille dans toutes les rues et les passages enserrant la grand-rue.

Si l'ancienne fabrique de papier peint Réveillon avait dû se séparer de la moitié de ses ouvriers, la manufacture de glaces de la rue de Reuilly avait repris son développement interrompu par la Révolution. Depuis longtemps, une grande partie de la fabrication était assurée en province, à Saint-Gobain [1] et à Tourlaville, pays du fondateur de la manufacture royale devenue « compagnie ». La vieille maison du Faubourg continuait pourtant à employer de deux cents à deux cent cinquante ouvriers. Le polissage s'effectuait à Saint-Gobain et à Chauny où de nouvelles machines, mues par la force hydraulique, imitaient par un mouvement de va-et-vient le travail à la main. Une machine à vapeur avait été essayée rue de Reuilly, puis un manège à chevaux, pour lancer les lourds polissoirs mais les résultats n'avaient pas été très bons. Le douci continuait donc de s'y faire entièrement à la main ainsi que l'étamage qui utilisait la plus grande partie du personnel.

– Le Faubourg est en train de changer! répétait Ethis. Le règne des grandes fabriques et des machines commence. Vous verrez qu'un jour prochain on construira les meubles à la machine!

Cela mettait Riesener en fureur.

– On fabriquera peut-être des tables et des chaises à la mécanique mais cela n'aura plus rien à voir avec ce qu'on appelle encore aujourd'hui des « meubles ». La main de l'homme est irremplaçable pour galber le dossier d'un fauteuil ou marqueter un devant de commode. Crois-moi, il y aura encore longtemps des ébénistes au Faubourg!

1. Transformée en compagnie industrielle financée par des actionnaires, l'ancienne manufacture créée par Colbert devient la Société Saint-Gobain.

Ils avaient raison tous les deux. Aucune machine ne ferait jamais les sièges de Jacob ou les secrétaires de Riesener mais il était vrai que le Faubourg s'industrialisait et que les compagnons du bois n'y étaient plus les seuls composants de l'activité. Les manufactures de faïence et de porcelaine s'étaient multipliées depuis la Révolution. Caron et Lefèvre, des amis de Lenoir, employaient plus de cent ouvriers au 64 de la rue Amelot. L'Allemand Jean Nast établi au Faubourg depuis 1783 en occupait aussi une centaine et les frères Darthes qui logeaient dans la même maison qu'Antoinette, place d'Aligre, venaient de transférer leur manufacture installée depuis trente ans rue de Charonne au 90 de la rue de la Roquette, dans l'ancien hôtel de Montalembert [1].

Et puis, il y avait François Richard, l'ami d'Ethis, et son associé Lenoir dont la manufacture de coton prospérait rue de Charonne. Le Premier consul était venu en personne visiter leur installation, la première qui associait à Paris la filature et le tissage, ce qui ne les empêchait pas de faire tisser en Normandie et en Picardie où ils trouvaient une main-d'œuvre qualifiée.

Sans être devenu un assidu des soirées de la place d'Aligre, Richard venait parfois partager le souper du mercredi. C'était un convive agréable qui, malgré les affaires considérables qu'il dirigeait, paraissait n'avoir aucun souci. Il était gai, avait de l'esprit et, surtout, avait toujours mille choses à raconter. Très bien introduit dans les milieux gouvernementaux où, sous l'impulsion de Bonaparte, on s'intéressait de près aux entreprises industrielles, il était au courant de tout, même souvent de certains secrets de la vie familiale du Premier consul. Ses confidences faisaient les délices d'Antoinette et de tous les convives. Percier et Fontaine que leurs fonctions appelaient souvent aux Tuileries, à Malmaison ou à Saint-Cloud, savaient aussi beaucoup de choses mais ils étaient plus discrets. Les propos de Richard les pous-

1. L'hôtel du comte de Montalembert, émigré, fut adjugé 40 300 francs aux frères Darthes en l'an XII (1803). Terrains et dépendances couvraient plus d'un hectare.

saient pourtant aux confidences et l'on ne s'ennuyait pas ces soirs-là place d'Aligre.

Les grands ont ceci en commun, c'est que les incidents de leur vie, leurs manies, leurs tics même intéressent le monde. Les journaux, tous contrôlés, filtraient leurs informations et les potins du Consulat n'en étaient que plus savoureux. C'est ainsi qu'on apprit chez Antoinette que le Premier consul avait une passion pour les bains chauds, qu'il s'y précipitait immédiatement au saut du lit et qu'il exigeait de son fidèle Constant que la température de l'eau fût aussi chaude qu'il pouvait la supporter.

– Bonaparte nous fait damner avec ses salles de bains! raconta Fontaine qui venait de faire installer celle de Saint-Cloud. Percier a dû lui en dessiner une dizaine. Et il fallait qu'elle soit à la fois proche de sa chambre à coucher et de son cabinet car l'envie de se baigner peut lui venir aussi bien au milieu de la nuit que pendant une séance de travail.

– Le matin, tandis qu'il trempe dans l'eau presque bouillante, Bourrienne, son secrétaire, lui lit des dépêches et les journaux. C'est comme cela, continua Richard, qu'il a appris que nous avions, avec nos installations de province, 4 000 métiers en activité. Ce chiffre l'a frappé comme s'il s'agissait d'une armée et c'est alors qu'il a décidé de venir voir tourner les broches du faubourg Saint-Antoine. Je tiens cela de Bourrienne qui l'accompagnait lors de la visite et que j'eus le bonheur de traiter peu après au *Rocher de Cancale* où l'honorable Balaine sert des huîtres et des homards dont la qualité est aussi élevée que le prix. Ce ne fut point pourtant de l'argent perdu. Outre le plaisir de la conversation de M. Bourrienne, ce dîner m'a permis d'obtenir de larges facilités pour le règlement de l'acquisition des couvents de Traisnel et de Bon-Secours [1]. Du coup, nous allons ouvrir de nouvelles filatures dans les abbayes de Saint-Martin-de-Séez et chez

1. Richard et Lenoir n'eurent à payer en bons que les deux tiers de la mise à prix. Richard sera plus tard, en 1811, déchargé par un décret impérial de la somme de 55 412 francs qu'il devait encore.

les bénédictines d'Alençon en attendant Laigle, Caen et Chantilly.

Ethis, béat d'amiration, écoutait Richard parler de son succès fulgurant et de ses fabuleux projets.

– Quand tu as commencé à t'occuper du coton, pensais-tu aller aussi loin? demanda-t-il.

– Bien sûr que non. Ma chance, c'est le basin anglais. Et aussi d'avoir rencontré Lenoir qui est une sorte de génie de la mécanique. J'aimerais bien que vous le connaissiez tous un peu mieux mais c'est un homme malade qui n'aime pas sortir.

– Parlez-nous donc encore de Bonaparte, coupa Antoinette que les machines à filer la laine et les métiers à tisser intéressaient peu.

– C'est vrai que l'homme est fascinant. Infatigable en campagne il conduit l'administration de la France avec la vigueur d'un capitaine qui sait tenir les armées ennemies à la pointe de son épée. Mais nos amis qui ont approché le grand homme en savent sur lui plus long que moi.

– Qui sait vraiment quelque chose sur ce diable d'homme qui s'est fait roi comme d'autres se font curés ou rôtisseurs! dit Alexandre Lenoir. Celui qui le connaît le mieux est peut-être le mamelouk Roustam qui tient le miroir quand Bonaparte se rase et qui lui présente sa culotte de casimir blanc. C'est lui qui lui met ses bottes et le garde pendant la nuit. A l'extérieur il fait l'office de piqueur et suit le Premier consul dans tous ses déplacements. Porteur de la bouteille de campagne, du manteau et de la capote, il galope dans les parades vêtu d'un superbe costume oriental et, aux armées, du costume des grenadiers de la Garde. Isabey l'a peint avec son maître, un maître, hélas! dont il ne veut pas parler.

– Ma chère Antoinette, dit à son tour Fontaine, ce sont là des mièvreries sans signification. Ce qui est important c'est le travail considérable qui se fait à la commission de la Justice et au Conseil d'État. Animée par Bonaparte et dirigée par Cambacérès, la commission rédige le Code civil qui régira les rapports des Français entre eux. Et il paraît que cela marche au pas de charge, comme si le

Premier consul avait hâte d'en finir pour passer à d'autres travaux.

Comme chaque fois, la conversation revint sur le bois, le style nouveau, les bronzes inspirés des campagnes orientales ou des emblèmes de l'Antiquité qui changeaient l'aspect des meubles.

C'était le moment où Riesener philosophait, où Fontaine et Percier défendaient les lignes nouvelles qu'ils imaginaient pour Jacob...

Il y avait justement beaucoup à dire à propos des Jacob. La maison de la rue Meslée venait d'être bouleversée par un deuil qui remettait en cause son organisation et même son existence à un moment où les commandes n'avaient jamais été aussi nombreuses et où sa renommée s'étendait jusqu'aux pays les plus lointains. Georges, l'aîné des enfants, était mort brutalement. François-Honoré ne pouvait assumer seul la direction d'une entreprise qui employait maintenant plus de trois cents ouvriers.

– J'ai été voir cet après-midi mon vieil ami Georges, dit Riesener. Il est évidemment très frappé par la mort de son fils et le voilà obligé de reprendre du service pour sauver la maison. J'espère que sa santé tiendra. Lui qui se disait si heureux d'avoir laissé les ateliers à ses fils pour pouvoir vivre une vieillesse tranquille!

Riesener avait certes de la compassion pour Jacob, mais dans le fond de son âme n'enviait-il pas le patriarche, fondateur de la dynastie, d'être amené à se succéder à lui-même? Pour lui Riesener, maître incontesté de Louis XVI, l'aventure était terminée. Pour Jacob, elle continuait, avec un fils dont le talent égalait le sien...

Antoinette devinait toutes les pensées qui assaillaient son beau-père. Elle demanda pour faire diversion :

– Ils ne peuvent pas garder la marque de « Jacob frères ». Vont-ils reprendre l'ancienne estampille « Iacob »? Au fait on n'a jamais su pourquoi le « J » s'était changé en « I »...

– Mais si. Il s'agit d'une maladresse du ciseleur qui a fait sauter un bout de lettre, et Georges a dit que c'était le sort qui l'avait voulu. Il refusa tout net de refaire le moindron. Cela n'enlève rien à la beauté des meubles et surtout des sièges qu'il a signés pendant cinquante ans! Pour la nouvelle estampille, François-Honoré a choisi de prendre le nom des « Desmalter » en souvenir d'une terre, « Les Malterres » que possédait son aïeul à Cheny [1].

Cela dit, Riesener se leva. Cette discussion l'agaçait, il annonça qu'il allait se coucher.

1. De 1803 à 1813, l'estampille sera libellée : « Jacob. D. R. Meslée », quelquefois simplement « J.D. ».

Chapitre 9.

LA MORT DU MAÎTRE

Les Caniolle habitaient dans l'un des petits immeubles qui entouraient le marché Beauvau. Antoinette connaissait bien Armande Caniolle qu'elle rencontrait chez les commerçants du quartier. C'était une petite femme discrète, toujours pressée, ne se mêlant jamais aux conversations qui animaient chaque matin la petite place. Son mari rentrait souvent à l'heure où les compagnons du bois gagnaient leurs ateliers. Lui non plus ne parlait à personne. Un salut en passant et c'était tout, il s'engouffrait dans la porte de sa maison ou filait d'un pas vif, sans se retourner, vers le Faubourg et la Bastille. On avait appris depuis peu qu'il était de la police secrète. Cela expliquait sa réserve. Les policiers n'avaient jamais été très populaires dans le Faubourg, non qu'on les craignît mais parce qu'ils exerçaient un métier « qui sentait mauvais ». Qu'ils fussent en uniforme ou en civil, les gens du bois méprisaient naturellement ces auxiliaires du pouvoir qui travaillaient dans l'ombre et entretenaient, disait-on, la délation.

Jean-François Caniolle ne gagna pas de faveurs à la révélation de son état. De lui on disait en riant : « Ce n'est pas un homme du bois, c'est l'homme à Dubois. » Dubois était alors chef de la police.

Et puis un jour, Antoinette croisa Armande Caniolle en larmes, serrant contre elle sa petite fille d'une dizaine d'années. Il lui sembla lire dans le regard de la femme une quête de sympathie. Elle s'arrêta :

– Que vous arrive-t-il, madame Caniolle? Rien de grave j'espère?

– Si, c'est terrible. Mon mari est dans un état grave. Il a été blessé d'un coup de poignard et d'une balle de pistolet en arrêtant Cadoudal. Son camarade Étienne Buffet, père de quatre enfants, a été tué.

Antoinette trouva quelques mots de consolation qui parurent toucher Armande Caniolle.

– Je vous suis reconnaissante de vous être arrêtée. J'avais besoin de parler à quelqu'un et je suis heureuse que ce soit vous. Tout le monde vous aime dans le quartier! Je sais bien que mon mari y est mal considéré. Son métier est ingrat mais il l'exerce avec humanité. Puisqu'il faut des gens de police, autant qu'ils soient comme lui, honnêtes et braves.

– Mais vous n'avez pas à vous justifier, ma pauvre amie. Ce Cadoudal et ses acolytes voulaient, à ce qu'on dit, tuer le Premier consul. Celui-ci est assez populaire dans le Faubourg pour que chacun compatisse à votre douleur. Pour ma part, j'espère que les médecins vont très vite guérir votre mari. Je vais acheter *Le Moniteur* pour lire tous les détails de l'affaire. M. Caniolle va sûrement être décoré...

– Je me moque bien des décorations. Ce que je veux, c'est qu'il vive! Merci encore de vos bontés. Elles me donnent du courage.

Quelques heures plus tard Paris apprenait la grande nouvelle: Georges Cadoudal était arrêté ainsi que le général Pichegru!

Le complot tenait l'opinion publique et surtout la police en haleine depuis des mois. Il ternissait l'aura du Premier consul qui n'avait jamais été aussi brillante, qu'en cette année 1804. Dès l'ouverture de la session de l'an XII, le Code civil avait été adopté en entier et Murat, l'époux de Caroline, l'une des sœurs de Bonaparte, venait d'être nommé gouverneur de Paris. Tout semblait sourire au Premier consul, inquiet seulement des conspirations qui se tramaient contre lui.

Le complot le plus dangereux était celui qu'inspirait

Georges Cadoudal, l'ancien chef des chouans réfugié en Angleterre depuis sa défaite par Brune en 1799. Le comte d'Artois l'avait nommé lieutenant général du Royaume, un titre virtuel qu'il entendait bien rendre effectif en capturant Bonaparte que les Anglais étaient prêts à mettre sous bonne garde.

Cadoudal, la police le savait, était à Paris. Pire, il avait réussi à attirer de son côté les généraux Pichegru et Moreau qui s'étaient illustrés dans les armées de la République avant d'essayer de détrôner Bonaparte, rival exécré.

Caniolle raconta un mois plus tard à Antoinette et à Riesener, lorsqu'il fut autorisé à quitter l'hôpital de l'Hôtel-Dieu où il avait été soigné, tous les détails de l'opération de police dans laquelle il avait failli perdre la vie. Ce jour-là, le policier, promu commissaire, avait tenu à venir remercier Antoinette de l'aide morale qu'elle avait apportée à sa femme. Cette visite n'enchantait pas tellement le vieux maître, non plus d'ailleurs qu'Antoinette qui n'entendait pas se lier à un personnage de la police. Mais Jean-François Caniolle était là, il fallait bien le recevoir poliment. Tous deux ne le regrettèrent pas car l'homme sut se montrer aimable et surtout passionnant. Il racontait bien et c'était une qualité qui ne pouvait laisser Antoinette indifférente. Quand Caniolle fut parti, elle reconstitua son récit – un vrai roman – en s'aidant des exemplaires du *Moniteur* qu'elle avait conservés, afin de l'envoyer à sa sœur qui, maintenant, se morfondait à Bordeaux où son mari avait été muté. « Pas de fioritures, se dit-elle, je rédige cela comme un rapport, en y mettant tout de même un peu de chaleur. »

« L'affaire commença le 18 ventose rue de la Montagne-Sainte-Geneviève. Tout passant un peu curieux qui serait monté dans l'après-midi vers Saint-Étienne-du-Mont eût pu remarquer que les petits rideaux à carreaux rouges et blancs du cabaret qui faisait le coin de la rue du Clos-Bruneau s'entrouvraient souvent pour permettre à plusieurs consommateurs attablés d'inspecter la rue. Le cabaret du *Bon Coing* et celui des *Barreaux verts*, un peu plus loin, étaient eux aussi remplis par des clients qu'un observateur eût facilement reconnus, malgré le soin qu'ils prenaient à paraître naturels, comme appartenant à la préfecture de police. Un rémouleur qui depuis le matin affûtait les mêmes couteaux et un commissionnaire, une lettre à la main, qui faisait mine de chercher une adresse introuvable, pouvaient difficilement cacher qu'ils appartenaient aux services de M. Dubois.

« Deux inspecteurs nommés Buffet et Caniolle descendirent de la Montagne vers quatre heures, chacun d'un côté de la rue. Le premier tenait son mouchoir comme s'il allait éternuer et l'autre sa canne sur l'épaule. Cela voulait dire qu'un cabriolet guetté depuis longtemps venait d'apparaître sur la place Saint-Étienne et se tenait rangé le long de la rue des Sept-Voies. C'était une voiture de louage jaune clair et portant le numéro 53 peint en lettres noires. Aussitôt, la plupart des faux clients des cabarets sortirent, prêts à intervenir au premier signal.

« Pendant ce temps-là, dans l'arrière-boutique d'une fruitière, des hommes parlaient à voix basse et se partageaient des armes tandis que Mme Lemoine, la propriétaire, faisait le guet dans son magasin. Au fond, une jeune fille qu'on appelait Denise faisait un paquet de hardes au milieu desquelles elle avait caché, dans un bas, une grosse somme en pièces d'or anglaises. L'homme qui semblait être le chef se nommait Georges Cadoudal. Âgé d'une trentaine d'années, il donnait des directives à trois autres complices : Joyaut, Burban et Gaillard.

« Les conspirateurs ignoraient que la police était au courant de leur projet : enlever en plein Paris l'usurpateur Bonaparte alors qu'il se rendrait à Saint-Cloud. Il était convenu que Cadoudal l'attendrait à la tête de soixante-dix Bretons qui arrêteraient sa voiture lorsqu'elle arriverait sur le quai de Chaillot. On tuerait les chevaux avant d'attaquer l'escorte à cheval, homme contre homme, à la loyale.

« Bonaparte livré aux Anglais, Pichegru et Moreau devaient appeler les armées sous le drapeau royal tandis que le comte d'Artois et le duc de Berry, arrivés de

Londres achèveraient par leur présence d'entraîner le peuple à acclamer la restauration monarchique.

« Les arrivées successives de conjurés venus d'Angleterre dont les Polignac, Pichegru, le marquis de Rivière et Pierre-Jean Cadoudal, le frère de Georges, n'avaient pas surpris la police et les arrestations s'étaient multipliées sans toutefois toucher les vrais chefs du complot. Pourtant, Querelle, l'un des conjurés arrêtés, préféra parler plutôt que d'être condamné à mort. Ses indications permirent de nouvelles arrestations dont celle de Louis Picot, le domestique de Cadoudal, mais son maître courait toujours, qu'on savait prêt à déclencher son plan insensé.

« Le Premier consul commençait à s'énerver. Impatient sur toutes choses, il l'était encore plus à propos de ce complot qui le menaçait dans sa personne et gênait ses projets immédiats d'assurer une assise à sa légitimité. Dubois et son adjoint Réal, conseiller préposé à la surveillance de la tranquillité publique, passaient des moments douloureux dans le cabinet de Bonaparte chaque fois que celui-ci les convoquait pour leur demander la raison de leur impuissance à découvrir la retraite de Cadoudal, dit Larive, dit Masson, dont le signalement détaillé était affiché sur tous les murs de Paris.

« Des troupes avaient été appelées, les barrières fermées et le mur d'octroi jalonné de sentinelles. Tout cela pour s'emparer d'un homme qui continuait à se promener impunément dans les rues de Paris. Une loi spéciale avait même été promulguée qui menaçait des pires sanctions " les receleurs de Georges Cadoudal et des soixante brigands soudoyés par l'Angleterre pour attenter à la vie du Premier consul ".

« Au début de février, la police crut s'emparer du Chouan. Georges avait été logé rue du Puits-de-l'Ermite où il se cachait avec Pichegru, Gaillard, Joyaut, Russillon, Rochelle et Burban. Hélas! quand Réal se présenta avec une armée de policiers, l'oiseau s'était envolé. Le 10 février, une arrestation, celle de Bouvet de Lozier, rendit l'espoir à Dubois. Dans une déclaration maladroite, le prisonnier avait compromis Georges, sans y prendre garde, en le désignant sous le nom de Larive. Il en fut tellement désespéré qu'il se pendit dans sa cellule. Entendant du bruit, un porte-clés se précipita et le sauva de justesse. Prévenu, Réal arriva aussitôt et réussit à obtenir une confession complète de Lozier qui, dans son délire, précisa les détails de la conjuration, indiqua le rôle de chacun et raconta comment Pichegru et Moreau étaient mêlés à l'affaire.

« C'était plus que suffisant pour déclencher l'offensive policière. Les deux généraux furent arrêtés les premiers tandis que la souricière s'organisait rue de la Montagne-Sainte-Geneviève où Cadoudal et ses amis fourbissaient leurs armes sans savoir que leur cachette était éventée. »

A ce point de l'histoire, Antoinette reconstitua le plus fidèlement possible le récit de Jean-François Caniolle :

« Nous guettions discrètement la maison de la fruitière où nous vîmes pénétrer une jeune fille sans doute dépêchée pour prévenir Cadoudal que le cabriolet l'attendait sur la place. Peu après, en effet, Georges sortit de la boutique bientôt suivi par ses trois amis et une jeune fille qui portait un sac. Le groupe disséminé remonta la rue en direction de la place Saint-Étienne-du-Mont sans se méfier des faux passants qui semblaient ne pas faire attention à ces gens pressés.

« L'intention de Cadoudal, on le sut après, était d'échapper aux recherches entreprises depuis deux jours dans le quartier et de gagner un refuge qui lui avait été ménagé chez un parfumeur de la rue du Four. C'est ce parfumeur qui avait chargé un homme sûr, Le Ridant, de lui procurer un cabriolet. Malheureusement pour Cadoudal, la chance était du côté de la police : Le Ridant s'adressa à un loueur du passage de la Main-d'or dans le faubourg Saint-Antoine, qu'il croyait bien connaître et qui mit d'autant plus d'empressement à lui fournir la voiture qu'il était l'un de nos agents secrets. Goujon, c'est son nom, instruisit tout de suite ses chefs, ce qui nous permit de surveiller la rue de la Montagne avec le soin que vous savez.

« Avec mon pauvre collègue Buffet, nous suivions Cadoudal, prêts à nous saisir de lui au moment où il monterait dans le cabriolet dont nous distinguions les lanternes allumées et le capot rabattu sur le devant. Soudain, Georges bondit vers la voiture et nous nous précipitâmes sur lui. Je poussai alors un cri qui alerta les autres agents : je venais d'être poignardé à l'épaule ! Buffet de son côté était assailli par Joyaut et ses compagnons tandis que le cabriolet s'élançait à fond de train vers la rue Saint-Jacques.

« Pour moi, il y avait plus de peur que de mal. Mon manteau m'avait protégé et le poignard m'avait à peine blessé. Tandis que les amis de Cadoudal s'enfuyaient à la vue du renfort qui arrivait, je m'élançais avec Buffet à la poursuite du cabriolet en criant : " Arrêtez-le ! Arrêtez-le ! " Goujon aurait dû choisir un cheval moins rapide : fouetté par Le Ridant, la bête avait des ailes et descendait la rue de la Liberté, l'ancienne rue Monsieur-le-Prince. Un encombrement au carrefour de l'Odéon l'obligea tout de même à ralentir et, suivis par un collègue, nous parvînmes à rattraper la voiture.

« C'est alors que le drame survint. Buffet, avec un rare courage, se jeta à la tête du cheval pour l'arrêter. Il y parvenait quand Georges qui tenait un pistolet à la main l'ajusta au front et tira. Mon pauvre camarade s'affaissa mortellement blessé tandis que Cadoudal tentait de s'enfuir par la droite. Je m'étais emparé d'un gros bâton en passant devant un chantier et le poursuivais quand un second coup de pistolet m'atteignit au côté. Je tombai à mon tour et vis dans un éclair Georges qui courait vers la rue de l'Observance. Ivre de rage et malgré la douleur je repris la poursuite le bâton levé. Un attroupement inespéré fut fatal au meurtrier que je réussis à rejoindre au moment où il essayait de se frayer un passage. Mes forces décuplées par le désir de venger Buffet, j'abattis mon gourdin sur sa tête. L'homme chancela et fut aussitôt maîtrisé par mes collègues et des passants. Je m'évanouis et me retrouvai à l'hôpital de l'Hôtel-Dieu tandis que Paris apprenait la nouvelle : Cadoudal était pris !

« Voilà, madame Antoinette et monsieur Riesener, l'histoire d'un modeste agent de la préfecture de police. Ni plus ni moins brave qu'un autre. Un bien mauvais métier tout de même! Mes enfants comme ceux d'Étienne Buffet seront élevés aux frais de l'État. Puisse cette faveur permettre à mon fils de choisir une autre profession. Moi, me voilà commissaire! Buffet, lui, est mort... »

La suite, Antoinette l'apprit comme tous les Parisiens par la lecture du *Moniteur*. Le préfet Dubois était lyrique : « L'arrestation de Georges a électrisé tous les cœurs; il est impossible de rendre l'espèce d'enthousiasme qu'elle a produit : une demi-heure à peine après l'opération, tout Paris en était instruit et l'on peut assurer que la joie est universelle. »

Arrêtés, tous les conjurés tombèrent sous la main de la justice, Pichegru, l'officier perdu, s'étrangla dans la prison du Temple avec sa cravate. Douze des quatre-vingts prévenus furent condamnés à mort. Le général Jean-Victor Moreau ne fut condamné qu'à deux ans de prison.

Il y avait longtemps que les sinistres charrettes du bourreau n'avaient conduit des condamnés à travers les rues de Paris mais le même spectacle attire les mêmes spectateurs. Ceux qui s'écrasaient en place de Grève le 25 juin étaient les frères des voyeurs sanguinaires de la Terreur. Georges avait demandé la faveur d'être exécuté le premier. Elle lui fut refusée. Tous ses compagnons montèrent les degrés sans faiblesse. Quand vint le tour de Cadoudal et qu'il fut arrivé sur la plate-forme, il s'écria : « Camarades! Je vous rejoins! Vive le Roi! » Ce fut son dernier mot. Il résumait et expliquait toute sa vie.

Bonaparte avait eu si peur que, onze jours après l'arrestation de Cadoudal, il décida de frapper un grand coup pour mettre fin aux menées royalistes. Il lui fallait une victime expiatoire : il choisit le duc d'Enghien qu'on alla arrêter en territoire étranger, à Etteinheim, dans le duché de Bade. Amené à Vincennes dans l'après-midi, on le réveilla à minuit. A deux heures du matin il était condamné à mort. A trois heures, il était fusillé dans les fossés du fort!

Les charges retenues contre Louis-Antoine-Henri de Bourbon ne reposaient sur rien et son assassinat – il s'agissait bien d'un assassinat – suscita un grand mouvement d'opinion. Mais la peur l'emporta, chacun se rendait compte que les lois de la République étaient impuissantes à protéger le droit des citoyens et se demandait avec inquiétude si ce crime d'État n'était pas le signal d'une persécution générale contre tous ceux qui n'étaient pas partisans du régime autocrate qui s'instaurait.

Bonaparte n'en avait cure. Il avait voulu faire peur et y avait réussi. Le vent de panique qui souffla sur Paris et la France dans les milieux royalistes et républicains d'opposition avait fait place nette. Le Premier consul pouvait réaliser son rêve : se nommer empereur.

Le 18 mai, jour où le Sénat avait décrété le sénatus-consulte organique par lequel le titre d'empereur était déféré à Bonaparte, était justement celui où le clan de la place d'Aligre se réunissait. Antoinette se réjouissait de ce hasard : on allait pouvoir discuter à chaud d'un événement si considérable qu'il n'était pas possible, tant la surprise était grande, d'en mesurer les conséquences.

Elle aimait, dans les grandes circonstances, tâter le pouls du Faubourg. Dès que la nouvelle fut connue elle passa chercher Marie à *L'Enfant à l'oiseau* et entreprit en sa compagnie le tour des ateliers. Les deux femmes commencèrent par celui d'Emmanuel Caumont, rue Traversière. Il y avait longtemps qu'Antoinette avait rencontré ce jeune homme courageux qui avait repris l'établi et les outils de son père au pire moment de la crise. Lucide, il avait choisi de fabriquer des meubles à la nouvelle mode, et Ethis qui lui avait acheté quelques guéridons avait dit à sa mère qu'il réussissait assez bien. Le tas de planches et de feuilles d'acajou qui bouchait à moitié le passage prouvait que c'était vrai.

– Bonjour Emmanuel, je vois que les affaires marchent! Quand j'étais venu vous voir après la mort de votre père, vous sembliez inquiet.

– Je le suis toujours, mais heureusement le travail ne manque pas. Savez-vous que c'est toujours un plaisir de vous revoir, mademoiselle Œben... Excusez-moi, vous restez pour moi la fille du grand Œben.

– Il ne me déplaît pas qu'on m'appelle mademoiselle. Cela m'arrive d'ailleurs de moins en moins souvent!

Elle rit et prit dans la main un petit bronze finement ciselé qui se trouvait sur l'établi.

– C'est joli, que représente cette dame qui semble voler dans le ciel?

– La Renommée. Je l'aime bien. Je n'en dirais pas autant des bronzes lourdauds dont on affuble maintenant tous les meubles. Tenez, je vais vous montrer la console-jardinière à laquelle il est destiné. Vous tombez bien, c'est un meuble dont je suis fier.

Il l'entraîna avec Marie dans le fond de l'atelier où la fenêtre vitrée donnant sur le passage éclairait une console d'acajou dont la grâce tranchait sur le volume massif d'un meuble d'appui que de multiples ornements de bronze en forme de sphinx ailés n'arrivaient pas à réveiller.

– La Renommée va être placée là, sur le devant, entre deux patères à figures de femmes sur fond clair. Les déesses antiques qui terminent les colonnettes ne s'imposaient pas mais enfin...

– Votre meuble est superbe, ne le dépréciez pas. C'est vous qui l'avez dessiné?

– Non, hélas! C'est une commande de Jacob. J'aime bien travailler pour le vieux Georges et son fils. Ils savent reconnaître le travail bien fait et demeurent exigeants bien qu'ils soient surchargés de commandes... Comment va Ethis? Votre fils me donne aussi du travail de temps en temps. Il semble réussir dans le commerce et c'est tant mieux. Nous autres, artisans, nous avons besoin qu'on vende nos meubles. Tout le monde aime Ethis au Faubourg car il n'exploite pas ceux qui travaillent de leurs mains, « les hommes mécaniques », comme on disait naguère...

– Il ne manquerait plus que ça! En d'autres temps, Ethis serait sans doute devenu ébéniste; son père qui, pourtant, n'avait jamais touché un outil de sa vie, lui a toujours appris le respect du travail manuel. Et puis j'étais là moi aussi et vous savez que je suis née dans un nid de copeaux!

– Les copeaux d'Œben étaient de l'or, madame Antoinette!

Antoinette n'était pas venue chercher des compliments ni échanger des lieux communs. Elle voulait savoir ce que les jeunes de la génération de Caumont pensaient de l'ascension impériale du général Bonaparte.

– Que dit-on dans les ateliers à propos du dernier sénatus-consulte? lança-t-elle.

– Que cela ne change pas grand-chose. Bonaparte était déjà le maître absolu de la France! Un autre que lui se serait fait proclamer empereur, le Faubourg se serait soulevé et sa colère aurait gagné Paris. Mais Bonaparte jouit d'un état de grâce. Parce qu'il a été pauvre. Parce qu'il fait triompher le drapeau tricolore sur les champs de bataille d'Europe. Et surtout parce que depuis qu'il est là le travail a un peu repris et que le pain ne manque pas dans les boulangeries. Il y a bien sûr encore des Jacobins pour pleurer la République et une liberté qui, hélas! n'a jamais été qu'un beau mot... Tout de même, dix ans après avoir guillotiné le rois Louis, se retrouver avec un empereur!

– La Révolution semble évidemment aujourd'hui n'avoir servi à rien mais voyez, Caumont, tout ce qu'elle a changé! Je suis sûre qu'il en restera quelque chose, ne serait-ce cette Déclaration des droits de l'homme qui n'a pas dépassé le stade de l'idéalisme mais que les peuples n'oublieront peut-être pas...

– Vous avez raison, seulement les jeunes comme moi qui n'ont connu de la Révolution que la misère, la douleur des mères et l'odeur du sang, ne demandent qu'à pouvoir gagner leur vie en travaillant et élever une famille. Si l'empereur exauce ces désirs, le Faubourg sera pour lui! Ma liberté, c'est quand je serre dans ma main droite la poignée de ma varlope et que, de la gauche, j'appuie juste ce qu'il faut pour que le copeau s'enroule comme un ressort sur l'arrondi du contre-fer. Les grands principes on s'en occupera plus tard. Quand on aura goûté, nous aussi, aux joies simples de la vie.

Antoinette l'avait écouté en silence, heureuse et émue. Heureuse parce qu'elle retrouvait dans les paroles du jeune homme une lucidité semblable à celle qui ne l'avait jamais quittée, même dans les moments les plus tragiques; émue car elle sentait bien que sous la désinvolture des propos se cachait la générosité et la sensibilité des gens du bois, compagnons au parler franc et au cœur d'or.

– Caumont, lui dit-elle, vous êtes un vrai, comme votre père. Vous avez raison d'essayer d'oublier un passé récent qui ne vous a apporté que des désillusions. Mon mari répétait souvent ce mot de Necker: « Les monarques sont presque toujours sages, vertueux et intègres quand ils prennent le pouvoir. C'est après que ça se gâte. » Profitez des débuts de Napoléon!

Antoinette s'en rendit compte en visitant plusieurs ateliers: la désignation de l'empereur était bien accueillie dans le Faubourg. Quelques commandes du Mobilier national et la promesse qu'elles seraient suivies de beaucoup d'autres n'étaient certes pas étrangères à cette acceptation d'un régime qui remplaçait celui qu'on avait pris l'habitude d'appeler la République. Il fallait convenir en tout cas que Napoléon Bonaparte bénéficiait d'un courant d'opinion favorable dans les milieux populaires.

La soirée tint ses promesses. Alexandre Lenoir ne se reconnaissait que dans un parti, celui des œuvres d'art. Il dit qu'il attendrait pour se prononcer de connaître le point de vue de l'empereur sur son musée.

– Je me dois de souligner, ajouta-t-il, que si la Révolution a détruit une quantité d'objets d'art et d'œuvres irremplaçables, si elle a vendu à l'encan notre patrimoine sous le ridicule prétexte que la France le devait à ses rois, le citoyen Bonaparte, qu'il convient maintenant d'appeler par son prénom – Napoléon –, s'est évertué de reconstituer ce patrimoine en s'attribuant celui de l'admirable Italie. Il a fait main basse sur des tableaux merveilleux, des statues sublimes et des monuments somptueux. L'honnête homme que j'étais avant 89 aurait désapprouvé cette friponnerie mais le conservateur de musée que je suis devenu ne peut que s'en réjouir. Mais dites donc, Fontaine, et vous Percier, un empereur, cela se couronne. Je pense que vous avez déjà taillé vos crayons pour imaginer sur le papier cette auguste cérémonie. De son côté, l'excellent David doit préparer le tableau de sa vie. On s'est souvent moqué de ses opinions fluctuantes autour de cette table, et voilà que l'Histoire offre à sa fringale le seul plat auquel il n'aurait jamais rêvé goûter : le couronnement d'un empereur de France!

Alexandre Lenoir maniait l'ironie comme d'autres la plume ou le pinceau. De sa voix bien posée mais qu'il rendait grave ou aiguë à l'occasion, il savait se montrer incisif, théâtral, charmeur ou simplement brillant. Antoinette lui disait que cette voix était l'agent principal de son pouvoir de séduction et qu'elle n'aurait jamais, sans ce timbre enchanteur levé les yeux sur lui. Quant à la raillerie dont il ne pouvait s'empêcher d'émailler ses propos, elle ne manquait pas d'agacer ses amis, à commencer par les frères siamois Percier et Fontaine qui se sentaient quelque peu courtisans en face d'un homme aussi libre et indépendant. Si Percier préférait tirer sur sa pipe sans répondre au persiflage de Lenoir, Fontaine, lui, aimait quand cela lui chantait tenir tête à son ami. C'étaient les moments que préférait Antoinette parce qu'ils constituaient les meilleurs morceaux des « festins de l'esprit » qu'elle était fière d'organiser et d'animer.

– Mon cher Lenoir, reprit donc Fontaine en souriant, vous semblez nous reprocher de vivre avec notre temps et même de le façonner dans les modestes limites de notre talent. Ne serait-ce pas là une forme de jalousie? Venant de quelqu'un qui ne s'est intéressé qu'au passé, cela est fort excusable...

– Touché! marqua Lenoir bon joueur. Alors dites-nous

ce que vous préparez pour asseoir Napoléon dans sa nouvelle dignité.

– Un trône! J'y ai travaillé cet après-midi avec Percier et je peux même vous donner la primeur de ce projet qui doit bien entendu être approuvé par Sa Majesté impériale avant d'être réalisé par les Jacob.

Il tira d'un carton à dessins qu'il avait déposé en arrivant une grande feuille de papier qu'il étala sur la table.

– Louis XVI se contentait d'un fauteuil, Napoléon aura pour poser son fondement impérial ce siège étrange et tarabiscoté dont nul ne pourra dire qu'il pêche par une excessive simplicité.

Toutes les têtes se penchèrent sur le dessin où l'on reconnaissait la minutie et le souci du détail de Percier.

– Voilà, dit ce dernier, le projet que nous allons présenter à l'empereur. Je me demande bien ce qu'il va vouloir enlever ou rajouter. Vous voyez ce beau dessin? Il va nous le rendre tout griffé de sa plume impatiente. Mais il ne s'agit là que du fauteuil de sacre. Il reste encore à imaginer les carrosses, celui du pape en particulier, les costumes. Et n'oublions pas Notre-Dame. Des centaines d'ouvriers travaillent déjà à démolir des maisons qui sont presque collées à la face est. Il va falloir aussi enlever la chapelle du Chapitre et badigeonner les murs...

– Quand je pense qu'il y a dix ans, nous nous battions, Ethis et moi pour sauver quelques morceaux de statues que des énergumènes brisaient à coups de masse. Ils pensaient que c'étaient celles de nos anciens monarques et ils décapitaient les rois de Judée!

C'est Lenoir qui venait de parler, trop heureux d'avoir trouvé un sujet se prêtant à quelques-unes de ces paraboles dont il avait le secret:

– Vanité, tout est vanité... Les plus grands artistes de notre époque vont, des mois durant, ne s'intéresser qu'au court moment d'éternité qu'un petit Corse a décidé de s'offrir en se faisant couronner empereur. On va badigeonner les voûtes de Notre-Dame, qui n'existeraient peut-être plus si l'adjudicataire de l'an VI, c'était hier, n'avait pas été insolvable. La cathédrale lui avait été adjugée 45 000 francs! Dieu ne pouvait tout de même pas laisser faire une chose comme ça. Il a ruiné l'acquéreur et s'est arrangé pour que Notre-Dame devienne la propriété du département de la Seine. Peut-être savait-il déjà que Napoléon rêvait de s'y faire couronner par le pape! Mais voyez-vous, ce qui m'ennuie, ce n'est pas tant ce siège d'or à boules d'ivoire que je trouve plutôt réussi, que le fait qu'on va badigeonner les architraves et les piliers de Notre-Dame. Ce désir simpliste d'effacer le passé ne va pas avec la volonté de rendre à la France son église et son bon vieux droit divin. Votre Napoléon me fait penser à ces gens qui se lavent les mains sans arrêt. Cela cache une conscience pas très nette. Non! On ne peut pas à la fois se réclamer de l'antique et récurer les gargouilles!

Quand ses hôtes furent partis, Antoinette se dit qu'elle restait sur sa faim. Elle espérait que l'empire allait susciter chez ses amis un large mouvement d'opinion et la conversation avait tourné autour d'un fauteuil doré et d'un lessivage de murs. Elle en déduisit, et cela corroborait les avis qu'elle avait recueillis l'après-midi dans les ateliers du Faubourg, que la France était encore trop lasse pour s'intéresser à son gouvernement et qu'elle prenait l'empire naissant comme un malade se laisse administrer un vésicatoire.

Les gens du bois, toujours prêts à s'enflammer pour les grandes fêtes carillonnées et les liesses populaires ne firent cependant pas grand cas de la célébration du couronnement. Les ors, les escadrons de cavalerie, les carrosses de gala ne faisaient rien à l'affaire : il manquait à Napoléon, pourtant populaire dans les faubourgs, le mystère de la tradition. La présence même du pape, qu'on savait forcée, n'enlevait pas à la cérémonie son caractère fabriqué et parvenu qui déplaisait au peuple plus qu'à la bourgeoisie.

L'estampille de Jacob sur un trône ne remplaçait pas des siècles d'Histoire!

Louis David et les inséparables Percier-Fontaine s'étaient pourtant donné beaucoup de mal. Jamais le couronnement d'un roi n'avait été marqué d'un tel cérémonial. Bien que la somme demeurât secrète, Fontaine révéla à ses amis que les cérémonies et les fêtes du couronnement avaient coûté 85 millions. Mais il y a des choses qui ne s'achètent pas et le peuple de Paris qui n'avait pu entrer ni aux Tuileries ni à Notre-Dame ne retint finalement du triomphe de César que le fait, non négligeable d'ailleurs, qu'on avait distribué 13 000 volailles et que des fontaines de vin avaient coulé dans les carrefours. Une chanson de circonstance avait même été créée et diffusée dans les quartiers. Trois violons payés par l'Hôtel de Ville avaient fait danser devant la fontaine Trogneux. Là où en 93 on chantait *Ça ira*, un artiste venu du Boulevard s'était époumoné pour faire reprendre en chœur le *Te Deum* du populaire. A l'heure où le pape lançait sous les voûtes de Notre-Dame *Vivat imperator in aeternum*, les apprentis du faubourg fredonnaient :

Vive, vive Napoléon,
Qui nous baille
D' la volaille,
Du pain et du vin à foison,
Vive, vive Napoléon.

Ce n'est pas sur ces immortelles paroles que le nouvel empereur devait asseoir sa légende. Une légende qui pourtant allait bon train depuis le début du Consulat et que l'éclat des victoires ne pouvait que renforcer. Napoléon d'ailleurs tenait beaucoup à cette adhésion populaire. Attentif aux besoins des classes laborieuses, il veillait à leur assurer des subsistances et du travail. Cela expliquait l'attachement que lui portaient les ouvriers du bois.

Charles Delacroix mourut dans la dernière semaine d'octobre 1805, trois jours seulement après avoir quitté la préfecture de Bordeaux. La voiture qui le ramenait avait à peine eu le temps de s'arrêter devant le portail de sa maison de Charenton-Saint-Maurice qu'il fut pris d'un malaise et se plaignit de violentes douleurs au bas-ventre. Transporté dans un fauteuil du salon, il expira peu après dans les bras de Victoire. Ses quatre enfants étaient autour de lui. Eugène, le plus jeune, avait cinq ans et demi. Très émotif, il pleura un père qui n'était pas le sien mais qui l'avait toujours traité comme ses autres enfants. Haut fonctionnaire sous cinq régimes et ancien ministre, Charles Delacroix eut de dignes et officielles funérailles. Il avait durant sa vie été souvent critiqué pour sa versatilité mais c'est grâce à cette souplesse politique qu'il avait finalement pu servir l'État jusqu'à l'âge de soixante-trois ans, après avoir échappé à la guillotine et à une sanglante opération. Dans son discours, le représentant du ministre de l'Intérieur passa sous silence le premier miracle mais insista sur le courage extraordinaire du grand homme devant la maladie.

Victoire Œben, sa femme, surmonta assez facilement sa douleur. A Antoinette venue assister aux obsèques, elle glissa : « C'est mon dernier rôle de préfète, on va pouvoir enfin se retrouver, ma grande sœur! »

La mort de Charles n'empêcha pas Lucie de fêter peu après son seizième anniversaire. Un déjeuner de gala avait été prévu place d'Aligre et toutes les femmes de la famille devaient mettre la main à la pâte pour célébrer l'événement. Comme chaque fois, le choix du menu avait fait l'objet d'interminables discussions. Finalement l'offre d'Alexandre Lenoir d'une oie farcie de chez Chevet avait mis tout le monde d'accord. Il ne restait à Antoinette, Marie et Lucie qu'à s'occuper des entrées et des desserts, ce qui nécessita tout de même trois jours de préparatifs appétissants et odorants.

Antoinette aurait dû être parfaitement heureuse à la veille de cette fête qui allait réunir autour de sa fille tous ceux qu'elle aimait. Pourtant, depuis un peu plus d'une semaine, elle avait du mal à cacher la tristesse qui l'envahissait dès son réveil et la laissait, tout le reste de la journée, en proie à la morosité et au découragement. C'était d'autant plus surprenant que son tempérament – elle l'avait montré bien souvent au cours de sa vie – ne révélait aucune tendance à la mélancolie. Antoinette était une lutteuse qui savait faire front à l'adversité. Et voilà qu'elle sombrait au moment où rien ne menaçait son bonheur!

Deux journées durant elle avait réfléchi : « Il se passe quelque chose que je ne comprends pas, qui me rend malheureuse. Je sais que je ne suis plus jeune, que mes cheveux sont devenus plus gris que blonds et que, sans la générosité d'Ethis et de Réveillon, j'aurais beaucoup de mal à élever ma fille. Mais enfin! J'ai connu des périodes autrement difficiles dans mon existence! » Elle avait ainsi frappé à toutes les portes de son esprit cartésien sans obtenir de réponse. Elle avait frappé à toutes les portes sauf une : celle d'Alexandre Lenoir. Comme elle était douée d'un esprit clair et qu'elle ne manquait pas de courage, cette source occultée finit par se faire jour un soir où elle cherchait le sommeil.

« Alexandre! C'est Alexandre! pensa-t-elle. Depuis longtemps je ferme les yeux pour ne pas voir, mais Lenoir n'est plus le même. Ses rapports avec moi ont changé. Il demeure certes affectueux et prévenant mais il est sûr que d'autres pensées le préoccupent. A-t-il une autre femme dans sa vie? C'est possible mais je ne veux rien savoir. Ce qui compte, c'est l'évidence : je vais avoir cinquante-deux ans, Alexandre n'en a que quarante-quatre. C'est un homme encore jeune et je deviens une vieille dame! Voilà les faits, il me reste à en tirer les conséquences. M'est-il encore permis de lutter, de " défendre mon bonheur " comme on dit? »

Durant des jours Antoinette ne cessa guère de s'interroger. Son caractère la poussait à se battre et la raison lui soufflait de ne pas s'engager tout entière dans un combat dont l'issue n'offrait guère d'espoir.

Elle vit plus souvent Alexandre afin d'essayer de percer

ses sentiments réels, de sonder son esprit toujours prompt à se jouer des questions embarrassantes. Avec une habileté qui l'étonna elle-même elle s'arrangea pour créer des situations qui pouvaient l'engager à se découvrir, pour parler incidemment de leur âge respectif et du poids que prendraient les années dans leur vie future.

Bien vite, Antoinette dut s'avouer qu'elle prenait un certain plaisir à ce jeu qui lui révélait chaque jour un peu plus le détachement de son amant, enfin un certain détachement car Alexandre demeurait l'ami attentif qu'il avait toujours été. Elle s'aperçut aussi que l'enjeu de sa réflexion lui paraissait moins important. Elle se prit même à sourire en constatant qu'elle se sentait soulagée L'angoisse s'estompait. C'était comme si la mécanique de son cerveau, bloquée par quelque grain de sable, s'était soudain remise à fonctionner.

La logique de la situation lui apparaissait, cruelle certes mais évidente : pour garder l'essentiel des relations qui la liaient à Lenoir, l'affection, la confiance, la complicité d'une conversation ininterrompue depuis des années, il lui fallait s'amputer, lui rendre la liberté de sa vie personnelle, demeurer l'amie irremplaçable en cessant d'être la maîtresse. Elle aimerait Alexandre d'une autre façon, voilà tout; comme elle l'avait aimé durant des années après l'arrestation de Valfroy. Ce serait difficile? Quelle femme n'a pas rêvé un jour d'avoir pour meilleur ami et confident un homme intelligent, fort, capable de la protéger et avec qui elle n'aurait pas de rapports physiques? « Ma vie de femme a jusqu'ici été pleine de passion, mes souvenirs m'aideront à mener une seconde existence qui aura d'autres charmes. Il me reste maintenant à faire part de ma décision à Lenoir. J'espère qu'il me comprendra... » Elle sourit en pensant que seule une femme était capable de faire ce qu'elle allait faire. Jamais en tout cas Alexandre n'aurait eu la lucidité, ni le courage, d'agir ainsi sur leur destinée. Sans elle, les choses auraient traîné, installant le mensonge, la défiance dans leurs relations. Ils auraient fini par se quitter sans retour, en se détestant...

– Allons Antoinette, dit-elle tout haut : tu as peut-être des cheveux blancs et ton corps n'a plus la sveltesse de ses vingt ans mais tu n'as rien perdu de ta force et de ta dignité. C'est peut-être de l'orgueil mais l'orgueil a du bon s'il sécrète du bonheur. Tiens, voilà des réflexions dont je devrais bien faire part à Lucie. A seize ans, il faut commencer de l'armer pour la vie. Mais je crois qu'elle est douée, je n'aurai pas trop de mal...

Forte de ses belles résolutions, elle commença le soir même – c'était le plus facile – de parler à Lucie de sa destinée de femme. Le moment lui paraissait bien choisi : elles étaient seules en train de piler des avelines dans le mortier pour faire des macarons. Lucie chantait, elle-même avait retrouvé sa belle humeur.

– Ainsi, ma chérie, commença-t-elle, te voilà presque une femme. J'ai du mal à l'imaginer, pour moi tu restes la petite fille fragile de la Révolution, comme disait ton père, celle pour qui on se battait afin qu'elle ait du lait et du pain. Mais, Dieu merci, tu as surmonté toutes les privations et tu es une jeune fille jolie, attirante et, ce qui ne gâte rien, plutôt intelligente. Je vais te répéter ce que ta grand-mère, une femme merveilleuse, m'a dit lorsque j'avais ton âge : le bonheur résulte rarement des coups de tête. Méfie-toi des emportements propres à la jeunesse et ne fais jamais une bêtise ou ce qui risque d'en être une, si tu n'en as pas vraiment envie. Tu es encore à l'âge où il est préférable d'être trop sage que pas assez...

– Mais je suis très sage, chère maman... Et bien que cela ne soit en aucune façon la sottise imprudente dont tu parles, il y a une chose qui me ferait infiniment plaisir. J'aurais dû déjà t'en faire part mais l'occasion ne s'est pas présentée...

– Tu m'intrigues. Quel est donc ce désir?

– J'aimerais inviter Emmanuel Caumont à mon anniversaire!

Antoinette en lâcha son pilon de saisissement. Elle s'attendait à quelque caprice et se voyait soudain confrontée à un problème qui rendait dérisoires les belles phrases qu'elle avait préparées. La vie heureusement lui avait appris à maîtriser ses réactions. Tandis qu'elle paraissait encore sous le coup de l'étonnement, elle réfléchissait : « Attention, se disait-elle, pas de colère intempestive ni de morale inutile. Évitons les banalités et voyons ce que cache cette invitation surprenante. » Elle regarda Lucie dont les yeux rougissaient en même temps que son visage et la serra contre elle :

– Je ne vois pas *a priori* pourquoi je te refuserais d'inviter Caumont, mais avoue que j'ai de quoi être étonnée. Nous n'avons pas vu plus de deux ou trois fois ce garçon qui n'est pas un familier et que tu ne connais pas.

En disant cela, Antoinette savait bien qu'elle prêchait le faux pour savoir le vrai : si Lucie avait tellement envie d'inviter le jeune ébéniste, c'est qu'elle l'avait revu et qu'il n'était pas un étranger pour elle. La confirmation ne tarda pas :

– Bien sûr que je connais Emmanuel. Je suis amoureuse de lui depuis longtemps.

– Depuis longtemps ? coupa Antoinette en souriant. Tu n'as tout de même que seize ans !

– Oui, depuis le premier jour où nous avons poussé la porte de son atelier, il y a presque cinq ans, tu ne te souviens pas ?

Antoinette se souvenait très bien avoir alors remarqué l'émoi de sa petite fille devant le jeune homme beau et fort qui reprenait avec courage l'atelier du père et maniait la varlope avec une élégance de violoniste. Elle se rappelait même avoir pensé en s'en amusant : « Tiens voilà Lucie amoureuse ! » Aujourd'hui, il lui fallait voir les événements avec plus de sérieux.

– Quand vois-tu Emmanuel ? Et depuis combien de temps ? Pourquoi ne m'as-tu parlé de rien ?

– Oh ! Ne va pas croire des choses... Simplement, quand je passe au coin de la rue Traversière, je vais lui dire bonjour. Je ne reste pas longtemps mais il a toujours des choses à me raconter, il m'explique qu'il exerce un métier passionnant et qu'il ne pourrait pas se passer de respirer l'odeur du bois. Il dit qu'en travaillant l'acajou il a l'impression de sentir la forêt du Brésil où l'arbre a été abattu. Il dit aussi que cet acajou rouge a des veines pleines du sang des Indiens qui vivent là-bas. C'est vrai que le bois est doux quand il est bien poli...

Antoinette, de l'inquiétude, était passée à l'émotion. Pour un peu, elle aurait pleuré, en écoutant sa fille lui chanter le refrain du bois qui avait bercé toute sa jeunesse et qu'elle aimait toujours aller réentendre au fond des cours du Faubourg. Elle aussi avait été, à quinze ans, amoureuse d'un compagnon de Riesener, un Allemand blond aux yeux bleus qui parlait à peine le français mais qui faisait vibrer les vitres de l'atelier de l'Arsenal de sa voix chaude en évoquant les eaux tumultueuses du Rhin et le vert des sapins de la Forêt-Noire... Et avant elle! Combien de filles du Faubourg le parfum de la sciure et le bruit de la scie avaient-ils rendues amoureuses? Antoinette n'avait pas suivi la tradition. Fille et belle-fille des deux plus grands ébénistes du siècle, elle avait aimé un fou du ciel puis un gentilhomme financier... Et voilà qu'aujourd'hui, Lucie, sautant une génération, se retrouvait prise par la magie du bois et le charme de ses artistes. Tout cela dans le fond était logique. Sa fille commençait peut-être une belle aventure...

Antoinette revint pourtant sur terre. Lucie n'était encore qu'une adolescente et Caumont avait près de dix ans de plus qu'elle. Elle avait de l'humour et cette évocation de la différence d'âge la fit tout de même sourire. La jeune fille guettait sur le visage de sa mère la réaction qui puisse la laisser espérer. Le sourire d'Antoinette dont elle ne pouvait comprendre la raison lui fit croire qu'elle avait gagné la partie.

– Tu me comprends, maman? Je vois que tu ressens tout ce que je ressens. Quel bonheur! Mais tout de même, une invitation d'anniversaire, ce n'est pas si important. Ce ne sont pas des fiançailles!

– Non mais cela en aura tout l'air. Tout le Faubourg dira le lendemain que la petite fille Œben va épouser Emmanuel Caumont!

– Et après? Les commères de la place d'Aligre pourront bien dire ce qu'elles voudront, je m'en moque.

– Bon! Ton Emmanuel sera invité. Mais pas par toi, par moi! Il faut tout de même sauver les apparences. Je passerai le voir et lui demanderai, comme s'il s'agissait d'une idée fortuite, s'il veut venir se joindre à nous.

Antoinette qui s'attendait à une explosion de joie fut déçue. Lucie la regardait d'un air peiné.

– Maman tu me déçois. Cette hypocrisie, cette crainte absurde du qu'en-dira-t-on ce n'est pas toi du tout. Tu aimes répéter que tu as toujours été une femme libre. Je suis sûre que c'est vrai mais voilà que parce qu'il s'agit de ta fille, tu te conduis comme une bourgeoise parvenue éprise de bonnes manières. Si vraiment la venue d'Emmanuel Caumont te gêne autant, je préfère y renoncer.

C'était exactement le discours qui, contre toute apparence, pouvait faire le plus plaisir à Antoinette. Allons, sa fille avait du caractère! En plus, elle avait raison. Ce respect des convenances était ridicule et même indigne. Elle éclara de rire, ce qui détendit l'atmosphère.

– Je préfère que tu tiennes à mon image de femme libre, tu sais bien que je ne me supporte que comme ça. Alors si tu veux nous irons toutes les deux inviter l'ébéniste de ton cœur. Je ne voudrais tout de même pas qu'il se figure que c'est ma fille qui décide de tout à la maison. Ah mais!

Tout finit dans les rires. Bientôt une odeur suave de noisettes grillées emplit le logement. Les premiers macarons de la fête brunissaient doucement dans le four en laissant éclater leur tunique de sucre en un réseau serré de craquelures.

Emmanuel Caumont avait accepté avec empressement l'invitation des Valfroy. Le charme de Lucie ne le laissait pas indifférent. Sans jamais penser qu'il pourrait un jour épouser la petite-fille d'Œben, aristocrate malgré l'indifférence qu'Antoinette comme sa fille accordaient à cette distinction de nouveau appréciée, il éprouvait du plaisir à bavarder avec la jeune fille et l'encourageait, tout naturellement, à passer le voir dans son atelier. Lucie d'ailleurs ne se faisait pas prier. Si elle n'avait pas été si jeune, Emmanuel se disait qu'il l'aurait bien emmenée un dimanche goûter aux jambons de la mère Saguet à la barrière de la Gare, où l'on met le couvert sur de petites tables de bois entre les plants de laitues du jardin. En attendant que ce rêve d'escapade puisse devenir une réalité, s'il le devenait jamais, Emmanuel s'arrangeait pour enfiler l'une de ses belles chemises de coton rayé de bleu les jours où Lucie avait des chances de passer.

Le déjeuner d'anniversaire constituait pour le jeune homme une péripétie dans sa vie laborieuse. Il n'ignorait pas la qualité des hôtes habituels de la place d'Aligre. Leur choix, qui ne devait rien à la fortune, n'était dicté que par l'intérêt de leur conversation et il savait bien que sans Lucie il n'aurait eu aucune chance d'être reçu chez Antoinette. Il savait aussi car il n'était pas sot qu'il allait subir dans ce logement modeste où soufflait l'esprit un examen de passage plus difficile que s'il avait été l'invité de Murat aux Tuileries. Il en était inquiet et son plaisir d'avoir été invité par Lucie se mêlait à la peur de gâcher par quelque maladresse une fête et un avenir sentimental qui pour être incertain n'était plus du seul domaine du rêve.

Il s'était ouvert de ses craintes à Lucie la veille de la fête. La jeune fille avait éclaté de rire.

– Mais que croyez-vous donc? Nous sommes des gens du Faubourg, comme vous. Le fait que vous soyez ébéniste de talent vaut pour nous toutes les médailles et les parchemins. Votre père était un ami de Riesener et de mon grand-père. N'ayez aucune honte à manier la gouge et le ciseau. Et dites-vous que si je vous aime bien – elle rougit en prononçant ces mots qui étaient presque un aveu –, c'est parce que vous êtes un homme du bois. Si vous voulez être apprécié de la famille, un conseil: parlez-leur de votre métier et, pour le reste, soyez vous-même. Et puis je serai là, avec Ethis qui vous trouve un garçon très bien...

Elle se tut et regarda Emmanuel qui était vraiment

beau dans son pantalon de toile et la large chemise échancrée sur une poitrine lisse et musclée contre laquelle il devait être agréable de se blottir. Leurs yeux se parlèrent une seconde, pas plus, mais se dirent beaucoup de choses. Lucie bougea la première et dit en riant :

– Ethis d'ailleurs exagère! A demain, monsieur Caumont, et soyez à l'heure, la bonne cuisine n'attend pas. Maintenant je me sauve...

Le lendemain, un dimanche, le froid piquait dur. Il avait neigé les derniers jours et la place d'Aligre ressemblait à un bois pétrifié avec ses marronniers couverts de givre. Réveillon s'était fait conduire le matin par une voiture de louage et le cheval, pourtant ferré à glace, était tombé en arrivant. La pauvre bête, liée aux brancards, n'arrivait pas à se relever. Comme le cocher, à moitié ivre, commençait à la cingler de coups de fouet en jurant, un attroupement se forma.

– Il faut le détacher! disait l'un.

– Ne battez donc pas cette malheureuse bête! lançait un autre.

Personne pourtant n'avait le courage d'approcher le cheval affolé qui lançait ses sabots dans tous les sens ni de maîtriser l'énergumène dont le fouet sifflait aux oreilles de qui l'approchait. Alerté par le bruit, Ethis qui était venu de bonne heure avec Marie et le petit Bertrand descendit en trombe en disant :

– Je vais dire deux mots à cet ivrogne!

Malgré Marie et Antoinette qui essayaient de le retenir, et trop heureux de pouvoir libérer une énergie trop longtemps contenue, Ethis redevenu subitement Traîne-sabot l'impétueux se jeta sur le cocher, lui décocha un violent coup de poing et s'empara du fouet. On entendit des « Bravo Ethis! » mais personne ne bougeait. Enfin un dernier arrivant s'offrit à aider Ethis. C'était Caniolle, l'agent de la police secrète.

– Tenez le cheval par la bride, parlez-lui pendant que je le détache, cria-t-il.

Ethis fit de son mieux. Il caressa les naseaux de la bête en la calmant.

– Allons mon beau cheval, tiens-toi tranquille... Là, tout doux...

– Que quelqu'un aille chercher de la sciure ou de la cendre, cria Caniolle en libérant la dernière bricole. On va essayer de le relever.

– Regardez cette bonne bête. Elle nous regarde comme si elle comprenait qu'on ne lui veut que du bien, lança Ethis.

– Elle est plus facile que le cheval qui emmenait le cabriolet de Cadoudal! répondit en riant l'homme de la secrète.

Le cocher dégrisé et peu soucieux de se frotter de nouveau à Ethis aida à la manœuvre. Caniolle lui dit qu'il était interdit de maltraiter les animaux et que la prochaine fois il aurait affaire à la police, puis il serra la main d'Ethis et disparut...

– Je ne vous donne pas de pourboire! dit sévèrement Réveillon en payant l'homme qui ne demandait qu'une chose : quitter au plus vite ce lieu où l'on ne laissait pas les cochers fouetter leurs chevaux.

Ethis constata en remontant qu'il avait perdu un bouton de sa belle veste de velours beige en se colletant avec le cocher. Gentiment, Lucie s'offrit à aller le chercher. En bas elle rencontra Emmanuel qui arrivait un paquet sous le bras.

– Bonjour monsieur l'Ébéniste, dit-elle en souriant. Je vous trouve bien élégant dans votre habit mais vous auriez dû mettre un manteau.

– J'y ai bien pensé mais le mien est si usé que je n'aurais jamais osé me présenter à votre mère...

– Alors, pour vous réchauffer, venez chercher avec moi dans la neige le bouton qu'Ethis a perdu en se battant comme un chiffonnier avec un patachon ivre.

Les deux jeunes gens fouillèrent du regard le champ de bataille souillé de cendre où les écarts du cheval avaient labouré le sol. Ils étaient près l'un de l'autre et s'amusaient à se frôler en marchant.

C'est lui qui trouva le bouton, brillant comme un sou neuf à cinq pas dans la neige. Lucie garda un instant dans la sienne la main qui le lui tendait. Elle sentit un frisson la parcourir et se dit que ce premier contact, pas si fortuit qu'on pouvait le croire, laissait dans son cœur la marque d'un engagement.

Les femmes avaient dressé la table dans la grande pièce dont on avait enlevé les meubles les moins beaux ou inutiles. Ceux qui restaient étaient des chefs-d'œuvre estampillés Œben ou Riesener. Emmanuel en souligna l'incomparable élégance en homme du métier, sans la moindre nuance de courtisanerie qui eût déplu dans ce milieu où la simplicité ne le cédait qu'à la franchise. Alexandre Lenoir enchaîna en répétant ce qu'il avait bien souvent dit dans cette pièce : Un meuble quand il atteint la réussite absolue est beau en soi et doit beaucoup moins qu'on ne le croit au cadre où on le présente. C'est le cadre qui doit aux meubles et non pas le contraire, affirma-t-il.

L'oie farcie que Lenoir devait à son ami Chevet était un miracle de saveur et de tendreté. Le célèbre traiteur avait glissé dans sa panse un tas d'ingrédients plus délicats les uns que les autres. Dosé par un cuisinier médiocre, ce mélange eût été un lamentable gâchis. Là, les petites truffes noires répondaient à leurs sœurs, les blanches du Piémont, et les raisins confits d'Espagne aux jubis de la Provence. On y trouvait de minuscules boudins blancs allongés sur des lits de morilles hachées et des châtaignes rôties émiettées dans une farce de veau. Parfois, sous la dent, craquait un lardon réduit sur la cendre ou un cerneau de noix enrobé de sucre roux.

Dans de pareils cas, Lenoir qui se piquait d'épicurisme ne manquait jamais de se livrer à quelque improvisation philosophique qui faisait les délices d'Antoinette et d'ailleurs de tout le monde car le sauveur de statues ne manquait pas d'esprit. Avant d'en arriver à un parallèle subtil entre la sculpture et l'art de la gastronomie, il ne laissa pas passer le magnifique sujet de dissertation que lui offrait l'oie de M. Chevet.

– Sous sa croûte dorée par les soins attentifs de nos cuisinières, l'oie que nous savourons a évidemment perdu certaines des qualités qui en ont fait un volatile sacré. Cependant, comment ne pas se rappeler, en laissant fondre dans sa bouche une cuisse où perle le jus suave de la cuisson, qu'une oie sauva Manlius et Rome en entendant le bruit que faisaient les Gaulois escaladant le Capitole? Tout le monde connaît cette histoire mais savez-vous que Rhadamante, le roi de Lycie, vénérait tellement les oies qu'il ordonna à tous les sujets de ses États de ne plus jurer par les dieux mais seulement par les oies? J'ai lu quelque part qu'un médecin érudit et fort célèbre, Jules-César Scaliger, professe une grande admiration pour l'intelligence des oies : « L'oie, a-t-il écrit, est un modèle de prudence, elle baisse la tête pour passer sous un pont quelle que soit sa hauteur. J'ai vu, écrit-il encore, des oies si prévoyantes que traversant les pentes du mont Taurus qui sont remplies d'aigles, chacune prenait une pierre dans son bec car se sachant bavardes elles ne voulaient pas qu'un cri intempestif vînt alerter leurs ennemis. »

Le repas fut aussi gai que succulent. Réveillon avait apporté un panier plein de vénérables bouteilles de vin de Bourgogne. Chaque cachet de cire qui sautait avec le bouchon faisait monter l'ambiance d'un ton et Antoinette dut à un moment faire signe à Ethis qui jouait à l'échanson de cesser de remplir les verres. Emmanuel avait bien improvisé son rôle, faisant preuve d'esprit de repartie et distribuant à chacun les compliments qui pouvaient lui faire plaisir. Tout en jetant de temps en temps un regard du côté de Lucie, il eut la sagesse d'observer à son égard une certaine retenue et Antoinette lui sut gré de ne pas jouer à l'amoureux transi.

Seul de toute l'assemblée, Riesener sembla ne pas partager la gaieté générale. Il n'avait à peu près rien mangé ni bu. Souvent ses yeux se fermaient comme s'il était las du bruit et du monde. Il n'avait répondu que par monosyllabes aux propos admiratifs d'Emmanuel Caumont et, finalement, Antoinette qui veillait sur tout son petit monde, lui proposa de l'aider à monter se coucher, ce qu'il accepta d'un sourire reconnaissant. Quand elle vint reprendre sa place, elle semblait inquiète.

– Riesener me fait peur, dit-elle. Il a beaucoup maigri et semble avoir perdu le goût de vivre. Je vais écrire dès demain à mon frère Henri-François car je crains le pire.

– Il n'est pas si âgé, remarqua Marie. Mon père est a peine plus jeune et il se porte très bien, il paraît même qu'on songe à lui pour devenir maire du VIIIe arrondissement [1].

– Mon beau-père tient tellement à la consécration de sa réussite qu'il ne mourra pas avant d'avoir obtenu un titre officiel!

C'était bien sûr Ethis qui venait de parler, s'attirant immédiatement une observation d'Antoinette. Ni l'un ni l'autre pourtant ne portaient dans leur cœur Eugène Bénard dont l'avarice et surtout la jalousie qu'il montrait à leur égard leur étaient insupportables.

– Riesener vient d'avoir soixante et onze ans, précisa Antoinette. C'est un âge respectable mais les dix dernières années d'inactivité lui ont beaucoup pesé. Il n'a jamais pu se faire à l'idée que ses meubles avaient cessé de plaire!

– C'est pourtant le plus grand! dit Emmanuel. Il n'est pas possible que l'homme qui a réalisé autant de chefs-d'œuvre meure oublié...

– Il mourra déjà pauvre! ajouta Réveillon. C'est un scandale que rien, même la mode, ne peut justifier.

– N'oublions pas, coupa Antoinette, que nous fêtons l'anniversaire de Lucie. N'attristons pas cette belle journée par des propos moroses. Je sais que vous avez apporté des cadeaux pour ma petite fille, ce serait peut-être le moment de les lui offrir. Jean-Henri Riesener, pour sa part, lui donne le petit bureau bonheur-du-jour qui a appartenu à ma mère.

On applaudit le vieux maître et chacun vint déposer son offrande autour de la reine de la journée qui se trouvait seule chacun s'étant reculé, assise sur son tabou-

1. Le VIIIe arrondissement comprenait depuis 1795 les quartiers suivants: Quinze-Vingts, Faubourg-Saint-Antoine, Popincourt et Marais.

ret comme sur un trône au milieu de la pièce. Lenoir avait apporté un pendentif et sa chaîne venus d'on ne sait quelle récupération post-révolutionnaire. Lucie les mit tout de suite à son cou et embrassa Alexandre. Réveillon, fidèle à la tradition, remit à la jeune fille une enveloppe contenant une feuille pliée en quatre. « Bon pour une belle robe », lut-elle tout haut. Ethis et Marie apportèrent un carton fermé par un ruban bleu. Il contenait, enveloppée dans du papier de soie, une magnifique chemise de nuit en soie brodée. Antoinette avait taillé et cousu la robe que portait Lucie avec beaucoup de panache. Le tissu, une fine percale blanche, venait de la fabrique Richard-Lenoir. Antoinette de Valfroy n'avait pu donner que son temps, son goût et son talent, mais pour sa fille c'était l'essentiel.

– Maman, déclara-t-elle, a travaillé des jours et des nuits pour faire la robe que je porte aujourd'hui. C'est mon plus beau cadeau!

Restait Emmanuel Caumont qui discrètement avait évité de se mêler à la famille. Il alla enfin chercher dans la petite pièce d'entrée l'objet qu'il avait apporté, enveloppé dans une toilette [1], et l'offrit, ainsi caché dans l'étoffe aux quatre oreilles à Lucie qui devint rouge comme une pivoine.

Il fallut l'aider pour desserrer les nœuds et enfin apparut le cadeau du jeune ébéniste : une petite console en bois doré entièrement sculptée dans la masse. Un singe ailé posé sur une dentelle de nuages en festons soutenait la tablette. Les motifs, entièrement ajourés, extraits à la gouge du cœur d'un peuplier, se terminaient en pointe vers le bas, achevant de donner à ce triangle d'or des proportions parfaites.

Lucie prit la console dans ses mains fines et l'éloigna un peu de ses yeux pour en admirer les détails. N'importe qui pouvait juger de sa beauté et imaginer le travail considérable qu'avait dû représenter la sculpture d'un tel

1. Petite pièce de coton dans laquelle les marchands et les artisans enveloppent leur marchandise pour la livrer.

ouvrage. Antoinette et même Lucie qui avaient vécu au milieu des œuvres d'Œben et de Riesener et entendu si souvent les ébénistes et les sculpteurs parler de leur art, voyaient autre chose que l'agencement des éléments et le fini des détails : le talent. Celui qui avait conçu cette composition arachnéenne ne pouvait qu'être un ouvrier suprêmement habile, un véritable artiste du bois, une « fine lame » comme on désignait dans le Faubourg ceux dont la technique atteignait la virtuosité.

– C'est magnifique ! s'exclama Lucie. Venez Emmanuel, que je vous embrasse.

La jeune fille déposa deux baisers sonores sur les joues de son ami et ajouta :

– Ainsi vous avez fait cela pour moi ?

– Pour qui voudriez-vous que je passe autant d'heures à fignoler dans le bois fragile, jusqu'aux plumes des ailes, un singe volant venu tout droit des bronzes du siècle passé ?

– Monsieur Caumont, votre habileté est prodigieuse ! dit Lenoir. Vous deviendrez un grand artiste. Permettez-moi d'ajouter que votre animal ailé est aussi bien de notre temps que d'hier. Jacob en pose souvent à l'extrémité des bras de ses fauteuils et ils sont beaucoup moins bien sculptés que les vôtres.

– C'est parce que les sculpteurs de Jacob ne sont pas amoureux ! lança Ethis.

Il se fit un silence. Emmanuel et Lucie échangèrent un bref regard et Antoinette, qui n'entendait pas aventurer la conversation sur un sujet aussi délicat, fit habilement diversion :

– Il faut absolument que Riesener voie votre console. Cela va lui faire plaisir de savoir que les jeunes sont encore capables de bien travailler le bois. Montez donc tous les deux la lui montrer. Il est très fatigué mais cela va lui redonner du courage.

Quand les deux jeunes gens eurent quitté la pièce, Antoinette se tourna vers Ethis.

– Qu'est-ce qu'il t'a pris de parler d'amoureux ? Je vois clair aussi bien que toi mais je pense plutôt à calmer cette jeune passion qu'à en attiser le feu. Ta sœur n'a que seize ans!

– S'ils s'aiment, et il est évident qu'ils s'aiment, personne, même pas toi, ne pourra les empêcher de se l'avouer.

– Peut-être. Mais ce n'est pas à toi de leur en donner l'idée! Tiens-le-toi pour dit. Je n'ai pas envie de marier Lucie aussi jeune!

On en resta là et comme la nuit commençait à envahir la place, chacun rentra chez soi, Emmanuel le premier qui pensait que la journée avait été assez fertile en événements et qu'il était sage de la terminer sur l'intervention inattendue d'Ethis.

Comme toujours, Alexandre Lenoir fut le dernier à prendre congé. Antoinette songea un instant à le prier de venir dans sa chambre afin de lui faire part de sa décision mais elle pensa à temps que ce n'était ni le jour ni l'heure de parler d'une affaire aussi grave. Elle laissa Lenoir lui baiser le bout des doigts et s'en aller : c'était la journée de Lucie qu'elle allait maintenant avoir toute à elle. « Peut-être plus pour longtemps », songea-t-elle avec un peu de mélancolie.

Antoinette décida finalement de ne rien dire pour le moment à Lenoir. « Il est plus intelligent, pensa-t-elle, de laisser nos rencontres intimes s'espacer. Cela ne fera d'ailleurs qu'affirmer un état de fait que je n'ai pas cherché. Petit à petit d'autres relations s'établiront entre nous, je le souhaite. Il sera toujours temps de s'expliquer. Et puis j'ai d'autres soucis... »

Ces soucis se situaient à l'étage au-dessus, chez Riesener qui n'avait pas quitté sa chambre depuis l'anniversaire de Lucie. C'est à peine s'il se levait quelques heures dans la journée pour ranimer le feu quand Antoinette n'était pas là ou pour faire un peu de toilette. Le médecin n'avait pas décelé de mal déclaré et le maître ne se plaignait d'aucune douleur. Simplement, il baissait chaque jour un peu plus, comme une lampe qui use ses dernières gouttes d'huile. Rien ne l'intéressait, il refusait le plus souvent de recevoir ses amis.

Son fils était arrivé de Lyon et s'occupait de lui avec beaucoup de tendresse. Henri-François avait installé une planche à dessin dans la chambre et travaillait une grande partie de la journée devant la fenêtre. Il avait bien essayé de peindre mais l'odeur des couleurs incommodait Riesener. Alors il dessinait, mettait en place des projets de tableaux et, surtout, faisait des croquis du malade, alité ou dans son fauteuil. En accumulant silhouettes et profils, il lui semblait qu'il rattrapait les années durant lesquelles il n'avait pas vu son père.

La seule chose qui intéressait Riesener était son œuvre. Il avait demandé à Lucie de lui rapporter de l'atelier de l'Arsenal les anciens livres de commandes et les vieilles factures pour dresser la liste des meubles qu'il avait conçus et construits au cours de sa vie. Sa mémoire chancelante redevenait précise et sûre quand il s'agissait de décrire, en quelques mots, un secrétaire en nacre de perles livré en octobre 1784 aux Tuileries pour les petits appartements de la reine, ou le bureau d'acajou de voyage à piétement dévissable commandé par le roi en mai 1780.

– Tu vois, disait-il à son fils, je fais cela afin qu'Antoinette et toi puissiez conserver le souvenir de ce que j'ai fait. Je vais aussi dresser la liste de tous les meubles que je n'ai pas vendus ou que j'ai rachetés aux ventes de Versailles. C'est la seule chose que je vous léguerai. Ces pièces, reconnues hier pour des chefs-d'œuvre, ne valent presque rien, mais peut-être qu'une autre génération s'intéressera aux travaux des ouvriers du roi et que ces meubles, témoins du goût de la monarchie défunte, retrouveront grâce auprès des acheteurs. A moins que vous ne préfériez garder ces commodes, ces secrétaires, ces bureaux qui ont meublé Versailles! J'aurais voulu vous laisser de l'argent, j'en ai gagné beaucoup!... Mais je vais mourir pauvre. Comme André-Charles Boulle. Georges Jacob, lui, a su conserver sa fortune mais il lui faut faire attention : son fils voit trop grand. Les commandes affluent, alors il engage sans cesse de nouveaux ouvriers, loue des ateliers et ne se rend pas compte qu'en développant son affaire il la rend plus fragile. Vois-tu, nous sommes des artisans, nous savons transformer des planches rugueuses en meubles d'apparat mais nous n'entendons rien aux histoires d'argent...

Antoinette et Henri-François le laissaient parler, vivre ses derniers jours au milieu de ses souvenirs et des sublimes reliques dont il aimait caresser les formes exquises aux couleurs de miel. Sa main d'or, aujourd'hui amaigrie, avait conservé la finesse de son toucher. Un jour où Antoinette le regardait, à la dérobée, passer sa paume hésitante sur le glacis d'une petite table qui avait autrefois appartenu à la reine et qui lui servait maintenant de chevet, elle vit des larmes qui coulaient de ses yeux mi-clos. Elle sut à ce moment que le vieux maître allait mourir. Il ne tomberait pas, comme le grand Boulle, la tête dans les copeaux mais s'endormirait pour toujours sur l'oreiller de toile blanche brodé aux initiales de Marguerite Œben, dans le grand lit d'acajou qu'il avait construit de ses mains, conformément à la tradition, avant d'épouser la veuve de son patron.

Pendant ce temps, Henri-François dessinait un nouveau portrait de son père. Antoinette lui fit signe et ils s'approchèrent du mourant qui semblait vouloir parler.

– Je vais aller rejoindre Marguerite, murmura-t-il. Et la reine! Et tous ceux qui ont aimé mes meubles...

L'allusion à la malheureuse Marie-Antoinette était si inattendue qu'Henri et sa sœur se regardèrent, étonnés. Ils s'avancèrent encore pour entendre le murmure qui sortait péniblement de la bouche de Riesener :

– Antoinette, il faudra laisser Lucie épouser son ébéniste, le fils Caumont, c'est un artiste...

– Et toi, Henri, tâche d'avoir un fils. Pour que le nom continue...

Ce furent ses dernières paroles. Jean-Henri Riesener, ouvrier du roi, s'éteignit à quinze heures le 6 janvier 1806. Il était âgé de soixante et onze ans.

Antoinette descendit prévenir Lucie qui chantonnait en regardant les gravures du *Journal des Demoiselles.*

– Riesener vint de mourir, ma chérie.

Elle serra contre elle la jeune fille qui avait éclaté en sanglots et lui dit :

– Il serait bien qu'Emmanuel Caumont fasse le cercueil. Va tout de suite le lui demander. Nous n'avons plus de menuisier ni d'ébéniste dans la famille.

La disparition de Riesener avait été durement ressentie dans le Faubourg. Avec lui, une époque finissait, celle des seigneurs du bois à qui les commandes des rois et des princes avaient permis de donner libre cours à leur génie, sans trop se soucier des contingences financières. Cela durait depuis François Ier. De la libéralité des monarques qui pensaient que la beauté n'a pas de prix, étaient nés des chefs-d'œuvre dont les temps nouveaux rendaient la création chimérique. Le grand Georges Jacob n'avait survécu qu'en adaptant sa production à une industrialisation dont le développement devenait une nécessité. Lui-même disait que ses plus beaux meubles, il les avait faits pour le roi.

Les artisans du Faubourg qui, durant des siècles, avaient dû leur prospérité à l'élan donné par les artistes du Louvre et de l'Arsenal, se sentaient un peu orphelins dans ce monde qui changeait d'harmonie, où la mort de Riesener résonnait comme un dernier avertissement. Les commandes impériales passées au Faubourg par Napoléon désireux de ne pas s'aliéner la popularité des ouvriers n'étaient pas celles des nobles et des notables suivant le goût du roi jusque dans leur façon de se meubler. On savait dans les ateliers qu'une époque était révolue, qu'il allait falloir s'adapter à celle que certains appelaient déjà « l'après-Riesener ».

Place d'Aligre aussi, la mort du maître avait marqué. Antoinette perdait son second père et tous les habitués du mercredi un phare qui éclairait depuis des années leurs entretiens hebdomadaires. Curieusement, les plus touchés étaient Fontaine et Percier, responsables avec David du changement de cap qui avait rejeté Riesener et les derniers grands du XVIIIe siècle sur les falaises du passé. Dieu sait que le vieil ébéniste ne les avait pas ménagés ces dernières années, pourtant ils n'avaient jamais cessé d'admirer et d'honorer son talent. Occupés par les travaux gigantesques que leur confiait l'Empereur, depuis quelque temps ils n'honoraient plus aussi souvent les dîners d'Antoinette, mais depuis la mort de Riesener ils se faisaient une règle de n'en manquer aucun.

– Nous tenons à être près de vous dans ce moment pénible, avaient-ils dit. Vous aider à maintenir une tradition qui tenait autant à la personnalité de Riesener qu'à la vôtre est une manière de rendre hommage à celui dont le fauteuil reste vide. Nous avons un remords, celui de ne pas lui avoir assez dit combien ses remarques, véhémentes mais légitimes, nous avaient été utiles. Il ne nous a pas empêchés de suivre un courant irrésistible mais il nous a fait éviter bien des excès. Nous ne l'oublions pas. Si le sort a été injuste pour lui, soyez sûre, chère Antoinette, que ses chefs-d'œuvre ne demeureront pas longtemps oubliés, ni son talent qui était immense.

Antoinette avait donc maintenu ses réunions du mercredi. Il faut dire que Fontaine et Percier leur apportaient beaucoup. Tous les projets de Napoléon, et Dieu sait s'ils étaient nombreux, passaient par leurs mains. Que ce soit l'ouverture d'une large rue bordée de maisons à arcades le long du jardin des Tuileries [1], l'achèvement des quatre ailes qui entouraient la grande cour du Louvre ou le difficile rétablissement de Versailles dans sa splendeur primitive, c'est à Percier et Fontaine que l'Empereur faisait appel. Les deux compères n'arrivaient donc jamais l'esprit vide place d'Aligre où l'on savourait, semaine après semaine, dans leur jus le plus frais, les fruits de la formidable imagination impériale.

1. La rue de Rivoli qui s'arrêtait à la rue de l'Échelle et que Visconti prolongera plus tard.

Ce soir de février 1806, Percier avait des choses particulièrement intéressantes à raconter. La veille, le 13, il avait été prié à déjeuner aux Tuileries par Napoléon qui voulait l'entretenir d'un projet dont il était question depuis Henri IV : la réunion du palais des Tuileries au Louvre.

– Un déjeuner avec l'empereur n'est pas un moment de détente! commença Percier. Il mange à une vitesse surprenante et expédie si bien le service que vous sortez de table la faim au ventre et ivre de paroles car, s'il touche à peine aux plats, il ne cesse de parler.

« Je veux, me dit Napoléon, déblayer l'espace qui sépare les deux palais, ménager un grand terrain avec des portiques dans l'axe des deux entrées, et placer aux extrémités deux arcs monumentaux, l'un dédié à la Paix, l'autre à la guerre! »

J'étais surpris, continua Percier, car nous travaillions depuis des mois à un plan qui raccordait les deux palais, plan difficile à réaliser car l'axe des Tuileries et du jardin n'est pas le prolongement de celui du Louvre. La nouvelle idée de l'Empereur me paraissait donc meilleure. Je le lui dis sans trop insister car il pouvait encore changer dix fois d'avis avant le premier coup de pioche. Napoléon m'entendit, demanda qu'on débarrassât la table et l'entremets auquel nous n'avions pas touché, fit convoquer le grand maréchal du palais et lui dicta un plan qui tenait compte du projet de la grande rue à arcades et se résumait, dans l'immédiat, à un arc de triomphe élevé entre les deux palais. Cet arc de triomphe sembla d'un coup accaparer toute l'énergie créatrice de l'Empereur : « A partir de cet instant, me dit-il, vous ne travaillez plus que sur ce projet. Je veux avoir les premiers dessins dans les quarante-huit heures! »

Comme je lui faisais remarquer que c'était là un délai bien trop court et que nous devions rendre le surlendemain un travail pour l'extérieur, il partit dans une grande colère en criant qu'il ne nous avait pas nommés l'année précédente architectes du Louvre et des Tuileries pour que nous acceptions des commandes de particuliers, et qu'il exigeait son projet dans le temps qu'il avait décidé! Napoléon se leva et quitta la pièce sans prendre congé, me laissant éberlué sur ma chaise...

– Alors, qu'avez-vous fait? demanda Antoinette.

– Nous nous sommes mis au travail et devrions à cette heure être penchés sur nos planches à dessiner au lieu de bavarder. L'Empereur aura son projet après-demain. Nous sommes contents de nous. Quel rêve pour des architectes que de construire un monument aussi important dans l'un des plus beaux sites du monde? Il sera établi sur le modèle des arcs romains, de Constantin et de Septime Sévère par exemple; mais aux trois ouvertures classiques nous en ajouterons une quatrième, longitudinale, qui donnera à l'arc son originalité [1]. La décoration sera plus riche et plus délicate que celle des monuments antiques. On y sentira dans les sculptures le goût et la finesse des œuvres de la Renaissance et aussi l'influence du style Louis XVI. Peut-être en souvenir de Riesener...

En prononçant ces derniers mots, Fontaine avait eu un sourire pour Antoinette qui le remercia silencieusement d'un signe de tête.

– Quand verrons-nous ce projet? demanda Lenoir qui devenait curieux dès qu'il s'agissait de monuments.

– Mercredi prochain si l'Empereur l'accepte. Peut-être jamais s'il le refuse. Mais je ne vous ai pas tout dit. Il faut que notre arc soit dominé par quelque statue remarquable, sculptée dans l'Histoire. Ce sera la seule que nous ne demanderons pas aux artistes de notre temps.

– Je crois avoir deviné, dit Alexandre Lenoir. En tout cas je sais ce que, moi, je planterais au sommet de votre arc de triomphe.

– Vous êtes le mieux placé, vous, le fondateur du musée des Monuments historiques, pour choisir l'œuvre grandiose qui fera passer notre modeste création. Voyons

1. Ce sera l'arc de triomphe du Carrousel, chef d'œuvre de Percier-Fontaine, construit en moins de deux ans grâce aux fonds provenant de la conquête de la Hollande.

si votre idée rencontre la nôtre. Et si elle est meilleure, nous sommes prêts à la retenir!

– Vous n'avez pas pu ne pas songer aux chevaux de bronze attribués à Lysippe ou Zénodore. J'explique pour les néophytes que l'empereur Théodose les enleva du temple du Soleil pour les transporter à Constantinople. Ces chevaux qui décidément enchantent les conquérants furent pris par le doge Dandolo et ornaient depuis le XIIIe siècle la façade de San Marco à Venise. Puisque notre empereur les a fait venir à Paris en 97, autant leur faire prendre l'air. Je crois qu'ils ne dépareront pas votre œuvre.

– Vous avez gagné. Et je suis sûr que Napoléon ne verra pas d'inconvénient à montrer au monde que les chevaux d'Alexandre et de Flavius sont désormais à Paris!

Ce soir-là, Antoinette avait invité Emmanuel Caumont considéré maintenant comme le fiancé officiel de Lucie. Le jeune homme, intimidé, avait écouté ces gens célèbres et instruits avec la ferveur d'un enfant admis pour la première fois à la table des grands. Il n'aurait sans doute pas ouvert la bouche si Fontaine ne s'était adressé à lui :

– Et vous, jeune homme, qui avez la chance d'avoir retenu la tendre attention de Lucie, que pensez-vous de ce branle-bas artistique qui vous concerne puisque vous êtes ébéniste et même sculpteur... Nous avons admiré la console que vous avez offerte à votre fiancée. C'est plus que bien. Il faut continuer dans cette voie...

Emmanuel qui tremblait depuis le début du souper d'avoir à répondre à une question de ce genre, se sentit soudain libéré. C'était comme si un autre parlait à sa place, d'une voix ferme, exprimant ses propres pensées sans crainte et avec clarté :

– L'opinion que vous manifestez de mon modeste talent me touche beaucoup et je vous en remercie. Venant de vous elle ne peut que m'encourager. C'est vrai que j'aime sculpter le bois. Je possède tous les outils de mon père et Mlle Œben, pardonnez-moi, je l'appelle toujours ainsi, m'a dit qu'elle me donnerait les gouges du maître Riesener. Mais, pardonnez mon audace, vous me conseillez de persévérer dans un art menacé de disparition. Je gagne ma vie en construisant des meubles nouveaux, inspirés de vos créations, où la sculpture est reléguée, quand elle n'est pas complètement supprimée, à un rang secondaire. Les bronzes l'ont remplacée. Sans doute conviennent-ils mieux à la forme rectiligne d'aujourd'hui mais ils rendent, hélas! inutile le métier de sculpteur. Celui-ci va s'éteindre. Si un jour la mode revient à l'ornementation directe du bois, il n'y aura plus d'ouvriers pour le sculpter.

Il se fit un silence. On se regardait, étonné par l'intervention du jeune homme qui aurait pu aussi bien, quelques semaines auparavant, être le fait de Riesener. Fontaine le premier prit la parole. Il semblait jubiler.

– Me croirez-vous si je vous dis que votre réponse m'enchante? Enfin un jeune qui voit plus loin que le bout de son nez et qui réfléchit à son métier! Vous avez raison mais laissez-moi vous dire que les modes passent plus vite que les métiers. La réaction actuelle aux abus de la rocaille n'aura qu'un temps et les gens retrouveront vite le goût de l'arabesque et des motifs ouvragés. Napoléon veut associer son règne à un style imposant, majestueux. Le retour à l'antique et l'acajou conviennent à son désir de grandeur comme la marqueterie de Boulle et l'ébène convenaient à celui de Louis XIV. Mais vous vivrez après l'Empereur et votre heure viendra de rendre de l'élégance aux meubles d'aujourd'hui qui, je le confesse, en manquent singulièrement.

– Merci, monsieur Fontaine. Vous me rendez la foi. Mais puisque vous parlez des goûts de Napoléon que vous êtes avec M. Percier les premiers à connaître, parlez-nous-en, si vous le voulez bien. Tout le monde met en avant les choix de l'Empereur. Napoléon aime ceci, Napoléon veut cela... Mais en fait personne ne pourrait dire dans les ateliers ce qu'il souhaite réellement.

– Ah! Les goûts de l'Empereur! Combien nous serions heureux, Percier et moi, de les connaître vraiment...

Parfois nous pensons être en mesure de les anticiper à propos d'un projet et crac! nous devons constater que nous nous sommes trompés! Tout au plus nous en appréhendons les grandes lignes. Autant il exige du grandiose lorsqu'il s'agit des pièces d'apparat, autant il demande de la simplicité pour ses appartements privés. Les meubles par exemple sont pour lui des instruments de travail destinés à écrire, à supporter des cartes d'état-major, à se reposer entre deux batailles ou deux décisions importantes. Le cadre de son activité est partout le même. Quand un meuble lui plaît, il en fait exécuter immédiatement des copies pour Saint-Cloud, Compiègne et Fontainebleau.

– Comme les fameux guéridons qui lui servent aussi bien pour écrire que pour déjeuner! précisa Ethis qui ajouta : Vous savez que mon idée d'en faire fabriquer au Faubourg pour les vendre m'a permis de monter mon commerce. Emmanuel est mon principal fournisseur. Sur ce plan-là, au moins, il ne se plaint pas des goûts de Napoléon. Que voulez-vous, c'est un nom qui fait vendre! Je dis à un client : « Laissez-vous tenter par ce guéridon que l'Empereur fait faire par Jacob et qu'il possède à dix ou quinze exemplaires, dans toutes ses résidences, c'est une pièce historique! » S'il hésite, j'ajoute que c'est le seul meuble qui suit Napoléon dans toutes ses campagnes. L'idée de déjeuner sur la table impériale ou de jouer au taquin sur le guéridon où le général en chef dresse ses plans de batailles vainc ses dernières résistances, il achète! Grâce à mon ami Richard, le filateur, je vends maintenant une vingtaine de guéridons par mois aux Anglais. C'est en partie grâce aux lords que je vais bientôt pouvoir réaliser mon rêve : acheter un cabriolet!

Chacun félicita Ethis pour sa réussite et Percier, avant de prendre congé, raconta une dernière histoire :

– Même pour les éléments décoratifs, l'Empereur exige la simplicité. Il y a quelques mois, nous lui avions soumis une aquarelle représentant des candélabres dont il nous avait demandé d'étudier le projet. J'ai conservé ce dessin qui nous est revenu des Tuileries avec cette note : « Simplifier les ornements, c'est pour l'Empereur. » Ainsi a-t-il la phobie des garnitures chères aux tapissiers. Après avoir arraché violemment les glands de passementerie qui ornaient un rideau il a dicté une « ordonnance irrévocable » pour ses fournisseurs et le Mobilier national : « Sa Majesté fait connaître qu'Elle ne veut pas de glands dans ses appartements. »

Le lendemain, dans la soirée, Antoinette se rendit chez Alexandre Lenoir rue des Lions. Il y avait près d'un mois que les deux amis ne s'étaient pas rencontrés dans l'intimité. Ainsi l'avait-elle voulu, constatant tout de même avec un petit serrement de cœur qu'il n'avait pas trop insisté pour la voir. Maintenant sa décision était prise : elle allait lui dire que leurs relations devaient désormais changer de nature.

L'attitude chaleureuse d'Alexandre ne facilita pas les choses. Il reçut Antoinette avec une tendresse à laquelle elle n'était plus habituée.

– Enfin vous me revenez ! Que je suis heureux de vous retrouver dans ce cadre où nous avons été tellement bien ! Comme je vous ai aimée et comme je vous aime encore ! Notre histoire est très belle, elle m'a apporté le bonheur. Je ne vois pas comment je pourrais me passer de vous...

Antoinette faillit flancher. Ces paroles douces la ramenaient dix ans en arrière ; elle revivait en les écoutant la folle journée de Notre-Dame et leur première étreinte. Elle se laissa embrasser comme naguère mais se dégagea bientôt en souriant.

– Mon cher Alexandre, c'est parce que notre histoire est belle et que moi non plus je ne saurais me passer de vous, que j'ai beaucoup réfléchi tous ces temps et suis arrivée à cette conclusion que si nous voulons rester amis et continuer d'apprécier cette merveilleuse complicité qui nous unit depuis si longtemps, il faut que nous nous voyions autrement qu'en amants.

Il l'écoutait, pâle, visiblement déconcerté. Il entrouvrit les lèvres deux fois mais aucun son ne sortit de sa bouche. Enfin il murmura :

– Je ne comprends pas... Que s'est-il passé pour que vous me teniez ce langage? Qu'ai-je fait pour mériter un traitement aussi cruel?

– Vous n'avez rien fait, mon ami, mais moi j'ai fait quelque chose, quelque chose d'irrémédiable : j'ai vieilli!

– Vous êtes folle, Antoinette. Vous avez toujours votre allant et votre jeunesse d'il y a dix ans. Vous pensez peut-être aux cheveux qui font grisonner votre tête mais je les aime vos cheveux gris! Loin de m'écarter de vous, ils m'émeuvent et me rapprochent. Dites-moi vite que tout cela n'est qu'un mauvais rêve et venez vous blottir dans mes bras. Je vous aime Antoinette! Je vous aime!

– Mais moi aussi je vous aime, et c'est pour que vous m'aimiez toujours, jusqu'à la fin de ma vie, que j'ai décidé de vous parler. Non pas pour rompre mais pour commencer ensemble un autre voyage que notre différence d'âge ne viendra jamais interrompre. J'ai cinquante-deux ans. Pour une femme, c'est déjà la vieillesse. Vous n'en avez pas quarante-quatre. Pour un homme, c'est l'âge le plus beau, celui de la force, de l'intelligence, des succès.

– Mon plus grand succès, c'est d'être aimé de vous!

– Bon! Alors, Alexandre, je vais être obligée d'être plus directe. Je ne mets pas en cause votre sincérité, elle est éclatante, mais permettez-moi de vous poser une question : si vous ne me trompez pas, n'avez-vous pas envie de le faire quand vous rencontrez une femme qui a vingt ou trente ans de moins que moi? Répondez-moi franchement!

– Qu'allez-vous donc chercher mon amie? Il n'y a jamais eu entre nous de ces crises de jalousie qui gâchent tant d'unions!

– Merci, vous m'avez répondu. Aujourd'hui, il n'est pas ou plus question de jalousie. Il m'importerait assez peu, dans le fond, que vous ayez de jeunes maîtresses. Je pourrais, fermant complaisamment les yeux, acheter les moments que vous me consacreriez avec un enthousiasme de moins en moins vif. Je gagnerais peut-être ainsi quelques années d'illusions. Si j'étais sotte, c'est sans doute ce que je ferais, mais j'ai une cervelle qui fonctionne assez bien et qui me dit que je paierais très cher ces mois de faux bonheur.

– Comment cela?

– Un prix exorbitant : mon cher Alexandre, je vous perdrais! J'ai donc conclu un marché avec moi-même : quelques ultimes moments de plaisir sensuel contre votre attachement perpétuel! J'y gagne, vous aussi.

– Mais pourquoi se presser? Il sera toujours bien temps de réfléchir à cela. Rien ne menace aujourd'hui l'amour que nous nous portons...

– Que voilà bien une réaction d'homme! Retarder les échéances, refuser les conclusions d'une sagesse élémentaire pour reculer une décision difficile... Cette décision, pour qu'elle soit porteuse d'intérêts, il faut la prendre tout de suite, avant que la crise éclate. C'est comme un testament : il faut y songer avant l'agonie...

– C'est du roman tout cela, rien qui résiste au bon sens. Revenez sur terre et dans mes bras Antoinette. Oublions cette conversation...

– Non! Si nous voulons demeurer des amis proches, des confidents liés par l'estime et l'affection... et pourquoi pas une certaine forme d'amour, il nous faut cesser d'être amants pendant que vous me désirez encore. Sinon, quand vous me rejetterez – car vous me rejetterez d'une façon ou d'une autre –, il ne pourra rien rester de notre alliance, que du dégoût, des rancœurs, de la haine. Maintenant je vais m'en aller, mon chéri. Réfléchissez à ce que je viens de vous dire et vous comprendrez que j'ai raison : pour être difficile à accepter, notre renoncement est la solution de sagesse, la seule qui puisse assurer la survie de notre liaison.

– Vous savez convaincre Antoinette. Croyez pourtant qu'il n'est pas facile de vous perdre! Vous m'avez assené un sérieux coup de maillet, ma tête est comme tuméfiée.

Vous me demandez de réfléchir, je vais le faire dès que j'en serai capable. Pour l'instant, je ne peux m'empêcher de penser que votre proposition est folle et qu'il est déraisonnable de se faire volontairement du mal. Vous aussi, Antoinette, je vous demande de réfléchir!

Antoinette ne s'attarda pas. Elle venait d'accomplir une démarche pénible dont dépendait l'orientation de sa vie et avait hâte de se retrouver chez elle, auprès de Lucie que l'amour rendait encore plus jolie et dont la gaieté allait lui être d'un grand secours en ce soir d'automne où elle avait plus envie de pleurer que de rire.

La jeune fille avait tellement de choses à lui raconter que la soirée se passa sans tristesse. Antoinette éclata même de rire quand Lucie lui fit part de la dernière trouvaille d'Ethis. Ayant appris que Biennais, le tabletier, fournissait à l'Empereur du bois d'aloès et de santal pour alimenter les brûle-parfum disposés dans toutes les pièces de ses résidences, il avait acheté avec Emmanuel un lot de bois orientaux qui, découpés en bâtonnets, se vendaient fort bien dans sa boutique et chez les confrères qu'il approvisionnait. Il avait même fait imprimer des prospectus qui vantaient les bienfaits des règles d'hygiène qu'appliquait Napoléon : « Comme l'Empereur, vivez dans une atmosphère saine et parfumée grâce aux bois de l'Orient. »

– Je crois qu'Ethis ne va pas tarder à s'acheter son cabriolet! dit Lucie. Quant à Emmanuel, les travaux que lui confie son futur beau-frère lui permettent d'économiser en vue de notre mariage. Je sais bien que ce n'est pas demain que j'épouserai Emmanuel mais cela nous rend heureux d'y penser.

Comme elle s'y attendait, Antoinette qui n'avait jamais retrouvé un bon sommeil depuis l'emprisonnement de Bertrand, dormit mal cette nuit-là. Elle revivait sans cesse sa conversation avec Alexandre et se demandait si elle avait eu raison de choisir la rupture. A force de vouloir être maîtresse de sa vie, ne s'en remettait-elle pas trop à la raison, c'est-à-dire à « sa » raison? N'était-elle pas en train de s'enferrer dans une erreur qu'elle regretterait durant des années? Quand elle s'endormit, au petit matin, elle était prête à remettre en question sa fière théorie et à s'abandonner au laisser-aller d'Alexandre.

Elle fut réveillée par des coups frappés à la porte. Lucie étant sortie, elle se couvrit d'un châle pour aller ouvrir. Un commissionnaire apportait une énorme gerbe de fleurs de chez Germont, le fleuriste du Palais-Royal, fournisseur de la cour impériale, connu à Paris pour la fraîcheur de ses bouquets et leur prix exorbitant. L'emballage avec son papier soyeux et ses rubans était à lui seul une œuvre d'art. Antoinette décacheta d'abord l'enveloppe qui était jointe à l'envoi. Avant de reconnaître l'écriture elle avait deviné le nom de l'expéditeur : seul Alexandre était capable, parmi ses amis, de faire une telle folie. S'il lui envoyait parfois des fleurs, c'était pourtant la première fois qu'il avait recours à Germont. Lenoir n'était pas riche, il avait dépensé une fortune, l'équivalent d'un souper chez *Beauvilliers*, pourquoi?

« Pour me supplier de revenir sur ma décision... », pensa Antoinette en tirant une carte de bristol de son enveloppe. Le cœur battant elle lut les quelques lignes qui allaient décider de sa vie :

Je n'ai pas dormi cette nuit en pensant et repensant aux projets que vous formez sur l'avenir de nos relations. Je sors meurtri de cette épreuve mais touché par vos arguments. Puisque vous êtes sûre qu'il nous faut rompre l'amour pour gagner l'amitié, je me rends, triste mais aussi heureux de vous garder pour la vie. Ces roses ne sont pas les dernières que je vous envoie mais j'ai voulu qu'elles soient les plus belles pour sceller notre nouvelle union. A mercredi, je vous embrasse.

Alexandre.

Antoinette relut une nouvelle fois la carte puis s'essuya les yeux avec son mouchoir de batiste, un cadeau d'Ethis; elle pleurait, moins son amour tari que les dix années de sa vie dont elle venait de refermer le livre. Et puis elle se reprit, se parlant tout haut à elle-même comme dans les moments difficiles :

– Allons, ce n'est pas la première fois que tu tournes la page! C'est toi qui l'as voulu, alors pas de regrets inutiles! Les pleurnicheries n'ont jamais été ton refuge. Respire plutôt ces roses magnifiques et dis-toi qu'elles vont parfumer le reste de ton existence. Dis-toi aussi qu'il ne doit pas y avoir tellement de femmes dont l'amant est disposé à se ruiner pour leur envoyer des fleurs le jour où on leur dit qu'il faut rompre! C'est à moi, maintenant, de montrer à Alexandre qu'il a eu raison de m'écouter!

Cette année 1806 était décidément fertile en événements qui influaient sur la vie du quartier. La mort de Riesener d'abord, bientôt suivie par celle de Lenoir-Dufresne, l'associé de François Richard dont l'entreprise cotonnière prenait des proportions imposantes. La fabrique de la rue de Charonne groupait maintenant 137 ouvriers au couvent de Traisnel, tous occupés à construire les machines que Richard disposait un peu partout chez les artisans de ses fiefs normands et picards. Le reste de l'effectif parisien, 900 ouvriers environ, travaillait à la filature. L'extension des affaires des manufactures Richard-Lenoir semblait ne pas avoir de limites. Chaque fois que François venait souper place d'Aligre, cela lui arrivait environ une fois par mois, c'était pour annoncer la création de nouvelles fabriques ou l'arrivée de mécaniciens anglais spécialisés dans l'usinage des métiers à tisser.

– Songez que mes cinq filatures totalisent maintenant près de 100 000 broches et occupent 3 000 ouvriers. Au tissage, j'en emploie près de 8 000! avait-il dit à Antoinette le jour où il était venu lui annoncer la mort de Lenoir.

– C'est une énorme responsabilité, avait-il ajouté, et je ne sais pas comment je vais me débrouiller seul. En tout cas la maison continuera de s'appeler « Richard-Lenoir »!

En disant ces derniers mots, François, à la stupéfaction d'Antoinette, s'était mis à pleurer. Tandis qu'elle essayait de le réconforter, intimidée par cet homme de quarante ans considéré comme l'un des hommes les plus entreprenants de l'Empire et que la disparition de son ami plongeait dans une affliction qu'il ne cherchait pas à dissimuler, il murmura :

– Pardonnez-moi, madame de Valfroy, mais c'est un frère que je perds!

– Je vous comprends, François, mais n'ayez pas honte de vos larmes. Elles prouvent qu'on peut être un homme d'industrie très puissant et ne pas avoir le cœur sec. Votre travail vous permettra de mieux supporter le moment pénible que vous vivez.

Un autre événement, pas tragique celui-là, avait étonné le clan de la place d'Aligre : Eugène Bénard, le père de Marie, venait enfin d'être nommé maire du VIIIe arrondissement.C'était pour le fabricant de papier peint de la rue de Montreuil, successeur de Réveillon, la consécration sociale à laquelle il prétendait depuis longtemps. Son attitude au moment du mariage de sa fille avec Ethis avait tendu les relations entre les deux familles. Marie, surtout depuis la naissance de Bertrand, s'était reportée vers Antoinette si bien que, sans être fâchées, les deux familles ne se fréquentaient guère.

Par égard pour Marie, on commenta sans malignité place d'Aligre la promotion de M. Bénard. Seul Ethis qui n'avait jamais oublié l'opposition du papetier à son mariage ni son refus de l'aider à monter son magasin, se permit une réflexion peu aimable.

– Faute d'avoir gagné une médaille ou un galon durant la Révolution, mon beau-père gagne enfin une distinction sous l'Empire! Riche, il était assoiffé de considération. Le voilà maire, espérons que cela le rendra plus généreux!

– Cela me fait tout de même plaisir pour maman! avait ajouté Marie qui, sans jamais l'avouer, partageait les sentiments d'Ethis.

La famille avait tout de même été invitée à la réception

donnée à la mairie pour célébrer l'événement. Pour la circonstance, Antoinette avait mis sa plus belle robe en soie indienne et s'était acheté un chapeau rue Saint-Antoine, chez *Magnelienne*, dont les créations faisaient fureur depuis qu'elle avait passé un an à Londres chez *Partridge*, le chapelier de Sa Majesté. Antoinette était vraiment belle et ne paraissait certes pas ses cinquante-deux ans. Pour une fois elle avait voulu redevenir Mme de Valfroy et, pauvre, se présenter comme une grande dame chez les riches beaux-parents de son fils. Pour parfaire son entrée, il lui fallait une escorte digne de son élégance. Ethis lui avait trouvé le cavalier idéal :

– François Richard, le plus gros manufacturier de l'arrondissement, est bien entendu invité. Tu connais sa réputation et sa prestance, on l'appelle le Brummell parisien, je vais lui demander de venir te chercher en voiture et de te donner son bras pour venir chez les Bénard.

Ethis n'avait pas eu de peine à convaincre sa mère et comme Fontaine avait lui aussi été invité, c'est entre les deux hommes les plus importants et les plus célèbres de la réunion qu'Antoinette fit une entrée de reine.

Très impressionné, le nouveau maire s'inclina et, durant toute la soirée, n'eut que des amabilités pour Antoinette. Celle-ci qui avait beaucoup plus l'habitude des salons que le pauvre Eugène Bénard, embarrassé dans son écharpe tricolore, y répondit avec une grâce exquise. Elle se permit même le plaisir de présenter au maire et à sa femme le fiancé de Lucie, éblouissant dans un habit de velours prune.

– Vous connaissez ma fille Lucie. Voici son futur mari, Emmanuel Caumont.

– Toutes mes félicitations! Le maire fit un rond de jambe et poursuivit : Que faites-vous, monsieur, dans la vie?

– Je suis ébéniste.

Devant l'étonnement mal maîtrisé d'Eugène Bénard, Antoinette continua, malicieuse :

– Eh oui! dans la famille nous n'en finissons pas d'être

ébénistes. Quand nous ne sommes pas aristocrates comme mon cher mari! Mais c'est pareil, la noblesse du bois a toujours plutôt fait bon ménage avec l'autre.

Georges Jacob et son fils étaient là, bien entendu. Ils firent fête à Antoinette et lui parlèrent de Riesener avec beaucoup d'affection.

– C'était le plus grand! dit Georges. On a été injuste à son égard mais il n'y a rien à faire contre le temps et la mode. Tenez, j'ai appris récemment que le serre-bijoux de la comtesse de Provence, une pièce superbe par l'équilibre de ses formes et l'élégance de ses décorations, l'un des chefs-d'œuvre de Riesener, a été proposé il n'y a pas longtemps par un antiquaire à l'administration du Garde-meuble. Daru, malgré sa préférence pour ce meuble unique, n'a pu que transmettre le refus de l'Empereur. Il m'a raconté la scène. Napoléon, après avoir examiné le dessin du serre-bijoux a dit: « Écrivez en réponse que Sa Majesté veut faire du neuf et non acheter du vieux. »

– Je trouve cela logique, dit Antoinette. L'Empereur fait ce qu'ont fait les rois auxquels il a succédé. Louis XIV n'a plus voulu des meubles Renaissance ni des pieds tournés de Henri IV et de Louis XIII; Louis XV et Louis XVI ont adopté le style léger, élégant de leur époque. Napoléon veut lui des meubles Napoléon, ceux que vous fabriquez si bien, mon cher Georges, avec votre fils.

– Un seul ébéniste ancien trouve grâce à ses yeux, ajouta Jacob-Desmalter, c'est Boulle. L'Empereur a fait placer une commode Boulle dans sa chambre de Fontainebleau et deux autres dans les appartements du deuxième étage. Deux grandes armoires à sujets de chasse et de pêche sont destinées à recevoir les cartes dans le cabinet topographique. Napoléon m'a demandé de restaurer deux meubles d'appui à écaille rouge incrustée de cuivre et d'étain. Il voudrait même que nous en fassions des copies! Les tendances décoratives des meubles de Boulle sont pourtant bien éloignées de celles de l'Empire!

– Oui, remarqua son père, mais ce sont des meubles monuments dont la majesté convient à l'Empereur comme elle convenait à Louis XIV. Sans doute préfère-t-il emprunter au Roi-Soleil plutôt qu'à Louis XVI!

On parla longtemps encore de meubles et de bois. Antoinette rentra enchantée place d'Aligre. Finalement cette réception qu'elle craignait comme une corvée avait été agréable et le gros Eugène, serré comme un saucisson dans son habit, lui avait paru plutôt sympathique. Elle le dit à Marie qui ne cacha pas son contentement de voir son père pris pour une fois en considération. Ethis, lui, ne put s'empêcher de se moquer :

– Du train où vont les choses, je vous parie que mon cher beau-père ne tardera pas à être anobli!

Jamais la popularité de Napoléon n'avait été aussi grande au Faubourg. Si l'Empereur avait des ennemis, ce n'est pas chez les gens du bois qu'il fallait les chercher, ni même chez les ouvriers des manufactures, coton, verre ou papier, dont le sort n'était pas enviable mais qui, au moins, avaient du travail et pouvaient nourrir leur famille.

Sans avoir retrouvé leur activité du siècle dernier, les ateliers d'ébénisterie réussissaient à vivre. Les maîtres qui avaient la chance de profiter des commandes impériales produisaient des meubles du nouveau style dont la qualité première devait être la simplicité. Ils n'étaient pas destinés à la famille impériale mais à ceux qui gravitaient autour du soleil dans les demeures officielles : ministres, grands officiers, maîtres de suite et même domestiques de rang supérieur. Dès qu'un atelier était favorisé par le choix du Mobilier national, la nouvelle faisait le tour des cours et des passages. C'est qu'une commande nécessitait l'embauche de quelques ouvriers et qu'il restait au Faubourg un certain nombre de compagnons sans emploi. Ainsi se repassait-on le nom des trois fils du vieux menuisier Simon Mansion, tous établis rue Saint-Nicolas, ou celui de Jean-Antoine Burns, un rescapé de l'Ancien Régime, ou encore celui de François-Ignace Pabst dont l'atelier du 195, grand-rue avait survécu à tous les régimes dans des circonstances miraculeuses.

Ceux qui ne recevaient pas de commandes, c'étaient les plus nombreux, se débrouillaient en travaillant pour l'exportation. Chose curieuse, ils étaient souvent obligés de se remettre à l'ancien : les Anglais en effet étaient fous de meubles Louis XVI, voire Louis XV, et ne voulaient pas entendre parler de l'antique napoléonien.

Le succès appartenait à ceux qui, à l'exemple de l'Empereur, étaient capables d'une activité considérable. C'était le cas de Caron et Lefèvre, porcelainiers rue Popincourt, des frères Darthes, faïenciers, qui occupaient 150 ouvriers dans leur manufacture du 90, rue de la Roquette, l'ancien hôtel de Montalembert, et surtout de Richard-Lenoir dont la réussite prodigieuse n'avait pas d'autre exemple.

Pour une fois les infatigables Fontaine et Percier n'étaient pas impliqués dans l'une des grandes affaires architecturales de l'Empire [1]. L'architecte Chalgrin et son rival Raymond avaient été choisis pour édifier place de l'Étoile un gigantesque et massif monument destiné à perpétuer le souvenir des victoires de l'armée française. C'est ainsi que le 15 août 1806 fut posée la première pierre de l'arc de Triomphe. Dans le même temps, se déroulait sur l'esplanade des Invalides l'Exposition des produits de l'industrie qui attirait une foule considérable et permettait aux 1 422 exposants de faire triompher l'esprit d'invention qui marquait la naissance de l'ère industrielle. François Richard était l'un de ceux-ci, il avait invité Antoinette et Lucie à venir visiter cette grande kermesse de la mécanique.

En dehors de l'industrie textile et des machines à filer dont les ouvriers de Richard assuraient la démonstration permanente, la dame et la demoiselle du Faubourg, comme les appelait Alexandre Lenoir, retrouvèrent parmi

1. Ils seront tout de même plus tard appelés à y participer.

les exposants un bon nombre d'habitants du quartier dont les activités relevaient plus ou moins directement du bois.

Depuis des années, Antoinette avait perdu de vue Pierre Saumon dont le père, un charpentier de la rue Saint-Nicolas, était le voisin de Marguerite Lacroix avant qu'elle épouse Œben. Lui-même, de cinq ans plus âgé, l'avait courtisée et elle l'aurait peut-être épousé si Pilâtre de Rozier n'avait fait irruption dans sa vie. Pierre avait succédé à son père et réussi à passer sans trop de mal à travers tous les récifs de la Révolution. Son métier avait été moins touché que ceux du meuble : on peut se passer d'acheter une commode mais on ne peut pas laisser un toit s'écrouler ou les marches d'un escalier pourrir. Il avait aussi travaillé à l'aménagement de la salle du manège pour abriter la Convention et fabriqué des affûts de canons, ce qui lui avait permis de faire manger ses cinq enfants à peu près à leur faim.

Le charpentier, pourtant, s'ennuyait à répéter les mêmes gestes. A l'équarrissage des pannes et des chevrons, il préférait dessiner puis réaliser des drôles de machines où les pièces de fer renforçaient les palans et les rouages taillés dans le noyer et l'ébène. Il présentait au Champ-de-Mars une lourde mécanique dont le squelette en mouvement ne risquait pas de passer inaperçu. Entre deux tours d'une grande roue il vit Antoinette et arrêta tout pour venir l'embrasser.

– Il y a au moins un ou deux ans que je ne t'ai pas vue! Sans mes coupables activités inventives, cela aurait pu durer encore longtemps. Et nous habitons tout près l'un de l'autre! J'ai appris pour Riesener... J'aurais dû te faire signe mais... Mais je ne l'ai pas fait, ce qui n'empêche pas que je suis heureux de te revoir. C'est ta fille? Je ne l'aurais jamais reconnue!

– Montre-nous donc ta machine. Tous ces bras qui montent et qui s'abaissent! Et ces roues... Explique un peu!

– Ma machine vient d'avoir la médaille d'argent et Richard-Lenoir est intéressé. Elle peut être utile aussi bien dans une filature que dans n'importe quelle manufacture : elle procure un double mouvement de rotation et de bascule pour faire à la fois le service de différentes usines... Tu comprends?

– Pas du tout mais si Richard s'intéresse à ton invention, c'est qu'elle sert à quelque chose! Je suis contente pour toi.

Antoinette et Lucie continuèrent leur visite et reconnurent d'autres familiers du Faubourg : Verdier et Husson, les jeunes faïenciers de la rue de la Roquette qui, diversifiant leur industrie, présentaient un minimum qui pouvait rivaliser avec celui qu'on importait d'Angleterre; Duchet qui fabriquait et vendait de la colle forte rue Traversière et qui venait de recevoir une médaille d'argent de deuxième classe, et encore Auguste Jaquemart fabricant de savon rue de la Roquette et qui se lançait avec le fils du chimiste Darcet dans la production de soude artificielle...

Non, cela n'allait pas mal pour le Faubourg au cours de cette année-là, sixième du siècle, qui devait être encore marquée par la mise en eau régulière des fontaines, une nécessité attendue depuis longtemps. Désormais, la fontaine Basfroi, au coin de la rue de Charonne, la fontaine de la Petite-Halle, en face de l'ancienne abbaye, et enfin la fontaine du marché Beauvau, place d'Aligre, dont le mince filet d'eau s'arrêtait constamment de couler, étaient reliées à la nouvelle pompe de Notre-Dame. La distribution de l'eau à Paris était un vieux problème qui n'avait jamais été résolu. Alors que presque toutes les maisons de Londres étaient desservies par des robinets installés dans les cours, Paris en était encore à faire appel aux porteurs d'eau pour suppléer les fontaines publiques le plus souvent à sec. Napoléon, dès le Consulat, avait considéré qu'il s'agissait d'une question urgente et n'avait cessé de penser aux fontaines de Paris en attendant la réalisation d'un projet considérable qui devait enfin permettre à Paris de devenir une ville propre et salubre : le détournement des eaux de l'Ourcq et de la Beuveronne vers la capitale grâce à un canal aboutissant au bassin de la Villette.

Enfin on apprit le surlendemain du 14 octobre 1806 que l'Empereur avait remporté à Iéna une grande victoire sur les Prussiens. C'est le jour où Ethis prit possession de son cabriolet, symbole de réussite auquel il rêvait depuis longtemps. Ce n'était pas une voiture de grand luxe mais la caisse était solide et les roues ne tournaient pas en faisant des huit comme celles de la vieille charrette d'Alexandre Lenoir. Emmanuel avait promis de refaire les côtés de la carrosserie qui portaient les traces visibles d'un long service dans les embarras de Paris, et un ancien « vainqueur » établi sellier à l'entrée du Faubourg, rue Saint-Sabin, devait regarnir le siège arrière enfoncé jusqu'à l'essieu. Ethis n'avait pas attendu ces embellissements pour venir faire évoluer son équipage autour de la place d'Aligre. Si la voiture n'était pas dans un état de fraîcheur indiscutable, le cheval, lui, était assez fringant. François Richard avait revendu pour une bouchée de pain à son ami un bricolier flamand bai clair, trop léger pour faire tourner le manège qui entraînait les métiers à tisser mais fort à son aise entre les brancards d'une voiture légère.

– Il faut fêter l'événement! dit Ethis à Antoinette. Je t'emmène demain soir avec Lucie chez *Lemblin* au Palais-Royal. Si Emmanuel veut venir par ses propres moyens, il sera le bienvenu mais on ne peut pas être plus de quatre dans le cabriolet.

– Vas-tu au moins savoir diriger le cheval? demanda Antoinette pas très rassurée. Avec tous les fous qui brûlent le pavé sur leurs phaétons autour du Palais-Royal je te demande d'être très prudent!

– Sois tranquille! J'ai assez conduit les voitures d'Alexandre avec leurs lourds chargements de pierres pour me débrouiller. Le cheval qui s'appelle « Coco » mais que je vais baptiser « Vainqueur », c'est plus glorieux, est une bête paraît-il tranquille et obéissante.

Le lendemain, les Valfroy partirent donc au trot vers cette kermesse permanente qu'était redevenu le Palais-Royal, tout de même plus calme et surtout mieux fréquenté depuis que les policiers de Dubois surveillaient les galeries et les alentours. Ethis ne trouva évidemment pas un anneau de libre pour attacher « Vainqueur » et il dut avoir recours à l'un des voituriers accrédités par les cafés du quartier pour s'occuper de son modeste attelage.

Il faisait encore très beau en ce jour du mois d'octobre et le Palais-Royal était plein d'une foule joyeuse, bigarrée et fourmillante où les gens du peuple qui avaient gardé de la Révolution les culottes longues de coton rayé et les blouses ouvertes côtoyaient les jeunes élégants en habits à basque et en bottes à revers. Les grisettes étaient ravissantes qui ramenaient sur le bras droit les plis pendants de leur tunique de linon pour se dessiner une silhouette à l'antique tandis que les femmes riches ou raffinées affectaient de donner une touche d'anglomanie à leurs toilettes de Vénus callipyge. Lucie avait pour elle ses seize années, bientôt dix-sept, pour enlever la robe blanche la plus simple qui soit. Antoinette avait sacrifié à la mode anglaise en arborant le spencer de doux lainage azurin que lui avait vendu Parisot, le marchand de *La Belle Fermière.* Quant à Ethis et Marie, ils étaient tout simplement bien habillés, avec le goût discret qui avait été celui de Bertrand de Valfroy et que son fils adoptif prenait pour modèle en toute circonstance.

Emmanuel Caumont les attendait à l'entrée du café *Lemblin,* sanglé dans le velours comme s'il avait dû se marier sur l'instant. C'était pour lui une promotion que d'être admis dans la famille Valfroy qui était d'abord celle d'Œben et de Riesener. Aussi prenait-il soin d'être à la hauteur de l'estime qu'on lui portait. Il n'avait aucun mal à y parvenir car il était naturellement distingué. Antoinette avait dit à Lucie : « Tu as bien choisi, c'est un seigneur du bois. » Dans sa bouche, cela valait toutes les richesses du monde.

Lemblin était le lieu à la mode où il était de bon ton, depuis un an, de venir prendre sa demi-tasse en parlant à un ami ou tout simplement à un voisin de banquette des affaires du jour. Sans être un habitué, Ethis s'y rendait assez souvent pour y rencontrer des confrères antiquaires et marchands de meubles ou y traiter une affaire. « Paris est comme ça! avait-il dit à Antoinette. Pour réussir, il faut se montrer là où il faut, quand il le faut. » Elle avait ri et s'était récriée mais, dans le fond, elle était très fière de l'incroyable chemin parcouru par son fils.

Pour l'instant Ethis n'était pas mécontent de montrer aux siens qu'il était connu dans ce lieu célèbre où l'on ne mangeait pas, où l'on buvait à peine mais où l'on parlait beaucoup.

– Nous verrons sûrement Lemblin tout à l'heure, dit-il quand tout le monde fut assis autour d'une table de marbre et qu'on eut commandé le café le plus parfumé de Paris.

– Ce que je suis contente! s'exclama Lucie. Je ne suis venue qu'une fois, avec toi déjà, au Palais-Royal mais j'étais bien petite. Est-ce que le café *Lemblin* existait déjà?

– Mais non! Il y a à peine un an qu'il est ouvert. Lemblin me plaît parce qu'il a réussi tout seul à monter le café le plus élégant de Paris. Il était garçon à *La Rotonde*. A force d'économies, il a pu racheter ce café à un certain Peron qui alors servait surtout les cochers. Avec l'aide de l'architecte Alavoine, un ami de Fontaine, il a métamorphosé l'établissement et triplé le prix des consommations. Puis il a repris le numéro 101 voisin du sien dans la galerie de Chartres. Aujourd'hui il faut quelquefois attendre un quart d'heure pour avoir une place. C'est le rendez-vous de tous les officiers de l'Empire quand ils passent par Paris et aussi celui des journalistes, des financiers, de tous ceux qui se flattent de politique. Mais buvez donc votre café avant qu'il refroidisse... Tenez, voici le patron!

Un petit homme rondouillard vêtu à l'ancienne mais avec recherche vint saluer Ethis qui lui présenta sa famille.

– La baronne de Valfroy, ma femme, ma sœur, et le maître ébéniste Emmanuel Caumont dont l'estampille est maintenant recherchée par tous ceux que Jacob n'a pas le temps de satisfaire. Si un jour vous avez besoin de beaux meubles, ajouta-t-il, prévenez-moi, je vous conduirai chez lui, à l'enseigne du *Bon Bûcheron* au faubourg Saint-Antoine.

Lemblin promit et partit vers une autre table tandis qu'Emmanuel stupéfait questionnait Ethis :

– Qu'est-ce que tu as été lui raconter? D'abord je n'ai pas d'enseigne...

– Tu en auras une. Je sais que l'habitude s'en est perdue mais raison de plus pour donner un nom à ton atelier. J'ai inventé *Le Bon Bûcheron* en parlant mais si tu préfères autre chose... Je vais maintenant m'occuper de toi et faire reluire ta renommée. Pas question de végéter en attendant une commande du Mobilier qui ne viendra peut-être jamais. Il faut aller de l'avant, comme Lemblin qui serait resté serveur toute sa vie s'il n'avait pas décidé un jour d'en sortir! D'abord, je veux que ma petite sœur épouse un ébéniste célèbre. Il n'y a plus de roi, de reine ni de princes pour distinguer les bons ouvriers, alors il faut faire savoir au monde que tu as du talent!

On rentra par le chemin des écoliers. Obéissant à son nouveau maître, Vainqueur prit la rue Saint-Honoré au petit trot puis le faubourg jusqu'à la place de la Concorde dont le centre demeurait vide depuis qu'en 1800 le Premier consul avait fait enlever la statue colossale de la Liberté dont le plâtre doré s'écaillait lamentablement. Assise sur le socle de l'ancienne statue de Louis XV envoyée à la fonte en 92, la Liberté n'avait pas résisté aux intempéries!

Antoinette voulait voir où en était la construction de l'arc de triomphe du Carrousel dont Percier et Fontaine parlaient avec l'angoisse des bâtisseurs. Les travaux avaient commencé. On voyait déjà trois des huit colonnes corinthiennes de granite rose provenant du Château-Vieux de Meudon s'élancer vers le ciel. Trois quarts d'heure après la voiture avalait la rue de Cotte et débouchait place d'Aligre. En cours de route, les femmes avaient décidé d'improviser un souper. Comme il n'était pas question un dimanche soir de courir tout Paris pour chercher un traiteur ou un boucher ouvert, le repas fut préparé avec le morceau de lard qui pendait dans la réserve de Marie et les pommes de terre d'Antoinette. Lucie confectionna un biscuit de Savoie et Emmanuel tint à offrir le vin, ce qui lui fut facile car, si les bouchers étaient fermés, les cent quatre-vingts marchands de vin, cabaretiers et gargotiers que comptait le territoire du Faubourg restaient ouverts le dimanche. Pour être modeste, le souper fut gai et détendu. Antoinette était heureuse de voir sa fille dévorer des yeux son bel ébéniste, Ethis ruisselait de plaisir en pensant que « sa » voiture attendait à la porte et Marie souriait de savoir que son grand enfant de mari avait réalisé son rêve.

– Il y a des journées comme celle-ci où la vie semble n'être faite que de joie et de douceur..., dit Antoinette pensive. Pourtant comme je serais plus heureuse si Valfroy était avec nous.

– En tout cas, lança Ethis, nous savons maintenant qu'un café chez *Lemblin* et une soupe au lard chez soi sont compatibles avec un plaisir de bon aloi. Je lève mon verre au souvenir de ceux qui ne sont plus là et aux amoureux qui n'attendent qu'un geste de la Dame du Faubourg pour se marier...

Tous les regards se tournèrent vers Antoinette qui sourit et détourna malicieusement la conversation :

– Ne crois-tu pas Ethis que le brave Vainqueur mérite aussi qu'on célèbre ses vertus ? Va donc lui offrir un peu d'avoine et d'eau de la fontaine !

Depuis la mort de son mari, Victoire Delacroix venait souvent voir sa sœur : « Je joins l'agréable à l'agréable, disait-elle, je viens bavarder avec toi et prendre une bouffée d'air parisien. »

Victoire qui s'était ennuyée toute sa vie auprès du préfet-ministre s'ennuyait maintenant seule avec ses enfants, dans sa maison de Charenton-Saint-Maurice. Ses escapades au Faubourg étaient des moments de bonheur pour Antoinette qui avait été privée de sa sœur durant de longues années. Les lettres, plus ou moins régulières, n'avaient jamais permis l'échange de confidences. Aujourd'hui, les confessions, les aveux mêlés d'éclats de rire et les repentirs émaillaient de nouveau la conversation comme au temps de la jeunesse.

Ce jour-là, pourtant, Victoire était morose :

– Décidément, je t'envierai toute la vie. Quelle chance as-tu d'être à Paris, au milieu de la famille et des amis ! Moi, je me morfonds dans ce trou en attendant je ne sais quoi. Charles n'était pas un boute-en-train mais il y a des soirs où je préférerais l'avoir à mes côtés. Le seul avantage de mon veuvage, c'est d'être débarrassée de toutes les contraintes de la représentation et de ne plus être obligée de fréquenter les bonnes femmes des notables.

– Tu m'agaces, toujours en train de te plaindre. Vois donc le bon côté des choses. Sans être riche, tu vis largement...

– C'est vrai, je ne compte pas trop et j'ai les moyens de louer une voiture lorsque je veux venir à Paris. Ce serait parfait si je pouvais vivre près de toi. Mais tu me vois abandonner la maison ! Eugène est toujours fragile et il a besoin de grand air.

– A propos d'Eugène, as-tu des nouvelles de son père ? Tu as vu comment l'évêque de la fête de la Fédération célèbre maintenant l'empereur-Dieu ? Le voilà prince de Bénévent ! Prend-il des nouvelles de son fils ?

– Jamais directement mais je sais qu'il se fait renseigner. J'espère qu'il l'aidera dans la vie, même s'il ne se fait jamais connaître.

– Diras-tu plus tard à Eugène qui est son vrai père ?

– Non ! J'ai beaucoup réfléchi et je m'abstiendrai. Eugène aimait beaucoup Charles qui a été très bon pour lui, comme pour moi. Je ne peux pas détruire ce père dans sa mémoire pour lui offrir en échange un superbe indifférent qu'il ne pourra que haïr.

– Et toi, tu le détestes ton Talleyrand ?

– Non ! Il m'a apporté deux choses : une éclaircie dans ma vie à ce moment bien sombre et surtout le fils que je souhaitais. Pour le reste, je savais ce qui m'attendait. J'assume la responsabilité de ma faiblesse. Et toi, ta vie sentimentale? Le bel Alexandre est-il toujours à tes pieds?

– Ma vie sentimentale n'est que... sentimentale. Lenoir est resté mon ami mais il a cessé d'être mon amant.

– Il t'a quittée, l'imbécile?

– C'est moi qui ai rompu avant qu'il me quitte un jour. Je crois qu'il a été un peu malheureux, surtout que cette rupture, je l'ai su depuis, a coïncidé avec le départ de la jeune et superbe Mlle Lange qu'il rencontrait quand son riche mari, le banquier Simons, était en voyage. Elle s'est installée au Bossey près du lac Léman... Mon don juan s'est vite consolé. Il file m'a-t-on dit le parfait amour avec une danseuse de l'Opéra.

– Cela te fait de la peine?

– Non. Les choses se passent comme je l'avais prévu. Tu me diras que je m'intéresse de près aux amours d'Alexandre. C'est vrai mais ce n'est ni par jalousie ni par déception. Seulement par intérêt... disons psychologique. Alexandre est adorable avec moi, il est là tous les mercredis, m'offre des fleurs de chez Germont et je ne suis pas malheureuse.

– Tu m'étonneras toujours, ma grande!

Sur cette constatation, Victoire éclata de rire et la conversation tourna sur les amours des enfants. Sa fille aînée, Jeanne Delacroix, était folle d'un jeune avocat de Vincennes: « Tu vois on recommence! » soupira Victoire. Antoinette annonça les fiançailles de Lucie et la moue qu'esquissa sa sœur en apprenant qu'Emmanuel était ébéniste faillit déclencher une vraie scène.

– Et alors? s'emporta Antoinette. N'es-tu pas toi-même la fille d'un homme du bois? Ma parole, les ronds de jambe dans tes salons grotesques t'ont monté à la tête. Emmanuel Caumont, le fils d'un ami de Riesener, est jeune, beau et il a du talent. Je sais qu'on ne devient jamais riche dans les ateliers du Faubourg mais on est souvent heureux. Alors, si le fiancé de Lucie te déplaît, dis-le, nous ne t'inviterons pas à la noce!

Surprise par cette colère subite, Victoire était passée du rire aux larmes et s'était précipitée dans les bras de sa sœur.

– Tu as raison, je suis une idiote! Mais tu as mal interprété ma réaction. J'ai été surprise, voilà! Tout compte fait j'aimerais mieux que Jeanne épouse un ébéniste plutôt qu'un avocat!... Tu me crois? Je ne voulais vraiment pas te faire du mal! Là, embrasse-moi!

Antoinette ne demandait pas mieux et Victoire fit le dernier pas vers l'oubli de sa fâcheuse grimace:

– J'aimerais bien le connaître, ce beau jeune homme. Pourquoi ne viendriez-vous pas tous dimanche à Charenton? Que Marie et Ethis amènent Bertrand. Il jouera avec Eugène.

Ainsi allait la vie avec ses deuils, ses joies, ses difficultés qu'Antoinette balayait d'un geste en souriant: « Mes enfants, ce ne sont pas que des petits soucis. Quand on a connu la Terreur et qu'on lui a survécu on sait ce que sont les vraies souffrances! »

Autour d'elle, la famille restait unie, cimentée par la fidélité des amis toujours groupés dans le clan du mercredi: Alexandre Lenoir, Fontaine, Percier auxquels se joignaient parfois François Richard et même Parisot l'actif habilleur de *La Belle Fermière* qui parlait de son grand rêve: créer un magasin où l'on pourrait trouver tout ce qu'il faut pour se vêtir, de la blouse d'ouvrier à l'habit élégant coupé aux mesures du client, sans oublier les uniformes, tous les uniformes... « Les gendarmes comme les maréchaux viendront s'habiller chez moi! » affirmait-il avec conviction. On se moquait un peu de lui mais sa foi était si grande qu'on finissait par y croire.

Et puis il y avait Réveillon, le fidèle, qui faisait partie de la famille depuis toujours. Entre deux crises de goutte il louait une voiture et arrivait place d'Aligre pour bavarder. Il avait maintenant plus de quatre-vingt un ans et n'apparaissait plus aux dîners du mercredi. Il en souffrait et se faisait raconter par Antoinette tout ce qui s'y était dit. Toujours généreux, il aidait sa filleule comme il l'avait toujours fait et gâtait Lucie en disant : « Que veux-tu, je n'ai jamais aimé que les jeunes filles. Ta mère est bien trop vieille pour moi maintenant ! »

Depuis la mort de son père, Henri-François Riesener s'était fixé à Paris. Il habitait rue Saint-Paul, tout près de la Bastille, et venait souvent voir sa sœur. Lui aussi était devenu un assidu des réunions du clan. Il avait gardé de son passage à l'armée un certain désenchantement dû peut-être à des séquelles physiques, ce qui ne l'empêchait pas de vouer un attachement profond à l'Empereur. A la demande de son médecin Corvisart, Napoléon avait autorisé son ancien soldat devenu portraitiste connu à le dessiner aux Tuileries le temps d'un déjeuner. Rentré dans son atelier, Henri Riesener avait tiré de ce crayon un portrait sur toile de bonne venue. Il en avait aussitôt fait un double qu'il avait été montrer à son ancien maître, David.

– C'est l'un des portraits les plus ressemblants qu'on ait faits de l'Empereur ! jugea le maître. Laisse-le-moi, je l'offrirai de ta part à Sa Majesté. Si Elle daigne partager mon sentiment, tu pourras faire et vendre autant de copies que tu voudras. Ce n'est peut-être pas de l'art tel qu'on le rêve mais il faut bien manger !

Henri remercia David qui avait ajouté à ses compliments quelques mots aimables sur son père, et retourna travailler au portrait du comte de Cessac, une commande en cours. Un mois plus tard, il reçut un mot de David : « Napoléon trouve ton portrait excellent, il le garde. » Riesener aurait préféré que son tableau lui fût payé mais le jugement de l'Empereur rapporté par David valait de l'or. Il y avait beaucoup de gens à Paris qui souhaitaient accrocher chez eux le portrait de Napoléon. Les demandes affluèrent [1].

Le peintre avait souvent fait des croquis de Lucie qu'il trouvait jolie et promit à sa nièce qu'il lui offrirait son portrait peint à l'huile, dans un beau cadre, lorsqu'elle se marierait. Un jour où, seul avec elle, il esquissait encore

1. Il fera plus de cinquante copies de son tableau.

une fois son fin profil sur une feuille de papier, la jeune fille se mit soudain à pleurer. Étonné, Henri posa son crayon et lui demanda la raison de ce chagrin.

– Que se passe-t-il? Ce n'est tout de même pas ton fiancé qui t'a fait des misères. Il t'adore et le montre à tout le monde...

– Non, il ne m'a pas fait de misères, répondit-elle en reniflant comme une petite fille. Il ne m'a pas fait de misères mais il m'a fait un enfant!

La réplique était involontairement drôle et Henri ne put s'empêcher de rire. C'était d'ailleurs un bon moyen de désamorcer la petite tragédie qui se jouait derrière le front lisse de la jeune fille.

– Cela te fait rire! éclata-t-elle. Tout le monde va me montrer du doigt, je vais déshonorer le nom de mon père... Comment dire cela à maman et comment va-t-elle réagir? Je suis la plus malheureuse des filles, je voudrais être morte!

– Comme tu y vas ma belle! dit Riesener devenu sérieux. Sais-tu que cela est arrivé à bien d'autres filles avant toi? Si tu veux mon avis, je crois qu'Antoinette ne va pas prendre ça trop mal. Certes elle ne va pas te féliciter, mets-toi à sa place, mais elle comprendra. Elle n'avait, hélas! plus de mère pour l'admonester, mais sa liaison avec Pilâtre... je pense que tu es au courant?...

– Oui, mère m'a tout raconté. Cela a été une belle histoire d'amour...

– Sans doute. Je voulais te dire que cette liaison à l'époque a fait beaucoup parler et qu'il n'aurait pas fallu alors hasarder la moindre remarque devant ta mère. Ceux qui s'y sont essayés ont été vertement remis en place. Il est vrai, et c'est ce qu'elle te dira, qu'elle avait plus de seize ans...

– Dix-sept dans quelques mois, oncle Henri!

– Bon, dix-sept... Elle en avait plus de vingt et pouvait se juger maîtresse de sa vie. Et puis, c'est aussi ce qu'elle te dira, elle s'est arrangée pour ne pas avoir d'enfant! Pilâtre devait sûrement avoir plus d'expérience que ton Emmanuel.

– Si tu savais comme il est ennuyé, le pauvre!

– Il ne manquerait plus qu'il ne soit pas ennuyé, le bougre! Je crois qu'étant donné les circonstances, tu vas être obligée de te marier plus tôt que prévu. Je ne pense pas que ce soit une punition trop dure?

– C'est le bon côté de la catastrophe.

– Maintenant, ma petite fille, il va falloir prendre ton courage à deux mains et aller le plus vite possible annoncer la joyeuse nouvelle à ta mère.

– J'avais pensé que tu...

– Pas question! Antoinette, cela se comprend, le prendrait très mal, comme un manque de confiance. Et puis quand on est capable de faire un enfant...

– Ce n'est pas difficile, tu sais...

– Ne te moque pas de moi, s'il te plaît. Je disais que lorsqu'on est capable d'être mère on doit avoir le courage d'assumer ses responsabilités. C'est toi qui parleras à ta mère. Je suis sûr d'ailleurs que tu le feras avec beaucoup de diplomatie. Ne lui dis même pas que tu m'as mis au courant : elle doit être la première à apprendre qu'elle va être grand-mère!

Le soir même, Lucie alla rejoindre Antoinette dans sa chambre. Elle était assise devant la grande glace ovale d'Œben et brossait ses cheveux en se regardant d'un air un peu nostalgique.

– Donne, maman, dit Lucie, je vais te démêler.

Elle prit le peigne et la brosse.

– Comme tes cheveux sont fins et beaux, maman...

– Ils sont surtout gris, de plus en plus gris, mais comment pourrait-il en être autrement? Attention tu me fais mal!

Lucie voyait le visage de sa mère dans le miroir et elle se disait que dans un instant cette image tendrement aimée allait par sa faute se décomposer, prendre les traits de la douleur, de la colère, de la peine sûrement. Elle hésitait encore à lancer les mots qui lui semblaient sacrilèges. Enfin elle parla en fixant Antoinette qui elle aussi la regardait dans le miroir.

– Maman chérie, pour la première fois de ma vie je

vais te faire vraiment de la peine. Depuis quelque temps, je suis malade, j'ai envie de vomir, je...

– Tu es enceinte, Lucie. J'essayais de ne pas y croire mais depuis hier, j'avais deviné...

C'est en vain que Lucie scrutait le visage de sa mère : il demeurait inchangé, toujours empreint de douceur. Seules les petites rides des coins de la bouche, Lucie les connaissait par cœur, s'étaient peut-être légèrement creusées. Antoinette immobile ne disait rien, elle semblait réfléchir mais, en fait, laissait vagabonder ses pensées dans une sorte de rêve dont elle savait très bien comment s'évader.

Le sourire vint avant les mots :

– Rassure-toi ma Lucie, je ne vais pas tempêter ni te faire des reproches dont la seule conséquence serait de te blesser... Pourquoi? Tout simplement parce que j'accepte une situation que je me refuse à confondre avec le malheur. Nous avons pleuré ensemble la mort de ton père, ne pleurons pas la naissance d'un petit... Tu es bien jeune mais Emmanuel est un homme solide qui saura te soutenir, te guider et t'aimer. Et puis, tu ne sors pas du couvent, les années terribles que tu as vécues t'ont forgé le caractère. Enfin, je pense que si tu tiens un peu de moi tu seras une femme et une mère responsable. Maintenant, il va falloir vous marier. Je néglige tout ce qu'on pourra raconter, cela n'a guère d'importance, mais les maîtres et les compagnons du bois dont tu vas être solidaire sont, même s'ils ne savent pas, des puritains plus attachés à la rigueur des mœurs que les bourgeois et les nobles. Il est inutile de les choquer. Quand l'enfant viendra, ils joueront le jeu si vous êtes mariés et ne feront aucune réflexion...

– Mais, maman, il n'est pas question que nous ne nous mariions pas, je ne sais pas pourquoi tu me dis tout cela.

– Je me le dis à moi-même sans doute. Tu sais que dans les moments cruciaux j'aime bien parler tout haut.

– Merci, ma mère chérie. Tu as été merveilleuse! Je

n'osais pas espérer que tu réagirais d'une manière aussi généreuse...

– Ce n'est pas de la générosité, c'est un peu d'intelligence mêlée à beaucoup d'amour!

Le mariage fut vite réglé. Eugène Bénard reçut le consentement des époux à la mairie du VIIIe arrondissement. Il fit un petit discours gentil et fit signer les témoins sur le registre de l'état civil : le maître Georges Jacob et le menuisier de sièges Victor Sellier établi au 30 de la rue du Faubourg, premier patron du marié, pour Emmanuel Caumont, Ethis de Valfroy et Alexandre Lenoir pour la mariée. Bien qu'on ne pratiquât guère dans la famille, Lucie tint à rendre visite au nouveau curé de Sainte-Marguerite qui bénit le mariage dans la plus grande simplicité. C'était un homme bon qui avait tout compris et qui voulait faire plaisir à Mlle Œben dont il connaissait l'influence dans le quartier.

Ce n'est que le mercredi suivant qu'on fêta en famille le mariage de Lucie. Un souper du clan comme un autre mais tout le monde était là, même Réveillon qu'on garda coucher le soir place d'Aligre car il était trop fatigué pour reprendre une voiture et rentrer chez lui rue des Bons-Enfants. Chacun avait apporté son cadeau mais c'est le vieux papetier qui une fois de plus combla la famille devenue sienne.

– J'ai une surprise pour toi, Lucie. Et aussi pour ton mari, bien sûr. Antoinette m'a dit que vous alliez habiter au-dessus dans l'ancien logement que louait Riesener. Eh bien! vous n'aurez pas à payer de loyer. Je l'ai acheté pour vous, il vous faudra seulement passer un jour chez le notaire.

C'était un cadeau royal et chacun applaudit. Antoinette y alla de sa larme et embrassa longuement son parrain, Lucie balbutia un remerciement et alla elle aussi étreindre Réveillon qui ajouta :

– Ethis avait eu la vieille maison des Thirion, il était juste que je t'assure aussi un toit. J'ai de l'argent pour vivre jusqu'à plus de cent ans. Comme je n'irai pas jusque-là, il me reste de quoi vous faire plaisir!

L'enfant, un garçon, arriva au monde sept mois après le mariage mais personne ne s'en étonna au Faubourg où, sans qu'on le fît jamais remarquer, on était fier que la petite-fille d'Œben, fille de baron, ait choisi de revenir au sein de la grande famille du bois en épousant un enfant du quartier. On baptisa le nouveau-né Jean-Bertrand pour honorer la mémoire de son arrière-grand-père et celle de son grand-père. La tradition reprenait ses droits après les bifurcations sentimentales d'Antoinette dans le ciel de Pilâtre de Rozier et dans le blason des Valfroy dont l'avenir du nom dépendait maintenant d'Ethis, l'enfant trouvé de la Bastille.

Jean Caumont avait un an et un mois quand le cercle de famille s'agrandit une nouvelle fois avec la naissance du petit Léon Riesener le 21 janvier 1808. Henri-François avait fini par se fixer. Il avait épousé un an auparavant Félicité, une jeune fille à la beauté éblouissante, pauvre mais cultivée, dont la jeunesse avait été bouleversée par un drame. Son père, Pierre Longrois, était au début de la Révolution garde-meuble du château de la Muette, résidence royale préférée de Marie-Antoinette. Il était encore en place quand la commune de Passy organisa en 1790 dans le château devenu bien national un banquet monstre pour 15 000 fédérés. Un an plus tard, le domaine subissait de graves mutilations. Seul demeurait debout en 92 l'un des bâtiments où Pierre Longrois avait réussi à mettre en sûreté les plus beaux meubles qu'il avait sauvés du vandalisme. Il ne faisait que son métier et la petite Félicité continuait de jouer à cache-cache dans les salons dorés où étaient empilés bureaux d'Œben, commodes de Molitor, consoles de Riesener et sièges de Georges Jacob.

Tout aurait pu bien se passer, tout se serait probablement bien passé si Alexandre Lenoir avait reçu la mission de sauver les meubles à la place des statues. Hélas ! au lieu d'être félicité pour sa conscience professionnelle, Pierre

Longrois fut dénoncé sous la Terreur et arrêté comme agent trop zélé de la royauté. Condamné à mort, Thermidor aurait pu le sauver mais il fut guillotiné le 6, trois jours avant la chute de Robespierre.

Félicité, à six ans, avait vécu au côté de sa mère cette épreuve épouvantable. Seuls son mariage et la naissance du petit Léon avaient réussi à lui rendre un équilibre moral. Antoinette n'était naturellement pas demeurée insensible au drame vécu par sa jeune belle-sœur devenue une familière de la place d'Aligre où sa conversation était appréciée. Elle parlait d'art et de sculpture avec Lenoir, d'architecture et de décoration avec Percier et Fontaine. Elle était même capable, le mécanicien anglais Miln ayant un temps installé l'une de ses machines à filer dans une aile du château, de discuter des nouvelles techniques du coton avec François Richard.

– La jeunesse nous pousse! disait Antoinette en riant. Et elle ajoutait : Voilà les garçons qui arrivent dans cette famille où il n'y avait que des filles! Comme j'aimerais savoir ce que feront dans la vie tous ces jeunes... Bertrand de Valfroy a huit ans, Eugène Delacroix en a dix, Jean Caumont a déjà doublé le cap de la première année et Léon Riesener vient de naître! Rien que pour cela j'aimerais vivre jusqu'à quatre-vingts ans!

– Et pour le reste alors? avait rétorqué Lucie. Ne nous dis pas que la vie t'échappe, tu es la plus jeune d'entre nous!

– Dis que je m'efforce de rester assez jeune pour vous intéresser encore mais mon existence a été tellement pleine que je me dis, à certains moments, qu'elle ne peut plus m'apporter grand-chose...

– Tu fais ta coquette, maman. Tu sais très bien que tu tiendras à la vie jusqu'à ton dernier souffle et que tu as encore un bon bout de chemin à parcourir avec nous!

Ethis qui s'était bien « embourgeoisé » comme disait sa sœur Lucie en se moquant, et qui jusque-là s'était montré un admirateur fervent de l'Empereur, trouvait de plus en plus souvent des occasions de réveiller le révolté qui sommeillait toujours en lui. Napoléon, au sommet de sa gloire, distribuait les dépouilles des peuples vaincus à ses frères, à ses généraux, à tous ceux qu'il faisait princes, ducs, comtes ou barons. C'est ce qu'il appelait « changer le plan de noblesse qui n'était que féodal et élever sur ses débris une noblesse historique fondée sur l'intérêt de la patrie ». Ces nominations dont la liste s'allongeait chaque jour dans *Le Moniteur* avaient le don de rendre Traîne-sabot furieux. Un mercredi, rompant l'usage qui voulait que les réunions du clan demeurent sereines, Ethis prit subitement la mouche à propos d'une anecdote rapportée par Fontaine selon laquelle les généraux, invités par l'Empereur le soir de la bataille d'Eylau, avaient trouvé un billet de mille francs sous leur serviette.

– Comment, s'écria-t-il, ces chefs dont la vertu militaire est si grande, n'éprouvent-ils pas un sentiment de nausée devant les récompenses en argent dont on les accable ! J'ai lu l'autre jour que les dotations annuelles versées aux nouveaux nobles se montaient à trente millions de francs ! Je trouve cela scandaleux et me demande pourquoi nous avons fait la révolution ! Napoléon a dit qu'il fallait que trente maisons de ducs s'élèvent en même temps que le trône ! Où sont-ils nos généraux en guenilles de l'armée du Rhin !

– S'ils ne sont pas morts, dit Lenoir qui s'amusait bien, ils sont aujourd'hui maréchaux, ducs de ceci ou de cela et dotés de revenus confortables. Mais ne te mets pas en colère. Il est normal qu'un empereur veuille asseoir sa grandeur sur un clergé dévoué et une noblesse empanachée. On m'a dit qu'à Saint-Cloud et aux Tuileries où ils sont priés d'être assidus, les braves qu'un titre de maréchal comble davantage que celui de prince ou de duc d'une petite ville d'Italie, doivent se dépouiller de leurs tenues militaires et abandonner tout aspect soldatesque. L'Empereur, à sa cour, veut ses ducs en costume de ducs : pas de bottes de campagne, des bas de soie !

– Tout cela est ridicule ! s'écria Ethis, si c'est cela l'Empire, je ne suis plus bonapartiste. Mais le peuple accepte tout. Il va bien avec les généraux, c'est un troupeau !

– Un troupeau de généraux, tiens c'est amusant. Je vois bien qui est le berger mais où est le chien? L'inconvénient de faire partie d'un troupeau, même d'un troupeau couronné sur le foirail de la gloire, c'est qu'on court le grand risque de finir ses jours à l'abattoir. A moins que Napoléon ne cesse de se croire invincible, ce qui est peu probable, notre prince d'Essling, nos ducs de Trévise ou de Reggio peuvent s'attendre à sentir bientôt le souffle du boulet!

– Dites donc, coupa Antoinette que les apologues d'Alexandre Lenoir plongeaient toujours dans le ravissement, j'ai l'impression que notre clan est en train de devenir le centre d'une redoutable conspiration.

– Et pourquoi pas! cria Ethis décidément fort échauffé.

– Parce qu'une conspiration, pour réussir, doit être conduite par un général. C'est l'usage. Or je ne vois ici que des artistes paisibles, des hommes et des femmes de réflexion, des manufacturiers et commerçants avisés. Pas trace d'un galon. Ton titre de « vainqueur de la Bastille » me paraît un peu juste pour entraîner les foules!

Sur cette dernière intervention qu'un sourire complice d'Antoinette avait récompensée, Lenoir plia sa serviette et dit qu'il allait rentrer se coucher. Mais il était en verve et ajouta encore :

– Dommage que le général Malet soit arrêté, nous aurions pu l'inviter. Et avec lui les généraux Guillet et Guillaume! C'est à croire qu'il n'y a que des généraux en France, ceux qui font la guerre avec Napoléon et ceux qui complotent contre lui. Tout compte fait, Antoinette, nous n'avons pas besoin de militaires. Quand ils ne sont pas sur des champs de bataille, ce sont des gens insupportables!

Fontaine qui ne parlait jamais pour ne rien dire s'intéressa à la conversation :

– Je trouve, moi, que la réaction d'Ethis est significative. L'Empire vit dans la munificence, le maître, tout-puissant, règle à cinq cents lieues de Paris la police intérieure de la France et surveille jusque dans les plus petits détails l'activité des théâtres impériaux mais les ouvriers indigents recommencent à s'inscrire nombreux dans les quartiers et les nouveaux contingents appelés par anticipation se chiffrent à quelque trois cent mille hommes. Les mères finissent par avoir peur, surtout depuis qu'a filtré la vérité des 10 000 cadavres français ensevelis à Eylau sous la neige. L'opinion se montre déjà moins docile et, surtout, il y a un signe qui ne trompe pas : Talleyrand vient de demander à être relevé de ses fonctions de ministre des Affaires étrangères. Jugerait-il que le traité de Tilsit signé au prix des victoires d'Iéna, de Friedland et aussi du sang versé à Eylau n'apporte aucun résultat définitif? Serait-il le premier rat à quitter le navire? Certains se le demandent tout bas...

Antoinette s'étonna :

– Quel pessimisme! Vous ne nous avez pas habitués à tenir des propos aussi vifs sur la politique de Bonaparte!

– La politique ne m'intéresse guère mais il s'agit là moins de politique que d'une crainte purement subjective que je me garderai de manifester ailleurs qu'ici. Il est vrai que l'Empereur, au sommet de sa puissance et de sa gloire, me paraît souvent fragile, comme entraîné malgré lui dans un enchaînement guerrier qui inquiète ses sujets les plus fervents. Pour ce qui m'intéresse plus directement, sa frénésie de construire, il semble de plus en plus pressé de réaliser des idées qui, hélas! ne relèvent pas toutes du meilleur goût. Et puis, tous ceux qui l'approchent sont frappés du changement qui s'est opéré dans sa personne comme dans ses manières. Son regard a toujours la même profondeur mais son visage s'est empâté et les rides de son front trahissent de graves préoccupations. Le corps lui-même a perdu la sveltesse et l'élégance des temps du Consulat. Un commencement d'obésité fait paraître ses jambes trop grêles. Bref, à quarante ans, il ne les a pas encore tout à fait, Napoléon semble déjà vieilli.

– Comment ne le serait-il pas après tout ce qu'il a fait en si peu d'années!

C'est Félicité qui eut ainsi le dernier mot, traduisant l'opinion de beaucoup de femmes qui dans les milieux modestes et ouvriers demeuraient très attachées à l'Empereur. Seules les mères ayant des fils en âge d'être appelés à combattre voyaient maintenant d'un autre œil les entreprises du monarque universel.

Lucie habitait avec son mari et le petit Jean-Bertrand l'ancien logement de Riesener, au-dessus de celui où elle était née. Henri-François avait laissé aux jeunes mariés les meubles de son père afin de leur permettre de s'installer. Pour l'instant, il ne souhaitait reprendre de son héritage que le lit où l'ébéniste du roi était mort et le fauteuil qui avait toujours été le sien depuis son mariage avec Marguerite Œben. Cependant Emmanuel entendait respecter la tradition des gens du bois: l'ébéniste se devait de fabriquer de ses mains le lit conjugal. Avant même que le mariage fût décidé, il en avait choisi l'acajou avec un soin minutieux. Ethis et lui avaient fait le tour des marchands de bois de Bercy et il avait finalement retenu des planches épaisses à la couleur franche et au grain fin dont le poids était assez léger pour attester son degré de séchage.

L'avancée du mariage et la naissance de Jean-Bertand avaient naturellement précipité la mise en chantier du lit. Comme Emmanuel devait, pour vivre, assurer d'abord les commandes, il travaillait le plus souvent tard dans la nuit. Après avoir hésité, consulté Fontaine et Percier plus habitués à dessiner les lits d'apparat de la famille impériale que la couche d'un ouvrier du faubourg, Lucie et lui avaient choisi un lit-bateau, à la mode du jour, dont la forme rappelait celle du lit que Jacob-Desmalter était en train de créer pour la Malmaison. Très gentiment, Percier en avait adapté le plan en simplifiant à l'extrême les sculptures et les appliques de bronze doré.

C'était un lit aux chevets légèrement enroulés, destiné à être adossé contre le mur dans le sens longitudinal. Lucie avait tenu à ce qu'il soit surmonté d'un baldaquin soutenu à la polonaise par un cerceau de bois sculpté. Pas question, hélas! d'utiliser une pièce de soie brochée ou un velours brodé. François Richard consulté avait dit qu'il se ferait une joie d'offrir le métrage nécessaire d'un nouveau tissu de coton dont la finesse était telle qu'on le prenait pour du foulard lyonnais.

Emmanuel n'avait jamais construit de grand lit et devait à chaque instant résoudre des problèmes techniques. Toute l'allure du meuble dépendait de la grâce des courbes qui devaient s'envoler, à chaque extrémité, dans le chatoiement des veinures du bois. Le découpage des différentes parties à la scie à chantourner était délicat, la moindre déviation de la lame eût gâché la pièce de bois. Dieu merci, le jeune ébéniste n'était pas seul, tout le Faubourg était prêt à aider « le fils Caumont qui faisait son lit de mariage ». Il n'avait qu'à sortir et pousser la porte de n'importe quel atelier pour qu'un maître ami vienne lui donner la main.

Le bois heureusement était de la meilleure qualité. Sans être trop sec, ce qui l'eût rendu fragile, il résistait bien à l'outil. Le ciseau et le bédane affûtés au fil le pénétraient sans blesser les fibres, et les assemblages s'unissaient dans un enchâssement parfait. Le jeune ébéniste travaillait dans une sorte d'état de grâce qui décuplait son habileté. Jamais encore il n'avait ressenti, en pliant le bois rouge à ses volontés, cette jouissance charnelle dont les vieux compagnons lui avaient parlé. Quand il rentrait dans la nuit place d'Aligre et qu'il se couchait auprès de Lucie, il lui disait à l'oreille en souriant : « Je t'ai encore trompée avec l'acajou de notre lit. »

Au bout de deux mois de travail, l'ébénisterie était achevée. Il restait encore à sculpter sur les deux rampants extérieurs une tête de cygne surmontée d'une feuille d'acanthe, selon le modèle de Percier, et à fixer sur le pourtour du châlit les roses de bronze doré que Nagler, le fondeur-ciseleur de la rue de Cotte, avait préparées.

Emmanuel avait toujours aimé sculpter le bois. Son père était une « fine lame », il lui avait appris à manier la gouge et le fermoir, à pousser l'outil de la paume ou à défoncer un panneau à la masse. C'est dire que le fils Caumont mit du cœur à l'ouvrage pour sortir les quatre cygnes des blocs d'acajou qui terminaient encore, comme des moignons, les gracieux bras des chevets.

Quand les cygnes et les feuilles d'acanthe eurent trouvé leur place, Lucie fut enfin admise à venir admirer le chef-d'œuvre.

– Magnifique! s'écria-t-elle en caressant le bois poli et poncé, encore vierge de cire. Comme je suis fière de toi! Tu t'es tué au travail mais tu as réussi. Te rends-tu compte du privilège qui m'est accordé : coucher jusqu'à la fin de mes jours dans le lit qu'a fabriqué mon mari!

– Je suis sûr que c'est pour cela que tu as épousé un ébéniste! dit Emmanuel en serrant Lucie contre lui.

– C'est vrai, mais aussi pour autre chose: me faire aimer dans ce lit qui sans toi ne serait rien que de beaux morceaux de bois!

– Alors, tu l'aimes notre lit d'acajou?

– Je crois en effet que je vais l'aimer beaucoup.

Il était temps pour Lucie de s'occuper de la literie. Retenue depuis longtemps déjà, Louise, la meilleure matelassière du Faubourg, s'installa un matin sur la place avec son attirail, une cardeuse à bascule et un cadre de bois. Il restait chez Antoinette deux vieux matelas dont la laine une fois rebattue servirait à gonfler l'enveloppe de toile forte destinée à garnir le nouveau lit.

C'était toujours une attraction quand la Louise débarquait dans la rue ou dans une cour. Entourée d'un nuage de poussière, elle transformait en chantant d'informes amalgames en laine vaporeuse qu'elle savait mieux que personne pousser sans la tasser dans la housse. Dès son arrivée, les enfants la cernaient de leurs cris et se moquaient d'elle en mimant son geste de balançoire. Elle riait puis, lorsqu'elle en avait assez, se levait brusquement et distribuait des taloches. Elle avait soixante-dix ans, la mère Louise, et faisait ce métier depuis au moins soixante. Elle avait aidé sa mère avant de prendre sa place et répétait qu'aujourd'hui le travail n'était plus rien.

– Ah! mes bonnes gens, si vous aviez connu le cardage à la main entre deux planches à clous! Ça c'était terrible!

Et Louise, l'une des premières profiteuses des progrès du machinisme, remettait en route sa mécanique en lançant l'un des cent dix refrains sur Napoléon, les uns pour, les autres contre, qu'elle prétendait connaître par cœur :

Au secours, au secours, on appelle mon garçon,
J' sais bien qu' c'est pour la nation
Comme il dit Napoléon.
Mais je maudis le canon, le canon, le canon,
Qui tue nos pauvres garçons.

Le lit terminé fut transporté démonté dans une voiture à bras jusqu'à la place d'Aligre. Emmanuel avait recouvert les pièces d'une couverture mais les deux chevets, trop hauts, dépassaient; les cygnes semblaient regarder, hautains, les amis et les curieux qui arrêtaient tous les dix pas le char conjugal afin de jeter un coup d'œil sur le fameux lit de Lucie dont tout le Faubourg célébrait la magnificence. Certains ajoutaient aux compliments quelques propos grivois auxquels Ethis, qui poussait à l'arrière, n'était pas embarrassé pour répondre.

Les assemblages étaient si précis et si coulants que le lit fut remonté en quelques instants sous le baldaquin que Lucie avait installé avec l'aide de Barranger le tapissier de la rue Saint-Bernard. L'effet était superbe. L'acajou brillait de tous ses feux sur le nouveau papier peint de la chambre. Enlacés, Emmanuel et Lucie reculaient de temps en temps pour mieux admirer le chef-d'œuvre. Sans rien dire, Ethis alla chercher dans son berceau le petit Jean-Bertrand et l'installa au milieu du lit. Trop petit pour apprécier la beauté de la chambre de ses parents, il eut le bon goût d'adresser un joli sourire à sa mère qui s'écria en riant :

– Tu vois Emmanuel, ton fils trouve le lit à son goût!

– Eh bien, ma douce, nous en profiterons pour lui faire un petit frère.

Et la vie continua, axée sur la nouvelle génération. Antoinette jouait avec bonheur son rôle de grand-mère, ce qui ne l'empêchait pas de demeurer animatrice attentive du clan et de devenir, hors de chez elle, celle à qui l'on faisait de plus en plus souvent appel pour recevoir un conseil, écrire une lettre difficile ou intercéder en faveur des plus démunis. Tout naturellement, sans que cela fût dit, les gens du bois cherchaient auprès d'Antoinette à retrouver la tutelle désintéressée qu'avait accordée durant des siècles l'abbesse de Saint-Antoine-des-Champs à son peuple d'artisans. Ce titre de « Dame du Faubourg » que ses proches lui avaient donné pour plaisanter devenait peu à peu une réalité. L'abbaye détruite, le quartier restait attaché à ses racines.

Chapitre 10.

LE BAL DE L'EMPEREUR

Il y avait maintenant des années que Pierre Fontaine et Charles Percier fréquentaient le « salon rose d'Antoinette », comme ils appelaient la grande pièce de la place d'Aligre où la fille d'Œben recevait ses amis. Cependant, en dehors de leurs travaux dont ils parlaient volontiers, ils demeuraient muets sur tout ce qui concernait leur vie privée. Antoinette elle-même, à qui l'on se confiait facilement, en était encore à s'interroger sur les liens qui unissaient les deux hommes. Beaucoup les croyaient frères, ils n'étaient qu'amis de très longue date. Surtout, ils se complétaient admirablement dans l'exercice de leur profession commune. Fontaine, les deux hommes l'avaient souvent expliqué à leurs amis, saisissait d'un seul coup d'œil l'ensemble de l'ouvrage projeté et en faisait rapidement une esquisse. Percier, après avoir discuté et éventuellement corrigé le projet, le fixait dans un admirable dessin exécuté avec une extraordinaire minutie.

Fontaine et Percier étaient pourtant dissemblables sur bien des points. Le premier était un homme actif qui aimait voyager et parler. Levé de grand matin, c'est lui qu'on rencontrait sur les chantiers, dans les bureaux où des démarches étaient nécessaires, chez les clients privés ou officiels qu'il fallait visiter. Il était en quelque sorte le ministre des Relations extérieures de l'atelier d'architecture où Percier, d'humeur plutôt casanière, mettait au point les projets. Ils avaient raconté qu'au moment du Consulat, Bonaparte avait voulu se séparer de Percier qui, disait-il, ne faisait rien et qu'on ne voyait jamais. Fontaine avait eu beaucoup de mal à convaincre le Premier consul qu'un homme qui ne venait pas aux Tuileries n'était pas forcément un fainéant et que, sans Percier, il serait incapable de poursuivre les travaux en cours.

On les savait célibataires mais personne, par discrétion, n'avait abordé ce sujet dans les conversations du mercredi. Antoinette que ce mystère agaçait, questionna pourtant un soir les deux architectes qui, arrivés les premiers, se trouvaient seuls avec elle.

– Ce n'est pas de la curiosité et je ne vous en voudrai jamais si vous ne me répondez pas. Elle sourit et continua : Et puis, si, j'avoue que je suis un peu curieuse à propos des gens que j'aime. Puisque vous faites partie de ceux-là, permettez-moi de vous demander pourquoi vous ne vous êtes pas mariés.

Percier, malgré sa tendance à s'isoler dans son métier, savait causer mieux que personne. On appréciait place d'Aligre les charmes de sa conversation. C'est lui qui répondit, l'œil malin :

– Ma chère Antoinette, c'est une vieille histoire. Il n'y a pas de mystère et puisque le comportement social de nos modestes personnages vous intéresse, je vais vous la raconter. Libre à vous, ensuite, de nous considérer comme des êtres bizarres, ce que nous sommes sûrement.

– Je vous écoute, susurra Antoinette.

– Eh bien, voilà! Cela remonte aux années de notre jeunesse alors que nous vivions ensemble, avec un autre étudiant nommé Bernier, à l'Académie de France à Rome. Nous formions un trio inséparable et nous fîmes un jour le serment solennel de ne jamais nous marier. Jusqu'à maintenant aucun d'entre nous n'a été parjure et je doute que cela change!

– Et pourtant, si vous aviez rencontré une femme brillante qui vous ait inspiré de tendres sentiments...

– Mettons que nous ne l'avons pas rencontrée! coupa Fontaine.

Antoinette comprit qu'elle ne devait pas insister. D'ailleurs Ethis arrivait en faisant grand bruit.

Un autre jour, c'est Pierre Fontaine qui se livra à la curiosité de tous en annonçant :

– Mes amis, j'ai une grande nouvelle!

– Vous vous mariez! lança étourdiment Lucie.

Fontaine éclata de rire :

– Non, ma belle, je ne me marie pas mais j'ai une fille!

– Une fille!

Stupéfaits tous les présents avaient lâché la même exclamation en même temps. Percier s'amusait dans son coin, Fontaine continua :

– Oui, je viens d'adopter une petite fille adorable. Voilà qui rassurera partiellement Antoinette qui me voudrait à tout prix accablé d'une famille. Je viens d'engager une nourrice et m'installe avec tout mon monde, la vieille bonne et le valet-cocher, dans un charmant hôtel que je me suis fait bâtir à la Muette, dans la commune de Passy. J'espère qu'un jour vous me ferez le plaisir de venir nous voir pour faire la connaissance de Pauline.

Pour une nouvelle, c'était une nouvelle. Le voile se déchirait un peu plus sur le mystère Percier-Fontaine mais il restait encore bien des points obscurs qu'Antoinette se promit d'éclaircir.

– Mes avatars ne doivent pas nous empêcher de faire le tour des nouvelles du jour, raison première de nos réunions. Eh bien, si vous voulez je commence en vous apportant sous la foi du secret la dernière idée monumentale de l'Empereur.

Les oreilles se tendirent.

– Voilà : Mon confrère, M. Célerier, architecte de la Ville, vient de se voir confier la mission de construire une fontaine triomphale sur l'emplacement de la Bastille. Jusque-là rien d'étonnant, l'Empereur ne songe qu'à couvrir Paris de fontaines, ce qui n'est pas une mauvaise chose. Mais il exige que cette fontaine géante ait la forme d'un éléphant! Pourquoi un éléphant? Sans doute parce que l'éléphant a participé à la gloire des conquérants de l'Antiquité. Napoléon doit rêver d'Annibal. Pourvu qu'il ne perde pas un œil dans sa dernière bataille!

– Un éléphant à la Bastille... Cela me laisse rêveur, commenta Lenoir qui voyait l'un de ses successeurs hériter un jour pour son musée de cette masse écrasante.

– Comme bien souvent, avec des fortunes diverses, j'ai essayé de faire comprendre à l'Empereur que ce n'était pas sa meilleure idée. Il m'a vertement remis à ma place en me lançant : « Dites que je n'ai aucun goût ! » Quatremère de Quincy [1] a tenté lui aussi de le dissuader mais notre souverain tient à son éléphant. Le sculpteur Bridan passe ses journées au jardin des Plantes pour dessiner son modèle. Il m'a montré une lettre de Napoléon adressée depuis Madrid au ministre de l'Intérieur : « Je suppose que l'éléphant sera très beau et de telles dimensions qu'on puisse entrer dans la tour qu'il portera. Qu'on voie comment les Anciens les plaçaient et de quelle manière ils se servaient des éléphants. » Voilà où nous en sommes, je vous tiendrai au courant de la suite donnée à cette grosse affaire !

Un an plus tard, les enfants du quartier regardaient le pachyderme grandir doucement sur le terrain vague qui séparait le Faubourg de la porte Saint-Antoine. Comme l'Empereur avait dû renoncer à son idée de faire venir les canons pris à Friedland et aux insurgés espagnols pour la fonte de la statue, l'architecte Alavoine avait entrepris de construire une maquette grandeur nature de l'éléphant, faite de bois et de plâtre. *Le Moniteur* en avait publié les dimensions : 16 mètres de haut sans la tour et 24 avec celle-ci. Un escalier à vis était prévu dans une patte et une plate-forme d'observation tout en haut. L'ensemble devait être badigeonné de couleur bronze en attendant que fût fondue la véritable fontaine.

D'autres projets de l'Empereur étaient en voie de

1. Savant archéologue, intendant des arts et monuments.

réalisation. Le « temple de la Gloire » commençait de s'élever au bout de la rue Royale sur les fondations de la nouvelle église de la Madeleine dont la construction avait été arrêtée à la Révolution. « Par temple, avait spécifié l'Empereur, j'entends un monument tel qu'il y en avait à Athènes et non pas à Paris. » Il voulait y placer l'armure de François Ier prise à Vienne, les statues du Tibre et du Nil, de Rome et le quadrige de la porte de Brandebourg rapporté de Berlin.

La bataille de Wagram venait d'être gagnée et le « nouveau Charlemagne », comme le nommait le cauteleux Cambacérès, avait fait le 14 novembre 1809 une entrée triomphale à Paris. Tout le Faubourg s'était précipité à l'Hôtel de Ville pour apercevoir l'Empereur caracoler à la tête de ses braves. Napoléon n'affichait pourtant pas le visage serein d'un vainqueur. Depuis le complot Malet et l'arrestation à Schönbrunn d'un jeune patriote allemand qui voulait le poignarder, Napoléon s'était rendu compte qu'il était à la merci du premier illuminé venu et, avec lui, l'Empire dont il ressentait la fragilité. Peut-être pensait-il, en répondant distraitement de la main à ceux qui l'acclamaient, qu'il lui fallait à tout prix un héritier pour assurer la dynastie.

Depuis quelque temps, le bruit courait à la cour et dans les communs de la Malmaison que l'Empereur avait décidé de divorcer afin d'épouser une princesse étrangère capable de lui faire des enfants. L'intendant de la maison de Joséphine avait même rapporté à Percier qu'il avait entendu Napoléon dire à Cambacérès : « C'est un ventre qu'il faut que j'épouse ! »

L'annonce officielle du divorce n'en fut pas moins un événement considérable. La raison d'État n'était pas l'affaire du peuple et ce n'est pas Napoléon qui allait changer cet état d'esprit aussi vieux que la France elle-même. Mais Joséphine, dont la générosité était connue, faisait partie de la légende napoléonienne. Elle était aimée et admirée, sa répudiation offusquait les femmes surtout qui vouaient à l'impératrice une sorte de vénération. Antoinette qui, selon son habitude, avait été prendre le pouls du Faubourg entendit plusieurs épouses de maîtres ou de compagnons proclamer que cette mauvaise action porterait malheur à Napoléon qui allait perdre avec Joséphine la chance qui l'avait toujours accompagné dans ses entreprises.

Ce n'étaient pas là des considérations susceptibles de faire revenir l'Empereur sur une décision mûrement réfléchie et quand, après avoir pensé un moment épouser la sœur du tsar Alexandre, il jeta son dévolu sur l'archiduchesse Marie-Louise, les choses ne traînèrent pas. Il n'y avait pas un mois et demi qu'il avait prévenu la malheureuse Joséphine de sa déchéance que l'ex-petit lieutenant d'artillerie devenait petit-neveu de Louis XVI et de Marie-Antoinette!

Tous les rois et les reines, les anciens comme les nouveaux, avaient été priés de venir à Paris pour entourer le couple impérial. Le roi et la reine de Bavière, le roi de Saxe et de Wurtemberg, les rois et les reines de Naples, de Westphalie et de Hollande étaient les hôtes d'une France dont le maître n'avait jamais été aussi glorieux.

Pour célébrer ce maître et son mariage avec la fille de son propre empereur, l'ambassadeur d'Autriche, prince de Schwartzenberg, avait décidé de lui offrir le bal le plus beau jamais donné à Paris, un bal comme seuls les Viennois savent les organiser.

L'hôtel qu'habitait le prince au 40 de la rue du Mont-Blanc [1], pourtant immense – c'était celui de Mme de Montesson qui y avait donné des fêtes somptueuses durant le Consulat –, parut trop exigu à son propriétaire pour abriter tous ses invités. Il convoqua donc pour le conseiller les architectes de l'Empereur. Comme d'habitude, c'est Fontaine qui se présenta l'un des premiers jours de juillet 1810 chez l'ambassadeur.

1. Reprendra son nom de rue de la Chaussée-d'Antin en 1816 après s'être appelée de 1791 à 1793 rue Mirabeau-le-Patriote (Mirabeau était mort en 1791 au nº 42).

– Sa Majesté nous accable de besogne, dit-il, et je suis obligé de vous prévenir que nous ne pouvons accepter aucune tâche importante. J'espère que Votre Excellence nous comprendra.

– Il ne s'agit pas d'une construction mais simplement de m'aider à recevoir mon monde. Je donne un bal le 1er juillet en l'honneur de votre Empereur et je compte inviter cinq ou six cents personnes. Il faut agrandir les salons, peut-être ouvrir des passages donnant sur l'hôtel d'à côté qui m'appartient aussi...

Fontaine visita l'hôtel de Montesson, se promena dans les jardins qui s'étendaient jusqu'à la rue Saint-Nicolas-d'Antin et dit :

– Nous sommes à la belle saison, au lieu de percer des ouvertures qui feraient beaucoup de dégâts, je vous propose de monter deux tentes qui abriteront une partie de vos invités et leur offriront de la fraîcheur.

– Mais je ne veux pas organiser une fête champêtre, monsieur Fontaine! Les personnages de la plus haute société seront là et il me faut du luxe et du confort!

– C'est bien ainsi que je l'entends. On peut monter des tentes superbes, les doubler à l'intérieur des plus riches tentures, les décorer de statues, de miroirs, de candélabres... Si vous le souhaitez, mon ami Percier va vous faire un projet à l'aquarelle qui vous donnera une idée du cadre somptueux qu'il est possible de réaliser dans votre jardin.

Percier et Fontaine qui n'étaient mondains ni l'un ni l'autre devinrent ainsi les maîtres d'œuvre de la fête qu'on appelait déjà à la Cour et dans les ambassades « le bal du siècle ».

– Ce qui m'ennuie dans cette affaire, dit un jour Fontaine à Antoinette, c'est que je vais être obligé d'assister à cette réunion. Mon ami Percier est un ours, pour rien au monde il ne changerait la moindre de ses habitudes et il refuse catégoriquement d'abandonner un soir sa table à dessiner. J'y pense, vous serait-il agréable, Antoinette, de m'accompagner? La réunion sera, j'en suis sûr, très brillante et vous rappellera les grandes fêtes de votre jeunesse. Et puis, pour tout vous avouer, vous me rendriez service : je ne connais pas de femme plus belle et plus distinguée que vous à qui je puisse offrir mon bras...

Antoinette sourit : elle savait pertinemment que Fontaine et Percier n'entretenaient pas de relations suivies avec la gent féminine. N'importe, la proposition lui faisait plaisir. C'était une occasion unique d'assister à un bal pour lequel on allait s'arracher les invitations aux Tuileries et à Saint-Cloud. Et puis, Antoinette était trop femme pour ne pas avoir envie d'apercevoir Napoléon qu'elle n'avait jamais vu et l'Impératrice dont les journaux disaient qu'elle avait un visage aimable et que son teint de blonde et ses yeux bleus étaient vraiment très rares. Enfin, accompagner Fontaine qui était une célébrité, ne lui déplaisait pas. Elle ne joua donc pas les coquettes, ce n'était pas son genre, et répondit sans hésiter :

– Je vous dis oui avec le plus grand plaisir. Seulement je vous préviens, je ne possède pas de robe somptueuse et mes modestes bijoux paraîtront bien ternes à côté des colliers, des broches et des pendentifs des ducs et des princes. Mais je vous promets de me faire toute petite.

Le 1er au soir, Ethis conduisit donc sa mère à l'hôtel de Montesson tout illuminé. Sa voiture réparée et repeinte ne faisait pas trop pauvre au milieu des attelages qui faisaient la queue pour déposer les invités. Ethis, comme un cocher stylé, sauta de son siège et aida Antoinette à descendre. Tandis qu'elle le remerciait d'un sourire et qu'il eût dû, ainsi qu'il l'avait prévu plaisamment, la saluer avec respect, il la prit dans ses bras et l'embrassa.

– Tu es trop belle, je n'ai pas pu m'empêcher. Et tant pis si des gens s'étonnent de voir un cocher embrasser sa maîtresse !

Mais personne ne faisait attention à eux et Fontaine qui était là depuis plus de deux heures pour mettre la dernière main à la décoration, se précipitait.

– Vous êtes superbe, chère baronne. Venez, tout va

bien, je ne vous quitte plus de la soirée. Vous savez, je n'ai pas tellement l'habitude de sortir des dames, mais ce soir je suis fier de vous avoir à mon bras.

Et il lui présenta un jeune homme blond fort séduisant :

– Le comte de Turpin-Crissé qui est un aquarelliste de talent et qui a fait de merveilleux dessins de Malmaison.

Et il ajouta, quand celui-ci se fut éloigné après avoir galamment baisé la main d'Antoinette :

– C'est le chambellan de Joséphine qu'il a suivie dans sa retraite du château de Navarre, près d'Évreux, où l'Empereur a relégué son ancienne épouse. Avec des larmes dans la voix, paraît-il. Le comte est aussi depuis peu l'amant de la proscrite, son consolateur...

– Ah! fit Antoinette, troublée de se voir d'un coup plongée dans les secrets de l'alcôve impériale. Mais il est beaucoup plus jeune qu'elle...

– Remarque bien féminine! Oui, Lancelot, c'est son prénom, a vingt-sept ans. Avouez qu'il est très séduisant, ce valet de carreau avec ses fins cheveux ramenés en coup de vent sur le front!

– Tout à fait, mais ne rêvez pas mon cher Fontaine...

Il rit et Antoinette remarqua qu'il était devenu tout rouge. Elle regretta sa réplique qui était la première entorse à une convention tacite du clan. Déjà d'autres groupes tourbillonnaient autour d'eux et Fontaine, quand ils croisaient quelqu'un de connaissance, ne manquait pas de présenter la baronne de Valfroy, un nom qui faisait son petit effet dans cette assemblée où les Français étaient pour la plupart des nobles de fraîche date.

Antoinette était aux anges. Ces dizaines de lustres illuminés, ces centaines de chandelles disposées à profusion sur les candélabres de cristal répandaient une lumière brillante que reflétaient d'innombrables miroirs. Les toilettes étaient somptueuses ou très simples mais le plus souvent de bon goût. Antoinette remarqua que les femmes de la nouvelle aristocratie avaient beaucoup appris depuis le Directoire. Les hommes, eux, arboraient presque tous des uniformes brodés d'or et il était bien difficile de distinguer dans ce chatoiement de couleurs, de galons et de médailles, la nationalité de chacun.

– Dire, confia Antoinette à Fontaine, que tous ces beaux officiers se retrouveront demain ou dans un mois sanglants et couverts de boue sur les champs de bataille !

– Eh oui ! Beaucoup même, qui se saluent et se présentent les élégantes qui les accompagnent, se retrouveront en ennemis et échangeront des boulets comme aujourd'hui des amabilités. Voyez-vous, Antoinette, quand je vois les guerres qui se succèdent et qui tuent tant de jeunes hommes, je me félicite de n'être pas soldat. Sans doute récolte-t-on moins de lauriers à bâtir qu'à détruire mais je préfère mille fois être un constructeur qu'un sabreur !

– J'aime vous entendre parler ainsi. Je ne peux m'empêcher d'éprouver un malaise devant ce spectacle étrange qui ressemble, si vous clignez des yeux, à une mêlée de bataille avec ce rouge qui domine et ces diamants qui jettent des feux comme les canons.

Soudain, un remous sembla entraîner l'assistance vers l'une des portes d'accès.

– Tiens, il se passe quelque chose, dit Fontaine.

– C'est l'Empereur et l'Impératrice ! lança une voix.

Napoléon entrait en effet. Sa tenue d'officier de la Garde, la plus simple sans doute de l'assistance, contrastait avec la robe somptueuse de Marie-Louise, toute souriante à son bras. Il était difficile, dans cette forêt de têtes où étincelaient des diadèmes, de distinguer les traits de l'Impératrice. Antoinette, faussant compagnie à Fontaine, réussit tout de même à s'approcher et put observer un court instant le couple à la fois nouveau et déjà prisonnier de sa légende.

L'Empereur qu'elle n'avait vu que représenté sur des gravures ou figuré sur le tableau d'Henri-François Riesener, lui parut gros, presque empâté. Elle se souvint des propos récents de Fontaine remarquant combien Bonaparte avait vieilli. C'était vrai : l'homme qui tenait l'Europe à bout de bras après en avoir maîtrisé tous les rois, paraissait fatigué, comme épuisé par tout ce qu'il avait fait en quelques années. Antoinette se dit qu'il faisait bien plus que ses quarante et un ans.

Marie-Louise, elle, resplendissait de jeunesse et de grâce. Derrière cette impression première, Antoinette distingua vite les défauts : le nez est trop long, se dit-elle, et les yeux de porcelaine, si bleus soient-ils, sortent un peu trop de leur orbite. Enfin, c'est tout de même une belle femme mais il lui manquera toujours le charme de la créole.

Accaparés par le maître de maison et conduits dans un salon privé, l'Empereur et l'Impératrice disparurent de la foule, et Antoinette vint retrouver Fontaine qui paraissait s'ennuyer en conversant avec une dame un peu forte qu'il présenta comme la baronne Toussard, avant d'entraîner la Dame du Faubourg vers l'un des nombreux dressoirs chargés de victuailles et de pâtisseries derrière lesquels des valets servaient des vins de Grinzing et de Champagne.

Vers minuit, un orchestre d'une cinquantaine de musiciens cachés jusque-là par un rideau de velours commencèrent à jouer une valse et tous les regards se portèrent vers le parterre de gazon qu'on avait transformé en salle de danse en le recouvrant de parquet. A la cinquième mesure, un couple commença de tourner avec beaucoup d'élégance, épousant le rythme ternaire de la musique dans un mouvement large et harmonieux : « C'est la reine de Naples et le prince Esterhazy qui ouvrent le bal », dit une dame. Antoinette aurait bien voulu danser mais elle ne connaissait pas la valse, cette danse viennoise qui commençait de faire fureur à Paris. Et puis, Fontaine l'avait prévenue : il ne dansait pas du tout. Elle se contentait donc de regarder, charmée par la musique, intéressée par le spectacle mouvant qui déroulait ses fastes dans le décor enchanteur.

– Que je suis loin de mon Faubourg! confia-t-elle pensive à Fontaine qui lui apportait une flûte de cristal remplie de vin de Champagne. Si ceux des Quinze-Vingts et des Enfants-Trouvés qui ont fait la Révolution voyaient cette richesse étalée devant tous ces nantis par les Autrichiens, je me demande ce qu'ils penseraient.

– Ils ne verraient que Napoléon et applaudiraient celui qui a pris le trône de Louis XVI. Moi, ce que j'aimerais bien connaître, ce sont les impressions de Danton, de Robespierre, de Saint-Just et des autres qui se sont envoyés mutuellement sous le couperet de Sanson pour sauver la République!

La République, c'est le dernier mot qu'entendit Antoinette car une bousculade la pressa contre un géant en uniforme de général et lui fit renverser son verre.

Un peu plus loin, sur la droite, à l'opposé de l'endroit où se trouvait l'Empereur qui maintenant allait et venait, causait, souriait aux uns et aux autres, une lueur avait jailli d'une tenture de voile dans le couloir qui menait aux salons de l'hôtel. La flamme d'une bougie, agitée par un courant d'air, avait frôlé le rideau et l'avait enflammé. Déjà, le comte de Beinhem avait versé une carafe d'eau sur le feu qui semblait éteint. De son côté, Dumanoir, le chambellan de l'Empereur, grimpé sur une table, avait arraché la légère trame qui risquait de propager l'incendie et avait étouffé sous ses pieds les dernières étincelles.

L'affaire semblait terminée, la musique avait repris. Sans la fumée qui envahissait peu à peu les salons, personne n'aurait pu croire qu'un feu venait de menacer les invités de l'ambassadeur d'Autriche. L'Impératrice, après avoir fait un tour, avait regagné l'espèce de trône qu'on lui avait préparé. C'est en allant de son côté qu'Antoinette s'aperçut avec terreur que le feu s'attaquait aux plus hautes tentures qui se rejoignaient en plissés harmonieux au centre du plafond. Bientôt de grandes flammes jaillirent, hors de portée de ceux qui tentaient d'intervenir.

Déjà des flammèches tombaient sur l'orchestre et les musiciens s'enfuyaient en essayant de protéger les instruments. Il était temps, le plafond venait de s'effondrer sur le piano-forte, les partitions enflammées s'envolaient comme des oiseaux de feu vers les cintres et allumaient d'autres foyers. L'Empereur qui avait conservé tout son calme et donné quelques ordres brefs aux officiers qui l'entouraient, conduisait l'Impératrice jusqu'à la rue. Il demanda à Murat de la reconduire aux Tuileries et revint vers le grand salon où le sinistre prenait des allures de catastrophe depuis qu'une porte malencontreusement ouverte sur l'extérieur avait donné passage au vent.

L'épouvante était devenue générale chez ceux qui n'avaient pas encore réussi à s'enfuir. Les femmes hurlaient, les officiers essayaient d'enrayer la panique et canalisaient la foule vers les issues. Malgré l'ambassadeur qui l'exhortait à partir au plus vite, Napoléon demeurait auprès de ses généraux. Il ne consentit à quitter la salle que lorsqu'il eut constaté qu'il n'y avait pas moyen d'arrêter l'incendie.

Dans la confusion générale où les premiers pompiers arrivés se mêlaient aux sauveteurs bénévoles et aux invités, le feu ne trouvait aucune résistance. L'eau qu'on versait à pleins seaux dans la fournaise se dissipait instantanément en vapeur qui, s'ajoutant à l'épais rideau de fumée, empêchait maintenant de distinguer les malheureux isolés dans les flammes. On se cherchait, on appelait les siens, on se précipitait avec fureur à travers les rangs où râlaient des blessés piétinés. Derrière, on apercevait parfois une robe de soie qui s'enflammait comme une torche. Le spectacle n'était pas moins affreux sur le perron où beaucoup de malheureux, tombés, étaient écrasés par les suivants presque tous blessés et brûlés par des tisons.

Antoinette, malgré ses efforts désespérés, n'avait pas réussi à gagner le portail où la chance de survivre était tout de même beaucoup plus grande que dans le fond de la salle. Tous ceux qui n'avaient pu s'enfuir à temps happés, les uns après les autres, par les flammes qui couraient, se faufilaient le long des tentures et des tables, comme dirigées par les Furies à la recherche de nouvelles victimes. Deux fois déjà, la malheureuse avait réussi à éteindre, avec la serviette qu'elle tenait serrée sur son visage, le feu qui avait pris à sa robe quand un morceau du plafond dont le brocart n'était plus qu'une flamme s'abattit sur elle, Antoinette sut qu'elle était perdue. Elle hurla, mais son cri, étouffé par la fumée, cessa bientôt et elle s'écroula comme une torche abandonnée sur les débris brûlants de la tente où la fête, à cette heure de la soirée, aurait dû resplendir des feux du plaisir et de l'élégance.

Au même instant, sa veste arrachée et le visage noirci, Fontaine cherchait désespérément Antoinette qu'il avait perdue de vue depuis le commencement de la panique. Faisait-elle partie des invités demeurés prisonniers des flammes? Il ne pouvait le croire et allait et venait, au hasard, dans les derniers mètres de l'entrée encore épargnés par l'incendie. La sortie heureusement avait été dégagée et il essayait de reconnaître le visage d'Antoinette sur les corps des blessés qu'on emportait. C'était la reine de Naples sauvée, alors qu'elle était à terre, par le grand-duc de Wurtzbourg, c'était la reine de Westphalie sévèrement brûlée, c'était le prince Kourakin, ambassadeur de Russie, évanoui sur une planche, qu'on tirait vers la sortie... Antoinette, hélas! ne pouvait pas être parmi ces rescapés. Cédant alors au désespoir et à l'épuisement, Pierre Fontaine s'effondra dans un fauteuil à demi brûlé qui se trouvait là et se mit à pleurer. Il se serait sans doute laissé dévorer à son tour par le feu si des sauveteurs ne l'avaient pas entraîné en même temps que la fille de l'ambassadeur d'Autriche hors de la fournaise.

A l'entrée, le diplomate éperdu embrassa celle qu'il croyait morte dans les flammes mais ne savait pas ce qu'était devenue sa femme qu'une charpente enflammée avait, en tombant, séparée de lui. Ce ne fut que le lendemain qu'on retrouva son corps carbonisé ainsi que ceux de la princesse de Leyen et d'une femme inconnue qu'Ethis identifia grâce à la médaille qu'elle portait au cou et que le feu avait épargnée. Ce bijou avait déjà été retiré une fois du corps d'un homme brûlé vif dans la nacelle de son ballon en feu: c'était la médaille que portait Pilâtre de Rozier lorsque son aérostat s'était écrasé sur les côtes de la Manche [1].

Près de cent personnes trouvèrent la mort au cours du bal tragique offert au couple impérial. Beaucoup virent un mauvais présage dans ce coup du destin. Au Faubourg on ne considéra celui-ci que dans son essence la plus simple : Antoinette la Dame du Faubourg, la mère généreuse, la fille de la scie et du rabot, aristocrate du bois par la naissance et baronne par le hasard, avait achevé son passage dans la vie. La tragédie était trop intense pour qu'on la noyât dans autre chose que des larmes.

Place d'Aligre, personne ne pouvait croire qu'Antoinette ne monterait plus jamais l'escalier dont les marches creusées racontaient toute son histoire. Les enfants avaient été courageux, ils n'avaient pas pleuré durant l'inhumation qui, grâce à l'intervention du maire Eugène Bénard, avait pu se faire dans le cimetière Sainte-Marguerite, désaffecté depuis la création du Père-Lachaise. Entourant la famille, tous les amis étaient là, les derniers maîtres qui avaient connu Œben, les compagnons de Riesener, les jeunes aussi qui ressentaient la disparition de la Dame du Faubourg comme un deuil personnel. Les plus vieux avaient ressorti les bannières des jurandes et les compagnons du tour de France, dont la communauté était interdite depuis l'Empire, avaient attaché les rubans symboliques au pommeau de leur canne, comme pour bien montrer que les gens du bois demeuraient étroitement unis. Les vainqueurs de la Bastille arboraient leurs insignes et leurs médailles pour soutenir Ethis. Lucie, pâle, presque exsangue, s'appuyait sur le bras d'Emmanuel Caumont qui avait construit un deuxième cercueil depuis son entrée dans la famille. Réveillon, qu'Ethis était allé chercher le matin avec sa voiture, était là aussi : « Dire que ma petite Antoinette part avant moi ! » répétait-il. Il était âgé de quatre-vingt-cinq ans et il avait presque fallu le porter jusqu'à l'église, trop petite pour contenir le flot des ouvriers au

1. Voir *Les Dames du Faubourg.*

Faubourg descendu des ateliers de Charonne et de Picpus, des cours du Marais et des Quinze-Vingts.

Les fidèles du mercredi étaient là bien entendu, serrés comme autour de la table que n'animerait plus jamais celle qui avait réussi la gageure de réunir dans un modeste logement du Faubourg tant de gens d'esprit et de grande renommée. Seul manquait Pierre Fontaine qui souffrait de cruelles brûlures mais qui, surtout, était complètement abattu depuis la soirée tragique. Tout le monde avait beau lui répéter qu'il n'avait rien à se reprocher, l'architecte s'estimait responsable de la mort d'Antoinette qu'il n'aurait, disait-il, jamais dû quitter d'un pas.

Quand chacun eut jeté sa poignée de terre du Faubourg sur le cercueil, Lucie et Marie se rendirent compte que personne parmi les membres du clan n'avait envie de quitter les autres.

– Venez, dirent-elles, c'est aujourd'hui mercredi. Si Antoinette pouvait s'exprimer elle vous demanderait de vous asseoir à votre place habituelle. Nous allons parler d'elle. Ce ne sera pas triste...

Le soir, quand Lucie demanda à son frère de lui donner la médaille recueillie sur le corps de sa mère, Ethis, les larmes aux yeux, fit non de la tête.

– Je ne suis pas superstitieux mais cette médaille a déjà été liée deux fois à une mort tragique. J'ai pensé à la jeter dans la Seine puis, finalement, je l'ai vendue au poids de l'or à un bijoutier du pont Neuf et j'ai remis la somme au curé de Sainte-Marguerite pour les indigents.

– Tu as bien fait Ethis. Il y a d'autres manières de se souvenir de maman qu'en portant un bijou maléfique

Et la vie continua... Sans Antoinette mais pourtant près d'elle. La mort parfois ne suffit pas à vous séparer d'un être exceptionnel dont la personnalité franchit le barrage de l'au-delà. Il ne se passait pas d'heure sans que le nom d'Antoinette soit prononcé, ses idées invoquées, son exemple mis en avant. « Qu'aurait fait Antoinette? »,

« Antoinette n'aimerait pas ça! », « Antoinette avait bien raison... »

Les mots, hélas! ne sont que des pansements. Dessous, la plaie saigne et fait mal. Les plus touchés étaient Ethis et Alexandre Lenoir. Le premier considérait qu'Antoinette lui avait donné plus viscéralement la vie en le sauvant et en l'éduquant qu'en le mettant physiquement au monde. Lenoir, malgré la rupture des derniers mois, se rendait compte qu'il avait perdu l'amour de sa vie et que ses aventures de danseuses n'avaient rien de commun avec l'alliance du cœur et de l'esprit qui l'avait uni à Antoinette. Ils se réfugiaient furieusement dans le travail. Ethis, qui s'était réconcilié avec son beau-père, parcourait le labyrinthe du Faubourg à la recherche d'artisans actifs et inventifs susceptibles de l'aider par leur production à créer de nouveaux emplois destinés aux chômeurs de l'arrondissement dont le nombre ne cessait d'augmenter. « Des idées, il faut avoir des idées! » répétait-il... Lenoir, lui, avait entrepris de réorganiser son musée et surtout, ce qui devait lui être reproché, de redonner vie à des éléments de sculpture disparates en les amalgamant pour en faire des monuments certes nouveaux mais, hélas! aussi parfois monstrueux, telles ces quatre têtes qui soutenaient la châsse de Sainte-Geneviève greffées à chacun des angles du tombeau de Diane de Poitiers.

L'appartement d'Antoinette était demeuré clos depuis sa mort. Lucie qui habitait au-dessus disait qu'elle ne pourrait jamais plus en franchir la porte et aucun des membres du clan n'avait émis l'idée d'y reprendre les réunions du mercredi. Ce n'est que deux mois plus tard qu'Ethis et Marie décidèrent de s'y installer.

– On ne peut pas laisser mourir ce logement qui a déjà toute une histoire! dit-il à sa sœur. Tu verras qu'il ne te fera plus peur quand nous l'habiterons avec le petit Bertrand. Et puis, Marie va avoir bientôt besoin de toi...

– Tu veux dire que...

– Oui, tu as deviné. Marie attend un autre enfant, j'aimerais bien que ce soit une fille...

– Voilà enfin une bonne nouvelle! Deux bonnes nouvelles car je n'osais pas te dire de venir t'installer place d'Aligre. La vieille maison du Faubourg n'est pas loin mais j'aimerais tellement mieux te savoir avec nous. Et puis, Antoinette aimera nous savoir réunis...

– Tu parles comme si elle devait entrer tout à l'heure pour nous dire que le pot-au-feu du mercredi sent merveilleusement bon et qu'il est temps de venir l'aider à mettre la table.

– C'est vrai, pour moi elle est toujours là. Il m'arrive de lui parler, de lui demander conseil...

Elle se mit à sangloter et Ethis la prit dans ses bras.

– Allons, petite sœur, cesse de pleurer. Tu sais ce qu'elle nous disait quand notre père est mort : « Ne pleurez pas, il n'aimerait pas ça ! »

Un pauvre sourire éclaira la figure baignée de larmes de Lucie.

– Tu as raison, tu viens de m'annoncer deux choses agréables, c'est à elles qu'il faut penser. Dis donc Ethis, quand tu habiteras en bas, est-ce que tu reprendras les soupers du clan ?

– Non ! Sans Antoinette ce n'est pas possible. C'est elle qui faisait vivre les réunions du mercredi. Le charme est rompu, il faut le savoir. Cela ne veut pas dire tout de même qu'il ne faut plus voir nos amis, ni même ne pas les inviter de temps en temps à venir partager le pain autour de la grande table d'Œben. Marie est une bonne cuisinière et tu n'es pas manchotte. Dans un petit moment il va falloir revivre. Antoinette...

– Aimerait !

Le frère et la sœur se regardèrent et sourirent.

– Oui, Antoinette aimerait nous voir rire! dit Ethis.

Il n'était évidemment pas question de vendre ou de louer la maison Thirion qu'Ethis et Marie quittaient avec peine. Antoinette avait fait resurgir de ses murs des messages étranges datant de plus d'un siècle et qui venaient de ses ancêtres. On s'était intéressé un moment avec Réveillon à ces signes du passé, on avait projeté d'explorer plus à fond le grenier mais la vie de tous les jours avait étouffé celle d'hier et l'on n'avait plus parlé du grenier ni des richesses qu'il devait receler. Et voilà qu'au moment de partir et de transformer cette maison d'ébénistes en resserre, Ethis se sentait envahi par un trouble profond. Lui, l'enfant trouvé sans parents, sans racines, éprouvait soudain l'envie de s'accrocher au fil ténu qu'Antoinette avait commencé à démêler. Ses pensées étaient encore confuses mais il se disait que s'il réussissait à faire parler la maison Thirion et à mettre au jour de nouveaux souvenirs, il se créerait lui-même, et pour ses enfants, ce passé que le destin lui avait refusé. « Je le ferai aussi pour Antoinette, se dit-il. Elle m'a tout donné d'elle au présent, c'est à moi et à moi seul de découvrir le passé. »

Quand le déménagement fut terminé, les meubles qu'on laissait rangés dans une pièce et le sol nettoyé pour recevoir les guéridons, les tables à jeu et les sièges « genre Jacob » qui ne tenaient plus dans la réserve du magasin de la Bastille, Ethis dit à Emmanuel Caumont :

– Si tu veux bien m'aider, nous allons monter au grenier et chercher dans toutes les vieilleries qui y sont accumulées les souvenirs se rattachant aux ancêtres d'Antoinette. Lors d'une première visite, quand nous nous sommes installés, nous avons déjà découvert une canne de compagnon qui remonte à plusieurs siècles et que les jeunes ébénistes de la famille se sont repassés de génération en génération, pour accomplir leur tour de France. Il n'y a pas de raison pour que nous ne trouvions pas autre chose.

Dans la petite pièce du haut qui servait elle-même de débarras, l'échelle était toujours en place qui menait au grenier par une trappe lourde que les deux hommes eurent du mal à soulever.

– Dire que ce bois a peut-être deux ou trois cents ans! C'était du bon chêne, dit Emmanuel.

– Il faut tout de même faire attention aux planches du parquet. Je me souviens que certaines d'entre elles sont complètement vermoulues.

La quête commença dans la poussière et les toiles

d'araignée, au fond du grenier, la partie qu'Ethis et Marie n'avaient pas explorée dix ans auparavant. Il y avait, empilés les uns sur les autres, des ballots de vieilles nippes dont l'étoffe se déchirait dès qu'on la tendait quelque peu, des caisses remplies d'écuelles et de vieilles marmites rouillées, des lames de scies usées jusqu'à n'être plus qu'un fil, des outils brisés dont le manche avait été enlevé, ce que regretta Emmanuel.

– Dommage, on aurait pu retrouver des noms gravés sur le bois.

Dans un coin, Ethis fit la première trouvaille intéressante en dégageant l'épaisse couche de papier réduit en poussière qui recouvrait plusieurs objets.

– Des jouets, ce sont des jouets! s'écria-t-il en soulevant une sorte de petit chariot en bois qu'un papa ébéniste avait dû jadis construire pour l'un de ses enfants.

Les roues finement ouvragées ne tournaient plus sur leur essieu rouillé, mais le chariot dont le constructeur avait même pris le soin de sculpter l'arrière et les côtés était charmant. Ethis dont le cœur était toujours prêt à s'ouvrir en était tout ému.

– Je vais le rapporter à Bertrand, dit-il. Il est trop grand pour jouer avec mais je lui raconterai une belle histoire à propos de notre découverte.

Un vieux jouet inutilisable, c'était quand même peu pour s'être sali une bonne heure dans les débris des vies qui s'étaient succédé sous le toit de la maison Thirion. En fouillant encore ils trouvèrent une arbalète et un pistolet à pierre complètement rouillé.

– Objets d'antiquité, je prends! dit Ethis en riant.

Les deux beaux-frères allaient arrêter là leurs recherches infructueuses et rendre à son sommeil le vieux grenier quand Emmanuel, surgissant d'un nuage de poussière, cria qu'il avait mis la main sur une collection de motifs sculptés dans le bois.

– Il y a de tout, des pieds de fauteuil, des têtes d'angelots et de monstres, et un tas de panneaux destinés sans doute à embellir des devants d'armoires et de buffets. Tout cela a dû être sculpté à l'époque du roi Louis XIV.

– Peut-être par Boulle. Te souviens-tu du tableau de marqueterie qu'Antoinette gardait précieusement dans sa chambre et qui y restera? Nous l'avions trouvé Marie et moi en même temps que la canne. Cela nous redonne du courage, fouillons encore un moment... Tiens, dans ce coin, le plus sombre et le plus sale, où personne n'a dû mettre la main depuis cent ou peut-être deux cents ans.

– Je ne vois rien, dit Emmanuel qui le premier avait plongé dans l'épaisseur des toiles d'araignée. Toujours les mêmes cochonneries!... Ah! Voyons pourtant ce que cachent ces lambeaux de couverture...

Il tira à lui un petit tableau couvert de saletés sur lesquelles il était impossible de discerner ce qu'il représentait.

– Rapportons-le à la maison, dit Ethis, je sais comment il faut le nettoyer.

Ils rentrèrent harassés place d'Aligre où Marie et Lucie les attendaient. Les deux femmes poussèrent des cris d'horreur en voyant dans quel état le grenier des Thirion leur rendait leurs maris.

– N'entrez pas! Déshabillez-vous sur le palier, nous allons vous préparer des bains!

– A condition qu'ils aillent avant chercher de l'eau à la fontaine! dit Lucie.

Une heure plus tard, sous le regard attentif des trois autres, Ethis commençait à l'aide d'un linge propre et d'un peu d'eau savonneuse à faire surgir de la macule du temps les formes colorées de ce qui semblait être un portrait de femme. Il avait auparavant décollé de l'envers une petite feuille de papier complètement jaunie dont tous les coins étaient tombés en poussière dès qu'il les avait effleurés. Deux lignes d'une écriture fine dont la moitié des lettres avaient été mangées par la moisissure, apparaissaient mais il fallait attendre le grand jour du lendemain matin pour essayer de les déchiffrer.

Curieusement, la poussière solidifiée avait dû protéger les couleurs qui, à part quelques craquelures, retrouvaient un éclat de jeunesse. Le tableau fut enfin visible dans son ensemble, il représentait le visage d'une femme, belle mais un peu triste, qui arracha le même cri à Lucie et Marie : « Elle ressemble à Antoinette ! »

Hormis la coiffure et les bijoux, sans doute italiens, qui éclataient sur le décolleté de la robe, les traits de l'inconnue présentaient une analogie frappante avec ceux d'Antoinette. La bouche bien dessinée dégageait, à cause d'un pli imperceptible de la commissure droite, la même touche de scepticisme. Les yeux surtout semblaient lancer devant eux l'étrange rayon vert où Antoinette puisait l'essentiel de sa séduction.

– Je vais chercher le portrait qu'a peint Henri-François. On distinguera mieux les ressemblances, dit Ethis.

Un long moment, les jeunes gens se penchèrent sur les tableaux où deux femmes qui n'existaient plus que par le pinceau de deux peintres semblaient se regarder et se sourire.

– Je suis sûre que l'inconnue que nous avons sortie de l'ombre était une ancêtre d'Antoinette, dit Ethis. C'est la seule explication possible de cette étonnante ressemblance et aussi de la présence du tableau dans la maison Thirion.

Le débris de papier, qui avait dû être une étiquette collée au dos de la toile, fut placé avec de grandes précautions entre deux plaques de verre afin qu'il ne se désagrège pas complètemeent. Le texte presque illisible était écrit en latin ou en italien. En dessous, d'une autre écriture, quelques mots de français devaient indiquer à qui avait appartenu le tableau. On pouvait déchiffrer : « ... part... sœu... Abb... cham... »

– Il doit s'agir de l'abbaye Saint-Antoine-des-Champs ! dit Lucie. Pour le reste, il faudrait une loupe puissante et encore, je ne sais pas si nous parviendrions à lire.

– Dès demain matin, décida Ethis, je porterai tableau et papier à Alexandre Lenoir. C'est bien le diable s'il ne découvre pas le fin mot de l'histoire.

Ethis rendait souvent visite à celui qui l'avait aidé, presque autant que les Valfroy, à sortir de la rue où il avait toujours vécu et à épanouir son intelligence. Il lui vouait une grande reconnaissance et une affection filiale qui résistaient à tous les aléas de la vie. En retour, Alexandre Lenoir considérait Ethis comme son fils. Il était fier de la transformation quasi miraculeuse de « Traîne-sabot » et de sa réussite. Les liens étroits qui existaient depuis vingt ans entre le conservateur et la famille Valfroy n'avaient pu que fortifier l'admiration d'Ethis pour son maître. Il n'entreprenait jamais rien d'important sans lui demander conseil.

– Tiens, Ethis! tu tombes bien, dit Alexandre en accueillant son ancien assistant. Tu vas me donner la main pour transporter le bas-relief que j'attribue à Jean Cousin mais qui est peut-être de Pierre Bontemps. Je veux voir l'effet qu'il produirait accolé au monument du cœur d'Henri III. Mais tu le connais ce bas-relief! Rappelle-toi le mal que nous avons eu pour l'arracher aux vandales qui voulaient l'envoyer en poussière au laboratoire de chimie [1]!

Comme au temps où ils sauvaient ensemble les statues, Lenoir et Ethis chargèrent *Le Réveil des Nymphes* sur un chariot et poussèrent en riant celui-ci jusqu'à l'urne monumentale venue de l'église Saint-Louis des jésuites, rue Saint-Antoine. Le mariage des deux sculptures ne s'imposait peut-être pas mais comme Lenoir semblait le trouver réussi, Ethis s'abstint de tout commentaire. D'ailleurs, il avait hâte de montrer sa trouvaille.

– Je voudrais bien que vous examiniez un petit tableau que j'ai découvert dans le grenier de la vieille maison du Faubourg. Et surtout les restes d'une étiquette qui l'accompagnait.

Alexandre Lenoir, installé à son bureau, défit le paquet apporté par Ethis et regarda longuement, en l'éloignant un peu de ses yeux, le portrait.

– C'est un très beau et très vieux tableau, dit-il. Sûrement d'un maître italien. Je ne vois pas de signature

1. Beaucoup de chefs-d'œuvre de la statuaire française furent alors réduits en poussière de marbre qui servait à faire de l'eau gazeuse.

mais tu m'as dit qu'il était accompagné d'une étiquette.

– Plutôt de fragments d'étiquette. Jugez plutôt.

Avec un air gourmand, Lenoir qui flairait une énigme a résoudre, souleva la plaque de verre pour mieux lire les quelques mots qui apparaissaient sur le papier jauni. Il prit dans un tiroir une grosse lentille et commença à déchiffrer.

– Le début est écrit en italien, dit-il. Cela ne va pas simplifier le travail. Je lis *Per mi gen... llo Ann... Suo vieccho amoro... Jacopo Il Tinto... Venezia... 580.* Donne-moi ma plume que je transcrive. On essaiera après de boucher les vides...

Tout en recopiant ce qu'il avait pu déchiffrer, Alexandre marmotta :

– ... Il Tinto... Ce n'est pas possible qu'il s'agisse du Tintoret. Et pourtant, la date semble correspondre... Il faut en tout cas vérifier le prénom. Si Il Tintoretto s'appelait Jacopo, tu as mis la main sur un tableau de valeur. Passe-moi le grand livre qui se trouve en haut de la bibliothèque ; *Vite de piu eccellenti pittori e scultori* de Giorgio Vasari. C'est la bible de tous ceux qui s'intéressent aux géants de la peinture italienne.

Il feuilleta le livre et s'écria :

– Bravo ! Le Tintoret s'appelait bien Jacopo. Jacopo Robusti ! J'ai gagné. Et toi aussi mon cher Ethis. Te voilà propriétaire d'un tableau de maître ! Maintenant, essayons à l'aide de la loupe de distinguer encore quelques bribes de lettres qui nous permettraient de reconstituer la phrase. Tiens je crois voir MO devant LLO. Et une barre qui pourrait bien être celle d'un D. Cela pourrait donner *modello,* ce qui serait logique. Ce serait la dédicace d'un peintre à son modèle. On peut aussi avancer que ces trois traits presque complètement effacés et dont on ne devine l'existence qu'à travers la lentille grossissante sont des T ou des L. Ou bien encore les deux, ce qui ferait *gentille. A mi gentille modella...* cela se tient très bien. Après, Ann, cela ne peut signifier que le prénom Anne. Pour le reste c'est visible : *Suo vecchio amoroso.* Tu comprends ce que cela veut dire... Attends maintenant que je regarde le tableau de plus près.

Il promena la lentille sur le bas du portrait et poussa encore un cri de triomphe.

– Tiens, regarde, dans la dentelle du col, presque au milieu : n'est-ce pas un T? Certains artistes alors aimaient cacher leur marque dans un détail. Voilà, ton tableau est identifié!

– Je vous admire, mon maître! Ce que cela est passionnant de pouvoir percer le secret des chefs-d'œuvre! J'aimerais en être capable mais...

– Mais quoi? Il te faut apprendre, il faut lire, il faut regarder, il faut imaginer le vraisemblable! Si tu veux devenir un grand marchand de meubles et d'œuvres d'art, tu dois étudier. Je te prêterai des livres et nos amis Fontaine et Percier pourront t'enseigner un tas de choses... Dans le domaine que tu as choisi, l'ambition et la vraie réussite passent par la connaissance! Mais dis donc, il y a encore du français sur ton étiquette, montre un peu. A la loupe on arrive à lire ou plutôt à deviner : Appartient à sœur Anne (Thirion). Abbaye Saint-Antoine-des-Champs.

– Thirion, c'est le nom de la maison, le nom qui lui est resté à travers les siècles dans la mémoire du Faubourg. La canne de compagnon du tour de France retrouvée elle aussi dans le grenier porte le nom de Denis Thirion. Ainsi, Anne Thirion aurait été la sœur ou la femme de Denis. Comment aurait-elle pu aller à Venise, y connaître Le Tintoret et être religieuse à l'abbaye? Ah! si Antoinette était là! Avec les souvenirs et les histoires que lui avaient racontés sa mère et sa grand-mère, elle réussirait à renouer tous les fils de cette extraordinaire histoire qui, c'est étrange, me touche comme si c'était vraiment celle de ma famille!

– C'est ta famille, Ethis! N'en doute jamais. Oui, c'est vrai qu'Antoinette aurait élucidé les points qui nous paraissent obscurs. Mais puisque tu as cité son nom, laisse-moi te parler un peu de ta mère. Tu sais les liens très forts qui nous ont rapprochés elle et moi après la mort de ton père. Nous ne l'avons jamais extériorisée mais c'était une vraie passion. Si tu savais combien elle me manque! Et puis, cette mort affreuse! Souvent je la vois dans mes rêves et c'est atroce. Le jour venu, je pense à Antoinette avec plus de sérénité et je me dis qu'elle nous a quittés en pleine beauté, en possession de toute son intelligence et de son esprit. Elle qui avait si peur, non pas de mourir mais d'être un jour diminuée intellectuellement, elle nous laisse une image d'elle radieuse et malgré tout heureuse. Elle disait souvent qu'en moins de cinquante ans elle avait vécu trois existences normales. Finalement, quand on meurt, c'est cela qui compte : être assez lucide pour savoir qu'on a utilisé avec plénitude les jours que Dieu nous a permis de passer sur la Terre. Je suis sûr qu'Antoinette a eu cette pensée quand elle s'est rendu compte que rien ne pouvait la sauver des flammes... Tu vois, cela m'a fait du bien de te parler d'elle. Il n'y a qu'avec toi que je peux le faire!

Il avait parlé sans regarder Ethis, perdu dans les souvenirs qui l'assaillaient. Quand il redressa la tête, il s'aperçut qu'Ethis pleurait doucement. Il lui prit la main et la serra très fort.

– Je t'ai fait pleurer, mon pauvre Ethis, mais ce n'est ni mauvais ni triste : ce sont des larmes du cœur, celles qui soulagent...

Vulnérable dans sa sensibilité d'artiste, Fontaine avait été longtemps choqué par le drame qui avait coûté la vie à Antoinette et dont il se sentait responsable. Et puis, les mois passant, guéri de ses propres blessures et pressé par l'Empereur qui exigeait la poursuite de ses projets, il avait repris le travail avec une sorte de rage qui inquiétait Percier et ses amis. Il habitait depuis longtemps l'hôtel d'Angivilliers, rue de l'Oratoire, à deux pas du Louvre.

tous les jours à cinq heures, il gagnait vite son atelier installé au rez-de-chaussée et travaillait toute la matinée. A midi, après un repas frugal, il allait visiter ses chantiers et ses clients puis gagnait l'hôtel de la rue Saint-Maur où grandissait sa petite fille adoptive. L'été dans le jardin, l'hiver dans l'un des salons de la maison, il jouait avec Pauline et travaillait à ses livres. Il aimait écrire et avait déjà publié l'année d'avant, avec Percier, un important in-folio illustré intitulé *Description des cérémonies et des fêtes qui ont eu lieu pour le mariage de S. M. l'Empereur Napoléon Ier avec l'archiduchesse Marie-Louise.* Maintenant, il s'était remis à la rédaction d'un autre livre qui lui tenait à cœur et qui comportait de nombreuses aquarelles : *Choix des plus célèbres maisons de campagne de Rome et de ses environs.* Il s'agissait, avec Percier, de mettre en œuvre les innombrables études et dessins rapportés jadis d'Italie. A dix heures, sa voiture venait le chercher et le ramenait rue de l'Oratoire où il préférait coucher pour être à pied d'œuvre le lendemain matin.

La rue Saint-Maur n'était qu'à dix minutes en voiture de la place d'Aligre et Fontaine qui n'avait pas voulu revenir durant plusieurs mois dans la maison d'Antoinette, ne passait plus maintenant une semaine sans venir retrouver un moment Ethis, Emmanuel et leurs femmes. Ce n'étaient plus bien sûr les longues veillées d'autrefois. Le clan avait perdu son âme, ni Lucie ni Marie ne pouvaient remplacer Antoinette. Pourtant, lorsque Fontaine et Percier étaient libres ou que Lenoir arrivait sans prévenir, les deux belles-sœurs improvisaient un souper. On retrouvait ainsi parfois, l'espace de quelques heures, la chaude atmosphère des réunions du mercredi. Il y avait toujours quelqu'un pour dire avant de se séparer :

– Antoinette aurait été heureuse !...

Antoinette aurait surtout été heureuse de la naissance d'Antoinette-Émilie, le 10 septembre 1811, dans la chambre où elle avait elle-même mis Lucie au monde, la chambre où elle avait aimé et tremblé, la chambre de la famille Œben dont la grande glace ovale dessinée et sculptée jadis par le maître reflétait encore les vieux papiers peints de Réveillon, inusables comme celui qui les avait fabriqués. Marie avait accouché sans histoire d'une jolie petite fille dont le prénom était convenu depuis longtemps. C'est pour pouvoir l'appeler Antoinette qu'Ethis avait souhaité une fille. Maintenant que l'enfant était là, dans le vieux berceau une nouvelle fois habillé d'un blanc douillet que son parrain François Richard avait fait tisser spécialement sur ses métiers de la rue de Charonne, l'ancien vainqueur de la Bastille ne quittait plus la pièce, attentif au moindre cri du bébé, toujours prêt à la prendre dans ses bras et à clamer qu'il était le plus beau de tout le quartier, de tout l'arrondissement et même de Paris tout entier.

La mère riait et traitait Ethis de grand fou. « Il était temps, disait-elle, d'avoir un deuxième enfant : j'ai trente-quatre ans et Bertrand, le garçon, en a déjà onze ! »

Bertrand avait les cheveux blonds et certains traits fins de sa mère. D'Ethis il avait hérité une solide carrure et un ton malicieux qui lui donnait beaucoup de charme. Son charme, il en jouait depuis longtemps dans les ateliers du Faubourg où le « fils Œben » était connu comme le loup blanc. Survivance des vieux usages ou désir instinctif de ne pas oublier le nom du maître, Bertrand était pour la communauté du bois le « fils Œben » comme Antoinette était restée malgré son mariage la « fille Œben ». Cela n'était pas pour déplaire au jeune garçon qui, depuis toujours, affirmait qu'il serait ébéniste, qu'il ferait son tour de France malgré l'hostilité du régime impérial envers tout ce qui s'apparentait au compagnonnage. Bertrand connaissait tous les tours et les détours du Faubourg, ses passages, ses cours, ses ateliers. Beaucoup d'ébénistes qui avaient connu sa grand-mère ou, pour les plus jeunes, qui avaient vécu avec Ethis les premières secousses de la Révolution, lui faisaient une petite place sur un établi afin qu'il s'amuse à raboter, à découper et à râper des chutes de bois. Il rapportait alors triomphalement à la maison ses chefs-d'œuvre et quelquefois une grosse « poupée » à l'un des doigts, qui protégeait la coupure qu'il s'était faite avec un ciseau trop bien affûté.

Ce goût pour le travail du bois ne plaisait pas trop à sa mère et irritait fort son grand-père, le nouveau maire de l'arrondissement qui envisageait un avenir plus noble et plus lucratif pour Bertrand. En revanche, Ethis voyait d'un bon œil son garçon s'orienter vers un métier qu'il aurait voulu apprendre.

– Si Bertrand veut être ébéniste et sculpteur, il le sera! disait-il. Je suis d'ailleurs certain qu'avec du talent et de l'intelligence on peut réussir dans ce métier qui va prendre bientôt un essor considérable. Et puis, je suis là pour l'y aider, son oncle Emmanuel aussi!

Seulement, il ajoutait à l'adresse de son fils qui se voyait déjà apprenti chez Emmanuel ou chez les Jacob :

– Dis-toi bien pourtant que tu n'apprendras pas le métier et que tu ne partiras pas faire ton tour de France avant d'avoir reçu au collège une solide instruction! J'ai trop souffert de mon ignorance et j'ai eu tellement de peine à acquérir une modeste teinture de connaissances que je ne te laisserai jamais t'engager dans la vie sans une bonne culture générale!

La question justement se posait de savoir où Bertrand allait recevoir cet enseignement. Jusque-là, il avait été un bon élève de l'institution qu'un carme, M. Fleurizelle, avait rouverte tout au bout de la rue Picpus mais, pour continuer des études il devait fréquenter un établissement plus sérieux. Ce n'était pas tellement facile à une époque où les structures de l'enseignement, démantelées à la Révolution, commençaient juste à se réorganiser.

Il y avait bien le Lycée impérial, l'ancien collège Louis-le-Grand où Molière, Voltaire, Robespierre et Camille Desmoulins avaient été élèves, mais on n'y entrait que sur recommandation. Eugène Delacroix, le fils de Victoire, y avait été admis en qualité d'interne deux ans auparavant mais il était le fils d'un ancien ministre et préfet. Ethis s'appelait bien de Valfroy, mais l'ancien « vainqueur » ne pesait pas lourd aux yeux de l'administration impériale. Restait Eugène Bénard, le beau-père auquel Ethis n'aimait guère avoir recours et puis, surtout, Fontaine et Percier qui avaient sûrement le bras assez long pour faire admettre Bertrand sur les bancs du lycée de la rue Saint-Jacques.

Alexandre Lenoir qu'on avait mis aussi à contribution n'eut même pas à intervenir, une lettre circonstanciée de Fontaine au ministre avait suffi à faire inscrire le garçon parmi les privilégiés internes de l'école impériale. Bertrand, lui, ne considérait pas comme une chance la perspective de quitter sa famille, ses camarades et son Faubourg pour aller étudier et vivre dans les classes et les dortoirs du lycée de la rue Saint-Jacques. Enfin, l'idée de retrouver son cousin et la certitude qu'il ne ferait pas renoncer son père lui firent faire contre mauvaise fortune bon cœur et il endossa sans trop de déplaisir l'uniforme de drap bleu des lycéens de l'Empereur en rêvant à son départ futur, un beau matin de printemps, une chanson aux lèvres et, sur son épaule, la canne de compagnon des Cottion et des Habermann.

Le souffle joyeux apporté par la naissance de la petite Antoinette-Émilie n'avait pas eu le temps de balayer l'immense tristesse engendrée place d'Aligre par la mort de sa grand-mère qu'un nouveau deuil vint frapper la famille. Un coursier envoyé par Mme Réveillon vint prévenir Lucie et Ethis que le camarade de jeux de Marguerite Œben, le parrain d'Antoinette, l'ami de toujours qui n'avait cessé d'affirmer qu'il possédait une seconde famille place d'Aligre, était mort dans la nuit en dormant. L'une des plus belles pages du roman du Faubourg était tournée. L'ancien petit commis de mercerie devenu grand patron de l'industrie parisienne naissante, celui qui avait permis aux frères Montgolfier et à Pilâtre de Rozier d'ouvrir la conquête du ciel, l'amateur d'art qui avait vu son œuvre, la Folie Titon, saccagée au cours de l'émeute qui devait être point de départ de la Révolution, abandonnait un monde auquel il ne s'intéressait plus guère. Son immense richesse avait fondu avec la dépréciation des assignats qui, ironie du sort, avaient été imprimés par les presses de Courtalin, sa première manufacture. Son inépuisable générosité avait eu raison des restes de sa fortune qui lui avaient juste permis d'atteindre, en continuant de vivre en seigneur, l'âge respectable de quatre-vingt-six ans.

Pour Lucie, c'était l'un des derniers maillons de la famille de sa mère qui venait de céder. Il ne lui restait plus que sa tante Victoire qu'elle voyait rarement et son oncle, le fantasque Henri-François qui peignait les dames de l'Empire en rêvant à de lointains voyages.

– Tu vois, dit-elle à Ethis, nous voilà bien seuls... Tous les liens qui nous rattachent au passé cèdent les uns après les autres. Je suis triste...

– Ne dis pas cela ! Si tu avais été comme moi un enfant trouvé, sans père ni mère, tu saurais ce que c'est qu'une existence sans racines et tu comprendrais mon obstination à me raccrocher aux souvenirs que m'ont légués mes parents adoptifs. Les morts font mal mais elles ne changent rien à la passionnante histoire qu'ont vécu ici, dans notre Faubourg, tous ceux qui nous ont précédés. Antoinette savait ce qu'elle faisait en nous aidant à découvrir sous les combles d'une vieille maison les bribes d'un passé devenu déjà une légende. Aujourd'hui, notre tour est venu d'éclairer les enfants et de leur dire qui a été leur grand-père, l'irréprochable M. de Valfroy, et leur grand-mère, la rayonnante Antoinette... Je ne le dis pas à Marie qui tremble à l'idée que son fils puisse un jour quitter la maison mais je suis heureux, et fier, que Bertrand ait envie d'emporter la canne de compagnon de Jean Cottion dans son tour de France. Pour ce qui est de Réveillon, il va bien nous manquer ! Et dire que c'est en jouant l'enfant insurgé chez lui que j'ai connu Antoinette ! La Révolution aura au moins eu une conséquence heureuse : elle m'a permis de trouver un père, une mère. Et une sœur... Viens ma petite Lucie que je t'embrasse !

Après la flambée des commandes impériales, le marasme s'installait à nouveau dans le Faubourg. La plaie saignante de la conscription envenimait la vie sociale et n'encourageait pas le commerce, à commencer par celui des meubles. Surtout, le blocus décrété contre l'Angleterre avait tari l'une des principales sources de commandes. Rares étaient les menuisiers et ébénistes du Faubourg qui n'avaient pas travaillé, par marchands interposés, pour l'exportation vers le royaume où la haute société méprisait la lourdeur du style napoléonien mais raffolait de l'élégante légèreté du Louis XV et du Louis XVI. Ethis qui avait expédié beaucoup de meubles aux sujets de Sa Majesté grâce à l'entremise de son ami Richard, commençait à se plaindre et envisageait de se créer d'autres sources de revenus dans des activités différentes. Emmanuel Caumont, de son côté, avait éprouvé des difficultés heureusement surmontées provisoirement grâce à la part qu'il devait à Fontaine et Percier du fonds de 350 000 francs de commandes dégagé par le décret du 9 mai 1811 en vue de « faire travailler les ouvriers du bois qui à Paris, n'étaient point occupés ».

Revenant de la rue Saint-Maur où il était allé embrasser sa fille, Fontaine était passé place d'Aligre annoncer la bonne nouvelle. Après s'être fait prier un petit peu, il avait accepté l'invitation à souper de Lucie dont le logement ne lui rappelait pas, comme celui du premier étage, le souvenir d'Antoinette qui le poursuivait comme un remords. Une fois de plus les deux belles-sœurs se surpassèrent et avaient réussi avec peu de chose, des saucisses et des pommes de terre, à préparer un repas appétissant quand Alexandre Lenoir arriva lui aussi à l'improviste en posant précautionneusement sur la table un paquet bien enveloppé.

– C'est une surprise! Et je suis content que notre ami Fontaine soit des nôtres pour en profiter.

– Des asperges! s'écria Lucie qui s'était empressée de déballer un petit panier où, bien rangées, les tiges blanches montraient leurs diadèmes d'émeraude comme pour se rendre plus séduisantes. Et ce sont des vertes, celles que je préfère!...

– J'étais tout à l'heure à Argenteuil, dit Lenoir. J'allais prendre possession de quelques vieilles pierres, vestiges du couvent des bénédictines qui recueillirent jadis la pauvre Héloïse, et j'en ai profité pour faire le tour des maraîchers. On m'a proposé ces premières asperges et j'ai pensé que nous pourrions les déguster ensemble. Mais ce n'est pas tout, il y a encore dans ma voiture trois bouteilles de ce vin d'Argenteuil élevé tout exprès pour les accompagner.

Lenoir méritait des compliments. Il les reçut et continua :

– Comment, mesdames, allez-vous nous préparer ces délicieux légumes ?

– A la vinaigrette tout simplement, dit Lucie.

– Et pourquoi pas à la flamande avec un hachis d'œufs durs dans du beurre fondu ? rétorqua Marie qui avait plus d'une recette dans son sac.

– Ah ! mesdames, vous reprenez là une vieille querelle qui réjouit encore, après plus d'un siècle, les fines gueules dont je m'honore de faire partie.

– Racontez ! lança Lucie. Vous en mourez d'envie. Et vous savez bien que vos histoires qui enchantaient Antoinette nous plaisent tout autant.

– Puisque vous insistez, voici mon anecdote qui remonte au temps de Louis le Bien-Aimé. Fontenelle, homme d'esprit et fin gastronome qui, je vous le rappelle, est mort centenaire pour montrer à ses contemporains que les deux qualités jointes font la vie plus longue, avait, à chaque saison, de fréquentes disputes avec son ami et commensal habituel, l'abbé Terrasson. Le prélat aimait les asperges à la vinaigrette, Fontenelle, comme Marie, les préférait à la flamande. Le cuisinier de Fontenelle faisait donc deux assaisonnements différents. Un jour, en se mettant à table pour le dîner, l'abbé tombe le nez dans son assiette, victime d'une apoplexie. L'histoire veut que Fontenelle appelle alors son maître d'hôtel et lui lance : « Allez tout de suite dire en cuisine qu'on les prépare toutes au beurre ! »

Le ton était donné. Pour la première fois depuis la mort d'Antoinette, la place d'Aligre retrouvait, un soir, l'atmosphère gaie et chaleureuse du clan. On s'extasia sur la fraîcheur des asperges, on mangea les saucisses de bon appétit et l'on écouta avec passion les dernières nouvelles que Fontaine avait glanées dans les résidences impériales.

Quelques jours auparavant avait eu lieu à Notre-Dame le baptême du roi de Rome. Fontaine n'y était pas mais Duroc, pour lequel il travaillait, lui avait raconté les à-côtés de la cérémonie, ces petits faits dont la presse n'avait pas parlé mais qui n'avaient pas échappé au fidèle des fidèles, le Maréchal du Palais. « Son inquiétude, dit Fontaine, commence à percer sous le masque du dévouement. » Il continua :

– Le plus vieux et le plus brave des compagnons de l'Empereur est angoissé par l'attitude de Napoléon. Il ne me l'a pas dit mais j'ai senti sa crainte de voir son maître persécuté, obsédé par l'idée fixe de la conquête. Tout l'entourage sérieux et proche de Napoléon essaie de le dissuader d'entreprendre la campagne de Russie pour laquelle il reconstitue et prépare la Grande Armée. Le baptême du roi de Rome qui scelle sa dynastie aurait encore accentué sa monomanie. C'est au moment où, aux yeux de tout son peuple, il atteint le sommet de sa puissance que ceux qui l'ont toujours soutenu et servi le voient s'engager, avec terreur, dans l'aventure glacée des plaines russes. La naissance et le baptême de son fils semblent légitimer et affermir son ambition. Celle-ci éclatait sous les voûtes de Notre-Dame quand, revêtu de sa tenue impériale pourpre, blanche et or, pompeuse à l'excès, il présentait à bout de bras son fils à Dieu et aux hommes. Rien n'arrêtera Napoléon, mais jusqu'où pourra-t-il aller?

– Vous me semblez bien pessimiste, dit Lenoir. Si l'Empereur réussit à regrouper l'armée de 600 000 hommes dont on parle, avec ses 200 000 chevaux et ses 12 000 canons, je ne vois pas qui pourra lui résister.

– L'obstacle n'est pas l'armée de l'empereur Alexandre mais l'éloignement, le froid, la neige. Enfin, le génie et la chance de Napoléon lui donneront peut-être encore une fois raison. Je le souhaite parce que, sinon...

– L'aveuglement de l'Empereur avide de nouvelles conquêtes me paraît en effet menaçant mais sa tyrannie à l'intérieur du pays ne l'est pas moins. A force de poursuivre tous les esprits indépendants, Napoléon a fait taire les talents, les écrivains bien en cour ne sont que de fades courtisans. Il paraît qu'il s'étonne de la pauvreté des œuvres présentées aux prix décennaux mais la dictature n'a jamais favorisé les lettres. Pour pouvoir décerner un prix d'Histoire, il a fallu remonter à Rulhière mort en 1791. Quant au prix de tragédie accordé au grotesque Baour-Lormian, il fait rire tout le monde, même Lancival et Raynouard les écrivains favoris de l'Empereur. Il y a bien Chateaubriand mais il s'en défie comme du diable. Et il ne faut pas lui parler des amis de Mme de Staël, Benjamin Constant, Sismondi, Barante, voués à l'exaspération impériale. Libraires et imprimeurs sont soumis à une inquisition permanente et la presse à la censure. Allez parler avec tout cela de création littéraire!

Ethis piaffait. L'énergie qu'il sécrétait comme d'autres la bile ne trouvait plus à s'exprimer depuis que la crise avait ralenti les affaires, au Faubourg comme ailleurs. Si le blocus touchait finalement peu l'Angleterre contre laquelle il avait été décrété, il plongeait toute l'Europe dans un marasme voisin de la souffrance. On ne trouvait plus ni sucre, ni thé, ni café. Le sel commençait même à manquer en Hollande où il était indispensable pour une industrie importante du pays, la préparation des harengs. *Le Moniteur* avait beau écrire que la graine d'asperge séchée et torréfiée avait le goût du café et que le thé de tremble valait celui des Indes, il n'y avait pas de queue chez les épiciers qui vendaient ces produits de substitution.

Ethis piaffait mais il était surtout inquiet de voir le nombre des faillites se multiplier dans le quartier. On venait d'en compter treize dans le bois et l'ameublement, trois dans les fabriques de papier peint et deux dans les filatures. François Richard lui-même dont l'entreprise était maintenant énorme grâce aux plantations de coton créées dans le royaume de Naples, avait été sauvé de la faillite grâce à un prêt de un million et demi, consenti par le gouvernement afin de ne pas accroître démesurément le chômage.

L'Enfant à l'oiseau, le magasin d'Ethis qui avait connu

le succès durant des années, végétait et, avec lui, l'atelier d'Emmanuel Caumont son principal fournisseur. Les deux beaux-frères avaient fait le projet de s'associer pour créer dans le Faubourg un grand magasin de meubles fabriqués en série et vendus à des prix accessibles. Ils avaient même pensé vendre le tableau du Tintoret – tant pis pour l'ancêtre – afin de s'installer; mais l'époque n'était propice ni à l'ouverture d'une boutique importante ni à la vente d'un tableau de maître.

– Il faut tout de même que nous fassions quelque chose! répétait Ethis. Nous n'allons pas attendre de ne plus avoir un sou et d'être inscrits aux indigents pour chercher le moyen de gagner notre vie!

Seul le magasin de vêtements *A la Belle Fermière* de Pierre Parisot, l'ami d'Ethis, demeurait achalandé. Les Parisiens de revenus moyens n'achetaient plus de meubles mais ils continuaient de s'habiller. Ce succès persistant donnait à penser à Ethis.

– Les meubles ne se vendent plus et il ne faut pas s'entêter, disait-il. Mais je ne peux tout de même pas ouvrir une boutique de vêtements à deux pas de celle de Pierre, nous fermerions vite tous les deux! Il faut donc trouver autre chose, peut-être une nouveauté, un accessoire à la mode... Regardez, ceux qui ont été assez malins pour fabriquer ou vendre des corsets à baleines et à busc, lorsque les femmes, pour être dans le ton, se sont mises à se comprimer le ventre et les hanches, ils ont fait fortune! On m'a assez dit que j'étais un touche-à-tout, je vais essayer d'utiliser ce méchant défaut!

Ethis, qui avait dû vendre son beau cabriolet, se mit à parcourir à pied les rues de Paris à la recherche d'une idée ou simplement d'un fait anodin, d'une remarque qui déclencherait sa mécanique inventive. Il revint un soir du Palais-Royal, persuadé qu'il fallait fabriquer et vendre des gilets. C'était pour les hommes la dernière mode de les porter droits, à revers, en châles ou en croisure. Toutes les fantaisies étaient permises y compris dans le choix des tissus qui pouvaient être de toutes textures et de toutes couleurs, à pois, à dessins, à fleurs ou en points de tapisserie.

– Jusqu'à présent, seuls les tailleurs coupent des gilets pour leurs clients. C'est trop cher pour les jeunes élégants peu fortunés, les plus nombreux. Je vais voir Richard et lui demander de me montrer les étoffes qui conviendraient et au besoin de les fabriquer.

Le lendemain, Ethis rapportait de chez Richard-Lenoir une dizaine d'échantillons d'étoffes susceptibles de séduire les amateurs de gilets et une autre idée qui, selon lui, devait mettre la famille à l'abri du besoin en attendant que reprenne la vente des meubles. Pour tout dire, il avait inventé les bretelles élastiques! Richard lui avait montré un nouveau tissage qui donnait au tissu une certaine souplesse, lui permettant, quand on cessait de l'étirer, de reprendre aussitôt sa forme primitive.

Plusieurs fois de suite, Ethis avait tendu la bande d'étoffe et l'avait regardée se rétracter. Il semblait fasciné par cette élasticité!

– A quoi joues-tu? demanda Richard intrigué. C'est un de mes ouvriers qui a découvert ce point et je pense qu'on lui trouvera une utilisation pratique.

– Je crois bien que je l'ai trouvée, cette utilisation! Si l'on réussissait à tisser les bandes plus étroites, on pourrait en faire des bretelles!

– C'est vrai, aujourd'hui beaucoup d'hommes retiennent leurs pantalons avec des sangles qui les engoncent et les transforment en manches à balais. Un peu de souplesse les rendrait plus confortables. Ton idée n'est pas bête!

Le soir, Ethis avait longuement parlé avec Marie des idées qui lui trottaient par la tête. Il voyait son magasin vidé de la plus grande partie des meubles et rempli de gilets multicolores que les élégants pourraient assortir à dix sortes de bretelles artistement présentées le long d'une baguette de bois pendue horizontalement au plafond.

– Que risquons-nous? dit-il. Nous avons la boutique, et la première mise de fonds sera minime puisque Richard me fera crédit. Reste la fabrication des gilets et des bretelles. Parisot doit connaître un tas de couturières capables de faire ce travail.

– Tu abandonnerais complètement la vente des meubles? demanda Marie.

– Non. J'en garderai quelques-uns dans la boutique et je pourrai toujours prendre les commandes quand elles se présenteront. Crois-tu qu'Emmanuel acceptera de délaisser son atelier pour m'aider? Je sais bien qu'il préfère les beaux meubles aux gilets à col châle mais il faut vivre!

– Monte le voir tout de suite, il n'est sûrement pas encore couché. Si tu veux mon avis, ton idée est merveilleuse. Antoinette m'avait bien dit que tu n'arrêterais jamais de m'étonner. C'est pour cela que je t'aime!

– Pour cela seulement?

– Non, tu as d'autres qualités qui me plaisent mais je ne te les dirai pas, tu deviendrais vaniteux.

Ethis avait retrouvé le sourire en même temps que l'occasion de se démener pour réussir son affaire. Emmanuel, bien sûr, avait été d'accord, tous deux couraient Paris à la recherche de tailleurs en chambre et de couturières adroites.

– Il faut que nous soyons prêts dès que nous aurons les tissus, lançait Ethis qui imaginait déjà une armée de grenadières de l'aiguille à ses ordres pour satisfaire les clients qui se pressaient devant les étalages de *L'Enfant à l'oiseau.*

Son but ne se bornait pas d'ailleurs à vendre sa fabrication dans son propre magasin. Il envisageait de fournir les meilleures boutiques d'habillement de Paris, à commencer par *La Belle Fermière.* Il devait bien ça à son ami Parisot qui l'avait beaucoup aidé et lui avait prêté l'argent nécessaire aux premières payes des ouvriers et des ouvrières.

Et cela marcha! Ethis encore une fois avait gagné son pari. Des messieurs venaient de l'autre bout de Paris chercher un gilet à fleurs et repartaient avec une ou deux paires de bretelles en supplément. Bientôt il ajouta les cravates au catalogue de la maison. Napoléon avait lancé la cravate royale à flots de points d'Alençon à l'occasion du Sacre, mais c'était un accessoire de grand uniforme et les hommes portaient maintenant couramment la cravate blanche nouée en chou. Les plus raffinés arboraient la cravate longue ou courte à nœud compliqué, à la manière de Brummell qui, malgré le blocus, faisait la mode à Paris.

Devant ce succès, Ethis mourait d'envie d'étendre son activité aux vêtements féminins mais il ne voulait pas concurrencer son ami Parisot. Celui-ci pourtant ne vendait pas le linge de dessous disparu avec la mode du Directoire mais dont la vogue renaissait. Chemises et jupons, que les femmes exigeaient maintenant finement travaillés et brodés, constituaient un nouveau marché dont l'intérêt n'avait pas échappé à Ethis. Prudente. Marie avait mis son mari en garde.

– Attends un peu, laisse ton affaire s'installer tranquillement avant de la développer inconsidérément. Souvent un petit commerce ou une industrie modeste gagne de l'argent alors qu'une grande entreprise s'étouffe et conduit à la faillite. Ton projet de lingerie est excellent mais il faut bien le préparer...

– C'est que, vois-tu, je voudrais acheter une nouvelle voiture. C'est indispensable pour faire le tour des couturières et livrer la marchandise. Les locations finissent par coûter cher et mangent une partie du bénéfice.

– Alors, va, ouvre ton rayon de lingerie mais fais attention. D'ailleurs, ne crois-tu pas que Lucie et moi serions de bon conseil? Nous allons nous occuper des dessous de ces dames!

Eugène Bénard, le père de Marie, s'était tout à fait réconcilié avec son gendre à qui il reconnaissait enfin de réelles qualités. La réussite de sa reconversion l'étonnait et le maire de l'arrondissement la citait souvent comme un exemple dans ses discours. Eugène Bénard lui aussi connaissait la griserie du succès. Il venait d'être nommé membre de la Légion d'honneur et créé chevalier d'Empire. Cela amusait beaucoup Ethis qui éclata d'un rire sonore quand il apprit peu après que son beau-père se faisait appeler maintenant Bénard de Moussignières.

– Enfin, ma chère Marie, le baron et la baronne de Valfroy – car n'oublie pas que tu es baronne – vont pouvoir sans déchoir recevoir ton papa, M. de Moussignières. Remarque que je l'aime bien, Eugène. Et puis, dans le fond, pourquoi un maire honnête et estimé n'aurait-il pas droit d'être récompensé au même titre que les militaires. Ils sont princes, ton père n'est que chevalier, la hiérarchie des honneurs est respectée. Vive le VIIIe arrondissement, vive Bénard, vive l'Empereur!

– Mon grand frère, tu es complètement fou! s'exclama Lucie en éclatant de rire. Heureusement, ta folie a du bon. Sans elle, et sans toi, je ne sais pas ce que nous serions devenus. J'ai appris tout à l'heure que Claude Maheu, le marchand ébéniste du passage de la Boule-blanche vient de faire faillite. C'est au moins la dixième depuis le début de l'année. Le bureau des indigents ne sait plus où donner de la tête. Nous savons, Emmanuel et moi ce que nous te devons!

Emmanuel Caumont s'était fait facilement à son nouveau métier. Sans joie, il avait abandonné son établi et rangé ses outils puis, entraîné par l'enthousiasme d'Ethis qui le considérait comme son associé, il avait vite pris de l'intérêt à la confection des gilets. Habitué à dessiner et à préparer des calibres de pièces d'ébénisterie, il créait maintenant des modèles de gilets et découpait des patrons pour les ouvrières à domicile. Garçon intelligent, travailleur et artiste, il était devenu l'ornemaniste de la maison. Ethis, qui s'occupait essentiellement de la partie commerciale, disait volontiers que sans lui, et c'était vrai, il n'aurait jamais réussi à exploiter ses idées.

Tout allait donc bien chez les Valfroy où Marie élevait sans histoire son deuxième enfant, la petite Antoinette-Émilie. C'était une exception au Faubourg où la crise et les levées successives n'entretenaient pas un climat de sérénité. L'Empereur y était cependant encore populaire. Il avait habitué le peuple aux guerres et aux victoires. Pour les ouvriers, la lente préparation de la campagne de Russie n'était que les prémices d'une expédition comme il y en avait eu beaucoup. Peu d'entre eux d'ailleurs savaient où se trouvait l'empire du tsar considéré hier encore comme un allié fidèle. Les journaux, tous soumis à la censure, annonçaient une promenade de santé dans un pays épouvanté par la puissance de la Grande Armée. Comment les paisibles gens du bois auraient-ils pu s'inquiéter quand, le 23 juin, *Le Moniteur* annonça que l'Empereur avait mis en branle sa formidable force : 550 000 hommes groupés entre la Vistule et le Niémen.

On s'intéressait plutôt au fameux éléphant factice de la Bastille, enfin terminé. Toutes les dimensions du projet adopté par l'Empereur avaient été respectées, l'eau jaillissait bien de la trompe du pachyderme impérial, l'escalier se vissait dans la patte avant droite mais le monument qui une fois badigeonné de couleur marron pouvait faire croire qu'il était en bronze, n'était qu'un stuc fragile promis à une rapide détérioration. De mauvais esprits voyaient un symbole dans ce colosse aux pieds plâtreux dont les journaux célébraient la grandeur [1].

A deux pas de l'éléphant, alors que l'Empereur s'enfonçait dans les steppes à la poursuite d'un ennemi invisible, un complot s'était tramé contre le pouvoir. L'inspirateur en était encore le général Malet. Comment le bouillant militaire avait-il pu conspirer alors qu'il était en état d'arrestation ? Mansuétude coupable ou négligence après dix-huit mois de séjour à la Force et à Sainte-Pélagie, il avait été transféré faubourg Saint-Antoine, dans la maison de santé du Dr Dubuisson où il était censé être surveillé. Or, non seulement il faisait bon vivre dans cette maison plus accueillante qu'une prison, mais le général eut la surprise d'y retrouver d'autres chevaux de retour de la sédition, dont les frères Polignac et le marquis de Puyvert compromis dans l'affaire Cadoudal.

Que peuvent faire des conspirateurs réunis sous le même toit sinon conspirer ? De leur pseudo-prison, Malet et ses amis avaient mis au point un plan diabolique qui faillit réussir le jour où, après s'être évadé, il réussit à faire croire aux troupes de la caserne Popincourt, la plus proche, puis aux chefs de la préfecture de police, que

1. Ce colosse de plâtre restera en place jusqu'en 1840, délabré, abri de milliers de rats. Victor Hugo fera le refuge de Gavroche de « ce cadavre grandiose d'une idée de Napoléon ».

l'Empereur était mort en Russie et que le Sénat, après lui avoir confié le commandement des armées, venait de proclamer la République!

Une maladresse avait mis fin à ce rêve insensé dont la réalisation partielle montrait tout de même la fragilité de la défense du trône impérial. Le Faubourg apprit toutes les péripéties de l'événement en même temps que l'arrestation des coupables. A voir l'attroupement devant la maison de santé, au coin de la rue Picpus, on pouvait se rendre compte de l'intérêt que portait à l'affaire l'ensemble de la population, les uns pour exprimer leur indignation, les autres pour se divertir de l'énorme farce. Une farce qui devait tout de même, un peu plus tard, envoyer Malet et ses amis devant le peloton d'exécution.

Un éléphant de plâtre, un complot avorté, le Faubourg ne vivait pas une actualité exaltante mais les habitants d'un quartier sont plus concernés par les petites choses qui s'y passent que par les grandes dont ils ne savent rien. Comment aurait-on pu, cour des Trois-Frères, deviner qu'à Wilna où elle faisait halte depuis vingt jours, la Grande Armée était déjà désorganisée, qu'elle avait perdu 50 000 hommes, déserteurs, morts de faim ou de dysenterie? Et cela avant même d'avoir combattu le premier Russe! Comment les compagnons qui vivaient chichement de quelques commandes officielles auraient-ils pu deviner que l'Empereur et ses braves ne se couvraient pas de gloire à Smolensk, à Borodino et à Moscou investi, vidé de ses habitants avant d'être incendié, mais qu'ils soutenaient des batailles sanglantes et devaient reculer devant l'hiver et les assauts des cosaques? Comment le Faubourg encore dévoué à Napoléon, aurait-il pu deviner que la décadence était amorcée et qu'elle allait se poursuivre avec une rigueur impitoyable?

Après le froid de l'automne il y eut la glace, les bivouacs sous la neige et la retraite sur la route de Smolensk balisée par les corps qui tombaient. Des 150 000 hommes qui avaient marché sur Moscou, il en restait 13 800 dont 150 cavaliers. Et puis, ce fut la Bérézina, le dramatique passage des ponts sous la mitraille de Koutouzov et l'infernal cortège des rescapés.

A Smorgoni, l'Empereur décida de quitter l'armée afin d'arriver à Paris avant que la nouvelle des désastres eût ébranlé le moral et la fidélité du pays. Le 6 décembre à dix heures du soir, avec Caulaincourt, Lobau et Duroc, Napoléon quitta son dernier quartier général après avoir fait partir le 29e bulletin. Il laissait le commandement à Murat.

Le soir où Napoléon, après avoir brûlé les étapes, arrivait aux Tuileries et se faisait donner tout de suite par Savary, ministre de la Police, des explications sur la conspiration du général Malet, Alexandre Lenoir, confortablement calé sur l'ottomane que Riesener avait fait construire jadis dans son atelier pour Antoinette, lisait et commentait *Le Journal de l'Empire*. Il excellait dans ce genre d'exercice et Ethis, comme sa femme, l'écoutait attentivement en buvant une tasse de tisane de menthe.

– C'est à se demander, remarqua Alexandre, si la campagne de Russie n'est pas le fruit de nos imaginations. Tous les bruits qui circulent dans les milieux officiels que je fréquente sont alarmants. On parle d'une véritable déroute. Eh bien, ce n'est qu'à la page deux qu'un bref communiqué du quartier général donne des nouvelles, d'ailleurs excellentes, de la Grande Armée. En revanche, le journal nous annonce dans un long article que tout va mal en Angleterre où l'opposition whig gagne sans cesse contre le prince régent. Je lis que la misère y augmente dans des proportions effrayantes. Le rédacteur compare le sort prospère et le contentement des ouvriers français aux révoltes causées en Angleterre par l'établissement des machines industrielles.

– Il y a sûrement du vrai là-dedans! dit Ethis qui s'accordait parfois le droit de rouspéter contre le régime mais qui n'aimait pas qu'on attaque Napoléon en qui il voyait encore, comme beaucoup d'autres, le défenseur de la Révolution.

– Tu as raison, il y a toujours un peu de vrai dans

toutes les opinions mais là, je crois qu'on nous monte le bourrichon! Tiens, voilà qu'un autre auteur, un certain M.D., s'extasie sur la magnificence de la récolte qui mûrit sur le continent. Et devine comment se prépare la même récolte en Angleterre? Désastreuse! Le blé manquera cette année. A moins que la Providence n'ait évité dans la distribution des moissons de donner sa part habituelle à notre perfide voisine, je dis que ce monsieur M.D., le journal qui l'emploie et le gouvernement qui encourage la publication de telles sornettes, nous prennent pour des imbéciles. Et vous verrez que si les nouvelles s'aggravent, ce que je ne souhaite pas, la presse officielle, mais il n'y a qu'elle, nous servira de plus en plus ce genre d'inepties. Comme ils sont loin les grands principes de la Révolution!

– Ont-ils jamais existé ailleurs que sur le papier? observa Lucie. Moi je n'oublie pas que c'est en leur nom qu'on a failli guillotiner mon père et que celui de notre tante Félicité est mort sur l'échafaud!

– Je ne vous contredirai pas sur ce point, continua Lenoir, mais oyez plutôt, mesdames, les nouvelles de l'étranger. « Le prince et la princesse Antoine de Saxe sont de retour à Dresde. Les eaux d'Aix-la-Chapelle ont réuni un grand nombre de personnes distinguées : la reine Hortense, Mme de Montmorency, des princesses... » Ou encore : « Le roi de Westphalie a placé son quartier général à Pultisk. Sa Majesté »... l'encre a bavé, on lit très mal mais je crois qu'il s'agit de Jérôme Bonaparte, « jouit d'une santé parfaite ». Voilà qui nous fait bien plaisir. Et pour finir je ne voudrais pas vous cacher cette révélation : « S.M. le roi de Rome a passé la dentition du premier âge. L'auguste enfant tiendra toutes les promesses qui reposent sur sa tête. » Vois-tu dans toutes ces nouvelles, mon cher Ethis, un signe qui rappelle la Révolution? Un enthousiasme qui encourage le patriotisme?

– Quand je vous écoute, dit Ethis, je me dis que vous avez raison mais je ne peux pas m'empêcher d'admirer l'Empereur!

– Eh oui! Savoir se faire admirer... C'est peut-être ça le

génie! C'en est au moins une forme. Ce qui est extraordinaire, c'est que le renom, la popularité de ces êtres d'exception durent alors même que les actions qui les ont motivés sont depuis longtemps entachées par des fautes, des trahisons ou simplement une dégradation de l'intelligence. Napoléon peut engloutir son armée dans les glaces de l'empire russe, il demeurera pour la multitude le prodigieux stratège d'Arcole, de Wagram et d'Austerlitz!

En fait, si le système napoléonien paraissait encore intact, l'insuccès de la campagne de Russie fut vite percé à jour. Les esprits avertis comprenaient que l'irrésistible ascension du sous-lieutenant de Brienne était terminée et la décadence commencée. Les affaires d'Espagne, de Russie et maintenant le pape qu'il retenait captif dans les ors de Fontainebleau, autant d'erreurs qui pesaient lourd dans le destin du surhomme qui, vieilli avant l'âge, obsédé par une gloire qui ne lui souriait plus, continuait à vouloir tout asservir à sa volonté.

Dans ce climat malsain, alourdi par la menace de la coalition de tous les grands pays européens, la vie économique de la France ne pouvait que se dégrader. Au Faubourg, une nouvelle vague de faillites allongeait chaque jour la liste des indigents. A nouveau les ateliers fermaient, et avec eux, des cabaretiers et des commerçants, comme Robert frères et Paradis, importants marchands de bois, qui avaient leur magasin au 47 de la rue de Charenton et leur chantier à la Râpée.

Le soir du 10 octobre, Lucie rapporta une nouvelle qui, sitôt connue, avait bouleversé le quartier : Jacob-Desmalter allait être déclaré en faillite! Si Jacob, le patriarche du bois, et son fils Jacob-Desmalter fermaient, n'importe quelle catastrophe pouvait survenir. Trois ans auparavant, les ateliers de la rue Meslée employaient jusqu'à 350 ouvriers dont une partie travaillaient pour le Garde-meuble et la famille impériale. Qu'une entreprise aussi prospère, fournisseur de l'Empereur, parée de l'estampille la plus célèbre d'Europe soit contrainte de déposer son bilan, semblait impossible à tous les maîtres et artisans.

Et pourtant les ébénistes, menuisiers de sièges, tourneurs, bronziers et ciseleurs qui travaillaient chez Jacob étaient tous rentrés chez eux, la plupart habitaient le Faubourg, en confirmant l'incroyable nouvelle.

Le lendemain, on ne parlait que de ça dans les cours et les impasses du vieux quartier du meuble :

– Si Jacob ferme, comment voulez-vous que nous survivions! disaient les uns.

– C'est l'arrêt des exportations vers l'Angleterre qui est la cause de tout! affirmaient les autres.

– Tout n'est pas perdu, soutenaient les plus optimistes. Les Jacob ne manquent pas de relations et il est impossible que l'Empereur laisse faire, sans rien dire, une chose pareille. Avec tous ceux qui travaillent en sous-traitance pour Jacob-Desmalter, cela va faire au moins cinq cents ouvriers sur le pavé!

– Ah! si l'impératrice Joséphine était encore là! regrettaient les femmes. Elle connaissait bien le vieux Jacob qui avait meublé sa première maison de la rue Chantereine. Elle serait sûrement intervenue.

Hélas! le renom de Jacob, son illustre passé et toutes ses œuvres qui garnissaient les résidences impériales ne purent rien pour enrayer la machine judiciaire. *Le Journal de Paris* daté du 15 octobre 1813 publiait la déclaration de faillite de la maison Jacob-Desmalter qui entraînait la mise sous scellés et l'inventaire de tous les biens. L'arrêt du tribunal de commerce précisait qu'il convenait de comprendre dans l'actif les ateliers, les réserves de bois, les meubles dont la fabrication était achevée et ceux en cours et aussi les appartements personnels avec leur contenu.

Cette condamnation à mort de la plus prestigieuse fabrique française de meubles, assortie de la saisie des biens personnels, était si inattendue et si sévère qu'on se demandait si elle n'avait pas des raisons cachées. Les bruits les plus fous circulèrent, on parla d'une vengeance de Savary à qui le fils Jacob aurait refusé d'offrir douze chaises de salle à manger, d'un geste de mauvaise humeur de Napoléon lui-même à la suite d'une livraison défectueuse... En fait personne n'en voulait aux Jacob, simples victimes d'une administration judiciaire nouvelle et déjà malade de sa bureaucratie.

Fontaine et Percier étaient atterrés. Les deux architectes étaient devenus au cours des ans les amis des Jacob qui avaient si souvent exécuté les meubles dont ils avaient imaginé et dessiné les formes. Sans doute auraient-ils pu, en d'autres temps, intervenir auprès du gouvernement ou même de l'Empereur en personne mais Napoléon et son entourage avaient d'autres préoccupations.

Quelques jours après la déclaration de faillite, Fontaine passa spécialement place d'Aligre pour faire part à ses amis d'une aggravation des sanctions qui le révoltait : Georges Jacob qui avait cédé depuis longtemps ses droits de participation à ses deux fils pensait ne pas être concerné par la mise en faillite de la maison qu'il avait créée. Certes, le coup moral qui lui était porté était terrible mais François Desmalter était encore jeune, il avait trop de talent pour ne pas repartir un jour vers un nouveau succès professionnel... Et voilà que la chute de la maison Jacob se passait encore plus mal qu'il ne l'avait soupçonné.

– C'est affreux! annonça Fontaine. En vertu de quelque papier mal enregistré en son temps le vieux Georges est déclaré solidaire de la faillite de son fils!

– Cela est-il si grave? demanda Lucie.

– Terrible! Georges Jacob est contraint de quitter l'appartement de la rue Meslée qu'il occupait depuis 1775 en y abandonnant tout son mobilier. Où va-t-il aller avec sa femme Germaine qui est malade? A soixante-quatorze ans, c'est une épreuve inhumaine! Le malheureux va en mourir!

– Vous savez que je suis républicain, dit Ethis, mais je suis obligé de penser qu'un roi n'aurait jamais laissé un ouvrier du Louvre ou de l'Arsenal finir ses jours comme un réprouvé!

– C'est sûrement vrai, Ethis, mais je ne peux croire que l'Empereur soit au courant de la situation de Jacob. Je n'ai jamais rien demandé à Napoléon, ni pour moi ni pour mes proches, mais je saisirai la première occasion pour lui dire ce que l'administration dont il est si fier a fait d'un des plus grands artistes de son règne!

L'occasion ne devait pas tarder. Fontaine et Percier travaillaient depuis des mois sur un projet auquel l'Empereur attachait la plus grande importance : la construction d'un palais monumental qu'on nommerait palais du roi de Rome, susceptible d'abriter la cour, les ministres, les bureaux du gouvernement, les officiers de la maison impériale et au moins dix rois à la fois s'il prenait plaisir à l'Empereur de les inviter. Avec les communs, il s'agirait d'une véritable ville bâtie sur la colline de Chaillot et dont le parc s'étendrait jusqu'à Boulogne, englobant le château de la Muette, Bagatelle et une partie du Bois. C'était tellement grandiose que Percier y avait vu dès le début un déchaînement de mégalomanie mais il avait obéi aux ordres et dessiné avec son ami Percier une suite de planches où les innombrables colonnades du palais surgissent comme une forêt de marbre au-dessus d'un ensemble de terrasses, de rampes verdoyantes et de soubassements d'arcades.

Les expropriations et achats de terrains s'étaient faits rapidement. Il en avait coûté deux millions de francs au Trésor et Napoléon avait ouvert un crédit de trente millions pour les travaux qui avaient commencé dès la fin de 1811 par la construction d'un portique à trois arcades donnant sur le quai, face au superbe panorama de l'École militaire.

– Achèverons-nous un jour ce palais qui serait le plus grand du monde? se demandait Fontaine qui, parlant des travaux à ses amis de la place d'Aligre, racontait combien les terrassiers avaient du mal à creuser des fondations dans le sous-sol crayeux de Chaillot.

En fait le sort du palais du roi de Rome s'était joué dans les glaces de la Bérézina. Revenu de la campagne de Russie, l'Empereur avait annoncé à Fontaine qu'il avait réfléchi et réduit ses ambitions :

- L'argent de l'État doit dans sa plus grande part aller à

l'armée. Je voudrais donc un palais moins grand que celui de Saint-Cloud mais plus grand que celui du Luxembourg. Le palais du roi de Rome sera un second palais, après le Louvre. Ce ne sera pour ainsi dire qu'une maison de campagne à Paris car on préférera toujours passer l'hiver aux Tuileries. Je ne veux pas d'une chimère mais d'une chose réelle. Je passerai un jour prochain visiter les travaux.

« Seul avec l'Empereur qui aura oublié pour quelques heures les soucis de la politique en jouant au grand bâtisseur, voilà un instant rêvé pour lui parler de Georges Jacob qui s'étiole dans une institution pour vieillards sans fortune à deux pas du chantier, à Chaillot, pensa Fontaine. Et si je faisais venir Georges et que je le présente à Napoléon en lui racontant sa triste fin? Cela serait encore mieux! »

Par bonheur, l'Empereur était de bonne humeur quand il vint un matin du début de décembre voir l'immense chantier de son rêve réduit à l'état d'un grand pavillon.

– Heureusement, Sire, que nous n'avons pas eu le temps de démolir les cinq cents maisons prévues, votre palais aurait été construit dans un désert. Les cent qui ont été abattues suffiront pour bâtir selon votre dernière décision, dont vous me permettrez de louer la sagesse.

– Vous trouvez? Montrez-moi les nouveaux plans.

L'Empereur se fit expliquer la position exacte du bâtiment central, mesura lui-même en enjambées les distances et se crotta les bottes. Satisfait, il allait remonter en voiture quand Fontaine fit signe d'approcher à Georges qui attendait, mêlé aux ouvriers.

– Sire, permettez-moi de vous présenter le meilleur des menuisiers-ébénistes français. C'est Georges Jacob qui a meublé toutes vos résidences. Je sais que vous appréciez son talent.

L'Empereur regarda dans les yeux le vieil ébéniste comme il regardait les plus braves de ses grenadiers sur le champ de bataille. Jacob qui ne savait trop quelle attitude prendre esquissa une sorte de garde-à-vous.

– Je connais votre nom, monsieur Jacob, ce que vous

faites est très bien, vos œuvres contribuent à la grandeur de l'Empire.

Fontaine qui attendait autre chose de Napoléon qu'un compliment banal enchaîna aussitôt :

– Sire, si je vous présente cet ouvrier qui a construit votre trône et le berceau du roi de Rome, c'est parce qu'il est malade et ruiné. Ses ateliers qu'il dirigeait depuis quarante ans, où il employait encore l'an passé plus de trois cents compagnons, viennent d'être déclarés en faillite. Privé, à soixante-quatorze ans, de tous ses biens, il a dû abandonner l'appartement qu'il occupait avec sa femme, malade elle aussi. Tous deux vivent maintenant dans une institution charitable. Si vous ne faites pas quelque chose pour eux, ils mourront bientôt dans la misère et le chagrin. David, notre grand artiste pour lequel Jacob a travaillé toute sa vie, m'a autorisé à joindre son nom prestigieux à ma requête.

L'Empereur parut touché, il posa quelques questions sur les circonstances d'une faillite aussi regrettable et dit avant de monter la marche de sa voiture :

– Votre infortune est grande, monsieur Jacob, et surtout injuste. Je vous promets d'intervenir et de vous secourir. Fontaine me reparlera de votre cas et nous verrons comment y remédier.

Quand Fontaine raconta l'entrevue à ses amis de la place d'Aligre, il ajouta :

– C'est l'Empereur lui-même qui m'a reparlé de Jacob. Celui-ci pourra dès demain regagner son appartement de la rue Meslée. Au moins pourra-t-il passer chez lui les dernières années qui lui restent à vivre.

– J'en suis heureux, dit Ethis. Antoinette qui aimait beaucoup Georges Jacob aurait apprécié votre intervention...

Il y eut un silence comme presque toujours lorsque l'on évoquait le souvenir de la dernière Dame du Faubourg. Fontaine ajouta :

– C'est aussi en pensant à elle que j'ai arrangé cette rencontre...

Ce jour-là, place d'Aligre, Henri-François Riesener était

là avec sa femme Félicité. Le petit Léon qui venait d'avoir cinq ans jouait dans la pièce d'à côté avec son cousin Bertrand. Félicité était aussi brillante que jolie. Elle plaisait beaucoup aux deux femmes de la maison qui admiraient sa vivacité d'esprit et son intelligence. C'est elle qui relança la conversation sur l'infortune des Jacob.

– Mon père n'était pas ébéniste mais il gardait les œuvres des meilleurs avec une conscience exemplaire. Il les connaissait et les aimait. Souvent il me parlait d'eux, de leur vie, de leur style. La fin de Georges Jacob me rappelle ce qu'il m'a dit peu de temps avant de périr sur l'échafaud : « Il semble qu'une malédiction pèse sur les grands artistes du bois. Boulle, le grand Boulle qui avait gagné tellement d'argent en travaillant pour le roi et pour la cour, est mort ruiné après l'incendie de son atelier du Louvre et de ses collections. A la mort d'Œben, l'inventaire de sa succession se soldait par un déficit, et pourtant lui aussi avait meublé le roi et les princes. Plus près de nous, regardez Riesener qui après avoir fabriqué tant de chefs-d'œuvre pour Louis XVI et la cour se voit rejeté parce que son genre n'est plus de mode. Il a été riche mais il mourra pauvre ! Et voilà qu'aujourd'hui il faut ajouter le nom de Georges Jacob au trio des grands artistes du bois morts ruinés ! Je ne crois pas aux malédictions mais il faut bien avouer que cette similitude dans le malheur a quelque chose d'étrange... Qu'en pensez-vous, monsieur Fontaine ?

– La malchance n'explique pas tout, coupa Ethis. Riesener a souvent répété ici que les artistes du bois étaient de piètres gérants de leurs affaires. Pour Jacob, alors au sommet de sa gloire, il a même dit qu'un jour la multiplication des ateliers et l'accroissement du nombre de ses ouvriers lui joueraient un mauvais tour. Il a même prononcé le mot de faillite possible, ce qui était prophétique. Les artistes peintres ne courent pas les mêmes risques, ils travaillent seuls ou avec quelques élèves. Leur art n'est pas industriel et échappe à la tentation d'un développement suicidaire.

– Et toi, Ethis, remarqua Félicité, ne crains-tu pas, avec toutes tes occupations, de tomber dans le même piège?

– Non, je me suis fixé des règles et des limites. Tous mes employés travaillent à la pièce et à domicile. Je ne leur commande et ne leur paye que ce qui m'a été commandé ou que je suis sûr de vendre. Il faut savoir, dans les temps que nous vivons, rester petit pour pouvoir durer.

– Ethis, dit Fontaine, votre lucidite m'étonne et j'admire votre sagesse. Que ne pouvez-vous en faire profiter l'Empereur! Comme Jacob, il voit trop grand pour ne pas nous mener à la faillite!

Chapitre 11.

COMPAGNON DU TOUR DE FRANCE

Faillite... Un mot terrible qui n'avait pas la même signification dans les ateliers du Faubourg et les allées du pouvoir. Ici, il était la conséquence de quelques factures impayées, là il concernait le bilan impérial où le nombre des morts l'emportait chaque jour davantage sur celui des appelés. Les sénatus-consultes se suivaient qui jetaient dans la guerre des Français de plus en plus jeunes : 250 000 appelés en janvier 1813, 180 000 en avril, 280 000 en octobre, 300 000 en novembre... L'année 1814 débutait sous les plus mauvais auspices. Le corps législatif lui-même renâclait et, fait inouï, votait une adresse qui demandait des garanties à l'empereur ! L'écho de la colère du maître avait franchi les murs de la salle du trône, on se répétait dans Paris ses anathèmes : « Vous avez voulu me couvrir de boue, je suis un de ces hommes qu'on tue mais qu'on ne déshonore pas... Qu'est-ce que le trône ? Quatre morceaux de bois recouverts d'un morceau de velours. Tout dépend de celui qui s'y assied... Est-ce le moment de me faire des remontrances quand 200 000 cosaques franchissent nos frontières ? Vous aurez la paix dans trois mois ou je périrai... »

Car on en était là. Le désastre de Leipzig après celui de la Bérézina avait produit en France une impression terrible. La nouvelle que MacDonald s'était sauvé à la nage et que Poniatowski, après avoir arrêté durant trois heures l'effort des troupes de la coalition, était mort noyé dans l'Elster, montrait aux plus aveugles combien la situation était grave.

La mise en activité, le 8 janvier, des 30 000 hommes de la garde nationale sous le commandement en chef de l'Empereur qui avait pris le général Moncey comme major général, toucha les quartiers ouvriers où jusque-là la popularité de Napoléon était demeurée à peu près intacte. François Richard sortit pour l'occasion son uniforme de commandant de la 8e légion, titre qu'il devait à l'Empereur lui-même. Il l'endossa sans enthousiasme, d'abord parce qu'il ne se sentait pas une âme de soldat, ensuite parce que ses affaires allaient très mal depuis l'institution d'une taxe sur l'entrée du coton en France. Lui aussi se voyait menacé par la faillite et la ruine alors que quelques mois auparavant il employait encore près de 20 000 personnes dans ses cultures et ses manufactures.

Cette fois, les affaires d'Ethis subissaient malgré la légèreté de leur organisation, le contrecoup des événements. Les gens du Faubourg comme les bourgeois parisiens pensaient moins aux gilets à fleurs qu'à la menace qui pesait sur la capitale. L'enfant trouvé n'avait pourtant pas perdu son âme de « vainqueur ». Il croyait encore à l'Empereur qui, avec son armée dépecée, accomplissait des prodiges dans la campagne de France. Il laissa éclater sa joie quand il lut dans *Le Moniteur* que dix drapeaux russes, prussiens et autrichiens pris à Montmirail, à Vauchamps et à Montereau avaient été remis à l'Impératrice et que les sabres des généraux ennemis prisonniers étaient exposés dans les salons des Tuileries où Marie-Louise et la cour faisaient de la charpie.

– Vous voyez bien, disait Ethis, que tout n'est pas perdu !

Le Faubourg avec lui reprenait espoir et voyait s'estomper les craintes d'une douloureuse bataille de Paris.

En repartant aux armées, Napoléon avait ordonné que, quoi qu'il arrivât, on empêchât sa femme et son fils de tomber entre les mains des ennemis dont les dernières défaites n'avaient, hélas ! guère entamé les forces. Prudents, ils craignaient toujours les retours du génie de l'Empereur et savaient que leurs généraux, dans toute leur vigueur, ne valaient pas Bonaparte dans sa décadence. Mais ils avaient pour eux le nombre et l'armement. Les victoires françaises étaient plus spectaculaires qu'utiles. Bientôt Marmont et Mortier livraient avec l'énergie du désespoir les dernières batailles sous Paris tandis que l'Impératrice et le roi de Rome quittaient les Tuileries pour le château de Blois avec Cambacérès et Joseph. Talleyrand, lui, restait. La dernière berline verte aux armes impériales avait à peine franchi les grilles du palais qu'il faisait préparer son hôtel de la rue Saint-Florentin pour y accueillir le tsar.

Il n'y avait maintenant plus rien à espérer. Le prince de Wurtemberg marchait sur Vincennes pour débusquer les Français des bords de la Marne et pour tourner les hauteurs de Charonne et de Belleville. Les Russes attaquaient les villages de Romainville et des Prés-Saint-Gervais tandis que la garde prussienne se préparait à occuper la butte Montmartre. La guerre était aux portes du Faubourg qui, sans consignes, sans chefs et sans armes retrouvait le courage des grandes heures de la Révolution et se pressait vers la barrière du Trône où quelques bataillons de vétérans, soutenus par un détachement de dragons et une batterie de la garde nationale, tentaient d'arrêter les innombrables troupes de Wurtemberg.

Ethis était de ceux qui voulaient se battre jusqu'au bout mais il eut juste le temps de se joindre, au coin de la rue Picpus, à la poignée de braves qui, conduits par les élèves de l'École polytechnique, s'opposait à une avant-garde de cosaques. Il s'arma d'un fusil pris à un soldat mort et lutta avec les autres. Surpris, les Russes reculèrent... Cet effort sublime et dérisoire signait sans doute l'un des derniers sursauts de la France de Napoléon. Bientôt les masses ennemies déferlaient dans la grand-rue du Faubourg. Blessé à l'épaule, couvert de sang, le « vainqueur de la Bastille » avait réussi à se traîner à temps pour ne pas être piétiné écrasé par les chevaux des cosaques jusqu'à l'entrée du dépôt de fourrage de la Ville dont il connaissait heureusement tous les recoins pour y avoir joué aux soldats lorsqu'il était enfant. Il se reposa un moment contre le portail en regardant, désespéré, les cavaliers du tsar s'engouffrer dans le vieux Faubourg en poussant des cris de victoire, puis réussit en rampant à gagner une réserve de foin. Épuisé, il se laissa tomber et s'évanouit.

Ethis n'avait prévenu personne de sa décision de se joindre aux volontaires du quartier. Place d'Aligre, c'était l'affolement. Marie était en pleurs et Lucie n'arrivait pas à la calmer.

– Je suis sûre qu'il a été se battre place du Trône et qu'il est mort avec tous ceux qui ont été écrasés par les cosaques. Mon Ethis, mon fou d'Ethis!...

Le déferlement des troupes ennemies dans le Faubourg avait plongé tout le quartier du bois dans un abattement profond. On savait le désastre possible, on ne l'imaginait pas si proche. Une fois encore les familles se réunissaient à l'abri des cours et des passages pour échanger des nouvelles et compter les disparus. La bataille de la barrière du Trône prenait des dimensions épiques. Le retour des morts et des blessés dans les voitures du loueur Quélen de la rue de Cotte, transformées en ambulances, dramatisait encore les scènes d'angoisse et de désespoir.

Marie, qui avait voulu descendre, allait comme une folle d'un groupe à l'autre pour demander aux rares rescapés s'ils avaient vu Ethis. Les réponses étaient vagues, certains l'avaient aperçu un fusil à la main, haranguant ceux qui hésitaient à entrer dans le carré formé par les polytechniciens. L'ouragan passé, personne ne se souvenait de personne...

Emmanuel Caumont essayait de voir plus froidement la situation.

– Il y a une chose certaine : Maintenant, tous les morts et les blessés ont été ramassés. Ethis n'en fait pas partie, donc il doit être encore là-bas. Sans doute a-t-il réussi à se mettre à l'abri. Je vais y aller voir.

– Je t'accompagne, dit Marie qui avait retrouvé un certain calme.

- Moi aussi bien entendu, ajouta Lucie. Nous allons le retrouver!

Le gros de la troupe passé, seuls quelques véhicules des troupes alliées remontaient encore la grand-rue suivis parfois de traînards ou d'estafettes à cheval qui ignoraient les regards méprisants et haineux que leur lançaient de rares passants. Il ne fallut pas plus de dix minutes à Emmanuel et aux deux femmes pour rejoindre le lieu du combat jonché d'armes, de caisses de munitions et d'équipements. Les seuls corps qui demeuraient sur place étaient ceux des Russes fauchés par les balles des volontaires. Sans doute les ennemis qui avaient emmené leurs blessés reviendraient plus tard chercher les morts. Les deux femmes s'étaient retirées à l'écart pour échapper à ce spectacle qui, sur une centaine de mètres carrés, étalait toute l'horreur des champs de bataille. Emmanuel, lui, avait été voir si Ethis ne gisait pas parmi les ennemis tués.

– Ethis n'est pas là! dit-il soulagé. Donc il est vivant. Blessé peut-être mais vivant. Nous allons passer en revue tous les endroits où il aurait pu se réfugier

Ils questionnèrent les habitants dont les portes s'ouvraient sur le Faubourg, mais personne n'avait remarqué un blessé essayant de se mettre à l'abri. « Nous avions d'ailleurs verrouillé l'entrée! » dirent-ils presque tous.

– Il ne nous reste plus qu'à revenir, dit Emmanuel. En continuant naturellement notre recherche.

Le dépôt de fourrage était assez éloigné du lieu du combat et ils étaient passés devant en arrivant sans songer à s'y arrêter. Pourtant, en apercevant le grand portail entrouvert, Lucie eut un espoir.

– Ethis m'a emmenée là plusieurs fois, quand j'étais petite. Il voulait me montrer les endroits où il se cachait, enfant des rues, pour jouer et même pour dormir. Il est tout à fait possible qu'il se soit réfugié dans l'un de ces bâtiments qu'il connaissait comme sa poche.

C'est là en effet qu'ils découvrirent Ethis étendu sur le côté dans le foin rougi de sang. Il était pâle et avait les yeux entrouverts.

– Je vous attendais, murmura-t-il. Mais que vous avez été longs à venir! Je commençais à me demander si quelqu'un aurait l'idée de venir me chercher ici! Je m'y suis traîné, mais maintenant je ne peux plus bouger. J'ai l'épaule fracassée et ai perdu beaucoup de sang.

Marie n'avait pas attendu la fin pour s'agenouiller, lui prendre la main et éclater en sanglots: « Mon Dieu! répétait-elle, dans quel état es-tu! »

– Restez là toutes les deux, dit Emmanuel, je cours chercher une voiture et on va le transporter aux Quinze-Vingts. Si je trouve un médecin, je le ramène avec moi. En attendant, essayez de trouver de l'eau et rafraîchissez-lui le visage, mais ne touchez pas à son bras qui a l'air de ne plus saigner!

Ethis fut soigné par un élève de Corvisart qui avait eu un pied gelé durant la campagne de Russie et avait dû abandonner l'armée. Il retira avec adresse la balle qui s'était logée dans l'épaule.

– Tu as de la chance! dit-il en couvrant d'une voix bourrue mais chaleureuse les gémissements d'Ethis. Les os ne sont pas touchés et ton bras refonctionnera bientôt comme avant. Se faire blesser à la barrière du Trône! On n'a pas idée. As-tu été à l'armée?

– Non, jamais, mais c'est ma spécialité de recevoir de la mitraille dans le faubourg Saint-Antoine. La première fois, c'était au cours de l'émeute chez Réveillon! répondit Ethis dans un pauvre sourire. Une fois à la jambe, une fois au bras... j'espère que je m'arrêterai là!

C'est sur son lit d'hôpital qu'il apprit le lendemain la signature de la capitulation de Paris. Il sourit tristement et demanda : « L'Empereur? » Alexandre Lenoir venu lui rendre visite lui répondit :

– Il ne fait aucun doute que Napoléon va être obligé d'abdiquer. Quand je pense que tu as failli te faire tuer par les cosaques en luttant à un contre cent! Tu vois Ethis, je préfère mes statues aux hommes, elles sont belles et n'ont pas de ces gestes insensés qui font les héros morts. Encore que les sculpteurs adorent glorifier ceux-ci dans le marbre..

Ethis était rentré chez lui, place d'Aligre, à peu près remis de sa blessure. Il commençait à pouvoir se servir de son bras et pouvait faire des petites promenades dans le quartier où, heureusement, les troupes alliées ne faisaient que de rares incursions. Il allait jusqu'au magasin où Emmanuel se morfondait, les clients étant devenus aussi rares que les partisans de Napoléon. A part les inconditionnels, comme Ethis, qui avaient encore le courage de défendre l'Empereur cloîtré à Fontainebleau en attendant de gagner son ridicule royaume de l'île d'Elbe, le maître d'hier ne comptait plus guère de fidèles. Ceux qu'il avait faits princes l'abandonnaient, c'est encore dans les faubourgs que son image gardait le plus de prestige. En face des Bourbons qui s'apprêtaient à revenir, elle représentait le dernier symbole de la Révolution. Et puis, les gens de Saint-Antoine n'oubliaient pas que l'Empereur leur avait épargné la misère par les commandes officielles et les aides des bureaux de bienfaisance.

Ethis allait mieux mais il était triste. La lecture des journaux qui, hier encore, encensaient Napoléon et qui, maintenant, consacraient des colonnes entières à la gloire du roi de Prusse, au tsar et à l'empereur d'Autriche, le mettait en fureur. Il allait d'atelier en atelier dire ce qu'il pensait de tous ceux qui retournaient leur veste. Chez lui, il était plus calme, il modérait ses éclats car Marie et Lucie, après l'avoir soigné avec amour, lui manifestaient sans retenue leur mauvaise humeur. Elles n'excusaient pas son acte de folie et il devait écouter, penaud, les deux femmes lui reprocher son irresponsabilité.

– Comment as-tu pu, avec deux enfants que tu prétends aimer et une femme qui, paraît-il, t'est chère, aller te jeter dans un combat perdu d'avance, où personne ne te demandait de t'engager? C'est un vrai miracle que tu sois encore vivant. Imagine ce que nous serions devenus si tu étais mort! Ce n'est pas la peine de travailler comme un diable pour nous faire une vie plus agréable si tu cours te faire embrocher par les cosaques à la première occasion venue. Recommence une fois encore cette folie et je pars avec les enfants!

Et sa sœur Lucie insistait :

– As-tu pensé à la réaction d'Antoinette si elle avait été là? Elle ne t'aurait jamais pardonné! On peut être un illuminé à quinze ans mais l'être encore à quarante, ce n'est pas supportable. Qui donc croyais-tu étonner en allant tirailler à la barrière du Trône?

Ethis acceptait les semonces car il les savait justifiées. En attendant que la colère des femmes s'apaise, il se demandait lui aussi ce qui avait pu le pousser à accomplir un acte dont il reconnaissait l'inutilité. Ce n'était pas le patriotisme, sentiment qui ne l'avait jamais beaucoup troublé, ce n'était même pas un acte de dévotion pour l'Empereur, il n'aurait tout de même jamais été jusque-là. Alors? Alors il se disait que l'enfant violent et révolté dont Antoinette et Bertrand de Valfroy avaient réussi à endiguer les fureurs gardait dans son âge mûr des impulsions difficiles à maîtriser. Il n'en était pas tellement mécontent, mais il se jura pourtant de réfléchir à deux fois avant de commettre une nouvelle folie.

La chaude soirée de la place du Trône oubliée, le Faubourg avait vite retrouvé son calme. Privé de la presse de ses thuriféraires, Napoléon voyait son image s'étioler. Le bouquet impérial se fanait dans son vase doré. Faute de nouvelles, on oubliait, entre la barrière et la Bastille, le parfum de poudre et d'encens qui avait longtemps charmé le quartier du bois. L'Empereur nu n'était déjà plus d'actualité, la popularité cédait la place à l'indifférence, la question importante était maintenant de savoir si le retour des Bourbons allait permettre au vieux faubourg du bois de retrouver un minimum d'activité. Pour l'heure, celle-ci était tombée avec l'Empereur. Encore une fois, artisans ébénistes et menuisiers se croisaient les bras devant leurs établis vides de tout bois à raboter, à sculpter ou à chantourner.

Les grandes industries installées au Faubourg subissaient elles aussi le choc de la défaite. Sauvée par deux fois de la faillite, l'entreprise de Richard-Lenoir avait dû fermer ses ateliers les uns après les autres. Riche à millions quelques mois auparavant, François Richard avec ses machines menacées de saisie et ses plantations inaccessibles n'était plus qu'un homme pauvre à la recherche de nouvelles idées. Comme les Jacob, comme les manufacturiers de glaces qui avaient dû licencier, comme les fabricants de faïence de la rue de la Roquette.

C'est dans ce climat de découragement que le Faubourg apprit l'arrivée à Paris du comte d'Artois. Rares furent ceux qui se déplacèrent jusqu'à Notre-Dame pour apercevoir le frère de Louis XVI gagner les Tuileries à la tête d'un brillant cortège. C'est à peine si, le lendemain, les lecteurs du *Moniteur* s'étonnèrent en apprenant qu'à côté des Mortemart, des Montmorency et des Rohan, le journaliste de service avait distingué la présence de Marmont, Ney, Oudinot, Moncey et Kellermann.

Quinze jours plus tard, l'entrée de Louis XVIII suscita un peu plus d'intérêt mais le nouveau roi arrivant par Saint-Ouen, les gens du quartier ne se levèrent pas assez tôt pour aller contempler sa voiture tirée par les huit chevaux blancs habituellement attelés au carrosse de Napoléon. Ethis, pourtant, l'éternel badaud, avait emmené son fils Bertrand au Carrousel, plein comme les jardins et les terrasses du château d'une foule enthousiaste.

– Tu vois, lui dit-il, cette foule qui acclame le roi aujourd'hui est la même qui, le 10 août 1792, demandait la tête de Capet et, le 2 décembre 1804, applaudissait l'Empereur et l'Impératrice. Ces gens que tu vois accueillir avec des cris de fête la duchesse d'Angoulême, l'orpheline du Temple, ont applaudi il n'y a pas si longtemps à la décapitation de son père et de sa mère...

A quinze ans, Bertrand était un grand garçon fin et intelligent. Au contact d'Antoinette et de ses amis, son esprit s'était ouvert de bonne heure et il comptait parmi les meilleurs élèves du Lycée impérial qui n'avait pas encore été débaptisé. Il avait écouté Ethis avec le sourire un peu moqueur qu'il devait à sa mère et l'entraîna vers un groupe de jeunes filles vêtues de blanc et parées de fleurs de lis qui, un peu plus loin, appelaient en chantant la bénédiction de la « fille de Saint Louis » :

– Les paroles que t'inspire cette foule inconstante me paraissent fort sages, dit-il à son père, mais crois-tu qu'elles s'accordent avec ta participation déraisonnable à la bataille de l'autre jour?

– Tu n'as pas tort... Tout de même, il y a une grande différence entre les deux cas. La foule d'aujourd'hui est veule et stupide, celle de la barrière du Trône était inconsciente mais généreuse!

Bertrand serra fort le bras de son père.

– Mon père, je t'aime et je t'admire comme tu es... Et tu es un homme bien!

Ethis s'arrêta, regarda son grand fils et essuya une larme.

– Tu vois, Bertrand, il faut que nous parlions plus souvent. Moi aussi je suis content de toi. Tiens, je vais t'avouer quelque chose : les quelques mots que tu viens de dire ont beaucoup plus de chance de m'assagir que les jérémiades des femmes!

Bras dessus, bras dessous, les deux complices rentrèrent au Faubourg, non sans s'être arrêtés au passage chez *Fusch,* le cabaretier de la Bastille qui vendait le blanc aigrelet de ses vignes du Petit-Charonne et des saucisses grillées.

– J'espère que ta mère ne va pas encore me servir une soupe à la grimace! dit Ethis en arrivant place d'Aligre.

L'odeur qui embaumait l'escalier les rassura. Des rires fusaient de la cuisine où Marie et Lucie mitonnaient un ragoût de mouton aux haricots. Tandis que Bertrand embrassait sa tante, Marie se jetait dans les bras d'Ethis.

– Je t'aime, mon mari terrible!

Place d'Aligre, la situation devenait difficile : le magasin *L'Enfant à l'oiseau* ne vendait ni meubles, ni lingerie, ni gilets. Les économies du ménage Valfroy fondaient aussi vite que le pain augmentait.

Ethis se débattait comme un beau diable, imaginait de nouvelles affaires avec Pierre Parisot victime lui aussi de la crise. Ils envisageaient de se lancer dans la fabrication de corsets, redevenus à la mode depuis quelques années. *Le Journal des Dames* était plein de ces accessoires et vantait la « forme Médicis qui efface le ventre et les hanches ». Les médecins s'étaient mis de la partie et signalaient les dangers d'un laçage trop étroit. Un nommé Bratel avait lancé « le corset à la Ninon » sans baleines, un busc assurant la rigidité. Ethis, lui, pensait utiliser le tissu que lui fabriquait Richard pour ses bretelles.

– Les hommes n'achètent plus de bretelles mais les femmes ne se passeront pas de corset. La mode est à la taille de guêpe, profitons-en !

L'idée n'était pas mauvaise mais difficile à réaliser. Il fallait du temps pour trouver des ouvrières spécialisées et surtout des capitaux. Heureusement, Emmanuel Caumont reçut une commande inespérée qui permit à la famille de respirer et d'attendre des lendemains plus prospères. Jacob-Desmalter ne pouvait utiliser ses ateliers, toujours sous séquestre, ni prendre de commandes en son nom. Cependant sa réputation était si grande que beaucoup de clients, et non des moindres, continuaient à faire appel à lui. Pour les satisfaire, il s'adressait aux meilleurs artisans menuisiers ou ébénistes. C'est ainsi qu'Emmanuel avait repris avec joie le chemin de son atelier de la rue Saint-Nicolas afin de fabriquer vingt-quatre chaises et fauteuils du genre Louis XVI et quatre meubles d'appui destinés au général Schwarzenberg.

– D'autres commandes suivront, avait dit Jacob-Desmalter. Les princes et les maréchaux de la coalition profitent de leur séjour à Paris pour meubler leurs châteaux à la française. Mais ils ne veulent pas entendre parler du mobilier de l'Empire ! Heureusement, mon père a conservé dans un vieil atelier-débarras de la rue de

Montreuil, celui de ses débuts, tous les gabarits et les dessins des sièges qu'il avait fabriqués au temps du roi Louis XVI. Vous allez donc, mon cher Caumont, faire un retour en arrière. Ces messieurs sont ce qu'ils sont, mais ils nous permettent de manger à notre faim.

Après avoir été l'obligé d'Ethis, Emmanuel sauvait la famille et cette idée doublait le plaisir qu'il éprouvait en empoignant le bédane de la main gauche et le maillet de la droite pour ouvrir des mortaises bien nettes dans les angles de pieds. Allons, il n'avait pas perdu la main en dessinant des gilets ! Il était même capable d'éprouver encore un petit frisson de jouissance quand les tenons d'un devant de bergère glissaient sans effort dans le hêtre et s'y fixaient si parfaitement qu'une simple cheville pouvait remplacer, comme il se doit sur un siège de bonne famille, le vulgaire encollage.

On avait donc retrouvé un roi. Au début, cela avait paru un peu bizarre après toutes ces années qui avaient suivi la décapitation de Capet mais le Faubourg, finalement, semblait se résigner et accepter ce Bourbon qui ne faisait pour l'instant que réparer les pots cassés par Napoléon sur la fin de son règne. Et puis, comme disait Alexandre Lenoir, qu'aurait-on pu mettre à sa place ? La république ? Il n'y avait pas de parti ni d'hommes d'État républicains. Un Bonaparte ? On en sortait et le carré de rois qui faisaient la loi en France n'en voulaient sous aucun prétexte. Le tout était de savoir quel genre de royauté préparaient Louis XVIII et ses conseillers parmi lesquels on retrouvait de grands personnages de l'Empire.

L'exemple venant d'en haut, les notables de moindre importance se ralliaient sans vergogne à la Restauration. C'est ainsi qu'Ethis apprit un jour que son beau-père, Eugène Bénard, le chevalier d'Empire, avait été anobli une seconde fois par le décret royal du 2 août 1814.

– Mon cher beau-père aura vraiment été l'homme de tous les régimes. Mais après tout, il est un bon maire et je ne vois pas ce qu'on gagnerait à en changer. Quant à l'anoblissement, c'est le fruit mûr qui tombe dans le panier de la fidélité convertible. Le bon Eugène n'a plus qu'à attendre un nouveau changement pour devenir marquis !

Le lendemain, Emmanuel rapporta une triste nouvelle : Georges Jacob venait de mourir dans son appartement de la rue Meslée retrouvé depuis six mois, veillé par sa femme Jeanne-Germaine et son fils Jacob-Desmalter. Le hasard l'avait fait s'installer hors des limites du Faubourg, mais le vieux maître était resté très attaché au quartier de ses débuts. Ami de Riesener et de Fontaine, il venait plusieurs fois l'an place d'Aligre assister aux soupers du mercredi, chez Antoinette qu'il avait connue toute jeune. Avec Georges Jacob disparaissait le dernier des géants d'une époque, celle des ébénistes des rois, qui avaient su faire franchir au métier du bois les frontières d'un art authentique.

Ethis fut touché par cette disparition d'autant plus inattendue que Fontaine avait quelques jours auparavant dit que le maître, heureux d'avoir pu rentrer chez lui, avait retrouvé toute sa santé. Il y avait bien les ateliers qui demeuraient fermés mais il attendait avec espoir que, l'honnêteté des Jacob enfin reconnue, son fils puisse réembaucher ses compagnons et reprendre son activité. Ethis annonça qu'il se rendrait le lendemain à l'enterrement de Georges.

– Je n'oublierai jamais, dit-il, qu'il m'avait pris en amitié et qu'il m'a encouragé et aidé quand j'ai voulu ouvrir mon magasin. Il m'a même confié des petits meubles à vendre, ce que la maison Jacob n'a fait pour personne d'autre.

– J'irai bien sûr avec toi, ajouta Emmanuel. J'ai surtout eu affaire à son fils mais les quelques fois où je l'ai rencontré, il m'a parlé de mon père, le vieux Caumont comme il l'appelait ; il avait débuté avec lui, apprenti chez Louis Delanois...

L'église de Saint-Nicolas-des-Champs [1] était bien trop

1. Cette église possède encore douze sièges d'acajou fabriqués dans les ateliers Jacob pour la salle capitulaire. Sans doute un don du menuisier à sa paroisse.

petite, le 6 juillet 1814, pour contenir le monde du bois venu du Faubourg et de la rue de Cléry enterrer leur compagnon. Jeanne qu'il avait épousée à seize ans disparaissait dans ses voiles de deuil, entourée par son fils Jacob-Desmalter et son petit-fils Alphonse. Derrière, dans les travées, juste après la famille, les ouvriers de la maison – certains y avaient leur établi depuis plus de trente ans – formaient une sorte de haie d'honneur et d'affection. Ils étaient tous là les compagnons des seize ateliers de la rue Meslée qui avaient fabriqué, rien que durant les quinze dernières années, pour près de dix millions de francs de meubles dont un tiers destiné à l'exportation. Tandis que le curé de la paroisse disait la messe des morts, Ethis et Emmanuel essayaient de mettre des noms sur toutes ces figures empreintes de tristesse, celles des menuisiers et des ébénistes, les plus nombreuses, mais aussi celles des sculpteurs, des doreurs, des polisseurs, des mouleurs, fondeurs, ciseleurs, serruriers-mécaniciens et tapissiers. La réunion de tous ces compagnons autour du cercueil du maître, permettait de mesurer l'importance du temple que Georges Jacob avait réussi durant sa vie à consacrer au Meuble, dieu lare qu'ils vénéraient autant que le fils du charpentier Joseph. Leurs prières pour le mort rejoignaient celles que leur dictait cette foi du menuisier, chevillée dans le chêne depuis le fond des temps : « Faites que rouvre bientôt cette maison, honneur de notre métier et de nos talents, qui nous fait vivre avec nos familles. Vous savez, Dieu tout-puissant, que Georges Jacob fut un honnête homme et un honnête ouvrier ! »

La longue file des gens du bois suivit le corps de Georges jusqu'au nouveau cimetière du Père-Lachaise. En attendant que fût gravée la dalle de pierre au nom de la famille, le fossoyeur planta dans la terre une simple croix de bois de hêtre, celui dont Jacob faisait ses sièges. François-Honoré, dit Jacob-Desmalter, avait tenu à la raboter et à l'assembler lui-même au petit matin. Son visage était grave mais il ne pleurait pas. A Fontaine et

Percier, les fidèles amis venus lui dire leur tristesse, il dit doucement :

– J'ai juré à mon père, avant qu'il passe, que l'estampille des Jacob continuerait après lui et que la maison dont il était si fier reprendrait bientôt son activité. Je sais tout ce que vous avez fait pour le maître, il vous doit ses six derniers mois de sérénité, je n'ose pas aujourd'hui vous demander de m'aider à respecter mon serment...

C'est Percier qui répondit :

– Pourquoi ? L'estime et l'admiration que nous avons portées à votre père, vous les partagez depuis longtemps. Nous espérons reprendre bientôt une collaboration stupidement interrompue. Il faut que les ateliers Jacob-Desmalter revivent. Nous allons nous y employer. David malheureusement ne pourra guère nous aider car il n'est pas en odeur de sainteté. Le nouveau gouvernement lui reproche davantage d'avoir été député montagnard et régicide que sa dévotion à Napoléon... Mon crédit et celui de Fontaine ne semblent heureusement pas menacés. Vous pouvez compter sur notre aide.

Finalement le Faubourg révolutionnaire s'accommodait de la Restauration comme il s'était accommodé de l'Empire. Seule une disette grave aurait pu le réveiller de sa léthargie mais, au contraire, l'activité commerciale et artisanale, brisée par le blocus et la désastreuse campagne de Russie, donnait des signes de reprise. Les maîtres de Saint-Antoine avaient conservé leur prestige et les commandes commençaient à revenir. Les ateliers se réveillaient au bruit des scies et des maillets, les marchands regarnissaient leurs boutiques en évitant les meubles napoléoniens que les événements n'engageaient pas à proposer aux acheteurs. Puisqu'on avait retrouvé un roi, ceux-ci semblaient préférer tout naturellement les styles anciens.

Ethis, avec son flair de la mode, guettait ce renouveau avec impatience. Il avait renoncé aux sous-vêtements et aux colifichets pour être prêt à aider le vieux Faubourg à retrouver sa vocation.

– Napoléon parti, disait-il à Emmanuel, il n'y a plus

d'avenir pour le genre d'ameublement qu'il a encouragé. Un nouveau style verra le jour mais, en attendant, les gens vont se reporter sur les meubles des siècles précédents. Il faut leur offrir ce qu'ils demandent!

– Tous les vieux secrétaires et les commodes marquetées vont ressortir des greniers, remarqua Marie.

– Je ne crois pas. Ceux qui ont les moyens de se meubler ou de se remeubler ne vont pas vouloir de cabinets usagés ni de sièges branlants. Il va falloir leur fabriquer des commodes du temps de Louis XV ou de Louis XVI avec des tiroirs qui glissent bien, des marbres neufs et des bronzes sortant de la dorure. Je ne sais pas ce qu'en pensent les autres, mais je suis sûr que j'ai raison. Mon cher Emmanuel, il faut se mettre au travail, embaucher quelques bons compagnons, pas trop, et copier les Œben, les Carlin, les Weisweiler, les Riesener. Je crois que Jacob-Desmalter a de beaux jours devant lui en remettant en fabrication les modèles créés par le vieux Georges au siècle dernier.

– Il en est conscient, coupa Emmanuel. Je travaille sur sa commande en utilisant les anciens gabarits de son père! Mais ce n'est pas tout de fabriquer et d'embaucher, il faut de l'argent pour payer les ouvriers et pour acheter le bois. Or je te rappelle que nous vivons sur l'avance que m'a consentie Jacob!

– Je le sais mais je sais aussi que l'argent ça se trouve. Peut-être que mon beau-père...

– Non! interrompit Marie. Je ne veux rien demander à mon père. D'abord parce que tu méprises ouvertement son goût ridicule des honneurs, ensuite parce qu'il a sacrifié une bonne partie de sa fortune à ses rêves de condition sociale. Il a vendu sa part de la fabrique de papier peint et la fonction de maire n'enrichit pas un honnête homme.

– Tu as raison. Ne misons pas nos espoirs sur la couronne du chevalier Bénard de Moussiguières. Mon ami Richard attend un nouveau prêt du gouvernement qui ne vient pas. Je ne peux compter sur lui...

– Et si nous vendions le portrait de l'aïeule? dit Lucie.

Alexandre Lenoir nous a dit qu'il valait une certaine somme. C'est peut-être le moment de faire appel à la seule famille qui puisse nous tirer d'affaire!

– Bon Dieu! je l'avais oubliée, ta grand-mère d'Italie. Je vais dès demain aller trouver Lenoir et lui demander de nous aider à en tirer le meilleur parti.

– Tu pourrais aussi voir Fontaine qui connaît tous les amateurs de Paris. Et puis, avec tous ces princes russes, autrichiens ou prussiens qui semblent tant se plaire à Paris, c'est bien le diable si tu ne trouves pas l'acheteur fortuné que nous cherchons!

Huit jours plus tard, le petit tableau du Tintoret était vendu par l'intermédiaire d'une actrice de la Comédie-Française, amie d'Alexandre Lenoir, au comte de Bombelle, ministre d'Autriche à Paris, qui voulait l'offrir à son protecteur Metternich. Mlle Baucourt qui triomphait chaque soir dans le rôle d'Angélique avait réussi, en jouant de son charme et en s'appuyant sur une estimation forcée d'Alexandre revêtue de cachets officiels, à tirer 18 000 francs du portrait de l'amoureuse de Denis Thirion. C'était très bien payé et la Baucourt reçut un cachet de 2 000 francs pour avoir joué une si bonne pièce au diplomate. Elle remercia par un sourire en disant qu'elle aurait tenu le rôle pour rien : elle était bonapartiste et détestait les Autrichiens.

Les seize mille francs qui restaient ne constituaient pas un capital énorme mais il était suffisant pour acheter du bois et engager Tombert, un compagnon qui avait longtemps travaillé chez Jacob et qui sculptait admirablement le bois. Avec le travail, la gaieté était revenue place d'Aligre. Les avances des anciens clients d'Ethis qui avaient retrouvé le chemin de *L'Enfant à l'oiseau* afin de changer le décor impérial de leur maison contre la grâce d'un salon à la reine, permettaient de vivre convenablement tout en assurant la trésorerie de l'affaire.

A la fin du printemps, l'atelier reçut le renfort d'un apprenti. Après trois années de lycée, Bertrand avait déclaré qu'il était temps d'apprendre le métier s'il voulait commencer son tour de France à dix-huit ou dix-neuf ans. Sa mère poussa les hauts cris et dit qu'il était trop doué pour arrêter ses études et qu'il pouvait avoir une autre ambition que celle de devenir un ouvrier du bois. Ethis savait que Bertrand réaliserait coûte que coûte son rêve, il s'insurgea :

– Tu es bien comme ton père ! Le travail manuel ne te paraît pas digne ! Et moi, qu'est-ce que j'étais quand tu m'as épousé ? Pas même ouvrier, je ne savais rien faire, qu'aider Alexandre à transporter des statues ! Aujourd'hui, es-tu malheureuse ? Regrettes-tu notre vie ? Si le petit veut être ébéniste, il faut le laisser faire. Et accepter qu'il parte sur le tour de France. Il ne deviendra peut-être jamais riche mais il sera un homme !

– C'est le tour de France qui te fait peur, maman ? dit Bertrand en prenant sa mère dans ses bras. Mais aujourd'hui il s'agit d'une grande promenade ! Ce n'est pas comme il y a deux ou trois siècles quand il fallait faire presque tout le chemin à pied. Maintenant il y a des voitures, des coches d'eau...

– Il paraît que les jeunes qui appartiennent à des sociétés rivales se battent comme des chiffonniers quand ils se rencontrent en chemin et qu'il y a souvent des morts !

– C'est moins dangereux que d'aller se battre contre les cosaques à la barrière du Trône ! lança inconsidérément Ethis qui se vit gratifier d'un regard assassin.

Bertrand calma sa mère en l'embrassant tandis qu'Emmanuel vantait les bienfaits d'un tour de France qu'hélas ! il n'avait pu entreprendre à cause de la Révolution. Lucie surenchérit et n'hésita pas à appeler les mânes d'Antoinette à la rescousse :

– Antoinette aurait été tellement heureuse de voir Bertrand devenir un grand ébéniste ! Et de le voir partir la canne de Jean Cottion sur l'épaule...

Finalement, comme toutes les mères qui s'étaient trouvées dans le même cas, Marie s'était rendue.

– Vous êtes tous contre moi, j'espère que vous avez raison et qu'il n'arrivera rien à mon petit. Mais tout de même...

– Je te signale, maman, que je ne pars pas demain matin et que je vais au contraire revenir à la maison. Je ne suis pas mécontent d'abandonner le dortoir et la nourriture du collège pour mon bon lit de plumes et ta succulente cuisine.

Tout finit par un grand éclat de rire. Le lendemain à six heures, on marchait avec le soleil, Bertrand gagnait en chantant l'atelier d'Emmanuel. Sitôt arrivé il fut prié de prendre un balai et de nettoyer le sol puis d'allumer le feu pour faire chauffer la colle.

– Ici, lui dit Emmanuel, tu es un apprenti comme un autre et tu feras toutes les tâches d'un apprenti, c'est-à-dire d'abord les corvées. Tu apprendras aussi le métier. Dis-toi que Riesener, les Jacob et moi n'avons pas débuté autrement!

Bertrand répondit qu'il était prévenu et prit le balai de bon cœur.

Ethis avait réussi à remplir d'une façon satisfaisante son carnet de commandes. Il prenait contact avec des clients éventuels, rentrés dans les fourgons de Louis XVIII et essayait de retrouver la filière qui lui avait permis naguère d'exporter des meubles en Angleterre. Surtout, il informait les nombreux diplomates de l'alliance séjournant à Paris qu'il était « en mesure de leur vendre des meubles de toutes les époques fabriqués dans les meilleurs bois par les ébénistes et les menuisiers les plus habiles du monde ».

Ce travail de promotion qu'il était le premier à avoir entrepris portait ses fruits. Déjà Emmanuel devait se décharger d'une partie des commandes sur des ateliers voisins. Tout cela n'empêchait pas Ethis de suivre les événements avec la passion qui lui était habituelle. Alors que le Faubourg demeurait indifférent à la politique indécise du roi tenaillé entre ses ultras et l'opposition bonapartiste, Ethis lisait la presse, comparait les commentaires des principaux titres et essayait de lire entre les lignes. Son grand plaisir était d'en discuter avec Alexandre Lenoir et Fontaine lorsqu'ils passaient place d'Aligre.

Les journaux avaient annoncé avec un retard de plusieurs jours le départ furtif de Napoléon de l'île d'Elbe et son débarquement à Golfe-Juan. L'événement était si inattendu et si considérable que le peuple du Faubourg, tiré de son apathie, commença à s'y intéresser. Le nom de Bonaparte qui avait presque complètement disparu des conversations y reprenait la première place. Les uns suivaient avec jubilation l'avance de Napoléon, d'autres pensaient que ce retour spectaculaire ne pouvait qu'aboutir à un échec après avoir déclenché une nouvelle guerre, certains enfin riaient de l'énorme farce que jouait l'empereur déchu aux royalistes, au tsar, aux princes d'Autriche et d'Allemagne.

Ethis avait bien changé qui, aujourd'hui, se rangeait du côté des rieurs et des sceptiques mais se demandait si ce nouveau coup d'éclat n'allait pas replonger l'art et l'industrie du bois dans le marasme des dernières années de l'Empire. Ce sentiment d'inquiétude se fit encore plus vif lorsque Lenoir vint annoncer, le soir du 19 mars, que Louis XVIII venait de faire ses malles pour retourner en exil avec une précipitation et un affolement qui rendaient cette seconde émigration irrésistiblement grotesque.

Alexandre Lenoir, plus voltairien que jamais, voyait dans les circonstances inouïes qui avaient marqué le retour de « l'Aigle », une occasion supplémentaire de mépriser la majeure partie de ses contemporains.

– J'ai conservé, dit-il, quelques titres du *Moniteur* de ce mois. Si un jour j'écris mes mémoires, ils y figureront en bonne place. Oyez plutôt, braves gens du Faubourg, Jacobins, bonapartistes, révolutionnaires et royalistes de tout ordre, voilà qui prouve que le papier de presse peut tout supporter sans déchirer l'aveuglement du lecteur-citoyen. Je vous lis les titres dans l'ordre chronologique de leur parution, du 3 mars à aujourd'hui :

« L'anthropophage est sorti de son repaire. »

« L'ogre de Corse vient de débarquer à Golfe-Juan. »

« Le tigre est arrivé à Gap. »

« Le monstre a couché à Grenoble. »

Remarquez que jusque-là le personnel royaliste ne croit

pas au danger. Seuls, paraît-il, les augustes participants au Congrès de Vienne s'émeuvent. Et puis, peu à peu, le doute s'installe à la cour et dans les salles de rédaction qui en sont des dépendances. Les qualificatifs deviennent moins sauvages :

« Le tyran a traversé Lyon. »

Les plumitifs de l'officiel *Moniteur* apprennent alors le ralliement de Ney qui avait promis à Louis XVIII de lui livrer Bonaparte pieds et mains liés. Nouvelle sourdine :

« L'usurpateur a été vu à 60 lieues de la capitale. »

« Bonaparte (tiens, on l'appelle par son nom) s'avance à grands pas mais il n'entrera jamais à Paris ! »

« L'Empereur (il a retrouvé son titre) est arrivé à Fontainebleau. »

Je peux vous dire à quelques mots près le titre du journal de demain : « Sa Majesté impériale a retrouvé son château des Tuileries au milieu d'une foule enthousiaste ! » Si je me suis trompé, je vous offre à souper chez *Bancelin* !

– Il y a quelques années, dit Ethis, une telle lecture m'aurait mis en rage mais l'enfant terrible devient sage. Il a écouté les leçons de sa chère femme et de sa douce sœur, il ne croit plus à rien et n'ira sûrement pas se faire trouer la peau pour tous ces illusionnistes !

– Voilà, Ethis, mon élève, comment j'aime t'entendre parler. Ah ! si les saints et les hommes illustres dont nous avons sauvé les statues du dépotoir de la Révolution pouvaient nous raconter leur véritable histoire et nous avouer comment ils ont gagné l'éternité par le génie du sculpteur ! Peut-être regretterions-nous d'avoir arraché leur marbre aux vandales qui étaient peut-être des justiciers de Dieu...

C'était là le genre de discours qui, naguère, plongeaient Antoinette dans le ravissement. Aujourd'hui, Ethis plus que Marie et Lucie qui considéraient Lenoir comme un aimable plaisantin, y prenait plaisir. Il enviait son maître de pouvoir jongler ainsi avec les mots et les idées. Il disait à son fils Bertrand :

– Tu es trop jeune pour comprendre et goûter tout ce que cache la conversation d'Alexandre Lenoir mais essaie tout de même d'en faire ton profit. Quand le tour de France t'aura mûri l'esprit, c'est comme lui que j'aimerais t'entendre raisonner. Si j'ai gagné un peu de sagesse en vieillissant, c'est à Lenoir que je le dois!

Le Faubourg était balayé d'un vent chaud dû plus à la saison estivale qu'à la passion. L'opinion ne suivait plus. Comment la France aurait-elle pu croire que Napoléon, aidé par Benjamin Constant, était vraiment décidé à faire ce qu'il avait toujours refusé : une part à la liberté. Personne ne prenait au sérieux l'« Acte additionnel aux constitutions de l'Empire » rédigé par l'ancien ami de Mme de Staël promu conseiller d'État.

– C'est un bateau de papier perdu dans l'océan de difficultés où se débat l'Empereur! disait Lenoir. Songez qu'il doit faire face à la coalition qui se reforme et qui, cette fois ne le lâchera plus, avec pour seul atout un peuple découragé et la pauvre armée que Davout essaye de reconstituer. Je ne parle pas de la trahison permanente de Fouché, maître de la police et de tous les secrets impériaux, qu'il doit subir pour ne pas sombrer tout de suite. Avec à Paris le duc d'Otrante, car il l'a fait duc, et Talleyrand au Congrès de Vienne, Napoléon ne peut plus s'en sortir.

Ethis avait du mal à admettre un jugement aussi pessimiste.

– Mais l'Empereur n'est pas seul. Il lui reste ses fidèles comme Caulaincourt, Ney, Drouot, Davout et même Masséna qu'il n'aime pas, paraît-il, mais qui est un soldat loyal.

– Eh oui! Et toute une armée de dignitaires aveuglés par leur vanité, mais ce n'est pas avec eux qu'il réussira à vaincre les armées étrangères qui se pressent déjà aux frontières. A propos, Marie, il paraît que votre père s'est rallié à l'Empereur?

– C'est hélas! la vérité. Ethis a essayé de l'en dissuader mais mon pauvre père est incorrigible. Il se livrerait au diable pour garder sa mairie où il se croit indispensable. Le pire, c'est qu'il n'agit pas par intérêt...

Ethis l'interrompit :

– Il m'a tout de même dit qu'il s'était toute sa vie rangé du côté du pouvoir et que cela ne lui avait pas mal réussi. J'ai trouvé cela désagréable et je lui ai prédit qu'il regretterait cette dernière volte-face. On s'est quittés fâchés une fois de plus!

– Tu vois bien que tu n'y crois plus à ton Napoléon! dit Lenoir en souriant.

Le Faubourg qui avait assisté à tant de changements depuis vingt-cinq ans se moquait de tout cela. Le retour de l'Empereur n'avait pas trop affecté la reprise du travail et l'on se disait avec fatalisme qu'il ne servirait de rien de s'inquiéter à l'avance d'événements sur lesquels on ne pouvait avoir aucune influence. C'est ainsi qu'une manifestation organisée au champ de Mai à l'occasion de la remise des drapeaux aux troupes nouvellement formées ne suscita pas l'intérêt escompté. Ce n'était, raconta Fontaine qui y avait assisté pour les besoins de sa charge, qu'une froide et pâle réminiscence de la fête de la Fédération de 1790 et de la distribution des aigles. Comment aurait-il pu en être autrement alors que l'Europe coalisée s'apprêtait à écraser le héros de la fête!

L'écho de la défaite de Waterloo ne releva pas le Faubourg de son indifférence. D'abord on ne l'apprit qu'avec plusieurs jours de retard, ensuite Napoléon avait perdu d'autres batailles et personne ne pouvait préjuger des conséquences qu'elle pouvait entraîner. En fait, ce n'est que le jour où l'armée anglo-prussienne fut annoncée aux portes de Paris que le quartier du bois commença à s'émouvoir. On apprit du même coup que le général Exelmans avait remporté une victoire à Versailles et que Davout, commandant de la défense de la capitale, venait de demander à l'ennemi les conditions de la reddition de Paris. Personne ne comprenait ce qui se passait à quelques kilomètres de la Bastille. Si l'on avait gagné pourquoi se rendre? Et si l'on se rendait qu'allait-il advenir de l'Empereur et de son gouvernement?

Le 8 juillet, Ethis apporta *Le Moniteur* qui annonçait une nouvelle stupéfiante : le retour de Louis XVIII, prévu dans la journée!

– On n'en finit pas d'entrer et de sortir aux Tuileries en ce moment! Cette fois je n'irai pas! dit-il.

– Tu as tort, dit Alexandre Lenoir qui venait d'arriver. Les Prussiens font sécher leur linge sur les grilles du palais et campent au Carrousel. C'est toujours un spectacle divertissant que celui de soldats faisant leur petit ménage au sortir du champ de bataille. Je suis sûr que les Parisiens vont accourir et, pourquoi pas, acclamer les vainqueurs de Waterloo comme ils applaudiront demain les trois monarques alliés qui doivent dîner chez le roi. *Asinus asinum fricat!*

– Ce qui veut dire, monsieur le Savant? questionna Lucie.

– L'âne se frotte à l'âne. C'est une admirable maxime qui illustre parfaitement les temps intéressants que nous vivons.

– Vous serez toujours aussi cynique! lança Marie. Savoir l'ennemi dans le palais des Tuileries ne prête pas aux discours plaisants.

Alexandre éclata de rire.

– A suivre votre raisonnement, chère Marie, nous n'aurions pas eu souvent l'occasion de plaisanter depuis le jour historique où Ethis a pris la Bastille. Tenez, la preuve que je ne suis pas l'être indigne que vous pensez, je songe avec horreur aux innombrables ânes de tous les pays d'Europe qui sont morts de s'être frottés les uns aux autres, sans même savoir pourquoi, depuis un quart de siècle. Tout cela pour en arriver au sinistre gâchis d'aujourd'hui! Non, vous avez raison, il n'y a ce soir aucune raison de se réjouir. A moins que ce ne soit pour ne pas pleurer. A propos, belles dames, m'offrirez-vous à souper pour me faire oublier les tristesses du jour?

– Vous savez bien que vous avez votre couvert mis quand vous le souhaitez. Et cela ne date pas d'hier!

– C'est vrai, la maison a toujours accueilli le célibataire que je suis avec beaucoup de chaleur. J'ai vécu avec vous tous les tourments et les joies de la famille mais je ne peux tout de même pas m'installer à table sans vous demander votre permission.

– Ce qui m'intrigue, dit Marie, c'est que vous arrivez presque toujours les soirs où nous avons eu envie, Lucie et moi, de nous mettre en cuisine. On ne vous voit jamais les jours de brouet maigre ou de soupe au lait.

– Le flair, ma chère, le flair! Je sens le fumet de votre cuisine à l'autre bout de Paris et j'accours. C'était pareil, n'est-ce pas Ethis? au temps où nous chassions l'œuvre d'art. Je ressentais à une lieue le moindre coup de marteau sur le marbre d'une statue comme si je l'avais reçu moi-même. Alors nous sautions dans la voiture et fouette cocher! nous allions sauver dans quelque abbaye un buste ou un bas-relief promis à la destruction. Je préfère, Dieu merci, exercer mes dons de voyant à propos des mets succulents que vous préparez dans le secret de votre cuisine et qui pourraient être servis à des anges, si ceux-ci rendaient encore visite aux Terriens comme au temps de Loth.

– En somme vous les avez remplacés. Le faisan que nous allons goûter convient-il, *a priori,* au chérubin Alexandre?

– Un faisan! Dieu tout-puissant, merci encore une fois d'avoir dirigé mon nez et mes pas dans la bonne direction en ce soir de juillet. Mais comment avez-vous pu vous procurer un faisan durant ces événements qui gênent le ravitaillement de Paris?

Marie, d'un geste du menton, désigna Ethis :

– C'est grâce à votre élève, maître Lenoir. Nous voyant en difficulté, il a été voir l'un de ses amis, ancien « vainqueur de la Bastille » bien entendu et braconnier habile qui exerce sa coupable profession sur les terres des religieux de Saint-Maur.

– Vous allez déguster ce faisan en lieu et place du banquier Laffite, annonça Ethis. Son cuisinier l'avait retenu pour un dîner offert par son maître à un confrère saxon de passage à Paris mais mon ami Victor n'a pas hésité à me le donner quand il a su que nous n'avions pas mangé de viande depuis deux jours.

– Et l'on trouvera encore des gens pour affirmer que la prise de la Bastille fut un acte inutile! s'écria Lenoir. Mais je suis venu aussi pour vous annoncer une bonne nouvelle. L'ennemi bivouaque dans nos palais mais la Justice poursuit sa marche imperturbable de tortue : un concordat vient d'être homologué qui permet à Jacob-Desmalter de réoccuper ses ateliers. Ses créanciers avaient depuis longtemps reconnu sa parfaite probité ainsi que celle du vieux Georges...

– ... Qui n'aura malheureusement pas pu assister à la reprise de sa maison! soupira Lucie.

Lucie et Marie avaient préparé le faisan de M. Laffite à la braise, dans la grosse cocotte bardée de lard et de tranches de bœuf très minces. L'oiseau était tendre et délectable. Lenoir qui ne débarquait jamais les mains vides avait apporté deux bouteilles d'un cru de la haute Bourgogne :

– Encore mon don de divination! L'honorable M. Brillat-Savarin, expert comme vous le savez dans l'art du bien-manger, a longuement médité sur les qualités de l'oiseau dont nous allons faire notre bonheur et il a dit à peu de chose près que ce mets de haute saveur doit être dégusté avec justement ce vin de Bourgogne que j'ai choisi sans savoir quel mets il accompagnerait. Coïncidence? Petit bienfait de Dieu en faveur d'honnêtes chrétiens qui savent goûter les bonnes choses qu'il a créées? A savoir... En attendant, monsieur Caumont, soyez assez aimable pour remplir nos verres!

Victoire Delacroix était morte quelques mois auparavant après une courte maladie. Elle avait vécu repliée dans sa maison de Charenton et, depuis la mort de sa sœur, n'était presque jamais plus venue à Paris. Eugène, en revanche, qui faisait des études classiques au Lycée impérial en même temps que Bertrand, était devenu un habitué de la maison. C'était un grand garçon mince aux traits fins dont la distinction frappait à la première rencontre. La disparition de sa mère l'avait profondément atteint et l'on avait cru un moment que sa santé fragile ne supporterait pas un tel choc, mais il avait découvert place d'Aligre l'affection et la chaleur qui le sauvaient. Il y retrouvait son cousin avec lequel il s'entendait bien et parlait de ses projets. Il voulait devenir peintre et Bertrand ébéniste. Tous deux dessinaient. Bertrand n'était pas maladroit mais Eugène montrait des dispositions exceptionnelles et donnait de vraies leçons à Bertrand dont il faisait des portraits très réussis qui étonnaient l'oncle Henri.

– Tu es doué, lui disait-il. Je n'ai jamais rencontré un garçon de ton âge dessiner d'instinct aussi parfaitement que toi. Il faudra quand même que tu prennes des leçons. Les conseils d'un bon maître te feront gagner du temps. Si tu veux vraiment devenir un artiste, je t'aiderai à entrer dans l'atelier d'un peintre qui t'enseignera les côtés techniques du métier que tu mettrais des années à découvrir seul.

– Je ne souhaite que cela, mon oncle. J'ai bien travaillé au lycée et je suis prêt à suivre tes conseils. J'aurais bien aimé être poète mais c'est avec un crayon et des couleurs que je rendrai le mieux ma pensée. Quant à l'imagination, j'en déborde, elle est je suis sûr aussi indispensable au peintre qu'au poète!

– Je veux pourtant te mettre en garde. Tu ne gagneras pas tout de suite de quoi vivre et même plus tard, quand tu auras réussi, tu ne rouleras pas sur l'or.

– Mais toi, mon oncle, la peinture t'a nourri avec ta famille...

– Mal! J'ai dû peindre tellement de tableaux contre mon gré! Aujourd'hui je n'ai presque plus de commandes, la mode des portraits du début de l'Empire est passée, et je crois que je vais être obligé de m'expatrier. On m'offre une situation: peintre officiel à la cour de Russie...

– Tu vas t'en aller si loin? Laisser Félicité et ton fils Léon?

– C'est pour les faire vivre que je pars. Je vais gagner là-bas beaucoup d'argent!

Un mois plus tard Henri Riesener prenait le chemin de Moscou après avoir placé Eugène chez Pierre Guérin dont l'atelier était aussi célèbre que les tableaux qu'il exposait au Salon. Quelques années auparavant, il avait eu Géricault pour élève et venait d'être nommé membre de l'Institut. Le chemin lumineux d'Eugène Delacroix s'ouvrait dans l'enthousiasme de la jeunesse. Celui de l'aventure, le dernier, bifurquait pour Henri Riesener vers les neiges moscovites...

Lucie avait vainement essayé de retenir son oncle en lui montrant qu'il était monstrueux d'abandonner sa femme et son enfant de sept ans pour aller travailler à l'autre bout du monde. En fait, Henri quittait sa famille comme il avait jadis quitté celle de ses parents pour aller combattre en Italie et en Égypte.

– Il n'y a rien à faire, dit Ethis. L'oncle Henri est un aventurier et l'envie de partir balaye pour lui, à certains moments, toute autre considération. S'il n'était pas parti pour la Russie, il aurait été ailleurs. Mais il reviendra!

– En attendant, la pauvre Félicité va se retrouver seule. Jamais je ne lui pardonnerai cet abandon!

L'embarquement de l'Empereur à bord du *Northumberland* pour Sainte-Hélène permettait enfin à ses ennemis de souffler et à Louis XVIII de s'asseoir sur son trône sans crainte d'en être délogé. L'activité du Faubourg, ralentie durant les Cent-Jours, reprenait et Ethis avait pu racheter un cabriolet. L'atelier de son beau-frère et associé Emmanuel Caumont avait dû être doublé par un vaste local loué dans la rue Traversière à un ancien fabricant de colle qui s'était retiré dans sa maison de Charonne. Trois nouveaux établis y avaient été installés, dont un pour Bertrand qui se révélait un ouvrier adroit et commençait à rendre des services. Il ne reparlait plus du tour de France mais sa mère, en le voyant prendre de l'âge et des muscles, savait bien qu'il n'avait pas renoncé et attendait, anxieuse, le moment où il lui annoncerait son départ. Un décret annonçant que désormais la grand-rue du faubourg Saint-Antoine se nommerait faubourg Royal fit la joie de tout le quartier. Comme si l'on pouvait débaptiser le Faubourg! La décision était si saugrenue que personne ne songea un instant à la prendre au sérieux. Le décret passa aux oubliettes populaires.

Fontaine, par respect de la mémoire d'Antoinette dont la mort atroce le culpabilisait encore, demeurait fidèle à la place d'Aligre. Il ne se passait pas de semaine sans qu'il allât voir « ses deux petites sœurs », comme il appelait Marie et Lucie. En fait, il aimait bien, après une rude journée passée en visites ou devant sa planche à dessiner, se retremper dans la chaude atmosphère du logement d'Ethis et Lucie, et parler avec Emmanuel Caumont des meubles en vogue. Percier et Fontaine qui avaient dessiné tant de sièges et de lits sous l'Empire regardaient avec une certaine nostalgie le style qu'ils avaient créé avec David tomber en disgrâce au profit d'un genre Louis XVI dont on exagérait les détails.

– Refaites les meubles d'hier si la clientèle le demande, disait Fontaine, mais bon Dieu! ne les surchargez pas de perles et de raies de cœur!

Caumont et Ethis se défendaient :

– Ce sont les meubles de l'Empire qui pèsent des tonnes avec leurs formes massives et leurs énormes bronzes!

– Ils représentaient au moins un style alors que vous cherchez désespérément le vôtre. Remarquez que c'est un peu de notre faute. Durant ces vingt dernières années ce sont les dessinateurs qui sont devenus créateurs de meubles, les ébénistes se contentant de les exécuter. Cela a entraîné une uniformité des modèles, pas heureuse, je le concède. Il n'existait pas, avant, deux commodes identiques, l'invention, la fantaisie de l'ébéniste empêchaient le rabâchage..

– Ce sont les protestations de Riesener qui recommencent à l'envers! dit avec malice Lucie. J'étais petite mais je me rappelle encore mon grand-père je l'ai toujours appelé ainsi, défendre ses commodes et ses bureaux.

Ethis, lui, ne s'intéressait pas trop à ces discussions. Il préférait sentir le vent, être le premier, avec Emmanuel, à exploiter une mode nouvelle, même s'il ne s'agissait pas vraiment d'un renouvellement de style. Il se rappela que durant le Blocus certains ébénistes avaient essayé de remplacer l'acajou devenu rare par des bois clairs, l'érable ou le citronnier. Puisque maintenant les gens souhaitaient des meubles plus légers, plus gais, pourquoi ne pas lancer la mode des bois indigènes? Félix Rémond, un ébéniste normand venu très jeune à Paris et qui avait travaillé chez Molitor, avait déjà réalisé quelques pièces de ce genre pour le Garde-meuble impérial. Il restait à exploiter commercialement l'usage de ces bois clairs. Ethis s'y employait fébrilement tout en continuant de vendre des commodes et des sièges inspirés directement du Louis XVI. Avec beaucoup de gentillesse, Fontaine aidait Emmanuel Caumont à créer des petits meubles, psychés, coiffeuses, guéridons d'après ses modèles du temps de l'Empire en en allégeant les formes et en les décorant, non plus par des bronzes dorés envahissants mais par des incrustations en filets ou en rosaces de différents bois plus foncés comme l'ébène ou l'amarante.

Ainsi, l'usage des bois clairs, né de l'absence de l'acajou cubain dont l'Angleterre contrôlait le commerce et qui répondait au désir de nombreux clients soucieux de vivre dans une atmosphère plus légère et surtout plus gaie, contribuait à élaborer sinon un style, du moins une ébauche de style inspirée des formules du Directoire.

Une fois encore, Ethis avait vu juste. Les guéridons en bois de frêne ou en loupe d'orme incrustés de citronnier, de racine d'if et de délicats filets d'ébène se vendaient très bien sous l'estampille d'Emmanuel, « E. CAUMONT », qui rêvait de la voir fleurir sur des meubles plus somptueux et des ensembles qui lui permettraient de donner libre cours à son talent. Comme pour Ethis, ce n'était pas encore la renommée, la grande qui vous installe au Walhalla de l'ébène, entre Œben et Jacob, mais la réussite qui donne du cœur à l'ouvrage et vous permet de faire vivre votre famille dans l'aisance.

Le succès d'Ethis arrivait au moment où son beau-père voyait s'effondrer tout espoir d'obtenir un poste de préfet, ultime objectif d'une carrière dont les échelons se confondaient avec les régimes successifs qu'il avait servis. Son dernier ralliement à l'Empereur lors des Cent-Jours et son élection à la Chambre étaient cette fois un faux pas. Louis XVIII qui l'avait anobli disgracia Eugène Bénard pourtant prêt à changer son écharpe tricolore contre la cocarde blanche. Il eût été facile à Ethis de triompher, de prendre sa revanche, mais l'enfant trouvé était un seigneur. Il ne s'était pas gêné pour railler l'homme de tous les régimes quand celui-ci avait des pouvoirs mais maintenant que sa carrière politique se trouvait ruinée, il n'aurait pour rien au monde accablé son beau-père, et Marie lui en était reconnaissante.

Alors que, tout à leur tâche, Ethis et Emmanuel ne s'intéressaient que de fort loin aux embarras de la monarchie restaurée, face aux ultras, aux libéraux et aux vétérans de l'Empire réduits à la demi-solde, ils reçurent leur première commande officielle. Et quelle commande! Ils la devaient à Fontaine qui vint un soir leur annoncer la bonne nouvelle.

– Un navire de la Royale vient de rapporter une tranche de bois de teck qui mesure, tenez-vous bien, deux mètres quatre-vingt-dix de diamètre! Embarrassé, le ministre de la Marine m'a fait demander ce qu'on pouvait en faire. Tout de suite, j'ai répondu : une table. Et j'ai pensé que l'atelier du maître Caumont pourrait prendre en charge la construction de cette table selon le projet que le Garde-meuble m'a prié de réaliser. Qu'en dites-vous mes amis?

Les deux beaux-frères restaient muets. Emmanuel, inquiet, se demandait s'il serait capable d'exécuter un meuble aussi considérable et Ethis soupesait les avantages que leur association pourrait retirer de cette commande prestigieuse. C'est lui qui le premier donna libre cours à son enthousiasme :

– C'est merveilleux, monsieur Fontaine! Emmanuel va faire un chef-d'œuvre. Comment vous remercier...

– Ne me remerciez pas. Dites-vous qu'Antoinette éclaterait de joie, si elle était là, de vous voir entreprendre un pareil travail. Mais attention! Il s'agit d'une entreprise difficile qui n'a rien à voir avec les guéridons que vous fabriquez, très joliment d'ailleurs. Tenez, regardez le dessin rapide que j'ai fait tout à l'heure. Vous verrez que transformer cette bûche géante de chêne de Malabar en table d'apparat n'est pas une chose simple. Sachez qu'elle est destinée au salon bleu des grands appartements du roi!

Le jeune Bertrand, qu'on n'appelait plus à l'atelier l'apprenti mais l'aspirant, suivait la scène passionnément. Il regardait le croquis de Fontaine par-dessus l'épaule de son père et murmura :

– Nous allons faire cette table à l'atelier! Quelle chance! J'espère, Emmanuel, que tu me feras participer à cette œuvre?

– Bien sûr mon garçon, on aura besoin de toi. Tiens, tu sculpteras les montants en forme de sirènes!

C'était évidemment une plaisanterie car les sirènes imaginées par Fontaine étaient de véritables statues de bois que seul un très bon sculpteur pouvait exécuter. On rit et Emmanuel poursuivit :

– Ces six sirènes ailées vont être la difficulté de l'affaire. Je ne suis pas un mauvais sculpteur mais je connais mes limites, je ne suis pas capable de mener à bien un pareil travail. Il faudra trouver quelqu'un... Dans quelle sorte de bois voyez-vous ces montants, monsieur Fontaine? Pas en teck j'espère...

L'architecte sourit

- Non, Dieu merci! Il faudra qu'Ethis trouve des blocs d'orme assez importants. Ce ne sera pas facile mais je lui fais confiance.

On discuta longtemps sur le dessin de Fontaine, sur la ceinture de la table prévue en orme sculpté elle aussi et sur le plateau lui-même, d'un seul morceau, qui devait bien peser plus de cinq cents livres. De quoi rêver... Toute la famille rêva la nuit durant. Bertrand, lui, se vit juché sur la table au milieu du salon bleu des Tuileries, sa canne de compagnon sur l'épaule, applaudi par toute la cour, le roi en tête. Étreint par l'émotion, il perdait l'équilibre et tombait de son piédestal. Cela le réveilla et il entendit sa mère l'appeler pour lui dire qu'il était l'heure de se lever et de rejoindre l'atelier.

La table de Malabar devint la grande affaire de la place d'Aligre. Percier avait fourni une suite de dessins aquarellés très fouillés et des plans cotés qui laissaient peu de place à l'improvisation mais dont la précision allait beaucoup faciliter la tâche d'Emmanuel. Un matin une voiture à deux chevaux conduite par des marins vint livrer rue Traversière le plateau de teck, ce qui causa un grand branle-bas dans le quartier. La pièce de bois ne passait pas par la porte, il fallut faire le tour par le passage et casser une fenêtre pour l'introduire dans l'atelier. On l'installa sur deux établis en attendant de savoir comment on allait l'attaquer pour parfaire sa circonférence et diminuer son épaisseur.

Ethis avait fini par dénicher à Bercy, dans les réserves d'un marchand de bois, les billes d'orme que le sculpteur devrait transformer en sirènes après que les ébénistes les auraient dégrossies et travaillées dans la forme. Il fut plus difficile de trouver un artiste assez habile pour se charger du travail. Durant l'époque napoléonienne la sculpture avait pratiquement disparu des meubles et, comme cela était arrivé plusieurs fois au cours des siècles, on avait cessé de former des apprentis et les « fines lames » étaient rares. Emmanuel finit par circonvenir un vieil artisan qui avait été autrefois l'un des compagnons de Riesener et qui avait abandonné depuis longtemps la sculpture, faute de travail. Bernard Cagnard, établi avec son fils Charles au 105 de la grand-rue du Faubourg dans la cour du Bras-d'or, fabriquait des tables à jeu inspirées de Leleu et de Riesener. L'idée de reprendre ses gouges, soigneusement rangées dans des trousses, le tentait mais il avait peur de ne plus être à la hauteur.

– Il y a plus de dix ans que je n'ai pas touché mes outils

de sculpteur. Tiens, regarde la paume de ma main droite, il n'y a plus trace du moindre durillon... Et puis les tables se vendent, et je ne veux pas laisser tomber le fils.

– Je vous comprends, monsieur Cagnard, mais je trouve qu'il est dommage, pour une fois que l'État commande un meuble sculpté, d'être obligé de refuser. Regardez au moins les dessins de Fontaine. Ce n'est pas un meuble ordinaire que nous allons faire! Vous seul pouvez sculpter ces sirènes. Si vous refusez il faudra que nous cherchions en province. On m'a dit qu'à Orléans il y avait encore un bon sculpteur...

Finalement, le maître Cagnard se laissa convaincre :

– C'est pour l'amour de l'art et du bois, tu sais, car je vais avoir du mal à retrouver mon coup de gouge... Enfin, il faut montrer aux gens du Garde-meuble qu'il existe encore à Paris un sculpteur digne de ce nom!

Il fallait aussi se faire aider pour la préparation de la bille de teck. Ethis engagea Jean-Simon Schaeffer, ébéniste et mécanicien au 137, près de la rue Cotte, spécialiste pour le sciage des bois des îles. Et l'aventure commença, dans un climat d'enthousiasme mêlé d'anxiété, comme chaque fois qu'un artiste entreprend une œuvre qui sort de l'habitude. Bertrand était certainement le plus passionné, il participait enfin à une vraie création et tout en dégauchissant les pièces d'orme devant servir d'entablement, il pensait au jour où il partirait pour son tour de France, jour qu'il sentait approcher avec une délicieuse appréhension et qui marquerait sa véritable entrée dans le monde du bois.

Ainsi passaient les jours, les semaines, sans autre souci que le ravitaillement qui redevenait difficile à Paris pour les gens pauvres car l'hiver était rude et les transports fonctionnaient mal. Les Valfroy et les Caumont n'étaient pas pauvres et comptaient parmi les marchands-ébénistes les plus prospères du Faubourg; pourtant les femmes devaient recommencer à compter car les économies des mois précédents fondaient à mesure que la table de Malabar prenait forme. Le Garde-meuble, en effet, ne faisait aucune avance et ne réglait qu'après livraison.

Entre-temps il fallait payer le bois d'orme et les ouvriers. Heureusement, Ethis avait refusé d'arrêter tous les autres travaux pour ne se consacrer qu'à la commande royale.

– Il faut, disait-il, profiter au contraire du prestige qu'elle nous apporte et continuer de servir la clientèle habituelle. Tant pis si nous prenons un peu de retard!

C'était la sagesse et la situation précaire de Richard-Lenoir rappelait à Ethis que la prospérité pouvait être la chose la plus inconstante de la vie. François Richard n'avait dû qu'à une intervention du fils du général Rapp, qu'il avait naguère obligé, de ne pas être déporté en raison du zèle dont il avait fait preuve à l'égard de Napoléon. Aujourd'hui il demandait l'octroi d'un nouveau prêt pour ne pas être contraint de fermer ses derniers ateliers en activité, mais le ministère se faisait tirer l'oreille : il devait à l'État plus d'un million de francs!

Au printemps de 1818, la table fut enfin achevée. Il avait fallu des jours et des nuits à Bertrand pour la poncer avant de la confier au vernisseur venu travailler à l'atelier car il n'était pas question de la transporter. Fontaine était enchanté du résultat et répétait que Jacob n'aurait pas fait mieux, ce qui était un compliment énorme pour qui savait l'admiration qu'il portait au maître et à son fils, ses collaborateurs attitrés.

Il fallait bien sûr fêter cet événement. Les femmes décidèrent que les agapes ne pouvaient se dérouler que dans l'atelier où la table avait été construite et trônait encore pour quelques jours avant de prendre place dans les appartements du roi. Cela nécessita un grand déménagement mais ce repas sur le lieu de travail jouissait du mérite de renouer avec l'une des plus anciennes traditions des gens du bois.

C'était le premier dimanche de mai, Ethis et Bertrand étaient partis le matin de bonne heure en voiture chercher des brassées de feuillage nouveau et d'aubépine; deux grosses marmites pendues dans l'âtre du logement de la place d'Aligre laissaient filer dans une franche senteur de girofle l'écume d'un pot-au-feu géant.

Les hommes avaient décoré l'atelier comme un jardin,

sur la table protégée par une grande feuille de frêne recouverte de copeaux neigeux, ils avaient posé un énorme bouquet de lilas dont le parfum se mêlait à celui de la sciure fraîche et à l'odeur si caractéristique de la colle forte dont l'âcreté aurait pu gêner des non-initiés mais qui ne risquait pas de surprendre les invités.

Établis servant de dessertes, planches posées sur des tréteaux, immenses nappes damassées et sièges de tous styles empruntés aux ateliers voisins, les « agapes du chef-d'œuvre » ne se différenciaient guère des repas de fête du compagnonnage des siècles passés. La même fraternité coulait du tonnelet de vin des coteaux parisiens et la gaieté rassemblait comme jadis tous ceux qui avaient aidé à la réalisation du meuble exceptionnel que constituait la table du roi. Seule différence peut-être, la joie était celle du travail mené à bien et non la fierté de savoir qu'il était destiné à Louis XVIII dont tout le monde se moquait bien.

Fontaine et Percier présidaient le banquet auquel Alexandre Lenoir avait été convié ainsi que Félicité Riesener dont le mari peignait toujours les princes et les généraux à la cour de Moscou. Eugène Delacroix qui venait d'entrer à l'école des Beaux-Arts était là lui aussi et dessinait la tablée d'un crayon si agile qu'on oubliait la main qui le dirigeait. Eugène s'était placé dans un coin où il pouvait embrasser toute la scène. Lucie lui portait sa part de chaque plat mais il y touchait à peine, accaparé par son dessin qui remplissait maintenant toute la feuille de papier et dont il travaillait les détails. Un par un, les maîtres et les compagnons présents qui savaient tous ce qu'était un dessin, se déplaçaient pour aller voir de près le jeune homme travailler. Tous hochaient la tête, fascinés par son extraordinaire facilité, et revenaient s'asseoir en disant : « C'est prodigieux ! »

Fontaine et Percier connaissaient Eugène Delacroix et son talent mais ils étaient subjugués par les progrès qu'il avait faits ces derniers mois. Ils lui avaient demandé s'il s'était mis à peindre et il avait souri :

– Oh oui ! La peinture est toute ma vie. L'imagination

chez moi passe par la couleur et, sauf quand je veux saisir une scène comme aujourd'hui, le dessin ne me sert qu'à déterminer les lignes de la composition et la place des figures. L'esquisse se fait le plus souvent directement sur le plateau au moyen du vague et en laissant les détails...

A vingt ans, il parlait de son art comme un vieux maître mais avec toute la fantaisie et l'enthousiasme de la jeunesse. Ébloui, Fontaine glissa à Marie qu'un très grand artiste, le meilleur de son temps sans doute, était en train de naître; Alexandre Lenoir dit qu'il n'avait jamais rencontré quelqu'un d'aussi doué, sauf peut-être David... Justement on parla de David, de sa vie à bascule entre l'art au service du roi et le chantre des messes révolutionnaires, entre le cachot à la mort de Robespierre et les palais impériaux.

– J'ai toujours défendu David, dit Lenoir. Sa consternante versatilité politique n'est qu'une petite tache dans le grand tableau de sa vie. Sans elle, sa carrière de peintre et sans doute sa vie auraient été interrompues à quarante ans. Je lui sais gré tout de même d'être resté fidèle à Napoléon et d'avoir choisi l'exil en Belgique plutôt que de solliciter sa grâce auprès de Louis XVIII. Ah! je n'oublie pas le portrait de Juliette Récamier à demi étendue sur son lit d'acajou dont la forme antique épouse les plis d'une longue tunique blanche...

– Qui admirez-vous le plus, dit Marie, David ou Mme Récamier? Comme tous les hommes vous avez été amoureux d'elle, peut-être l'êtes-vous toujours!

– Naturellement!

– Vous l'avez bien connue? demanda Lucie, curieuse.

– J'aurais voulu la connaître mieux mais, hélas! ma passion n'était que l'une des innombrables qu'elle suscita mais auxquelles elle ne céda jamais. Pour moi comme pour tant d'autres elle a su transformer en amitié l'amour que je lui portais. A ce propos, j'aime le compliment que lui fit un jour Montlosier: « Vous pourriez, comme le Cid, dire cinq cents de mes amis. » Aujourd'hui elle fait face avec dignité à des revers de fortune et l'on m'a dit hier qu'elle voulait se retirer à l'Abbaye-aux-Bois. Ses cinq cents amis en feront le salon le plus intelligent de Paris.

Tard dans la soirée, on parlait encore de bois exotiques, du style neuf qui avait bien du mal à prendre racine dans le Faubourg balayé durant de longues années par des vents contraires, des nouvelles machines à scier et à détailler le bois de placage qu'un ingénieur anglais essayait dans le secret d'un atelier du cul-de-sac de la Forge-Royale. Tandis qu'on emplissait les verres une dernière fois, Bertrand, le plus jeune de ceux qui avaient travaillé à la fabrication de la table, demanda un discours au maître Emmanuel Caumont. Sur l'air des lampions, l'assistance reprit l'invite et, malgré ses protestations, Emmanuel dut improviser une adresse à ses amis. Il s'en tira très bien, n'oublia personne dans ses remerciements et rendit hommage à son frère et associé, le « vainqueur » Ethis dont, dit-il, l'activité et l'enthousiasme sauvaient le Faubourg d'une torpeur inquiétante. Il annonça enfin le prochain départ de son aspirant compagnon pour le tour de France, annonce saluée par une longue ovation. Marie, seule n'applaudit pas. Du coin de son mouchoir elle s'essuyait les yeux.

C'est Bertrand, le plus instruit de la famille, aussi celui qui avait la plus belle écriture, qui fut chargé de rédiger la facture de la table pour l'administration du Garde-meuble. Les mots comme les chiffres en avaient été pesés. Il s'agissait de décrire le meuble livré en des termes rigoureusement conformes au devis, faute de quoi le relevé risquait d'être renvoyé et repoussé le délai de règlement, déjà fort retardé.

La facture était bien présentée. Ethis la lut tout haut pour la famille :

« Une table en bois de teck dit chêne de Malabar, exécutée selon les dessins et directives de M. Fontaine, architecte en chef de S.M. et comportant : pieds à socle plein avec fortes roulettes de cuivre, six montants formés par des sirènes ailées, ceinture avec double baguette, gorge et corniche, coupe au milieu du socle, le tout en bois d'orme poncé et verni comme le plateau de teck massif d'un diamètre de 2,77 m. Pour 4 000 francs. »

La table partie pour le palais des Tuileries laissa un grand vide dans l'atelier, vide bientôt comblé par la livraison du bois nécessaire à la confection d'un mobilier composé de deux canapés, deux bergères, six fauteuils et six chaises destiné à la vicomtesse de Gontaut. Cette commande importante, Ethis et Emmanuel la devaient cette fois à Lenoir. La joie et l'enthousiasme qui marquent dans les ateliers le commencement d'un nouveau travail manquèrent cette fois de chaleur. Bertrand partait le surlendemain pour Nîmes, première étape de son tour de France, et Marie n'était pas la seule à avoir le cœur gros. Bertrand lui-même se demandait s'il avait raison d'entreprendre ce voyage aventureux et s'il ne ferait pas mieux de rester travailler avec Emmanuel à la commande de Mme de Gontaut... Mais il était trop tard, tout le quartier était au courant de son départ et il serait mort de honte s'il avait dû annoncer son renoncement. D'ailleurs, la fièvre de l'action avait raison des pensées puériles qui l'avaient un instant effleuré. Son bagage réduit tenait dans une toilette de fort coton que lui avait donnée Richard. Pliée et attachée d'une certaine façon, elle pouvait se porter sur l'épaule comme une grande musette. Il avait été convenu que sa mère lui enverrait une malle de vêtements par la poste quand il serait arrivé à Nîmes. Il comptait s'arrêter en route pour visiter les pays et les villes traversées, au gré de sa fantaisie et de la disponibilité des places dans les diligences.

Le maître ébéniste Dulong qui avait son atelier au 20 rue du Figuier-Saint-Paul, de l'autre côté de la Bastille et qui, comme beaucoup, avait travaillé autrefois pour Riesener, lui avait délivré son passeport d'aspirant qui lui permettrait tout au long du voyage de se faire reconnaître, d'être admis dans les « cayennes », hébergé jusqu'à ce que le « rouleur » lui ait trouvé du travail. Dulong était très fier d'avoir effectué son tour de France trente ans auparavant, il s'intéressait avec dévouement aux jeunes Parisiens tentés par l'aventure et aux « passants » qui souhaitaient s'arrêter un temps dans la capitale.

– A la minute même où s'ébranlera la diligence qui doit le conduire à Sens, puis à Lyon, avait-il dit à Bertrand, tu te sentiras un homme libre... Ou plutôt, afin qu'il n'y ait pas de confusion avec ce beau mot assaisonné à toutes les sauces depuis quarante ans, tu te sentiras un homme libéré, soudain étranger à l'enchaînement des contraintes extérieures. Tu seras, comme je l'ai été, compagnon du Devoir de liberté, c'est-à-dire un gavot. Pourquoi ? Parce que j'en suis un et que je te recommande à mes amis. C'est un hasard qui t'entraînera à te battre contre ceux du Devoir car, si stupide que cela paraisse, on se bat entre sociétés rivales. J'essaye toujours de lutter contre cette déplorable habitude qui devient du fanatisme mais, surtout dans le Sud où tu vas, on continue de s'assommer ! Enfin, les choses ont peut-être changé ! Il arrivera bien un jour où ces jeunes ouvriers qui ont le même idéal : honnêteté et travail, finiront par s'entraider. Tout de même, ne t'affole pas, tu ne vas pas à la guerre ! Ce que tu ne trouveras pas dans la société rivale tu l'auras chez les tiens : l'entraide, l'amitié, l'accueil... Tes compagnons te donneront un nom que tu garderas non seulement durant ton voyage mais toute ta vie durant. Moi, c'était « Charollais-le-Résolu » parce que ma mère était de Charolles. Parfois, on m'appelle encore comme cela et j'en éprouve du plaisir.

Bertrand écoutait, posait des questions, essayait de déchiffrer le passeport que venait de lui remettre Dulong et qui lui paraissait incompréhensible.

– Tu comprendras plus tard ton « affaire [1] ». Elle est écrite uniquement en initiales. C'est l'un des éléments d'un rituel auquel tu auras à cœur de te conformer,

1. Passeport du compagnon qui « présente son affaire en arrivant chez la mère ».

surtout quand tu seras reçu compagnon. Bonne chance petit! Je me revois à ton âge quittant ma famille... Écris souvent à ta mère. C'est dur, tu sais, le tour de France pour les mères!

Le 14 mars, Bertrand quittait la place d'Aligre. Il n'avait pas voulu que ses parents le conduisent au Palais-Royal d'où partait la malle-poste. Il voulait, comme Jean Cottion dont il portait la canne sur l'épaule, remonter le Faubourg à pied, marcher en sifflotant pour se donner du courage, faire bonne figure auprès des gens du bois qu'il croisait et qui lui souhaitaient bonne chance. Il savait que s'il avait été au côté de Marie dans le cabriolet d'Ethis, il aurait pleuré sur son épaule.

Le voyage se déroula sans encombre. On n'était plus, Dieu merci, au temps où la malle du courrier de Tours était dévalisée au bout du pont Neuf, ni même à celui de Marivaux qui faisait débuter son chef-d'œuvre *Marianne* par le pillage du carrosse de voiture allant de Paris à Bordeaux et racontait, sans qu'aucun lecteur pût trouver le fait invraisemblable, que cinq voyageurs avaient été tués avec le cocher et le postillon. Bertrand qui avait pensé un moment s'arrêter à Sens préféra continuer. A Lyon même il ne demeura que quelques jours chez un cousin de Lenoir qui lui avait donné une lettre de recommandation. Ce cousin qui fabriquait des soieries était très ennuyeux. N'aurait été sa fille Adrienne qui avait dix-huit ans et de jolis yeux, Bertrand serait reparti dès le lendemain. Il avait hâte de joindre la première étape de son tour de France, Nîmes, où il devait présenter à la mère la lettre de recommandation du maître Dulong.

Il quitta la malle-poste à Avignon et se demandait s'il allait faire à pied les dix lieues qu'il lui restait à parcourir quand un jeune homme qui attendait assis sur une borne du relais de poste l'apostropha :

– Tope [1]!

Bertrand ignorait tout du rituel des compagnons. Il

1. Le topage est le dialogue de reconnaissance de deux compagnons.

savait pourtant que le topage risquait de dégénérer en bataille si les deux inconnus se révélaient appartenir à des sociétés différentes. Il répondit prudemment : « Bonjour, je suis aspirant ébéniste mais ne suis pas encore affilié [1] ! »

L'autre éclata de rire :

– Je te prenais pour un vieux compagnon, un partant allant chez son nouveau bourgeois. Où te rends-tu ?

– A Nîmes chez ceux du « Devoir de liberté ».

– Bravo ! Je suis un « renard de liberté [2] » et je vais aussi à Nîmes. Nous allons faire le chemin ensemble et je te conduirai chez la mère. Une voiture de poste part dans une heure. D'où viens-tu ?

– De Paris !

– Et tu fais ton tour ! Il est rare que les Parisiens quittent leur ville pour aller voir ce qui se passe dans les provinces. J'ai toujours eu l'impression qu'ils se croient supérieurs et qu'ils nous méprisent...

– Mais non, il y a à Paris des gens bien, comme ailleurs, et aussi pas mal d'imbéciles...

– Comme ailleurs !

Ils rirent, mangèrent de bon appétit le jambonneau que le renard venait de sortir de son sac.

– Nous sommes, je crois, dans le pays du vin, dit Bertrand. Viens, nous allons trinquer à notre rencontre. Mais avant, dis-moi ton nom.

– Paul Véron, dit « Vivarais-le-Cœur-content », compagnon charpentier sur le tour ! Je suis natif d'Annonay où je rentrerai dans six ou sept mois pour remplacer le père qui se fait vieux. Et toi ?

– Je m'appelle Bertrand Valfroy. Un jour je te raconterai mon histoire et celle de ma famille mais c'est long et compliqué. Mon père est marchand de meubles faubourg Saint-Antoine. C'est un « vainqueur de la Bastille ». Et je suis un peu le petit-fils du grand Riesener...

1. L'« affilié » est le jeune admis dans une société du Devoir de liberté.

2. Renard : se dit d'un charpentier qui fait son tour de France.

Paul Véron émit un léger sifflement et ne posa pas d'autre question. Le passé d'un compagnon lui appartient, il n'en dit que ce qu'il veut.

Ils prirent leurs places sur le toit de la voiture, les moins chères et les plus inconfortables durant la nuit et quand il fait froid mais les plus agréables lorsque le soleil brille. Bertrand découvrait la Provence, ses vignes et ses champs d'oliviers. Il se félicitait d'avoir rencontré Paul, compagnon de voyage agréable dont la présence, la chaleur de la voix et un drôle d'accent un peu rocailleux lui faisaient oublier son appréhension. Pour la première fois il allait vivre hors de sa famille, travailler chez un inconnu. Il allait aussi devoir gagner sa vie. Tout cela lui faisait un peu peur...

Vers les six heures ils arrivèrent chez la mère qui fit aussitôt chercher le premier compagnon de la ville et le « rouleur [1] ». Ce dernier qui s'appelait Martin Clésio était un compagnon menuisier d'une trentaine d'années. Son visage ouvert et son bon sourire plurent tout de suite à Bertrand. Quant à Paul, il était déjà passé à Nîmes au début de son tour et se trouvait en pays de connaissance.

– Ainsi tu arrives de Paris! dit le rouleur. C'est rare de vous voir débarquer sur le tour, vous, les gens la capitale. Tu vas voir, Nîmes est une ville accueillante. C'est toi qui l'as choisie comme ville du devoir?

– Oui, sur les conseils du maître ébéniste Dulong, connu faubourg Saint-Antoine chez les compagnons sous le nom de Charollais-le-Résolu. Voici sa lettre de recommandation.

Il jeta un coup d'œil au passeport, le tendit au premier de la ville puis à la mère.

– Demain, dit-il, je te ferai la conduite jusque chez ton bourgeois. C'est un bon ébéniste qui donne aussi des cours de dessin. Tu logeras chez lui et il te nourrira. Mais

1. Rouleur ou rôdeur, celui qui est chargé des arrivants et des partants qu'il conduit chez un nouveau patron ou qu'il reconduit jusqu'à la sortie de la ville. Fonction exercée à tour de rôle par les compagnons de la société.

montre donc cette drôle de canne que tu portes. Ce n'est pas une canne de compagnon. Tu ne recevras celle-ci que lorsque tu seras reçu...

– Cette canne a fait trois tours de France. Le premier remonte, c'est gravé dessus, à 1470. Son premier propriétaire s'appelait Jean Cottion, c'est lui qui a fondé la communauté des ouvriers libres du faubourg Saint-Antoine. Nous avons retrouvé la canne dans le grenier d'une maison familiale. Je l'ai prise en guise de porte-bonheur mais je ne m'en servirai pas avant d'être reçu compagnon.

– Elle est émouvante, cette relique des premiers compagnons, prends-en soin et ne la promène pas quand il risque d'y avoir du grabuge car un « dévorant » te le volerait. Maintenant, viens que nous te donnions l'accolade. La mère va apporter les bouteilles d'arrivants afin que nous choquions les verres. Ce soir tu coucheras et tu souperas chez elle. C'est comme ça le premier jour... Et puis il va falloir que tu fasses connaissance avec notre rituel. Pour l'instant, il te suffit de savoir que tu dois le respect à la mère et que tu ne dois pas te présenter devant elle en tenue négligée, en tablier ou en chemise et sans cravate le dimanche!

La vie avait repris son cours place d'Aligre. Marie, un moment affligée par le départ de Bertrand, s'était ressaisie. A l'atelier, on s'affairait autour de la commande de Mme de Gontaut. L'absence de l'aspirant s'y faisait sentir et Caumont avait dû engager un jeune compagnon pour le remplacer. Une première lettre de Bertrand expédiée peu après son arrivée à Nîmes avait rassuré la famille. Elle en annonçait une seconde, beaucoup plus détaillée, qu'on attendait avec impatience.

S'il n'y avait plus table ouverte le mercredi, comme au temps d'Antoinette, l'hôtel d'Aligre, comme l'appelait Lenoir, continuait de recevoir la visite des vieux amis, à commencer par Fontaine et Percier qui sans le dire veillaient sur la bonne marche de la boutique et de l'atelier, auxquels ils envoyaient beaucoup de clients.

Ethis, de son côté, était toujours aussi actif. Il ne se passait rien d'un peu important dans le quartier sans qu'il en fût aussitôt informé. Il avait fait ainsi la connaissance d'un curieux personnage qui venait de s'installer dans d'anciens locaux des Quinze-Vingts, appelés *L'Enclos des Mousquetaires.* Des mousquetaires de l'industrie naissante avaient pris la place des anciens bretteurs de la Maison du roi. Brown et Picfort d'abord, qui y avaient monté le premier mule-jenny en France, et un certain M. Burdan qui fabriquait les plus beaux fils de coton. Il avait fait faillite en 1813 et le troisième mousquetaire venait de prendre sa place : un certain Nicolas Appert qu'on disait un peu sorcier depuis qu'on l'avait aperçu suant sang et eau devant d'immenses chaudrons dans lesquels il ne pouvait faire que la cuisine du diable. En réalité M. Appert était un homme célèbre dont tous les savants, de Chaptal à Gay-Lussac, connaissaient et encourageaient les travaux qu'il poursuivait dans sa maison-atelier-laboratoire de Massy. Cet ancien confiseur de la rue des Lombards était tout simplement en train de bouleverser la façon de se nourrir avec ses bouteilles à large goulot dans lesquelles il réussissait à conserver, d'une année sur l'autre, à peu près tous les produits frais consommés par l'homme.

Quittant Massy, il continuait dans le Faubourg ses recherches et commercialisait ses inventions.

– C'est un homme fantastique ! avait raconté Ethis. Il a inventé le moyen de conserver tous les légumes, les viandes et même le lait et la crème. Je vais l'inviter à venir souper un de ces soirs. Il en sera ravi car figure-toi, Lucie, qu'il a entendu parler de notre maison. Il paraît que les réunions de la place d'Aligre sont célèbres dans certains milieux et que des gens très en place disent que malheureusement il s'agit de réunions très fermées où n'est pas admis qui veut !

– Ethis, tu dis des bêtises ! interrompit Lucie. Comment veux-tu qu'on nous connaisse dans un monde qui nous est tellement étranger, qui habite les quartiers élégants et qui aurait peur de se salir en foulant le pavé de nos rues.

– Détrompe-toi. Appert lui-même m'a affirmé qu'il y a une foule de gens qui connaissent le nom d'Antoinette Œben et du baron de Valfroy. Je pense que nos vieux amis Lenoir, Percier, Fontaine et Richard ne sont pas étrangers au renom flatteur dont jouit la famille. Certains de nos clients, qui connaissent depuis longtemps la boutique *L'Enfant à l'oiseau,* m'ont souvent demandé s'il était vrai que des personnages aussi célèbres que Fontaine ou Richard dont l'Empereur avait visité la manufacture de Charonne, fréquentaient assidûment notre maison. Mieux, il paraît qu'un journaliste du *Constitutionnel,* Évariste Dumoulin, voudrait consacrer un article au « salon du Faubourg » dans sa suite sur les quartiers de Paris.

– Quel malheur qu'Antoinette ne puisse voir cela ! C'est son œuvre et il sera bon qu'un journaliste, et peut-être un jour, un romancier, raconte cette histoire. Quant à ce bon M. Appert qui peut vous faire manger des fraises et des haricots verts au mois de janvier, j'aimerais bien le connaître. Invite-le, il ne déparera pas notre liste des hôtes illustres. Bien entendu, il faudra prévenir Alexandre Lenoir qui se prétend fin gastronome et qui l'est d'ailleurs. Il aura sans doute mille questions à lui poser.

Marie et Lucie attendaient un vieillard chenu s'aidant d'une canne qu'elles se proposaient d'aider à monter l'escalier. C'est un homme tout à fait alerte, souriant et plein d'entrain qui frappa à leur porte.

– Bonjour mesdames. Vous me faites un grand honneur de recevoir un voisin solitaire toujours plongé dans ses livres, ses marmites et ses recettes de cuisine. Car c'est un cuisinier qui vient dîner chez vous ce soir, un cuisinier un peu particulier dont les plats se mangent six mois, un an ou même deux après avoir été cuits. Je me suis d'ailleurs permis de vous apporter quelques échantillons de ma fabrication.

« Tenez, dit-il, en sortant des bocaux de verre et des boîtes de métal du cabas qu'il portait à la main, voici un bocal de truffes dont vous pourrez user quand il vous plaira. Elles ont été récoltées durant la saison, il y a six mois. Là ce sont des conserves de fruits, abricots, pêches, groseilles. Enfin, j'ai apporté pour que nous y goûtions ce soir un bocal de foie gras arrivé de Colmar il y a plusieurs mois.

On s'extasia sur la saveur du pâté dont Lenoir affirma qu'il était meilleur que tous ceux qu'il avait mangés jusque-là.

– Vous êtes un bienfaiteur de l'humanité, monsieur Appert, dit-il. On ne s'en rend pas compte dans ce pays et c'est bien dommage. J'ai lu, en leur temps, les propos louangeurs que Grimod de La Reynière a tenus sur vos inventions. Cet avis paru dans *L'Almanach des gourmands* est fort intéressant mais il aurait mieux valu que le gouvernement l'assortît de mesures propres à vous aider dans vos recherches.

– Le gouvernement, monsieur, me donne parfois des médailles d'argent ou même d'or sur la demande de mes collègues du Conservatoire des arts et manufactures. Mais il ne m'aide guère autrement, alors que les Anglais qui appliquent mes méthodes de conservation disposent de moyens considérables. Ils sont maintenant en avance de vingt-cinq ou trente ans sur nous. Si j'ai été le premier à fabriquer des conserves destinées aux marins, conserves dont nous avons prouvé, mon ami le grand chirurgien Tenon et moi, l'innocuité totale en ce qui concerne le scorbut, ce sont aujourd'hui les industriels anglais qui les vendent dans tous les grands ports du monde [1] !

– Me permettrez-vous de visiter vos ateliers de fabrication? demanda Ethis.

– Naturellement, vous entrerez par le numéro 17 de la rue Moreau. Mes voisins directs sont les aveugles des Quinze-Vingts. Je leur donne un peu de travail, ils sont

1. Voir l'excellent livre que Rosemonde Pujol a consacré à Nicolas Appert (Denoël).

habiles, malgré leur infirmité, pour l'épluchage des fruits et des légumes. Venez, je vous montrerai mes nouveaux autoclaves qui me permettent d'économiser du temps et du combustible! Mais assez parlé de ma modeste personne. Je sais que je dîne, fort bien mesdames, dans l'un des temples du faubourg des meubles. Racontez-moi l'histoire de votre famille qu'on m'a dit être apparentée au grand Riesener.

– Et à Œben mon grand-père, dit Lucie. Tenez, voici son portrait.

Durant toute la soirée on ne parla plus que de bois, de meubles et du tour de France que venait d'entamer le plus jeune ébéniste de la maison. Nicolas Appert était visiblement heureux au milieu de cette famille simple où le goût du beau et du travail bien fait dominait et justifiait la vie. Il promit de revenir mais dit qu'il voulait auparavant inviter tout le monde chez lui, dans son « antre ».

– Vous composerez vous-même votre menu en arrivant, seule la table sera mise à l'avance! Mais, aujourd'hui, je m'en vais car il se fait tard et, si je suis encore un homme, j'ai tout de même près de soixante et dix années!

A la même heure, chez le maître Garadot, menuisier-ébéniste à Nîmes, Bertrand montait se coucher après une rude journée de travail. Cela faisait déjà un mois qu'il avait quitté la place d'Aligre et les soirées familiales commençaient à lui manquer. Il aurait, ce soir-là, donné cher pour retrouver son lit soigneusement refait le matin par sa mère...

– Allons, se dit-il en ouvrant la porte de la petite chambre où ronflait déjà « Marseillais-la-Bonne-Conduite » reçu compagnon depuis peu et qui partageait sa vie simple chez le bon M. Garadot, ce n'est pas le moment d'avoir des états d'âme, demain nous devons terminer la nouvelle porte d'entrée de la Maison carrée.

Il se déshabilla, souffla la chandelle et s'endormit du sommeil des justes compagnons du Devoir de liberté.

Le chantier de réfection de la Maison carrée groupait de nombreuses entreprises. L'atelier de Bertrand avait été chargé de refaire la porte d'entrée du monument. En bois de noyer massif, épaisse de quatre pouces, avec de belles moulures de cuivre embrevées dans les traverses et les battants, elle avait été achevée la veille. Il s'agissait maintenant de la transporter à pied d'œuvre et de la sceller dans la pierre impériale qui, depuis le Ier siècle, dressait vers le ciel ses trente colonnes corinthiennes.

Hercule Garadot, dont la stature imposante supportait vaillamment le prénom, savait parler de sa ville dont il connaissait l'histoire aussi bien que M. le Conservateur des ruines. Bertrand, fasciné, l'avait écouté décrire, avec son accent de soleil, la fine sculpture des chapiteaux, de la corniche et de la frise, la délicatesse des rinceaux :

– Mis au jour depuis peu, tiré des entrailles de la terre, ce temple est l'un des monuments les plus beaux et les mieux conservés que les Romains ont laissés en Gaule. Quel honneur pour nous, modestes compagnons du Languedoc, de contribuer à la restauration d'un tel chef-d'œuvre!

Garadot terminait ses envolées lyriques par un grand geste en direction de ses compagnons qui l'écoutaient respectueusement :

– Vous tous, à commencer par Vivarais-la-Vertu et Médoc-la-Rose-d'amour, sans oublier Marseillais-la-Bonne-Conduite et notre pigeonneau [1] parisien qui sera bientôt reçu compagnon du Devoir de liberté, vous avez travaillé pour l'amour du beau. Je vous en remercie.

C'est vrai qu'elle avait belle allure, la porte des compagnons. Par la justesse de ses assemblages et la beauté de son fini, c'était un chef-d'œuvre de menuiserie.

– Longtemps, continuait le maître, les gens de la partie comme les simples visiteurs admireront votre travail! Demain, quand la porte sera en place, nous tiendrons une assemblée chez la mère avec tous les drilles [2] de la ville, nous boirons en règle [3] des bouteilles de vin frais et

1. Aspirant chez les menuisiers-ébénistes.
2. Surnom donné primitivement aux compagnons charpentiers et étendu aux compagnons du Devoir de liberté.
3. Boire conformément aux rites de la société.

chanterons. A propos de chanson, je me suis laissé dire, le Parisien, que vous avez une jolie voix et que vous composez même des couplets. Eh bien, écris-nous donc une chanson sur notre porte afin que nous la reprenions en chœur!

La lourde porte installée, qui mettait à coup sûr les tableaux du musée à l'abri des voleurs, dix-huit compagnons en veste et en cravate se retrouvèrent chez la mère. Il faisait très chaud, la tenue conforme au règlement des assemblées pesait lourd sur les épaules.

– Je propose, dit Beauceron-la-Vertu, le plus ancien des compagnons, que nous nous mettions à l'aise. Jetons nos vestes et nos cravates bas. Si quelqu'un arrive et nous prend à l'amende, nous la paierons et en boirons notre bonne part!

Le premier de ville entra peu après, salua l'assemblée et compta les présents.

– La mère, dit-il, apportez dix-huit bouteilles de vin. Nous les boirons en règle et gare à l'amende pour ceux qui se tromperont, même d'une seule syllabe.

Arrivé à la dernière phrase de son discours, sa langue fourcha, il prononça le nom de maître Jacques à la place de celui de Salomon [1]. On se regarda et une voix lança :

– La mère, apportez deux bouteilles de vin aux frais du premier compagnon qui a péché contre le règlement en portant mal sa santé!

C'était la loi : quand le premier compagnon commet une faute, il paie le double. Raison de plus de rire et de s'amuser... C'est à ce moment que Bertrand fut prié de lancer le refrain qu'il avait écrit la veille au soir dans sa chambre. Ému, déjà un peu gris, « le Parisien » se jeta à l'eau :

Splendide monument aux colonnes si fines,
Aux chapiteaux fouillés dans la pierre d'Italie,

1. Maître Jacques, considéré comme fondateur du compagnonnage du Devoir. Les « Enfants de Salomon » sont les compagnons du Devoir de liberté.

Tu nous as révélé des hommes la folie
De vouloir imiter tes formes palatines.

Par Salomon, beaux drilles, nous te rendons hommage
En offrant à tes pierres l'amour de notre ouvrage.

Le froid guettait ton cœur noble Maison carrée
Il fallait des frimas protéger tes statues.
De la scie, du rabot, Vivarais-la-Vertu
A fermé de bon bois ton beau manteau troué.

Par Salomon, etc.

Chanté sur l'air des *Belles Vivandières,* l'hymne à la Maison carrée comportait une bonne dizaine de couplets ou Hercule Garadot et chacun des compagnons du Devoir de liberté était célébré comme il le fallait. Le refrain était repris en chœur et chacun voulait une copie de la chanson. Tard dans le soir, on chantait encore chez la mère. Bertrand que tout le monde avait félicité s'était créé en moins d'une heure une réputation de poète qui allait le suivre tout au long de son tour de France. Il rayonnait de bonheur, bien loin de son Faubourg qui, la veille, avait failli lui arracher des larmes de désespoir.

A Paris, Louis XVIII gouvernait mollement, laissant à ses ministres courtisans le soin de naviguer au plus près entre les entreprises des comploteurs bonapartistes et ultras. L'assassinat du duc de Berry, espoir de la continuité monarchique, avait permis à ces derniers de prendre le gouvernement, mais cette réaction laissait le Faubourg assez indifférent, surtout les gens du bois qui retrouvaient une clientèle chez les émigrés rentrés pour la plupart dans des hôtels vidés de leurs meubles. Les ateliers avaient donc du travail, on y fabriquait deux sortes de meubles : des interprétations plus ou moins heureuses des styles de l'Ancien Régime et des créations en bois clairs ou en acajou issues du Directoire et de l'Empire. Jacob-Desmalter, dans ses ateliers retrouvés de la rue Meslée, demeurait fidèle à la tradition familiale et travaillait l'acajou aussi bien que l'érable moucheté incrusté de filets d'amarante. Comme lui, Emmanuel Caumont aurait préféré ne pas remettre sa scie et son rabot dans les traces des géants du XVIIIe mais l'atelier, grâce à la boutique d'Ethis, s'était créé une bonne réputation dans l'« ancien » et les commodes « genre Riesener ou Molitor » se vendaient trop bien pour qu'on cessât de les fabriquer.

Toujours aussi actif et inventif, Ethis avait perdu, avec l'âge, son impétuosité dévorante. A quarante-cinq ans, il ressemblait plus à un bourgeois arrivé qu'à la tête brûlée de la Folie Titon. Marie et lui s'ennuyaient du fils dont chaque lettre suscitait la joie, l'inquiétude et la tristesse. Ethis parlait à tout le monde de Bertrand « qui faisait des armoires, restaurait des chefs-d'œuvre et troussait des vers à l'autre bout de la France ».

– C'est un artiste, disait-il. Je travaille pour lui, vous verrez quand il rentrera comment il développera notre affaire ! Et il est poète par-dessus le marché ! Il paraît que ses chansons recopiées circulent dans toute la France et sont reprises en chœur de Brest à Marseille par tous les compagnons du tour de France !

Que son fils fasse des vers l'impressionnait plus que les travaux d'ébénisterie qu'il décrivait par le menu dans ses lettres. C'était pour lui le signe d'un esprit supérieur et Marie devait tempérer son enthousiasme quand il comparait Bertrand à ce M. de Lamartine qui venait de publier ses *Méditations poétiques* avec un énorme succès.

L'autre petit génie de la famille, Eugène, semblait devoir réaliser les espoirs de son entourage. Victoire n'était plus là, elle qui avait tellement cru dans la destinée d'un fils dont personne aujourd'hui, en dehors d'Ethis et de Marie, ne se souvenait qu'il était très certainement l'enfant naturel de M. de Talleyrand. Elle ne pouvait pas constater que les dons et la beauté d'Eugène n'avaient fait que s'épanouir depuis le temps où, petit garçon, elle s'amusait à retrouver dans ses traits d'une finesse presque excessive ceux du visage de l'ancien Monsieur d'Autun devenu ministre du Directoire.

A l'école des Beaux-Arts, où il semblait, on le dira plus tard, bénéficier d'une mystérieuse protection, il avait, depuis longtemps, délaissé l'académisme professé par son vieux maître Guérin, pour suivre avec passion l'impulsion nouvelle donnée à la peinture par Gros et surtout par Géricault auquel il vouait une admiration sans borne.

Il avait montré à Alexandre Lenoir et à Fontaine ses premières grandes toiles.

– Je sais que ma *Vierge des moissons* et ma *Vierge du Sacré-cœur* sont encore inspirées des maîtres italiens de la Renaissance mais ce n'est qu'un travail d'école. Je pense à d'autres tableaux pour les prochains Salons. On pourra peut-être me dire qu'ils ressemblent à des Géricault. Ce sera le plus grand compliment qu'on puisse me faire. Son *Radeau de « la Méduse »* est un inimitable chef-d'œuvre et aussi l'œuvre d'un novateur incontestable !

Lenoir et Fontaine qui connaissaient le jeune homme depuis qu'il crayonnait ses premiers dessins furent stupéfaits : « Eugène, dirent-ils ensemble, n'a pas fini de faire parler de lui. »

Lettre de Bertrand à ses parents.

Montpellier, le 30 juillet 1818.

Mes chers parents,

Comme vous le voyez, j'ai quitté Nîmes et mon bourgeois, M. Garadot. Je garde un bon souvenir de cette ville superbe et de ses ruines romaines. Je n'oublierai jamais que j'ai participé à la construction de la porte de la

Maison carrée, une belle aventure que je vous ai déjà racontée. Je me fais à ma nouvelle vie, même si vous me manquez beaucoup, je suis heureux dans ma société où règne l'entraide et l'amitié. Heureusement, mon compagnon de travail, Marseillais-la-Bonne-Conduite, n'a pas voulu me laisser partir seul, nous avons donc fait le voyage ensemble et j'espère que le rouleur de Montpellier nous placera chez le même patron. Ce soir nous soupons et couchons chez la mère.

Avant de vous raconter notre voyage, je veux vous parler du départ qui a été une cérémonie extraordinaire. Bien que cela se fasse moins de nos jours, les compagnons ont tenu à nous offrir une conduite en règle. C'est un honneur dont je suis fier. Du coup, nous avons mis nos malles au roulage et nous avons décidé de faire à pied la dizaine de lieues qui nous séparait de Montpellier. Je n'oublie aucun détail car cette « conduite » vous montrera mieux que de longs discours l'esprit qui règne sur le tour de France.

La troupe s'est mise en route vers sept heures. Le soleil commençait à chauffer et la campagne était superbe. Marseillais et moi, les partants, marchions en tête avec le premier compagnon et le rouleur qui portaient nos deux « malles aux quatre nœuds » sur l'épaule, au bout de leur canne. Tous les compagnons, canne en main, rubans bleus attachés au côté qui voltigeaient au gré du vent, suivaient sur deux rangs et formaient une longue colonne. Les affiliés, comme on nomme les aspirants, fermaient la marche, précédés de deux corbeilles enrubannées portées par quatre d'entre eux. Dans l'une il y avait des verres et des bouteilles de vin, dans l'autre du pain et du fromage. Sur la serviette recouvrant les victuailles étaient posés l'équerre et le compas, symboles du compagnonnage, qui brillaient sous le soleil.

Alors que nous marchions, un geste du premier de la ville déclencha un chœur où les voix se mêlaient harmonieusement en suivant le rythme de notre pas cadencé. C'était une surprise : les compagnons avaient tous appris l'une de mes chansons et, ma foi, je dois dire sans forfanterie que j'étais heureux et que j'ai trouvé mes paroles plutôt bien venues. Arrivés à Bornis, le rouleur nous fit signe de tourner à gauche dans un champ. Toujours en chantant, compagnons et affiliés formèrent un cercle et plantèrent leur canne en terre. Protégés par cette clôture de fanions, on rompit le pain, on mangea le fromage de bon appétit et l'on trinqua avant de s'embrasser fraternellement et de se souhaiter mille bonnes choses. Les agapes s'achevèrent sur un dernier chant. L'heure était venue de se séparer. Marseillais et moi, les larmes aux yeux, car tout cela était émouvant, prîmes nos balluchons et nous éloignâmes du cercle pour prendre la route. Alors, tous les camarades se mirent à crier notre nom, à nous appeler. En vain car les partants doivent avancer fièrement sans se retourner. Voilà ce qu'est une conduite en règle sur le tour de France!

J'arrête là pour ce soir car il se fait tard. Je continuerai ma lettre dans quelques jours pour vous dire comment je suis installé chez mon nouveau maître et si je fais un travail intéressant. Je vais m'endormir en pensant à vous tous.

Le 5 août.

Je reprends donc mon bavardage de l'autre soir. Marseillais et moi sommes bien tombés chez M. Moulongin qui fabrique de beaux meubles Ils n'ont ni le fini ni l'allure de ceux qui sortent de l'atelier d'Emmanuel mais ce sont tout de même des pièces de bonne qualité J'ai raconté à mon nouveau bourgeois et aux compagnons qui travaillent avec moi l'histoire de la table en chêne de Malabar Ils ne voulaient pas croire que nous l'avons fabriquée pour le salon du roi. Louis XVIII est d'ailleurs ici presque un inconnu. Le moins qu'on puisse dire est qu'il ne jouit pas d'un grand prestige.

M. Moulongin est un brave homme, exigeant pour le travail mais cela n'est pas pour me déplaire. Il me donne vingt-six sous par jour, la nourriture et le coucher en plus. C'est suffisant pour s'amuser le dimanche. En plus de Marseillais-la-Bonne-Conduite, j'ai avec moi Marseillais-

Franc-Cœur et Vivarais-le-Cœur-content. Le premier est instruit et me prête des livres. Vivarais sait à peine lire, mais il a du cœur, du jugement et beaucoup de bon sens. Tous sont de bons ouvriers.

Je suis très content car il y a à Montpellier un maître de dessin. C'est M. Pradines, un vieil homme aux yeux rieurs qui porte longs ses beaux cheveux blancs. Il a fait son tour de France, son tour d'Italie et a vécu à Rome. Il dessine bien les meubles mais est surtout très fort en architecture. Ses dessins et lavis sont remarquables et j'espère que je ferai des progrès avec lui. Il me prend quatre francs par mois, ce qui n'est vraiment pas cher. Malheureusement, je n'ai guère de place pour travailler et mon lit me sert de table à dessiner.

Pour finir, une petite histoire du tour de France. L'autre semaine, un compagnon a quitté son patron avec lequel il ne s'entendait pas. Comme celui-ci avait refusé paraît-il de lui payer son dû, il est parti en laissant de graves malfaçons : il a collé les tiroirs d'un secrétaire qui avait bonne allure de l'extérieur mais qui, évidemment ne pouvait servir à rien. La société est contre ce genre d'agissements et le premier en ville a écrit à Bordeaux où le compagnon devait se rendre, afin qu'il soit réprimandé dans les règles devant l'assemblée...

La lettre arriva par la poste deux jours plus tard au Faubourg. Marie pleura ce qui mit Ethis en colère :

– Je ne te comprends pas. Nous recevons de très bonnes nouvelles du fils et tu inondes le parquet de tes larmes. Il faut au contraire se réjouir!

– Vous, les hommes, vous avez le cœur sec. Tu ne comprends pas que je sois émue en apprenant comment vit Bertrand, loin de nous? Je sais qu'il n'est pas malheureux mais c'est plus fort que moi, les larmes me viennent aux yeux quand je vois cette lettre, une lettre que tu vas aller faire lire à tout le quartier, fier comme un coq de village. Tiens, tu ferais mieux d'aller lui acheter le livre de M. Lamartine. Je vais répondre à Bertrand et nous le lui enverrons en même temps que la lettre.

Penaud, Ethis embrassa Marie sur le front et s'en fut aussitôt chez M. Lambresacq qui tenait librairie rue Saint-Antoine, à côté de l'église des jésuites.

Quand elle fut seule, Marie monta tout de suite au deuxième étage pour faire lire la lettre de Bertrand à Lucie. Les deux femmes lurent et relurent chaque passage en les commentant. Tout finit par un fou rire, interrompu par un appel qui venait de l'escalier. C'était M. Nicolas Appert avec son éternel cabas.

– Je pense que votre fils qui est sur le tour de France mange convenablement chez les gens du Midi mais il sera peut-être content d'améliorer le menu des compagnons avec ces quelques boîtes préparées à son intention. Il y a des pâtés de volaille, des haricots blancs, des fèves des marais et des fruits. Mes nouvelles boîtes en métal permettant d'expédier mes fabrications sans risque.

Marie remercia le brave M. Nicolas qui au lieu de s'enrichir comme ceux qui en France et en Angleterre exploitaient son invention, préférait chercher dans sa cuisine-laboratoire des Quinze-Vingts les moyens de la perfectionner.

– Vous êtes trop bon, monsieur Appert, dit Marie, mais puisque vous êtes là restez donc dîner avec nous. Justement on va fêter l'arrivée d'une bonne lettre de Montpellier. Notre autre vieux célibataire Alexandre Lenoir doit venir et vous vous entendrez bien tous les deux!

Ce soir-là encore, le souper fut gai. On y mangea modestement un honnête plat de lentilles à la reine, les plus petites qui sont aussi les meilleures. Une saucisse de Lyon bien dodue cuite dans le jus les accompagnait. Comme toujours place d'Aligre, le meilleur n'était pas dans l'assiette. Bien que la chère y fût excellente elle n'atteignait jamais la qualité et l'intérêt des conversations. Lenoir donna des nouvelles de Fontaine et de Percier qui n'étaient pas passés depuis longtemps au Faubourg.

– Ils sont entièrement occupés par la construction de la chapelle expiatoire que le roi leur a commandée rue d'Anjou, sur l'emplacement de l'ancien cimetière de la Madeleine où Louis XVI et Marie-Antoinette furent inhumés après leur exécution. C'est une sorte de nécropole gréco-romaine à laquelle nos deux amis attachent une grande importance. J'ai vu les plans et je dois dire que je trouve ce monument un peu lourd. Enfin, il paraît que pour un architecte c'est une bénédiction d'avoir à bâtir un tel ensemble historique.

Il fallut insister pour que Nicolas Appert acceptât de raconter son récent triomphe à la Société d'encouragement pour l'industrie nationale :

– Tous les savants étaient là et le rapport de Bouriat lu du haut de la chaire de la grande salle des Arts et Manufactures m'a paru beaucoup trop élogieux. Pensez que ma méthode est maintenant officiellement désignée sous le nom d'« appertisation ». Voilà que la gloire me tombe dessus à soixante-dix ans !

Ethis, lui, parla du dernier prêt consenti à son ami Richard que tout le monde appelait Richard-Lenoir, comme il le souhaitait pour perpétuer le souvenir de son ancien associé. Ce prêt du gouvernement sauvait une fois de plus la filature de la rue de Charonne mais son fondateur, naguère riche à millions, était virtuellement ruiné puisqu'il était toujours débiteur de 1 257 000 francs envers l'État.

– Ce pauvre Richard finira dans la misère, dit Ethis. Lui qui a tant fait, tant travaillé, tant créé ! Qui se souviendra dans cinquante ans des progrès qu'il a fait faire à l'industrie cotonnière [1] ?

On parla aussi bien entendu de meubles. Appert, venu par hasard dans le quartier des ébénistes, s'était tout de suite intéressé à la communauté attachante des gens du bois qui avait adopté ce nouvel arrivant simple et discret qu'on disait savant et qui passait son temps à préparer une cuisine gargantuesque. Quand il rencontrait Ethis et Emmanuel Caumont, il avait toujours mille questions à

1. Ethis se trompait. Si Nicolas Appert n'a pas été honoré comme il le méritait, Richard-Lenoir est demeuré une célébrité dans son quartier du faubourg Saint-Antoine où un boulevard porte son nom depuis 1859.

leur poser sur les outils, les scies mécaniques utilisées de plus en plus dans les ateliers pour certains ouvrages, ou les bois exotiques qu'il voyait décharger non loin des Quinze-Vingts. C'est ainsi qu'Ethis lui apprit qu'un de ses voisins établi au 30 dans le Faubourg, un nommé Victor Sellier, fournisseur du Garde-meuble à la fin de l'Empire, venait d'inventer le « canapé confortable » sans bois apparent. « D'ailleurs, dit Ethis à Emmanuel, nous devrions nous inspirer de cette trouvaille et fabriquer des sièges douillets agréables à la vue et à l'usage. »

Le temps passait. Le Faubourg travaillait et se souciait peu de politique, se contentant de délaisser une presse privée de liberté et de rire des manières de la cour où le roi goutteux imposait une étiquette copiée sur l'ancienne splendeur. Les vieux hochaient la tête en apprenant que le maître des cérémonies aux Tuileries n'était autre que Dreux-Brézé, celui de 89 et de Mirabeau!

– L'Histoire se répète! disait Ethis devenu philosophe.

En fait, on avait ressorti pour Louis XVIII tout l'attirail des simagrées qui faisait déjà sourire avant 89 : les saluts, pirouettes, génuflexions et même, avec l'honneur du tabouret, celui plus incroyable des « battants » : la porte était ouverte à un ou deux battants selon la qualité du visiteur.

Loin de tout cela, Bertrand poursuivait son tour de France avec Marseillais-Franc-Cœur. De Montpellier, il avait gagné Béziers où il travaillait aux pièces chez un maître avare et désagréable. Heureusement il logeait et mangeait chez la mère, comme tous les autres aspirants et compagnons. Il lui en coûtait vingt-deux sous par jour et la bonté des hôtes lui faisait oublier l'aigreur du bourgeois. Tout le monde mangeait à la même table, M. Durand, mari de la mère des compagnons se comportait en vrai père de famille. Il servait chacun et veillait à ce que les repas se déroulent dans un calme de bon aloi et que les conversations soient empreintes de politesse. Le pain et le vin étaient offerts à discrétion. N'aurait été l'attitude de son patron, Bertrand serait resté plus longtemps à Béziers. Au bout de deux mois, il partit pour Bordeaux avec Marseillais, lassé lui aussi des brimades d'Harpagon.

Leurs malles au roulage, les paquets sur l'épaule au bout de la canne, les deux amis, conduits un moment par les compagnons, prirent la route à pied en chantant. Carcassonne, Alzonne, Castelnaudary..., couchers à la belle étoile ou le plus souvent chez un habitant du même compagnonnage toujours prêt à aider les jeunes qui sont sur le tour, la route s'ouvrait devant eux chaude, belle et accueillante. De temps en temps une dizaine de lieues sur une voiture de poste aux places les moins chères, celles du toit dont on descend couvert de poussière, ou à bord d'un bateau de poste sur le canal. La vie était belle. Ils ne s'arrêtèrent pas à Toulouse car leur société de compagnonnage avait quitté la ville depuis quelques années, et continuèrent vers Montauban et Castelsarrasin. Des noms qui chantaient aux oreilles de Bertrand qui avait lu *Les Quatre Fils Aymon* au lycée.

A la sortie d'Agen, Marseillais et Bertrand eurent très peur. Une troupe de dévorants venait à leur rencontre. C'étaient des charpentiers, enfants de Soubise, qui fêtaient la Saint-Joseph. « Vont-ils nous toper, nous assommer ? » demanda Bertrand. « Peut-être pas, marchons et saluons-les de la canne, répondit Marseillais qui en était à sa deuxième année du tour et qui était aguerri. Ils firent ainsi et passèrent sans autre mal que d'avoir essuyé quelques quolibets sans méchanceté.

– Pourquoi être toujours obligé d'être sur le qui-vive ? dit Bertrand. Le compagnonnage serait une si belle institution sans cette scission imbécile qui fait des ennemis de jeunes gens avec qui vous avez envie de fraterniser !

– Malheureusement, c'est comme ça et nous n'y pouvons rien, répondit Marseillais en haussant les épaules. Pensons plutôt à ces quatre-vingts lieues que nous aurons parcourues pour arriver à Bordeaux. Ce voyage, nous ne l'oublierons jamais!

Après avoir marché longtemps dans la ville, ils arrivèrent enfin chez la mère des compagnons qui leur ouvrit ses bras et les serra sur sa grosse poitrine. Ils durent encore embrasser son mari, le gros père Bertrand. C'était la règle. « Maintenant nous allons fêter les arrivants! » dit la mère à la foule des compagnons qui, en ce dimanche d'avril, étaient tous dans la maison, rasés de frais et cravatés.

– Ah! vous deux, dit la mère en remontant de la cave les bras chargés de bouteilles, je vous signale qu'ici personne ne se tutoie, on se dit vous chez moi comme au travail!

Cela aussi c'était la règle. On ne la transgressait qu'entre amis intimes, en voyage ou quelquefois durant le travail. Jamais chez la mère.

Lettre de Bertrand à ses parents.

Bordeaux, le 18 avril 1819.

Mes chers parents, ma petite Antoinette-Émilie,

Me voici installé à Bordeaux et je peux enfin vous donner des nouvelles. Tout va bien, je suis en excellente santé et, si vous n'étiez pas si loin de moi, je serais parfaitement heureux.

Autant mon bourgeois de Montpellier était désagréable, autant celui d'ici est brave et paternel. Il plairait beaucoup à papa. Comme lui il s'est battu en 89, comme lui il a été blessé à une jambe, comme lui il ne rêve aujourd'hui que de vivre et travailler dans le calme. Le patron, M.

Desvignes, nous fait travailler en association, soit à deux avec Marseillais-Franc-Cœur, soit à trois en nous adjoignant Vivarais-la-Rose qui couche dans la même chambre que nous, qui aime la lecture et qui me passe ses livres. M. Desvignes fait très peu de meubles, il est menuisier spécialisé dans l'aménagement et la devanture des magasins. Pour moi, c'est nouveau et, si je préfère construire des meubles, ce travail ne me déplaît pas. Comme je suis le meilleur dessinateur, c'est moi qui trace et qui prends en fait la direction du travail. Le patron l'a remarqué et m'a dit que j'étais très habile et qu'il ne comprenait pas que je ne fusse encore reçu compagnon. « Je vais en parler au premier de la ville », me dit-il. Ainsi l'autre dimanche, j'ai été reçu au milieu de tous les compagnons. Me voilà possesseur de rubans à attacher à la boutonnière les jours de cérémonies et d'assemblées générales ainsi que d'une canne. Cette canne, semblable à celle de tous les autres compagnons, pose un problème : « C'est que je possède déjà une canne, ai-je dit au premier. Celle d'un ancêtre qui a fait son tour de France à la fin du quinzième siècle! »

Il a cru que je me moquais de lui et m'a dit d'aller chercher ma canne. Quand il a vu les sculptures, les noms gravés et les dates il s'est écrié qu'il n'avait jamais pensé qu'un tel objet puisse encore exister. Il a fallu que je raconte toute l'histoire telle qu'Antoinette l'avait reconstituée et la façon dont la canne avait été oubliée et retrouvée dans un grenier. Finalement, après en avoir discuté avec le rouleur et les anciens du compagnonnage, il m'a dit avec émotion :

« Cette canne est un objet inestimable qu'il faut conserver avec soin et amour. Il n'est pas souhaitable que vous voyagiez avec, d'autant plus qu'elle ne ressemble pas à celles que nous portons aujourd'hui. Et puis, vous risquez de vous la faire voler ou briser dans une bataille comme il en survient, hélas! trop souvent. Je vous propose donc de la faire rapporter chez vous à Paris. Nous trouverons bien un ami voyageur qui s'en chargera. Cela dit, Valfroy, comme il faut vous donner un nom, je propose qu'on vous appelle

sur le tour de France, et plus tard, Parisien-la-Canne. Et comme cela sonne trop bref, qu'on y mette un peu d'or, l'or symbolique que représente la canne du plus ancien compagnon du tour de France que l'on connaisse. Votre nom sera " Parisien-la-Canne-d'or ". Vous porterez donc la canne et les rubans de notre compagnonnage, et un surnom. Faites respecter ces symboles. Grandissez toujours plus à vos propres yeux et aux yeux de ceux qui vous regardent. Vous êtes maintenant le point de mire des affiliés, des aspirants, vous devez leur servir d'exemple. Guidez-les dans le chemin de l'honneur, du travail, de la droiture, de la vertu! »

Tous les compagnons m'ont alors embrassé et vous ne serez pas étonné si je vous dis que j'ai pleuré en ressentant l'extraordinaire pression du cercle d'amitié qui m'entourait. Cela dit, Bordeaux est une ville gaie où l'on ne s'ennuie pas. Le dimanche nous partons faire des repas champêtres et j'apprends même à danser. La semaine je travaille dur car, après ma journée, je suis des leçons de dessin chez un maître menuisier, M. Roussel, qui a du talent et me fait faire des progrès. Dites à Eugène qu'il n'est plus le seul artiste de la famille!

Bertrand, c'était vrai, s'amusait beaucoup le dimanche. Ce qu'il ne disait pas, c'est que la cause de ce bonheur avait un nom : Pauline, la fille cadette de M. Desvignes, une brune délurée de dix-huit ans dont l'accent chantait et qui n'avait pas tardé à remarquer le jeune Parisien qui s'était joint aux compagnons de son père. Elle n'avait pas eu de mal à embraser ce cœur tendre en mal d'affection. Bertrand n'était pas un puceau timoré. Une voisine, la veuve d'un capitaine des lanciers demeuré accroché, le front troué d'une balle, à la rambarde du pont de la Bérézina, l'avait gentiment déniaisé un soir de l'été dernier. Cette expérience ne s'était pas renouvelée, de par la volonté de la dame. Bertrand avait ensuite connu des jeunes filles du quartier qu'il avait embrassées dans l'ombre des passages qui reliaient le Faubourg à la rue de Montreuil mais ces amourettes n'avaient jamais dépassé les sages limites des extases de jeunesse. Pauline arrivait donc à point dans l'univers sentimental du jeune compagnon. M. et Mme Desvignes qui connaissaient la prudence de leur fille laissaient faire. Peut-être se disaient-ils que ce garçon sympathique dont le père tenait un magasin de meubles à Paris ne ferait pas un mauvais parti.

Ce dimanche-là, les deux jeunes gens avaient semé les amis après le déjeuner champêtre et s'étaient éloignés du côté des bois de La Souye. « Ne vous occupez pas de nous, avait dit Bertrand à Marseillais-Franc-Cœur, nous vous rejoindrons. » Marseillais avait souri d'un air entendu et fait un grand salut avec son chapeau haut de forme tout neuf. Certains qui ne connaissent pas les habitudes des compagnons du tour peuvent se les figurer vêtus d'habits usés par le travail ou défraîchis par les voyages. Quelle erreur! Le dimanche et les jours de fête, chacun sort de sa malle son costume au pantalon long étroit, son gilet de piqué et sa redingote de drap ou de velours. Le long ruban bleu et blanc des compagnons du Devoir de liberté pendu au revers et le chapeau planté droit sur la tête, sans oublier la cravate plus ou moins bouffante sur le plastron blanc de la chemise, voilà le compagnon prêt à aller danser ou à se rendre à une assemblée.

Bertrand qui n'avait pas emporté beaucoup de vêtements de Paris s'était vite senti gêné par l'élégance de ses amis. Une lettre de change, expédiée par Ethis, lui avait permis de s'habiller chez un bon tailleur de Bordeaux et Pauline n'avait pas à rougir de son chevalier servant qui, ce jour-là, se laissait aller à ces confidences qui préludent le plus souvent à une déclaration en règle.

Tenant en caressant doucement les mains de Pauline, Bertrand parla longuement du Faubourg, de ses parents, d'Antoinette et des gens illustres ou simplement intelligents qui fréquentaient l'appartement de la place d'Aligre La jeune fille fermait les yeux et appuyait de plus en plus son buste frêle sur l'épaule du garçon. C'est tout naturellement qu'il lui murmura je t'aime.

– Je sais bien que ce n'est pas original mais les

hommes et les femmes, depuis qu'ils existent, n'ont jamais trouvé d'autres mots. Je t'aime, je suis heureux quand je suis avec toi.

Pauline sourit et lui tendit ses lèvres :

– Tiens-tu le même langage à toutes les filles que tu rencontres dans les villes où tu passes ?

– Cela ne m'est encore jamais arrivé depuis que je suis sur le tour et je n'ai pas envie de dire « je t'aime » à quelqu'un d'autre que toi. C'est sérieux, tu sais...

– Moi aussi je t'aime, Bertrand, et je n'ai pas non plus envie de dire cela à d'autres garçons.

Bertrand avait pendu sa veste à la branche d'un arbre et serrait contre lui le jeune corps de Pauline allongée sur l'herbe de la clairière. Le temps n'existait plus, ni les autres dont les rires lointains arrivaient étouffés, presque inaudibles. Ils n'entendirent pas des gens qui approchaient en faisant craquer le bois mort sous leurs souliers. Ce n'est que lorsque l'un des jeunes hommes s'arrêta et cria « Tope ! » que Bertrand se rendit compte qu'il était à la merci de quatre dévorants, des tailleurs de pierre du Devoir qu'on appelait les « loups-garous » et qui avaient à Bordeaux, la réputation d'être de sacrés batailleurs.

Bertrand avait souvent pensé qu'un jour ou l'autre il serait amené à se mesurer aux compagnons ennemis. On lui avait raconté, chez les mères où il était passé, des combats sanglants qui avaient opposé quelquefois de véritables armées de compagnons. Il y avait eu des morts, des blessés et il y en aurait encore. La stupidité de ces combats faisait frémir Bertrand qui n'était pas un lâche et possédait les moyens physiques de se battre mais qui souhaitait ardemment n'être jamais placé dans l'obligation de se défendre. Et voilà que le moment redouté arrivait alors qu'il goûtait au bonheur d'aimer !

Il se leva d'un bond et dit :

– Il est défendu à ceux du Devoir de liberté de toper. Passez votre chemin, je n'ai nulle envie de me battre aujourd'hui ! D'ailleurs vous êtes quatre et je suis seul Laissez-moi appeler mes amis.

– Non. rétorqua l'autre, un trapu à tête de bœuf. Nous

allons nous battre à deux puisque tu ne veux pas toper.

Aussitôt, il se défit de sa veste et se précipita sur Bertrand qui, heureusement, avait prévu une attaque brusquée et jeté sa jambe droite en avant. Si le pied avait porté en plein sur le tibia de l'autre, la bataille eût été terminée à peine commencée. Malheureusement la semelle dévia et ne fit qu'effleurer son genou, ce qu'il fallait pour décupler la hargne du loup-garou qui, agitant ses bras musclés par le travail de la pierre et, donnant de furieux coups de pied, déborda Bertrand et l'obligea à reculer pour se protéger et se remettre en garde. Un coup reçu en plein estomac gênait le Parisien pour respirer mais n'entravait pas sa souplesse naturelle qui lui permettait d'esquiver et même d'ajuster de franches volées sur la face de son adversaire.

Pauline, un moment hébétée par la brusquerie de l'attaque, s'était mise à hurler dans l'espoir d'être entendue par les amis. Tout en criant « Au secours! », elle voyait avec terreur le tailleur de pierre prendre le dessus sur Bertrand qui continuait pourtant à se défendre avec courage devant les trois autres dévorants, témoins passifs de la bataille. Alors, arriva l'imprévisible qui transforma en drame un combat qui n'aurait dû se solder que par de sévères contusions. Dans un sursaut, Bertrand réussit à placer un violent coup de poing sur l'œil gauche de son adversaire qui s'effondra, l'arcade sourcilière ouverte, le visage en sang. Hélas! emporté par son élan, le Parisien le suivit dans sa chute et sa tête, en touchant le sol, heurta une pierre tranchante. Tandis que l'autre se relevait en titubant, il demeurait inanimé sur le terrain, la tempe ouverte, les bras en croix, comme mort.

Pauline se précipita comme une folle, s'agenouilla près de Bertrand en essayant de le réveiller : « Ce n'est pas possible, tu n'es pas mort, dis-moi mon chéri que tu n'es que blessé!... »

Stupéfaits, les dévorants se penchaient eux aussi sur le corps inerte du Parisien. L'un d'eux avait ouvert sa chemise et posé sa main sur son cœur, un autre lui avait pris le poignet et cherchait son pouls. Tous deux se relevèrent en même temps en disant : « Son cœur bat, il n'est pas mort ! »

A ce moment arrivèrent en courant tous les gavots emmenés par Marseillais-Franc-Cœur. En voyant le dévorant ensanglanté et Bertrand étendu, ils comprirent tout de suite ce qui s'était passé. A la lueur de colère qui passa dans leur regard, Pauline crut qu'ils allaient fondre sur les quatre tailleurs de pierre mais l'heure n'était pas à la revanche, il fallait s'occuper du blessé.

– On ne peut pas le soigner ici, dit Breton-le-Résolu, un loup arrivé depuis peu à Bordeaux.

– Coupons les branches et construisons une litière ! proposa Marseillais.

– C'est la meilleure idée, trancha Pauline Faites vite !

Tous les compagnons, gavots et dévorants confondus, sortirent leur couteau et rapportèrent bientôt des brassées de fines branches de saule et de frêne qu'ils tressèrent sur deux solides brancards coupés à grand-peine dans la forêt. Dix minutes plus tard, la civière était prête. Avec d'infinies précautions, deux compagnons y allongèrent Bertrand que Pauline tenta vainement de ranimer en rafraîchissant son visage avec l'eau d'une gourde.

Le dévorant, triste héros du drame, dont l'œil tuméfié saignait toujours répétait : « Je ne voulais pas cela, je suis fautif mais je fais le serment aujourd'hui, de ne jamais plus me battre ! »

Deux loups-garous voulurent porter les premiers la civière mais Marseillais s'y opposa : « C'est à nous de ramener notre ami ! »

Lentement, la colonne des compagnons s'ébranla sur la route de Bordeaux. Aux chants joyeux de l'aller succédait un silence accablé. On entendait seulement Pauline sangloter. A Marseillais-Franc-Cœur qui la tenait par le bras elle murmura : « Je l'aime trop pour qu'il meure mon Parisien ! Il vivra et il sera mon mari... »

DU MÊME AUTEUR

Aux Éditions Denoël

CHEZ LIPP.
LES DAMES DU FAUBOURG.
LE LIT D'ACAJOU (Les Dames du Faubourg, II).
LES VIOLONS DU ROI.
LE GÉNIE DE LA BASTILLE (Les Dames du Faubourg, III).
RÉTRO-RIMES.

Aux Éditions Fayard

HÔTEL RECOMMANDÉ, roman.

En collaboration avec Jacqueline Michel

DE BRIQUES ET DE BROCS.
DRÔLES DE NUMÉROS.

Aux Éditions Albin Michel

SI VOUS AVEZ MANQUÉ LE DÉBUT.

Aux Éditions Philippe Lebaud

LE LIVRE DU COCHON, en collaboration avec Irène Karsenty.

Aux Éditions d'Art, Joseph Forêt

HENRY CLEWS, préface d'André Maurois.

COLLECTION FOLIO

Dernières parutions

3945.	Alain Finkielkraut	*L'imparfait du présent.*
3946.	Alona Kimhi	*Suzanne la pleureuse.*
3947.	Dominique Rolin	*Le futur immédiat.*
3948.	Philip Roth	*J'ai épousé un communiste.*
3949.	Juan Rulfo	*Le Llano en flammes.*
3950.	Martin Winckler	*Légendes*
3951.	Fédor Dostoïevski	*Humiliés et offensés.*
3952.	Alexandre Dumas	*Le Capitaine Pamphile.*
3953.	André Dhôtel	*La tribu Bécaille.*
3954.	André Dhôtel	*L'honorable Monsieur Jacques.*
3955.	Diane de Margerie	*Dans la spirale.*
3956.	Serge Doubrovski	*Le livre brisé.*
3957.	La Bible	*Genèse.*
3958.	La Bible	*Exode.*
3959.	La Bible	*Lévitique-Nombres.*
3960.	La Bible	*Samuel.*
3961.	Anonyme	*Le poisson de jade.*
3962.	Mikhaïl Boulgakov	*Endiablade.*
3963.	Alejo Carpentier	*Les Élus et autres nouvelles.*
3964.	Collectif	*Un ange passe.*
3965.	Roland Dubillard	*Confessions d'un fumeur de tabac français.*
3966.	Thierry Jonquet	*La leçon de management.*
3967.	Suzan Minot	*Une vie passionnante.*
3968.	Dann Simmons	*Les Fosses d'Iverson.*
3969.	Junichirô Tanizaki	*Le coupeur de roseaux.*
3970.	Richard Wright	*L'homme qui vivait sous terre.*
3971.	Vassilis Alexakis	*Les mots étrangers.*
3972.	Antoine Audouard	*Une maison au bord du monde.*
3973.	Michel Braudeau	*L'interprétation des singes.*
3974.	Larry Brown	*Dur comme l'amour.*
3975.	Jonathan Coe	*Une touche d'amour.*
3976.	Philippe Delerm	*Les amoureux de l'Hôtel de Ville.*

3977.	Hans Fallada	*Seul dans Berlin.*
3978.	Franz-Olivier Giesbert	*Mort d'un berger.*
3979.	Jens Christian Grøndahl	*Bruits du cœur.*
3980.	Ludovic Roubaudi	*Les Baltringues.*
3981.	Anne Wiazemski	*Sept garçons.*
3982.	Michel Quint	*Effroyables jardins.*
3983.	Joseph Conrad	*Victoire.*
3984.	Émile Ajar	*Pseudo.*
3985.	Olivier Bleys	*Le fantôme de la Tour Eiffel.*
3986.	Alejo Carpentier	*La danse sacrale.*
3987.	Milan Dargent	*Soupe à la tête de bouc.*
3988.	André Dhôtel	*Le train du matin.*
3989.	André Dhôtel	*Des trottoirs et des fleurs.*
3990.	Philippe Labro/ Olivier Barrot	*Lettres d'Amérique. Un voyage en littérature.*
3991.	Pierre Péju	*La petite Chartreuse.*
3992.	Pascal Quignard	*Albucius.*
3993.	Dan Simmons	*Les larmes d'Icare.*
3994.	Michel Tournier	*Journal extime.*
3995.	Zoé Valdés	*Miracle à Miami.*
3996.	Bossuet	*Oraisons funèbres.*
3997.	Anonyme	*Jin Ping Mei I.*
3998.	Anonyme	*Jin Ping Mei II.*
3999.	Pierre Assouline	*Grâces lui soient rendues.*
4000.	Philippe Roth	*La tache.*
4001.	Frederick Busch	*L'inspecteur de nuit.*
4002.	Christophe Dufossé	*L'heure de la sortie.*
4003.	William Faulkner	*Le domaine.*
4004.	Sylvie Germain	*La Chanson des mal-aimants.*
4005.	Joanne Harris	*Les cinq quartiers de l'orange.*
4006.	Leslie kaplan	*Les Amants de Marie.*
4007.	Thierry Metz	*Le journal d'un manœuvre.*
4008.	Dominique Rolin	*Plaisirs.*
4009.	Jean-Marie Rouart	*Nous ne savons pas aimer.*
4010.	Samuel Butler	*Ainsi va toute chair.*
4011.	George Sand	*La petite Fadette.*
4012.	Jorge Amado	*Le Pays du Carnaval.*
4013.	Alessandro Baricco	*L'âme d'Hegel et les vaches du Wisconsin.*
4014.	La Bible	*Livre d'Isaïe.*

4015. La Bible — *Paroles de Jérémie-Lamentations.*
4016. La Bible — *Livre de Job.*
4017. La Bible — *Livre d'Ezéchiel.*
4018. Frank Conroy — *Corps et âme.*
4019. Marc Dugain — *Heureux comme Dieu en France.*
4020. Marie Ferranti — *La Princesse de Mantoue.*
4021. Mario Vargas Llosa — *La fête au Bouc.*
4022. Mario Vargas Llosa — *Histoire de Mayta.*
4023. Daniel Evan Weiss — *Les cafards n'ont pas de roi.*
4024. Elsa Morante — *La Storia.*
4025. Emmanuèle Bernheim — *Stallone.*
4026. Françoise Chandernagor — *La chambre.*
4027. Philippe Djian — *Ça, c'est un baiser.*
4028. Jérôme Garcin — *Théâtre intime.*
4029. Valentine Goby — *La note sensible.*
4030. Pierre Magnan — *L'enfant qui tuait le temps.*
4031. Amos Oz — *Les deux morts de ma grand-mère.*
4032. Amos Oz — *Une panthère dans la cave.*
4033. Gisèle Pineau — *Chair Piment.*
4034. Zeruya Shalev — *Mari et femme.*
4035. Jules Verne — *La Chasse au météore.*
4036. Jules Verne — *Le Phare du bout du Monde.*
4037. Gérard de Cortanze — *Jorge Semprun.*
4038. Léon Tolstoï — *Hadji Mourat.*
4039. Isaac Asimov — *Mortelle est la nuit.*
4040. Collectif — *Au bonheur de lire.*
4041. Roald Dahl — *Gelée royale.*
4042. Denis Diderot — *Lettre sur les Aveugles.*
4043. Yukio Mishima — *Martyre.*
4044. Elsa Morante — *Donna Amalia.*
4045. Ludmila Oulitskaïa — *La maison de Lialia.*
4046. Rabindranath Tagore — *La petite mariée.*
4047. Ivan Tourguéniev — *Clara Militch.*
4048. H.G. Wells — *Un rêve d'Armageddon.*
4049. Michka Assayas — *Exhibition.*
4050. Richard Bausch — *La saison des ténèbres.*
4051. Saul Bellow — *Ravelstein.*
4052. Jerome Charyn — *L'homme qui rajeunissait.*

4053.	Catherine Cusset	*Confession d'une radine.*
4055.	Thierry Jonquet	*La Vigie* (à paraître).
4056.	Erika Krouse	*Passe me voir un de ces jours.*
4057.	Philippe Le Guillou	*Les marées du Faou.*
4058.	Frances Mayes	*Swan.*
4059.	Joyce Carol Oates	*Nulle et Grande Gueule.*
4060.	Edgar Allan Poe	*Histoires extraordinaires.*
4061.	George Sand	*Lettres d'une vie.*
4062.	Frédéric Beigbeder	*99 francs.*
4063.	Balzac	*Les Chouans.*
4064.	Bernardin de Saint Pierre	*Paul et Virginie.*
4065.	Raphaël Confiant	*Nuée ardente.*
4066.	Florence Delay	*Dit Nerval.*
4067.	Jean Rolin	*La clôture.*
4068.	Philippe Claudel	*Les petites mécaniques.*
4069.	Eduardo Barrios	*L'enfant qui devint fou d'amour.*
4070.	Neil Bissoondath	*Un baume pour le cœur.*
4071.	Jonahan Coe	*Bienvenue au club.*
4072.	Toni Davidson	*Cicatrices.*
4073.	Philippe Delerm	*Le buveur de temps.*
4074.	Masuji Ibuse	*Pluie noire.*
4075.	Camille Laurens	*L'Amour, roman.*
4076.	François Nourissier	*Prince des berlingots.*
4077.	Jean d'Ormesson	*C'était bien.*
4078.	Pascal Quignard	*Les Ombres errantes.*
4079.	Isaac B. Singer	*De nouveau au tribunal de mon père.*
4080.	Pierre Loti	*Matelot.*
4081.	Edgar Allan Poe	*Histoires extraordinaires.*
4082.	Lian Hearn	*Le clan des Otori, II : les Neiges de l'exil.*
4083.	La Bible	*Psaumes.*
4084.	La Bible	*Proverbes.*
4085.	La Bible	*Évangiles.*
4086.	La Bible	*Lettres de Paul.*
4087.	Pierre Bergé	*Les jours s'en vont je demeure.*
4088.	Benjamin Berton	*Sauvageons.*
4089.	Clémence Boulouque	*Mort d'un silence.*
4090.	Paule Constant	*Sucre et secret.*
4091.	Nicolas Fargues	*One Man Show.*

4092. James Flint	*Habitus.*
4093. Gisèle Fournier	*Non-dits.*
4094. Iegor Gran	*O.N.G.!*
4095. J.M.G. Le Clézio	*Révolutions.*
4096. Andréï Makine	*La terre et le ciel de Jacques Dorme.*
4097. Collectif	*«Parce que c'était lui, parce-que c'était moi».*
4098. Anonyme	*Saga de Gísli Súrsson.*
4099. Truman Capote	*Monsieur Maléfique et autres nouvelles.*
4100. E.M. Cioran	*Ébauches de vertige.*
4101. Salvador Dali	*Les moustaches radar.*
4102. Chester Himes	*Le fantôme de Rufus Jones* et autres nouvelles.
4103. Pablo Neruda	*La solitude lumineuse.*
4104. Antoine de St-Exupéry	*Lettre à un otage.*
4105. Anton Tchekhov	*Une banale histoire.*
4106. Honoré de Balzac	*L'Auberge rouge.*
4107. George Sand	*Consuelo I.*
4108. George Sand	*Consuelo II.*
4109. André Malraux	*Lazare.*
4110 Cyrano de Bergerac	*L'autre monde.*
4111 Alessandro Baricco	*Sans sang.*
4112 Didier Daeninckx	*Raconteur d'histoires.*
4113 André Gide	*Le Ramier.*
4114. Richard Millet	*Le renard dans le nom.*
4115. Susan Minot	*Extase.*
4116. Nathalie Rheims	*Les fleurs du silence.*
4117. Manuel Rivas	*La langue des papillons.*
4118. Daniel Rondeau	*Istanbul.*
4119. Dominique Sigaud	*De chape et de plomb.*
4120. Philippe Sollers	*L'Étoile des amants.*
4121. Jacques Tournier	*À l'intérieur du chien.*
4122. Gabriel Sénac de Meilhan	*L'Émigré.*
4123. Honoré de Balzac	*Le Lys dans la vallée.*
4124. Lawrence Durrell	*Le Carnet noir.*
4125. Félicien Marceau	*La grande fille.*
4126. Chantal Pelletier	*La visite.*
4127. Boris Schreiber	*La douceur du sang.*
4128. Angelo Rinaldi	*Tout ce que je sais de Marie.*

Impression Bussière
à Saint-Amand (Cher),
le 4 février 2005.
Dépôt légal : février 2005.
1er dépôt légal dans la collection : mai 1989.
Numéro d'imprimeur : 050499/1.

ISBN 2-07-038149-8./Imprimé en France.
Précédemment publié par les Éditions Denoël.
ISBN 2-207-23221-2.